BFF'S Forever:

Best Frenemies Forever

Series Books 1-3

BFF'S Forever:

Best Frenemies Forever
Series Books 1-3

Brenda Hampton

www.urbanbooks.net

Urban Books, LLC
300 Farmingdale Road, NY-Route 109
Farmingdale, NY 11735

BFF'S Forever: Best Frenemies Forever Series Books 1-3

ISBN 13: 978-1-945855-26-9
ISBN 10: 1-945855-26-6

First Trade Paperback Printing June 2018
Printed in the United States of America

10 9 8 7 6 5 4 3 2 1

Distributed by Kensington Publishing Corp.
Submit Orders to:
Customer Service
400 Hahn Road
Westminster, MD 21157-4627
Phone: 1-800-733-3000
Fax: 1-800-659-2436

BFF'S Forever:

Best Frenemies Forever
Series Books 1-3

by

Brenda Hampton

BFF'S

Best Frenemies Forever Series

Prologue

No words in the dictionary—not even the urban dictionary—could define how Cedric Thompson made me feel right about now. There was so much hatred in my heart for the man whom I used to love with every fiber of my being. Surely, we'd had our ups and downs, highs and lows, but lately things had gone beyond anything I had ever imagined. He'd become disrespectful. He ignored my demands and how dare he try to sit back and call all of the shots. I tried my best to get him to see why we needed to be together, but he wasn't trying to hear me. He wanted everything to be his way, or no way at all. That was why the time had come for me to finally have it my way.

Thinking about this fucking disease he gave me, I glared straight ahead while driving my car in the direction of his house. My vision was blurred from tears in my water-filled eyes. The scars that he'd left cut deep; I was damaged beyond repair. For days, I pondered about what to do with the man who told me that he loved me and said that I meant everything in the world to him. Yet, when it came down to it, his actions didn't show what his mouth confessed. I was a fool to believe anything he'd said. The shame was on me for putting myself in this predicament. That in itself was hard for me to swallow, and so was the baseball-sized lump in my throat that was stuck there. As much as I swallowed, it wouldn't go away. The pain in my heart lingered, and the only satisfaction I would get was when Cedric Thompson lay dead in his grave.

With black leather gloves on, I squeezed the steering wheel tight. I could feel beads of sweat dot my forehead, and when I looked in the rearview mirror, my smudged mascara cascaded down my face with tears. Anger was trapped in my eyes. I was so upset that I growled loudly and slammed my foot harder on the pedal. I saw the speedometer needle jump from 60 to

90 mph as my car flew down the highway. My legs trembled from the crazy thoughts in my head, but I couldn't help but to crack a tiny smile when a vision of Cedric's dead body flashed before me. Needless to say, I was eager to get this over with. It was time. Time for him to answer for all the dirt he'd done, and go stand before his Maker. Oh, how I wished I could be there to hear his explanation for being such an asshole. He may have manipulated or gotten over on me, but there was no getting over on his Maker. Cedric would have to answer for his actions, and the punishment would be more brutal than the way I intended to do away with him.

My car rocked as I made my exit, rolling over a few bumps on the road. I decided to slow down, because the last thing I needed was for the police to come after me. I was so sure that I would be questioned after my beef was settled, but I had planned this day for many months. I already knew what to do, when to say it and how to say it. I suspected that no fingers would point to me, and with all of the trifling bitches in Cedric's life, finding the killer would be like searching for a needle in a hoestack. Or, at least, that was what I hoped. I hoped that this would be the end. That I would never have to look back on this day, feeling sorrow or having regrets.

Instead of parking my car in the curvy driveway, I parked down the street. My eyes searched the neighbors' houses that were close by Cedric's. I had to be sure that no one saw me. The darkness enabled me to hide the shotgun by my side, so I raced toward the front door with my heart slamming hard against my chest. A hoodie was thrown over my head, and the baggy jeans I sported barely hung onto my butt. My white tennis shoes were the only things that reflected in the night, but I wore them just in case I needed to run.

While at the door, I pulled a black mask over my face. With the leather gloves still on, I reached for the brass doorknob, turning it. The door *clicked* and opened immediately. I was surprised by the easy access, but rich people were always leaving their doors unlocked. Thing is, I had no idea where Cedric was inside. I had spoken to him today, and I'd seen him already too. All I knew was he was here. Somewhere inside. Unaware that he was minutes away from sucking in his last breath.

I tiptoed across the floor then step-by-step I climbed the carpeted staircase that led me to Cedric's bedroom. I expected to find him in bed, possibly rocking the shit out of it or asleep. But when I pushed on the double doors, they squeaked. The king-sized bed was empty and so was the rest of his bedroom. I inhaled the smell of his masculine cologne, then I went into his walk-in closet to look around. His tailored business suits, in almost every color, were neatly hung. His expensive leather shoes were stored in separate compartments and an island with drawers sat in the middle of the floor. On top of it were several expensive watches, gold cuff links, and diamond earrings that I assumed cost a fortune. I swiped up the items, stuffing them into my pockets. Since he had made me a homeless woman, I had to get something out of the deal.

I took a few steps away from the closet, causing the floor to squeak. That was when I heard Cedric's voice and realized that he was downstairs.

"Jacoby," he shouted. "Is that you?"

Of course, I didn't respond. I held my breath as I heard his hard footsteps on the stairs. While peeking through the cracked door, I observed as Cedric went into Jacoby's bedroom, looking for him. I suspected that Jacoby would be here soon, so I had to hurry and finish the job. Then, I needed to get the hell out of there.

I made another move and took a few more steps to get closer to the door. I could see Cedric coming my way, dressed in a silk robe. He reached inside to scratch above his dick, and when he pushed on the door, he was met with the barrel of my shotgun, aiming steady at his face. His eyes grew wide then they squinted as if he were trying to figure out who I was. That was kind of hard to do, because every inch of me was covered in black, with the exception of my tennis shoes.

"Wha— what do you want?" Cedric stuttered.

He carefully eased his hands in the air, keeping his eyes locked with mine. Fear was trapped in his eyes, and I was delighted to see the scared look he presented.

I held my finger on the trigger and Cedric's eyes shifted to it. "Please," he begged. "Don't do this. I'll give you anything you want. Wha—what is it that you want?"

I released my finger from the trigger and placed it over my red, glossy lips, signaling for him to hush. When my finger returned to the trigger, I took a few steps forward, causing him to step back. As I moved, he moved. He kept squinting and searching into my eyes, trying to figure out who I was. At this point, I didn't give a damn if he recognized me or not. We halted our steps at the top of the stairs, and that was when I signaled good-bye with a slow wink. His mouth opened, but before any words came out I lowered the shotgun to his buffed chest and happily squeezed the trigger.

The force from the gun jerked me backward, but I remained standing. I got much pleasure in watching Cedric's body tumble down the stairs. His blood stained the clean carpet, and several of the rails broke loose as he tried to reach for them to break his fall. His body, however, landed on the cold, marble floor in the foyer. He lay there with his arms stretched wide, eyes gazing at the high ceiling. I moved slowly down the stairs, keeping a close watch on him as he gasped to catch his breath. Blood dripped from the corner of his dry mouth, and it also trickled from a deep scar on his forehead. I reached the bottom stair and stood over him with a wide smile that was visible behind the mask. His eyes fluttered, and wanting him to see who I was, I removed the mask and raked my fingers through my sweaty hair.

"Don't you know, Cedric? Too much pussy ain't good for you."

He strained to speak, but no words could be comprehended. His eyes fluttered a few more times before they shut and never opened again. His head tilted and the heaving of his chest came to a halt. I sucked in a deep breath then sighed from relief and grief. My mission was accomplished, or at least that was what I thought, until I saw someone staring at me through the glass front door. Right then I knew I was busted.

Chapter One

Evelyn

It had been a long day at work. I was completely exhausted. I breezed my Lincoln Navigator through the busy traffic in downtown St. Louis, trying to make my way home. My loft was on Washington Avenue. It was good to know that I was only ten minutes away from relaxation. My stomach was growling and my bed was calling me. I had worked overtime today so I could have extra money in my pockets to pay down the rising debt I found myself in. My girlfriends, Kayla and Trina, were the only ones who knew how messed up my financial situation was. But just so I didn't have to borrow any more money from them, I decided to pick up more hours at work. I also decided to do something else—something that I suspected my girls wouldn't approve of. That was find a man who could help me crawl out of my unfortunate situation. He was exactly what the doctor ordered. And there was no question that I had to give a little in order to get a whole lot. On-call pussy was what he wanted, but that didn't bother me one bit. I was willing and able to give him whatever, and for the past three months I realized how beneficial this relationship could be to me.

Minutes later, I entered the parking garage, parking my SUV into the reserved spot. That was the plus side of living in a loft apartment. I appreciated the privacy it offered. I used my swipe card to open the elevator that took me to my loft on the third floor. Dressed in a black pencil skirt and silver blouse, I sashayed down the narrow, carpeted hallway like a runway model. I had always wanted to be a model, and my slim figure had brought about many opportunities in the past. But then life happened. Moneywise, things didn't pan out for me.

What I settled for was being a customer service representa-tive, working for a white man who did nothing but boss our entire department around. It pained me to get up everyday and go to work, but I was blessed to have a job. Therefore, my complaints were kept to a minimum. I just had to put up with the bullshit until I could get the man in my life to save me by forking out more money.

I approached the bright red door to my loft with a smile plastered on my face; partially because I was home, but mainly because of the written note I saw taped to the door that instructed me to enter at my own risk. That meant Cedric was inside, waiting for me. I was delighted that he was there, only because we hadn't seen each other for almost two weeks. Our relationship was . . . complicated, but it was a relationship that I refused to tear myself away from.

I hurried to put the key in the door. The moment I walked inside, I was hit with the scent of Cedric's masculine cologne. A trail of pink and red rose petals were scattered on the hard-wood, shiny floors. The petals made a path that led straight to my bedroom door. The door was closed and there was another note taped on it. I squinted behind my silver-framed glasses and still couldn't read the note. Eager to see what was up, I put my purse on the kitchen island and removed my high-heel pumps. My hair was parted through the middle and making sure everything was in order, I teased the flowing, blond-tinted tresses of curls with the tips of my fingers. I didn't have time to freshen my makeup, but with it being M•A•C, I was sure that it still looked fresh. My light, silky skin glowed from the shimmery lotion I wore. It didn't take much for me to present myself as sexy.

As I neared the door, the words on the note became clearer: *SOMETHING GOOD AWAITS YOU! HURRY!*

I rushed to open the door, feeling as if I had entered para-dise. The strawberry-scented room was dim from the melting, flaming candles that burned on my nightstands. The trail of rose petals continued to the foot of the bed and a white sheet rested on the bottom half of Cedric's muscular frame. A smile was washed across his face, and as our eyes locked together in a trance, my heart started to race from excitement.

"What's up, sexy?" Cedric said, flashing his pearly-white teeth. "I hate to say it, but you know you looking more and more like my future wife, Evelyn Lozada, everyday. And not because of the first-name thing, baby, but because I said so."

My smile turned into a smirk as I started to undo my silky blouse. I pulled it away from my shoulders and began to create a pile behind me.

"I hate when you compare me to other women, and must I remind you that she doesn't have it like this." I flashed my goodies, hoping that Cedric appreciated what I was offering. "So, on another note, I'm glad you let yourself in. I'm highly interested in learning about the risk you mentioned at the front door, so why don't you tell me more about it?"

Cedric moved the sheet aside, exposing his flawless body that looked as if it had been dipped in creamy, milk chocolate. His dick stood at full attention, and as he relaxed sideways on his elbow, I walked to the bed and crawled my way up to him. Our eyes remained connected. When our lips finally touched, all I could do was shut my eyes and savor the taste of pure sweetness. My tongue danced with his, and like always, the lip-lock was intense.

Cedric held the sides of my face then backed away from me. "What did I ever do to deserve all of this?" he questioned.

"I could ask the same question, but I won't. I'll just say that we both should feel grateful and leave it there."

Cedric nodded then lay back on the bed. I straddled the top of him as he tucked a fluffy pillow behind his head and narrowed his light brown eyes to stare at me. His eyes scanned down my naked body. It didn't take much longer for his hands to roam. From the small curves in my hips to my plump ass that was just right, Cedric squeezed all of that and then some. I was so hungry for him that I reached for his package and positioned it to enter me. As my pussy lips sucked him into the heat I was packing, he closed his eyes. His hips started to grind in circles with mine, and the sound of my creamy juices being stirred played like theme music to our ears.

Minutes later, things sped up and we were going at it like two dogs in heat. The mattress squeaked and the loose headboard kept slamming against the wall. I was putting in some serious overtime, doing my best to please the one man who kept me satisfied more than any other.

"Yeah, you bad. Work that pussy on me, baby," Cedric said with a healthy portion of my ass gripped in his hands.

I rubbed the minimal hair on his buffed chest, and then gripped his broad shoulders so I could have something to hold on to when I increased my pace. I always got excited when he talked dirty to me, but there were times when he got too animated and went a little overboard.

"That's right, bitch!" he spewed through gritted teeth and smacked my ass. "Serve Daddy like you supposed to! Do that shit, girl, do it!"

By now sweat was raining down on my body. Per his request I was doing *it*. My pussy felt swollen from being beat by his mammoth-sized package that Cedric always used as a weapon. I was just about ready to cum. The moment my toes curled Cedric hurried to lay me on my back. He threw my long legs over his shoulders and broke into my insides like a thief in the night. For fifteen more minutes, we went at it. Then it happened: The same thing that happened every time we got together. It was always the one thing that brought our sex sessions to an end. I couldn't help myself from going there. I wanted to know what his wife had been up to, because I hadn't heard from her today.

"Why go there?" Cedric looked down at me with a blank expression on his face. "Why must you bring up her name every time we get together?"

"Because I can't help but to wonder how she would feel about all of this? I mean, do you fuck her as well as you screw me? I hate to keep asking, because one of you is lying. She says you do, you say you don't. What's really the truth?"

Cedric eased his dripping wet goodness from my insides, causing my coochie lips to lock. He released a deep sigh and shook his head.

"The truth is, all that shit you talking right now don't matter. I always try to do nice things for you, Evelyn, just so you'll recognize how much you really mean to me. You're pushing me away with your bullshit. Don't be mad at me when I tell you I've had enough."

As Cedric got dressed to go, I sat on the bed and pouted. Maybe I had been too hard on him, but then again, maybe not. After all, he was my friend's husband. Kayla would kill us if she knew about this, but this was not about me being in love with Cedric. I was in love with his money: Money that I needed right now and saw no other way to get it. Kayla had everything in life she wanted. Sharing a piece of her husband's dick wasn't going to cause her world to come tumbling down. She knew Cedric was no good, and after fifteen years of marriage all they did was put up with each other.

I honestly didn't view this situation as a big betrayal. I assumed that Cedric didn't love Kayla anymore and that she didn't love him. They stayed in their marriage because of their sixteen-year-old son, Jacoby. That in itself was the wrong reason.

Feeling kind of bad for bringing up Kayla around Cedric, I realized that I had some quick making up to do. But when I got out of bed, Cedric was dressed and ready to go. He was one fine man who knew how to turn up the heat in the bedroom. He also knew how to present himself as a professional businessman. The business suit he wore clung to his athletic frame that had been there since college. At thirty-eight, Cedric had his act together. I wasn't the only woman who craved him. Many people thought he was the real Columbus Short, and some women were foolish enough to run up to him for an autograph. So, not only did Kayla have her hands full with me, but she also had her hands full with tricks who desired to have her husband for his looks, and with those who wanted him for his money.

"I'm out," he said, glaring at me as I stood in front of him. He buttoned his suit jacket and backed away from me when I lifted my arms to place them on his shoulders.

"Evelyn, we're done for the night. Sex was good, but if you learn to keep your mouth shut you can always make it better."

He turned to walk away, but I followed him. "Forgive me," I said, knowing that he would. "I let the thoughts of Kayla get to me sometimes. I guess I shouldn't do that."

Cedric removed his keys from the living-room table then turned to face me. "I said it once and I'll say it again. Kayla is my concern, not yours."

"You're so right. From here on you will not hear me speak her name around you again. On another note, were you able—"

"Yes. The deposit is there. Check your account to be sure. If the money hasn't been deposited, let me know."

Cedric walked around me, making his way to the door. Knowing that the money was mostly likely in my account, the least I could do was send him off with a good-bye kiss. I hurried past him, just so he could get once last glimpse of my naked ass and come back for more. I reached for the doorknob to unlock the door, but Cedric stopped me when he inched close to me, pressing his body against my backside. He moved my hair away from my neck and planted a trail of soft kisses on it.

"I guess I'm forgiven," I said with a smile.

"Always," he whispered in my ear. "Especially since I can't resist that cute little dimple you have on your left ass cheek. Every time I see it, I just want to bow down and kiss it."

I wasn't sure if the dimple thingy was a compliment or not, but when Cedric squatted to kiss my ass I laughed. He laughed too then told me he needed to get going before he changed his mind about leaving.

"I'll call you tomorrow." He kissed my cheek and reached for the doorknob. I moved out of the way to let him exit.

"Tell Kayla I said hello."

Cedric glared at me then walked out. I watched as he smooth-walked his way to the elevator. Before it closed, I waved and he gave me a nod by tossing his head back.

Needing a shower, I closed the door and went into my bedroom. I turned my backside to the huge floor mirror that sat against my wall to check out the dimple on my ass. My ass and thighs were cellulite free, but Cedric was right. There was a dimple on my left cheek, and at thirty-six I didn't appreciate it. I frowned as I made my way to the bathroom to take a shower, but when I got out and checked my bank account, the money Cedric had deposited was there. That left a smile on my face. I wanted to call and thank him again, but instead I called Kayla.

"I'm in the middle of something," she whispered into the phone. "Can I call you back?"

I hoped that she wasn't in the middle of having sex. Just for the hell of it, I had to be sure. "You and Cedric are too horny for me. Why would you answer the phone during sex?"

"Uh, no. I'm at Jacoby's band concert. Don't you hear all the music in the background?"

"Oh, I do. Tell him that I'm sorry I couldn't make it. I'll make it next time. From what I can hear, though, the band sounds good. Is Cedric there too?"

"No. He hasn't made it yet. I'm not sure if he's coming. I don't care, either, but let me call you back, okay?"

"Sure. Sorry for interrupting. Don't forget to tell Jacoby what I said."

Kayla said she would and ended the call. I sat on the bed, thinking that if she didn't hold Cedric accountable for not being there for her and Jacoby, why should I care about all that was transpiring behind closed doors? As far as I knew, nobody suspected that anything was going on between Cedric and me. If he wasn't going to tell, neither would I. I was getting what I wanted; that was all that mattered. I swiped my hands together after I clicked the *send* button on my laptop to make my rental payment on time.

Chapter Two

Kayla

The school's auditorium was filled with plenty of parents, as well as grandparents and siblings, there to show support for the high school students in the jazz band. Jacoby had learned to play the saxophone years ago. His solo performance brought tears to my eyes. I sat proudly and my heart was filled with joy. There was a little disappointment too, as the chair next to me remained empty. Cedric said he would do his best to come, but I guess he couldn't pull himself away from his office chair that he was forever glued to. Either that or he could have been out somewhere wining and dining one of his tricks. I had a gut feeling that Cedric had been stepping out on our marriage, but after so many years together, some things weren't worth bringing to the kitchen table anymore. We had been there, done that before.

My main gripe was the relationship Cedric had with his son. Needless to say, I was disappointed. There was a time when the two of them were very close, but as Jacoby got older he started pulling away from Cedric. Jacoby barely wanted anything to do with him anymore, and they often walked around the house like two people who didn't know each other. I expressed my concerns to Cedric, but he blamed it on Jacoby's age. He said that as a growing teenager, Jacoby didn't want to be bothered and the two of us needed to back off and let him grow up. I agreed with that too, but there was much more to it that Cedric wasn't seeing. I figured it was up to Jacoby to tell him what was really going on with his attitude. I'd be lying if I said the way things were turning out didn't hurt.

The band instructor announced the last song of the night. That was when I looked up and saw Cedric walking down the stairs and making his way up to me. I wasn't sure if Jacoby saw him or not, but to be honest I was rather embarrassed by his late appearance. I crossed my legs, causing the slit in my ruffled yellow dress to slide over and show my cinnamon-brown skin. My metallic, pointed-toe heels matched my accessories, and my long, thin braids that flowed midway down my back were pulled away from my round face. My makeup was on like a work of art. The rich, plum lipstick I wore made me resemble Lauryn Hill, which was a plus because she was one of my favorite artists.

Cedric noticed me from all the brightness I added to the room. He displayed a forced smile before sitting next to me.

"You're late," I said with a little snap in my voice.

"Thanks for the announcement, but at least I'm here."

"Then maybe the standing ovation at the end of the concert should be for you. And by the way"—I turned my head toward him—"you should have showered before you came. The smell of sex can be calmed with hot water, you know."

Cedric held a smirk on his face and straightened his suit jacket. "And a loud mouth can always be silenced with a fist. Wrong place, wrong time, Kay. Silence yourself to prevent the embarrassment."

"You've already done that, and I welcome the idea of you putting your hands on me. You remember what happened last time you tried that mess. If I can recall, you lost a whole lot of sleep that night. Save your threats for that slimy hooker who didn't encourage you to wash up before you left her."

"Woman, would you shut up!"

The tone of Cedric's loud voice caused several people in front of us to turn around. It was a good thing that the band was louder than his voice, but I'd had enough. I got up from the seat I was in and went to sit in another one. I hated to carry on like this, but being around Cedric made me this way. There was a time when I loved him to death. I dropped out of college when I got pregnant with Jacoby. Shortly thereafter, Cedric and I got married. He finished college and jumped right into business with two other guys he'd met while in school. They all had computer science degrees that helped them create a profitable software development company that made them millionaires in less than five years.

Moneywise, we didn't have much to complain about, but everything else in our lives was a mess. The more money Cedric made, the more controlling, arrogant, and disrespectful he'd gotten. There were plenty of times that I wanted to leave him, but at this point I didn't have much to fall back on. I didn't want to start over and giving up all that I had didn't seem like the sensible thing to do. Then there was Jacoby. He was accustomed to the way we lived, even though he didn't always seem happy. He hated to hear Cedric and me arguing. I knew that the way we carried on was tearing him apart. That was why I did my best to hold my piece around him. The only time I confronted Cedric about my concerns was when Jacoby wasn't around. He still knew things weren't the best between his father and me, and the constant frowns on my face made my unhappiness quite clear.

The band was given a standing ovation after the concert was over. Cedric and I waited in the crowded hallway for Jacoby to put his instrument away and join us. Moments later he did. We both congratulated him on a job well done, and when he inquired about a critique of his solo performance, I quickly spoke up so Cedric didn't have to.

"It was awesome. Practice pays off and you are getting better by the day," I said.

Jacoby gave me a hug then he waited for a reply from Cedric. There was no doubt that he wanted his father's approval. For whatever reason, it meant more to Jacoby than my approval did. Cedric did what he knew best and lied.

"Yeah, that was the best I ever heard you play. Keep up the good work, son, I'm proud of you."

Cedric patted his back, but I suspected that Jacoby knew his father had only been there for ten minutes. Either way, we left the school together as a family. Jacoby and Cedric rode together in his Mercedes. I pulled off the parking lot in my black Jaguar. It was almost nine o'clock, but I figured Evelyn was still awake so I returned her call from earlier.

"Hello," she answered in a soft tone.

"Are you in bed already?"

"Yes, I am. I've been working a lot of overtime and I'm tired."

"I can understand that, but you've been sleeping a lot lately. You're not pregnant, are you?"

"Hell no, I'm not. I haven't had sex in almost a year. Besides that, you know I've had difficulties with getting pregnant."

"Well, you really need to take care of that D-thing because no woman your age should be without sex. I thought you were thinking about calling Marc again. He was real nice, Evelyn, and I don't think you gave him a fair chance."

"I did, but he failed the test. Nice, but broke. I'm already broke. The last thing I need is a broke man in my life."

"A rich man ain't all that, either, but you didn't hear that tad bit of information from me."

"Yes I did, and you, my sista, have no room to complain. Cedric is a for-real provider, and from what you say, he's pretty darn good in the bedroom too."

"That's fine and dandy, but his sexual capabilities don't matter right now. Do you know that he was late for Jacoby's concert tonight? And when he did get here, coochie was on his breath. Right after he sat next to me I could smell sex on him. Then again, maybe I'm saying these things because I'm upset about his tardiness. I don't know if he's been seeing other women or not, but it's hard for me to believe that he works late all the time."

Like always, Evelyn defended him. "Yeah, you need to stop exaggerating, Kayla. Cedric wouldn't dare come near you like that, and if he does have a little something on the side, so what. Any man who holds it down like he does should be allowed to do whatever he wishes. Instead of griping all the time, you need to be grateful that you're not in my situation—alone and broke. Let me know if you would like to trade places. I'm ready whenever you are."

"I'm not going to entertain your ridiculous comment about him being allowed to do whatever he wishes. The only reason I wouldn't trade places with you is because of my son. So, since we're on very different levels pertaining to this situation, I'm going to change the subject. Have you heard from Trina lately?"

"I spoke to her about two days ago. She just got back from an art show in New York. I'm surprised you haven't spoken to her."

"I've been busy. I'll call her tomorrow. Maybe we can meet for dinner, after church on Sunday."

"Who's cooking? You, me, Trina or Red Lobster?"

"The lobster sounds good, but I may be able to whip up something for us. I'll call to confirm before Sunday."

"Sounds good. Enjoy your evening and tell Cedric I said hello. Jacoby too."

"Will do. See you soon, Evelyn."

We ended our call, which left me in thought about my twenty-three-year friendship with Evelyn and Trina. Lord knows we all have had our ups and downs, but we remained very close. Sometimes, I questioned why because we didn't seem to have much in common. We didn't seem to understand each other at times. As we'd gotten older, the for-real support was lacking in every way possible. All we ever did was compete against each other, but when Cedric started bringing the money in, my whole life changed. I was able to afford the things that they couldn't. Where I lived—the Mansions at Williamson's Estates—couldn't even compare to the apartments they lived in. The cars I drove were very expensive, and while they shopped at the cheaper department stores, most of my clothes came from Saks or Neiman Marcus. I never thought that I was better than either of them, and even though I wasn't as happy as I should have been, I still viewed my life as a blessing. The plus side to our friendships was when I needed to vent, they were both there to listen. When my parents were killed in a car accident, I'll never forget how they stood by me. They were there when I had Jacoby, and since I had no siblings, it was good to have friends who I considered my sisters. Surely, things could be a little better between us, but maybe I was settling for so much BS because I feared having no one to turn to.

Minutes later, I entered the house and could hear Cedric and Jacoby arguing. I wasn't sure what it was about, until I walked into the kitchen and saw them standing face-to-face.

Cedric had a smirk on his face, but Jacoby's forehead was lined with thick wrinkles. I had never seen him look so angry, so I rushed in between them to try and calm the situation.

"What is going on in here?" I asked with a twisted face.

"What's going on is your rotten-ass son wants to be the man of the house. He thinks he can speak to me any way he wishes and I'm not having that shit."

Jacoby fired back. "No, what's really going on is your husband is full of shit! I may as well be the man of the house, because in no way is he representing one."

"One more word, Jacoby, and I swear I'm going to knock you on your ass. No matter how you feel about me, I'm your father and you will respect me!"

"As your son, you need to respect me too. And if you feel a need to get some shit off your chest and knock me on my ass then do it!"

Cedric squeezed his fist, but I placed my hand against his chest. "Stop this," I shouted then looked at Jacoby. "Go to your room and cool out. I'll be in there to talk to you in a minute."

"Yeah, you better get him the fuck away from me," Cedric said. "Listen to your mother, son, she's a very wise woman."

Jacoby shook his head and walked away. "If she was wise, she would leave your sorry ass and find a better man. Unfortunately, Pop, you ain't him."

Cedric rushed around me and ran up to Jacoby. My heart dropped to my stomach when he tightened his fist and punched Jacoby in his face. Several inches taller than Cedric, Jacoby staggered backward, almost falling. When Cedric punched him in his stomach, that was when Jacoby doubled over and dropped to his knees. Cedric stood over him, pointing his finger near Jacoby's face.

"Talk like that will get you killed up in here. Consider this a warning."

Anger crept across my face as I saw Jacoby in pain. I rushed up and pushed Cedric away from him. "You didn't have to put your hands on him!" I shouted. "Can't you deal with your son without invoking violence?"

"No, I can't and if you put your hands on me again, wife or no wife, you're going to see more violence."

Like always, I had to remain the sensible one here, so I ignored Cedric. He stormed away, mumbling underneath his breath. I helped Jacoby off the floor, but he snatched away from me. He held his stomach and limped up the half-circle staircase to his bedroom. I hated to see my family go out like this, and I was anxious to find out what had happened between them in the car. With questions heavy on my mind, I made my way up the steps, but held on to the rail because I felt dizzy. Jacoby's room was next to the bonus room that was used for entertainment. His door was closed, so I knocked.

"Not right now, Mother," he said. "I'm not in the mood to talk."

"Get some rest and we'll talk tomorrow for sure. I thoroughly enjoyed your concert. Keep up the good work, okay?"

There was no response, so I moved away from his door with much sadness in my eyes. As I walked through the double doors to our master suite, I could hear water from the shower running. Cedric's clothes were in a pile on the floor, right next to our California king bed that was accessorized with mahogany and gold silk sheets. With throw pillows on top and with four thick columns surrounding the bed, it looked made for a king and queen. In front of the bed was a fireplace with a TV mounted above it. A small sitting room was to the left, and our humongous walk-in closets were to the right. There was a time when I truly enjoyed being in this room with Cedric. Now, I hated it. I hated being in bed with him, wondering who he had been sharing another bed with. Our backs always faced each other's, and the last time we'd had sex was at least two, maybe three months ago. I could tell that things were getting worse by the day. After what had happened today, I wasn't sure how much more of this I could take.

By the time Cedric came out of the bathroom, I was already in bed with my nightgown on. My braids were tied down with a scarf. I had the remote control in my hand, flipping through the channels.

With a towel wrapped around his waist, Cedric went into his closet to hang his clothes. Minutes later, he got in bed and turned his back to me.

"Aren't you going to tell me what happened between you and Jacoby?" I inquired.

"Why should I tell you? You've already decided to take his side, so what happened between us doesn't really matter."

"I haven't taken anyone's side. All I said was that I didn't appreciate you putting your hands on him."

"And I don't appreciate you telling me how to be his father. You heard that insulting shit he said to me. If you think that it's okay for him to speak to me like that then you're just as fucked-up in the head as he is."

I put the remote down and glared at the back of Cedric's head. "If you want to be his father then you should have started your journey a long time ago. You can't wait until now to show up. He's not hearing you and he's definitely not down with you putting your hands on him at sixteen. Quite frankly, neither am I."

Cedric turned around and tossed the cover aside. "I refuse to stay in this room and listen to your bullshit about how I'm such a bad father. Yo' ass wasn't complaining when I bought that BMW for him last year, you weren't complaining when I paid for him to go to Italy with his classmates, nor were you complaining when I spent almost fifteen thousand dollars on a lavish sixteenth-birthday party that you wanted to have for him, just to impress your friends. Bad parents don't do that kind of shit, so get your facts straight first then we can talk on a level in which you need to be on."

Cedric headed to one of the guest rooms. I shouted out to him as he stomped down the hallway. "You can't buy his love, Cedric. It takes more than money to raise a child and he needs way more than that from you."

He stopped in his tracks, turning to look at me. "Since I have all of the money, why don't you step up your game through nurturing and guiding? After all, we are in this shit together, aren't we?"

I wanted to tell him to kiss my butt, but by then he had already closed the door. I seriously could not go on like this. Something had to change about this situation because I was starting to feel as if I were losing my mind up in here.

Chapter Three

Trina

The room was nearly pitch black, but I could see Lexi claw the sheets and suck in a deep breath. Her silky-smooth legs were wrapped around my neck and the sweet taste of her pussy always left me satisfied.

"More," she said in a soft whisper. "Then it's my turn to do you."

Giving her what she asked for—more—I slipped my tongue deeper into her hot pussy that covered my lips with a light glaze. Lexi rocked her lips against my mouth, and minutes later she expressed her excitement for me.

"I love you so much, Trina. No man has ever made me feel this way."

I knew exactly how Lexi had felt. Been there, done that, and what a waste of time it was. Day by day, I found myself being more attracted to women. I was even attracted to my girl, Evelyn, but if she and Kayla knew my situation they would never have anything to do with me. Even my own mother disowned me and so did my brother. I had no one but Kayla and Evelyn. They were considered my best friends. Still, there were some things I didn't want them to know. They often questioned me about why I rarely brought my male companions around, but to keep their concerns to a minimum I threw some of my male coworkers in the mix and introduced them to my girlfriends. From my coworker Keith to JaQuan, I toyed with them and made them believe I was interested. Truthfully, the only thing I was interested in was tasting more of Lexi and getting her to cum again before the night was over.

Almost an hour later, Lexi and I sat in a bathtub filled with bubbles. She was between my legs and the back of her head rested against my breasts. I lathered her body with soap, using my hands instead of a towel. While massaging her firm breasts, she squirmed around and tilted her head. I placed a trail of delicate kisses down her neck and lowered my hand to touch her stiff bud that peeked out of her coochie lips. Soft music played in the background and two glasses of wine sat on the edge of the tub.

"If you love me like you say you do," Lexi said, "why do you continue to keep our relationship a secret? I'm ready to tell the world how I feel about you. I'm a little disappointed that we've been seeing each other for almost two years and you don't acknowledge me as your woman."

Right then, I removed my finger from Lexi's insides. Sometimes, she griped a little too much for me. It was the wrong time to have this conversation that we had had over and over again. I hated to repeat myself and the last thing I wanted to do was hurt her feelings.

"I already told you why I didn't want to tell anyone about us. I have a lot to lose if I do. I thought you understood why I don't want to go there. My decision to stay quiet has nothing to do with how much I love you. I do, but I know the consequences behind me admitting our situation to others."

Lexi pouted, but then she took my hands, rubbing them together with hers. She remained quiet for a while, but minutes later she stood to get out of the tub. Suds rolled down her blemish-free body and her heart-shaped ass was so perfect that I couldn't allow her to leave. I rubbed up and down her long legs then I separated her ass cheeks as they faced me. She backed up and squatted so I could taste her again. With my fingers in motion too, Lexi shivered all over and cried out my name. We finished up our sex session in bed, and by morning she was on her way out.

Unfortunately for me, though, Lexi bumped right into Evelyn as she opened the door to leave.

Lexi's eyes widened. She searched Evelyn from head to toe. Evelyn peeked through the doorway with a smile plastered on her face. "Is Trina here?"

From in the kitchen, I waved my hand in the air. "I'm over here, Evelyn. Come right in."

Lexi moved aside to let Evelyn in. The look in Lexi's eyes said it all. She was jealous. She couldn't hide it. The twitching of her eyes alarmed me. I had to remind Lexi who Evelyn was so she wouldn't trip.

"Lexi, this is my best friend, Evelyn. Evelyn, this is my coworker, Lexi. She brought me some papers to sign this morning and joined me for breakfast. I guess you're here for breakfast too?"

They spoke to each other, but Evelyn quickly turned her attention to me.

"If you could cook," Evelyn teased, "I would love to join you for breakfast. But all you're going to offer me is cereal and milk, so no thanks."

"You got that right," I said, laughing. "But you're welcome to a bowl of Honey Nut Cheerios. We just had some, and the orange juice—if you want some—is back in the fridge."

Evelyn shook her head, signaling no. She then sat at the kitchen table. I moved toward the door with Lexi who appeared irritated by Evelyn's presence. After I opened the front door, we stepped outside of my apartment.

"So, what's up with you and this Evelyn chick?" Lexi asked then folded her arms across her chest. "Are you sure the two of you are just friends?"

Lexi had no reason to be jealous of Evelyn, because she was just as pretty. The only thing with Lexi was her attitude. At thirty-one, she was five years younger than I was and she was a bit immature.

"I'm positive that the two of us are just friends. Now go before you miss your spa appointment. I'll call you later."

Lexi rolled her big round eyes that were nearly hidden behind her bangs. She tossed her straight, long hair to the side and rushed off with much attitude on display. She was a sexy biracial woman who stood about five feet two. I was happy to have her in my life, but unfortunately, she wasn't the only woman I was attracted to.

I tightened the belt on my sweatpants and pulled down my tank shirt that cut right underneath my breasts. A flowered tattoo flowed across my stomach and a belly ring was clipped to my navel. I always wore my hair short and layered, but it wasn't intact this morning. I hated that it wasn't styled, only because I didn't like to be around Evelyn when I didn't look my best. She was very critical, unlike Kayla, who wasn't— especially not of me.

I went back inside, locking the door behind me. Evelyn was on her cell phone talking to someone, but she rushed to tell the caller she would have to call them back.

"What's up with that Lexi chick?" Evelyn questioned then placed her phone on the table. "She had a real bad attitude."

"She's always like that, so don't take it personal. The people at work complain about her all the time and no one really likes her."

I hated to lie, but I'd gotten pretty used to it. Evelyn nibbled on her nails while looking around. "I like what you've done to this place, but it's a little too colorful in here. These bright yellow walls are working me. I know you got this artistic stuff going on, but you should consider toning it down in here. I feel like I'm back in the seventies or something."

"I knew you would like my orange sectional and purple chairs, but how about you do you and let me do me? I'm sure you didn't come over here to talk about my weird paintings on the walls and how outdated my furniture is. What brings you by this early in the morning?"

Evelyn crossed her long, smooth legs, and then reached into her purse for a cigarette. After she lit it, she whistled smoke into the air and licked her perfect lips. "First of all, I stopped by to see you because I haven't seen you in a few weeks. I also wanted to find out if you were going to Kayla's house for dinner tomorrow. I've been trying to reach you all night, but your phone kept going to voice mail. I came here to check on you in person, just to make sure everything was okay."

I got up from the chair and went to check my phone. It was off the hook. With all the ruckus I caused with Lexi last night, we probably knocked the phone in my bedroom off the hook. I went to my bedroom, and sure enough the phone didn't have a dial tone. I put it back on the charger and then joined Evelyn again in the kitchen. I hated for her to smoke in my apartment. She kept fanning her hands in the air to clear the smoke.

"I don't have much else to do tomorrow, so I guess I will confirm with Kayla today that I'm coming to dinner. I assume she wants us to bring a dish, but whatever you do, please do not make any of that spaghetti you made the last time. That mess was awful."

Evelyn laughed and pursed her lips. "I made it taste bad on purpose. This time, though, I'm going to make a seven-layer salad and call it a day."

I looked up, pondering about what I had in the fridge to put together. Trying to see what, I got up and opened the stainless-steel door to the fridge.

"I . . . I guess I'll make a cheese tray with veggies. I may add some fruit to it too, unless I go to the grocery store and get something else."

"Uh, please do. I like to watch my weight, but my weekends are for splurging. Why don't you make lasagna? The last one you made was fire."

"I would love to make one, but do you see this figure I got?" I put my hands on my waist and twirled around. I was more fit than Evelyn and Kayla, only because I spent a lot of time at the gym working out. The muscles in my arms and abs were tight. "I don't want to ruin what I have going on with this body. When I weighed two-hundred-plus pounds in the eighth grade, you and Kayla couldn't stop teasing me. It took me years to get my weight under control, and lasagna is the last thing I need right now."

"Fine," Evelyn said, throwing her hand back at me. "Stick with the veggie tray and keep that muscle-packed, hourglass figure you got. You sure do have way more hips and ass than I do, but some men like all this slimness, so I'm good."

"Some men," I said, sitting back at the table. "Not all."

"Well, the one who matters does."

"Who may that be this month? And when are we going to meet him?"

"Maybe tomorrow. I may invite him to come with me tomorrow, so please be on your best behavior."

"I will, so no worries."

Evelyn and I sat for the next hour or so talking. I wasn't paying much attention to the conversation, because I was thinking that I didn't want to go to dinner tomorrow by myself. If I did, Evelyn and Kayla would surely question me about why I didn't bring a date. I kept thinking about who to call, Keith or JaQuan. I suspected that they were getting tired of playing this game with me. Both of them had been trying to get closer, but I wasn't having it. I pretended to be interested, but realistically, all they were good for was helping me keep up this front. The date thing wasn't the only thing on my mind. So was Evelyn. Sometimes, I felt uneasy in her presence, considering these crazy feelings I had. I felt terrible for eyeing her sexy lips as she spoke. When she got up to get something to drink, I admired her ass that was fitted into a stretch skirt. I wanted to see her naked—taste her and make love to her like I did Lexi last night. I'd had these feelings for a while—well, more so after I ended a bad relationship with my ex. It was so hard for me to keep this secret, but I had to. I couldn't tell Evelyn that all I wanted was one day with her. Just one. After that, I would want no more.

Evelyn stood and reached for her purse. "Well, it's been real, my friend, but I need to get to the cleaners to pick up my clothes. I wanted to go shopping today, but window shopping won't do."

"I agree. I'm down to my last hundred bucks. I just paid rent and the hundred dollars is all I have left until I get paid again."

Evelyn laughed. "At least you have that. I'm a broke bitch right now, but if I keep on working overtime it should help me get back on my feet. I don't want to borrow any more money from Kayla. I have yet to pay her back the two grand I already owe her."

"I know. I owe her twelve-hundred dollars and she told me to pay her back when I can. I was thinking about hitting her up for a few hundred tomorrow. I need something to help me make it to my next payday."

Evelyn and I let out a deep sigh at the same time. Our financial situations sucked, but I was thankful to Kayla for being there for us. She was a jewel. I really did appreciate our friendship.

After Evelyn left, I picked up the phone, trying to secure a date for tomorrow. Keith wasn't home so I called JaQuan.

"Did I catch you at a bad time?" I asked as I heard loud music in the background.

"No. I'm just stuck in traffic. There was an accident on the highway and nobody is moving."

"Sorry to hear that, but . . . uh . . . I have a question for you. Are you busy tomorrow?"

"Not really. Why? What's up?"

"I wanted to know if you would attend a dinner engagement with me. It's at my girlfriend's house and she invited me to come over."

"Which one of your girlfriends? The rich one or the snobby one?"

"The rich one. The one who is married to Cedric."

"I liked that dude. We had an interesting time at the baseball game that day and he seemed real down-to-earth. I wanted to talk to him about a business venture I'm interested in—so, yeah, I can do that. What time would you like for me to pick you up?"

"Around ten o'clock in the morning. If you don't mind, I'd like to go to church first. Then we can meet up with everyone for dinner."

"That's fine. See you tomorrow, Trina, and thanks for asking me to go with you. You must be my good-luck charm because traffic is finally moving again. Way to go, huh?"

"Yeah. See you soon, JaQuan. Be safe."

The next morning, JaQuan was right on time picking me up. He complimented the brown dress I wore that melted on my curves like a chocolate candy bar. My hair was layered and the makeup I wore dolled-up toffee-colored skin. The gold strappy heels I wore gave me much height; I was almost as tall as JaQuan, who stood almost six feet two. He was a head-turner too. Too bad it didn't do much for me. The good thing was that being around JaQuan was fun, because he was very comical.

We arrived fifteen minutes late for church, but were lucky enough to find seats that provided a clear view of the pulpit.

Pastor Clemons sat in his chair, watching as church folks filled the sanctuary from the first pew to the back. The announcements were being read, and a few minutes later the ushers began to take an offering. When the choir started to sing, several people stood, clapping their hands. The first lady, Cynthia, was always there to show her support. Even though her husband was the biggest player in the church, she stood by him. But the truth was, she wasn't on the up-and-up, either. She had flaws, like many of us who were there to cleanse our souls.

After the choir finished singing, Pastor Clemons approached the podium.

"Amen," he shouted.

"Amen!" the congregation shouted back.

"We have one of the best choirs in St. Louis. Don't forget to get your tickets for the annual concert. When I tell y'all this choir is going to set the roof on fire, I mean it!"

The congregation laughed and clapped their hands. My eyes were focused on Cynthia, who kept turning her head to the side, looking at me. I could see her staring, but I ignored her. JaQuan seemed to pick up on the constant eye gestures, and it didn't surprise me when he leaned in to inquire about Cynthia's actions.

I shrugged my shoulders. "I'm not sure. It looks like she's checking you out."

Of course, she wasn't. Because, like me, the first lady loved women and got excited whenever she saw me. She knew what I was capable of doing to her, and it had been almost a month since we'd had one of our sexual escapades. Cynthia told me that she wanted to call it quits because Pastor Clemons was starting to get suspicious. The last thing she wanted was to lose her status as the first lady. According to her, there were plenty of women waiting to take her place.

No matter what, though, I didn't attend church to see her. I didn't come to judge anyone. I was there to save myself. I knew the way I was living my life wasn't right, and I looked forward to asking God to forgive me, especially on Sunday mornings.

Church let out a few hours later. JaQuan left me standing on the stairs while he went to get the car. That was when Cynthia took the opportunity to approach me.

"Hey there, Sister Watson," she said while holding on to her wide-brim hat that was about to blow off her head. The sun was shining bright, but the wind was gusty. I leaned in to give her a hug and she hurried to whisper in my ear. "I need to see you. Can I stop by tonight?"

I backed away from her, forcing a fake smile. "I'll call you on Wednesday. Maybe we can get together for Bible study. Until then, give Pastor Clemons my love."

I moved quickly down the concrete steps, making my way to the car. Luckily, several other members of the church crowded around the first lady to talk. That way she couldn't come after me. I was glad about that. JaQuan already had a bunch of suspicion in his eyes. The last thing I needed was for him to dig deeper into what was really going on between me and the first lady at Stone Mount Baptist Church.

Chapter Four

Evelyn

To be honest, I was not looking forward to dinner at Kayla's house, but what the hell? I didn't want her to suspect anything between me and Cedric. The best thing I could do was show up with a man and pretend that he was my lover, instead of her husband. I hadn't spoken to Cedric since the other day, but like Trina, I was also low on cash. After rent was taken care of, that didn't leave me with any money to play with. I needed something in my pockets, especially since I saw these Jimmy Choo shoes I wanted yesterday while browsing the mall. Having nothing else to do yesterday, I went ahead and drove to the mall. I wished Trina had gone with me. It seemed as if she needed to get out and have some fun. But when you're broke, getting out and doing things was hard to do. I definitely knew where she was coming from, and I looked forward to the day when the two of us would get out of the ruts we were in.

Marc, the poor excuse of a man I elected to take with me as a date, said his car was in the shop, so I went to his house to pick him up. We had dated several years ago and still kept in touch. We made great phone buddies, but a relationship we could never have again. We couldn't seem to click and we argued more than anything. The only time we got together was when he needed to showcase me around his family and friends. I used him for the same reasons, so he wasn't too enthused when I called and invited him to attend dinner with me. There wasn't a chance in hell that I was going to this dinner alone. I had to show Cedric that I wasn't as hooked on him as he thought I was. I was hooked on his money more than anything, and maybe—just maybe—a little hooked on his sex too.

Marc had been running his mouth the whole time in the car. He looked decent in his jeans and polo shirt, but the smell of his breath was tearing up my nostrils. His bald head had a shine to it and his tinted sunglasses covered his hazelnut-colored eyes. His body was sculptured like a linebacker, and my only other complaint was his dingy tennis shoes that needed to be washed with Tide.

"Am I allowed to kiss you while we're here?" he asked as I was only five minutes away from Kayla's and Cedric's house.

"No, you're not. Do not hug or touch me, either. Just be friendly and say nice things about me."

"Now, that's going to be hard for me to do," he said with a smile. "I don't know too many nice things about you, so you may have to help me out with this."

I rolled my eyes, even though I figured Marc was joking around. A few minutes later, I pulled into the arched driveway in front of their two-story brick house. The bay windows were sparkling clean, the bushes were neatly trimmed, and beautiful tulips were starting to bloom. The grass was well manicured and the outside of their home looked fit for the cover of *Better Homes and Gardens* magazine. Three other cars were already there, but I wasn't sure who they belonged to. Before we exited the car, I reached in my purse to offer Marc a stick of gum.

"Thank you," he said, reaching for it. "I was going to ask if you had any gum. You must have read my mind."

Good thing he couldn't read mine. All I did was smile and check my beautifulness in the rearview mirror. The curls in my hair were working for me, my makeup was done to perfection, and the summer orange skirt I wore matched my thong sandals. My white sleeveless tank stretched across my breasts and a simple gold necklace I wore matched my hoop earrings. I felt great about my appearance, even though Marc had failed to acknowledge how spectacular I looked. That was another thing that I hated about him. He was so into himself that he didn't have anything good to say about anyone else. I could only laugh to myself. I guess the same could be said about me.

With the seven-layer salad in my hands, I rang the doorbell and looked through the double glass doors that viewed the loveliness of the house. The marble-topped foyer could be seen, as well as a hanging chandelier. I saw Jacoby walking down the circular staircase and then Kayla appeared with a welcoming smile on her face. As she opened the door, I checked her out. She had on a white linen jumpsuit, accessorized with silver jewelry. Her long braids were pulled away from her face and I couldn't deny that she had the prettiest round eyes I had ever seen. She was such a classy lady and her sweet perfume smelled a whole lot better than Marc's breath. I leaned in to air kiss her cheeks then I thanked her for inviting us.

"You remember Marc, don't you?" I said, looking at his lust-filled eyes that were glued to Kayla.

Marc reached for Kayla's hand, kissing the back of it. "Of course she remembers me. Hello, beautiful," he said.

Kayla blushed, but pulled her hand away from him. "Hi there, Marc. Come on back to the kitchen. We should be ready to eat in about another hour or so. Please make yourselves at home."

How I wished I could make this my home. Kayla had it made, yet she seemed so ungrateful. I never understood why she always seemed so unhappy, either. If I had it like this, all of my problems and worries would be solved. In addition to that, she had a good-looking man to wake up to every morning. Not a man in off-brand tennis shoes that were dirty like Marc's were.

Either way, we followed Kayla into the immaculate kitchen that was every woman's dream come true. A granite-topped island sat in the middle of the floor and the hardwood floors had a shine that showed my reflection. An apple pie was baking in the double oven, along with rotisserie chicken that I couldn't wait to tear into. Another salad was already on top of the island and so were an array of desserts, vegetables, pastas, and fruit.

Trina sat at the oval-shaped table next to a man who I had seen her with twice before. He was rather cute to me. I preferred to have him as my date than Marc. Cedric looked spectacular in his cargo shorts, Nike shirt, and cap. He looked up to speak then lowered his head to read the golf magazine that was on his lap. Trina introduced me to JaQuan, and then she got up to acknowledge me. I placed the salad on the island before I embraced her.

"Good seeing you again," she said. "I hope that salad you made is better than the one Kayla made."

"I doubt it," Kayla said.

"We'll just have to see about that, won't me?" I shot back, but was serious about my salad tasting much better than hers.

We laughed and walked over to the table to sit. The only person who hadn't joined us was Jacoby. He spoke to us in a dry tone then headed back upstairs.

I looked across the table at Kayla, who was sitting next to Cedric. "What's wrong with Jacoby? I've never seen him look so glum. Is that a bruise on the side of his face?"

Kayla and Cedric looked at each other. After rolling her eyes at him, she quickly spoke up.

"Jacoby and one of his so-called friends were wrestling and he got punched. Besides that, he's a sixteen-year-old with a chip on his shoulder."

"No, he's a sixteen-year-old who needs to get his shit together," Cedric added. "That's what his problem is."

No one at the table bought that bullshit. It was obvious that Cedric was responsible for the mark on Jacoby's face, but I wasn't going to question why Cedric wasn't getting along with his disrespectful son. That was their business.

The men at the table started a heated conversation about how the young men were conducting themselves these days. I didn't have much to add because I had no children and I didn't plan on having any, either. For whatever reason, Kayla didn't appreciate where the conversation was going. She kept rolling her eyes and sighing every time Cedric said something.

"Can we please change the subject?" she suggested. "I can tell you why I think many of the young men out there act the way they do, but I don't want to hurt anyone's feelings."

I could sense something between her and Cedric. Just to spark up a heated conversation between them, I encouraged Kayla to speak up when I added my two cents.

"I mean, I think it has a lot to do with these boys being fatherless," I said. "And some of the absent fathers need to take responsibility."

"I agree," Kayla said. "And some have fathers who don't know how to be fathers. It's a mess. I'm just doing the best that I can with Jacoby."

"Yeah, *we* are," Cedric said, correcting her. "I hear what both of y'all are saying, but there are some lazy women out there half-ass raising boys too. And when the men try to step up, they got issues with it. I think it's wrong to put the blame solely on the men, especially when some mothers need to get their shit together."

Of course the other men agreed, but I knew that Marc had no room to talk. He wasn't even paying child support. All he did was gripe about his son's mother begging for money, so he needed to shut the fuck up. Cedric was holding his family down, but I didn't necessarily see that father-and-son connection between him and Jacoby. And based on what Kayla had said, Cedric was slacking. I wasn't sure what was up with JaQuan, but maybe I would get to know a little more about him after dinner was over.

Trina and I got up to help Kayla in the kitchen. The men continued their conversation, but every now and then Cedric and I kept taking peeks at each other. I hoped we weren't being too obvious, but I wondered if he had those naughty thoughts swarming around in his head like I'd had. Needing some extra cash, I had to figure out a way to get him away from everyone before I left.

Dinner was ready and we all circled the island, holding hands. Trina blessed the food and everyone got a plate to pile it with food. Cedric filled our flute glasses with wine and Kayla made sure that we all had everything we needed. She was such a good host and she was at the top of her game when it came to being organized. Jacoby didn't join us, but as soon as we all sat at the table to eat, he came into the room with the same long look on his face.

"Do you mind if I go over to Adrianne's house?" he asked Kayla.

"I don't care, Jacoby. Only for a few hours."

Jacoby nodded and then turned to walk away. That was when Cedric spoke up. "She said only for a few hours. That doesn't mean you need to stroll up in here at midnight. If you do, you're going to find yourself on punishment."

Jacoby shrugged. "There is no reason for you to be co-signing, because I heard what she said. If I'm going to be late, like always, I'll call."

Cedric wasn't backing down. "If you heard what she said then that means don't be late. If you are, a punishment will be enforced. Period. End of discussion."

"Whatever. I'm out."

Cedric didn't appreciate his tone, and quite frankly, neither did I. He was about to get out of his chair, but Kayla reached for his arm. "Would you please stay seated and let him get out of here? I'm trying to enjoy dinner with my guests, and I don't have time to entertain a dispute between you and Jacoby."

Cedric snatched his arm away from Kayla and got up anyway. She didn't have enough power to tell that man what to do, and it was so apparent that he was the one in charge around here.

"Jacoby," Cedric shouted after him, halting his steps. "Don't you *whatever* me. You'd better listen to me when I speak. Understand?"

Jacoby's whole face was twisted. He didn't say another word, but the look in his eyes showed much hatred for his father.

"As I was saying," Cedric continued. "Since you got an attitude, you don't need to go anywhere right now. Go chill out in your room and think about how you need to get at me."

We all watched, holding our breaths. Kayla was so embarrassed that she dropped her napkin on the table and got up to go intervene. "Just let him get out of here, Cedric. We have guests right now and this is seriously the wrong time."

"Wrong time," Cedric said. "Maybe so. I'd hate for anyone to see me beat that ass, and just so you know, you're never too old for me to do it. Now, get the hell out of here before I change my mind."

Jacoby didn't flinch. He released a light snicker and walked away. Kayla and Cedric returned to the table, and it was obvious that things were very heated around here. Everyone's eyes shifted around the table and we were quite speechless. I was a little relieved when JaQuan spoke up and changed the subject.

"Well, on a more positive note, Trina and I are getting married," he said.

All heads snapped in his direction. Trina's jaw was dropped and her mouth was wide open. "What?" she shouted. "Uh, I don't think so. Where did that breaking news come from?"

JaQuan laughed and sipped from his glass of wine. "Calm down," he said, laughing. "I'm just kidding. Thought I'd say something that would get us off that rocky path and on to another one."

Trina didn't find any humor in what JaQuan had said. She turned to him and got to the point. "I didn't find your little joke funny. Next time, I would appreciate if you wouldn't include me in it."

JaQuan shrugged his shoulders and didn't seem to trip. I didn't know what was going on, but this setting wasn't working for me. I was so glad that Marc had kept his mouth shut, but I guess my thoughts were too soon.

"Kayla, I must admit," he said, "the food is dynamite and you truly outdid yourself. You're going to have to invite me over here more often, or I need to invite you to my crib so you can come cook for me."

I dropped my fork. His comment was very disrespectful and all Cedric did was stare at him from across the table. Kayla blushed, obviously loving the attention. "Thank you, Marc. I will invite you over again—and wait until you taste my meat loaf. I'll cook that next time."

He was all smiles and had the audacity to lick his lips. "That's what's up. I would love to come over here again. And FYI, I cook too. Maybe I can show you a few of my good recipes and you can hook me up in return."

"Sounds good to me. I love it when people hook me up."

They laughed, but neither I nor Cedric heard shit funny. He cocked his head back, looking at Kayla's ol' disrespectful ass. "Hook you up? Really? Well, before you hook him up, you need to hook me up. Hook me up with some daily meals, some back rubs, and with some pussy. Can you handle that for me, Mrs. Wifey?"

Before Kayla could respond, Cedric looked across the table at Marc, who had paused from eating his food. "This dinner will probably be over with real soon. Until then, watch what you say to my wife. I don't appreciate the disrespect and the fact is, she won't be hooking you up, nor will you be hooking her up with shit. No one comes here unless I invite them . . . so it doesn't look like you'll be visiting us anytime in the near future."

I was a little jealous about Cedric's "wife" comment. Did he really care? Maybe he was jealous, but why? Marc was very out of line. He couldn't compete with Cedric, and I always admired how Cedric handled himself. Listening to him put Marc in his place made my pussy wet. He'd have to take care of that little problem for me real soon.

"I didn't mean any disrespect," Marc said. "I was just complimenting her food. It's been a long time since I had a meal like this one, and the women I've dated can't touch this. Her cooking makes me feel like I'm at home . . . like when I'm at my mother's house. That's all I was saying and it wasn't about me trying to hook her up with anything else."

"Thank you for clearing that up, Marc," Kayla said, rolling her eyes. "I don't know why anyone would assume we were talking about anything other than food."

She played clueless, but Cedric and I knew better. Marc did as well. I felt as if the stanky-breath fool insulted me. I knew where he was going with his comment about not having a good meal, and it was his way of not saying anything nice about me as I had asked.

"It's a good thing that we never got around to dating each other," I said. "Because had we done so, you would know that I can cook my butt off. I do so at times, especially for the men who mean a lot to me."

I couldn't help but to look at Cedric, referring to how well I cooked for him. Right then, though, I felt someone's foot rub against my leg. I thought it was Cedric's foot, but he had an irritated look locked on his face like he was so done with this dinner. My eyes shifted from one person to the next. Trina was the only one looking at me. I blinked fast and the foot rubbing stopped.

"Is that you?" she questioned. "I thought you were JaQuan. Forgive me."

Everyone looked at us, not knowing what was going on. My leg didn't feel like JaQuan's. Trina needed to correct herself, because she was about to get cussed out for rubbing her feet on me. I got back to my food, admitting to myself that everything was delicious. JaQuan and Trina raved about the food, but the last thing Kayla needed was for me to swell her head even more. She definitely wouldn't get any praise from me.

The next hour was filled with jabs, conversation, and laughter. Once dinner was done, the men headed downstairs to the entertainment room to play pool while me, Trina, and Kayla stayed in the kitchen to clean up. I couldn't help but to ask Kayla what was going on between her and Cedric. Whatever was going on she pretended like everything was all good.

"We're just a married couple who have minor issues that can be worked out. It's really nothing, but I'm hoping that him and Jacoby reconcile their differences soon."

"I hope so too," Trina said. "It seemed like things were about to turn ugly."

Kayla refused to go any further. She continued to stack the dishes in the dishwasher while I packed up the leftovers and put them in the fridge. Trina cleared the table and wiped it down, along with the countertops.

After the kitchen was spotless, we joined the men downstairs. I kept thinking of a way to get Cedric alone, but he seemed immersed with shooting pool.

For the time being, I sat on the leather sectional and watched a reality TV program with Trina and Kayla. We couldn't stop talking about how ridiculous the women were, but to be honest, the reality shit was going on right in this room.

Cedric must've read my mind when he told Kayla he was going upstairs to return a business phone call. I saw it as the perfect opportunity for me to step away, and while Marc and JaQuan started another game of pool, and Trina and Kayla's eyes were glued to the TV, I announced my departure.

"I'm going outside to smoke." I knew Kayla wouldn't allow me to smoke in her house. "I'll be right back."

"Hurry, because I'm not going to rewind this until it's over," Kayla said. "You're going to miss the new chick getting slapped. I think it's coming up next."

"I'm sure y'all will tell me all about it when I get back."

They assured me that they would.

I made my way upstairs to find Cedric. The moment I reached the top stair, he was standing by the kitchen counter, waiting. He placed one finger over his lips, as a gesture for me to be quiet. He then nudged his head toward the garage door and walked toward it. I followed. Inside of the five-car garage was a fleet of lavish cars that belonged to him and Kayla. The only spot that was empty was the spot where Jacoby parked his car. Cedric unlocked the car and he opened the back door to his Rolls-Royce that provided plenty of room in the back-seat.

"Are you serious?" I whispered to him. "We're just going to talk, aren't we?"

"Ay, that's all I want to do, unless you have something else in mind like *hooking me up*."

We laughed and I got in the backseat with him. Talking wasn't in our plans. His hands eased up my skirt, and the moment his fingers slipped into my wetness, I turned on my stomach. Cedric unzipped his pants and flipped up the back of my skirt. He moved my thong to the side and filled my hot pocket with his hard, thick meat that always guaranteed me an orgasm.

"You know I'm jealous," Cedric whispered in my ear while long stroking me from behind. My ass was hiked up and the sounds of my pussy juices made him aware that he was hitting the right spot.

"Jealous of who or *whaaaat*?" I moaned. "You have *noooo* reason to be jealous. I'm the one who is jealous. Jealous of Kayla for getting a piece of this whenever she wants to."

"You can have a piece whenever you want to. Just ask for it. And the next time you come over here, leave the broke-look-ing joker at home. He's an embarrassment and I know you can do much better."

"I can. That's why I'm doing it with you and not with him."

Cedric tore into my insides and rushed me to the finish line so we could hurry to go back inside. The car rocked fast from the speed of our action, but as soon as I opened my mouth to react to him busting my cherry, the garage door lifted. Cedric covered my mouth with his hand and we dropped low on the floor in the backseat. My pussy was dripping wet from a mixture of our juices, and the feel of Cedric's dick still in me felt spectacular.

For whatever reason, I was hoping that Kayla would see us. It wasn't that I hated her or anything like that. I had just lost a lot of respect for an ungrateful bitch who didn't realize or appreciate what she had. Cedric peeked through the tinted windows and whispered to me that it was Jacoby, not Kayla. He waited until Jacoby was inside before he hit me with a few more strokes that tickled my insides and gave me something more to smile about. He had definitely gotten what he wanted, but now it was time for me to get what I wanted.

"Before we go back inside, I need to ask you for a favor. I know you're getting tired of me, but until I find another job, I don't—"

"How much," Cedric said then planted a kiss on my cheek.

"Several hundred dollars. Whatever you can spare is fine with me. Anything will help me right about now."

"I'll transfer the money into your account in the morning. And don't be ashamed to ask me for money. We have to look out for each other."

No doubt we did. I was very appreciative of Cedric's generosity. Like always, he came through for me and I intended to always come through for him.

Ten minutes later, Cedric and I entered the house as if nothing had gone on between us. We returned to the basement together, telling Kayla and Trina that he took me to his office to show me his collection of autographed baseballs he had from several St. Louis Cardinals players.

"Evelyn didn't believe how much my balls were worth," Cedric said. "I had to prove to her, as well as show her that they were worth a lot."

His balls were definitely worth a lot—to me they were. I was on a serious high from what had transpired, but when I checked my account the next morning, I was pissed. Cedric had only deposited a hundred dollars, when I clearly said *several* hundred were needed. I called to chew him out, but unfortunately for me his voice mail came on. Cheap bastard. I thought . . . oh, no, he didn't. I checked my account again, realizing . . . oh, yes, he did.

Chapter Five

Kayla

These ongoing arguments between me and Cedric were getting on my nerves. They were embarrassing and we were starting to lose too much respect for each other. I wanted to calm things down and see if we could somehow start working on our marriage that was falling apart. I knew that Cedric would never agree to counseling, but we had to do something to get our lives back on track. Jacoby was being affected by this. I couldn't sit by much longer and watch our family being torn apart.

Cedric was at work, so I decided to take him lunch so we could talk. I wasn't sure how late he was working tonight, and I was ready to get some of my concerns off my chest. When I arrived at his office, dressed in a long, multicolored sundress and sandals, the bubbly receptionist directed me to go ahead on back to his office.

"He should be in there," she said, checking me out from head to toe. She also looked envious of me, but she didn't have to worry about me being envious of her. She was a trashy-looking white chick who one of Cedric's partners had offered the position to. I wasn't sure if Cedric's partner, John, was involved with her or not, but he did have a wife who I knew very well.

As I approached the door to Cedric's office, I could hear him speaking to someone over the phone. He spoke in a light whisper, but busted into a fit of laughter a few times. I heard him refer to the caller as "sweetheart" and not knowing if he was flirting or not, I entered his office with a forced smile on my face. He was leaned back in his chair with the phone up to his ear. The noticeable hump in his pants surprised me and the smile on his face vanished.

He slowly sat up, clearing his throat. "Uh, let me call you back later. I need to take care of something right now."

Not waiting for a response, Cedric put the phone down and looked at the bags in my hand.

"I thought you might want some lunch," I said. "But if you're busy, I can always come back."

"Nah, I'm good. That was just someone I'm trying desperately to close a business deal with. Have a seat and thanks for thinking of me."

"I always think of you, Cedric. Whether you know it or not."

I sat in the chair in front of his desk and opened one of the bags. I pulled out a turkey sandwich, some chips, an apple, and a diet Coke. I baked some chocolate chip cookies too, so I laid those on the desk as well.

"I feel like a school kid," he said with a smile. "Please tell me what I did to deserve this, Mom?"

"Sarcasm will get you nowhere with me. Now eat up and let's talk about what has been going on with our marriage."

Cedric bit into the apple and leaned back in his chair. He gazed at me from across his desk, narrowing his eyes. "You look nice," he complimented. "But as far as our marriage goes, what about it?"

"I can't believe you have to ask." I opened my can of diet Coke and took a sip. "We've been arguing day in and out. I don't think you're happy anymore, and I'm here to ask if you want a divorce."

Cedric sat silent for a few seconds. He bit into the apple again and chewed. "No, I don't want a divorce. I admit to not being completely happy, but you're not happy, either."

"No, I'm not. We really need to do something about this because I don't like how we're treating each other. I'm willing to do whatever I must do to correct our problems, but you need to tell me what it is that you need from me. Then I'll share what I need from you. We have to work at improving on the things that are hindering us from growing together in a respectful and healthy marriage."

"I would love to talk about all of that, but why talk about it here? You know that I have work to do, Kay. We'll have to discuss this when I get home."

"That's fine, only if you're coming home at a decent hour. Are you working late tonight?"

"As of right now I'm not. But I'll do my best to be there by seven."

"Seven o'clock is fine. That way I'll have time to talk to Jacoby before you get there and see if he'll go hang out with his friends tonight so we can have some privacy."

"Sounds like a plan."

Cedric and I ate lunch together in peace. Before I left, he gave me a peck on the lips and patted my ass as I walked out the door. He didn't know that I had an earful for him tonight. Maybe it was a good thing that we didn't have our conversation on his job, because I expected things to get heated.

When I arrived home, I waited for Jacoby while watching TV in the family room. He was late, and when I called his cell phone he told me that he stayed after school.

"After I get done with band practice, do you mind if I go to Adrianne's house for dinner? Her mother invited me to come over and then we want to go to the mall. I promise not to stay out late, and I'll have my cell phone available if you need to reach me."

"I don't mind. Have a good time and tell Adrianne's mother I said hello."

"I will."

I sat on the couch thinking about Jacoby. He was a good kid. Any bad behavior that he had been representing was due to what was transpiring at home. He had a look in his eyes like he hated his father. I was going to do my best to change things around.

By seven o'clock, Cedric wasn't there. He finally came home close to eight. I waited for him to eat dinner then he joined me in the family room. Still dressed in his suit, he sat on the couch next to me and wiped his mouth with a napkin.

"Okay, Kay, tell me what's on your mind."

"I plan to, but I would like to start with you telling me what you expect or want from me. I assume I'm making some mistakes. I don't know what they are unless you tell me."

Cedric's cell phone rang and he pulled it from his pocket to see who it was. He winced then slipped the phone back into his pocket. "For the most part, my only problem with you is how you interfere in my relationship with Jacoby. I don't appreciate how you take his side all the time, and for so many years you have tried to tell me how to be a father. That's an insult to me. I don't need your assistance and your behavior has caused me to put up a wall between me and my son. I'm real pissed about it too. What I need for you to do is back off and support me sometimes."

"I can do that, okay. I do understand where you're coming from and I have made some mistakes pertaining to that. Forgive me for not being supportive. I hope it's not too late for the two of you to fix things."

Cedric shrugged. "We'll see. I was thinking about asking him to join me next weekend on a business trip so we can talk. Just me and him, without you."

"That's fine with me. I'm sure I can find something to do while the two of you are away."

"I'm sure you can too, but whatever you do, please don't invite Marc over here to feed him. Don't invite Trina over here, either."

My brows shot up. I was surprised to hear Cedric say that about her. "Why wouldn't I invite Trina over here? She's my best friend and she is always welcome into my home."

"She should be welcomed, but not when I'm not here. I prefer to keep my eyes on her, if you know what I mean."

"No, I don't know what you mean. Please explain yourself to me, because I don't know why you feel a need to keep your eyes on Trina."

Cedric stood and stretched. "Baby, come on. You've been knowing Trina for many, many years. Don't sit there and tell me that you don't know she's gay."

My eyes bugged and mouth opened wide. "What? Have you lost your doggone mind? Trina is far from being gay. Why would you say that about her?"

"Because I know a gay woman when I see one. Like always, she didn't have no connection with her date and they barely talked to each other. They didn't even touch and he was almost like some kind of prop for her. In addition to that, I've never seen her checking me out. Whenever a woman doesn't look at me, I know something is wrong with her."

I pursed my lips and threw my hand back at him. "If you think Trina is gay because she doesn't look at you, you're a fool. She doesn't show interest because you just happen to be married to her best friend. Stop being so arrogant and full of yourself, Cedric. Some women may not find you attractive, and I've never heard either of my BFF's rave about you."

"Just because they don't rave, it doesn't mean they're not interested. You need to start paying closer attention to things, and only when you open your eyes will you really see what is going on with your friends."

"Right now I'm not interested in what is going on with my friends. I'm more interested in what is going on with my husband. I want to tell you some of the things I need from you too, and I hope that you don't take me the wrong way."

Cedric didn't respond. He sat back on the couch and faced me to listen.

"First, I've suspected for a long time that you've been having extramarital affairs. I don't have any proof that you have been, but if you are, I want you to end whatever it is that you have going on outside of our marriage. I also want you to think before you speak. Some of the things that you say to me are very harsh. I don't appreciate being disrespected by my own husband. You already know how I feel about your relationship with Jacoby, and I hope you're willing to do whatever to correct it. Lastly, I appreciate you for providing for us, but in addition to money, I need to be shown some love too. You rarely do anything spontaneous or kind for me anymore. I would be very appreciative if we could have sex more often. Is that asking for too much?"

Cedric pulled off his jacket and laid it on the arm of the couch. He looked at me with much seriousness in his eyes. "I'm going to say this to you one time and one time only. I am not cheating on you and I will never cheat on you. There are times when I flirt with women, talk to women or even have dinner with women. Sometimes, I do that shit to enhance my business relationships with them, but you have my word that I have not been intimate with any other woman than you.

"As for my mouth, what can I say other than it gets slick at times. You knew that before you married me, and depending on the situation, there are times when I can't control what I say. I will, however, try to control myself, but I can't make you any promises. I will work things out between me and Jacoby, but just remember what I said and back off. When it comes to us having sex, that's on you, baby. You've been the one holding back on the pussy, and I need to be presented with some spontaneous, thrilling shit too. You are just as boring as I am in the bedroom, so don't blame me for our sex life not being what it should be."

"I thought it wasn't what it should be because you've been intimate with other women. I want to believe you, Cedric, but it's so hard to when I know you have conversations with them, they call you, and you're always coming home late."

"Baby, I am late because I work hard to keep all of this you see around you. You need to stop assuming things and accusing me of doing stuff that I'm not doing. You have never caught me doing anything. It's so unfair to me if you're thinking all of that craziness in your head. That's where the problem lies between us. You need to get that craziness out yo' head and start giving me some credit."

Could I have been wrong about him? That was a possibility, especially since I had never caught him in the act doing anything. I had definitely been assuming a lot, only because my gut had been signaling that something was very wrong.

For now, I had to trust what Cedric had said. We agreed to work on our marriage and see what we could do better to repair it. The repair process started that night. While Cedric was in the shower, I hurried into my closet to put on something sexy. I opted for a ruby red, lace negligee with diamond studs that lined the breasts area. The negligee revealed most of my privates, including my nipples that were visible through the lace. The crotch section slipped between my shaved coochie lips, and the mountains on my smooth ass looked squeezable. I wanted to spice things up, so I lit some candles then dimmed the lights. I sprayed my body with dashes of sweet perfume, and then put on some slow, jazzy music to set the mood.

Cedric opened the doors to the bathroom with shock in his eyes. I smiled while lying sideways on the bed, where he had a clear view of my ass. He moistened his lips with his tongue then dropped the towel that was around his waist to the floor. His dick rose to its full potential and he glided up to the side of the bed.

"Now, that's what I'm talking about," he said, reaching out to rub my ass. He squeezed and massaged it, right along with my thick thighs. I had to turn my body around to face him, just so he could look between my legs and see what his touch was capable of doing to me. While he appeared to be in a trance, I switched positions on the bed and opened my legs. I felt the crotch of my negligee ease further into my slit and I suspected that Cedric got a glimpse of my moist folds.

"Sometimes," he said, "I forget how sexy you really are."

I felt the same way about him, but didn't say a word. Cedric rubbed his fingers against my walls then he pushed his fingers further inside, causing me to tighten my eyes and suck in a heap of air. I was on fire as he rotated his fingers inside of me, and my creamy fluids trickled between the crack of my ass. Seconds later, Cedric replaced his finger with his steel. It had been a while since we indulged ourselves, so I jerked slightly backward from the feel of his pleasing muscle.

"Don't act like you can't handle this," he said. "You've had it in your possession for years. You already know what to do with it."

Darn right I did. And once I got comfortable, I spread my legs wider, gripped his tight butt, and grinded my hips in circles. My glaze covered Cedric's entire shaft, and I toyed with my own clit while he watched. His eyes were filled with lust, and his deep strokes slowed as he attempted to calm his heartbeat and catch his breath.

"I—I don't know what to say about you, Kay. Other than you doing it, baby, you straight-up got that pussy doing the damn thing."

He didn't have to tell me, because I already knew it. I purposely stepped up my game. I wanted to let Cedric know that there was no reason for him to seek sexual pleasure elsewhere, especially when I was capable of providing him with all of the loving he needed. But I wasn't the only one at the top of my game. So was he. He had lifted me up from the bed and held me in his arms. My legs were secured around Cedric's waist as he backed me up to the wall and slammed his dick into me. I was going crazy as our naked bodies slapped together. My backside was being banged against the wall and when a picture fell, we both ignored it. I focused on the way he sucked my breasts and squeezed them. The way he grinded inside of me, milking my pussy for all that it could give to him. I wanted to give him more, but the dick was so good that my body weakened in his arms. My legs trembled and my fists pounded into the wall as I neared another orgasm.

"Give it to me, baby," Cedric said while lifting me to his broad shoulders. I held on tight and sprayed his lips with juices. He cleaned me up, but we were back at it again.

This time, I was bent over a chair, trying to catch my breath. We were still going at it when Jacoby came home. He knocked on the bedroom door to let us know he had made it in. I hoped that he didn't hear me screaming at the top of my lungs for Cedric to "fuck me harder," but I couldn't control the excitement my husband brought to the bedroom. This was long overdue. We had exhausted ourselves and Cedric wound up falling asleep with his dick resting comfortably inside of me.

The next day, I drove to Trina's apartment to see her. She seemed kind of quiet during dinner on Sunday, and she was known for always being the one who kept the conversation flowing. She also whispered to me that she needed to borrow some money, but I forgot to follow up with her. My mind was on other things that night, and they were also on what Cedric had said about her. He couldn't have been more wrong. If Trina was gay, I was born a dog.

I arrived at her apartment around noon. Trina did most of her art projects from her extra bedroom that she had turned into a studio. Her apartment was rather small, but she had given the place new life with colorful pictures and furniture. I knocked on the door. A few minutes later she opened it. She looked surprised to see me and she had a paintbrush in her hand. Her sweatpants had paint blotches on them and the tank shirt she wore revealed her toned arms. A scarf was wrapped around her hair, keeping it intact.

"What's been up with you and Evelyn's pop-up visits? First her, now you."

She widened the door to let me in. I could tell her comment was playful because she and Evelyn always showed up at my house unannounced too.

"I see you're busy painting and everything, but I stopped by because I wanted to find out what was going on with you. You also mentioned that you needed some money. How much?"

Trina closed the door and invited me into her living room to sit. "I'm doing okay. I just wish I didn't have to bother you about money all the time, but you know I don't have anywhere else to turn."

"I know and trust me when I say it's no bother. If the shoe were on the other foot, I know you'd do the same thing for me. Now, how much do you need?"

"Just a couple hundred dollars."

I removed my checkbook from my purse and wrote Trina a check for three hundred dollars. She smiled when I handed it over to her.

"Thank you. Now is there anything that I can do for you? You never ask me or Evelyn for anything. I want you to know that we're here for you as well."

"I get that, and all I need sometimes is somebody to talk to. I had some concerns with Cedric, but the two of us worked it out last night. I'm feeling much better now. I have a feeling that my marriage is back on track."

"That's good to know. After all that appeared to be going on with him and Jacoby, I thought Cedric found out about your little secret. He still doesn't know, does he?"

Hearing Trina speak of my secret caused my heart to drop to my stomach. This was something we weren't supposed to talk about. It was one of those things that needed to stay in the past.

"No, he doesn't know and he will never know that Jacoby isn't his son. They've had some issues lately that I expect them to work out real soon."

"I hope they do. You know, I always said your decision not to tell them the truth would come back and bite you in the butt one day. I hope I'm wrong."

Thinking about it was starting to give me a headache. I hurried to change the subject, and thought about what Cedric said to me about Trina last night.

"I know you're wrong, but anyway, can I tell you what Cedric had the audacity to say to me last night? It nearly floored me and I couldn't stop laughing."

"What? What did he say?"

"He said that he thought you were gay. His reason was because you never pay him any attention, and he said that you never show a connection with the men you bring around us. Now, tell me how full of himself my husband really is."

Trina shook her head and laughed. "Very much so full of himself. I don't see how you put up with his arrogant self, and for him to think such a thing is crazy. I am strictly dickly. There isn't anything that a woman can do for me. Period."

We high-fived each other and laughed again.

"I do think your husband is extremely fine, but I'm not the kind of person who will fall all out over a nice-looking man. I think that Cedric's ugly ways are what makes me not compliment his fineness, yet he may be onto something when he mentioned my connection with men. I tend to choose the wrong men. JaQuan and I had a disagreement before we got to your house, so we weren't speaking to each other that much. I'm not sure if I'm going to keep seeing him, and when I go into the studio tomorrow, I may call it off with him. I don't like how aggressive he is. When we have sex, he doesn't put enough into pleasing me."

"Yes, that's something that is very important, so I do know where you're coming from. I'm delighted that my arrogant and full-of-himself husband knows what he's doing in the bedroom. That's definitely a plus. Pertaining to the gay thing, I hope I didn't offend you. But in my opinion, I think two women sexing each other is so nasty. How can a woman give another sexual pleasure? I try not to judge people who get down like that, and I felt insulted when he spoke about you in that manner."

"I'm not offended at all. I think gays are pretty darn disgusting too. But what other people do in the privacy of their own homes is not any of my business. If they like it, I love it."

"Well, I don't like it or love it. But you're right. It has nothing to do with me."

Trina called me crazy and we continued to share good conversation. What I'd said didn't appear to bother her, but my friends were known for going back on things and calling you out on it later. I wasn't sure if Trina would throw this back at me later, but I was positive that somewhere down the road she would tell me that I hurt her feelings.

I left Trina's house around three o'clock. I wanted to get home to cook for Jacoby and Cedric, but when I got in the car I sat for a while, thinking. When Cedric and I were in college, I wanted to be with him so badly that I stopped taking my pills and did my best to get pregnant. But while I was seeing him, I had also been seeing someone else. His name was Arnez, but I didn't have feelings for him like I had for Cedric. Cedric had a good head on his shoulders, and I suspected that he would do right by his child and take good care of him. Arnez was a thug. He dropped out of college, had several other baby mamas and he started doing drugs. I knew Jacoby was his son, but I told Cedric the child was his. I stuck to my lie and the only people who knew the truth were Trina, Evelyn, and Arnez. They promised me that they would take my secret to their graves with them. I prayed that they would.

Chapter Six

Trina

As soon as the G-word left Kayla's mouth, my stomach tightened and my palms started to sweat. I did my best not to have a reaction that would alarm her, and the only thing that I could do was laugh. After she left, though, I cried. Cried because I didn't want to lie to her, but I had to. Why? Because, Kayla said it herself—being with another woman was nasty and she didn't understand how a woman could find sexual pleasure with another. She didn't get how we could love one another, so therefore, it would be a cold day in hell before I ever told anyone the truth.

Since I knew Cedric was suspicious, I had to do something to change his mind. That opportunity presented itself a few days later as I was sitting at a restaurant in the Central West End with the pastor's wife, Cynthia. Cedric walked in, but I hurried to shift my head in another direction.

"Who is that?" Cynthia asked. "You act as if you know him and don't want to be seen."

I had slumped down in my chair, but I wasn't sure if it had done me any good. Cedric kept looking around, but then he walked over to a table to join another woman. She wasn't all that great-looking and she definitely didn't have anything on my friend. I guess it could have been a business lunch, but there was too much smiling going on between them.

"Are you going to pay attention to what I said or are you going to focus on him?" Cynthia asked with snap in her voice.

"I heard everything you said, Cynthia. Just so you know, that's my friend's husband. I'm making sure everything is good, okay?"

"Oh, I see."

Cynthia turned in her seat to get a glimpse of the seemingly happy couple. I wanted to get the hell out of there, but if Cedric was going to be all up in my business, I had no problem getting in his.

"You said that you wanted to end things between us," I said to Cynthia. "Now you're singing a new tune. All I question is why?"

"Because I've been missing you, that's why. I'm having a difficult time moving on and I'm sure you can understand that, can't you?"

"I guess, but as long as you accept that I'm still involved with other people. You seemed a little irritated about me telling you that. I don't know why, especially since you're presenting yourself at church as being happily married."

"It's all for show, Trina. I seriously hate that man. I wish he would roll over and die so I can collect the money from his insurance policy. If you only knew the horrible things my husband has done. Then for him to stand there every Sunday morning and act like everything is all good is ridiculous."

Cynthia had some nerve. She was fake as all get-out and for a first lady, she had the sharpest tongue I had ever witnessed. Her bluntness was a real turnoff for me, but since I was only interested in sexual pleasure, I dealt with the crap.

"Pastor Clemons isn't the only one pretending. You should take a look in the mirror. The bottom line is we all have our issues. None of us are perfect. Not even him."

"I get that, so don't you start defending his actions. I hate speaking to you about him because you always act as if I'm the one in the wrong, not him. I say fuck him, and if you continue to take his side, fuck you too."

"Whatever, Cynthia. This isn't about who is right or who is wrong. You need to realize your own mistakes and stop blaming him so much for all that is going on between the two of you."

"I'm not blaming—"

Cynthia paused and looked behind me. When I turned my head, I saw Keith from work heading our way. He stood tall, was dark as midnight and handsome as ever. As always, his hair was cut into a sharply lined fade, and the artistic, colored tats on his muscular arms were what got my attention more than anything. I appreciated a creative man. I also admired one who sported a sexy goatee. With baggy jeans on, a leather belt holding them up, and a tank top that stretched across his ripped chest, I was so done with Cynthia. This conversation wasn't getting us anywhere.

Keith came up to the table. He was right on time. I introduced the two of them and invited Keith to join us, even though he said he was there waiting for his brother to show up. Cynthia was pissed. She stood up and snatched her purse off the table.

"When you have time, we'll talk further about what's going on. Enjoy the rest of your evening." She looked at Keith and shook his hand. "Nice meeting you, Keith. And, only if I wasn't married." Cynthia winked at him, laughed, and then walked away.

Keith blushed, but didn't say a word. I hated jealous women, and between Cynthia and Lexi I had my hands full. I enjoyed being with them, but they were both immature women who wanted to have our relationship their way or no way at all.

"So, why haven't you been to work?" Keith asked, turning the chair around, straddling it. "I haven't seen you around in several days."

I had been trying to avoid JaQuan. Thankfully, he had given up on calling me. "I've been working from home. Been getting a lot done and I'm preparing for the art show at the end of the month."

"Yeah, I am too. Been working my ass off. I'm looking forward to selling a lot of paintings that weekend. I need to get rid of some of the work I have stuck up in my house and there is plenty of it."

"I feel you. I'm anxious to get rid of some of my paintings too."

Keith's cell phone rang. He said it was his brother calling, so he answered. I looked over his shoulder at Cedric who was now clinking wineglasses with the lady. They were very talkative, but I was sure to get his attention, especially since Keith was now sitting with me.

"It's okay," Keith said. "If you're going to be that late, don't worry about it. Right now, I'm sitting across the table from a beautiful woman whose company I'm enjoying."

I smiled and he paused to listen to his brother. After Keith ended the call, he told me his brother wasn't going to make it.

"That's too bad," I said then laughed. I laughed loud enough for Cedric to turn his head, but he didn't.

"No, actually it's pretty good. After we get a quick bite to eat, maybe you'll invite me to your place so I can check out some of your paintings. Or I can always take you to my crib for you to check out mine."

I was so excited to see Cedric look away and lift his finger to get the waiter's attention. That was when I giggled and told Keith I would love for him to come to my place. Seduction was visible in my eyes, and from afar, I could finally see Cedric looking.

"Then let's hurry up and get this meal started," Keith teased. "How hungry are you?"

"Real hungry. So hungry that I think we should skip our meal and head out right now to my place."

Keith was all for it. He helped me finish the wine that Cynthia and I had been drinking and then we stood to go. I pretended to be tipsy. I giggled loudly again, and when I looked in Cedric's direction his eyes were glued to me. I smiled at him and held Keith's hand as I made my way over to the table where Cedric sat. He appeared uptight by my presence. I guess he figured I would call Kayla to tell her where he was. But friend or not, I didn't get down like that. I did my best to stay out of other people's business, and it had to be something real serious in order for me to get involved.

"I thought that was you over here, Cedric," I said, nearly rubbing my body against Keith's. "How are you?"

"I'm good. And you?"

"Fine. But . . . uh . . . this is Keith. Keith, this is my best friend's husband, Cedric."

They shook hands, but Cedric didn't dare introduce me to the woman sitting across the table from him with shock in her eyes. I didn't know if the *best friend's husband* announcement caught her off guard, or if jealousy had her eyes locked in that position.

"Enjoy the rest of your evening," Cedric said, trying to rush us off.

I looked up at Keith, who towered over me. I winked and turned my attention to Cedric again. "You bet we will. You have a wonderful evening too. Tell my girl I said hello, and I'm looking forward to dinner again. This time, you all can come to my place. Maybe I'll talk Keith into cooking something real delightful for everyone."

Cedric nodded. "Maybe so. Be sure to talk to *her* about it and let me know."

I started to check his ass for referring to his wife as *her*, but I left well enough alone. I had shown him that it was possible for me to make a connection with a man, and I was so sure that Cedric's eyes were still on us as we left the restaurant, appearing real cozy. My only problem was: How I was going to get out of this? Yes, Keith was fine-slash-sexy as fuck, but I didn't want to have sex with him. He was looking forward to something. I could tell by the glare in his eyes.

We stood next to my car with no breathing room in between us. "I guess I'm following you, right?" he said.

"I guess you are. Go get your car and I'll be right here waiting for you."

"My car is parked in the parking garage around the corner. I may be a minute, but I'm coming."

"Sure. I'll be waiting right here in my car. Hurry."

Keith walked away, and as soon as he was out of my sight, I hurried into my car and sped off. Almost ten minutes later, he was ringing my cell phone. I didn't answer, but the next time I saw him I was sure I had some explaining to do.

Within thirty minutes I was home. Unfortunately for me, though, Cynthia was parked outside in her car waiting for me and Lexi was waiting in her car. I was not in the mood to explain myself to anyone, and I certainly didn't want them going at it with each other. Their personalities would clash, so I just kept it moving, hoping that they didn't see me.

My only other options were to either go to Evelyn's place or Kayla's. By the time I sat around with them talking and wasting time, I was sure Lexi and Cynthia would be gone. Then again, maybe not, especially since Lexi was more persistent than Cynthia was.

I made up my mind and drove to Evelyn's place. I squeezed my car in between two vans, but as I got ready to exit
the car my cell phone rang. It was Keith calling again. I felt
terrible for dissing him like I did, so I answered as if I were in
a rush.

"Please, please forgive me," I said in a fake panic. "As soon
as you left, my sister called and said my father had been
rushed to the hospital because of a heart attack. I'm here now,
trying to see what's going on. Can I call you back later?"

"Su—sure, Trina. Take care and if you need anything let me
know."

"I will. Thanks."

I shut my phone off and sighed from relief. I wasn't sure if
he believed me or not, but it was the best I could do for right
now. As for my father, he was a deadbeat any damn way. I
hadn't seen him in years, so I didn't feel bad about the lie I
had told.

I opened the car door to get out. But the moment my heel
touched the pavement, I spotted a familiar car coming in my
direction. There weren't too many people driving around in a
steel-gray Mercedes with tinted windows and a personalized
license plate. At first, I assumed that Kayla was behind the
wheel. But, when Cedric got out, my brows shot up. Shock
washed across my face as I watched him smooth walk his way
to the elevator and swipe a card to get in. I wasn't sure if he
was heading to Evelyn's loft or not. Security was tight in her
building and she had to personally let her guests in.

Cedric, however, had his own access. I was curious about
what was going on, so I waited for fifteen minutes until I got
out of my car and went to the elevator. I punched in Evelyn's
code. A few seconds later she appeared on the screen.

"What's up, *chicka*?" I said. "I just stopped by to see what
you were up to. Do you feel like company?"

Evelyn raked her fingers through her hair. Her eyes were
shifty. I could tell something was up, and it didn't take long
for me to realize that Cedric was there with her. *Why?* was the
real question.

"You know what," she said, then released a fake cough. "I'm
not feeling well right now, Trina. Can I call you tomorrow? I
really want to get some rest."

"No problem. I'll call you tomorrow—or better yet, I look forward to seeing you at lunch. Until then, I hope you feel better."

Evelyn displayed a fake smile then she disappeared from the screen. I got in my car and left. All kinds of thoughts were swarming in my head. Was I wrong for thinking that Cedric and Evelyn were fucking? I mean, why else would he be here at eight o'clock in the evening? And whatever happened to his date? Maybe she got upset with him or maybe she wasn't his date after all. I was left with plenty of questions, but maybe they were questions that I didn't want answers to. Kayla surely had her hands full. It was in my best interest to keep quiet and not hit her with accusations. If she said she and Cedric were getting back on the right track, I had to accept that and let them work on their marriage.

Chapter Seven

Evelyn

I was in bed watching TV when I heard the door squeak open. I heard his shoes hit the floor, and when Cedric stood in the doorway to my bedroom, I wasn't surprised or excited about seeing him. The last deposit into my account had me shaken up. I had been leaving him plenty of messages, but he hadn't returned my phone call. To say I was upset would've been an understatement. He could tell by the blank expression on my face that I wanted him out.

But as soon as I opened my mouth to speak, that was when someone buzzed me from outside. It was Trina. I had to hurry to the door and get rid of her. I was pleased that she didn't question me and I was glad that she didn't push to come in.

After turning her away, I moved away from the screen and rolled my eyes as I walked past Cedric in my white silk robe. He grabbed my wrist and swung me around.

"What in the hell is wrong with you?" he asked. "Why all the attitude?"

"You know what's wrong with me," I hissed. "If you don't, check your cell phone and see. Better yet, check my account and you'll really see."

I snatched my wrist away from him and rushed into the bedroom. Cedric came after me and pushed me on the bed. I fell on my stomach, right on the edge of the bed. He lay on top of me, pressing his body against mine so I couldn't move.

"I've been busy. I didn't have time to answer all thirty-nine of your bullshit messages. How dare you get upset with me about money? If I could calculate all that I've given you, you know damn well that you have no reason to be talking shit.

You make me feel as though all I'm good for is feeding your damn bank account. Can't we get together one fucking time without you asking me for money? Just one time, Evelyn, and you don't always have to ask to receive."

"Shut the fuck up talking to me and get out of here. You're not the only one who gives a lot and—"

"No, you shut the fuck up! All you give me is pussy and a goddamn headache, every time I leave here. I don't know why I keep coming here and fucking with you like this. I'm much better off at home with Kayla. At least she don't gripe as much as yo' ass do."

I tried to turn around and slap the shit out of him for comparing me to Kayla. The comparisons hurt, but as I tried to express my anger, he continued to hold me down. He lifted himself just a little and pulled my robe up to expose my ass. He then lowered himself and slithered the tip of his curled tongue down the crack of my butt. His touch tickled and felt good at the same time. My resistance stopped when he separated my butt cheeks and started to taste me while down on his knees. My breathing slowly increased and my eyes fluttered then shut.

"I—I'm so sorry for stressing you," I whined between deep breaths. "I get—get lonely at times and I need you here with me. I want more, Cedric, *waaaay* more of you—this, all of it. I'm so jealous that Kayla has you, and all that you give to her and—and I wish this could be about us and she—she was no longer in the picture. You're *soooo* good to me, and my *puuuussy* gushes over the way you make it feel. I l*ooooove* how you do that shit, and I'm . . . I'm *cuuuumming!*"

Cedric held my hips and licked faster as I covered his lips with my sweet icing. It took a few minutes for me to regroup then I rushed off the bed to rip off his clothes. I dropped to my knees and sucked his dick into my mouth. It soothed the back of my throat, and it wasn't long before he sprayed my mouth with his fluids. I swallowed his energy drink then fell back on the bed. Cedric stood at the end of it and spread my legs wide. He beat his dick on my pussy to get hard again. It grew to great heights, and as he slipped it into me, he rocked our bodies at a fast pace that caused my firm breasts to wobble around. I couldn't get enough of this man. My need for his overly satisfying dick was starting to supersede my need for his money.

Cedric spread my legs even wider and he grinded so hard that I was on the brink of cumming again. "You like this shit, don't you, bitch!" he shouted. "I appreciate all that bullshit you be talking, but don't be jealous. This dick ain't going nowhere but in this juicy pussy, inside of that pretty ass of yours and back in your mouth. Until then, throw that pussy to me so I can catch it."

I threw it and Cedric caught it. We indulged ourselves that night, and by morning I could barely walk straight. I was scheduled to meet Kayla and Trina for lunch, and when I limped into the restaurant, feeling as if Cedric's dick was still inside of me, they both stared at me.

"What's wrong with you?" Kayla asked, wincing. "Are you all right?"

I plopped down in the chair and crossed my legs to calm the soreness. "Nothing is wrong with me. I'm just tired and my boss has been working me like crazy today."

"Are you still sick?" Trina asked. "You looked terrible last night. I was worried about you."

"I'm feeling a little better. I was so out of it last night. I meant to call you, but I knew I'd see you today." I picked up the menu, looking at it. "Have y'all ordered yet? I only have five bucks on me, so I may have to order some soup or something."

"No problem," Kayla rushed to say. "You know I got you. Order whatever you want to."

In that case, when the waiter came over to take our orders I ordered a cheeseburger and some fries. I hadn't splurged like that since our dinner engagement, and I didn't even have money to buy groceries. While we were sitting at the table, I used my phone to check my bank account status. Maybe Cedric would surprise me and throw some money in my account. But when I checked, all I saw was red. My account was at a negative thirty dollars. Payday was tomorrow, so I released a deep sigh, trying not to trip.

"Okay," Kayla said, rubbing her hands together. "I need y'all help with something."

She reached into her purse and pulled out several vacation brochures. "I want to surprise Ceddy with a vacation. The other day we talked about sprucing up our marriage and I think we should start with a relaxing vacation. Tell me which one of these resorts looks and sounds the most interesting. It's been a while since we've been on a vacation together and he really needs one."

Was she seriously over there bragging about a vacation when my ass was broke? She knew Trina didn't have any money, either, and how dare Kayla be so selfish and make this lunch meeting all about her? Trina picked up the brochures to look at them, but I didn't even bother. I pretended to be occupied with something on my phone, and then I sent *Ceddy* a text message, telling him how spectacular last night was.

"You can never go wrong with Hawaii," Trina said. "But these vacation packages for Sandals look very interesting too. What do you think, Evelyn?"

"I think . . ." I paused when my phone alarmed me that I had a message. When I looked at it, Cedric had sent me a picture of his hard dick. I snickered and read his comment: Still hard, thinking about last night. Can't wait 2 see you again!

My pussy thumped from the thought. I smiled then continued with the conversation. "As I was saying, I think Cedric wouldn't have a good time. Instead of spending his money, why don't you just plan something simple? Most men like to keep it simple. The vacation thing is more about you, Kayla, than it is about him."

Her face scrunched from my comment. "No, it's not. And it'll do us good to get away. All I asked was for you to help me choose. I don't think you know Cedric enough to comment on what he would or wouldn't like. All you know about him is what I tell you."

Was this bitch a fool or a damn fool? I knew Cedric better than she did. If she believed that he was trying to work on their marriage, I felt sorry for her. I didn't get how a woman could spend years and years with a man, yet be so blind and not see what was going on around her. Kayla was setting herself up for a huge downfall. One day I was going to have a little pleasure of watching her come down from the high horse she had been on.

I only had an hour for lunch, but after spending thirty to forty minutes talking about what Ceddy had been up to, I was ready to go. I gobbled down my burger and finished every last fry. I was so full from eating so much that my stomach felt tight. I air-kissed Trina and Kayla's cheeks before telling them I had to get back to work.

"You look like you need to go back home and get some rest," Trina said. "Don't you have some vacation time left from work?"

"I do, but my vacation isn't scheduled until later this year. I said I'll be fine, and I only have a few more hours left anyway."

"Well, go ahead and get out of here," Kayla said. "If you want me to, I'll stop by later to bring you some soup and flu medicine. I know you say you're fine, but you don't look well to us."

"Whatever, Kayla, do what you wish. I gotta go. I'll see the two of you soon."

I walked off, but as soon as I made it back to the office a sheen of sweat covered my forehead. My stomach felt queasy. I rushed to the bathroom and could feel vomit creeping up my throat. The toilet was piled high with my lunch and with the orange juice I drank earlier. I wiped my mouth with a napkin then splashed water on my face to cool off. I left the bathroom to tell my boss that I needed to go home, but he asked me to come into his office and close the door.

"Have a seat, Evelyn, this won't be long."

I took a seat and stared at Mr. Payne from across his desk. He was a grumpy old white man with a toupee sitting crookedly on his head. His gray eyes were frightening, and the buttons on his shirt were about to pop off due to his potbelly that could be seen a mile away.

"You can go home, but unfortunately, you may have to stay there. Today will be your last day. We can't keep employing people who we consider troublemakers. We've gotten too many complaints about you, Evelyn. Too many and I've ignored those complaints for long enough."

I sat in shock with my eyes bugged and my jaw dropped. Tears welled in my eyes, but I blinked to clear them. "Complaints? What complaints are you talking about?"

"Letters that show you've been harassing some of your coworkers. One coworker said you keyed her car and scripted your initials, another one said you flattened her tires and wrote her a nasty letter. I don't know what you have against the white women who work here, but this obviously isn't the place for you."

I seriously could have fallen out of my chair. I had no idea what he was talking about and this whole damn thing sounded like a setup. "Mr. Payne, if you received that many complaints about me, why didn't you say anything to me? You never questioned me or gave me a warning. I have no clue what you're talking about and I have never done anything to anyone in here. I'd like to see the letters you're talking about. I would also like to talk to the people who complained about me. Something isn't adding up here. I have nothing against white women, period."

Mr. Payne reached inside of his desk drawer and pulled out two letters. He gave them to me. All I could do was shake my head. The letters referred to the women as white sluts who I hated with a passion. According to the letter, I threatened them and promised to do more damage if they told on me. The letters had my signature and it was so identical to mine that it was scary.

"This . . . this is not from me." I wiped a slow tear that trickled down my face. "I swear it isn't me. Why would I write something like that and then sign my name to it?"

"I don't know, but either way, I need for you to go. We'll investigate this more, but for now you need to vacate the premises until this matter is resolved."

I surely wanted to tell Mr. Payne to kiss my ass, but I figured there was a possibility that I would have to come back and kiss his. It was times like this when I wished that I could afford a lawyer. EEOC was another option too. But for now, I packed up my belongings and left without causing a scene.

While in the car, I wondered who had written those letters. Who in the hell was out to get me and why? Had the white women conspired to do harm to me? They were all so jealous of me, and I saw the way many of them looked at me with jealousy in their eyes. But the other women were all haters too. I never befriended any of them. All I ever did was go to work and come home. My measly paychecks were nothing to brag about, and the headache all of this had caused wasn't worth it.

For now, I needed Cedric more than I had ever needed him before. I had to ask him for more money. He was the only one who could save me. I reached for my cell phone and punched in his number.

"I'm on my way to a meeting," he said. "Make it quick."

"Are you coming over tonight? I need to talk to you about something very important."

"Talk or play? I'm sure we won't be talking all night, will we?"

"No. We can play too, just come, okay?"

"See you around eight or nine, maybe sooner. It depends on whenever I can get out of here."

"Okay. I'll be waiting."

I drove home in a daze. I hoped that Cedric would be able to help me. This would be the first time I had to ask him for a staggering amount like fifty-thousand dollars to make up for the losses I was about to incur. Damn!

Chapter Eight

Jacoby

I tried not to poke my nose where it didn't belong and stay out of grown-folks' business, but sitting on the sidelines was something that I couldn't do. I was so upset with my mother for acting as if she didn't have any fucking sense at all and I hated my father with a passion. I saw right through his bullshit. I wondered why my mother hadn't opened her eyes and realized how much she was getting played. This was ridiculous. I was so upset the other night when I heard the two of them fucking. I mean, what good was that going to do? What was the purpose and what kind of marriage were they representing? I was so outdone and had felt this way for a very long time. Thing is, I was told to keep my mouth shut. My mother wasn't trying to hear it and neither was Cedric. That's why I was doing what I could do to change this situation around and it started with Evelyn.

A blind person could see that she was fucking around with my father. Anyone paying attention would know and it was as if neither of them cared who found out. I'd seen them at dinners, at her house, at his office, and even at my house. She had the audacity to come into our home to fuck my father, and when my mother went to Atlanta last year, that same night, Evelyn was there. They thought I was asleep, but I wasn't. I saw it all, as I had seen it every time I went somewhere with my father. I didn't understand his obsession with women. It was as if he could never get enough.

Me, I'd had enough. I did my best to get Evelyn fired. I wanted her to feel some of the hurt I'd been feeling. She was out to destroy my parents, but I wanted to destroy her. This was just a start, and I assumed that her little situation at work would be dealt with real soon. I also wanted to get my father where it hurt, but I had to be careful with him. He was a smart man. He could always sense when something wasn't right. For now, the least I could do was have a man-to-man conversation with him. Let him know how I was feeling about all of this shit and encourage him to knock it off before it was too late. If I couldn't get through to him today, I wasn't sure where I would turn.

I had a half day at school, so I drove by my father's office to see if he was there. As I was looking for a parking spot, I spotted him leaving his office. He met up with a woman I had seen him with plenty of times before. The two of them shared brief words and a quick kiss before she got into my father's car. Before getting inside, his eyes scanned the parking lot while he unbuttoned his suit jacket. He then hung it on a hook in the backseat and I saw him unbutton his cuffs so he could raise his sleeves. Afterward, he got in the car and sped off. I followed closely behind. I figured they were headed to their usual place, which was in a nearby parking garage where she often gave him a blow job. There were times when they'd had sex too. I had pictures to prove it, and hurtful or not, I would one day show my mother who the real liar was.

My father parked his car in a reserved spot that belonged to him. My car was parked several rows over, but I could see him pull out the newspaper, as if he were reading it. The woman next to him disappeared. To his lap she went and there appeared to be some maneuvering around going on. Once things got settled, I watched from afar. I tried to give the motherfucker time to bust his nut, but then I thought it would be best for me to interrupt him.

I cocked my hat on backwards and eased my hands in my jean pockets as I made my way up to his car. I figured he saw me in his rearview mirror, because the newspaper lowered and the woman with him jumped up from his lap. As I bent over, he lowered his window. I glared inside. My father appeared calm as ever, but the woman wiped her lips and kept looking at me with bugged eyes.

"Can I help you?" Cedric said.

"We need to talk?"

"Right now? Can't you see I'm busy?"

"You're always busy, but it's either now or never. I prefer now because I have some shit that I need to get off my chest."

Cedric unlocked the car. "Get inside. Make this quick, Jacoby. I need to get back to work."

Work my ass. I sat on the backseat, behind him. I swear if I had a rope or something close to it, I would have used that opportunity to choke his ass. I was starting to hate him that much.

My father looked over at the woman sitting next to him. "Just in case you don't know, that's my son. His timing is way off, but I would be pleased if you wouldn't mind finishing what you already started."

The woman spoke to me then wiped her lips again. "Are you sure?" she said. "You . . . you want me to continue with your son in the car?"

He looked at me in the rearview mirror. "Why not? It ain't like he ain't never had his dick sucked before. I'm sure that he loves pussy just as much as I do. Right, son?"

I wanted to throw up. Whether I liked that shit or not, he didn't even have to go there with this trick. Her stupid ass didn't hesitate to drop back into his lap, and I kept thinking to myself what a fool she was.

My father pressed the back of his head against the headrest and closed his eyes. "What's on your mind, Jacoby? Speak."

I didn't hesitate. "What's on my mind is I want you to stop this. Don't you know how much damage you're doing to our family? And what about Mother? Why are you doing this to her? I mean, I don't get it. If you don't want to be with her, why don't you just divorce her? That way, we can all get on with our lives and you can do whatever it is that you want to do."

He opened his eyes and shrugged his shoulders. "I'm doing what I want to do regardless. And to answer all of your questions, I'll shoot one word to you and hope that you understand. Timing. Timing is everything. I'll divorce your mother when I get ready to. As for right now, I'm not ready to make that move."

The slurping sounds of the woman sucking his dick were very distracting. She lifted her head to reply to his comment. "I hope you're ready soon. You told me that you—"

He grabbed the back of her head and pulled her hair tight. "Keep your fucking mouth shut and stay out of this conversation between me and my son. You can do so by focusing more on making me bust this nut, and just so you know, I'm nowhere near that yet. Ya feel me?"

She nodded and resumed sucking his dick. "That's my girl," he said while patting the back of her head. "*Deeeeep*. Go deep."

I released a deep sigh and shook my head. We caught each other's eyes in the rearview mirror and I could see the smirk on his face. He was definitely getting a kick out of this.

"Don't look so disappointed, son. See, when you accrue all of the money that I have over the years, you'll be able to do this kind of shit too. It's called having power over the pussy. Women will flock to you and you'll be able to get them to do whatever in the fuck you want them to do. They will love your dirty drawers and all they'll want from time to time is a little cash and a hard, satisfying dick. That's all your mother ever wanted from me, so don't be upset with me if she got exactly what she asked for." He paused and shut his eyes. "Umph. You on to something, baby. I likes that shit—damn it, girl, slow down!"

He started lifting himself from the seat, pumping the woman's mouth that was full with his goods. He seemed so into it that I doubted he was paying me any attention. My fists were tightened. I swear that I wanted to knock him upside his head, just because. I wanted to scream and release all of this anger inside of me, but I figured that would do me no good. My father would never see things my way. He would never understand the damage behind his actions. I felt as if I had wasted my time, so I was ready to let him get back to "work."

I shook the headrest to make him open his eyes. When he stared at the rearview mirror, I looked at him and spoke. "Ju—just think about what I'm saying to you. Enough is enough, and I'm losing so much respect for you. There was a time when you were real good to me, man, but you've been on my back and coming down on me, knowing damn well why

I'm so angry with you. I can't control my anger. All of this is upsetting to me, and I . . . I want my parents to love, honor, and respect each other. That's all I want. If y'all can't do that then walk away from each other. I don't care who you're with, not even with Evelyn. My mother deserves better than this. Deep down, I think you know that."

He bit into his lip and squeezed his hands on the steering wheel. When the woman lifted her head, I turned mine to look out the window. I figured her mouth was filled with his semen, and I surely didn't want to see it.

"*Ahhhhh,*" he said then sighed. "I—I've always been good to you, son, but unfortunately, there are a few things that you don't understand right now. One day you will. When that day comes, you and I will be on the right path. I figured that you knew about me and Evelyn, but like all the rest, she don't mean shit to me. If anybody deserves better, it's me. I deserve better, and deep down, that's the only truth that I know."

I opened the car door and placed one foot on the ground. I then turned to the woman who appeared hurt by Cedric's words, but kept her mouth shut.

"I guess we all need to wake up and know our self-worth," I said, directing my comment to her. I then looked at the back of Cedric's head. "Money or not, you shouldn't treat people the way you do. And whatever it is that I need to understand, I wish someone would lay it on the line and tell me. As of right now, I don't get it. You're the worst fucking father on this earth and I wish that when your whole world come tumbling down, that I'll have a front-row seat."

"Well, for now, yo' ass is in the back. Thanks for the father-son talk, but I need to head back to the office. See you at home, son, and I wish you had more time. Time for my princess over here to give you some of that action that she just gave me. Maybe it'll help to knock off that chip on your shoulder, and trust me when I say that every man needs a little relaxation from time to time."

I didn't have anything else to say. I slammed the car door, feeling as if I could kill him.

Chapter Nine

Kayla

After Evelyn left the restaurant, Trina and I stayed for at least another thirty minutes or so. She was telling me about her experience with Keith and said that she was starting to feel something for him.

"I don't know what it is," she said. "He's different. When he came over last night, we made love. I was in another world with him, and I appreciated how he took his time with me. I think he could be the one."

"I'm glad to hear that, and I'll be so glad when either you or Evelyn get married. Sometimes, I feel so out of place in this friendship. I'm always talking about me and my husband, feeling as if the two of you can't relate. Aside from that, it'll be good for you to settle down. I'm pleased that you haven't given up on love."

Trina smiled and ate a piece of the pecan pie she'd ordered. "So, what's your take on Evelyn?" she asked. "She was so out of it today, wasn't she?"

"Yes, she was. I could tell something was wrong with her, but I guess she didn't want to say what it was. I'm going to stop by her place later to check on her. I'll probably take her some soup and orange juice, just in case she needs it."

"From the way she was looking she definitely needs it. I'm starting to worry about her a lot. I'm worried about you as well. I don't mean to pry, but are you sure your marriage with Cedric is on the right track? There is something about him that I—"

"I know. Something about him that you don't like. I get that, Trina, but Cedric is an awesome man and decent husband.

He's not perfect, but he's trying to do better. I don't say a lot to you and Evelyn about our situation because I don't want y'all judging me. I don't want you to despise him, either, and please know that I'm a big girl who is capable of dealing with the man I married. So, don't worry about me. I already told you that things are starting to get better. He sent me a dozen beautiful roses earlier, and I have a feeling that tonight is going to be real special for us."

Trina had a peculiar look on her face that I couldn't read. I wasn't sure why she was so worried about me, and I figured her opinion about Cedric had changed, especially after him saying that he believed she was gay. Maybe I shouldn't have said anything to her.

As I was in thought, she reached over and placed her hand on top of mine. "As your friend, all I'm saying to you is: Know who to trust and who not to. Keep your eyes and ears open and pay attention to your surroundings. Listen to your gut and don't allow love for anyone to destroy you."

"I appreciate the advice and the same goes for you."

Trina finished her pie. Shortly thereafter, we went our separate ways. I stopped by the grocery store to pick up a few things for Evelyn. Then I went home to check on Jacoby. He was there doing his homework while watching TV.

"I'm on my way to Evelyn's place," I said, standing next to him in the kitchen. "Do you want anything to eat before I go?"

He shrugged with such a disappointed look on his face. "I'll just throw a TV dinner in the microwave. And if you don't mind, I'd like to take Adrianne to the movies tonight."

"I don't mind, but you know it's a school night. Don't stay out too late and be sure to take your time on your homework."

"I will. And—uh—by the way, tell Evelyn I said hello."

"I sure will. But I want you to perk up. Things aren't that bad, are they?"

Jacoby stared at me for a few minutes and then he placed his hands behind his head. "Since we're living in this fantasy world, I guess things aren't bad at all. But what do you think?"

"I think I need to go see about my friend. Don't forget what I said, and no matter how bad you may think things are, I will always love you."

I started to walk away, but I turned around when I thought about Cedric. "Did your father speak to you about going on a business trip with him yet?"

"No. I don't want to go on a dumb business trip with him, and he can forget about asking me that crap."

I went back over to the table and touched Jacoby's back. "Don't be like that, Jacoby. Give your father a chance to make things right. He's trying. He really wants to make peace with you. He can't if you continue to have up a brick wall. So when he inquires about going places with him, at least think about it first."

"I don't have to think about anything because my answer will always be no. The peace that I get is when he's away from here. That's all the peace I need."

I released a deep breath and swallowed the lump that felt stuck in my throat. Jacoby was being difficult when he didn't have to be.

"You're going to ruin your relationship with your father, and one day you're going to regret it. For the sake of our family staying together and being happy, please reconsider and think hard about how you can improve your relationship with him. You are too stubborn, Jacoby. It's time to let go of the bitterness you have inside and move on."

Jacoby sucked his teeth and narrowed his eyes. "Move on? Really? If I am bitter, it's because he made me this way. I'm not as forgiving as you are, Mother, and I don't enjoy being around my father as much as you do. All he does is disrespect you when I go places with him. I don't like how he looks at other women and—"

"Stop it right there, okay? A married man is allowed to look at other women, as long as he doesn't touch. Hell, I look at other men, but it doesn't mean that I love your father any less. You're finding excuses as to why you don't want to get your relationship with your father on the right track. That's a shame, Jacoby. A darn shame and I'm real disappointed in you."

I walked off, but halted my steps when Jacoby shouted at me.

"Disappointed in me! Well, guess what? I'm disappointed in you too. The question is when are you going to wake the fuck up? When are you going to see my father for who he really is? I don't want to be around him, especially not when I have to go to so-called 'business meetings' with him and listen to him fucking other women in the next room. He's been doing more than just looking. I *have* lost all respect for him, and I'm about to lose it for you too!"

I rushed up to Jacoby and slapped him across his face. "Lower your voice and don't you ever speak to me that way! To hell with the movies. When you get done with your homework, go to your room and think about how you're going to work on that bad attitude of yours."

Jacoby got out of his chair and hurried past me. He went into his room, and not listening to a word I said, he ran out of the house and got into his car. I went after him, but couldn't catch him. Mad as hell, I hurried back inside to call Cedric.

"Yes, Kay," he said with a sigh, as if he were busy.

"I'm sorry to bother you, but Jacoby just ran out of here, upset. I tried to stop him, but I don't know where he's gone."

"What is he upset for this time?"

"I asked if he would join you on the business trip you mentioned and he said that he didn't want to go because your trips turn personal and women are involved. He then started yelling and cursing at me, so I slapped him. I don't know what is happening. . . ." I paused to wipe my tears. I had never put my hands on my son, but his words to me were so hurtful.

"Calm down, all right? Jacoby needs some time to get his head straight. I assure you that he'll be back soon. I keep telling you that he's just at that age right now where he wants to be the boss and he doesn't want to listen. I used to act the same way as a teenager, especially when things didn't go how I wanted them to. As for my business trips, he's just bitter and he'll say anything to upset you. Stop letting him get to you like that. The moment I get home tonight, I'll have a talk with him. I promise you that things won't get out of hand, and I'll listen to whatever he has to say."

I swallowed again and nodded. "Okay. I'll see you when you get home. I'm glad we had a chance to talk. I feel better."

Cedric laughed, only to make me laugh. "Good. Now can I get back to work?"

"Please do."

After we ended our call, I wasn't going to go over to Evelyn's place, but since I had already bought her fruit, soup, and juices, I decided to go. It was a little after five o'clock. Since she got off work at four, I assumed she was at home. With a grocery bag in my hand, I punched in her code. Minutes later, she appeared on the screen, looking at me.

"Yes," she said.

"Buzz me in. I have something for you."

"Whatever it is, I don't want it. I don't feel up to company right now, so please go."

I could tell Evelyn had been crying from the puffiness in her eyes. "I'm not leaving, so you may as well buzz me in. I want to know why you're so upset, and stop shutting me out like this. Have you forgotten that I'm your best friend?"

Evelyn disappeared from the screen then she buzzed me in. The elevator opened and I took it up to her floor. When I got off, I could see that her door was cracked. I opened the door and saw her lying on the couch in skimpy boy shorts and a white wife-beater. Her nipples were poking through it and her hair was wildly scattered on her head. Beads of sweat dotted her body and her entire place felt like heat was delivered straight from hell. I put the bag on the counter and walked over to the thermostat.

"What in the heck is going on with you?" I asked then clicked the thermostat on cool.

"Don't bother," she said. "My electric was turned off today. The air doesn't work."

"How . . . why is your electric turned off? Didn't you pay your bill?"

Evelyn sat up on the couch and wiped snot from her nose with a tissue. "I didn't have enough to pay it. I called for an extension, but they wouldn't give it to me."

"That's ridiculous."

I walked over to the windows to open them. There wasn't much of a breeze stirring, but it was so stuffy inside that I needed some fresh air. I sat on the couch next to Evelyn, clenching her hand with mine.

"If you needed some money for your electric bill, all you had to do was ask me. Now go get your bill and let me call the electric company to make your payment. They will turn it right back on, won't they?"

"Probably not until tomorrow. This has to be the worst day of my life. To make a long story short, I also got fired today. My whole world is tumbling down. I don't know what I'm doing wrong or what I can do to stop all of this crap from happening to me."

I felt horrible for her. I didn't understand why she hadn't told me things were this bad. "Fired? Fired for what? And your world is not tumbling down. Most things can be fixed and you're just going through a difficult time."

"I was let go because of coworker complaints. Obviously, the women there don't like me and they conspired to get me fired."

I shook my head and silently thanked God for being in a position where I didn't have to involve myself with some of the crazy people in corporate America. "That's terrible. But you'll find another job, so don't worry. Just go get your electric bill and let's get this thing paid for."

Evelyn wiped her nose again and dabbed her watery eyes. She stood up and went to her bedroom. I couldn't help but notice how shapely she was. And she was slim. Her body didn't have an ounce of fat on it. I had way more curves than she did, and according to her I was thick.

While she was in the bedroom getting her bill, I went into the kitchen to put up the groceries. I opened the fridge and the only thing inside was a bottle of diet Coke. It was empty as ever. I felt terrible for not realizing how badly my best friend had been suffering. I wish I had gotten her some more groceries, and I made a mental note to come back tomorrow to bring her some more things. I put the fruit and juice in the refrigerator then put the cans of soup in the cabinets. They were pretty bare too, causing me to shake my head even more.

Evelyn came back into the living room and sat on the couch. I poured her a glass of orange juice, but when I looked in the trash can to throw the bag away, I noticed a pregnancy test inside. I blinked several times, looking at the positive sign that was clearly visible. A smile washed across my face as I carried the orange juice over to her.

"What are you smiling for?" she said in a soft tone. She took the glass from my hand and gave me her electric bill.

"I'm smiling because I see somebody is about to be a mommy." My voice screeched and I reached over to give Evelyn a hug. "Why didn't you tell me? Oh my God, I can't believe you're pregnant! How could you consider this the worst day of your life, after finding out you're pregnant?"

Evelyn didn't appear as excited as I was. She slowly nodded and gazed at the trash can in the kitchen. "I—I just took the test today. I wanted to wait until the doctor confirmed it, before I said anything."

"Those tests are pretty accurate. I—I don't know what else to say, other than I'm so happy for you."

Evelyn shrugged and sort of rolled her eyes. "I'm sorry if I'm not as excited about this as you are, but this is a bad time for me. A child is not what I want to bring into this mess I have going on right now."

I reached for her hands again, holding them with mine. "Listen, I know you're going through a lot, but this will all work itself out. That child is a blessing to you and don't you ever forget that. I'll help you get back on your feet, but you have to promise me that you'll get back to work and get out of this slump you're in. I hate seeing you like this. It pains me that you didn't share with me what has been going on with you. Why didn't you tell me you needed help?"

Evelyn removed her hands from mine and plopped back on the couch. She massaged her forehead and closed her eyes. "Because, I get tired of coming to you for every single thing. You already have a full plate and I knew Trina had just hit you up for some cash. I suspect that Cedric doesn't know about all this money exchanging hands, and isn't he going to be upset with you for giving us his money?"

"At the end of the day, his money is my money too. He never questions what I do with it because he knows that I'm responsible. It's not like I'm out here blowing a lot of money. I'm very careful about how much I spend. You know how I used to run to the malls every day and do all that crazy stuff that rich women do? I don't go out like that anymore, because material things don't bring about the happiness my heart desires. Seeing my best friends on their feet and doing well makes me feel good. Knowing that my son's college is paid for delights me, and having a husband who I can trust is what's important. Now tell me, my dear, longtime, beautiful friend, how far in debt are you?"

Evelyn bit into her nails and widened her eyes as she looked at me. "I'm too embarrassed to say."

"Tell me. Now!"

"Almost two-hundred thousand dollars in debt, but that includes student loan money that I have yet to start paying on. Minus that and the interest money, about a hundred thousand in debt."

I put my hand on my hip. "With no mortgage, you should know better. But here's what I'm going to do."

I told Evelyn that I would give her twenty-five-thousand dollars for the next four months to help her. She agreed to call the student loan provider to make arrangements on her bill. She also agreed to find another job, and I offered to help with lawyer fees because the situation on her job sounded fishy. By the time I got ready to leave, she was all smiles. She appeared better and she seemed more upbeat about the baby.

"So what does Marc have to say?" I asked. "He is the father, isn't he?"

"He—he seems excited. I just told him today and he said that he hoped it would be a boy. I'm hoping for one too."

"Either one will suit me just fine. I can't believe I'm going to be an auntie, and with all that's been going on today, it's finally good to hear some exciting news. I got into a heated argument with Jacoby earlier, so I need to get out of here to see if he's made it home, okay?"

"Go handle your business. Thank you so much for every-thing, Kayla. I appreciate you more than you will ever know."

We hugged right at the door and then I left. I walked slowly to the elevator while punching Jacoby's number into my phone. It was almost seven o'clock. I wondered if he had made it home. He didn't answer his phone so I left a message, telling him to call me back. I was still looking down when the elevator opened. But when I looked up, Cedric was standing there with his hand in one pocket and his suit jacket was tossed over his shoulder. His stare was without a blink. So was mine.

"What are you doing here?" I questioned.

Cedric cleared his throat and swallowed. "I . . . uh . . . called Evelyn looking for you. She told me you were here. She didn't tell you?"

"No, she didn't."

"I'm not sure why, but after our conversation earlier, I came here to make sure you were okay."

I sighed from relief and smiled. "I'm fine. I feel a whole lot better, so let's go home."

I put my arms around Cedric's waist and rested my head against his chest. I asked how he'd gotten upstairs and he said he got on the elevator with a man who had a swipe card. The elevator took us back to the parking garage where we got in our cars and headed for home. I was glad to see Jacoby's car in the driveway, but when we went inside and Cedric tried to talk to him, Jacoby didn't want to hear it. He went into his bedroom and shut the door.

"I'm done," Cedric said, removing his clothes. "His ass will have to make the next move. I've had it with his disrespect."

"Don't give up on him just yet. He's going through a lot and we can't expect for this situation to change overnight."

"See what I mean?" Cedric went into the bathroom and turned on the shower. "You're always making excuses and stiking up for him. I wish you would just say he's wrong and stop trying to sugarcoat shit."

"I admit it, okay. He's wrong. That's what our talk was about earlier. I told Jacoby to stop being so bitter and to put forth some effort to work this out with you."

Cedric didn't say anything. I watched as he lathered his body with soap, and it was one sexy sight to see water running from his body to the drain. I removed my clothes and stepped into the shower with him. We faced each other. The silence was broken when Cedric gripped my ass and inched me closer to him.

"I do love you, you know," he said. "In the midst of every-thing that is going on, you're still my wife and I appreciate you for being there for me."

"I love you too, and I certainly do my best to please you."

Our tongues danced through the falling water that ran from the showerhead and drenched us both. Cedric lifted and positioned me for more action against the wall. I held on to his neck and rubbed the back of his waves. During my orgasm, I dropped my head back as he sucked my chocolate nipples, trying to arouse me even more. Wanting to please him too, I released my legs from his waist and squatted in front of him. He pulled on my braids and pumped his steel deep down my throat. I mas-saged the muscles in his ass, and when they tightened, he pulled out of my mouth and resumed in my pussy where I needed to feel him the most.

Around midnight, Cedric and I were cuddling in bed. We had just finished another long, lovemaking session and were on our way to sleep. I couldn't stop thinking about Evelyn. I wondered if she had called Trina to tell her about the baby. I decided to check with Evelyn first, before I ran off at the mouth and said anything to Trina. I did, however, feel as though it wouldn't hurt anything if I mentioned it to Cedric.

"Guess what?" I said while rubbing the sparse, smooth hair on his chest.

"I know. You love me, right?"

I laughed and so did he. "Yeah, I do. A whole lot, but that's not what I was about to tell you. I was going to tell you that Evelyn is pregnant. I found out today and I'm so happy for her. You know she's always had a difficult time getting pregnant, and this is a huge surprise to all of us."

For a few seconds, Cedric didn't respond. I felt his body get real tense, so I looked up at him. A blank expression covered his face and I got no reaction from him.

"Did you hear what I said?" I asked.

"No, I—I didn't. What did you say?"

"I said that Evelyn is pregnant. What were you thinking about since you didn't hear me?"

"I was thinking about some stuff with Jacoby, that's all. I didn't mean to ignore you, but . . . uh . . . I guess that's good news. You know how wild she is. I assume she probably doesn't even know who the father is."

I frowned and playfully pushed Cedric's chest. "That's not nice. You seem to dislike my friends and you never have anything nice to say about them. Evelyn is not like that anymore and she has settled down a whole lot. Marc is the father, and from what she told me he's pretty excited about the baby."

"Yeah, well, good for them. Now, turn out the light on your side. It's already late and I need to get some sleep."

I reached over to the lamp to turn it off. I was ready for some more action, but Cedric had turned on his side to face the wall. He pulled the cover over him, and a few minutes later he was out. As for me, I couldn't sleep. I had too much on my mind, including my doctor's appointment tomorrow that was only a checkup.

Chapter Ten

Kayla

I hated going to the doctor's office, because no matter what I came here to do they were always busy. And then when they called my name to go back into one of the rooms, I still had to wait at least another thirty minutes to an hour to be seen. My doctor, Kenneth Woodrow, was a doctor I'd had for quite some time. And no matter how crowded his office was, I was comfortable with him and didn't want to switch doctors. The plus side was he was a fine black doctor who I trusted. I waited for him to come into the room, and sat on the examination table while paging through a magazine. The nurse had already taken a sample of my urine and she had drawn blood as well. I had on one of those ridiculous wrinkled gowns with an opening in the back.

I heard a knock on the door and Dr. Woodrow entered. Normally, he would be grinning from ear to ear, but I guess today was a hectic day for him.

"Hello, Kayla," he said, closing the door behind him. "How are you feeling?"

"I feel great. Just here for my regular checkup. I wanted to make sure everything is good with me."

Dr. Woodrow sucked his teeth and opened my folder to look at it. He nodded and scanned his eyes down the papers inside. He licked his lips then his brows shot up.

"It's that bad, huh?" I teased.

He finally smiled. "No, no. Not bad, but certainly not good, either."

My heart fell way below my stomach because I had no clue what he meant by that. "Not good? What's going on?"

Dr. Woodrow pulled up a stool and sat in front of me. "You know I don't like to get into your personal matters, but we've known each other for a long time. How has your marriage been doing?"

"It's been . . . been okay. I mean, Cedric and I have had some issues, but nothing that can't be worked out. Why are you asking—"

"Any issues with infidelity?"

I was straightforward with Dr. Woodrow and was a little irritated as well. "No. Not at all."

He scratched his head and glared at me. "You have chlamydia, Kayla. I suggest that you and your husband use condoms from now own because you don't want to open yourselves up to anything else."

My brows shot up; I was speechless. I had an out-of-body experience and I wasn't quite sure I had heard what he'd said. Chlamydia was something that young people—teenagers—got. Not a grown woman like me who was married and had been so for many, many years.

"Look, Dr. Woodrow, there has to be some kind of a mistake. Maybe my urine test got mixed in with someone else. I'm going to need for you to go back out there and clear this mess up."

"I understand that you don't want to accept this, but it's apparent that someone in the marriage has been unfaithful."

Hearing his comment made my blood boil. I knew darn well that it wasn't me and I suspected that it wasn't Cedric.

"No, you don't understand that we don't get down like that. Please go find out what the hell is going on and correct this mess, now!"

Dr. Woodrow stood up. He left the room and I hopped down from the examination table to put my clothes back on. If the organization in his office was this screwed up then I was going to have to find me another doctor. How dare he come in here feeding me this crap about having chlamydia? I was seriously considering a lawsuit against him for getting it wrong.

Once I put my clothes back on, I paced the floor and waited for Dr. Woodrow to return. My thoughts were all over the place. The what-if's started to kick in. My heart was already racing and when Dr. Woodrow came back into the room the same gloomy look was on his face.

"I wish I was wrong about this, Kayla, but I'm not." He handed me a piece of paper that showed the results to my test. He started to point out why he was correct, but I snatched the paper from his hand.

"This is such bullshit," I said as tears rushed to the brim of my eyes. "I don't believe this. Cedric would never—" I couldn't even finish my sentence because my gut had already told me what the hell was up. Jacoby had told me too, but I chose to accept what Cedric said as if his word was above all.

"I would like to give you a full examination, just to make sure everything else is okay with you," Dr. Woodrow said. "I want to check for herpes—"

I was so embarrassed that I ran out of the room in tears. Everybody was looking at me and questioning if everything was okay. I was numb all over. By the time I reached my car, I was a wreck. I felt like Dr. Woodrow had just told me I'd had cancer. The pain I felt from Cedric's betrayal was unbearable. I couldn't wait to confront him with this, and instead of waiting until he got home, I drove straight to his office. I didn't bother to clear up the smudged mascara that was running from my eyes, nor did I bother to straighten my clothes. My lips trembled as I stood at the receptionist's desk, asking where I could find my husband.

"He—he's in a meeting right now," the receptionist said with caution. "I'm sure he'll be done shortly, so why don't you have a seat and I'll tell him you're here."

"Don't bother."

I stormed off to the boardroom that was at the end of the hallway. The door was closed, but when I swung it open, Cedric sat at a shiny, mahogany wooden table with at least a dozen other executives in business suits. Many of them were chuckling until the door flew open and they saw me standing there, distraught. Shock covered their faces. The room was now so quiet that you could hear a pin drop.

Cedric shot up from the chair like a rocket, but by the time he could make it around the table I took off my shoe and flung it across the room, hitting him in the head. I then charged into the room with tightened fists. I swung out wildly at him and pounded his body with my fists so hard that he had to crouch down in the chair.

"You dirty, nasty-dick motherfucker! How dare you do this shit to me! How dare you give me a goddamn disease from one of your trifling whores!"

I didn't care about putting our business out there. I wanted Cedric to feel my pain and embarrassment too. My arms got tired from swinging, so I picked up the leather binder on the table and smacked him with it. Papers scattered everywhere and so did some of the men who were in the room.

"Call security," one of the executives said to another. "Hurry!"

With the crazed and disturbing look in my eyes, I was sure that they thought I was strapped. I wished I were, but unfortunately I wasn't. Cedric had finally stood up and tried to push me away from him.

"Chill the fuck out!" he shouted while shielding his face. "Stop acting a damn fool and get a grip of yourself!"

He locked his arms around my waist and squeezed so tightly that I couldn't breathe. I started pounding my fists at his back and a few minutes later two security guards rushed into the room. They pulled me away from him and locked my arms behind my back.

With a busted lip, Cedric plopped down in the chair and took several deep breaths. "Get her the fuck out of here. Call the police and have her arrested."

"You bastard!" I shouted and tried to spit on him. The security guards had to drag me out of the room, because I continued to charge at him and had fallen on my knees. I never, ever thought I was capable of getting my clown on like this, but I couldn't control my actions. Not until he was out of my sight.

Almost an hour later, the security guards released me and told me to leave the premises. I was also told to never come back. Apparently, they were following the orders of my husband, who had obviously changed his mind about having me arrested.

While in the car, I cried until I couldn't cry anymore. I called Dr. Woodrow to apologize for my behavior earlier. He told me that he wanted me to come back in for a full examination. He also said he would call in my prescription to the nearest Walgreens.

Yet again, I was humiliated as I stood at the pharmacy counter to pick up my medicine. There I was . . . walking around like a classy bitch with chlamydia. Pussy was all fucked up. There was no doubt that I was dying to get my hands on Cedric again. This mess was far from over. I just didn't have time to deal with it tonight. So instead of going home, I called Trina to see if she was home. She wasn't there, so I contacted Evelyn. She answered and I asked her if I could stop by.

"Sure. I don't have any plans and I'll be here all evening," she said.

"I'm on my way."

When I arrived at Evelyn's place, she buzzed me right in. This time, it was me who needed comfort. I needed her to lend me an car, give me some advice, and show me some support. But unfortunately, when I broke the news to Evelyn, she appeared just as taken aback as I was. Even her eyes filled with tears and she covered her mouth.

"You have got to be kidding me, Kayla. Wha—did—was the doctor sure about that?"

"Yes! Very sure. I've been walking my dumb tail around here in denial, dissing my son and believing every single lie that Cedric has told me. I feel like such a fool. I swear to God that I could kill him right about now."

Evelyn still didn't have much to say. She got up from the couch and went into the kitchen to get some water. She didn't even bother to offer me any, which wasn't surprising because I had obviously forgotten how selfish my best friend was at times. So selfish that I didn't feel at ease talking to her about this anymore.

I snatched up my purse, tucking it underneath my arm. "I'm going home to talk to Jacoby. I'll call you later."

Not saying another word, she walked me to the door and opened it. "I hope everything will be okay. That's a shame what Cedric did to you and he knows better."

I shrugged and moved forward to make my way to the elevator. Evelyn called my name and I swung around with anger displayed on my face.

"I don't mean to bring this up right now, but please don't forget about the money you promised me. I'm really in need, okay?"

Well, ain't that about a bitch? I was in need too, but she obviously didn't care. "Sure, Evelyn. I'll be sure to take care of that for you."

"Thanks."

I walked off and heard her close the door before I even made it to the elevator. Something was going on with her, but I didn't have time to worry about her, especially when I was trying to deal with all of this.

This time, I drove to Trina's place to see if I would get a different reaction from her. I felt down and out and needed somebody to be there for me. But as soon as I parked my car in a parking spot at Trina's apartment complex, I saw her sitting in the car with the pastor's wife, Cynthia. I was getting ready to get out of my car and go speak to her, but then I saw Cynthia lean in closer to Trina. It looked as if they were kissing. I squinted to get a closer look, noticing that they were.

I covered my mouth and sat still as if cement had been poured over me. I watched as the two of them laughed and kissed several more times before eventually getting out of the car and going inside. Several lights were on, but then they went out. I was sick to my stomach and wanted to throw up. Why in the hell was all of this coming down on me in one day? My best friend was a dyke? I couldn't believe it. And the pastor's wife . . . oh my, God! Really? What in the hell was going on? Why didn't I see the people in my life for who or what they really were? A dyke? Damn!

I refused to let Trina get away with lies, and what excuse could she come up with now? I felt so betrayed. The only time Trina was being truthful with me was when she wanted my money. Only then would she speak the truth. All of this other mess was a lie. She was living one big lie and had me believing that she and Keith were in love.

The wrinkles on my forehead deepened with every step that I took to her door. I banged on the door, knowing that she would do her best to avoid answering it. Little did she know, I wasn't going anywhere. I banged so loudly that one of her neighbors opened her door and went off.

"Damn, she's not in there. Come back next week or next year, and stop bangin' so hard before you wake up my son."

I ignored the black woman who needed to take her crusty-looking tail back inside and mind her own business. Today wasn't the day to mess with me. Little did she know, she was about to catch hell. I continued to bang on the door, but Trina didn't answer.

"I know you're in there, Trina!" I shouted. "Open the door!"

"Bitch," the neighbor hissed. "Did you hear anythang I just said to you? I got a baby in here tryin' to sleep. Unless you gon' brang yo' ass up in here and stay with him all night then I suggest you stop knockin' on her door like dat and take yo' uppity-ass back where you came from."

I turned and shot daggers at her with the look in my eyes. "Would you like to hear my suggestion to you? Take yo' ass back inside and put a plug in your freaking ears, bitch. If not that, go run some bathwater so you don't hear me knocking. You look like you could use a hot shower—and a lengthy one at that."

As soon as the woman stepped forward, Trina opened the door. She was wearing a purple silk robe and had on a pair of house shoes. Her short hair was messy and not a drop of makeup was on her face.

"What is going on out here?" she questioned. "Kayla, why are you out here banging on my door like you're Five-O?"

I folded my arms across my chest. "Because I would like to speak to you now, if you don't mind."

"Please let that bitch get whatever she gots on her chest off of it," the woman said.

"And please gift wrap this bitch a dictionary, because she really needs one."

Trina pulled me inside and slammed the door. She turned on the light and stood looking at me like I was the crazy one. "What is it, Kayla? I was trying to get some rest. What is so important that you have to speak to me right now?"

"Don't play me like a fool, Trina. Where is she?"

Trina cocked her head back. "Where is who? What are you talking about?"

I figured she wouldn't be truthful with me. Hell, nobody was, so what did I expect? Instead of asking her again, I started to search her living-room closets.

"What are you doing?" Trina said, following behind me.

"I'm searching for the truth. That's what I'm doing."

"The truth about what?"

"You'll know when I find it."

I continued to walk around her apartment, searching every closet and looking underneath everything that I could see under.

"You need to leave, Kayla," Trina said. "Leave now or I'll have you arrested."

"Yeah, well, it won't be the first police threat of the day. Feel free to call whomever you wish to."

Trina stormed away from me and went into the other room. That was when I went into the bathroom and yanked the shower curtain aside. Inside stood Cynthia, covering her nakedness with a towel.

"I—I was just borrowing Trina's shower and—"

"Get out!" Trina said, pointing to the door. "How dare you come into my home as if you own it! Who in the hell do you think you are, Kayla? Who?"

I turned around and darted my finger at her. "I thought I was your best friend, Trina! The one who you share your freaking secrets with! The one who I could depend on when I needed you! The one who wouldn't lie to me about anything and the one person who I seriously thought I could trust! But who are you, Trina? Who in the hell are you, because you damn sure aren't my best friend!"

"I am that and then some! But—but I'm also gay!" Trina's voice softened. "I don't like men, but I do love women. So now you know, Kayla. Now . . . now you know my secret. So tell me. How does it feel to have a best friend who prefers to make love to women?"

I truly thought I was dreaming. God, please let me wake up from this dream and start this day all over again. But when I turned to look at Cynthia, it was all real. I looked at Trina and there she was staring at me, waiting for a response.

"You disgust me," I said, releasing deep breaths. "This is disgusting. How could you be over here having sex with the pastor's wife and then go to his church and call yourself a Christian? You're no friend of mine, Trina. I would be a fool to ever refer to you as one again. Don't you ever call me again, and as for you—" I turned to Cynthia. "You had better get on your knees and pray like hell for God to forgive you. What kind of woman are you? How dare you have others refer to you as the first lady of the church? How dare you?" I shouted.

I rushed out of the bathroom and bumped my shoulder with Trina's on the way out. She softly called my name, but I didn't bother to turn around. I got the hell out of there and drove to the nearest hotel so I could somehow or some way sort this mess out.

Chapter Eleven

Trina

I didn't feel so good after Kayla left. She didn't understand that this had nothing to do with her. It was more about not wanting anyone to know what was going on with me. I was so outdone that I made Cynthia put her clothes back on, and I asked her to leave. She, however, removed the towel from around her and straddled my lap as I sat in a chair.

"I'm not going anywhere and I'm here for you. Kayla is going to have to get over it. She has some nerves standing in judgment of us, and there are times when you can't help who you have feelings for. One day she'll understand. In the meantime, please don't let this stress you out."

"I can't help it. I feel bad for not being honest with her. I know that you'll be there for me, but I really need to be alone right now."

Cynthia removed herself from my lap and said nothing else as she got dressed. She kissed my cheek and headed for the door. "Hope to see you on Sunday," she said. "No matter what, we all still need Jesus."

She didn't lie about that, but hearing those words come from her kind of went in one ear and out the other. It was one thing to be gay, but then to be married and carrying on the way she was, wasn't right. I was participating in the mess too. I felt horrible for doing so. It was time to clean up the crap, but before I did anything I called Kayla to speak to her. She didn't answer so I left a message on her voice mail.

"I get that you're upset with me for not being honest with you, but please call me back so we can discuss this. I need to clear the air. After that, if you still don't wish to mend our friendship, so be it. At least hear me out and try to understand where I'm coming from."

I hung up and then called Evelyn to see if Kayla had called her. I hoped she hadn't, because I sure didn't want Evelyn to know my secret.

"She was over here earlier," Evelyn said. "But she left pretty upset about her and Cedric getting into it."

"About what this time? She needs to consider letting him go."

"Maybe this time she will. Apparently, he gave her a sexually transmitted disease. I'm not sure how he's going to explain that to her, but knowing him, he'll think of something."

"Are you serious?" I shouted. My heart went out to Kayla. Now I knew why she was so upset. Maybe this didn't have anything to do with me. She just caught me at a bad time. I was even more eager now to speak to her.

"That's awful. Do you have any idea where she's at? I tried to reach her on her phone, but she didn't answer."

"I have no idea where she's at, but I'm not looking for her right now. I'm trying to find Cedric, the one who I would love to give a piece of my mind."

"I want to get at him too, especially for doing Kayla like that. She recommended that we stay out of her business, but this is downright ridiculous."

"Yeah, it is. But look. I gotta go. I need to get out of here for a while and I'm supposed to meet Marc for dinner."

"Maybe we can hook up on Sunday. I have information about a job you might be interested in, so I'll pass that on to you."

"Fine. I'll call you on Sunday and we'll go from there."

Evelyn hung up, but unlike her, I was very interested in where Kayla was. So interested that I put on my sweatpants and a hoodie, got in my car and drove to her house. Jacoby was there. He opened the door to invite me inside.

"Is your mother home yet," I asked.

"Nope."

"Do you know where she's at?"

"Yep."

"Do you mind telling me?"

"She asked me not to tell anyone."

"Jacoby, please. I need to see her and it is so urgent that I do."

As we stood in the foyer, we heard the garage door open. I rushed around the corner to see who it was, but it was Cedric. He looked at me and at Jacoby, who was standing behind me.

"What's going on?" he questioned. "What are you doing in my house?"

"I'm here looking for Kayla. Do you have any idea where she's at?"

"No, I don't. But you can stay here and wait for her, if you'd like to. I'm sure she'll be coming home soon; after all, where else is she going to go?"

I turned around to Jacoby and addressed him first. "Please forgive me for saying this and I truly mean no harm." I faced Cedric and pointed my finger near his face. "You are such an asshole. You're married to a beautiful woman and all you can do is figure out ways to treat her like shit. I look forward to the day when you have to bow down to her and beg for forgiveness. I pray that whenever that day comes, she'll spit in your face and have the guts to tell you to go to hell."

Cedric casually removed his jacket and started to unbutton his crisp white shirt. "Are you done? If so, you can get the fuck out of my house. If not, for the first time, my son will have to witness me kick a woman's ass like she stole something from me. But then again, you're not really all woman, are you? You like pussy too much to be a woman, and there is a possibility that you even love pussy more than me. So, man-to-man, mind your own business. Don't worry about Kayla, because at the end of the day, I got her back and front, not you."

Before I could open my mouth, Jacoby tugged on my arm. I turned around and he nudged his head toward the door. I hated to go there like this with Cedric. It took everything I had in me not to chew him up further. Jacoby walked away and I followed. As soon we went outside, he told me where Kayla was. I gave him a squeezing hug and drove to the Embassy Suites by the airport.

Jacoby told me Kayla was in room 324, so I went to that room and knocked. Kayla asked who I was, but fearing that she wouldn't open the door, I put my finger over the peephole and whispered "room service." She opened the door. When she saw that it was me, she walked away from it.

I went inside and stood in front of her as she sat on a couch with her hands covering her face. Her braids were in a ponytail, and she wore a long pajama shirt that was almost down to her knees.

"What do you want, Trina? Why are you here?"

"First, I want to say that I'm sorry about what has happened between you and Cedric. I'm not going to say anything negative about him, but please figure out a way to deal with him. He's out of control. As for our friendship, the only reason I didn't tell you about me being gay was because I knew you would react the exact same way that you did. I was afraid of losing our friendship, and my being gay has nothing to do with how I've treated you as a friend. I may have lied to you about this, but it was because of my own insecurities. I didn't want anybody to know, so please do not go around spreading my business to other people, including Evelyn. When I'm ready to tell her, I will. In the meantime, if you would prefer to end our friendship like this, I'll have to deal with it. It won't be the first time I lost those closest to me because of my preferences, and I'm sure it won't be the last. The choice is yours, Kayla. Just let me know what's up either way."

Kayla lifted her head and took a deep breath. She shook her head and her eyes searched me. "You know what, Trina? I do not have time for any of this. The only thing on my mind is what in the hell am I going to do about my marriage. Who you love or who you have sex with is not important to me. I don't have time to sit here and talk about this with you, but I will say this: I don't trust you and I never will. I thought I knew who you were, but I don't. I've shared some of my deepest secrets with you, yet you lied to me when I inquired about you being gay. I'm in a place where I don't want to be around anybody. So why don't you just leave and go be with whoever you want to be with. It doesn't matter how I feel about what you're doing—and why are you so adamant about seeking my approval?"

"I don't need your approval; after all, I am a grown woman who will make my own decisions. After what happened today, I felt obligated to come clean about my situation, so that's why I'm here."

Kayla's eyes grew wider. "Obligated? Girl, please. The only reason you came clean was because you got busted in the midst of screwing the first lady. Don't stand there like you came here to express all this crap to me because our friendship means so much to you. The bottom line is, if it did, you had years . . . plenty of years to tell me what was going on with you. I've been running around here with you, claiming you as my best friend and I really don't know much about you. How many other women are you screwing at our church? I'm sure they all probably think I'm some kind of gay trick too."

Kayla's harsh words stung. I looked at her and made myself clear. "This conversation is over. I tried to get at you like a for-real woman would, but I see that you're so fucking bitter at your husband right now that your mind is real twisted. I'm going to get out of here before I disrespect you, as you have clearly disrespected me. Have a nice life, Kayla. I'll be praying that everything works out for you."

I turned to walk toward the door.

"Don't pray for me, pray for yourself," she shouted. "Pray that you get your head on straight and that God can deliver you from being a lesbian."

Unfortunately, she touched a nerve. I turned around and let her have it. "I would rather be a lesbian any day of the week than be a dumb, disease-infected bitch who allows her husband to fuck all over her. Get your own house in order before you start running up in mine, trying to advise me on the best way to conduct myself. Good-bye, Kayla, and good riddance."

I walked out, telling myself that I would never, ever speak to her again.

Chapter Twelve

Evelyn

I called. He wouldn't answer. I left messages. He wouldn't respond. I didn't want to go to their house because Kayla was there, so the only place I could reach Cedric was at his office. I was pissed. After Kayla left my place and told me about the disease incident, I rushed to my doctor this morning, only for her to tell me the same thing. This fool had given me chlamydia and now he didn't have anything to say about it. I still hadn't had time to tell him about the baby either. There was so much mess going on, and Kayla had the nerve to be running around here looking for sympathy and wanting some attention. I was still waiting for her to swing some money my way. As of yet, she hadn't given me one dime.

I knew darn well where I could get some money from, and Cedric was a fool if he thought he was going to dismiss me. He didn't know who he was messing with. I wasn't a passive trick like his wife was. I thought he knew that, but maybe he needed to be reminded once again.

I entered the lobby with my dark shades on. My hair was pulled back into a thick, curly ponytail. My makeup was painted on like artwork and I was rocking some bright red lipstick that moistened my lips. The fitted sleeveless dress I wore appeared melted on my small curves, and I stepped like a model in my five-inch heels. I lowered my shades, peering over them to look at the blonde-haired receptionist who always had an attitude.

"Would you let Cedric Thompson know that his baby's mama is here to see him?"

The receptionist's eyes grew wide. She picked up the phone and buzzed Cedric on speakerphone. "Excuse me,

Mr. Thompson. A woman is here to see you. Is it okay for me to send her to your office?"

"What woman? Is it my wife? If so, you need to call security."

"No, it's not your wife. But the woman says that she's your . . . uh . . . baby's mama."

Cedric paused then told the receptionist to buzz the door and let me through. I hadn't noticed the door before. Obviously, it was something new. I swished my hips from side to side as I made my way to Cedric's office. The door was wide open, and when I walked inside he was gazing out of the window with his hands in his pockets. He looked dynamite in a brown tailored suit, but too darn bad his dick was shooting fire.

"Close my door," he said without looking in my direction. I closed the door then proceeded forward and removed my glasses.

"I guess you already know that you're on my shit list and why, right?" I said.

"I don't give a damn about your shit list. And just so you know, you're on mine too."

I folded my arms across my chest. "For what? Please tell me why my name would be on your list then I'll tell you a gazillion reasons why yours is on mine."

Cedric turned to face me. His eyes scanned me up and down, before he walked up to me and stood within inches. "Because you're a fucking slut, that's why. And if you came here to tell me about your baby, I don't want to hear about it. Tell Marc to step up and be a man. I hope he's capable of providing for you, and all I can say is the two of you deserve each other."

He came off as a little jealous, causing me to reach out and slap his ass. He caught my hand in midair. He shoved me backward and I stumbled. "Don't bring that bullshit in here today, woman! I'm not in the mood! Since we're done talking, you can get the fuck out of here. Don't come back unless I invite you to."

I was very disturbed by Cedric's tone and his actions. He was showing his ass, but I wouldn't dare let him see how hurt I was by what he'd said.

"When all is said and done, this child is yours and you know it. Marc doesn't have to step up because, eventually, you'll have to do it. In a big way, I may add, so prepare yourself to deal with it. And one more thing before I go. No, two more things: Spreading diseases around town ain't really cool, and that nasty dick of yours will never get to touch this pussy again. If you even think about making things hard for me, I will go to your wife and tell her everything I know. I will make your life miserable, Cedric, so you'd better think long and hard about how you intend to play your hand going forward. Meanwhile, I'm broke. I need some money. I hope you don't mind kicking me out a little something, especially after all I've done for you."

Cedric leaned against his desk with a sly smirk on his face. "You're a real piece of work, Evelyn, and I finally get why I started fucking with you. I got a couple of things to add before you go too, so listen up real good because I'm not going to repeat myself again. You can tell Kayla whatever it is that you want to. I don't give a fuck, and our marriage has been over with for quite some time. Whatever you tell her won't matter to me not one bit. The baby, mine or not, will be better off aborted. Besides, I don't have kids with whores and I will never take care of a child who belongs to one.

"Finally, pertaining to your little situation with chlamydia, why are you and Kayla running up in here like the sky is falling and it's a big deal? Go pop some damn pills to clear that shit up and be done with it. It's not the end of the world and some people get caught slipping from time to time. I could tell something wasn't right with that other pussy when I was in it, and believe me when I say I feel awful for making you swallow, and, uh—well, you know what freaky you did. Anyway, forgive me. When we both get cleared up, maybe you'll have a change of heart and let me hit it again. Call me when you're ready. You know where to find me."

Cedric winked and walked around his desk. He picked up his phone, holding it in his hand. "Work without play is no good. I'm done playing, so now I need to get back to work. Get the fuck out of my office. If I have to listen to one more word from you, I'll have you removed from this building."

Okay. So I thought I was a bad bitch, but Cedric had the last word. As soon as I opened my mouth, security came and escorted me out. I still had so much to get off my chest, but it wasn't getting off anytime soon. I had to rethink my approach to this situation. It started with going to see Kayla so I could see where things between her and Cedric now stood.

I swerved in and out of traffic while trying to reach Kayla on my cell phone. I hadn't spoken to her since she'd left my place the other day. Whenever I called her home phone, Jacoby told me she wasn't there. I wondered if Trina knew where she was, but when I questioned her she had an attitude.

"No, I don't know her whereabouts, and quite frankly, I don't care."

"Since when? Have the two of you had some differences again?"

"Yes we have. This time, however, I don't think we're going to be able to repair our friendship. Kayla said some things to me that I didn't appreciate, so I'm going to leave her alone and let her do her."

"How many times have the two of you been down this road before? Y'all always make up and you know she's dealing with some crazy stuff right now. I don't get why you're tripping. We've been up and down throughout our friendship, and the least you can do is try to understand her situation and be there for her."

I was feeding Trina a bunch of bull. I liked when her and Kayla were at each other's throats. It was kind of hilarious to me, and they always tried to get me to pick sides.

"I hear what you're saying, but it's not like you've actually been there for her either, have you? Every time I talk to you, you're too busy and you don't seem to have time for me or Kayla."

"I have my own problems to deal with, Trina. You know I still haven't found a job and I'm looking forward to meeting with you so I can hear about that lead you mentioned. And I also didn't tell you this yet, but I'm pregnant. That's why I've been acting so standoffish. I have a lot of things on my mind, okay?"

"I'm surprised to hear you're pregnant. Congratulations to you. Do you know who the father is?"

"Hell, yes, I know who the father is. Why would you ask me that? Like . . . like I'm some type of confused whore who's been sleeping around with a bunch of men."

"I didn't mean it like that, but you have talked about several men that you've been seeing. Plus . . ." Trina paused for a few seconds. "Never mind. I got this lady over here who wants to buy some artwork. I'll call you later, all right?"

"Yeah, whatever, Trina. I wish you would be clear about what you want to say and stop beating around the bush."

"I don't want to assume anything and hurt your feelings. I could be wrong about this, but tell me the truth and be honest. Have you been having sex with Cedric?"

I didn't dare respond yet. I wanted to tell Trina what I had been doing, but now wasn't the right time. "I don't know where you're getting your information from, but I am highly offended by you asking me that. What kind of person do you think I am, Trina? I would never stoop low like that and have sex with my best friend's husband. Are you crazy for asking me something like that?"

"Maybe I am, but like I said, I gotta go."

She hung up on me. I couldn't help but to wonder where she had gotten her information from. I assumed that nobody knew about me and Cedric but us. I guessed Trina had been speculating, but she was definitely on to something.

Kayla had been missing in action, but while Cedric's foolish self was still at work I drove by their house to see if she was there. She wasn't, but Jacoby was outside washing his car. The music was blasting and he had on a pair of sagging jeans that showed his drawers. A wife-beater displayed the muscles in his arms, but there weren't many muscles to get me hyped. Jacoby was thin and very tall. He was a handsome young man, and I couldn't help but sit in my car for a few minutes, thinking if I wanted to include him in my next plan. I put my shades back on and got out of my car. I swayed my hips, locking his attention as he kept his eyes on me.

"Hi, Jacoby. I've been trying to reach your mother. Do you know where she is?"

"Yep," he said, then bent over to swirl the soapy rag on his car.

"Do you have any idea when she's coming home?"

"No, I don't."

I sighed, because I didn't appreciate how short he was with me. "Listen. I know she probably told you not to let anyone disturb her, but she needs us right now. The last thing Kayla needs is to be cooped up somewhere without family and friends. I would like to see her. Therefore, I would appreciate if you would tell me where I can find my best friend."

"Sorry, but I have specific rules to follow, and I'm going to follow them. All I can say is she checked out of one hotel and is now in another one."

"Which one, is the question. Please tell me."

Jacoby shook his head, signaling no. He continued to wash around his car, then he headed inside with several dirty rags in his hands. I followed behind him, still trying to persuade him to tell me where Kayla was.

"Jacoby, why are you ignoring me? You know how close your mother and me are. Don't you know that she needs me? What if she's suicidal and needs somebody to talk to? I'm sure you know the condition she's in, especially if you've been speaking to her."

Jacoby tossed the dirty rags in the trash can, and then he looked underneath the sink and got a few more clean ones. He held them in his hand and turned to face me. "I have been speaking to her every day. And you know what, Evelyn? She sounds like she's doing okay. All she needed to do was get away from my father for a while. Maybe she'll be able to rethink some things and do what is right for her future."

"Lord knows I hope you're right. She has gotten herself in a real big mess and this doesn't look like it's going to be an easy fix."

Jacoby shrugged as if he didn't care. He stood silent for a minute. His eyes narrowed like Cedric's often did sometimes. I stepped up closer to Jacoby, leaving very little breathing room in between us.

"You know what," I said in a soft tone. "You're looking more and more like your father every day. You had better be careful with that, because that would put you in a position to have any and everything you could possibly want."

Jacoby displayed a smug look on his face, identical to Cedric. "So, let me get this straight. You're saying that I have it going on just like my father does? Really?"

"You sure do. And let me repeat myself again: That means you can have anything you want. All you have to do is ask for it."

Jacoby inched forward, this time leaving no space between us. My breasts were pressed against his chest. I could feel his muscle swelling against me. Our eyes stayed locked together, and I was surprised when he slipped his arm around my waist.

"Anything," he said in a whisper.

I nodded and confirmed my words. "Anything. Especially for a young man who wears a size thirteen shoe."

"Fourteen," Jacoby said, while lifting me on the island. He parted my legs then moved in between them. The direction of his eyes dropped to my lips and mine dropped to his. I reached out to grab the back of his head, but as I leaned in to seal a kiss, he backed his head up.

"I—I can't help but to think about what positions I would like to put you in, Evelyn, but maybe I should let you decide."

Jacoby reached into his pocket and pulled out his cell phone. He turned it so I could see the pictures, and to my surprise, there were pictures of Cedric having sex with other women.

"What about that position?" Jacoby said, flipping through the pictures. "That's a good one right there. Or how about this one?"

My face was already cracked and had hit the floor. I looked at the picture of Cedric and me having sex. It was in his bedroom when Kayla was away in Atlanta.

"I say we go upstairs to my parents' bedroom and get busy. What say you?"

I jumped down from the island to gather myself. Jacoby was playing games with me and I certainly didn't appreciate it. "I say, you can take all of those pictures and shove them. I don't know what kind of game you're playing, but you're way out of your league."

I tried to move, but he remained in front of me. "I think I'm playing this game quite well for my age, and even though I may be my father's son, I don't want anything to do with his whores. What may be good for him is not good enough for me. So all I'm going to ask you to do is get the hell out of my mother's house and please figure out a way to check yourself on the major disrespect."

I was highly upset by the way he spoke to me, but he would never know it. I switched to my game face and displayed a smile.

"You mean, *your father's house*, because your mother's name is not even on it. And at least we agree that I have been good to your father. Sometimes, leftovers are. You can't knock it if you haven't tried it—and with that, I'm on my way home. If your mother calls, please tell her to reach out to me. And if you by chance have a change of heart about me, my door is always open."

Jacoby didn't respond. He just stared at me. That was when the smirk appeared and something eerie was trapped in his eyes. "How's the job coming along, Evelyn? You've been rather busy. I wondered if you were able to find another job yet."

"Why are you concerned about my job? I see your mother has been over here running her mouth again."

"No, honestly, she hasn't. I heard about your troubles through someone else. It's a shame what happened to you on your job and I hope you're about to find another one."

Jacoby walked off, leaving me puzzled about how he knew so much. First, the pictures of me and Cedric alarmed me. Then, with him bringing up my job, something wasn't adding up with this.

"Are you the one responsible for what happened on my job?" I asked.

Jacoby snickered and slapped the rag against his hand. "Ding-ding. I guess you are somewhat bright after all. It took you a minute, but you finally got it. You didn't think I was going to stand by and let you make me and my mother's life miserable, without you suffering any consequences, did you?

And trust me when I say this is just the beginning, especially if you don't do the right thing and end your friendship with my mother and stop fucking my dad. I know it's going to be difficult for you to tear yourself away from him, but believe me when I say he's no good for you. You deserve better, Evelyn. I do mean that from the bottom of my heart."

Jacoby opened the door to go back outside, but I rushed after him. This conniving fool had cost me my damn job and I was anxious to hear about his plans to destroy me. Prior to today, he was the least of my worries. Now all of that had changed. I still had something up my sleeve, though, and I was ready to pull it out like a weapon and use it.

I ran in front of Jacoby, stopping him dead in his tracks. I pointed my finger in his face and spoke through gritted teeth. "You listen to me, boy. If I find out that you had anything to do with me losing my job, you're going to be in big trouble. As far as Cedric is concerned, you don't have what it takes to be like him. The reason why you can't get along with him is because you're jealous. You wish that his blood ran through your veins, but your blood comes from a lowlife negro who isn't shit. So the next time you speak to your precious mother, be sure to inquire about your father. The question you may want to ask her is, which one is he?"

I stormed away, mad as hell. How dare this kid try to mess with me? After my conversation with Cedric, I'd just about had it with these people. Kayla and her entire family could go to hell. I was over this bullshit, and I had to figure out another way to get my hands on some money.

Chapter Thirteen

Kayla

Jacoby had been blowing up my phone, telling me to come home. I rushed out of the Renaissance Hotel, and as soon as I walked through the door, he was sitting on the couch in the living room, waiting for me. His eyes were puffy; he was roughly massaging his hands together. Fearing that something bad had happened, I hurried into the room and stood in front of him.

"No more bad news, please," I said tearfully. "What's going on now?"

Jacoby looked up at me. A tear sped down his face and dripped on his trembling knee. "I got a question for you," he said. "And please do not lie to me, Mother. I want the truth."

My stomach was already being squeezed in a tight knot. There was only one thing that could make Jacoby this upset. I hoped my secret was not about to come out.

"What is it?" I said softly.

"Who is my damn father? Is Cedric not my real father?"

"Absolutely, hell fucking no, I'm not," Cedric said from behind me.

I swung around and staggered as I saw him standing there. "It's time to come clean and get all of this shit out in the open. I'm glad you finally asked the question, Jacoby, and for a long time I was very confused myself. I was suckered into believing that your mother really and truly loved me, but then I discovered that it was all a lie. She used me, man, so that she could have all of this. She lied to you, for the sake of keeping her financial situation on lock. Then she turned around and made me out to be the villain in all of this. I'm just a monster that she created. There was no way for me to stay committed to a woman who hurt me as much as she did. I hope you see now, son, why I've conducted myself in such a horrible manner. Maybe I was wrong for taking some of this out on you, and all I can do is ask for your forgiveness."

My mouth hung wide open. Cedric was so good at manipulating people. I prayed that Jacoby wouldn't fall for the bullshit. But when I turned my head to look at him, the anger in his eyes had deepened. His stare was cold. He didn't dare take his eyes off me. I stood there, unprepared. I didn't know what to say, and I wasn't even sure if the truth was good enough.

"Do not believe that mess Cedric just told you. This has nothing to do with my financial situation and—"

"To hell with your financial situation!" Jacoby yelled. "Who in the fuck is my father?"

My whole body shivered from his tone. No matter how upset he was, he needed to calm down. "Don't raise your voice at me. I'll tell you who your father is, but we need to go somewhere away from Cedric—"

"Stop beating around the damn bush," Cedric said. "Tell Jacoby who his father is right now. As a matter of fact, fuck it. I'll tell him. His name is Arnez Jackson and he was one of my friends in college. He started doing some crazy shit, got himself in a whole lot of trouble, dropped out of school, and got on drugs. He came to me about three years ago, asking for some money and threatened to tell you that he was your biological father, if I didn't give the money to him. I didn't give him a damn dime, but someone else paid him a large sum of money to keep his mouth shut. I don't have to tell you who that person is. I'll just say that you're looking right at her."

I could barely breathe right now. I held my chest and looked at Jacoby with sorrow and much regret in my eyes. "I lied to protect you," I confessed. "Arnez had disappointed me so much and I wanted you to be raised by a man who I thought you could look up to and who could show you how to be a real man. I failed you, son. I'm so sorry for—"

Jacoby hopped up from the couch. He spoke through gritted teeth while looking at me and Cedric both. "Sorry my ass, Mother. I can't believe how pathetic the two of you are. I have wasted too much of my time, trying to get the two of you to act like grown people who should know better. Is it so damn hard to love and respect each other? Is it so easy to keep secrets from the ones you love? No wonder I've been running around here feeling as if I don't fit in. Cedric not being my biological father explains a lot, especially his ill treatment and his I-don't-give-a-fuck attitude. I can't say that I blame him, Mother. Only because you created this mess. I don't give a damn how you get out of it, but whatever you do, leave me the fuck alone. I'm done."

Jacoby rushed past me, and when I grabbed his arm he shoved me backward, almost knocking me on my ass. Cedric jumped in front of him, holding his shoulders and looking directly into his eyes.

"From the bottom of my heart, you will always be my son. I regret that it has come to this, but I'm delighted that the truth has finally come to the light. Take all the time you need to let this soak in. If you need me, I'll be right here."

Jacoby didn't respond. He opened the front door and left. I didn't bother to go after him, only because I knew he wasn't prepared to listen to my explanation for all of this. Cedric had definitely gotten what he wanted. I was anxious to wash that smug look off his face.

I smacked away several tears and was seething with anger as I spoke to him.

"If you knew about Arnez, why didn't you ever say anything to me? You know darn well that the only reason I didn't come clean about this was because of the kind of man Arnez was. You were broke back then, Cedric. My decision didn't have anything to do with money and you know it!"

"Yes it did, so wipe your tears, cut the drama, and stop acting. That's all I talked to you about—my plans to be wealthy. You knew I had everything lined up, and you had just as much faith as I did that we would one day have all of this and then some. The bottom line is you lied to Jacoby and you lied to me. Face it and stop trying to justify your actions. From day one I knew Jacoby wasn't my son. When I looked into his eyes all I saw was Arnez. But I went along with it, because at the time I did love you. For years, I had to live with your fucking lie and pretend that everything was all good. Now, you want to come down on me for the shit that I've been doing. You want to run up in my office, kick my ass, embarrass the hell out of me, and pretend that you've been the good wife. You can't pretend anymore, Kay. The shit has hit the fan. I expect for you to be out of my house and out of my life for good. My divorce lawyers will be in touch soon."

This time Cedric walked away. I had to admit that I was unprepared for all of this. I feared what was about to happen and it wasn't like I had anyone in my corner. The only person I was somewhat on good terms with was Evelyn. Maybe I could stay in one of her extra bedrooms for a few weeks, until I worked this out. I had to settle things down, get to my bank account and clear it out fast. I didn't have money to waste at hotel rooms and I knew Cedric was about to shut my life down. I had to admit my mistakes. Maybe I did break Cedric's heart. Maybe he was the kind of man he was because of me. The least I could do was apologize.

I walked slowly up the stairs and into our bedroom. Cedric was in the sitting area with his feet propped on the table in front of him. His hands were locked behind his head and he looked to be in deep thought.

"I don't even know if I should be apologizing or if I should be demanding an apology from you." I walked further into the room and stood by the fireplace. "We've both made some mistakes and you have no right to point the finger at me. In my heart, I still believe that we can somehow work things out. The last thing I want is a divorce. You say that you don't care anymore, but that's because you're angry right now. I will give you all the time you need to think this through, but please do not go rushing off to divorce me."

Funny. Just yesterday I couldn't wait to file for a divorce. I had an appointment scheduled with my lawyer and everything. Today was a new day. I still wondered if my actions had hurt him as much as he proclaimed they did.

Cedric lowered his arms to his elbows and licked his lips. "The damage is already done, Kay. I'm no good and I'll never be any good. You hurt me too bad and unfortunately, I'm not as forgiving as you are. Don't waste your time fighting for something that will never be. I assure you that this marriage will never be what you expect it to be, because the truth is, I don't love you anymore."

His words cut deep. I stood, feeling as if a sharp knife had been stabbed in my stomach. I wanted to drop to my knees as Cedric left the bedroom. And when I heard the door open and his car speed away, I cried my heart out. My husband and son were gone. I had no clue how to piece this all back together. I basically had to start all over, but I didn't know where to start. I was confused. Not in a million years did I see this day coming.

The next day, which was Saturday, I went to the bank to withdraw my money. Unfortunately for me, Cedric had transferred all of my money into another account. He was unaware of a small savings account I had for Jacoby that had almost ten grand in it. I took that money out, but I had to be very careful how I spent it. Basically, I had to make it stretch until I could find a way to stabilize my situation.

Once I left the bank, I checked out of the pricey room at the hotel and drove to Evelyn's place with my luggage in tow. I had plans to go back home and remove some of my expensive jewelry, but I was so sure that Cedric had changed the locks already.

A woman was going up on the elevator, so I got on and took it up to Evelyn's floor. When I knocked on the door, she opened it with a bowl of ice cream in her hand and a spoon was in her mouth. She glanced at my luggage and then she widened the door for me to come in.

"I need a place to stay," I said immediately. "Do you mind if I stay in one of your rooms until I can figure out what to do about my situation?"

"I've been trying to find out exactly what is going on with your situation, but you've made yourself unavailable."

"I know. I needed some time alone to think."

I rolled my luggage into the living room and left it there. I plopped down on the couch, along with Evelyn. I told her everything that had happened between me, Jacoby, and

Cedric. I also told her about my fallout with Trina, but I didn't mention that Trina was gay. I worked around that little situation, feeling that if Trina wanted Evelyn to know she would tell her.

"Wow, Kayla, I—I really don't know what to say. I'm surprised that you never thought Jacoby would find out who his real father was, and I'm more in awe to know that Cedric knew about it all this time and didn't say anything."

"Not one word. He put me on the spot, and Jacoby now thinks that I'm the worst person on this earth."

"I doubt that he thinks that, and like you said, he just needs time. As far as Cedric is concerned, I don't know what to say about him. It sounds like the marriage is over. Maybe it's a good thing that you're moving on."

"I never said anything about moving on. I intend to save my marriage and my family will not be torn apart because of this. I've been trying to put myself in Cedric's shoes, and a part of me understands where he's coming from. My lies may, indeed, have hurt him. It explains why he's changed so much over the years."

Evelyn rolled her eyes and threw her hand back. "Girl, please. Cedric is faking the funk. He's making excuses for his actions and is trying to justify why he's been an unfaithful husband. I don't know why you don't see that. It's part of his plan to make you feel like you're the one who has done wrong, when realistically it's him."

"I thought about that too, but there is no denying that I lied to him, Evelyn. And this wasn't just any ol' lie either. It was a lie that I knew would affect us deeply, so here we are."

"So, I guess you've forgiven him for the whole chlamydia thing, huh? It's okay that he's been having sex with other women, and you're perfectly fine with him taking the money out of the bank and changing the locks on the doors. And then the way Cedric told Jacoby that he wasn't his father was okay with you too. Forgive me for not understanding your feelings about this. I'm seriously over here scratching my head."

"You wouldn't understand any of this, because you're not Jacoby's mother and you're not the one married to Cedric.

You didn't witness the hurt in their eyes. I did. You don't know how much damage my lie has done to them. I do. Like Cedric said, some people just aren't as forgiving and they have their own way of dealing with things. Of course I'm upset about the chlamydia thing. I'm upset about the other women as well, but I have bigger fish to fry than to worry about hoes out here screwing my husband."

Evelyn pursed her lips and got off the couch. She put her empty ice cream bowl in the sink then she opened the fridge to get a bottled water. "Would you like something to drink? All I have is water, nothing else."

"No, I'm fine. I haven't forgotten about giving you the money I told you I would give you, but things have changed and I'm unable to help you out like I said I would. Right now, I have about ten grand to my name. The only thing I can afford is about fifty or sixty bucks to help you get some groceries. I'll be able to give you a few extra dollars for letting me stay in your room, but to be honest, Evelyn, I may need the money that I have to fight Cedric in court. I have a feeling that he's not going to back down and he's planning to leave me high and dry."

"Possibly, but here's the problem that I have. Marc is supposed to be moving in with me on Monday. He's supposed to help me with my finances, so I can't let you stay here. It wouldn't look right, but had you come to me sooner, maybe I could have made some different arrangements."

After all that I had done for her, I couldn't believe what she'd just said. "I won't be in the way. I only need to stay here for—"

"No," Evelyn said adamantly. "You *would* be in the way and I don't want Marc to be uncomfortable. He already gave me first month's rent, so I'm not going to renege on him."

I was in total disbelief. The expression on my face showed it. "I could stay on the couch and make sure I'm gone all day. Marc wouldn't even know I lived here and—"

"No, Kayla, that wouldn't work."

The tone of my voice rose. "So what do you want me to do, Evelyn? Sleep in my car?"

"Why not? It's big enough, but I doubt that you'll have to do that. Why don't you go make up with Trina? She has an extra bedroom, doesn't she? It's unfortunate that I can't help. Whether you know it or not, I'm deeply sorry that I can't."

This conversation with Evelyn left me speechless. In order for me not to cuss her out, I got off the couch, grabbed my luggage, and decided to go. I didn't even say good-bye. I proceeded to the door and didn't bother to close it after I walked out.

Chapter Fourteen

Trina

Whenever I was under pressure I threw myself into work. I had been trying to avoid too many people and it had been a minute since I had worked from the office. I suspected that Keith was eager to finish what we never got started and he'd still been trying to contact me.

Cynthia had also been ringing my phone, but I wanted to keep my distance from her. I avoided church altogether. When she came to my apartment last night I didn't answer the door. Lexi hadn't been bugging me as much, but she did call last night to inquire about my sudden distance. She said that she would stop by today to see me and when I heard a knock on the door, I was so sure that it was her. I looked through the peephole and saw Kayla standing there with her head lowered. I wasn't up to arguing with her, so I ignored her.

"Trina, I already heard you walking to the door. I came here to apologize and to ask you a few things. Please open the door."

For whatever reason, I couldn't stay mad at Kayla if I tried. Ever since we were in elementary school, I always managed to forgive her for all of the hiccups in our friendship along the way. Yes, we'd said some harsh things to each other over the years, we'd done some ugly things, and we'd kept many secrets from each other. But at the end of the day, I still cared for her. I still considered her my best friend—one that I was mad at but still loved with all my heart.

I opened the door, but refused to smile at her, even though I wanted to. She had a weary look on her face and was dressed in a pair of stonewashed jeans and a T-shirt. Her braids were wrapped in a bun and her gold hoop earrings matched her thong sandals.

"Apology accepted," I said to her and said no more.

Tears welled in Kayla's eyes and she reached out to embrace me. She wasn't what I considered an emotional woman, and whenever she cried I knew something deep was going on inside of her. "I'm so sorry for what I said to you," she said. "I—I don't know what got into me and I never should have treated you that way."

Seeing her cry made me cry, but I hurried to blink away my tears. "I'm sorry too. I was wrong for saying what I said to you as well. I knew you were going through some things and I apologize for not understanding your situation."

We backed away from each other. I invited her to come in and follow me. I went into my studio to finish painting, and she sat on one of the stools watching me.

"By the look in your eyes," I said, "I can tell there has been a lot going on. I'm all ears, so tell me what's been up."

Kayla told me about the situation with her family, and then she told me about Evelyn. I just shook my head, but deep down I knew the real reason why Evelyn had been acting funny. She had been fucking around with Cedric and she was also pregnant with his child. I wanted so badly to tell Kayla the truth, but she was already on the brink of losing it. I didn't want to cause her more pain. I felt horrible about not saying anything, and there I was—again—feeling as if I was betraying her. Thing is, I wasn't sure if it was my place to say anything. I didn't want to be the one to open up another can of worms, and I thought about what this would do to my friendship with Evelyn. We still got along well, but there was no secret that Kayla and I were closer. It had been that way for quite some time, only because Kayla had always been there for me, way more than Evelyn had been.

"So, that about sums up my drama," Kayla said. "And with that, I need a place to stay. I won't wear out my welcome and I will do my best to be out of here in a few weeks, no later than a month."

"It doesn't matter how long you stay. You're welcome to my guest room. But I have to say this to you, and I don't want to make you feel uncomfortable about this. My life goes on over here. I have several lady friends who come to see me from time to time and I'm not going to change my situation because you don't approve of it."

"Look. You do you and don't worry about how I feel. I doubt that I ever will approve, but so what, Trina. It has a lot to do about how I was raised and I can't change my way of thinking overnight."

"I get that and it's cool. All I ask is that you refrain from any negativity about my situation while you're here and please do not insult my guests. It's already hard enough being me. The last thing I need is a friend who constantly judges me."

Kayla told me that she understood. She went to her car to get her luggage and when she came back in she put her luggage in the guest room. She watched me paint for a while and complimented the work I had done.

"You have some serious talent," she said. "I'm surprised you don't have your own studio. You really should try to open up a store or something."

"What do you think I've been trying to do? It's kind of hard when you don't have money to do those things. If I had your money, I could've made big things happen by now."

Kayla dropped her head and looked down at the floor. "Tell me something, Trina. Have I been a good friend to you? Do you think I helped you enough, considering all of the money I was sitting on?"

I put my paintbrush down and wiped my dirty hands on my sweats. "Our friendship hasn't been all about what you can do for me, but it has been about what we can do for each other. It's my responsibility to make things happen for myself, not yours. There are times when I wanted to ask you for the money to help me get my business started, but this is something that I want to do for myself. If you had offered, of course I would have taken the money, but I'm glad you never did."

Kayla got up from the chair and walked over to the window to look out. "If the shoe was on the other foot, I would've wanted you to help me. I mean, that's what friends are for too, and it's kind of like a blessing that I could have passed on to others. Maybe that's why I'm in the situation I'm in right now. You have to admit that I've been a little selfish. Maybe that's why Evelyn has her issues with me, and I can honestly say that I kind of get her coldness at times."

"Okay. So you are a little selfish, but we do have to take responsibility for our own lives. I said it and now you know. Now if you don't mind, I would like to get out of here and go get something to eat. I'm starving and I'm not going to stay cooped up in here all night."

"Food, here we come," Kayla said.

Before we left, I called Lexi to see if she would meet us at Louie's in the Central West End. Kayla called to see if she could reach Jacoby. A sad expression was on her face and she told me that his number had been disconnected.

"I'm going to drive by the house to see if he's there," she said. "Afterward, I'll meet you at the restaurant, okay?"

"That's fine. Be careful and don't push so hard, Kayla. Eventually, he'll come around."

"I hope so."

Kayla left in her car and I got in mine, heading to the Central West End. It was warm outside, so I wore a pair of baggy jeans shorts and a half top that showed my midriff and tattoos. The shorts hung low enough where my belly ring showed and my preppy tennis shoes provided a casual look I was trying to accomplish. When I got to Louie's, I was seated at a booth in the far corner. It was packed and the music in the background was rocking. Flat-screen TV's were mounted on the walls and several people were there to watch the basketball play-offs.

I sat for at least thirty minutes, wondering where Lexi and Kayla were. But when I looked up and saw Keith, I put the menu up to cover my face. Unfortunately, he spotted me before I could hide myself.

"Trina, is that you?" he asked as he walked up to me with one of his friends next to him.

I lowered the menu and smiled. "Hey, Keith. What's up?"

"Nothing much. This is my boy, Dane. Dane, this is Trina. The amazing, beautiful woman I was telling you about."

"Oh, yeah," Dane said, extending his hand. "Nice to meet you."

"Same here."

"So . . . uh . . . are you here with someone?" Keith asked.

"A couple of my girlfriends will be here shortly—and as a matter of fact, here comes one now."

I saw Kayla coming my way. It didn't appear that she had any luck with Jacoby. I introduced her again to Keith then to Dane.

"Hello," she said, keeping it short, and then she took a seat next to me. "Why don't the two of you join us? I'm sure we can all fit in this booth, can't we?"

I didn't necessarily approve of Kayla asking them to sit with us and I wasn't so sure how Lexi would feel about it. Either way, they sat at the booth with us and everybody started ordering drinks and food. Minutes later, Lexi strutted in. She had a thing where she always wanted me to herself, so she was surprised to see the others sitting at the booth with us. I introduced her to everyone. Keith and Dane didn't know what was up, but Kayla appeared to be uncomfortable.

"I want to sit next to Trina," Lexi said.

In order for that to happen, Kayla had to move. She looked at me and I didn't say one word. In an effort not to make a scene, I hoped she would just get up and allow Lexi to sit where she wished. Thankfully, Kayla did.

"I'm sorry I'm so late, but I got held up at the nail shop. Trina, do you like my nails?"

"They're nice. Real nice, but why don't you go ahead and order your food? Everyone else has already ordered theirs."

Lexi picked up the menu, looking at it. Dane and Keith were talking and checking out the game and Kayla sat on the end stiff as a board. She kept looking around the restaurant at several gay people, and her eyes bugged when she saw two men kissing. Her nose winced at two ladies who stood by the bar with their hands in each other's pockets, but I did notice her smile at a man who waved at her from afar. When he walked away, she was back to looking stiff. Her arms were so tight against her and she made sure that Lexi didn't touch her. Lexi gave the waitress her order and then passed her the menu. As we all began to talk, Lexi placed her hand on my leg and started to rub it.

"I can't believe I finally met you," Dane said to me. "All my boy ever talk about is you. You got this fool feeling some kind of way about you."

Kayla smiled, but Lexi narrowed her eyes then rolled them. She squeezed my thigh then took my hand and put in on her lap. From underneath the table, she inched my hand up her skirt, trying to get me to feel her hot spot. I saw Kayla observing from the corner of her eye. She then picked up the glass of water in front of her, gulping it down.

"Yeah, Keith and I are good friends," I stressed. "It's good to know that he still has nice things to say about me."

"Always," Keith said, putting his cute dimples on display. "But I'm not letting you get away from me tonight. So you may have to say bye-bye to your girlfriends and come spend some quiet time with me."

Lexi pinched my thigh real hard and snapped her head to look at me. I mean, What in the hell did she want me to say? I wasn't about to put my business out there tonight, so I ignored her gestures that were very annoying; so annoying that Kayla stood up and tucked her purse underneath her arm.

"I'm not hungry anymore," she said. "I need some fresh air and I think I'm going to get out of here and go home. It was nice meeting you all. Trina, can I have the keys to your apartment? I will see you later."

I gave Kayla the keys and she walked off. Lexi questioned why Trina was going to my apartment and, not satisfied with my answer, she pouted. Keith kept pursuing me and Lexi was upset that I hadn't told him to back off.

"You invited me here," she said with an attitude. "But it's obvious that you don't have time for me tonight."

Lexi stormed off, leaving me in a position where I had to explain my silly friends. "I apologize, but I have friends who demand my attention. Don't take them walking out like that personal. I'm sure I'll catch up with them later."

Keith and Dane looked at each other then shrugged. They continued to watch the game and get their drink on. I did as well. I had a good time with the fellas and when we got ready to go, Keith reminded me about his invitation.

"Just for an hour or so," he pleaded. "I live nearby and you don't have to travel far."

I kept telling myself that I didn't want to be alone with Keith, but I also didn't want to go home and face Kayla, nor did I want to hear Lexi gripe about tonight. Therefore, I decided to take Keith up on his offer. Dane left in his car and I followed Keith to his house.

It was an old, historic house that had been remodeled in the inside. I loved how spacious it was and the old wooden staircase and the stained-glass windows revealed the real history behind the house. Keith showed me around, leaving me in awe. The ceilings were very high, and every single room had an old fireplace that Keith said dated back to the early 1900s.

"When I updated the place there were some things that I didn't want to change. There's a lot of history in the house and I've even been told that there are ghosts living here."

"Yeah right," I said, walking closely behind him. "I find it hard to believe that you live here all alone."

"My grandparents used to live here, but when they died they left the place to me. I had a roommate a while back, but he started stealing shit so I had to put him out. Ever since then, I've stayed here by myself. I'm hoping to one day raise a family up in here . . . have a wife and some kids, and do that happily-ever-after stuff."

Well, he was barking up the wrong tree with me. I didn't want any children and I surely wasn't trying to be nobody's wife. I kept my mouth shut, until he walked me into another spacious room on the third floor that was his studio. His beautiful artwork was all over the room. I was left breathless. I only wished that I had a place like this to do my work.

"Believe it or not," he said, "this used to be a ballroom. You see how high the ceiling is?"

I nodded and gazed up at the cathedral ceiling that was painted gold. Crown molding surrounded the room and the silk curtains that draped the windows made this one classy room.

"I can picture a ballroom being in here. And with all of this space you must be in heaven. Why do you even need the space at work?"

"I just go there when I get sick of being in here. It can get kind of boring at times, and it does me good to get out."

Keith began to show me some of his paintings, and he also showed me some of the invoices he'd gotten from orders. I wished I had it going on like him. Dude was straight-up making a for-real living off of his talents.

"I'll be glad when I get to your level. I mean, my work is good too, you know?"

"Very good," he complimented. "I've seen a lot of it, but it's nowhere near better than mine."

We laughed, and I had to admit that he was way more skilled than I was. I began to look through more of his paintings and as I browsed the room, he dimmed the lights. I turned around and Keith walked up to me. He eased his arms around my waist and pulled my body closer to his. Needless to say, I was real nervous because in that moment, I was forced to admit that I had some feelings for him.

"Do you have any idea how long I've waited to get you alone like this?" he asked.

"I do, but I'm not sure if I'm ready for this right now."

"Why not?"

I looked into his eyes that were so sexy and luring. "Because, I'm so unsure about a lot of things."

"I can tell and I have an idea what things you're speaking of. Just give me a chance, and whichever way you decide to swing with this relationship is fine with me."

I released a deep breath that caused my breasts to rise against his chest. He leaned in to kiss me and the moment our lips touched I was eager to get out of my clothes. I started to remove my shorts, but Keith stopped me by touching my hand.

"Wait a minute. I want to do this right. Give me a minute."

Keith walked away then pulled an old-fashioned, velvet-covered chair that I'd seen in one of his paintings, to the middle of the floor. He kept his eyes on me as he removed his clothes then he sat in the chair. On display was the beauty of his nakedness and those colorful tats that made him look like a work of art sitting there. I watched his dick grow from six inches to about a strong eleven. I was impressed.

"Okay, now it's your turn. But remove your clothes in an artistic way while I sit here and stroke my brush."

Keith held his dick and began to slow-stroke it with his hands. I wasn't sure how artistic I could get with removing my clothes, but I did so by going real slow and creating a small pile beside me. Keith's eyes were locked on my small breasts and then the direction of his eyes lowered to my shaved pussy that was already leaking. I rubbed my hands all over my naked body, and when I turned around he had a view of my picture-perfect ass that I was proud of. I squeezed my ass cheeks then I bent far over to entice him even more. With my head dropped, I looked between my legs. Keith gestured his finger in a come-here motion.

"Now all you have to do is back up to me. Don't turn around just yet."

I backed up and as he held his dick straight up, I held onto the arms of the chair and eased down on his hard muscle. It put a large gap between my pussy lips and I certainly could not take it all in at once. I worked with the tip first and as my insides moistened more, I was able to glide up and down on Keith's muscle with ease. He planted soft, delicate kisses against my back and stroked me at a smooth pace that made me hear music in my head, even though there was none.

"Now tell me," he whispered between the kisses he planted on my back, "how does that feel?"

I shut my eyes and poked out my breasts to form an arch in my back. I slowly grinded my hips to the music playing in my head, yet was unable to spill my guts and tell him how him being inside of me made me feel.

He lifted his hands to squeeze my breasts and with his lips, hands and muscle in action at the same time, I couldn't hold back my inner thoughts much longer. I revealed them in a soft whisper. "You feel damn good, Keith. Too good."

"So do you."

He released his hands from my breasts and lowered his fingers to my clitoris. He swiped it delicately like a paintbrush and the vibrations of his fingers caused me to gasp and widen my eyes. I squeezed his wrist, trying to calm the intensity of how he was making my whole body quiver.

"Let it go, baby," he said. "Get it all out and don't hold back on me."

I let the deep breath that I was holding escape from my mouth and released my hand from his wrist. His fingers moved faster over my clit and his tool was so far up in me that it brushed against every inch of my walls. Seconds later a flood of my juices drenched his vibrating fingers. I cried out *"Keeeeeith"* and bent over to drop my face in my hand. My emotions ran high because I didn't want this to feel so spectacular. I told myself that a man wasn't capable of pleasing me, but there I was, wanting more of Keith. I wanted him to stay inside of me, and when he lifted me up by my waist and tried to pull out of me I rejected his move.

"What are you doing?" I asked. "Stay there. I'm not finished."

"Neither am I."

Keith stood me up straight and got behind me. He turned me around and sat me in the chair. He then spread my legs, placing each of them on the arms of the chair. With my pussy in his view, he kneeled between my legs and leaned in to suck my breasts. His mouth was massaging them so well that the arch in my back formed again. I could feel heat from my mouth that stayed open, to the tips of my toes that were curled. Keith continued to massage my breasts, but now with his hands. A trail of his kisses flowed down my stomach, into my pieced navel, and landed right at my pussy. He pressed his thick lips against mine and used the tip of his curled tongue to separate my slit. With ease, he brushed again and again.

With a little force from his tongue, he sucked and fucked me to a new level. With his vibrations, he broke me down and made me cum all over his handsome face. I squirmed in the chair, causing it to tilt backward, but then Keith caught me. He lifted me and secured my legs around his waist. I loved a strong man and that he was. Eager to feel him, I was the one to put him back inside of me. But all he did was stand still and hold me up. He searched into my eyes that were filled with many questions that only I could answer.

"What?" he said. "Tell me what's wrong."

My eyes watered because I was so confused. I thought I was done with men, especially after my first love, BJ, had done me so wrong. He beat me and dared me to tell anyone.

He threatened to kill me, and raped me whenever I told him I didn't want to have sex. I hated him so much that I told myself that if love ever presented itself again, that love would be for another woman. Especially after my ex went to jail, I continued to pursue women. Now things had changed. I didn't know what I wanted going forward, but for right now, I wanted Keith.

"Nothing," I said after a hard swallow.

"Tell me," he repeated. "I want to know what you're thinking."

Silence soaked the room. I squeezed my arms around his neck and placed my lips close to his ear. "I—I'm thinking that I'm gay and—"

"No, you're not. Confused, unsure, hurt . . . but definitely not gay."

"How can you be so sure that I'm not?"

"Because . . ." Keith squatted and laid me back on the floor. "Because if you were gay, your pussy wouldn't be able to react to me the way it just did, your body wouldn't tremble like it has done all night, and if a woman was truly who you wanted to be with then you would totally reject me. There's still time to do it, and all you have to do is walk out that door and leave."

I replied to him by turning on my stomach and backing my ass up to him. He was crazy if he thought I was going to depart from this—there wasn't a chance in hell that I would. We displayed our artistic talents to each other for the next few hours, and I'll be damned if I didn't leave his house the next morning feeling like a brand-new woman.

Chapter Fifteen

Kayla

I had a difficult time sleeping last night. I left the guest room and went to go watch TV in the living room. That was where I fell asleep on the couch, hoping that Trina would come in and wake me. But by six o'clock in the morning, she still wasn't home. I assumed she was with Lexi. I was thankful that they hadn't come back here to finish up what had gotten started at the restaurant. Seeing what I saw made me very uncomfortable. I had a hard time accepting Trina's status and I felt kind of bad for walking out of the restaurant last night. But her girl Lexi was working me. She was so needy and she irritated the hell out of me. Surely Trina could do better and as far as I could see it, she had made some really bad choices with women.

Keith, however, was a different story. He was an extremely attractive man, but Trina didn't seem to be giving him much play. That was her loss because I would take him any day over that Lexi chick and Cynthia.

Thinking about my bad choices with men and about how much I didn't have much room to talk, I got up to take a shower. Like the rest of Trina's place, the bathroom was very colorful. Pink, yellow, green, and purple daisies accessorized the bathroom, and they were on the shower curtain and wallpaper too. The colors were a bit much for my taste, but all I needed right now was water.

While in the shower, I pondered my situation. I called Jacoby again and called home, but that number had been disconnected too. I was very worried about him, but as with anything, I suspected it would take time to heal. I had to give him space and not force this issue with him. But this was hard.

Harder than I ever thought it would be. I even wanted to reach out to Cedric again, but I changed my mind about doing that. For now, I decided to wait. Wait and see what the next move would be, good or bad.

After my shower, I went to the bedroom and changed into a comfortable silk nightgown that went all the way down to my ankles. I wasn't going anywhere today and the plan was for me to relax. I went into the kitchen to cook breakfast. When I glanced at the clock it was almost nine o'clock. Just as I got ready to call Trina, she came through the door. The look of *I just had sex* was written all over her face and her smile on display said it all. I could only imagine what probably happened between her and Lexi. I quickly washed the thoughts from my head.

"Good morning," she said with much pep in her step. She walked up to me in the kitchen and gave me a hug.

"What's this for?" I said, hugging her back.

"No reason. Just for being you."

Trina kept smiling as she headed down the hallway. She went into her bedroom then came out with clothes to take a shower.

"I'll take some sausage and eggs too. Burn my toast a little and kill it with strawberry jelly."

I shook my head and got busy with breakfast. By the time Trina came out of the bathroom, breakfast was on the table. I poured orange juice in two glasses, but Trina reached for a bottle of Ciroc vodka.

"You couldn't be serious," I said. "This early, Trina?"

"Yes. Now pass me the glass of orange juice. I need something strong this morning."

I gave her the glass and she filled it to the rim with vodka. We then blessed the food and sat at the table to eat.

"I guess I don't have to ask why you're just now coming in, do I?" I said, prying.

"No, Mother, you don't. But I will say that I had a very interesting night and a pretty interesting morning too."

"You don't have to tell me. It's written all over your face. And if being with Lexi makes you this happy, who am I to judge? I want to apologize for running out of the restaurant like I did last night. This may take me some time to get used to, but at the end of the day, you're still my best friend and I love you."

"*Awww*," Trina teased. "That's so sweet. I love you too, bestie, and I do understand how you feel about my relationships. But just so you know, Lexi is not responsible for this smile you see on my face this morning. Keith is."

I rolled my eyes and pursed my lips. "Whatever. You played that trick on me before, Trina. Told me how much you were feeling Keith and you weren't even thinking about him. That's too bad, because he is gorgeous. I don't like my men that dark, but I could see myself getting it in with a man like that."

"Yeah, well, you're not the only one, and I'm not lying to you this time. We got it in last night, and when I say we got it in, I really, really mean that he got it in there. *Waaaay* in there."

We laughed and I didn't know whether to believe her or not. "I don't believe you. You had me convinced that you were done with men, and now you're telling me that you spent the night with Keith. I think you're just saying that because you know how I feel."

"Truthfully, I don't care how you feel. And I'm telling you that Keith and I had amazing sex last night. We topped it off with more sex this morning. He took me to a level up here." Trina raised her hand up high to show me. "And I'm so high right now that I can't come down."

I looked at her from across the table, trying to feel her out. It didn't appear that she was lying to me, and when her cell phone rang, she smiled and hit the speakerphone.

"Hello," she said.

"Didn't I tell you to call and let me know you made it home?" Keith said.

"I was getting ready to do that. You called when I had my hand on the phone."

"I'm not buying it, but I'm glad you made it home. I had a great time last night and this morning. I'm looking forward to seeing you again real soon, but you make the call, all right?"

"Will do, and I will do so real soon. Enjoy your day and thanks for calling."

Trina punched the button to end the call. She looked at me and shrugged. "Now what? I told you I was with him, didn't I?"

"That just about confirms it, but here's what I want to know: What are you going to do about that obsessive chick who couldn't keep her hands off you? I'm sorry to say this, but she was working the heck out of me. I believe in love and everything, but she was showing too much love. And does Keith know what's—"

"Yes, he knows. He also knows how I feel about him, so I have some serious thinking to do. Lexi has been there for me for a long time. The last thing I want to do is hurt her feelings. She does have some growing up to do, but I like her."

"What about Cynthia? Have you seen or spoken to her?"

"I have, but she's back on her husband's team right now. She does that from time to time, so our relationship really isn't a consistent one. My biggest problem is Lexi. From the way I feel about Keith right now, she's bound to get hurt."

"Yes. And learn from me . . . do not hold back the truth from anyone. Once you feel sure about your feelings, tell Keith and Lexi what's up."

"I plan to. But I need to be sure about who I am and what I want."

Trina sipped from her glass then squeezed her eyes and rubbed her throat to soothe the burn. She bit into her toast and picked at the cheese eggs with a fork.

"Tell me something, Trina. How long have you known you were like this? I mean, you did a hell of a job hiding this from me and Evelyn, unless she knows too and hasn't said anything to me."

"No, she doesn't know. And what's so funny is I actually had a crush on her for a long time. I still think she got it going on, but there is much about Evelyn that turns me off too."

I was surprised to hear Trina confess her feelings for her. That made me a little tense. I tried not to interrupt and say the wrong thing. "I don't necessarily see that as a funny thing, and to me it sounds kind of weird. Did you ever act on those feelings and since you're being honest, did you ever feel that way about me?"

I could tell that my questions were making her uncomfortable, but I did want to know.

"Slow it down with your questions and let me finish what I was saying. I used to have a crush on Evelyn, but I don't anymore. I think you're a beautiful woman, but because I knew you were committed to Cedric, I never really thought about hooking up with you. I've been like this since me and BJ parted ways. What I never told anyone was that he beat me, raped me, treated me like shit, and threatened to kill me many times. If you remember, during that time I became distant with everyone. I told y'all everything was good, but it wasn't. Those black eyes you saw me with were not from car accidents or from me falling. When I broke my arm that time, I wasn't injured at the gym. BJ did all of that to me, and had he not gone to jail, I know he would've killed me. After that, I was done with men. I wanted no parts of them, so I started dating women and felt as if I could relate better to them."

I laid my fork down and wiped my mouth with a napkin. "I feel so terrible about this, because deep down I knew BJ had been abusing you. I never said one word to you, nor did I encourage you to leave him or go get help. I guess I was so wrapped up in my own—"

"Regardless, I wouldn't have listened to anything you said. There was nothing you could've done, so don't go blaming yourself. All I ask is that you keep what I've said to you this morning between us. I don't want Evelyn to know any of this, because that girl is the walking *National Enquirer* and she would put my business out there."

We laughed because Trina had spoken the truth. There was always one friend in the bunch who was out of control.

"I won't say a word, but what I would like to do is change the subject. I want to hear more about your time with Keith, and please tell me when you plan to hook up with him again."

Trina gave me explicit details of what transpired with her and Keith yesterday. I was blushing and shaking my head. I was so excited that I had to get me a drink too. We took the conversation over to the couch, laughing our asses off.

The conversation about Keith made me think of Cedric. He had always been a great lover and still was. But maybe that part of my life was over. I didn't know, but either way, today felt good. I got blasted with Trina. It had been a long time since we'd had such a fine time.

"You should not drink anything else," Trina said, snatching the glass from my hand. I had spilled some of the alcohol on the floor and she stumbled to the kitchen to empty my glass.

"I do—don't need anything else to drink," I slurred and wobbled as I stood up. "A—and neither do you!"

Trina turned up a bottle of Hennessy while standing in the kitchen. I shook my head and plopped down on the couch. "Call that bitch Evelyn over here so I can give that heefer a piece of my mind for dissing me," I said.

"It's *heifer*, not *heefer* and I'ma call her over here so the two of y'all can make up. Where . . . where my phone at?"

Trina slammed the Hennessy bottle on the counter and patted the pockets on her sweatpants. She stumbled back to the couch and fell back on it, next to me. She punched in Evelyn's number and a few seconds later she answered.

"Say bitch," Trina slurred. "Get on some clothes and come over here right now."

"Who is this?" Evelyn snapped.

We giggled and that was when I cleared my throat and yelled into the phone. "It's Big Daddy calling. Get over here now or else yo' ass is grass. I don't want no back talk, woman, ya hear me?"

"Trina and Kayla, stop playing. What is wrong with y'all this morning? Are the two of you drunk?"

Trina looked at me and held her hand in front of her mouth. "*Daaaamn*, are you drunk? I know I'm not, so she must be thanking that we—"

"I'm thinking that y'all are drunk and how pathetic that must be, especially since it's this early on a Sunday morning. What about church? Are either of you going?"

I slapped my leg and cracked up. "*Noooooo*, no church for me this morning, no siree. But I will be there next Sunday for sure."

"I see the two of you need a good old-fashioned cussing out. I'm on my way and y'all better have y'all's act together when I get there."

Trina tossed the phone on the floor and by the time Evelyn got there, we were acting like complete fools. The music was blasting and Trina was walking around like a chicken, flapping her arms and poking her neck out. Evelyn and I nearly died from laughing. It felt really good to have this much fun with my best friends. We still had issues, but the truth was . . . what frenemies didn't?

Chapter Sixteen

Evelyn

I was exhausted. Being with Trina and Kayla wore me out, and I was glad to get out of my place. I had been worrying myself sick about everything. The baby was on my mind and at this point, I wasn't sure if I should have it or not.

Yeah, it was my best friend's husband's baby, but so what? It wasn't like I tried to get pregnant by him. It just happened and I was left trying to figure this mess out by myself. There was no way in hell I wanted Kayla to stay here and I was delighted to see that Trina had let Kayla stay with her. That way, I didn't feel so bad about lying to her about Marc. The truth was, I hadn't seen him since we had left dinner that Sunday. He pissed me off by tossing so many compliments Kayla's way, and I viewed it as complete disrespect. He didn't even say anything nice about me like I had asked him to, and all he had done was embarrass me that day.

I so badly needed a drink, but because of the baby I didn't drink anything while I was at Trina's place. I had cut back on smoking too; didn't want to bring more problems to myself than I'd already had.

The day had come and gone. I had a job interview in the morning. I thought about my previous job, and when I thought about the possibility of Jacoby somehow sabotaging me, I realized that if he did, he probably did me a favor. I wanted out of that place and I got tired of kissing my boss's ass. By the way he treated me I should've been out of there. If Jacoby thought he had hurt me, he was sadly mistaken. He actually did me a favor, so that case was closed.

My interview tomorrow was for another customer service position. I liked working the phones and it always kept me busy. Hopefully, I'd get the job, and wanting to be well rested and ready to go in the morning, I shut it down right before ten o'clock. With my peach bra and panties on, I cuddled with the warm blanket and pulled it over my head. My eyes fluttered and I felt myself entering a deep sleep. What seemed like hours later, I felt something crawling on my leg. I kicked whatever it was with my feet and when I snatched the blanket away from my face, I looked up and saw Cedric standing at the end of my bed, scrolling the tips of his fingers against my leg. He was dressed in a suit, but his jacket and shirt were unbuttoned.

"What are you doing here?" I moved my legs to avoid his touch.

He snatched the blanket off me and tossed it on the floor. Without saying a word, he crawled on the bed and got on top of me. I resisted by trying to push him away, but he pinned my hands to the bed and maneuvered his body in between my legs. His lips touched the side of my neck and he pecked down it.

"Stop this," I said through gritted teeth. "I don't want you anymore, Cedric! Get up and get out of here. Now!"

He ignored my order and continued to peck down my neck. He started to grind his package between my legs and the harder it got, the more I resisted.

"No!" I shouted. "*Stooooop! Pleaaaase, stop!*"

Cedric halted his kisses and looked into my watery eyes. "You know this feel good to you, so quit pretending. I came here to tell you that it's over between me and Kayla. I filed for a divorce today and whether you wanted me to do that or not, it's done." He pecked my neck a few more times then stopped. "I—I've had time to think about how wrong I was about you and my baby. I'm excited about being a father. With Kayla out of the way, the two of us can be together. We can be good parents to our baby and you can let me take care of you like I want to. It's over, baby. I hope like hell that you're glad it's over."

I was speechless. I took several deep breaths and they slowed with every word that he spoke. Was it really over? Was it now my time to shine? I didn't quite know what to say, but the resisting stopped. My legs fell further apart and when Cedric released my hands, I used them to pull his shirt and jacket away from his chest. Without removing his pants, he unzipped them and stretched the crotch section of my panties over to the side. After putting on a condom, his dick filled me up. While he pushed deep strokes into me, I lowered my hands down into his pants and gripped his ass. My nails sunk into his flesh and I sucked his lips with mine.

"I'm so glad that Daddy's home," I said between sloppy, wet kisses. "I'm . . . so . . . glad . . . you're . . . home . . ."

"Me too."

Cedric tore into me like a maniac that night. He didn't leave until noon, causing me to miss my interview. Truthfully, I didn't even care. I had Cedric back on my team, and when I checked my account the money had been flowing again. I smiled and fell back on my bed, screaming "Yes!"

Later that day, I got a call from Trina that came from out of the blue.

"I need to speak to you as soon as possible. It's very important, Evelyn, and I can't go another day without getting this off my chest."

I wasn't sure if Cedric was coming back today or not, but I told Trina that we could meet. She wanted to meet at a downtown bar and grill that we used to meet at, but I thought that was odd because she knew I couldn't drink. I still agreed to it, and as soon as I put on some clothes I left.

When I arrived at the bar and grill, Trina was sitting at a booth in a pink-and-black sweat suit. There weren't too many customers inside and the lighting was so dim that I could barely see her. I made my way over to the booth, but immediately noticed the blank expression on her face when she saw me.

"I suspect this isn't going to be good by the look on your face." I eased into the booth and set my shades on the table.

"Unfortunately, it's not going to be, especially if what I suspect is going on winds up being the truth."

I had a feeling where Trina was going with this, but the first thing I needed was a cold soda. I flagged down the heavyset waitress with dirty-blond hair and asked her to bring me one.

I then opened my clutch purse and pulled out my compact mirror. I dabbed my lips with red lipstick then smacked them together.

"Okay, Trina, go. The floor is yours and I'm all ears."

She didn't beat around the bush. "Are you having sex with Cedric and is that his baby you're carrying? I want the truth, Evelyn, and I want you to tell me now."

I folded my arms across my chest, as if I were offended. "I don't know why you keep confronting me with this dumb shit, but to answer your question again, no. No, I'm not having sex with Cedric and I'm not having his baby. I told you that I was pregnant by Marc and we are still seeing each other."

Trina glared at me and sighed. The waitress brought my soda over to the table and asked if I wanted anything to eat. "We got hot wings, hamburgers, hot dogs—you name it, we got it," she said, smacking on gum.

"No, thank you. The soda will be fine."

The waitress looked at Trina. "What about you, cookie? Can I get you anything other than the milkshake you're drinking on?"

"Not right now. If I need anything else, I'll let you know."

"Okay," she said, then squinted to get a closer look at Trina. "Say, anybody ever tell you that you look like that chick from Destiny's Child? You know the brown one with the cute tush and not that Beyoncé."

"Who Kelly? Kelly Rowland?" Trina questioned.

"Yeah, Kelly. I like her a lot."

"No, that's the first time I heard that, but thanks for the compliment."

"No problem. Enjoy y'all's day and holler if you need anything."

She walked away and Trina picked up where we left off. "Marc, huh," she said. "Well, I need to let you in on something right now. I saw Marc at the grocery store last week. We talked and he said that he hadn't heard from you. When I mentioned a baby, he damn near fell on his ass because he hadn't a clue what I was talking about. So either he's lying or you're lying. I have a strong feeling that it's you."

I cut my eyes at Trina and looked away, thinking hard if I should tell her the truth. Eventually, I expected it to come out and if Cedric and I were planning to be together then maybe it was time to admit to the breaking news.

"Yes. Yes, I have been seeing Cedric and I am pregnant with his child. The last thing I ever wanted to do was hurt Kayla, but she has always had certain things that I wanted and desired to have for myself."

Trina had a look on her face that could kill. You would have thought that I just told her it was her husband. I didn't understand why she thought any of this was her business to begin with.

"I don't know if I should reach across this table and smack the shit out of you or if I should feel sorry for you. I can't believe that you have that much jealousy in your heart for Kayla—and for God's sake, Evelyn, she is supposed to be your best friend. What are you thinking?"

"You want to know what I'm thinking? Well, what I'm thinking is that Kayla may have been a good friend to you, but she hasn't been one to me. She knows—and has known for quite some time—how messed up my situation is, but all she does is sit back on her millions and get a kick out of me begging her for money. She shops at Saks while we shop at Target. She pretends like she doesn't know what's going on in our lives, and the first thing she always says is, 'Why didn't you tell me you needed something?' Why tell someone who already knows? If she really cared about us, she would offer to help us."

"Evelyn, you need to get it through your thick head that Kayla doesn't owe us anything. And please tell me what your messed-up financial situation has to do with your decision to fuck around with her husband? I'm not making the connection here. What you're saying sounds like a bunch of bullshit."

"Bullshit or not, it's the truth. If I had her money, you would be set. You would have everything you ever wanted and so would she. We've been friends for a long time. Shared our lifelong dreams, talked about our futures, and prayed for doors to open for all of us. They opened for her, but she never looked back. You can't deny that, Trina, and now that her world has come crumbling down, she has to come to us for help. I just couldn't find it in my heart to help her."

"Okay, fine, that's how you feel. But tell me again where Cedric comes into all of this. He's a lowlife bastard. I swear if I ever get some alone time with him, I could just . . . just kill him."

"Violence won't solve anything and you need to stop poking your nose where it doesn't belong. Cedric is my ticket to get out of the rut I'm in. He's been giving me money from time to time, but I'm so far in debt that it may take a while for me to get out of it. I didn't plan to get pregnant with his child, but it happened. All I can do is take this opportunity and run with it."

"Opportunity? You really see this as an opportunity?"

"Yes, I do. An opportunity to have some of the things in life that I've never had. For once, I just want a taste of the good life. I want to shop until I drop. I want to drive in fancy cars and live in a house like the one Kayla lives—or should I say, *lived in.* I want to know for a fact that the electric company can't turn off my lights, and I want to travel the world and see more than just the end of my street."

"You can have all of that one day, but this is not the way. Cedric is not going to be your ticket to anywhere but hell. Look at what he's doing to Kayla right now. She depended on him to take care of her and stick by her side, for better or worse. Now, she has to figure out a way to make it on her own. You can't trust a man like him and having his baby is not going to save you."

"It may or may not, but it's a start. I don't trust Cedric, but I'm going to milk him for every dime that I can, while I can do it. During the process, some people's feelings may get hurt and some things may have to come to the light. Meanwhile, I have to see about me. I need to take care of me and my child, and at any cost I will do it."

Trina rubbed her forehead and squeezed it. "If you've been feeling like this, why don't you tell Kayla? As long as we've been friends, you owe that to her. While she may have done some things that you disagree with, you should have gone to her and said something about how you felt. This is so awful,

Evelyn, and I don't think you realize how much damage this is going to cost all of us."

"If you want her to know, and if you're so worried about damaging your friendship with her, then you tell her. You consider yourself a true friend, so tell me, Trina: What's holding you back and keeping you from saying anything?"

"Because, it's not my place to say anything. I feel as though I'm caught in the middle."

"I'm giving you permission to get out of the middle. I won't feel betrayed if you tell her about this and it's just a matter of time before she finds out. Cedric has filed for divorce. I suspect that things are about to change real soon."

"Meaning? Are you planning to marry him or something? Is it really that serious?"

"Not hardly. But we will be spending more time together. At my place, as well as at his."

Trina's phone rang and when she looked down at it she decided not to answer. "I can't take any more of this right now. I don't know what I'm going to do, but all I can say to you right now is that you're wrong, Evelyn. So wrong for all of this. You have shown me what kind of friend you really are and this shit is scary."

"A good friend to friends who are good to me."

Trina didn't bother to reply. She left five dollars on the table and walked out. After she left, I reached for my cell phone to call Marc. I was ready to chew him out for talking to Trina, but I was startled when he said he hadn't seen or spoken to her.

"I don't know why she would lie on me like that, but either way, I need to call you back. I'm busy right now," he said.

I hung up and sucked my teeth as I thought about that lying bitch. She found out what she wanted. The question was, what was she going to do with the information?

Chapter Seventeen

Kayla

I was still feeling hung over from Sunday and it was Tuesday. Trina called last night and told me that she was spending the night with Keith. I hoped that she wasn't staying away from her apartment because I was here. The last thing that I wanted was to inconvenience her. I called her cell phone to check on her, but she didn't answer. As I was leaving her a message, a call interrupted. It was coming from an unknown number.

"Hello," I said.

"I want to meet my real father," Jacoby said. "Can you pull some more of your tricks to make that happen?"

I wanted to go off on him for speaking to me that way, but I had waited so long for him to call me that I didn't want to blow it. "I don't do tricks, but I can see what I can do to make that happen. Where are you?"

"I'm at Adrianne's house right now."

"How have you been?"

"Just fine, Mother. Perfectly fine and I couldn't be better."

His voice was filled with sarcasm and I hated it. "Have you been to school?"

"Of course."

"Have you been staying at home?"

"Yes, I have, but I've also been in and out. I'm trying to keep busy, but the thoughts of my father keep bugging me."

"I know and I get it. I take full responsibility for what I've done and I didn't want to hurt you like this. You have to believe me when I say that. It pains me that you believed what Cedric—"

"I couldn't care less about Cedric. All I want to do is look my real father in the eyes. I want to talk to him and possibly get to know him. You denied me that opportunity. I'm so angry with you for doing this."

"Fine. Then allow me to make this right. Give me a number where I can reach you and I'll call you back as soon as I reach him."

Jacoby gave me a number where I could reach him and hung up. My heart was heavy. I hadn't spoken to Arnez since I gave him a measly ten thousand dollars to stay out of our lives. He would have taken five and the truth was that he didn't give a damn about Jacoby. I wasn't even sure if Arnez would meet him, but to settle this once and for all, I kept my word to Jacoby and called Arnez.

"Is this who I think it is?" he said, obviously having my name and number locked in his phone.

"I'm not sure who you think it is, but it's me, Kayla. How are you, Arnez? Did I catch you at a bad time?"

"Nah, not really. I'm just sitting on this bed, playing with my musty nuts and waiting for you to call me."

The thought made me want to puke. Yet again, though, I had to be careful with my words. "My call is here, but I assure you that it has nothing to do with your musty nuts. I'm calling because my son wants to see you."

He laughed then started coughing. I guessed the fool was choking because it took a minute for him to get himself together. "Excuse me. Something got caught in my throat and I had to clear it. You said *your son*, but don't you really mean *our son*?"

"My son, your son, whatever, Arnez. Jacoby wants to see you."

"How old is he now? I forgot, so tell me again."

"He's sixteen. He recently discovered that Cedric wasn't his real father and now he wants to meet you."

"Discovered, huh? Why all the fancy words when you know we don't run around here discovering shit like that everyday. We may find out that a muthafucka lied about some shit, but a discovery is kind of pushing it, don't you think?"

"I guess, but either way he found out that you are his biological father. Are you up to meeting with my son or not?"

"Just from your attitude, I can tell yo' ass is in hot water. What has Cedric done to you now? It must be something real deep because ain't no way in hell you would be calling me for anything, unless something deep is going on."

"Whatever is going on between me and Cedric is our business, not yours. Now, I'm trying to be nice, Arnez. All I want to know is if you have time to meet with Jacoby?"

"Of course I do. I tried to meet with him years ago, but you wouldn't let me, remember? You pushed me away and told me you were embarrassed—"

"All you wanted was money, so stop with the lies. You got what you wanted and that was your drugs, whores, and freedom. Don't be mad at me because things didn't work out for you."

"I see you're still the same evil bitch that you've always been. Hell, yeah, I want to see my son, but not in your presence. Take my address down and bring him to me. I'm eager to see him."

I hated that some people brought out this ugliness in me. I had a feeling that this was a bad move, but I hoped that once Jacoby got one look at this drunk, crack-smoking idiot that he would run far away from him.

"What's the address?" I asked.

Arnez gave it to me and then ended the call. I paced the floor, still not a 100-percent sure about this. Realizing that I didn't have much of a choice, I called Jacoby back to give him the address.

"I want you to go with me," he said.

"I don't want you to go at all, so please reconsider doing this. Let Arnez be, please."

"No. Now, are you going with me?"

"I don't want you to go alone, but he doesn't want me anywhere near him. We don't get along and I don't want to cause any trouble."

"I'm asking you to go with me."

I scratched my head then told Jacoby I would meet him at Adrianne's house within the hour.

When I arrived at her house, Jacoby was already outside waiting for me. I got out to give him a hug. It felt good to see my son. His hug wasn't as tight as mine, but it didn't even matter.

"I'll drive too and follow you," he said.

I nodded and not wanting to prolong this, I drove to Arnez's place that was on Martin Luther King Avenue. I parked in front of an old brick house that looked as if it would fall down if the wind blew any harder. The porch was leaning and several of the windows were cracked. Black bars covered them and the grass that was supposed to be in front of the house was mud. I knew where Arnez lived was bad, but I didn't expect for it to be *this* bad. Jacoby got out of his car first with a nervous look deep in his eyes. I tried to be the brave one, but as I got out of the car a heavyset man rolled up to me in a wheelchair. He appeared to be barely hanging on and his gray beard looked as if it hadn't been shaved in ages.

"You got any change on you, ma'am? Maybe a quarter or something."

I wasn't sure what he could buy with a quarter, but as I was about to dig in my purse, Jacoby tugged on my arm, pulling me away from the man.

"Sho' nuff," the man said. "That's how I get treated? *Daaaam*, yawl colder than a muthafucka."

We kept it moving to the front door and the man kept on rolling down the street in the wheelchair. "Bubba!" a lady yelled at him from the other side. "Butch and them lookin' for you!"

Looking for him for what? I wasn't sure. But whatever it was, Bubba got out of the wheelchair and broke out running. It was a miracle and all I could do was shake my head at the foolishness.

"I figured he was full of it," Jacoby said, then knocked on the door.

My stomach tightened and when I heard the chain being removed I could feel beads of sweat forming on my forehead. I hoped and prayed that Arnez didn't look as bad as he did when I saw him last, but when he swung the door open, his appearance was even worse. I didn't understand how a thirty-seven-year-old man could look like he was damn near sixty. He used to be one fine man, but there was no doubt that drugs, alcohol, and too many women had done him in.

"Well, well, well," Arnez said as he opened the ripped screen door. "What do we have here?"

Jacoby almost looked frightened. He stood with his eyes locked on Arnez and hadn't said a word.

"I—I know you didn't want me to come with him," I said. "But I didn't want him to come alone. May we come in?"

"Fasho," he said, and then moved aside for us to enter. As I walked past him, he inhaled and sniffed his nose close to my neck. "Damn, woman, what's that sweet perfume you wearing? Alizé?"

"Alizé is a drink and you've obviously had too many," I said, staring into his beady eyes. He seriously looked like Eddie King from *The Five Heartbeats*. I didn't know whether to laugh at his joke or cry.

Arnez laughed, though. His hazel eyes were fire red and the wavy hair he once had was all gone. He was tall like Jacoby, but much, much thinner. His lips were black and his beard was scraggly.

Jacoby looked around at the old house that badly needed renovated. It needed to be cleaned too and the smell of piss infused the air. Spiderwebs were caked in the corners and the tile floors were filthy.

"Come on in here and have a seat," Arnez said.

We followed him into a spacious living room that had a card table sitting in the middle of the floor. A sunk-in dirty couch sat in front of a window, and on the table was a glass with brown liquid in it. A joint was next to it and several cards were spread out.

"Y'all have to excuse me, but I'm getting ready for my card game with the fellas in about an hour. Anyway," he said, holding out his hand to Jacoby, "I'm Arnez. Good seeing you, man, and all I can say is you sho'll look just like me."

What an insult. Jacoby shook his hand and nodded.

"Nice to meet you," was all he said.

We sat in the aluminum chairs and Jacoby continued to look around. I wondered what he was thinking and more than anything I hoped he was grateful.

Arnez opened his arms and held them wide. "This is my palace and I'ma show y'all the rest of the crib before y'all go. Can you believe yo' mama traded all of this in for a lousy muthafucka who wasn't shit? Man, I could tell you some stories about that punk Cedric, but I want to hear about you. What you got going on, nigga?"

Jacoby shrugged his shoulders and couldn't stop gazing into his father's eyes. I knew he saw himself, even though Arnez was looking a hot mess.

"What I got going on right now is school. I already know what college I'm going to and I'm majoring in computer science, like my da—like Cedric. I play basketball, but I'm not really that good at it, and I have a girlfriend named Adrianne. We've been together for a while and I honestly think that I may one day wind up marrying her. I also play the saxophone too, but I only do that in my spare time. I want to experiment with some other instruments too, mainly the trumpet because I like how it sounds. Other than that, my life is kind of boring. I write, read, and like to bowl. I'm an A-B student and that's pretty much it about me. What about you, though? Tell me about you."

I was real proud of Jacoby. And whether my secret had caused a lot of damage or not, at that moment I realized that I may have done the right thing. A lie was still a lie, but this one I wasn't going to beat myself up about anymore.

Arnez sipped the brown liquid from the glass and cleared his throat. "Well . . . I used to have stuff like that going on, but then life happened. It can be a muthafucka, you know, and that shit can shut you down so fast that you can't even predict what's coming. Right now, I'm just chilling. I've been in rehab, trying to get my act together and I'm doing pretty good right now. Been clean for about six months, but I kick back a li'l alcohol from time to time. Other than that, I get disability because I hurt my back a while ago and I can't really do much work."

"So, like, when you were my age, what were your dreams and aspirations? I know you went to college, so what did you go for and what did you want to do? How did you know my da—Cedric, and how did you meet my mother? When did you start doing drugs and do you have any more children? How is your relationship with them and why did you accept money—"

"Whoa . . . whoa, calm down," Arnez said, then laughed. "I see you got a lot of questions for me, and I'm going to answer them for you, but I must say this to you first. I don't know what brought you to my doorstep today, but I'm glad you came. I may not ever see you again, but this moment right here is one that we will never forget. What I want to say to you is whatever disturbs your heart about me and your mother, you gotta let that shit go. I'm not shit, I ain't never gon' be shit. Even back then yo' mama knew I was fucking up. She did right by taking you from me 'cause I didn't have my head on straight. I regret that shit too, man, but there ain't a damn thing I can do about it now. If Cedric done took care of you and made you a nigga like this, I'm grateful. I mean, I gotta back the fuck up and let that man continue to handle his business, 'cause I can't. That may sound fucked up, but on a for-real tip, you are better off. I hope you know that. And now to answer all this other bullshit you done hit me with . . ."

Arnez and Jacoby went back and forth talking. I kept my mouth shut and didn't say one word. There were times when tears filled my eyes, times when I laughed with them, and times when Arnez tried his best to drag me into the conversation.

"With yo' fine self," he said, rubbing his finger along the side of my face. I smacked his hand. "Yo' mama was *soooo* good-looking back then. She fine now too, but not like she was back then. When I busted that nut, I knew I had gotten her pregnant. I sprayed that—"

"Arnez, please. You were doing just fine, and I'm sure Jacoby is not interested in details about how he was conceived."

Jacoby folded his arms across his chest and nodded. "You know, actually, I would like to hear about it."

Arnez let out a cackling laugh and pounded his fist against Jacoby's. "My nigga. You are damn sure all right with me."

They continued their conversation and as promised, Arnez gave us a tour of the rest of the house. It was awful. I felt bad for him, but he was proud of the place he called home. He talked about fixing it up and told Jacoby that if he ever needed a place to stay that he was welcome to come there.

Jacoby didn't respond. Almost an hour later, we got ready to go. He and Jacoby shook hands again, hugged each other, and gave their good-byes. I watched as Jacoby walked to his car, and I turned to address Arnez before leaving.

"Thank you for that," I said. "It's what he needed and he has your number if or whenever he needs to reach you."

Arnez nodded and rubbed sweat from his head. "You did good, sugga, and I hope I didn't embarrass you too much. Jacoby got a bright future ahead of him and I can see that shit in his eyes. Now on another note: Why don't you hit me up with a few dollars? I'm broke as shit and my disability check ain't gon' get here for another week or two."

"Good-bye, Arnez. Maybe I'll call you tomorrow and take care of that for you, or maybe I won't. Whatever you do, don't hold your breath on it."

He laughed as I walked away and he watched as me and Jacoby got in our cars and drove off. I wasn't sure how Jacoby felt about today, but when we got back to Adrianne's house he came up to my car to talk.

"That was interesting," he said. "I appreciate you for calling him, but just let me chill out for a while, okay? I need time to think. Kind of get my head straight and let all of this settle in. I'm going home tonight, and just so you know, me and Cedric have been doing okay. He's been staying out of my way and I've been staying out of his. I don't know what is going on with the two of you, and I don't care to know. Work it out however you wish."

"I will."

I gave Jacoby another hug and he walked away to go into Adrianne's house. It was time for me to work out my situation with Cedric, but as soon as I got to Trina's apartment, a man was standing outside with papers in his hands.

"Kayla Thompson?"

"Yes."

He gave the papers to me and hurried to walk away. When I looked at the papers, the top read *Affidavit of Dissolution of Marriage*. My heart raced fast. I guess Cedric had finally made up his mind. I doubted that there was anything I could do to change it.

Chapter Eighteen

Trina

I was caught between a rock and a hard place. I didn't know if I should say anything or not to Kayla about what Evelyn had admitted to me, and when Kayla shared with me that Cedric had filed for a divorce, I felt terrible. I also saw it as a good thing. She could finally be rid of an asshole who meant her no good. Kayla would get the closure she needed and at this point, I felt as if there was no need for me to interfere.

I feared that if I told Kayla, she would fight for her man. She wouldn't want any woman, especially Evelyn, to have him. This thing would drag on forever and ever. Then again, maybe I was trying to justify my actions. I felt like a coward—a friend who should've known better. This was hard. Really hard, but I had to realize that I had bigger issues going on in my own life.

For the past few weeks, it had been all about Keith. We had been spending an enormous amount of time together. I had fallen head over heels for him. He was everything I needed the man in my life to be. He cooked for me, treated me with respect, lifted me up, and praised the work I'd done. He supported my endeavors and he continued to take our lovemaking sessions to new heights. I couldn't believe all of this was happening to me. It was almost frightening. I didn't know what to call myself these days: gay, straight, bisexual or what. All I knew was that I was giving my time to the one person in my life who was making me happy. Unfortunately, that person wasn't Lexi. I didn't know how to tell her when she stood outside of my apartment, begging and pleading for me to tell her where I was going, as well as who I had been spending my time with.

"Nobody," I rushed to say while walking to my car. "If there was somebody else, I would tell you."

"You never told me before." She hurried after me, damn near walking on the back of my shoes.

That pissed me off, so I spun around to face her. "All I said was that I had other friends. But I'm not in love with those friends, Lexi, nor do I have feelings for them like I have for you. So, back up. Stop tripping and go home. Please."

She rolled her eyes and tapped her foot on the ground. "Why can't I go with you? If you're not going to see anyone else, tell me why I can't go?"

I spoke through gritted teeth. "Because, I don't want you to. I need some time for myself and I'm on my way to the library. There's no need for you to be there with me, unless you're interested in reading some books. I doubt that you are, so go home and I'll call you when I'm done."

Lexi stood with tears in her eyes. I felt bad for her, but I didn't appreciate her stalking me. I turned to walk to my car, and as I got inside, she continued to stand there and mean-mug me. I drove off and went out of my way to Keith's house, just to make sure she wasn't following me. Almost forty-five minutes later, I arrived at his place.

He reached for my hand and rushed me to the third floor. "Come over here and look at this." Keith sat in a chair and stared at a painting in front of him.

I sat on his lap, observing the weird-looking painting that hadn't moved me at all."It's . . . I guess it looks okay. I really don't like how the colors blend in together and it looks sort of sloppy to me."

Keith cocked his head back. "Sloppy? Did you just have the nerve to call my work sloppy?"

"I did, but in no way was it my intentions to hurt your feelings. It's just my honest opinion. You know I'm entitled to it, especially since you asked."

"Yes, you are entitled to it, only if I'm entitled to do this."

Keith lifted my shirt and moved my bra away from my breasts. He nibbled on my nipples and already feeling the heat, I snapped my bra loose in the back.

"Aren't you tired of all this sex we've been having?" I teased then sighed. "I know I'm getting tired of doing it, but if we must go there again, so be it."

"Yeah, unfortunately, we must."

Catching me by surprise, he dipped his brush in paint and splattered red paint on my cheek. I tried to snatch the brush from his hand, but I wound up getting more paint on me. I jumped up from his lap and as I rushed to grab a cup full of black paint, he doused me with the cup of paint in his hand. It was a good thing that white sheets were on his floor. We made one big mess, but neither of us were disappointed when the time came for us to clean up in the shower. We stood face-to-face with our wet bodies pressed against each other. Keith ran his finger along the side of my face and searched into my eyes as I gazed up at him.

"You know, there comes a time in a man's life when he knows that he has finally found that special someone in his life. For these past few weeks, I've been feeling that way. I've been feeling real good about us and it's almost like I know I found my soul mate. But then the relationship is so young. We're both very excited and I don't know if these feelings will fade. I'm hoping that they don't, but I wanted you to know that I can't stop thinking about you while you're away. It's driving me nuts too, because I usually can't stand to be around nobody this much. But I like you a lot, Trina. I enjoy being around you and I hope the feeling is mutual."

"Trust me when I say it is. I'm glad I found you. Things in my life are very different now."

"Wait a minute. You didn't find me. I found you."

"No, no, no, my dear. I found you. I was the one who approached you at work, remember?"

"Yes, I remember well. I walked up to you and asked if I could use your stencils. You smiled, said yes, and then I asked for your number. You must be thinking of JaQuan."

I laughed and gave Keith a kiss. "Maybe I was, but I'm not thinking about him anymore."

"Good. Now turn around and bend over so I can spank that ass for being incorrect."

I never got a spanking that felt so spectacular. Afterward, Keith cooked dinner and we chilled in his room, which was on the second floor, to watch TV. His big bed was so comfy, topped with cushiony throw pillows and a thick comforter that we cuddled in. We chomped on buttered popcorn while watching an interesting drama movie that had us tuned in. When the doorbell rang, Keith looked at the clock.

"Damn, it's a little after eleven. Who could that be?"

He tossed the comforter aside and got out of bed to go see who it was. "I'll be right back," he said. "Pause the movie for me."

As he put on his robe, I paused the movie and waited for him to come back. I wondered who was at the door. I tried to listen in to see what was up. At first, all I heard was a female's voice. Then I heard a thud and a loud gasp. I heard a door slam too and that was when I rushed out of the bed to see what was going on. From the middle staircase, I looked over the rail and could see Keith squirming around in the foyer. He was squeezing his stomach and blood covered his trembling fingers as he tried to catch his breath.

"*Keeeeeith*," I screamed and rushed down the steps. I missed a few of them and my legs buckled underneath me. I went tumbling down the stairs, but I got back up and quickly rushed up to him. He looked to be in so much pain, so I pressed my hand on top of his wound, not knowing if it was a gunshot or if he had been stabbed.

"Hold on baby," I cried out. "Please hold on! I'm going to go get you some help, okay? Hold on!"

I scurried off the floor and rushed into the living room. My bloody hands trembled as I dialed 911 and yelled into the phone for assistance.

"Help me, please! My boyfriend has been hurt! I think he's dying!"

I screamed the address into the phone then threw it down and rushed to Keith's side again. "Who did this, baby? Can you tell me who did this and why?"

Keith's eyes fluttered and shut a few times. I kept shaking him and I continued to apply pressure to his wound to stop the bleeding. I wasn't sure if what I was doing would help, but he was losing more and more blood by the minute. In a panic, I rushed up from the floor and opened the front door. I was going to get him into the car and take him to the fucking hospital myself.

"Help me!" I screamed out then turned to face him again. His eyes were closed and I released a deafening cry that echoed throughout his entire house. "*Noooooo*! Please God, *noooooooo*!"

I tried to drag his body out of the front door, but he was too heavy. He opened his eyes and strained to talk to me.

"La—Lesi," he stuttered.

I wasn't sure what he was trying to say, but then it hit me. "Lexi!" I shouted. "She did this to you!"

He slowly nodded and closed his eyes again. Every single breath in me had escaped and left my body. I heard sirens coming from down the street and the blaring sounds knocked me out of my trance. I left Keith near the doorway and ran down to the middle of the street so the ambulance could see me. The paramedics moved quickly. They worked on him, he had lost so much blood. I wasn't sure if he was going to make it, but as they put him on the gurney, I squeezed his hand and kissed his cheek.

"Please don't die. Hang in there, baby, please hang in there."

The paramedics asked me to move out of the way so they could get him to the hospital that wasn't far away. I closed the front door and hurried to my car so I could follow the ambulance. They beat me there, but when I walked through the emergency room doors, I had to wait. He was in surgery. All I could do was pray for him and pray that I didn't have to go to that bitch Lexi's house and kill her.

The clock ticked away and there was still no news. At this point, no news was good news. I continued to get hit with so many questions about Keith. But pertaining to the man I cared so much about, I knew little about him. I mean, I couldn't answer much. All I knew was his first and last name, where he worked, what he did for a living, his birthday, and his address. I didn't know how to contact his parents, nor did I know how to reach out to his brother, who he was really close with. I had no idea who his insurance carrier was, or even if he *had* insurance. His phone was back at his house, as well as his wallet. I was sure those things would be helpful to me, but before I left the hospital, I asked the nurse if she could give me some kind of update on his condition.

"Please tell me something. Anything that you know right now would be helpful," I begged.

The nurse told me to wait, where I stood for a few minutes. She came back almost ten minutes later and touched my hand. "The doctors are still working on him. You have to believe that they're doing the best they can. Just say a little prayer and everything will be all right. As soon as I know something, I'll let you know."

I wiped my flowing tears and nodded. Wanting to go get Keith's information and call his family, I got in my car. I felt so horrible because this was all my fault. I should have told Lexi about my feelings for him. I knew how possessive she was and it was my fault that things had escalated like this. I reached for my cell phone in my purse and called Kayla. She answered my phone and I was so glad she was at my place.

"Kayla, Lexi stabbed Keith. I'm at the hospital. I really need somebody right—"

"Oh my God!" she shouted. "Is he okay? Where are you?"

"I don't know if he's going to make it, but I'm at Barnes-Jewish Hospital on Kings highway."

"I'm on my way."

Kayla hung up. I thought about calling Evelyn, but unfortunately, she just wasn't that kind of friend. She was trouble and right now I didn't need trouble. I put my phone back into my purse, and as soon as I started my car, I felt a sharp blade touching the side of my neck. I was getting ready to turn around, but Lexi told me not to bother.

"How dare you cry over a dumb-ass nigga like this? What happened to us, Trina! Huh! Is this how you want to play me!"

My whole body was stiff. I didn't dare move. I did, however, look in the rearview mirror at her. She appeared very unstable.

"Pu—put the knife down, Lexi. You don't want to do this and you've already done enough."

"Is that muthafucka dead? That's when I'll know if I've done enough!"

I had to think fast and do my best to calm her. I was nervous as ever and could feel sweat sliding down the side of my face.

"Yes, he is dead. I didn't want to tell Kayla that he was, but you killed him. It's all over with and you don't have to worry about him anymore. It's you and me, again; forever and just like it was before."

I could hear Lexi breathing heavy. Never in my wildest dreams did I expect for anything like this to happen. How was I to know that I had been sleeping with a crazy bitch like her? She was way off.

My eyes shifted as I looked around for a police officer, security guard or somebody to help me. Unfortunately for me, though, there weren't too many people close by us.

Lexi pressed the knife harder and I felt a sting. I could feel blood trickle down my neck and I had no idea how deep she had cut me. I did know, however, that I needed to do something fast.

"It can never be like it was before," she cried out. "You played me, Trina! I loved you with all of my heart and you *plaaaaayed* me!"

"I'm sorry, but please know that I loved you too. I still love you and I promise you we can work this out. But if you do something stupid, we can't. We can't be together if you do something stupid and I know you don't want that."

Right then, I saw a police officer pull his car near the emergency room entrance and get out. I lifted my hand, slamming it against the horn. It sounded off so loudly that Lexi jumped halfway over the seat and began swinging the knife around. She stabbed everywhere she could, missing my face and head by inches. I hurried to loosen my seat belt and tried to unlock the door with her all over me. The knife cut deep into my shoulder and when I fell out of the car, I yelled out for help. The policeman was already headed in my direction and before Lexi got out of the car, he pulled out his gun and aimed it at her.

"Put the knife down or I'll shoot," he yelled.

Lexi was too anxious to get at me. She ignored the cop's warning and in a rage, jumped out of the car to get at me as I lay on the ground. Once she raised the knife in the air, the officer fired one shot that whistled right into her chest, blowing it wide open. As her limp body fell on top of me, I covered my mouth with my hands and screamed out as loud as I could.

Chapter Nineteen

Evelyn

After meeting with Trina, I was kind of hoping my phone would ring or that Kayla would come knocking on my door to confront me. I prepared myself on what to say to her. It was along the lines of exactly what I'd said to Trina. Unfortunately, I hadn't had the opportunity to spill my guts yet. Kayla hadn't called, but Trina called about an hour ago, telling me she was at the hospital with her boyfriend Keith. She said he had been stabbed and that she had been injured as well. She didn't sound good at all. It seemed as if there was more to the story that she wasn't telling me. So trying to be nosy and to give her some support, I put on my summer dress and headed out.

The moment I walked out the door, the wind picked up and blew up my dress. It was kind of flimsy and I hoped nobody got a peek at my turquoise thong. After I left the hospital, I planned to stop by Cedric's house to see him. He'd been working from home lately and he said Jacoby wasn't always there. That was a good thing, because we did need some privacy.

I arrived at the hospital around nine o'clock that morning. I wasn't sure where Trina was, so I called her on my cell phone to see what was up. She directed me to go to the waiting room and said she would be there shortly. When I got there, I saw Kayla sitting in one of the chairs, paging through a magazine. I eased over to her because I didn't know yet if Trina had said anything to her. I wasn't sure if she would come out swinging on me, so I paid attention to her expression. She lifted her head and smiled when she saw me coming her way. She then stood up and when I approached her, she gave me a hug.

"It's about time you got here," she said.

I sighed, knowing that everything was good; at least for now, anyway. "Trina just called me this morning. What happened and how long have you been here?"

Kayla gave me the scoop about what had happened, but I was still a little confused.

"So, this backstabbing, no-good fool had a girlfriend? If that's the case, then he deserved what he got. A scorned woman is nothing to play with, and some men need to stop trying to date all these women at one time. I don't understand why Trina is sticking by him. If it were me, I would be out of here."

"That's not what happened. I'll let Trina give you the details of what happened. But I can assure you that you're barking up the wrong tree."

"I don't see how. We see this kind of stuff happening all the time. Man cheats, woman gets mad and kills him."

Kayla caught an attitude with me. "Again," she snapped. "That's not what happened. If you want to know the truth about something, I'll share this. Keith is really a good guy. He didn't deserve this and that's all I'm going to say."

"Well, I'm not sure if you know the meaning of a good guy. You think Cedric is a good guy, but we both know that he isn't."

Kayla cocked her head back and frowned. "Are you okay this morning? You're coming off real strong and your attitude is horrible."

"I'm fine. Maybe being pregnant has me on edge a little. You know how that goes."

Kayla smiled and lightly smacked her forehead. "Oh, forgive me. With all that's been going on, do you know that I forgot you were pregnant? We haven't spoken much lately, and I want you to know that you're always in my thoughts and prayers, no matter what."

This heifer was so fake. Now, how do you forget that your best friend is pregnant? That made no sense to me and this was an example of the problem I had with Kayla. If it didn't revolve around her, she wasn't interested.

As we were sitting in the waiting area, in walked a dark-skinned, attractive man with locks. I paused my conversation with her to take a look. He walked up to the snack machine and then to the soda machine. When he came over to us, I gazed up at his sexy self.

"Here," he said, handing Kayla a soda. "I figured you may want something to drink."

"Thank you," she said, and then turned to me. "Bryson, this is Evelyn. She's my and Trina's best friend. Evelyn, this is Bryson, Keith's brother."

"Nice to meet you," I said with a smile. He shook my hand and said the pleasure was all his.

Bryson gave us the scoop on Keith's condition. From what he said, Keith pulled through surgery and was now in serious, but stable, condition. His parents were with him. So was Trina.

He looked at Kayla. "She told me to tell you to go home, get some rest, and said she would call you later."

"Well, you tell her that I'm staying right here. I want to make sure she's okay. I'm not leaving until I know for sure."

Bryson smiled and walked away. If Trina wanted us to leave, I really didn't want to stay. But I did so anyway, just so she could see me there during her time of need. There was no telling when I would need her to be there for me. It did bother me, though, that Kayla had always seemed to be there more for Trina than she was for me. It had been this way for a long time, so I added that to my list of gripes about her.

About fifteen minutes later, Trina came into the waiting room looking worn-out. Her sweats were hanging low. Her tennis shoes were untied and she had on an oversized T-shirt that was too big. I couldn't believe she was up here representing herself like this in front of Keith's parents. I figured they weren't impressed by their son's choices in women. I cut her some slack, considering the situation, but still.

She came up to me and Kayla with a somber look on her face. The first thing she did was thank me for coming and then she sat in a chair across from us and crossed her legs. She started to tie her tennis shoes and then slowly shook her head.

"I can't believe all of this is happening," she said. "Keith is doing better, but he's not out of the woods yet. He lost a lot of blood and she stabbed him like three times in his stomach.

I don't know how he made it through this. The more I think about it, I can't help but to think about how all of this is my fault."

Trina covered her face and started to cry. Kayla rushed over to the seat next to her and hugged her. "No, it's not your fault. I know Keith does not believe that, either. Some people just do crazy things sometimes and this matter was beyond your control."

I sat there clueless. Now, why in the heck would Trina think this was all her fault? It was Keith's fault for being a player. Was she actually sitting there taking responsibility for him? I swear, I had some stupid-ass girlfriends. They needed to get their acts together. Maybe I was missing something, but this was ridiculous. Either way, I played along with it and offered my support too by going to sit next to her.

"I don't know why you see this as your fault, but it's not," I said, rubbing her back. "Calm down. You have to believe that Keith will make a full recovery."

Trina seemed to lean more toward Kayla, so I backed away. They looked at each other, and then Trina turned to me.

"Can we go somewhere and talk?" she asked.

I assumed she wanted to talk to me about my situation with Cedric, but I wasn't up to hearing it right now. "Later," I said. "We'll talk later, especially since I think I already know what it's about."

Trina stood up. "No, you don't know. Let's go somewhere and talk now."

She seemed adamant, so I stood up and followed her. We walked together to the cafeteria, where Trina sat at a table that was far away from others.

"Listen," I said, taking a seat in the chair across from her. "This is the wrong time to be bringing up my relationship with Cedric. If you're worried about me saying anything to Kayla, I won't. I told you I'm not going to tell her, but I'm shocked that you haven't said anything."

"I'm not going to tell her. I truly believe that you should be the one to come clean. But I didn't bring you here to talk about that. I wanted to tell you about a secret I've kept for a long time and through keeping that secret is why I'm here today.

Maybe me telling you this will make you spill the truth. And believe me when I say it's a very bad feeling when you know you're responsible for hurting the people you care about."

I shrugged. "Yeah, well, some of those people have hurt me too. But what's your secret?"

Trina swallowed the huge lump I saw forming in her throat. "Evelyn, I've been involved—meaning intimately involved—in relationships with women for the past several years. When my relationship with BJ ended, I made the decision not to ever date another man, because he had done me so wrong. I started seeing that chick, Lexi, and our relationship got real serious. I kept that relationship a secret and then I met Keith. To make a long story short and without getting into more details, Lexi was the one who stabbed Keith. She was shot dead on the parking lot outside yesterday, and the police shot her in her attempt to kill me."

I hadn't moved, hadn't blinked . . . nothing. Did she just tell me she was a dyke? This had to be a joke. I assumed that Trina had fabricated this story, making it so tragic that I would be convinced to tell Kayla the truth.

"That was pretty good, Trina, and it was also pretty low. I'm not going to tell Kayla what is going on, and if you think your little story about Lexi and Keith is going to move me then you're sadly mistaken. And the whole gay thing is ridiculous. You love dick too much to go that route and I know that for a fact."

"Do you? Really? I guess you may need to open your eyes and reflect on the last several years, then. You haven't seen me with many men, and if you have, there's been no connection between us. I hadn't talked about them and besides all of that, I would never, ever lie to you about something like this. As my friend, I wanted you to know the truth. I've been holding onto this for so long, and now other people's lives have been affected."

I was trying to read Trina. What I discovered from the look in her eyes was that she was telling the truth. All kinds of crazy thoughts swam in my head, and I kept thinking about the many times I got undressed in front of her, how many times I hugged her, and the many times she put her lips on my cheeks. I couldn't do this shit, and no best friend of mine could be this way and not tell me.

"So, let me get this straight," I said as more anger crept on my face. "You're a lesbian, but you're in love with Keith. Your girlfriend tried to kill him and then she tried to kill you. After twenty-plus years of friendship, you're coming clean today because you feel guilty for destroying other people's lives. Does that about sum up everything you've told me?"

Trina stared at me from across the table. "I knew you wouldn't get it, Evelyn. You just don't have it in you to understand—"

"Understand," I said, raising my voice. "No, I do understand, Trina, and I understand things very well. I bet any amount of money that Kayla knows about this and has known for some time. The two of you have never been real friends to me, and I'm always the one being left out and dismissed like I'm not shit! This whole BFF stuff is a bunch of bullshit and it has been so for a very long time. If friends come in the form of you and Kayla, guess what? *I . . . don't . . . want . . . no . . . friends!* To hell with you both and you can take your pussy-eating-ass back in there and tell Kayla what I said. The next thing you're going to be telling me is the two of you are fucking each other and you want to hook up for a threesome. That wouldn't surprise me one bit and the two of you deserve each other."

I stood and tucked my purse underneath my arm. "Give Keith my condolences. I hope that whenever he comes out of this, he realizes the kind of woman you really are and he runs like hell to get away from you."

I stormed off. Many people's heads were turned in my direction and whispers filled the room, but I didn't care. I got the hell out of there and called Cedric to see if he was home. He didn't answer, but I still drove to his house anyway.

I parked in the curvy driveway, right behind a car that I hadn't seen before. I assumed that the car belonged to one of Cedric's business partners, but when I got to the glass doors that viewed into the house, I could see Cedric sitting on the couch in the great room. His head was dropped back and his eyes were closed. I thought he was sleeping, but as soon as I lifted my hand to ring the doorbell, I saw the long, black hair of a woman whose head was in his lap. It was apparent that her mouth was going to be burning too, and Cedric simply could not get enough. I was already in a bad mood, but he would never see me act a fool and go crazy about him being with other women. It did sting a little, especially after he seemed so decent the other night and had come off like he was getting serious about us.

Instead of ringing the doorbell, I stood for a few minutes, watching the action. Cedric looked to be faking it and the woman kept looking up at him for approval. She appeared to be real young and she was probably the one who had given him chlamydia. I wondered if he was giving her money like he was me, and thinking about her cutting into his cash was what prompted me to ring the doorbell. Cedric snapped his head to the side and a few minutes later he tied his robe and came to open the door.

"I see that you're busy, but do you mind if I come in?" I asked.

"It would be nice for you to call. That way you don't interrupt me. What is it that you want this time, Evelyn?"

"For starters, did you know that bitch Trina was gay?"

I had to say something that would get his attention. He laughed and that was when I took the opportunity to ease inside. "I promise to be good and I have nothing to say to your midday trick," I said. "I'm going to your office, so meet me there as soon as you can."

Cedric shook his head as I walked away. I passed through the great room, eyeing the young chick as she stood and wiped her mouth.

"Do—"

"Evelyn, don't," Cedric warned. "Go to my office. I'll be there shortly."

I kept my mouth shut. Didn't want to say anything to the stupid broad who probably had no clue what she was getting herself into, like Kayla. I knew Cedric more than anybody did. He had taught me a lot, even within the last month. The truth was, Cedric didn't give a damn about anybody. His love was for the almighty dollar and that was it. Women were good for one thing and one thing only. That was sex. Love didn't live in his heart anymore and thanks to Kayla's lies it hadn't lived there in a long time.

See, he and I had a lot in common. That was why Cedric appreciated me, more than he did anyone. I wasn't the kind of woman who griped all the time about every little thing, but if I ever felt that he had crossed the line he would surely hear about it. The chlamydia thing crossed the line. And the way he spoke to me that day made me look at him in a different way. He showed his true colors. I had to prepare myself better for what was to come.

I sat on a comfy sofa in Cedric's office with my legs crossed. The bay window brought in much light, but some of the light was blocked by the silky brown curtains that draped down to the floor. His oak-wood desk was cluttered with papers and the bookshelf behind his desk was filled with books. Cedric was a brilliant man and even though he had his flaws, I admired a man who knew how to make millions. For that I gave him credit. Relationship-wise he wasn't shit. I saw a picture of him and Jacoby on his desk, but there were no pictures whatsoever of him and Kayla. Not even on the twenty-seven-inch monitor that sat on his desk or on the walls, where there were pictures of him and his business partners.

The door squeaked open and he came inside. A cigar dangled from the corner of his mouth and he tightened his robe before taking a seat behind his desk.

"You know I got work to do, so shoot. What's up?"

"Did you know Trina was a lesbian?"

"Yes. I've known for a long time. I'm surprised that it seems to be breaking news for you. I told Kayla that I thought she was, but she didn't believe me."

"So, Kayla didn't know?"

"She may know now, but as of a month ago she told me I was out of my mind for telling her something like that."

"Well, Trina told me about her status today. Her boyfriend was shot by her lover, and the police killed her lover for trying to kill her."

"What? I didn't know she had a boyfriend."

"It's that Keith dude. Anyway, enough about them. What's up with you and Miss Youngin'? Is she the one who gave us chlamydia?"

"Don't start that shit again, all right? Did you take your pills?"

"Of course I did and I can tell you this right now. We won't have sex again without using condoms. I mean it, Cedric, and when you come to me you need to be prepared. I know I will."

"Just like you were prepared the other night, right? Let that bullshit go, Evelyn, you're better than that and no need to be petty."

"It's not being petty. You should be more careful, especially since you enjoy sex so much. You're too old for me to be schooling you, so I'm going to move on to the next subject. That would be my living arrangements. Without me working, I can't keep up with the rent. I'm not sure if I'll be able to find a job soon or not, and with me being pregnant I don't know if I can handle work anyway. So, I've been thinking. You have plenty of room here, and as you can see from my reaction to your head blower, I won't get in the way. When the baby is born, I'll already have everything set up. I'll cook, keep the house clean for you, and I'll continue to make myself available to you sexually. Now, what man would want more than that?"

Cedric responded by shaking his head. "Sometimes, I wonder about you, Evelyn. There are times when I wholeheartedly admire you, and then there are times when I honestly believe you need to see a shrink. I see that you've put much thought into this, but let me stop you before you get ahead of yourself. Jacoby is my son, and in case you forgot, he lives here too. I get that you're pregnant, but since our last conversation I've given this situation more thought. I don't think it's a good idea for us to live together, or be together as a couple, because I have too many things going on that you won't approve of. I may decide to make arrangements for you and the baby to live in a better place that is suitable for the two of you. The loft that you have isn't bad, and if rent money is what you need, I'll see what I can do. Meanwhile, you do need to get back to work, because I will not be supporting you. As far as the pussy thing goes, you're not doing me any favors by making yourself available to me. So are many other women, so your pussy ain't a big deal."

Cedric occasionally irritated me by saying the wrong things. I stood and walked over to his desk. "It sounds like you're trying to leave me out in the cold, but I told myself that I wouldn't come here to argue with you, so I won't. But let's be clear about some things then we can figure out the correct way to move forward. Jacoby is not your son and you know it. You've been playing the fatherly role for too long to a child that isn't yours. It's time to give it up." I pointed to my stomach. "This baby here, however, is yours. He or she will be your first. He or she will carry on your legacy, so therefore, he or she will need to be your number-one priority. With that, all I'm asking is that you consider what I said. I thought it was a wonderful offer, but please know that the offer won't stay on the table for too long. Let me know what's up soon. As for now, I'm going to let you get back to what you call work."

"Thank you. Be sure to close the door behind you and try like hell to have a good day."

"Oh, you too."

I rolled my eyes at him and walked out, thinking that his ass may have been better off dead than he was alive.

Chapter Twenty

Kayla

So much had been happening that I hadn't made much time for myself. I was doing my best to be there for Trina, and being there for her helped push to the back of my mind all that was going on with my life. Trina told me about her conversation with Evelyn and the way she reacted was a shame. Then I thought about my reaction too and understood how Evelyn probably felt betrayed. Still, I left it up to them to settle their differences. When all was said and done I was sure they would.

The one thing I was glad about was that I had been speaking to Jacoby more. He'd been calling me and I'd been calling to check up on him. Everything seemed to be okay with him, but he did tell me that he thought a new relationship with Arnez wasn't the right thing to pursue now. I was glad that he had made that decision and it was a decision that only he could make. It took him to see Arnez in that condition for Jacoby to realize he wanted no part of it.

We talked about Cedric filing for divorce and Jacoby asked what I intended to do. Right then, I wasn't sure. I was on my way to see a lawyer, just so I could know what my options were. Unfortunately, I had signed a prenup back in the day, saying that if we ever divorced, what belonged to him was his and what belonged to me was mine. I signed that stupid thing, having no idea that Cedric would one day make all of this money. Surely we both had hopes that things would prosper, but I never envisioned that it would get to this level. Apparently, he did. He was always ten steps ahead of me and I regretted that he was in control of so many things, including my life.

Before meeting with the lawyer, I stopped by Cedric's office to see if he was there. I was banned from entering the building, but the receptionist told me that Cedric was working from home. Knowing that Jacoby was at school, I drove to the house so I could look him face-to-face and be sure that this divorce was what he really wanted. When I got there, however, I saw Evelyn's car parked in the driveway. I had no idea what she was doing there and the fact that she was kind of upset me. I drove past the house, but as I turned around at the end of the street, that was when I saw her coming out the front door. A mean mug was on her face and she shielded her eyes with glasses. She hopped into her car and sped off down the street, going real fast.

After she left, I pulled in the driveway. I went to the door and it was unlocked. I walked inside and looked around. I missed being here and this still felt like home to me. I heard Cedric talking to someone and made my way back to his office, where he was. When I opened the door, his conversation came to a halt.

"Clay, let me call you back," he said through speakerphone. "Give me a minute to look that up, okay?"

"Sure. Call me back when you check that out for me."

Cedric clicked the button to end the call.

"I just ran into Evelyn—well, not really ran into her, but she sped off before I pulled up. What was she doing here?"

"What do you think she was doing here?"

"I don't know. That's why I asked."

"Money, Kay. She came here to ask me for some money. I told her to get the hell out of here and she left upset. I guess since she hasn't been able to hit you up for cash anymore, she thought she could come over here and ask me. It's not going down like that and you know it."

I couldn't believe that Evelyn was that darn desperate—then again, yes, I could. She knew better, didn't she, and what nerve? I made a mental note to call her and go off on her for doing something so sneaky and ridiculous.

"Well, I'm glad you didn't give her one dime. I'll be sure to call and talk to her about her greed later."

"Don't worry about it. You know that people try to hit me up all the time for money and you've had experience with that too. I don't want her to feel embarrassed, so just let it go."

Cedric was right. Besides, I wasn't there to talk about Evelyn. I was there to talk about us. "I will let it go, but I don't want to let our marriage go. I received the divorce papers the other day and I can't tell you how much my heart is bleeding right now. I think this can be worked out, Cedric. I also think you're making a big mistake. I haven't been perfect, I've made plenty of mistakes, but so have you. Can't you forgive me, as I've forgiven you? I've been so miserable and I'm here to claim my life back again. I want to come home and be the best wife that I can be to you, and the best mother that I can be to Jacoby. Allow me to do that and let's end all of this nonsense today."

Cedric put his hands behind his head and swayed back and forth in his leather swivel chair. "I wish it were that easy, Kay, but it's not. I am not trying to hurt you by divorcing you and you need to be clear about one thing: Love. I don't love you anymore. I have not loved you for a very long time. I have no other choice but to set you free and get on with my life. I'm not going to make this hard for you and it's not like I'm going to leave you out there in the streets. I just don't want you here, living in this house with me anymore. My advice is that you consult with your attorney, have him check out what I proposed, and let's get this rolling as amicably and quickly as possible. Delaying this process will be the only thing that hurts. Don't continue to do that to yourself and one day you'll realize this divorce is for the best."

I stood in front of Cedric with tears streaming down my face. It had finally hit me that this was the end of us, of our family, of everything I had always wanted. I had given up so much for him, as well as for my son. This pain I wouldn't wish on my worst enemy and to hear Cedric say that he didn't love me anymore tore at my heart and soul.

"Please," I begged as tears rolled over my trembling lips. My hands were shaking and I felt as if I were on the brink of a nervous breakdown. My heart was heavy and I could hear it pounding rapidly against my chest. "Don't do this to me.

This is not about you giving me money and please know that money will not heal my broken heart. I still love you, Cedric, and you're just still bitter about me lying to you. That anger will pass and . . . and you will—"

"No. No, I won't forgive you and I will never forgive you. I know how hard this is for you, and if you need counseling I'll be happy to pay for it. But this is done, baby. This marriage is done and you will have to accept that."

I could barely catch my breath from crying so hard. Cedric was so cold. I couldn't bear to stand there and allow him to see me so broken like this. I wiped my flowing, salty tears and turned to face the door.

"I am sorry that it has to be this way, Kay, but you brought this on yourself."

I didn't bother to respond. Maybe I did bring this on myself and now my chickens had come home to roost. I staggered my way to the door like a zombie. When I got to the car, I dropped my head on the steering wheel and clenched my chest. "This isn't over," I said in a whisper. "By no means is this over with yet."

While sitting in my car thinking, I called Evelyn to see why she had stopped by to see Cedric. She didn't answer, but I left a voice mail, telling her to meet me at Trina's place. It was time to get to the bottom of this.

Chapter Twenty-one

Cedric

I was a man who, with no question, had a conscience. Seeing Kayla that way broke my heart, but the damage was already done. With all that had been going on with me and Evelyn, there was no turning back. With all the lies that Kayla had told, there was no way for me to ever forgive her. I couldn't go back to the life we once shared and things weren't always like this. But today was a new day. I wanted my freedom and I wanted her to go seek the happiness she deserved.

Thinking about all that had been transpiring, I massaged my forehead and lowered my head on the edge of my desk, lightly pounding it to knock out my headache. I wanted to go get some aspirin, but my body and eyes were so tired from not getting much sleep these days that I found myself fading. Resting my eyes caused me to enter into a deep sleep, but I woke up about an hour or so later.

My headache was still throbbing, so I got up to go to the kitchen. As I passed by the stairs, I heard the floor squeak from upstairs and thought it was Jacoby.

"Jacoby, is that you?" I yelled up the stairs. There was no answer and when I looked at the clock on the wall it was after six o'clock, so I figured he was home.

I jogged up the stairs and entered his bedroom. He wasn't there, so I turned off his TV that must have been on all day. I roamed his room being nosy, and when I picked up a picture that sat near his computer of us playing basketball, I smiled. Jacoby was a good kid and my son or not, I still intended to look out for him. I hated that he was caught in the middle of all of this, but I wanted him to know the truth about me not being his real father. I could have told him a while back, but in my world timing was everything.

I heard footsteps again, so I put the picture down and proceeded down the hallway to my bedroom. One door was already opened, but when I opened the other one, I was met with the barrel of a shotgun that was aimed directly at my face. The person holding it was in disguise. All I could see at first were the eyes behind the black mask that was pulled over the person's head. I tried to quickly decipher if the body behind the baggy clothes was that of a man or woman, but I couldn't.

"Wha—what do you want?" I asked in fear, with my hands in the air. "Take anything you—"

No response, so I continued to plead with my intruder. "Please," I begged. "Don't do this. I'll give you anything you want. What is it that you want?"

The intruder released one hand from the trigger and placed one finger against her lips, as a gesture for me to be quiet. The lips looked kind of familiar to me, but I still couldn't make them out. As she took several steps forward, I backed up. When she moved, I moved. I paid close attention to the sway of her hips, trying to get myself familiar with who they belonged to. I wasn't there yet, but I was getting there.

I stopped backing up at the top of the stairs and as the shotgun remained aimed at my face, it hit me. I knew who was behind the mask, but the moment I opened my mouth, she lowered the gun and squeezed the trigger. All I remembered was the loud, blasting sound that popped my eardrum. I saw fire spark from the gun and I felt myself tumbling down the carpeted stairs. The ceiling was spinning and my entire body was numb. My eyes watered, but I could see a blurred vision of the woman standing over me. She pulled the mask over her head and wiggled her fingers through her hair.

"Don't you know, Cedric," she said with a smile on her face. "Too much pussy ain't good for you."

After that, my eyes fluttered some more, and I saw darkness with a flash of white, bright lights.

Chapter Twenty-two

Trina

Thank God Keith was doing much better, but he would have to stay in the hospital for some days yet. I spent every hour that I could by his side, making sure that he would be okay. I was also very appreciative of Kayla being by my side, but as for Evelyn, she had seriously let me down. I don't know why I expected anything different from her. I should have prepared myself better for her reaction. I didn't know if we would ever be able to mend our friendship again, but I was at a point where I didn't care anymore.

Keith turned in bed and looked at me sitting in a chair with my legs pressed against my chest. The room was kind of chilly, but I did have a blanket over me to stay warm. Keith had beads of sweat on his forehead. He cocked his head from side to side while looking at me.

"You're still here," he said with a slight smile.

"Where else am I going?"

"I don't know. You could go to work, go for a walk, to the mall . . . something."

"Nope. I'd rather be here with you—that's if you don't mind."

"Of course not."

He licked his dry lips and looked around at the get-well-soon balloons and many cards. They were from coworkers, family, and friends. Keith had a lot of love, as well as support.

"Have my mother and father been here?"

"They were here earlier, but you were sleeping. Your mother said she would be back around seven and your dad said he was coming back tomorrow."

"That's cool."

Keith looked around the room again and then he stared out the window for a minute.

"Can I get you anything?" I asked.

"Nah, I'm just thinking. I never came that close to death and it's a scary feeling. I'm just grateful to be alive and see all of this around me."

I stood up and walked up to the bed. I took his hand, squeezing it with mine. "I'm grateful too and I wanted to tell you how sorry I am for putting you in the middle of my relationship with Lexi. I had no idea that she was crazy like that and you have no idea how horrible I feel for my mistakes."

"It's not your fault. I wouldn't necessarily say that Lexi was crazy. It's just that love can make you do some crazy things sometimes. I don't know if you told her about us or not, but maybe you should have. Then again, it may not have made a difference, because I'm sure that losing a woman like you wouldn't be easy for anyone."

"I'm glad you can see it like that, but to me she was crazy."

I told him about Lexi being shot and killed by the police. I also showed him the numerous stitches I'd gotten from where she stabbed me. He couldn't believe it. He chuckled and retracted on his statement.

"Maybe she was a bit coo-coo then, but all I'm saying is if the mind isn't as strong as the broken heart is, you'll have a problem. My suggestion: Always be honest with people. The truth may hurt, but it'll set you free every time."

Keith was so right. We talked for a while longer and I couldn't help but to think about the secret I was keeping from Kayla. Whether the truth about Cedric and Evelyn would hurt her or not, she needed to know. I wanted to set myself free and get all of what I had known about Evelyn's and Cedric's relationship off my chest. I didn't want a repeat of what had happened to Keith and this time there would be no blood on my hands. With that in mind, I stayed with him for a little while longer. I then prepared myself to go home and tell Kayla the truth.

I bent over Keith's bed, giving him a lengthy kiss. "I'm getting ready to go home and take care of a few things. I'll be back tomorrow, okay?"

"That's fine, but when you come back tomorrow will you do me a favor and bring me something real sweet?"

"*Daaang*, you got me. What more do you want?"

He chucked a little and held his stomach. "I didn't know I had all of you, but that's good to know."

"All of me and then some. And that's just a little something that I thought you should know. Now, as for the sweet thing you're in need of, tell me what you want and I'll bring it to you."

"Are you good at baking cakes?"

"It depends on what kind of cake you want. Duncan Hines, Betty Crocker . . . what?"

"Homemade. One of those homemade, buttery pound cakes with that light glaze on top. My grandmother used to bake those all the time. I would love to have one of those."

"I know exactly what you're talking about, but you told me to be honest with you, so I will. I can't go there like that and any cake that I make you will not be homemade. I will do my best to make you one very close to it, and are you sure you're supposed to be eating that kind of stuff already?"

"I would love to be eating you, but I'm settling right now, all right? Do your best on the cake and I'll appreciate whatever you bring me tomorrow, even if it's a Snickers bar."

I laughed and leaned in to give him another kiss before leaving. On my way home, I stopped at the grocery store to see what I could put together. I wanted to bake the cake from scratch, but I didn't have a good recipe. I did have my cell phone, though, so I looked up the ingredients on the Internet and filled my cart with the items I needed. I also got Duncan Hines cake mix, just in case the homemade cake didn't pan out for me.

As I waited in line to pay for my groceries, I spotted Cynthia waiting in another line. She was with another lady I recognized from church, but I didn't know her name. They appeared to be real chummy with each other. I turned my head to ignore them. What Cynthia had going on wasn't my business anymore, and it was so funny that I now found myself not attracted to her.

The clerk rang up my groceries and when the bagger put them into my cart I strolled out the door. I put the bags in my trunk, but as soon as I opened my car door, Cynthia came up to me.

"You're not going to speak," she said.

"Oh, hey, Cynthia. I'm sorry. I didn't see you."

"Yes you did. I saw you watching me in there, and don't be jealous because you were the one who started acting funny with me. You didn't expect for me to wait around for you to get your act together, did you?"

"No, I really didn't. And if you're happy, I'm happy. Just do yourself a favor and come clean with Pastor Clemons. I know the hurt behind what he has done to you is making you this way, but tell him how you're feeling inside and go to counseling. Maybe the two of you can work things out, maybe y'all can't. But what you're doing to yourself is no good. In the end. Somebody may wind up getting hurt."

Cynthia threw her hand back at me. "I hear enough preaching on Sundays. Thanks for the advice, but save it for someone who needs it. My husband and I will be just fine. I do appreciate your concern for him, especially since you're in love with his wife. Unfortunately, sweetheart, I'm taken."

She walked away, sashaying her hips from side to side. The other lady was eyeing me, trying to see what was up. She wasn't going to catch any hell from me. I was done; finished with that mess, and the only love on my mind right now was Keith.

I entered my apartment, wondering if Kayla would be there. She wasn't, but I was surprised to see Evelyn standing outside of my door.

"What are you doing here?" I asked in a snobby tone.

"I got a call from Kayla. She wanted me to meet her here so we could talk. I need to get some things off my chest too, so I thought it would be wise to stop by and chat with the both of you."

Without saying a word, I put the key in the door to unlock it. Evelyn took a seat on the couch while I put up the groceries and went to change into my jeans and a T-shirt. While in my bedroom, I kept rehearsing in my head how I was going to break the news to Kayla about Evelyn and Cedric. Then again, maybe Evelyn was here to do it. She said that she wanted to get some things off her chest, but that could mean anything. I pondered about what I could say to get this mess out in the open, just in case Evelyn wouldn't step up to the plate.

"They've been having sex . . . screwing each other . . . no, fucking," I mumbled. "He doesn't love her and I think. . . . no, I want you to stay strong, and screw him. Let them stay together . . . girl, fight for your marriage and to hell with Evelyn."

I didn't know how to break it down to Kayla, so I let out a deep sigh and returned to the living room where Evelyn was. Before I could say one word, Kayla came through the door. Her braids were gone and almost all of her hair had been cut off. I was surprised to see her hair shorter than mine, but the nearly bald cut looked decent on her. It showed the roundness of her face more and it also revealed her almond-shaped, pretty eyes. Her eyes showed sadness, though, and I could see the puffiness underneath them. It was obvious that today wasn't a good day. I assumed that she had just finished meeting with her attorney. Evelyn stood to look at Kayla, but she didn't say a word.

"So how did it go?" I asked, referring to her meeting.

Kayla appeared to be out of it. She walked slowly into the living room and sat on the couch. "How did what go?"

"The meeting with your attorney. What did he say?"

"I didn't go. I changed my mind about meeting with him."

My brows rose as I sat in the chair next to her. Evelyn sat back down too and started to question Kayla. "Why? What changed your mind?"

Kayla moved her head from side to side. "I . . . I just don't want a divorce. I'm not giving up and I'm going to fight to save my family."

"But you can't save your family, Kayla," I said. "What's done is done. Don't you think you should consider moving on?"

"I am moving on. I'm moving out of here by the end of the week and I'm going back home. I'm going home to be with my husband and son."

"I don't think so," Evelyn said. "That wouldn't be a good idea."

"Why not?" Kayla hissed. "And why are you always being so negative?"

Evelyn folded her arms across her chest. "I'm not always being negative, but the question is, Why did you ask me to come here?"

Kayla squeezed her forehead and frowned. "Forget it, Evelyn. I was thinking crazy stuff when I called and told you to meet me here. The truth is, how I feel about you right now doesn't really matter."

"Well, it matters to me. And now that we're all here, I have a few things that I want to say." She looked at me first. "I apologize for how I treated you at the hospital, but please understand that your news was very hard for me to swallow. I thought about it over and over again. And you know what, Trina? Do you. Who am I to judge you, when I have my skeletons too?"

She was right about that, but I wasn't worried about my friendship with Evelyn. There was a bigger issue and it revolved around her and Kayla. I figured the day would come when we would reconcile our differences, yet I was surprised that Evelyn had approached me first. Normally, I would be the one who reached out to her.

"Your apology is accepted and I apologize for saying some of the hurtful things that I said to you too. But we all need to stop with the lies. If we're going to call ourselves friends, then we need to start acting like real friends, instead of haters. Is there anything else that you would like to share with me or Kayla? Now is the time to do it."

Thank God the direction of Evelyn's eyes shifted to Kayla. "I don't know where to start, Kayla, but I owe you an apology too. This is so hard for me to say, but as your best friend, I have betrayed you."

Kayla appeared out of it. All she did was move her head from side to side and bite her nails.

"I saw you at my house today. I went there to get Cedric to change his mind, but he didn't want to do it. He said that he didn't love me anymore, and I can't believe that he . . . just . . . does not love . . . me . . . anymore."

Kayla was in a daze. She looked straight ahead and didn't even turn to look at me or Evelyn. What in the hell was going on?

"What did you see going on between him and Evelyn? Did you see something?" I questioned. Evelyn sat still and waited for Kayla to respond.

Kayla rubbed her hands together and stood up. She paced the floor then stopped to squeeze her forehead. "I didn't see anything, but something is going on. I can feel it. You know how you have this . . . this eerie feeling inside that something is wrong. He said she was there for money, but I think there's more to it. I really do, but I just can't . . . I can't put my finger on it."

I was trying to pull this out of Kayla, especially since she was speaking as if Evelyn wasn't even there. "Well, put your finger on it and touch it. Open your eyes and see it. What are you feeling? Say it, Kayla, say it and don't lie to yourself anymore. Don't ignore what you know. Your gut has been telling you things, but you've been ignoring it. Rewind the tape and play those images in your head. Ask yourself: What do you see?"

Kayla closed her eyes and tears cascaded down her face. When she opened her eyes, she locked them on Evelyn. "I see Cedric and I see you, Evelyn. I've seen the way he looks at you and I've seen the way you smile at him. I saw him at your place one day," Kayla paused, sucked in a deep breath and released it. "And . . . and I saw your earrings and nasty panties in his car. I saw his account where he transferred thousands and thousands of dollars into your account and I . . . I smell the scent of my husband when I walk into your home. So the questions are: Are you fucking my husband, and if so, why didn't either of my best friends tell me what in the hell has been going on behind my back?"

I sat speechless, figuring that Kayla must have known about my betrayal as a friend too. Evelyn swallowed hard and sat with teary eyes. She blinked and scooted to the edge of the couch. "I'll answer your question, but for the record, you have never seen my nasty panties in Cedric's car. Those panties must have belonged to someone else. As I said before, I do owe you an apology—not for fucking your husband, but for allowing him to fuck me and use me to hurt you. For that, I am deeply sorry and I truly hope that you will one day forgive me for interfering in your marriage when I shouldn't have."

The room fell silent. Kayla glared at Evelyn without a blink and her fists quickly tightened. My breathing halted and I felt as if cement had been poured over me—I couldn't move. I could see beads of sweat dotting Evelyn's forehead and a slow tear slid down her face. The only thing that transformed the moment was the unique ring from Kayla's cell phone. The sound snapped her out of thoughts and she hurried to answer.

"I'll call you back, Jacoby," she said through gritted teeth. Then her face fell flat and her eyes widened. "What! Oh my God! I'll be there soon! Stay there!"

Kayla cut her eyes at Evelyn and me. She snatched her purse from the table and bolted to the door.

"What happened?" I yelled and jumped from my seat. "Please say something before you go."

Kayla didn't respond. The door flung open and slammed against the wall. A cool breeze blew in and I was left standing their counting the mistakes I had made while trying to refer to somebody as a best friend. I was in no position to call myself that and shame on me.

I hurried to call Jacoby, just to see if he would tell me why Kayla rushed out of there. When he answered his phone, I could hear loud cries over the phone.

"What's wrong, Jacoby?" I rushed to say. "Please tell me what's happening."

He gasped and released staggering cries. "My fa—father, Cedric, is dead. I think my mother killed him! She was so upset that she—she killed him!"

I thought about Kayla's unstable demeanor that was similar to Lexi's. My mouth opened wide and I dropped the phone, seeing it crash to the floor and break into pieces like our lives.

"What did he say?" Evelyn shouted out to me. "Why are you looking like that?"

I slowly turned my head to look at her. My mouth cracked open and I was now the one in a daze because I feared what Kayla had done.

"She—she killed him. Kayla killed Cedric."

I was shocked by Evelyn's reaction. She crossed her legs and shrugged her shoulders. "Like I've always said, too much pussy ain't good for you and a mad pussy is never a good thing. I'm deeply sorry for Kayla's loss. It's unfortunate."

I didn't bother to respond. I hurried out the door, hoping and praying that we would all recover from our tragedies.

BFF'S 2:

Best Frenemies Forever Series

Chapter 1

Kayla

I was a nervous wreck. Jacoby's phone call about Cedric being shot had me driving like a bat out of the devil's lonely hell. I swerved in and out of traffic, trying to get to the place I once called home. Tears streamed down my face. I could barely see the road through my blurred vision. My heart raced like I was on the verge of a heart attack, and so many thoughts swarmed in my head.

No matter what Cedric had done to destroy our marriage, I didn't want him to die. He had been the worst husband ever, but in no way did I want to be a widow. I still had much love for him. Someway or somehow, I thought we could piece our marriage back together. But after today, that would be difficult. If he survived his injuries, I didn't know how I would be able to forgive him for having a relationship with my best friend, Evelyn. How could I forgive the lies and betrayal of what they'd done? It wouldn't be easy, but for now, I had to focus on Cedric.

When I spoke to Jacoby earlier, he said that someone called 911 and the police and ambulance were on their way. I couldn't stop thinking about who could've wanted to kill Cedric. Why would they want him dead? I had my issues with him, no doubt, but I'd never thought about killing him. I should have, though, especially after the way he treated me; kicking me out of the house, removing money from my bank account, and fucking my friend—that was a sure way to get me stirred up.

I couldn't say that I was totally surprised by Evelyn's announcement today, but I couldn't get that smirk she'd had on her face, while making her confession, off my mind.

I could sense Evelyn's fakeness.

I gazed at her without a blink and was ready to beat that bitch's ass! But for whatever reason, I couldn't move. I couldn't open my mouth. All I could do was stare in disbelief. I wanted to be wrong about the two of them, but her acknowledging the affair proved me right. Seconds later, my cell phone rang. It was Jacoby, crying hysterically and telling me that Cedric had been shot.

After Jacoby's call, I left in a hurry. I was on my way to see what was up. My car was moving at high speeds, but I needed to call Jacoby, again, to see what was going on. Unfortunately, he didn't answer. I called back several times, but got no response. I was only fifteen minutes away from Cedric's place, but I needed to know his condition. I needed to know if Jacoby was okay. Maybe he had done something to Cedric. They didn't get along that well, and these last few months had been hell for all of us. I hoped that he hadn't done anything this horrific, and the thought of it made my stomach turn. I was in deep thought, until I heard loud sirens. When I looked on the other side of the highway, a speeding ambulance had zoomed through traffic. That wasn't good. Was Cedric's dead body in there? Were the paramedics working hard to keep him alive? More tears fell, and I prayed all the way to my destination.

Upon arrival, I could see several police cars and plenty of my neighbors standing outside being nosy. Yellow crime scene tape squared the well-kept property and no one was allowed to cross the line. The front door was wide open. And when I looked around for Jacoby, he was nowhere in sight. I jerked the car in park and rushed to the first officer I saw. My legs wobbled and my heart raced faster, as I pulled on the officer's arm to get his attention.

"Where is my husband . . . my son? Please tell me what happened."

The officer could see how unstable I was. He pulled me closer to the house, as my neighbor, Betty, shouted to ask if I was okay.

"I hope so, and let us know how Cedric is. Meanwhile, please get Rich out of this. He didn't do anything but try to help, but the police keep questioning him."

I frowned because I was clueless to what she was talking about. That was until I looked into the back of a police car and saw her husband, Rich, sitting on the back seat while talking to an officer who sat in the front. Jacoby was inside of another car, and in another car was a white woman with dingy, blond hair. Her head hung low, and I couldn't see her face.

The officer held my arm and shook it. "Do you need an ambulance?" he said.

I shook my head, trying to come out of the daze I was in. "No, no, I don't. I need to find out what has happened to my husband, and why is my son in the back of the police car? I need to go see him."

I turned to walk away, but the officer grabbed my arm. "Come inside for a few minutes. If you're Mrs. Thompson, I need to speak to you."

"But I . . . I need to go see about my son. Why is he in the police car?"

"He's just speaking to one of the officers about what he saw. He'll be fine."

I moved my head from side to side and snatched away from the officer. I wasn't sure why he was trying to keep me away from Jacoby, and with him being seventeen the police had no right to question him without my consent. I stormed away from the aggressive officer who followed after me.

"Ma'am, I need to speak to you about your husband."

That got my attention, so I swung around to address him. "My husband? Where is he? Would someone please tell me where he's at?" I pounded my leg and started to cry even more.

"He's on his way to the hospital. We don't know his condition yet, but he was pretty bad when he left here in the ambulance."

I held my chest, squeezing it. That was when Jacoby got out of the police car and came up to me. He appeared frightened. The confusing look washed across his face upset me.

"Mama, this . . ." He paused to embrace me. And as my son who stood six two held me, he started to break down on me. "What has happened to our family?" he cried. "I thought you were the one who shot my dad, but I was wrong. I pray to God that he lives. God, please don't let him die. This is all my fault because I wished him dead, Mama. I prayed for his demise."

I looked around at the officers who were tuned in to Jacoby's every word. I didn't want him to incriminate himself, so I told him to be quiet. I rubbed his back and did my best to comfort him, considering how messed up I was.

"This is not your fault. I had my issues with Cedric too, but neither of us wanted him dead. As for our family, we'll be fine. Trust me, we will be fine, so don't you worry, okay?"

Jacoby nodded and backed away from me. He smacked tears away from his face then wiped down it with his hand to clear it.

"Rich saw her do it," he said. "He told me she did it, and I could've stopped her, Mama. I figured she would do something like this, especially after I talked to her that day."

My mind was going a mile a minute, trying to figure out what Jacoby was saying. But I couldn't comprehend anything because the officer behind me kept taking notes, and grabbing at my arm, asking me to come into the house. More sirens kept blaring, as more cars showed up. My nosy neighbors looking on didn't help either, and why were everybody's dogs barking? Maybe it was a good thing for us to go into the house, after Jacoby cleared himself of any wrongdoing.

I turned to the officer. "Officer, I will answer any question that you want me to, after I'm done speaking to my son. You say my husband is at the hospital, so we need to get there soon. Please allow me to get out of here to go see about him."

"Yes, we do need to get out of here," Jacoby said. "I'll fill you in, in the car and tell about what happened. But for now, let's go to the hospital to see what's up with my dad."

For whatever reason, the officer didn't want us to leave. "I'll arrive at the hospital in about thirty minutes," he said. "Hopefully, we'll be able to talk in private then."

"Sure," was all I said then rushed to my car with Jacoby.

On our way to the car, I took another glance at the white woman sitting in the police car with her head hung low. This time, two officers stood outside of the car, talking. I could barely see her, but when she swooped her frizzy hair behind her ears, my eyes grew wide. My mouth dropped open, and then I squinted to be sure that the woman was Cedric's receptionist, Paula Daniels. As I started to move in her direction, Jacoby called out to me.

"Let's go, Mama. Cedric needs us. I will tell you all about her in a minute."

I kept my eyes on her then slowly got into the car. As I drove off, she turned her head to look at me. Our eyes stayed connected, until she rolled hers and lowered her head again.

"Keep your eyes on the road, please," Jacoby said. "We will discuss her, but before we do, I want to ask if you're okay. You seem a little off."

"That's because I am. It's been a crazy day. The truth is, I don't know if I'm coming or going."

"I understand exactly how you feel. But before we get to the hospital, I need to tell you that Paula was the one who attempted to kill Cedric. She's been seeing him for quite some time, and he pushed her to the edge. He kicked her out of the house he purchased for her, and he also made promises to her that he failed to keep. I saw them together, numerous times— more recently in a parking garage getting it on. After that, I reached out to her. She told me what Cedric had done to her, and she threatened to kill him. I didn't take her seriously, but I should have.

"When I got home today, all I saw was Cedric's bloody body on a gurney. I thought he was dead, and at first, I assumed you had killed him. Forgive me for thinking that, but I knew how upset you were with him too. The truth is, Rich witnessed Paula walking toward our house with a shotgun in her hand. He followed her and called the police. By then, it was too late. Cedric had already been shot."

I was speechless. So much anger was inside of me. I couldn't believe that Cedric had been also having an affair with the receptionist, and then to buy her a house was crazy. I guess that explained why she always looked at me with envy in her eyes whenever I visited his office. It explained why she always had an attitude when I called to speak to him, and it explained why he always worked late hours. Then there were the Christmas parties, the company picnics, and the company milestones and celebration parties I attended with Cedric. I could always sense how fake Paula was. Deep inside, I always felt as if she was watching me, and for some reason, she seemed to hate me. I questioned Cedric about her attitude toward me, but he claimed that she treated everyone that way.

He made it seem as if Paula had been dating one of his partners, not him. I believed him because she didn't seem like his
type. But then again, what was Cedric's type? I really didn't
know because me, Paula, and Evelyn were like night and day.

Thinking about all of this, yet again, I felt like a fool. First
Evelyn, now Paula. I was starting to feel as if Cedric dying
wouldn't be such a bad thing after all.

"Mama, I know what you're over there thinking, but you may
want to speed it up so that we can get to the hospital. Going
twenty miles an hour, we'll never get there."

"All of a sudden, I feel as if there is no rush. I hate to say this,
but Cedric had this coming. I don't wish him bad, but you
must understand how betrayed I feel. And his receptionist
hasn't been the only woman. I just found out that he's been
screwing Evelyn too."

Jacoby sat quiet. He looked straight ahead then lowered his
head to look at his lap.

I slammed my hand on the steering wheel. "Please tell me
that you didn't know about that too. Did you know that he'd
been seeing Evelyn?"

There was a crisp silence for a few seconds then Jacoby
spoke up. "Yes, I knew. Found out awhile back. I confronted
her about her actions too, but she didn't see things my way. I
wanted to tell you but, as your son, I didn't want to see you
hurt. I felt relieved about the divorce, but you kept pushing to
make things work. Then there was a part of me that wanted
things to work out, too, because our family means everything
to me."

I felt horrible inside. I understood how Jacoby felt, but
no words could express how disgusted I was about the
whole thing. Everybody had been keeping secrets from
me, including my other friend, Trina, and now my own son.
Something inside of me wanted to turn this car around, park
it somewhere, and get the hell out of dodge.

"If you knew about Cedric's affair with Evelyn, I wish you
would have said something. I always had my suspicions too,
but it seems as if everyone wanted me to make a complete fool
of myself. When I kept defending Cedric, all you had to do
was tell me what he'd been up to."

"I did tell you." Jacoby raised his voice. "But you wouldn't listen, remember? I may not have been specific about Evelyn, but I told you Cedric was no good. I told you he'd been with other women, but all you did was yell at me. You told me that I was the one who needed to get my act together."

Jacoby shut me up with the quickness. He had mentioned Cedric's cheating ways to me before, but I chose to believe him and take his word that he wasn't cheating. I apologized to Jacoby. After that, I kept my mouth shut until we got to the hospital. Meanwhile, my thoughts about Cedric weren't good.

The hospital's emergency room was jam-packed. Two young men had been shot, and their families were all over the place, having a fit and praying to God for Him to save them. A child with a broken arm stood next to his mother in tears, and as she did her best to comfort him, a man in a wheelchair rolled in complaining about chest pains. I had already asked the nurse behind the counter where Cedric was, but all she said was for me to have a seat. When I pushed, she got antsy.

"Ma'am, all I can say right now is they're working on him. Please have a seat. The doctor will be with you shortly."

"Shortly as in a few minutes or a few hours? That's my husband back there. I would really like to know how he's doing."

I could see the young woman's eye twitch. "I repeat, the doctor will be with you shortly. There is nothing else that I can say right now."

I rolled my eyes and walked away. Jacoby walked next to me, and we both took seats in the waiting area. Even with a leather jacket on, I was cold. I had gotten all of my hair cut off earlier, and the short cut that I sported surely didn't keep my head warm. Jacoby kept looking at my hair, but he didn't say anything about it. I felt like a bad mother for putting him through so much. It wasn't until I reflected on all that we'd been through these last few months when I realized how much of a burden my marriage had been on our son. First, for Jacoby to learn that Cedric really wasn't his father was enough. Then for him to run around after Cedric's women, asking them to stay out of our lives, that had to be hurtful for him. All he wanted was a stable family, yet what we provided was a dysfunctional mess.

I reached over for his hand and held it with mine. "If Cedric survives this, I don't know where we go from here. But, I want you to let me handle this from now on. I know you feel as if I've been weak, and that's why you've taken things into your own hands. But I got this, trust me. Get back to your life as a teenager and try to have some fun. I don't want you to worry so much about me and Cedric, because—"

"I worry, because no matter what, the two of you are still my parents. I know Cedric isn't my biological father, but he has taken good care of me and you too. He has a high sex drive, and I do believe that your lies contributed to some of this as well. But none of us are perfect, Mama. If I forgive you, I have to forgive him too."

I swallowed and blinked to wash away my tears. "Thank you," was all I could say.

On the inside, I was too angry to forgive Cedric right now. I was too angry about what he had put us through. Yes, he'd provided for his family, but that was what he was supposed to do. I didn't share any more of my thoughts with Jacoby. And as I'd said before, I would handle this.

Jacoby got up to get a soda from the soda machine. He also said he needed to return his girlfriend, Adrianne's, phone call. He walked away to go call her, so I reached for my cell phone to check my messages. I had five messages from Trina. She wanted to know where I was, and she sent several text messages, asking for me to call her back. I really didn't want to be bothered, but I sent her a text, telling her that I was at the hospital waiting to find out Cedric's condition. The second I put the phone back into my pocket, I saw two of the officers from earlier enter through the sliding glass doors. I turned my head, but the one I had spoken to earlier had already spotted me. He wasted no time coming up to me.

"Do you have a few minutes to talk?" he said, scratching his bald head that was full of dents.

I sighed and got up from the chair. Before walking away, I looked around for Jacoby and saw him standing next to the bathroom, talking on his cell phone.

"This will only take a few minutes," the officer said.

I followed him into the hallway, in no mood to be questioned. Didn't they find out everything they needed to know from Rich, Jacoby, and the killer herself? This officer was barking up the wrong tree, and he had racist pig written all over that red, puffy face of his.

I eased my hands into my pockets and leaned against the wall. My blank expression alerted him that I didn't want to be bothered. "What is it that you want to ask me?" I said to the officer.

He pulled out a notepad and scanned his eyes up and down to look at it. "Are you and your husband separated or divorced?"

"Right now, I don't know what we are. But you may want to ask him that question if, or when, he comes out of this."

"I'm asking you. Some of my sources say that the two of you are separated, and that you were angry because your husband filed for a divorce."

My face twisted. "Of course I was angry. But are you implying that I had something to do with what happened?"

"I'm not implying anything. I'm just trying to get to the bottom of this, that's all."

"If you want to get to the bottom of this, go talk to that hoochie who was in the back seat of the police car. She can probably tell you more than I can, and please don't stop there. My husband has been screwing around with several women, so it wouldn't surprise me if they all conspired to do away with him."

"Well, that's why I'm here. Did you pay Paula Daniels to kill your husband? I mean, she doesn't seem like the kind of woman who could pull off something like this alone."

I chuckled and shook my head. "Why couldn't you see her doing it? Because she's a white woman, and they don't do things like that? You would like to believe that I paid her to kill my husband, but if I wanted to do so, you best believe that I would've picked up the doggone gun and shot him myself. You're wasting your time, Officer. Going this route will get you nowhere with me."

He ignored me and kept on with the questions. "Where were you today? Do you have an alibi? And just to let you know, we will be checking your phone records. If there are any conversations between you and Miss Daniels, we'll be in touch."

"I'm not going to answer another question from you. If you want to question me further, you will do so in front of my attorney. Meanwhile, stop showing sympathy for murderers. No matter what color they are, do what you must to keep them behind bars. If not, you're the one who has to live with it, not me. Thank you, Officer. Have a nice day."

I walked away with a mean mug on my face. How dare he go there with me? I figured he wanted someone else to go down for this, other than Miss Prissy whom he obviously felt sorry for. The more I thought about this, the more my anger took over. It got worse when I saw Trina come through the door, searching for me. I cut my eyes and moved in another direction. It wasn't long before she caught up with me down the hallway.

"Stop this, Kayla, and tell me what's going on. Did you attempt to kill Cedric?"

I turned to her and snapped. "Hell, no, I didn't, but I can think of a whole lot of people I wouldn't mind shanking right now. What do you want, Trina? Why do you keep bothering me?"

"If you didn't attempt to kill Cedric then who did?"

"It's none of your business, and if you think I did it then keep on believing that."

"Look, you don't have to get an attitude about it. I asked you that because Jacoby told me you killed him."

"Jacoby was mistaken. Now, tell me again why you're here?"

"I'm here because I'm your friend and you need my support. I get that you're still upset about the conversation that took place at my place earlier, but, at least, now you know the truth."

I pursed my lips and shook my head from side to side. I couldn't help the sarcasm. "Yeah, I do. And I'm so grateful to you for telling me everything. After keeping their little secret and protecting their feelings, thank you, Trina, for all that you've done. As for you being here for me, no, you're here because Keith is still in this hospital from being stabbed by your lover, Lexi. I'm sure you can't wait to get by his side, so don't go pretending to be such a supportive friend of mine, please. I wouldn't call it a friendship, would you?"

Trina narrowed her eyes and muffled her lips. I could tell she was trying to prevent herself from going there with me.

"I saw Keith earlier, so I didn't come back here to be with him. And I'm not going to argue with you about this friendship thingy; been there, done that. When you're ready to talk, call me. I'm here for you, like I've always been. Yes, I've made some mistakes, and I should have told you about Evelyn and Cedric. But I had my reasons for not going there. Reasons that you may or may not understand."

I wasn't the kind of woman to keep up a lot of drama, especially in a public place, but Trina needed to hear me loud and clear. "You mean, reasons that I will never understand. Now, get out of my face, Trina. I'm so done with this right now. You and Evelyn, both, can go to hell."

"I'm too blessed to go there, but do yourself a favor and get a grip. This attitude thing ain't you, and I must say that you don't wear it well. I won't share my reasons for not telling you about your cheating husband and backstabbing friend, but I will tell you this. They have a child on the way, so be prepared for Evelyn to go after Cedric's cash. I don't know if he'll make it or not, but whatever you do, tell her that he's dead. With her believing that he is, that may change the game, if you know what I mean. Meanwhile, I'll keep my distance, yet pray that everything will work out for you."

Trina walked away, leaving me stunned yet again. A baby? It didn't even dawn on me that the baby Evelyn was carrying was Cedric's. I thought it was her ex-boyfriend, Marc's, child. I mean, really? If I'd had a gun, I would have gone back there and made sure Cedric was dead. My anger turned into hate. I just couldn't stay there any longer.

Jacoby was still on his cell phone, talking to Adrianne. When I walked up to him, he told her to hold.

"What did the officer say?" he asked.

"Nothing important. But, uh, if you don't mind, I need to get out of here. I'm not feeling well, and being here is making me sick."

Jacoby frowned. "What about Cedric, Mama? Don't you care about him? Don't you want to know if he'll survive? I know you're upset about all of this, but he's your husband and—"

"And I'm his wife," I shouted. "I am his fucking wife and that bastard cheated on me, got another woman pregnant, and had the audacity to buy another one a house! To hell with Cedric, Jacoby! If you want to stay here, please do. As for me, I'm going home! I need to get the hell out of here and go home!"

Jacoby wiped away sprinkles of my spit that landed on his face. He slowly lifted his phone and told Adrianne he'd call her back. "Then go," he said to me. "Adrianne is on her way up here. I'll call you later to keep you posted on Cedric."

"Don't bother," I said, looking around at the many people staring at me as if I was crazy. It definitely wasn't my intention to put my business out there like this. I was totally embarrassed. "I'm sorry about this, but I . . . I can't do this."

I tearfully walked away and left the hospital. While inside of my car, I rested my forehead on the steering wheel and broke down. Tears wouldn't stop falling. I held my chest, wishing that the pain inside would go away. *Why me?* I thought. *Why did all of this bad news hit me like this in one day?* I felt as if I'd lost everything. Other than Cedric, there was another person to blame. Evelyn. I had to go see her, just to look her in the eyes and give her a piece of my mind.

Almost thirty minutes later, I arrived at Evelyn's loft. Like always, security was walking around, and I saw her car parked in the parking garage. Cedric had probably paid for her car, and I thought about keying the side of it. But after I parked, the security looked at me, smiled, and said hello. I spoke back, but I could tell that he was alarmed by how distraught I appeared. He watched my every move, and unfortunately for me, I wasn't sure if Evelyn would buzz for me to come inside. I took my chances and pushed the code to alert her that someone was there to see her.

Seconds later, her beautiful, blemish-free face appeared on the screen. Why did she have to always look so darn pretty?

It wasn't that I was jealous of her, but there was no denying that out of all of us, Evelyn always got the most attention from men. Even while we were in high school, most of the boys wanted to date Evelyn. It could have been because she was a slut, too; a slut who got her hands on my husband, and had the audacity to be pregnant by him.

"Hello, Kayla," she said with that same smug smirk from earlier. "What do you want?"

"We need to finish our conversation. Now that Cedric is dead, I think we should talk about what to do with your baby. You are carrying his baby, aren't you?"

Evelyn didn't say a word. She buzzed me inside, and on my way up in the elevator, I felt as if I wanted to throw up. I swallowed and bit into my trembling bottom lip. When the elevator parted, I looked straight ahead and saw Evelyn standing with the door wide open. Neither of us was smiling and seriousness was locked in our eyes. It was obvious that we were about to handle our business.

I stepped forward, but before Evelyn could say one word, I reached out and slapped her so hard that a new hairstyle formed on her head. My hand stung, and I watched as a red handprint swelled on the side of her cheek. Her forehead lined with wrinkles, and as her mouth dropped open, I turned to walk away.

"Thanks for the conversation," I mumbled. "It was well needed."

"You bitch!" she shouted. "You are going to pay for that! I swear to God that you will pay!"

I ignored her and got back on the elevator. Before it closed, I returned the same smug smirk that she had been representing all day. Whatever she had in store for me, I welcomed it. It couldn't be any worse than what she had already done to me.

Chapter 2

Trina

I was to the point where I'd had enough of Kayla's attitude. Evelyn's backstabbing ways, as well, were too much for me to handle. After Kayla left my apartment earlier to go see about Cedric, I politely asked Evelyn to leave. There were times when I felt as if I had the worst best friends ever. I understood that no one was perfect, but this was too much. I was tired of kissing Kayla's ass, and I always found myself trying to convince her what a good friend I had been. I truly felt as if it wasn't my place to tell her about Cedric and Evelyn, but I decided to poke my nose where it didn't belong and let it all come out today. My timing, however, was off. Evelyn was ready to spill her guts, and Cedric had been shot. Now, here we all were, mad at each other, again, and trying to blame each other for why things had turned out this way.

I waited in my car for a while, and right after I saw Kayla leave the hospital, I went back inside. While speaking to Kayla, I'd seen Jacoby on his cell phone, so I assumed he was still inside. Once I had a chance to speak to him, I was going to spend the night in Keith's room.

The moment I entered the hospital, I saw Jacoby sitting in a chair. Another family was gathered in a circle, conversing with a doctor. Seconds later, all hell broke loose. Cries rang out, screams echoed loudly and one lady fell to the floor.

"Noooo," she shouted. "Not my Rico! I can't believe he's gone!"

More chaos erupted, especially when one of the family members picked up a chair and threw it. Security was called, and Jacoby and I stepped aside until the chaotic situation

cooled down. He told me he still hadn't heard anything about
Cedric, so I walked to the check-in station to see what I could
find out. The nurse behind the counter looked as if she didn't
want to be bothered.

"I know you're busy," I said, deciding to lie about who I was.
"But my nephew and I have been waiting for quite some time
to see what's going on with my brother, Cedric Thompson.
Can you please check with someone to find out?"

"He arrived about forty-five minutes ago, and if the doctor
hasn't come out to speak to you, I'm sure it will be soon. As
you can see, we've had a lot going on this evening. The night
is still young."

To ask for patience, at this time, wasn't understandable.
Forty-five minutes or ten minutes, somebody could've come
out to say something. For now, our hands were tied so all we
could do was wait.

"I'm real worried about my mother," Jacoby said as I sat next
to him. "I've never seen her like this. The look in her eyes is
cold, and for her to walk out like that was crazy."

"I know, but she's been through a lot these past several
months. Give her time, okay?"

"I will. I know how she's feeling, but I feel so bad for Cedric.
After seeing him like that, I just can't get the thoughts out of
my head. I hope he'll be okay."

"Me too."

Jacoby updated me on what had transpired at Cedric's
house. And after he informed me of Cedric's affair with his
receptionist, I was numb. No wonder Kayla was so bitter. She
definitely had a lot on her plate, and I really wanted to be
there for her. I wasn't sure if she was going to head back to
my apartment, or if she was going back to the house she once
lived in with Cedric. I asked Jacoby to call her, but that was
when my cell phone rang. It was Evelyn. I could barely say
hello before she started yelling into the phone.

"You'd better get some control over your stupid-ass best
friend. Please tell her that if she put her hands on me again,
I'm going to press charges and have her arrested."

I rolled my eyes. Some people loved drama and Evelyn was one of those people. "What are you talking about, Evelyn? When did she put her hands on you?"

"She just came over here, claiming that she wanted to talk about the baby. Since Cedric is dead, I figured she would offer me some kind of money to help me take care of our child. I don't know what I'm going to do now, but whatever I decide, please tell her to stop hating because this baby doesn't have anything to do with it."

I wanted to call Evelyn all kinds of names for being so foolish, but I didn't want to waste my time with her. "Can I make a suggestion to you? Do yourself a favor and go see a shrink. If you thought Kayla had any interest in helping you with that baby, you're crazy as hell. I don't know what you're going to do, but please don't count on any funds from her."

"Yeah, whatever. I figured you would take her side, like you always do. Meanwhile, I'm the one over here suffering."

"Girl, bye. I don't know what you consider suffering, but trust me when I say you don't know the meaning."

"How could you say that? I'm pregnant, and now that Cedric is dead, there is no way for me to take care of this baby all by myself. I don't want to have an abortion, but what else am I supposed to do? Kayla's life isn't the only one affected. Just so you know, so is mine."

Thank God the doctor came out and called for us. Otherwise, I was about to let Evelyn have it.

"I gotta go. I'm at the hospital with Keith and he needs me."

"I see who your priority is, so go do you. Tell Keith I said hello, and if his brother, Bryson, is there, tell him I said hello too."

I lied and said I would then ended the call. Jacoby and I rushed up to the doctor who squeezed his eyes and rubbed them before speaking to us.

"For now, he's in serious condition, but stable. He lost a lot of blood, and all we can do is wait. He's a fighter, so I'm hopeful that he'll make it."

I sighed from relief and so did Jacoby. "Ca . . . can I see my father?" he asked. "Just for a little while. I want to see him. Let him know I'm here."

The doctor opened the door for us to come inside. We followed him to a space that was divided by white curtains. "Five or ten minutes," he said to Jacoby. "We want him to rest. It's the best thing for him right now."

Jacoby nodded. We moved behind the curtain and saw Cedric lying there looking casket ready. Tubes were in his nose and mouth. Dried up blood was on his face and hands. The sheets had a few blood stains too, and even though he wasn't dead, he sure did look it. IVs were in his hands and the beeping sound from his heart monitor sounded off. I felt bad for Jacoby who stood there motionless. Hurt was trapped in his eyes, as well as a little fear.

He reached out to touch Cedric's hand, which looked swollen. "Take care, Dad. Just wanted to let you know that I was here. I'll be back tomorrow. Hopefully, Mom will come with me."

To no surprise, Cedric didn't respond. I reached out to give Jacoby a hug, and after ten more minutes, we left. Adrianne was waiting for him in the waiting area. He said that she would drive him home.

"Be careful," I said to them. "Let me know if you speak to your mother. I'll let you know if she calls me."

With a sad look on his face, Jacoby left. I headed to Keith's room, looking like a bum in a plain gray sweat suit that was kind of dingy. I didn't want him to see me like this, but I had rushed out of the house to see about Kayla. A cap was on my head, covering my short, layered hair that needed perming. The only thing jazzy on me was my gold hoop earrings.

I entered Keith's room and saw him sitting up in bed watching TV. Bryson was there, too. He was talking on his cell phone, but excused himself before leaving the room.

"I thought you were going home," Keith said with his gown hanging off his broad shoulders. His muscles were exposed, and in a hospital bed or not, my man always looked sexy. "And where is the cake you promised me?"

"I haven't had time to cook anything. Needless to say, this day has been a day from hell."

Keith patted the spot next to him. "Come here. Tell me all about it. Based on our conversation from earlier, when you promised to tell Kayla the truth, I take it things turned ugly."

"More than ugly. Almost deadly."

Keith cocked his head back in shock. I sat next to him on the bed and began to tell him about the drama between me and my BFFs.

Chapter 3

Evelyn

A week had passed, and to no surprise, I hadn't heard from Kayla or Trina. I, at least, thought somebody would call to let me know about Cedric's funeral, but I guess they didn't want his baby's mama, me, showing up and causing a scene. I was livid. Called myself telling Kayla what was up with her no-good man and this was the thanks I got. It wasn't my fault that she had married a man like Cedric, and any woman in her right mind would've hopped in the bed with him and taken his money too. I was in need of cash, and since he'd offered to pay my rent, I couldn't turn him down. And even though I had to give a little something in return, sex wasn't necessarily a bad thing. Not with a man like Cedric anyway, because sex with him was always finger-licking good. That's what I was going to miss, and there was a tiny part of me that missed him already. I wondered who had shot him. Obviously, not Kayla since she was probably too busy running around, looking for sympathy. Trina would surely give it to her. The next time I saw either of them, I was going to let them have it.

For now, I had to make it to my appointment at the abortion clinic. I thought long and hard about this. It was in my best interest to terminate the pregnancy. I could barely take care of myself. Bringing a child into my unstable situation wasn't a good thing. I figured I would have to seek other alternatives regarding my financial situation. Now that Cedric was gone, my well had definitely run dry.

At first, I wasn't nervous about aborting the baby. But, the moment I walked into the waiting area and saw many others, my nerves started to rattle. I wasn't sure why they were there to see the doctor, and I hoped like hell that nobody knew what

I was about to do. I wrote my name on a clipboard and then took a seat. Seemed like everybody's eyes, including mine, roamed around the room. There were fake smiles on display, but I gave no expression in return. All I wanted to do was get this over with, but for the next couple of hours, all I did was sit, think, and wait.

Being there made me think about my parents, particularly my mother. She was so excited about sharing her second pregnancy with my dad, but he wasn't trying to hear it. The moment she showed him the pregnancy test that displayed a positive sign, he washed the smile right off her face. I remember sitting there, watching his fist pound straight into her stomach. She doubled over and fell to the floor. He began kicking her like he was punting a football in the NFL. Told her that she needed to get an abortion, or else he would beat the baby out of her. I wasn't sure what my mother decided to do, but whatever it was, there was no baby.

Dad got what he wanted and his abuse continued. My mother and I, both, caught hell. I despised her for allowing him to get away with so much, and I promised myself that I would never be like her. She lived broke and died broke. Her entire life revolved around my father, and neither one of them gave two cents about me.

The bubbly nurse interrupted my thoughts when she called my name. I followed her to a room where I went through a short counseling session and then I had an ultrasound. An hour later, I was being comforted by a doctor who handled my procedure then wished me well. I was asked to chill in a waiting area for at least an hour, but when no one was paying attention, I slipped out the door and left.

I had never experienced anything so gut wrenching. What I had done to my baby weighed heavily on my mind, but it was my choice—a choice that I had a feeling I would one day regret. I knew I would, especially since I had always wanted a child. Not now, though; when things were in order, when I was married to the man of my dreams, or when I knew that my child's father was capable of being there and providing for our child in a major way. Regardless, I figured that Cedric wouldn't turn his back on me or our baby. He wasn't that kind of man, but a dead man he was.

I was starting to feel depressed so I needed someone to talk to. I couldn't stop crying, and as I looked in the mirror at my puffy, red eyes, I felt shameful. I moved my long hair away from my face and tucked part of it behind my ears. I pictured my beautiful baby who probably would've looked just like me. No question, Cedric was a handsome man too, but my family had strong genes. I rolled my eyes at myself then flushed the toilet and washed my hands. My cell phone was on the counter, so I picked it up to call Trina.

"Hello," she said then laughed. It was a good thing to know that one of us was having fun.

"What's so funny?" I asked.

"Nothing. I was just laughing at something Keith said."

"Oh, I see. So, I guess you're with Keith. Is he out of the hospital or are you at his place?"

"Yes, he's out of the hospital, and I am at his place. Why are you asking?"

"Because I want to see you, spend some time with you. I haven't heard from you, and I'm a little disappointed that you kicked me to the curb because of Kayla."

"I haven't kicked you to the curb. And as a matter of fact, I haven't heard from Kayla. I'm giving the two of you time to chill out and get y'all selves together."

"I can't believe that you haven't spoken to her. I'm sure you went to Cedric's funeral, and I know you spoke to her then."

Trina paused for a while, and then she changed the subject. "What do you want to do? Meet me somewhere for drinks or have dinner tomorrow?"

"I'd rather not go out. Can you come over here today?"

"Not right now I can't. I'm getting ready to start cooking dinner for Keith. We have plans this evening."

"Well, put your sexual plans on hold. I'm coming over there, if that's okay. I promise not to stay long, but I really need for you to lend me your ear. I'm going through something right now, and I'm not sure about what direction I should go. So needless to say, bestie, I need your advice."

"Since when? I doubt that you will listen to any advice that I offer. Besides, Keith has only been home for a few days. We need some time alone."

I winced and rolled my eyes. "This is a life-or-death situation. I'll be there within the hour. Save some dinner for me, and if you're cooking chicken, like you always do, make mine extra crispy. I'm on my way."

I ended the call, and when Trina called back, I didn't bother to answer. Instead, I brushed my hair into a sleek, bouncing ponytail that showed my round face. I put on some ice-blue eye shadow and thickened my lashes with mascara. I added shine to my lips with a clear gloss and sprayed a few dashes of perfume over my clothes. The simple jeans and T-shirt that I previously had on wasn't suitable enough, so I changed into a gray stretch dress that hugged my curves. It was strapless and showed a healthy portion of my cleavage. I accessorized the dress with silver hoop earrings, and the five-inch heels I wore gave me much height. I was sure Trina wouldn't want her best friend looking like a bum around her man, but then again, he was probably used to her sporting sweat suits, jogging pants, and plain ol' T-shirts and jeans all the time. Now that she wasn't claiming her dyke status anymore, I hoped she jazzed herself up and tried to dress better.

I tucked my clutch purse underneath my arm and put on my game face, pretending as if today had never happened. I was so good at hiding my pain, and had learned to do so when my father chastised me about being such a wimp and a crybaby. *Nobody cares about crybabies, and most men won't give a damn about your tears,* he'd say. *Keep it moving and never let anyone see how hurt you really are.* That was what I did when he beat me and had sex with me, too. Pretended as if I wasn't hurt, when deep down I was.

I washed away my thoughts and headed to my car. It was a little chilly outside, but I didn't want to cover up and hide my sexiness. Maybe I'd go somewhere for a drink tonight and find me another rich man who could assist me in my time of need. That was definitely an option, because I was so sure that I didn't want to stay cooped up with Trina's boring self all night.

I stopped at the grocery store, and then arrived at Keith's house almost an hour later. I had never been there before, but awhile back Trina told me where he lived. I was impressed by the humongous, historic house that looked fit for a king.

Trina said Keith was just an artist, but I didn't know that artists were doing it like this. I rang the doorbell and could see Trina making her way to the door, through beveled, thick glass. As expected, she had on a pair of navy jogging pants and a half shirt that showed her midriff and tattoo that was drawn near her side. While she was definitely a shapely woman, her muscles always irritated me. I didn't think a woman should look so toned, but that was her preference, not mine. She opened the door, and the first thing she did was look at the card, balloon, and bottle of wine in my hand.

"Really?" she said. "Are you serious?"

"About what?"

"What's with the card, balloon, and wine, Evelyn?"

"The card and balloon is for Keith, and the wine is for dinner. What is wrong with me trying to do something nice?"

Trina removed the card from my hand, but she popped the balloon and left it on the porch.

"That doesn't need to come in here."

I was a little pissed, but I didn't want to argue with her about her jealous ways. She opened the door wider for me to come inside. I looked up at the high, cathedral ceiling and at the wooden staircase that traveled several floors up.

"Wow," I said with wide eyes. "This is nice. No wonder you're over here all the time. It sure as heck is a major step up from your tiny, junky apartment."

"Maybe so, but my apartment is much bigger, better, and cleaner than your loft is. It doesn't surprise me that you're impressed by Keith's house, especially coming from where you just came from."

I threw my hand back, ignoring Trina's comment. Besides, by the way she looked me over, I could tell her attitude was because she was jealous. I watched as she opened the envelope and pulled out the card. I tried to snatch it, but she pulled it away and started to read it.

"'Hope you're feeling better and welcome home. Trina will definitely take good care of you, but if she doesn't, be sure to let me know so I can hurt her.'" Trina pursed her lips and ripped the card in two. "You can be sure that I will take good care of him. This is going overboard, don't you think?"

"No, I don't, but I understand how insecure some women can be at times. It was simply a nice gesture. Nothing more, nothing less."

"I'm sure you said the same thing to Kayla about Cedric. But on another note, thanks for the wine. Dinner is almost done. I hope you can't stay long, and before we go to the kitchen, would you mind telling me why you're here again?"

I released a deep sigh and folded my arms. "Stop being so bitter and just enjoy my company. There was a time when we used to have so much fun. I would certainly like for our friendship to get back to what it used to be, but that's up to you. In addition to that, I had an abortion today. I've been feeling kind of bad and lonely. Wanted to spend some time with my best friend. Is there any harm in that?"

Trina hesitated before saying anything. I could tell that she wanted to reach out to me, but she held back. "I'm sorry to hear about the abortion. Even though I wish you wouldn't have gone there, I respect your decision. Now, do me a favor. Let's not talk about your situation with Kayla and Cedric tonight. I'm so done with that. Have a piece of chicken, drink a little wine, and then get your tail out of here so I can make love to my man. It's been awhile, so you can understand how hungry I am."

Trina laughed and so did I. "Then get your horny self in the kitchen and finish up. And where's Keith? I must tell him how much trouble you really are. Obviously, he doesn't know better yet."

I followed Trina, and when I made it to the kitchen, I damn near stumbled in the doorway. Keith sat at the table with his shirt off and many colorful tattoos were on display. His skin was a dark, luscious chocolate and was shiny and smooth. There was a small bandage at his midsection; I assumed that was where he had been stabbed. His fade was lined to perfection, and the second his eyes locked on me, I felt a trickle in my panties. I wasn't sure if it was blood from the abortion or a gathering buildup from me feeling excited. Keith was almost identical to his brother, Bryson. It was a tossup on who actually looked the best. I mean, I loved the look of Keith's numerous tattoos, but if Bryson didn't have as many, he would be voted the best looking in my book. Maybe one day I'd get a chance to see them both naked. Then I'd be able to confirm either way.

"Evelyn brought us some wine," Trina said, showing the bottle to Keith. He stood and a warming smile washed across his face. His teeth were straight, white, and perfect. I was a little jealous that my best friend had a man like this in her possession.

Keith thanked me for the wine. He moved at a slow place toward me, and then reached out to give me a hug. I purposely pressed my breasts against his muscular chest and held on to the embrace for as long as Trina would allow it. I could see her eyeing me from the corner of her eye.

"You're so welcome," I said. "I also brought you a ca—"

Trina cleared her throat. "Go ahead and have a seat. And I told you I didn't need a *can* of veggies, because I like mine fresh. Keith and I go to the Soulard Market every weekend to get fresh vegetables, don't we, baby?"

"Yeah, we do," he said.

He walked back over to the chair and stretched before sitting down. I couldn't help but to notice his sexiness in the black jogging pants he wore that tied at his perfect waistline. There was also a bulge in his pants. I wondered if his goodness was on the rise, due to our close embrace.

After Keith sat, so did I. Trina stood close by the stove. She was mashing some potatoes while frying chicken at the same time.

"This is almost done," she said. "Evelyn, if you would like to make a quick salad, I'd appreciate it. The lettuce, tomatoes, ham, and eggs are in the fridge. I boiled the eggs earlier. All you have to do is chop them."

"I didn't come over here to cook or prepare anything, but since I'm sure Keith is hungry, and so am I, then I'm going to put the salad together without complaining."

"Well, thank you," Trina said with sarcasm. "Besides, I want to keep you busy while you're here, just so you don't find yourself in that trouble you mentioned earlier."

I laughed and ignored Trina's remark. Truthfully, I could've found myself in trouble. Then again, so could Keith. He kept looking at me, and when I flaunted myself to the refrigerator to get the items for the salad, his eyes were all over me. I purposely dropped a tomato, just so I could bend over. I wanted him to get a clear view of what I looked like in that position.

"I'll be right back," Keith said. "I need to go make a phone call."

"Okay," Trina said. "Take your time. By the time you get finished, dinner should be good and ready."

Trina didn't lie. Within fifteen minutes, Keith returned to the kitchen. The table was set for three, and I took the honor of pouring the wine.

"Half glass or full?" I said while standing in front of Keith with a flute glass in my hand.

"Full," he said. "All the way to the rim."

"All you have to do is ask."

I filled his glass then sat it on the table in front of him. I figured Trina would only want her glass filled halfway, so I poured the wine and placed the glass in front of her. Before pouring my glass, I sat at the table and crossed my legs. I lifted my glass and toasted to good friends.

"May we all stay this close for many years to come."

Trina displayed a fake smile and Keith nodded. Minutes later, we tore into the food and kicked up a conversation that went on for quite some time. Trina directed more of her conversation to Keith, and truthfully, so did I. We talked about his career, his family . . . more so about his brother. Keith definitely had my attention when we discussed Bryson, so I elaborated more.

"Where did you say he worked?" I asked.

"I didn't, but he's a construction manager. The last two projects he worked on were the Stan Musial Bridge and Ball Park Village."

"I bet that was interesting. I have yet to drive across that bridge, but I have been to Ball Park Village. It's nice. Is he married? I saw him at the hospital when you were there, but I didn't get a chance to introduce myself."

Trina and Keith spoke at the same time: "Yes/no, he is/isn't married."

I laughed when Keith looked at Trina who insisted that Bryson was married.

"I'm sure Keith knows if his brother is married or not," I said to Trina.

She gave him an evil gaze, but smiled to play it off. "You're right," she said. "He's not married, but he's engaged, isn't he?"

Keith shrugged. "If you want to call it that, yes, he's been engaged for almost four years. I'm not quite sure if he's found exactly who or what he's looking for yet."

"I know," I said then took a bite of the chicken. "Many of us are still looking for the right one. It's hard to know exactly what you want, and we fool ourselves so many times, thinking and believing that we've found our soul mates."

"I truly believe that I have," Keith said, looking at Trina. "Make no mistake about it, I'm not confused in any way."

Trina smiled then leaned over to give Keith a kiss. I wanted to puke. He only said that because he knew she was pissed about something. Probably about how much he kept staring at me. To me, his eyes said it all. If I wanted him, I could have him. But for now, he had to say kind words to warm her little heart. Too bad he may soon break it.

"Awww," I said with a fake smile. "Isn't that so sweet? I'm glad you're not confused, because Trina was confused for a real long time. When she told me that she was down with women, instead of men, I was like, girl, please. Don't even come to me with that mess. I didn't believe she was trying to go there, but I guess she had an urge. I was totally shocked about the Lexi thing, and I'm sorry you got caught in the middle. I told Trina to always be honest about her feelings. If not, somebody was liable to get hurt."

Trina's face fell flat. I guess my little comment caught her off guard. She lowered her fork to the plate and killed me a thousand and one times with the look in her eyes.

"Just so you know, Keith knows that I used to date women. He knows all about my past relationship with Lexi, may she rest in peace. I don't recall you ever telling me to be honest about my feelings for anyone, especially since honesty isn't exactly your specialty."

I dabbed my lips with a napkin and remained calm as ever. Besides, I was sure Keith didn't want a loudmouth ghetto girl, and Trina was definitely representing.

"I don't know why you're raising your voice. All I did was express to Keith how confused you were about relationships. I've been confused before too, so it's really no big deal. I applaud him, especially if he knows what he wants. Most men don't, but I appreciate those who do."

Keith spoke up before Trina did. "I get what you're saying, and after our little incident, we have agreed to always be open and honest with each other. I doubt that Trina is confused by who she wants, and there was a legitimate reason why she felt a need to pursue relationships with women, rather than men."

"Well, she never shared that tad bit of information with me. And as long as the two of you are happy, that's all that matters. I'm good, but I could be so much better if you'd do me a favor and introduce me to your brother. If he's still confused, maybe I can help him settle his needs and desires, once and for all."

Keith looked at his watch. "Funny you should ask. I told him to drop by after work. He should be here shortly, and you two can have another opportunity to meet then."

"No," Trina said. "I mean, it's not right to introduce him to someone when he's already engaged to someone else. In addition to that, Evelyn is getting ready to go. I'm sure she didn't intend to stay this long."

Trina shot me a dirty gaze and tried to cover it up with a smile. I smiled back, but made it clear that I had nothing else to do.

"I didn't intend to stay this long, but what the hell? And as for Bryson being engaged, allow him to tell me his relationship status. Then we'll decide where to go from there. Who knows? He may not even like me. I might not be his type, so just relax."

"Oh, you're definitely his type," Keith quickly said. "No question about that."

"What is that supposed to mean?" Trina hissed. "Why would Evelyn be his type?"

Keith had put his foot in his mouth without even knowing it. Trina stared at him, awaiting an answer. So did I.

"What I mean is she seems nice. He appreciates nice women with pretty smiles."

His punk ass just lost a few points with me. If anything, he should've been honest and told Trina exactly why he thought Bryson would be interested. It was because I was sexy as hell, way more beautiful than Trina could ever be, and my personality was off the chain. I couldn't even count how many times I'd made Keith smile and laugh tonight. He knew that I was capable of bringing more excitement to his brother's life. Maybe to his too.

"Nice, huh," Trina said then turned to look at me. "Well, I hope your pretty smile gets you exactly what you want."

I displayed that smile she was referring to. "It always does."

Keith sensed an argument brewing so he quickly intervened. "Ladies, I didn't mean any harm. I meant nothing by stressing my brother's taste in women. Ultimately, he'll decide what to do with Evelyn, not me."

Trina didn't appreciate his words. She got up from the table with an attitude. "I'm going to do the dishes. After I'm done, I'm going to bed."

Keith got up and wrapped his arms around Trina as she faced the sink. "You want me to help? How about you wash and I dry?"

"No, I don't want you on your feet for that long. If Bryson is going to be here soon, why don't you go chill in the living room? Turn the TV on, and I'll bring in some more wine before going to bed."

"Are you sure?" Keith said. "I don't mind helping you clean up. I'm not that tired."

"I'm sure. If anything, Evelyn can help me then she can leave. Like I said, I'm a little tired and the bed is calling me."

I guess that was a hint, but whatever. Keith kissed her cheek, and when the doorbell rang, he gave her a light pat on the ass and walked away. She smiled, but I caught her rolling her eyes at me again.

Since I had just gotten my nails done, I wasn't about to help her with the dishes. I stood next to her with my arms folded. "You know, I really don't get why you're being so mean to me. One minute we're cool, and the next minute you're treating me like you don't want to be bothered."

"That's because I don't want to be bothered, Evelyn. You tend to say the wrong things sometimes, and the last thing I needed was for you to remind Keith about why he was stabbed. I already feel bad about the shit. I don't need you up in here talking about how confused I was."

"You act as if being confused is such a bad thing. I meant no harm by my comment, and excuse me if I rubbed you the wrong way."

"Well, you did. Now on another note, you need to forget about pursuing Bryson. From what Keith told me, he has enough drama with his girlfriend. I don't want you to involve yourself in anymore mess, so that's why I spoke up about it."

"Thanks for the warning, but I think I can handle Bryson."

"Just like you handled Cedric, right?"

"I didn't handle Cedric. Obviously, someone else did and good for her. He deserved whatever he got. Remind me to go put some flowers on his gravesite, whenever it dries. I'd hate to get mud on my shoes."

"Well, breaking news. You may want to sit down before I say this to you, but don't go buying flowers just yet. The woman you're speaking about didn't do a good job. Cedric is alive and well. Jacoby told me that he got out of the hospital yesterday and he's at home with his family."

I wanted to punch Trina in her face for lying to me. All she was doing was trying to upset me, because she was mad about the attention Keith had shown me tonight.

"Stop your lies, Trina. Kayla already told me he was dead and so did you. Did he come back from the grave?"

"We both were sadly mistaken. He's alive. Maybe not as alive and well as he could be, but I assure you that Cedric Thompson is alive. I don't mean any harm by saying this, but you should have waited before having that abortion."

The wicked smile on Trina's face cut me like a knife. I felt a hard jab in my stomach that was tied in a knot.

"Don't lie to me, Trina. This is nothing to play with. Is he really alive or is he dead?"

"Why don't you call his cell phone and see? Maybe he'll answer, maybe he won't. If he does, tell him I said I hope he feels better. I'm sure you'll stop by with some wine, a balloon, and a card. If you're planning on giving him a card, make sure you let me sign it."

I wasn't sure if Trina was messing with me. But just to be sure, I rushed to my purse to retrieve my cell phone. I dialed Cedric's cell phone number, and after three rings, a woman answered. I didn't recognize her voice, but I was sure that it wasn't Kayla's.

"May I speak to Cedric Thompson?" I said.

"Mr. Thompson is not accepting phone calls at this time. Would you like to leave a message for him?"

"You said that he's not accepting phone calls at this time. When will he be able to accept them?"

"As soon as he's better, ma'am. I can give him your message, and I'm sure he'll return it as soon as he's able to."

It still wasn't clear to me that Cedric was alive. "What I'm asking is, if I leave him a message, will he be able to get it? I thought Mr. Thompson was deceased."

"No, ma'am. He's alive. You can leave a message—"

I pushed the end button and stood with a stoned face. I could hear Trina whistling in the background. She had the audacity to giggle.

"Told you so," she teased. "Now, getting back to that card. Are you going to go purchase it, or shall I?"

I swallowed the oversized lump in my throat and tucked my purse underneath my arm. I was in no mood to entertain Bryson now, but the second I entered the living room, there was hope. Needless to say, Bryson was one fine motherfucker. I felt another trickle, especially when he stood and extended his hand to me.

"I'm Bryson, Keith's brother. I believe we met before, at the hospital. I can never forget a face as pretty as that one."

I was deeply hurt inside about Cedric being alive, but I couldn't help but smile at Bryson's kind words, as he towered over my short frame.

"Yes, I remember seeing you at the hospital. It is such a pleasure to see you again."

"Why don't you have a seat and join us for some drinks? I haven't had dinner yet, so maybe Trina can whip me up a plate and bring it to me."

Bryson looked over my shoulder at Trina. She winked at him and promised to bring his plate in a minute. Meanwhile, she stepped up to me and whispered in my ear.

"Whatever you do, don't turn around. Take what's in my hand, go to the bathroom, say good-bye, and then leave."

I wasn't sure what the hell Trina was up to. Whatever it was, I backed out of the living room and removed what was in her hand. When I looked at it, it was a maxi pad.

"You're bleeding," she said. "See, if I was a dirty friend, I would have let you flaunt yourself around, like you've been doing all night, and embarrass yourself. The least you can do is thank me. Your abrupt departure will let Bryson know you're not interested, unless you want to go back in there with that stain on the back of your dress."

I was floored. Without saying another word, I rushed to the bathroom to check my blood flow. Trina was right. I would've embarrassed myself big time. I was seconds away from turning around so Bryson could get a glimpse at my shapely behind. I hurried to clean up, and before I made a swift exit, I poked my head through the living room's wide doorway.

"Fellas, I'm sorry. I have an emergency, so I have to leave. Bryson, I hope to see you soon, and Keith thanks for letting me stay for dinner. Take care, okay?"

They looked confused. Bryson stood and offered to walk me to my car.

"No, please, I'm good," I said. "Stay. I promise you that we'll speak soon."

Trina rushed me to the door and I didn't say another word to the men. While on the porch, I whispered for her not to tell Keith about my little incident.

"Good-bye, Evelyn. Go home and see about yourself. And leave Cedric alone. Let that man rest and wash your hands to that situation."

I didn't reply. Trina knew I wasn't about to make that kind of promise.

Chapter 4

Kayla

The good thing was that Paula Daniels was behind bars. She confessed to trying to murder Cedric, and the focus had been taken off of me. Jacoby was delighted that Cedric was recovering well, but the unfortunate thing was that I wasn't.

I wanted to forgive Cedric for all that he'd done, but I couldn't. I couldn't find the right time to speak to him about his affair with Evelyn, and now that he was home, I didn't want to be in his presence. So instead of staying in the house, I moved my things out of Trina's apartment and went back to a hotel room. This time, I had money in my pocket, and I withdrew a substantial amount of money from Cedric's bank account; money that could assist me, until I decided what to ultimately do. The divorce papers that he'd sent to me, right before he was shot, awaited my signature. I wasn't sure if I would sign them, but for now, the papers sat on the table in the hotel room, along with several checks that I'd written to take care of his bills, along with mine. With Cedric unable to handle things, I took the initiative to make sure everything was taken care of. He was very organized, and as I searched his office, I found a list of his monthly expenses that needed to be taken care of. I also found a list of the numerous payments he transferred to Evelyn's account, and additional payments he sent to other women's accounts as well. I didn't know who any of the women were and some of the deposits into their accounts could have been work related.

The house that his receptionist lived in had Cedric's name on it. After he kicked her out, he'd planned on renting the place. At $5,000 a month, it was obvious that she hadn't been living in a shack. Evelyn was the one who had gotten duped. Her loft was nice, but in no way could it have been like the house Paula had lived in. Speaking of being duped, that applied to me too. There were hotel receipts from when Cedric was out of town. He paid for dinners, plays, cars, and then some. He damn sure wasn't cheap when it came to giving money to his mistresses, but they all were required to put up with his mess. What I discovered was there were plenty of women who seemed willing and able: willing to hurt me and destroy our family, like Cedric was.

Since Jacoby decided to stay at the house with Cedric, I felt a little better. I didn't want Cedric being alone, so what I did was hire a maid/nurse's aid, Cynthia, who was capable of taking care of him. Ever since he'd been home, I stopped by to check on him. Some days he didn't know I was there, other days he would see me but wouldn't say much. According to Jacoby, he said he and Cedric were starting to talk more. He said they had a few positive conversations, and Jacoby had asked me when I was coming back home. At this time, I wasn't sure.

I entered Cedric's house through the front door. Jacoby was sitting on the couch in the great room, watching TV with Adrianne. They both smiled when they saw me.

"Hey, Mama," Jacoby said, standing up.

So did Adrianne. She reached out to give me a hug. "Hello, Mrs. Thompson. How are you?"

"I'm doing okay. What are you all watching on TV?"

"ESPN," she said then playfully rolled her eyes. "We're going to the movies in a little bit. Would you like to go with us?"

"No, not today. Maybe some other time, but thanks for asking."

Cynthia came into the room to join us. She wiped her hand on an apron and nudged her head toward the kitchen. "May I speak to you for a minute, Kayla?" she said.

"Sure." I followed her into the kitchen, where she was preparing a meal. Whatever she had in the oven smelled delicious. I could tell it was something sweet. I'd definitely try whatever it was, especially since I'd lost so much weight in the past few months. My curves were starting to disappear and this was the smallest I'd been since college.

Much shorter than I was and a bit on the chubby side, Cynthia stood in front of me. She gave me a piece of paper and showed me Cedric's phone. "This woman called four times for Cedric. She didn't want to leave a message, but she sent a text telling him to call her, once he was better. I just thought you may want to know this. Also, another woman left a message for him. It was very sexual, and I assume she doesn't know what happened."

I took the phone, and sure enough, one of the numbers belonged to Evelyn. I guess she must have figured out that Cedric wasn't really dead. I thanked Cynthia for the information.

"No problem. Mr. Thompson has been asleep for most of the day, but the last time I checked on him, he was up watching television. I think he's starting to feel better, because I heard him laugh when speaking to Jacoby. You have a very loving son, but sometimes he walks around here in a daze. I ask if he's okay, and he says that he's fine. I think this whole thing with his dad is kind of troubling him. But it's good that he's been here for his dad. They seem to like each other's company, and all in all, you do have a good son. Your husband, however, is a little demanding. But that's okay. I know how to deal with him, and when I offer him my fist, he laughs."

"Thank you for the information, Cynthia. I think Jacoby will be fine, and he is a good kid. I wouldn't have him any other way. As for my husband, good luck with him. That's why I'm paying you extra, because I know he's a force to be reckoned with."

We laughed and Cynthia agreed.

"Now, what's for dinner?" I asked. "If you made some more of that delicious lasagna you made the other day, I'm staying."

She lifted her finger and switched it from side to side. "Listen, girlfriend, I may be an Italian woman, but I also like to experiment with soul food. I'm cooking a delicious pot roast, mac and cheese, candied yams, and greens. My cherry cobbler is in the oven, and I can't wait for you to taste that."

"I think you may have to leave the soul food to me, but we'll see. Let me go talk to Cedric. The conversation that I have with him will determine if I'll stay."

I walked past the great room where Adrianne and Jacoby seemed to be enjoying each other's company. As I slowly made my way up the stairs, I stopped to take a deep breath. I wasn't prepared to look face to face with Cedric since he'd been shot and today was no different. But after I paused, I continued up the stairs and into the bedroom. I was pleased to see him lying on his side, sound asleep. The TV was on, and I turned to see who the person was on TV yelling. It was a commentator on ESPN, talking about sports. I couldn't believe that his foolishness had caught my attention. So much so that when Cedric called my name, I barely heard him.

"Kayla," he called again. I turned and saw him adjusting himself to sit up in bed. "Do you mind helping me with a few of these pillows? Bring me some of those pillows at the bottom of the bed so I can prop myself up."

Just because I didn't want to come off as bitter, I did what he'd asked. I fluffed the pillows and placed them behind him. He appeared comfortable and smiled. "Thank you. And if you would please get me a glass of water, I would appreciate it. I think Cynthia has an ice bucket over there. My glass is right here on the nightstand."

I didn't budge. I folded my arms and stared at him. "I don't mean to be rude, but let me say this to you. I am not starring in a role for *Diary of a Mad Black Woman,* so, therefore, you won't find me around here washing your tail, cooking and cleaning, feeding you or massaging your back for you. It pains me to fluff your pillows and get you a glass of water, simply because I don't appreciate all that you've done to me. I don't have to recall everything you did, but just so you know, the baby is a hard pill for me to swallow, Cedric. So was the affair with your receptionist, and let's not talk about all of the others. I'm here to make sure you're being taken care of by Cynthia. Also to see about my son, and to make sure the bills don't get behind. If there is anything pertaining to the bills that you would like for me to take care of, please let me know."

Cedric let out a dry cough and then he wiped his mouth. He reached for his glass on the nightstand and reached out to hand it to me. "My mouth is dry. There is ice in the ice bucket and water in the bathroom. Would you please take care of that for me?"

I stood my ground. "No. I will let Cynthia know what you need, and since you're paying her well, I'm sure she will abide. Now, if there is nothing else pertaining to your finances, I'm going to go."

Cedric didn't say anything else, so I moved toward the door. When he called out my name, I halted my steps.

"There is one thing," he said then lightly chuckled. "No, two. Be sure to put aside some money to buy my baby some Pampers when he or she arrives, and buy yourself a wig, too. Your short haircut looks as bad as that attitude you got, and don't come here again until you figure out how to sympathize with me regarding this situation. Yes, I created a mess, but don't you stand there being all innocent and shit, like you're so gotdamn perfect."

This bastard had my blood boiling. Yet again, I was the one to blame for his fuckups. I wasn't sure when he was going to fess up and take responsibility for what he'd done. I already admitted to how hurtful my lies about Arnez being Jacoby's father may have been, but I wasn't going to take the blame for anything else. I marched over to the bed and poked at his wounded chest. He squeezed his eyes, revealing that he was in a little pain.

"Buy your own baby Pampers, and you can keep on paying for all of those hoochies' pussies too. I have lost all respect for you, Cedric. A huge part of me wish . . . I wish you would've died!" I choked back my tears, realizing how difficult it was for me to say that to him.

He appeared stunned too, and this time around, his voice softened. "Don't worry about my finances. All I want you to do is sign those divorce papers and free yourself. After you do that, I assure you that you'll feel a whole lot better. Now leave so I can get some rest. I've had enough arguments with you. Quite frankly, they're not worth my time."

I took a hard swallow and tried to gather myself to say something else to him that would hurt. Instead, I stormed toward the door and slammed it behind me. When I reached the bottom stair, I looked into the great room at Jacoby and Adrianne.

"Tell Cynthia I'm not staying for dinner. I hope the two of you have a great time at the movies. When you get home tonight, Jacoby, please call me."

"Will do, Mama. Holla tonight."

I left, feeling on edge. Every time Cedric brought up those damn divorce papers, it upset me. Every time I saw him, I wanted to scream at the top of my lungs and punch him a thousand and one times. But the truth was, for me to allow him to upset me like this, it proved that I still loved him. There was something inside of me that didn't want to let him go. I didn't want any of those other women to have him either, and I hated myself for still having feelings for him—no, for loving him. The hold he'd had on me needed a retirement date. I needed to retire him, but unfortunately, I didn't know how long his hold would last.

I was so wound up that, almost an hour later, I found myself following Evelyn as she made her way to the grocery store. She parked and hopped out of her car as if the paparazzi were waiting to snap a picture of her. She removed her shades and tossed her long hair from side to side. She was so busy trying to make sure everyone noticed her that she didn't even see me coming up from behind her. I tapped her shoulder. She swung around and frowned at my presence. Catching her off guard, again, I slapped the mess out of her.

"I'm not going to keep having these conversations with you," I said, pointing my finger near her face. "Stop calling my husband and leave us the hell alone."

I walked off, but this time, Evelyn came after me. I'd known her for many years, so I already knew that she didn't know how to fight. She was too worried about not looking cute, but that was the least of my worries.

"Your ass is going to jail," she shouted then slapped her hand against my back. "You're not going to keep slapping me and getting away with it!"

I turned around and grabbed her neck. I squeezed it as hard as I could, causing her to weaken and almost melt close to the ground. She squeezed her eyes and scratched at my hands so I would loosen my grip. I did and that was when she grabbed her own neck and rubbed it. She was doubled over, trying her best to catch her breath.

"I swear." She kept choking. "Yo . . . you are so in trouble. I am pressing charges today!"

"Do what you wish. Besides, I have money for a lawyer; how about you? Probably not, and trust me when I say it will be your word against mine. But if you want to resolve this little matter, and stop having these abrupt conversations, then leave me and my family the hell alone. The choice is yours."

People going into the grocery store had stopped to look. But no one was about to interfere when it came to two black women going at it. I saw one lady reach for her cell phone, so I pushed Evelyn one last time. She stumbled, but managed to stay on her feet. I walked to my car and listened to her numerous threats. All they did, for the time being, was make me laugh. I felt as if I'd gotten some kind of satisfaction.

Chapter 5

Trina

Maybe it was just me blowing things out of proportion, but Keith had me a little hot the other night when Evelyn stopped by. All of a sudden he seemed to perk up, and every time she got up from the table, I saw him gaze at her ass. I saw his eyes drop to her cleavage, and his comment about Bryson's taste in women rubbed me the wrong way. And then to imply that Bryson would be interested because of her smile, that was an insult to my intelligence. Really? That's the real reason I was mad, in addition to Evelyn's snide remarks.

Then again, like I'd said, maybe I was tripping. Evelyn was a nice-looking woman. What man wouldn't give her a double look? There was a time when I had her on my to-do list too, so I guess I could give Keith a pass. That night, however, I didn't give him a pass. I went to bed, while he and Bryson stayed up playing cards. They invited two more of their friends over, and by the time they all left, it was almost four in the morning. Keith came to bed that night, drunk and looking for some action. I was in no mood, and as horny as I was, I had to diss him for giving Evelyn too much attention.

I had been spending so much time at Keith's house that my poor little apartment was being neglected. Kayla had removed the majority of her things, and it had been a few weeks since I'd last heard from her. I wondered how she was, especially since Evelyn had called to tell me about another incident between them at the grocery store. I told Evelyn that I didn't want anything to do with what was going on between her and Kayla. I also reminded her that calling Cedric wasn't the brightest thing to do. She accused me of making her reach out to him, but it was the only way she would believe that he was alive. I figured she regretted the abortion, even though she hadn't yet admitted it.

For the next few hours, I stayed home and cleaned up. My apartment was a mess. Kayla didn't help me clean up while she was living here, and it was apparent that she was used to a maid cleaning up the big house she lived in with Cedric. I mopped the floors, washed the dishes, and took out the trash. I also cleaned the bathrooms, but as soon as I plopped down on the couch to rest, Keith called.

"Are you coming back over tonight?" he asked.

"Not tonight. I've been cleaning up all day, and I'm kind of tired. I'll stop by tomorrow. I'm going to the grocery store first, so let me know if you need for me to pick up anything for you."

His masculine, sexy voice transmitted through the phone and right into my ear. "All I want is my woman and some juicy oranges. A loaf of raisin bread would be good, too, but nothing would satisfy me more than being with my lady right now."

I took that as a hint that Keith didn't want to be alone tonight. He definitely knew how to put a smile on my face. He also knew how to get me to change my mind.

"How badly do you want to see your woman? She's tired, lazy, and a little groggy. She may not be good company tonight, but after she gets her beauty rest, she will feel so much better."

"Truthfully, I love her even more when she's tired, lazy, and a little groggy. Can't be up all the time, and trust me when I say I can handle it. Besides, the last time I checked, she rests pretty well when she's with me. Right in my arms and sleeping like a newborn baby."

I couldn't deny that. So instead of staying home, I told Keith that I would stop by the grocery store then come to his house.

Within the hour, I was at his place. Two bags of groceries were in my hand, and I unlocked the door with the key he'd given me. The downstairs lighting was dim, but when I looked up the staircase, I saw a light on in his bedroom. I could also see a sliver of light coming from the kitchen, so I made my way to it to put up the few groceries I'd had. As soon as I reached the kitchen's doorway, Keith startled me and crept up from behind. He slipped his arm around my waist and unhooked the button on my jeans. A burning candle was on the kitchen table, along with two plates topped with Chinese food that smelled pretty darn good.

"Since our dinner was ruined the other night, I thought I'd make it up to you. But first, you got to do a little making up yourself, if you know what I mean."

I dropped the bags on the floor and stood as Keith unbuttoned my jeans and pulled them down to my ankles. As I stepped out of them, he lifted my tank shirt over my head, and in one snap, he unhooked my bra. I stood in my yellow lace panties and could feel his naked body pressing against mine. When I tried to turn around and face him, he wouldn't let me.

"I need to work it out from back here, first. Then we'll seek another position."

While still in the doorway, Keith remained behind me. He massaged my tiny breasts together and placed a trail of delicate kisses along the side of my neck. My head was tilted and eyes were closed. I felt so lucky to be with him, and shame on me for acting so foolish the other night.

"Mmmm," Keith moaned while playfully biting my neck. "You smell like Pine-Sol."

I opened my eyes and couldn't help but to laugh. "I told you I'd been cleaning up. You wouldn't let me do anything else, but rush over here to see you."

"That's because I had something to give you. And as soon as you remove those panties, I'ma show you exactly what it is. I'm also going to be generous and let you feel it."

I lifted my arms and placed my hands on the back of Keith's head to rub it. "I like it so much better when you remove my panties. For some reason, when you do, my pussy tends to perform better."

Keith massaged my tight abs, twirled his finger around in my belly button then lowered his hand to cuff my pussy. He pulled the crotch section to my panties aside and pushed two of his thick fingers into my heated pocket. Almost immediately, I straddled my legs and ground my hips, as if his fingers were his dick easing in and out of me. He made it feel that way, and my wetness caused a heavy buildup of cream on his fingers. I was so wet, but there was something in his touch that always brought out the best in me.

Aside from our moans, we could also hear my juices being stirred. Keith added another finger, and he worked them inside of me so well that I was now on the tips of my curled toes. I pushed my ass in his direction, and I could feel his hardness fighting back. It grew against the crack of my ass, and the more I felt his growth, the more I wanted him inside of me. I yanked his fingers from my insides, lowered my soaking wet panties, and hurried toward the kitchen table. While bending over, I reached back to spread my ass cheeks apart. My moist hole smiled at Keith, who in return, stepped forward and positioned his dick to enter me. He loved to tease me, but I was in no mood for foreplay.

"Put it in there," I whined. "I want all of it, baby. Drive it all the way up in there."

"As wet as you are, I may skid on the icy road and hurt myself. Something tells me that I'd better take it easy or else."

"Yeah, well, something tells me that if you don't stop teasing me like this, you will hurt yourself. I won't take it easy on you, so you'd better take advantage of working this out from behind."

"I love tough talk, baby. Bring it on."

Keith assisted me in holding my ass cheeks apart, and then he plowed his dick far inside of me. He rocked me at a swift pace from behind, so fast that I had to reach out and hold on to the table. I felt every single inch of him gliding in and out of me, and the sounds of my pussy gushing echoed in the room. I did my best to keep up with Keith. Every time I pushed back, he answered with a long stroke that caused my legs to weaken.

"I know you ain't going to sleep on me, are you?" he said, holding my waist to keep me on my feet.

"Noooo," I cried out. "It's just that . . . that your dick feels so good that I'm melting. I can't help it that I'm weakening and melting like this."

Keith snickered. I had to admit that it was pretty funny too, but it was the truth. I was melting right in his hands, and when the tip of his head shaved against my clitoris, it was all over with for me. I damn near fell to my knees. The orgasm I had was that damn good. Keith had to pick up my trembling body from the floor. He carried me upstairs to the bedroom and laid me back on the bed. I had finally calmed down. That was when he lay over me and wrapped my legs around his back.

"I say to hell with dinner," he suggested. "Let's finish what we started, and this time, I want you to hurt me like you said you would."

I wasn't sure if I had enough energy to *hurt* him or not, but I rolled on top and gave it everything that I had. Even that didn't seem like enough, but whether it was or not, we spent the next couple of hours making love. Afterward, I fell asleep in Keith's arms. Just as he had predicted, I slept like a newborn baby.

By morning, I rolled over and yawned. I looked for Keith, but he wasn't in bed. I was naked and my body was sore all over. I also had a headache, so I sat up and massaged my forehead. Wanting to take a shower, I got out of bed and grabbed towels from the closet. I then looked in the medicine cabinet for aspirin, but there were none. I did, however, see two boxes of opened condoms. From both packages, one condom was missing. I thought that was kind of odd, especially since I felt as if we had developed a trusting relationship and had stopped using them. I provided the ones we had used in the beginning of our relationship, so there was no way for him to say that he'd used the condoms with me.

I closed the medicine cabinet and laid the towels on the counter. Not sure where my clothes were, I looked into his closet to get one of his T-shirts. It barely covered my ass, but for now it had to do. I walked down the stairs and could hear rap music coming from the kitchen. When I entered, Keith was standing by the stove, flipping pancakes. My eyes scanned down his backside that was without a stitch of clothing. Sexy, he was, but not sexy enough for me to forget about the condoms.

"Since we skipped dinner," I said, getting his attention, "I guess we're now on for breakfast."

Keith turned around and smiled. He licked his lips then wiped his mouth. "I don't know about you, but I ate pretty good last night. Got full, too, and it's been a long time since I felt that fulfilled."

"A long time as in maybe three weeks? We did indulge ourselves, right before . . . never mind."

I hated to talk about the incident with Lexi. It made me revisit how wrong I was for lying to her, and for almost causing Keith to lose his life.

"It's okay to talk about what Lexi did. I'm over it, trust me. I hope you are too."

"It may take me a little longer than you to get over it, simply because I don't like the fact that you got hurt."

"So did you. But there's no need for us to harp on the past. I'm all about the future, so I have a question for you. Come closer so I can ask you this."

I walked farther into the kitchen and stood by Keith. He lifted a fork and picked up a slice of his pancake. "Open your mouth and tell me how that taste. To me, it tastes rubbery. But maybe it's just me."

I laughed, thinking that he was about to ask me something else, like if I would marry him. Lord knows I wasn't ready for that. Even though I loved Keith, I still believed that even our relationship was young. Maybe after another five years, I'd be ready to walk down the aisle.

I opened my mouth and he put the pancake inside of it. It didn't taste rubbery to me. Actually, it tasted pretty good.

"You're good," I said with a nod. "Throw in two sausages, a slice of bacon, and some orange juice and you'll be on point."

Keith grabbed my waist and positioned me to face him. We shared a lengthy kiss then he spoke up again. "You know that's not really what I was going to ask you, right?"

"No, I didn't know, but spill it. What's on your mind?"

"I want you to move in with me. I miss you when you're not here, and I hate calling you all the time, begging and pleading for you to come over."

He was teasing me about the begging and pleading part, but he seemed serious about me moving in with him.

"I'm not so sure if I want to do that just yet. Give me some time to think about it, and I'll let you know, okay?"

Keith held a blank expression on his face. He didn't appear to like my answer. He let me go and turned to face the stove. He flipped another pancake and placed another one on a plate. "What's there to think about?" he said. "And why wouldn't you want to move in with me?"

"For starters, I don't want to rush into anything. Sometimes, I need my space and I assume that you do too. I also question if you're seeing somebody else, especially since you have open boxes of condoms in your medicine cabinet."

Keith's head snapped to the side. His brows curved inward and he cocked his head back. "Condoms? Yes, I do have open boxes of condoms, but in case you forgot, we used to use them."

"You're right, we did. But I was the one who always had them, not you. Not once did you ever use any of your condoms."

He quickly shot my comment down. "That's a lie. I know what I used and who I used them with. And for you to suggest that I've used them with someone else is stupid. As it is for you to question if I've been seeing someone else, when you know damn well that the only person I've been with is you."

"So, in other words, you just called me stupid? If I'm so stupid, then why do you want me to move in with you? That's stupid for you to ask, especially if you think I'm so stupid."

Keith turned to me with much frustration on his face. "You know what's stupid? This conversation. Obviously, you woke up on the wrong side of the bed. I don't have time to argue with you this morning, and forget about me asking you to move in with me. I shouldn't have ever asked."

"No, you shouldn't have, especially since you can't figure out why you have two open boxes of condoms. When you figure that out, maybe we can talk about moving in together."

I cut my eyes at him and walked away.

"Not interested," he said underneath his breath. "Silly shit, I swear."

I turned around and put my hand on my hip. "Silly? Now I'm stupid and silly. Wow, Keith. It's great to know how you really feel."

He laid the spatula on the stove then faced me. "You want to know how I really feel? I'll tell you how I feel. I feel as if, for some reason, you are holding back on this relationship. That makes me uneasy. You purposely came down here this morning to start an argument with me; that way you can go home and get some of the so-called space you need. I don't know what's preventing you from giving me your all, but maybe like Evelyn said the other night, you're still confused. If you are, just let me know. That way, I don't put my all into this relationship and wind up hurting myself again. Been there, done that before. Ain't trying to go there again, so your honesty about how you feel, as well as about how confused you may really be, would be much appreciated."

Did he seriously just go there and bring up Evelyn? No, he didn't. "I'm not holding back on anything. Just because I don't want to move in with you right now, it has nothing to do with me being confused. The problem is you not getting your way. You can't accept no, and that's all there is to it. I didn't purposely pick an argument with you. You're the one with condoms that aren't accounted for, so don't go turning this around like I don't have my head on straight. In addition to that, if you think Evelyn has a valid point, then why don't you call her up to chat? I'm sure you would like that, especially since you couldn't keep your eyes off of her the other night."

Keith nodded and sucked his teeth. "Okay, I finally get it. That's what this is all about. You've been holding that shit in since the other night. I'm glad you got that off your chest, and just so you know, Trina, I can look all I want to. It's a good thing that you never know what I'm thinking, as I am doing right now while looking at you. Lastly, I can accept no, if you say it. Now that you've said it about moving in together, I accept it. Forget it and let's move the hell on."

I wasn't sure how to take his comment, but more than anything, the thought of him thinking anything about Evelyn upset me. I rushed up to him, ready to smack some sense into him. But before I got within inches of him, he stepped back.

"Think before you act," he said. "I don't fight women, and if you ever put your hands on me in an offensive way, this shit is over. If I want a ghetto girl, I'll go get one."

"I'm sure if you want one with a pretty smile, you'll go get her too. I'm out of here, Keith. And save those rubbery pancakes and your condoms for the next woman you want to trick."

Keith walked around me and went to the closet. He removed my jeans and T-shirt from inside, and then made his way to the door. After opening it, he made a gesture with his hand.

"Get your clothes on and go. There are plenty of men who may want to spend their time arguing with you and dealing with your insecurities. Unfortunately for you, I'm not the one."

I continued to rant and change my clothes right at the door. And as soon as I stepped outside, Keith slammed the door behind me. It was a good thing that he'd shown his true colors before I decided to move in with him. I hurried to my car, thinking how badly he had screwed himself. I also wondered if I had done the same.

Chapter 6

Evelyn

To be honest, things were getting a little bit rough around here. Now that I no longer had Cedric to depend on for money, everything was behind. I had been on two job interviews, but neither of them panned out for me. One only paid eight dollars an hour, and the other one was too far away. The manager who interviewed me had nothing but jealously in her eyes, so I suspected that she wouldn't offer me the job anyway.

When I returned home, there was a note from the rental office on my door. I was almost two months behind on rent. The landlord gave me until the end of the week to come up with at least one payment. Not to mention that my car payment, light bill, and personal property taxes were due. I was now driving around with improper plates, and it was just a matter of time before the police would pull me over and give me a ticket.

The only thing that I could do, for now, was gather up some of my expensive clothes and purses that Cedric had given me money to buy, and see if I could sell them to a consignment shop. There was one in Ladue. From what I'd heard, they paid a nice piece of change for brand name clothes and purses. I piled the items into my car and headed to the consignment shop to see what I could get. I had so many items bunched in my hand, and when I placed them on the counter, the lady behind it looked at me like I was crazy.

"How may I help you?" she said in a snobby tone.

"I want to see what I can get for these items."

She lowered her glasses and winced at the items. "Are they real or knockoffs?"

I didn't want to insult this bitch, but she sure did insult me. Why would I even come here, if my items were knock-offs? I placed my hand on my hip, and rolled my neck around. "Where do you get off asking me if they're real? Do I look like I wear knockoffs? I think you'd better look again, because I only wear the real deal, sweetie. Thank you very much."

The old, angry-looking white woman sorted through the items, laying them flat on the counter. She kept looking at the labels. When it came to the purses, she kept looking inside and feeling the leather.

"I'm not sure about this one," she said, referring to my Michael Kors bag. I used the money Cedric had given me to purchase that one at Macy's.

"If you're not sure, then you need to question Macy's about selling counterfeit purses. I assure you that they're not getting their purses from Soho in New York."

"Maybe not, but since I'm not sure about that one, I can't give you a quote on it. As for the other items, how much do you want for them?"

I was desperate for money, so I didn't want to get on this bitch's bad side and argue with her about the purse. Instead, I quoted her on what I thought the ten items were worth.

"How about five . . . no, six thousand dollars?"

Finally, the lady laughed and removed her glasses. "That's funny," she said. "And now that you're done joking with me, how about telling me how much you really want for these items?"

I looked at her with a straight face. "I just told you how much I want, and since I'm not smiling, you know I'm not joking. In case you're not bright enough to know what these pieces are worth, please check the price tag on the one right there. I've never worn it, and it cost twelve hundred dollars. The others I may have worn once or twice and they cost the same, maybe even higher. I'm sure you already know how much the purses cost, and three of them should tally up to what I want. Got it?"

The woman was blunt. "What you want, you won't get here. Got it? This is a consignment shop, where our customers expect to pay a discount for brand name merchandise. The clothes are wrinkled, and I won't mention the stain I see on one of the dresses. Looks like the same stain Monica Lewinsky had on her dress, but I'm not one to assume anything. As for the purses, they are not in tiptop condition. The most I could give you for all of this is five hundred dollars. That's it."

I couldn't hold back, especially not after the Monica Lewinsky comment. "Bitch, are you crazy? Five hundred dollars? I should jump over this counter and knock some sense into you. At that price, you shouldn't be working here. You apparently don't know the value of these items. And stain or not, you know darn well that this stuff is worth way more than that. I could go stand on a corner and sell these items for more than that."

"Then I suggest you go do that because all I can offer you is five hundred dollars. Since you don't want to accept my offer, good-bye and thanks for stopping by."

How dare this snobby heifer treat me like this? I snatched up my items and stormed out of there. I tossed the items on the back seat and slammed the door after I got inside. My mind was racing a mile a minute. I couldn't think of anywhere else to get some quick money, other than to rob a bank. I had to laugh at how desperate I'd become, and the thought of robbing a bank was a bit much.

I started my car and breezed my Mercedes with improper plates on it through traffic on Lindbergh Boulevard. Just as I was about to get on the highway, my cell phone rang. I looked to see who it was, and surprisingly, it was Trina. I hadn't spoken to her since the other night, but I had planned on calling her so I could get Bryson's number to call him.

"Hello, bestie," I said in a joking manner. "It's good to know that I'm on your mind, or should I say your radar today."

"I'm not going to say all of that, but I called so we could talk. Keith and I had an argument, and I wanted to ask if you thought I was wrong about something."

This was interesting. Trina and Keith always seemed so chummy with each other. And while many couples had arguments, Keith didn't seem like the arguing type. As for Trina, that was a different story. She could be a real shit starter, if she wanted to be. I'd known that from experience.

"What happened? Tell me."

Trina told me about the condoms and about him telling her to leave. I wanted to laugh my ass off. I envisioned his foot traveling deep in her ass when he kicked her out. Either way, I gave my input to my friend who seemed distraught about what had happened.

"First of all, you had every right to be mad," I said. "I would have questioned those condoms too. At the end of the day, he needs to provide you with a legitimate explanation for the ones missing. He didn't have an answer; that's why he kicked you out and made you leave. He's hoping that you forget all about it, and that you'll miss him so much and come running back to him. If I were you, I wouldn't. I'd keep it moving and find someone else who has no problems with being honest."

Trina sniffed then blew her nose. "I agree. He made me look like the bad person, and then had the nerve to say that I was stupid and silly. That hurt. I never thought Keith would speak to me like that."

"I don't know why you thought he was so special. He's just like any other man, and to be honest, the last thing you need is another mentally abusive man in your life. The last one you had was both physically and mentally abusive, and you see where that got you. With that crazy bitch, Lexi. You definitely don't want to go there again."

"No, I don't. I don't get why relationships are so hard, but maybe it's time for me to step back and chill for a while. I need to get myself together before I start dating again."

"I agree. I feel the same way. I have so much going on right now that I can't even think straight. My bills are way behind, and I've been on four or five interviews. The job market sucks. I haven't found anything yet."

"Eventually, you will. And if you need to borrow a couple of dollars, let me know. I could spare twenty or forty dollars, but that's it."

I pursed my lips. What in the hell was I supposed to do with twenty or forty dollars? That was barely enough for me to get my nails and toes done.

"No, thanks, I'm good. At least until I get my unemployment check, so no worries. In the meantime, you need to chill and forget about Keith. I'm out and about right now, so if you want some company, let me know. I'll stop by to chat."

"I'm leaving in a few to go to the studio and get some work done. Whenever I'm this upset, I like to paint. You'd be surprised by what I come up with, when I'm feeling down like this. Painting always makes me feel better."

"Well, go do you. I'll call to check on you tomorrow."

"Thanks, Evelyn. I really do appreciate it. I know we've had our ups and downs, but at least we can still have a decent conversation with each other."

"You're right. I've known you since elementary school, and we've had way more ups than downs. You'll be okay. I'm sure that I will be too. By the way, have you heard from your attack dog, Kayla?"

"Don't say that about her. And no, I haven't heard from her. I've thought about calling her, but since I've been in touch with Jacoby, he says that she's doing okay. I'm giving her time to sort things out. She has a lot on her plate with Cedric. I assume that she doesn't want to be bothered."

"We all have a lot going on, but you already know how Kayla is. Her problems are always bigger than everyone else, and we're supposed to stop what we're doing to see about her. I haven't talked to her since the incident at the grocery store. I guess she hasn't been in the mood for another one of her so-called conversations that consists of her slapping me."

"No comment. I'm not touching that thing with you and Kayla. Maybe one day y'all will work it out."

"I doubt it. It doesn't matter to me either way, but I'm going to let you get out of there and go to the studio. Have fun and remember what I said to you about Keith. A dog will be a dog, and sometimes, you have to let him bark and dig his own grave."

Trina said good-bye. I hoped she had washed her hands of Keith, but I knew how my BFF's were. They didn't always want to walk away from relationships, even when they knew they should have.

I drove to my next destination, which was only five minutes away. That would be Keith's house. I hoped he was home.

I parked my car and strutted to the door. After ringing the doorbell, I waited for him to answer. Minutes later, I saw him coming down the stairs. He appeared upbeat and was dressed in a pair of white cargo shorts that were unzipped and hung low on his waist. They looked dynamite against his chocolate skin, but unfortunately for me, he had on a wife beater that covered up part of his chest. Still, the man was sexy as ever. *Trina had better get herself together—fast*. No man wanted to be involved with a woman who kept up a lot of foolishness. She whined too much, and he couldn't be happy about her appearance that didn't seem to be her priority. She never wore name brand anything. The least she could do was carry a name brand purse. Every real woman had at least one.

Keith swung the door open with a grin on his face. "What's up, Evelyn? Trina's not here. If you need to reach her, you may want to hit her up on her cell phone."

"Oh, I know she's not here. She told me earlier about the brutal argument the two of you had. Since I was in the neighborhood, I wanted to stop by to see if I could convince you to give me your brother's telephone number? The other day, Trina didn't seem as though she wanted me to have it. I don't know what's been up with her attitude, and I don't appreciate her being all up in my business. She's been acting real funny lately. I think it may have something to do with . . . never mind. Forget it."

As I predicted, Keith opened the door wider for me to come inside. He wanted to know what was really going on with Trina. I would happily fill him in.

"You don't have to stand out there. Come in."

"Are you sure?" I said already stepping inside. "I mean, you weren't busy, were you?"

"I was upstairs in my studio, painting. Whenever I have a lot on my mind, it's usually what I do."

Awww, they were like two peas in a pod. Trina had just said the same thing; they clearly had something in common.

"Your studio? You have a studio in here?"

"Yep. On the third level. Would you like to see it?"

See that and then some, I thought. "Yes, I would. Trina told me what a great artist you are. I thought the two of you worked together; and didn't you meet her at that, uh, studio on Delmar?"

"Yes, I did. I haven't been there in a while, though, but I may stop by next week to attend an art show."

I wanted to yawn. How boring. I focused on something other than his conversation, as he made his way up the stairs in front of me. His nail-gripping ass was right there, waiting on me to touch it. All I wanted to do was reach out and touch it, but Trina would kill me. I had a vision of his muscular body on top of mine, sweating while we fucked each other's brains out. I would put any amount of money on it that Trina didn't know how to utilize a man like this. Keeping him excited would be difficult for her. That was why he needed me.

By the time we made it to the third level, I was out of breath. I stood in the doorway, watching as Keith proudly showed me some of his paintings. There was no question that the man had talent. His studio had some of the most exquisite pieces of art I'd ever seen. I was in awe as I looked around the room. The smell of money was floating in the air and these pictures had to be worth a lot of money.

"Oh, my God," I said, walking up to a colorful painted picture of Miles Davis. "This is so beautiful. A friend of mine would love this! Miles is his favorite jazz player. I have never seen anything like this before."

"I sold the original to a museum in Atlanta. Unfortunately, that one there isn't for sale."

"I'm not trying to be nosy or anything like that, but how much does something like this cost? You have so many beautiful pieces in here. I wonder how much they're worth."

Keith shrugged and boasted about his work that was quite impressive. "Anywhere from five to thirty or forty thousand dollars. It depends on what I'm asked to do. I have some wealthy clients who pay high dollars for their artwork. They often refer me to others, so I stay quite busy."

"I see," I said, gazing around at the large room. "And it's a good thing that you love what you do. I wish I could discover what my real talents are. Maybe I would be able to make money like this, but for now, it is what it is."

Keith sat on a stool next to his work station. He invited me to have a seat on the couch in front of him. I did and crossed my legs.

"So, what is it that you exactly do, Evelyn?"

I didn't appreciate him getting all up in my business, but if we were going to get to know each other on another level, why not?

"Currently, I'm unemployed. I was working customer service, but I got laid off. I've been looking for work, but it's hard to find a job. Many economists claim the economy is recovering, but I'm not feeling it yet. My bills are behind, and everybody I try to borrow money from is in the same predicament."

"Yeah, that's too bad. But keep your head up, though. Things will get better."

I was sure that he would offer me a little something, but at least he gave me hope. He started to dabble on a sketchpad that was on his workstation. I admired a man who utilized his talents to make money; and, all the way around, he was so damn gorgeous to me.

"While at the door, you mentioned something about Trina's strange behavior," he said. "Do you mind elaborating on that?"

Keith's eyes scanned my moisturized legs, which were still crossed. Then his eyes traveled from my head to toe, before he looked at the sketchpad again and waited for me to reply.

"What I meant by that was I told Trina she needed to knock it off. No offense to her, but there are times when she chooses to be a drama queen for no reason. It irritates the heck out of me, and I reminded her that no man would put up with that mess. We had a little argument because she didn't like what I had to say to her. Please don't tell her that I'm sharing this with you, but she be acting a little off at times. I told her that she needs to go get herself checked out, and that's why I said she was confused the other night. She is confused. When I say that to her, she takes it personal."

Without looking up, Keith hit me with more questions. "Confused about what? What do you think she's confused about?"

"Honestly, I think she's confused about being with you."

He finally looked up and wet his lips with his tongue. "Why would she be confused about being with me?"

"I say that because when we talk about y'all's relationship, she always hesitates and brings up her past. She talks about her attraction to other women, and I'm not sure if she's satisfied with being with a man. I could be wrong. Trina is very hard to read, but she's been that way for a very long time."

Keith sat quietly for a while. I could tell he was in deep thought. His pencil scribbled faster and the frown on his face said that he wasn't too pleased. I wanted to turn his frown into a smile.

"What are you doing over there?" I asked.

"You'll see. In a few more minutes, you'll see."

Keith continued to dabble while I turned my head to look around the room. I noticed a beautiful painting of Aretha Franklin, but as I scooted forward to get off the couch, he stopped me.

"Don't move just yet. Give me about ten more minutes."

I smiled, figuring that he was creating a sketch of me. "Work your magic," I said. "Had I known that you were creating a sketch of me, I would have gotten myself in a better position."

"The one you're in right now is just fine."

I relaxed back on the couch and spread my arms on top of it. "Okay, if you say so. Have at it, if you will."

Almost ten minutes later, Keith turned the sketchpad around, showing me the picture he'd drawn. I was floored. It was the most awesome drawing of a person I'd ever seen. My mouth was wide open. I peeled myself off the couch and walked up to him.

"Tha . . . that is magnificent. You're so talented, Keith. How did you do that so fast? I kept moving around, talking; you make it look so easy."

Keith was all smiles. The way to any man's heart was to compliment his work. "It was easy, especially when I'm working on someone like you."

I cocked my head back in surprise. "What is that supposed to mean? Someone like me who—"

"Someone like you who is very attractive and funny. That's why I think you'll be great for my brother."

Now was the perfect time for me to make my move. I was close to him, and his masculine cologne drew me right in. I didn't want to let his compliment with regard to me go to waste. I placed my arm on his shoulder and gazed at the sketch in his hand.

"Yeah, I could be great for your brother, but something tells me that I could also be perfect for you too. I don't know why, but I have a feeling inside of me that says so."

Before Keith responded, I removed the sketch from his hand and placed it on his workstation. I stood in front of him and my other arm rested on his shoulder. The direction of my eyes traveled to his thick lips, but as I inched forward, he backed his head away from me.

"Uh, I don't think this is a good idea."

"I'm on the other side of the fence. I think it's a great idea."

I leaned in again. This time, my lips touched Keith's. I forced my tongue into his mouth, and as soon as I felt his, he jumped up from the chair.

"I think you need to go," he said.

I glanced at his hardness that was showing through his shorts. "You're doing a whole lot of thinking, Keith, but your thoughts are not beneficial to either of us. This time, I won't push. You know where I stand, and if you're ever in need of a real woman, who knows exactly what she wants, call me. If you decide not to, I will settle for your brother. Give my number to him, and we can go from there."

I picked up the sketch pencil and scribbled my number on the drawing he'd created of me. Keith stood in silence as I said good-bye and sauntered my way toward the door to exit. I walked down the stairs, and with a smile on my face, I opened the front door and headed to my car. Twenty minutes later, I stopped at a gas station to get gas and a lottery ticket. Rubbed the ticket and won $500. Somebody was definitely looking out for me, even more so when my cell phone rang and it was Bryson. No question about it, this was my lucky day.

Chapter 7

Kayla

I was sitting in the hotel lobby, having a few drinks at the bar and listening to a man playing some soothing music on a piano. The past few days had been peaceful, especially since I hadn't stopped by the house to see Cedric. Jacoby met me for dinner last night and he updated me on what had been going on at the house. According to him, Cynthia had been taking very good care of them, and Cedric was starting to move around. Jacoby asked me to free my mind of all the hatred I had inside of me. He stressed that if he could move on, I should be able to as well. He had no clue that I still loved his father. That was why I chose to minimize my visits. The last thing I needed was for Cedric to manipulate me again. If I continued to show up and show concern for him, he'd do just that. I felt like such an idiot for not putting closure to this yet, but I guess that timing was everything.

Later that night, I returned to my room. The first thing I looked at was the divorce papers that were still sprawled out on the table. I had picked them up a million and one times. Read them over, time and time again. Cedric didn't agree to give me half, but what he offered was a measly 20 percent for all of the headaches and setbacks he'd caused me. 20 percent was all that I was worth to him, not to mention that he'd get to keep the house. I basically had to start all over and make it work with 20 lousy percent.

Thinking about it, I tossed back another drink. The vodka burned my throat, but it relaxed me. Relaxed me so much that I fell back on the bed and started to laugh at this situation, instead of crying about it. This was it, the end, and it was time for me to get on with my life. I rushed up from the bed and straightened the pile of papers on the desk. I tucked them inside of my purse and snatched my keys off the dresser. I tossed back one more shot of vodka, and then stumbled to the door and left.

Feeling woozy, I plopped down in the driver's seat of my car and revved up the engine. The clock showed one minute after midnight, but I didn't care. I needed to sign these darn papers and deliver them to Cedric ASAP. Should have done this a long time ago, but today felt like the day that it needed to be done.

I swerved in and out of traffic, occasionally crossing the yellow and white lines. My eyes fluttered and felt real heavy. I didn't think I was that drunk, until I heard a loud horn that caused my eyes to shoot wide open. The man next to me lowered his window.

"Watch where the fuck you're going, you dizzy broad! You almost hit my freaking brand new car!"

I lifted my middle finger. "To hell with your car! I hope you have insurance!"

He shook his head and sped off in his Corvette. Who was he to say something to me, when he was driving that fast? I did slow down, but this time I was moving too slow. Other drivers blew their horns as well, yelling for me to get off the road. I honored their requests, just for a little while. My first stop was at Evelyn's place. Luckily for me, I didn't have to buzz for her to let me in. A resident and his girlfriend were going up on the elevator. I leaned against the wall, trying to rest my body that felt limp.

"Are you okay?" the man asked with his arm around his girlfriend's shoulder.

"Yeah," the woman said. "You don't look so good."

I threw my hand back at them. My voice slurred a little. "No, trust me, I'm fine. It's been a long day. I juss . . . just wanted to stop by to see an old friend of mine."

They didn't respond. Got off the elevator at the fourth floor, while I made my way up to Evelyn's loft. I straightened my jacket and patted my hair. The stylist trimmed it for me earlier, and no matter what Cedric said, I thought it looked pretty darn good. My pants didn't hug my thighs like they used to, and in less than a week, I was down another three pounds. Barely able to stand, and wobbling from side to side, I knocked on Evelyn's door. There was no answer, so I knocked harder. This time, I moved closer to look into the peephole. I squinted and blew my breath on the door.

"Trick, I know you're in there. Open the door, so I can tell you how much yo' ass done ruined my life. It's what you want to hear, isn't it?"

Just then, Evelyn snatched the door open. She had on a soft purple robe that cut right at her thighs. Her hair was covered with a scarf and her makeup-free face was blemish free.

"I can't believe this," she said, crossing her arms in front of her. "The perfect princess is at my door, drunk. If you came here to have one of your conversations, I'm not interested. I'm tired and I'm in no mood to keep fighting with you."

I forced myself to stand up straight, as if I had it all together. "That's because you can't fight. Not one lick, and you always needed me to help you when you got beat up by those other kids. I was always there to help you, but you sure as hell didn't help me. What you did was fuck me over and I will nevah, evah forgive you."

"I don't recall ever asking you to, so why don't you take your highly intoxicated ass elsewhere and leave me alone. You told me to stop calling Ceddy, so I did."

I laughed and slapped my leg. "Ceddy? That's my nickname for him, so I wish you wouldn't be a little copycat. But then again, that's what you've always been. Everything I have or have had, you want. You want to be me, Evelyn, but there is only one bad bitch out there who goes by the name of Mrs. Cedric Thompson. Or should I say went by that name because I"—I pointed to my chest—"I'm throwing in the towel. I came to tell you that you and your baby can have him. After today, he's going to be"—I paused and hiccupped—"be a free man. I, on the other hand, will be a free woman with twenty percent of his income."

Evelyn shook her head and gazed at me with disgust. "You're pathetic, Kayla. Truly pathetic. No wonder Cedric found himself curled up in my bed with me."

I reached out to slap Evelyn, but this time, she grabbed my hand and shoved me backward. I couldn't keep my balance and fell on the floor.

"If you're still out here in one minute, I'm calling security. Cameras are all over the place, and I assure you that, this time, you will be arrested."

Evelyn slammed her door. I barely had enough energy to peel myself off the floor but I managed. I stumbled back to the elevator and held on to the rail as the elevator went down to the parking garage. Somehow, I managed to get back into the car, and I drove myself to Cedric's place. Jacoby's car was parked in the curvy driveway. Adrianne's car was behind his. I wondered what she was doing over here this late; and if I were here, this would never be.

I put the key in the door and pushed it open. It squeaked, but inside of the house, there was nothing but silence. I used the railing to pull myself up the stairs. By the time I reached the second floor, I could see that Jacoby wasn't in his bedroom. Figuring that he was probably downstairs, I headed to the bedroom I once shared with my fake husband. I pushed on the double doors, watching as he lay there sound asleep. It must've been nice that one of us was resting well.

"Yo," I shouted loud enough for him to hear me. "Cedric, get up. I need to get at you 'bout something real important."

I staggered over to the bed. He didn't move, so I leaned down and placed my lips close to his ear.

"Get up!" I shouted. "Don't you hear me?"

Cedric jumped from his sleep and damn near fell out of the bed. He frowned at me and blinked several times to focus.

"What in the fuck are you doing?" he barked.

I put my hand on my hips and pursed my lips. "I . . . I'm doing what yo' grimy tail asked me to do. I'm signing these doggone papers so that we, you and me that is, can be free to fly like little birdies."

I turned in circles, and flapped my arms as if I were flying around the room. Cedric sat up in bed and turned on the lamp. I could see him shaking his head.

"So, here you go." I dug in my purse, trying to retrieve the papers. When I pulled them out, my purse fell on the floor and all of the contents inside scattered on the floor. I dropped to my knees, attempting to stuff my things back into my purse. But when I spotted a pen, I reached for it.

"Ah, ha!" I said with glee in my eyes. I held up the pen, showing it to Cedric. "There it is. Exactly what I was looking for. My little penny pen. Do you see it?"

Cedric didn't say a word. I plopped on the bed and slammed the messy papers on my lap. I scribbled my signature on the long line then tossed the papers at his face. I swiped my hands together then leaned in closer to him.

"Done. All done, and now you can move the hell on. Just make sure I get my twenty freaking percent because I have places to go, people to see, and a new life to go live."

Cedric reached out to grab my face. He held it close to his and our eyes searched into each other's. "I hate to see you like this," he said in a whisper. "No words can express how sorry I truly am, but after all that's happened, I know that saying I'm sorry will never be enough."

"Yeah, well, I . . . I'm sorry 'bout this too, but it is what it is."

I hiccupped again, and before I could back away from Cedric, vomit rushed up my throat. All I remember was it spraying in his face. After that, I blacked out.

I woke up in the morning, not knowing where I was. My head was banging, and the room I was in felt like it was spinning. I yawned and cracked my eyes wider to look next to me. That was when I saw Cedric. He was sitting up in bed with a food tray resting over his lap. A piece of toast was near his mouth and his glass of orange juice wiggled as the bed moved when I tried to sit up.

"Wha . . . How did I get over here?" I asked.

A wet rag dropped from my forehead, and I had on a tacky flowered nightgown that definitely didn't belong to me.

"I can't believe you don't remember."

Cedric seemed to have an attitude, but I was concerned about how I'd gotten there. I remembered driving last night, and I also remembered walking up the stairs. That was pretty much it.

"I don't remember everything, but I guess it doesn't really matter. I do know what I had to drink, and . . . What's that smell? Something smells funny."

"Maybe we didn't get a chance to clean up all of your puke. That could be what you're smelling."

I tossed the covers aside and sat up. "I vomited? Where?"

"All over the place."

"Stop lying, Cedric. You're just trying to make me feel bad."

"If you don't believe me, fine. Go ask Cynthia. I'm sure she'll tell you all about it, especially since she and Jacoby had to help me clean you up."

I got off the bed and looked down at the tacky nightgown again. Maybe that explained why I was wearing it. I left the room, and when I entered the kitchen, Cynthia was making breakfast.

"Good morning, Mrs. Thompson," she said.

"Kayla will suit me just fine, Cynthia. Now please tell me something. What happened last night? How did I get into this gown?"

She smiled at me from behind the island. "Do you really want to know?"

"Yes, I do. Please tell me."

Cynthia told me everything that happened last night. From me throwing up in Cedric's face, to him giving me a shower. She was the one who cleaned up my vomit and changed the sheets. And Jacoby was asked to help carry me to bed, because Cedric was too weak. Now, I felt really embarrassed. I apologized to her, and when I asked where Jacoby was at, she said he had already left with Adrianne. That reminded me about seeing her car parked outside last night, so I excused myself from the kitchen and went into another room to call Jacoby. He answered the phone, appearing to be out of breath.

"Where are you?" I asked.

"I'm at the gym with Adrianne. Are you feeling better?"

"Much better, and I apologize for whatever happened here last night. You already know that I have a lot of things on my mind, and even though alcohol isn't the answer, I used it to cope."

"No need to explain yourself, Mama. I can honestly say that I understand. I'm dealing with some things too, and trust me when I say that you're not by yourself."

His comment caught me a little off guard. I thought things were getting better for Jacoby. Apparently, something else was stressing him. "Do you mind telling me what else you're dealing with? Does it have anything to do with why Adrianne is here in the wee hours of the morning?"

"She's not always there in the wee hours of the morning. Sometimes, but not always."

"Sometimes is more than enough. You know that's something I didn't allow while I was here, and I definitely don't allow it when I'm not. With that being said, answer my question. What else are you dealing with?"

I heard Jacoby sigh. He wasn't trying to have this conversation with me this morning. "Whatever you say, Mama. And the only thing I'm dealing with is school. Can't wait until the semester is over."

"Why? Are your grades suffering? The last time we spoke about school, you said your grades had improved."

"They're up and down. But I'll work it out, like I always do."

"I'll make sure you do, and when I get back to the hotel, I'm going to look at your grades on parent portal. If anything isn't up to par, you know you're going to hear about it."

"I'm sure I will. Meanwhile, I'm trying to get my workout on. Can I hit you back later?"

I wasn't sure if his grades were the issue or not, but I left the conversation there. I told him to enjoy his workout, and asked him to call me later. After I ended the call, I went back into the kitchen where Cynthia was. She interrupted my thoughts.

"Don't look so worried," she said. "I hope you're in the mood for breakfast, because I made enough for everyone. I thought Jacoby and his girlfriend wanted something to eat too. Unfortunately, they didn't."

"All I want is some orange juice and something light, like a bagel. No cream cheese, because my stomach is upset."

Cynthia stopped what she was doing to pour me a glass of orange juice. She got me a bagel from the fridge and brought everything over to the table.

"Tell me something." I looked at Cynthia and thanked her. "How often does Adrianne spend the night? She's not over here during the week, is she?"

Cynthia hesitated to speak. I figured that she didn't want to get Jacoby in trouble, but with her not saying anything, I suspected that Adrianne had been spending plenty of nights here.

"I really don't want to interfere, Mrs. Thomp . . . Kayla, but the truth is, she has been over here quite often. Jacoby has skipped school a few days, too, and I have seen them in some"—she cleared her throat—"questionable positions."

I figured there was more to it, and I didn't know why I had a feeling that Adrianne was pregnant. Jacoby's behavior alerted me that something was really wrong. "Thank you for telling me that. I'll be sure to add a little something extra on your check. Is there anything else I should know?"

Cynthia pulled back a chair and sat down. She clenched her hands together and rubbed them. "No, not really, other than Cedric is getting better. He's been speaking to several people, including a few women who called to check on him. He's been walking around a lot at night, but during the day he uses his cane. I don't think your friend, Evelyn, has reached out to him again. But I haven't looked at his phone in nearly two days."

I placed my hand on top of Cynthia's. "Again, thanks for the update. You have my number, so be sure to call me if you think there is something urgent I need to know."

Cynthia nodded. She told me she had washed my clothes for me and went to the washroom to get them.

I finished my bagel and orange juice then made my way back upstairs with my clothes thrown over my shoulder. When I entered the bedroom, Cedric was now on his laptop, appearing to be occupied.

"Thanks for your assistance last night," I said. "I apologize for throwing up on you. By the way, I feel there will be no more drinking for me."

"I doubt that, but if that's how you want to cope with your pain, do whatever you wish."

I ignored Cedric's comment and went into the bathroom to change clothes. I used his wave brush to brush my hair then slipped into my heels, which I saw thrown in the corner. Unfortunately for me, one of the heels was broken.

I held the shoe in my hand and went back into the bedroom. "What happened to my heel?" I asked.

Cedric looked up and shrugged. "That probably happened when you were turning in circles, trying to pretend that you were a bird flying. You stumbled, and I do believe that was when you broke your shoe."

"I think you're exaggerating about some things. Why would I be turning in circles, trying to fly around like a bird?"

"Because you were celebrating. Celebrating this."

Cedric removed a piece of paper from the nightstand and reached out to give it to me. It was the last page of the dissolution of marriage agreement. My signature was poorly scribbled on the line.

"I didn't sign this," I said, handing the paper back to him.

"Yes, you did."

"It doesn't look like my signature."

"But it is. I saw you do it and you used this pen right here." Cedric lifted the pen and showed it to me. "Now, my question to you is if you were serious about it. Are we going to move forward with this divorce?"

"You're asking me as if I have a choice. You're the one who presented me with those papers, so I assume that you still want this to go as planned. Or have things changed?"

Cedric licked his lips then scratched his head. He rubbed the scruffy hair on his chin then shifted his eyes back to me again. "A lot has changed. I don't want the divorce, but I totally understand if you do. So, yes, I'll let you decide what to do. However you want this to pan out, I'll roll with it."

Honestly, I was stunned. It was funny what being so close to death could do to a person. Cedric had a big change of heart.

"Why would you let me decide, especially since you confessed to not loving me anymore? You couldn't stay married to a woman you didn't love; and what about your baby on the way? You know darn well how I feel about that, and we would have a very difficult time, trying to get that to work."

"Yes, we would, but I have a feeling that we would manage. We've been through a lot, Kayla, and I think it may be safe to say that our bad days are finally behind us. As for me not loving you anymore, you know I said that shit to upset you. The truth is, I do still love you. Very much. And I have a feeling that you still love me too."

See, I knew this would happen. Cedric was a master manipulator. He was saying anything right now to get me back on his team. Unfortunately, I felt it working.

I bit my nail and swallowed the lump in my throat. "I've been tricked before, Cedric. And I doubt that a bullet to your chest is going to change anything. You still have a baby to deal with, other women at your beck and call, and Lord knows what else. I don't want to keep going down this road. For you to—"

"I'm a changed man. I don't even believe that Evelyn's baby is mine, and there are no more women. The majority of them all scattered when they thought I was dead. The only person who has been here for me is you. While you haven't been at my beck and call, I know you've been here almost every day to check on me. That means a lot, Kayla, and I'm telling you right now that I want my family back."

This time, I nibbled on my bottom lip. I took another deep breath and narrowed my eyes to look at Cedric. "All we're going to do is argue. You're going to continue disrespecting me and—"

"I only argue and disrespect those who disrespect me. I went there with you because you did the same with me. Like I said, all of that is now in the past. Allow us a new beginning, and if there are some things that you need to get off your chest, do it now. Curse me the fuck out, if it makes you feel good. Slap me, hit me, beat the hell out of me if it helps. Let's get it all over with. Whatever you dish out, I'll take it like a man who wronged his wife. I'm not going to say much more, but once again, the ball is in your court. Take at least another week to think about this, and then let me know. I'm not going anywhere, and as you already know, I'll be right here, waiting."

I stood speechless. I couldn't even look at Cedric much longer, because I didn't want him to sense what I was thinking.

A huge part of me wanted to reconcile, but then there was something inside telling me to run like hell. Then, of course, there was this little thing with Evelyn. How I wished I could go tell her that Cedric and I would be together forever. That we survived this setback, and that our marriage was going strong. I wanted to send a message to all of his mistresses, letting them know that they could not tear apart what God had put together. This was my husband, and no matter what, I would be keeping my status. And that included the money. I wouldn't have to start over, and I could kiss that lousy 20 percent good-bye. All of those thoughts swarmed in my head. I was in no position to answer Cedric right now, so I left out of the room without giving him an answer. I told Cynthia good-bye and reminded her to tell Jacoby to call me later. I needed to get him straight again, but not as bad as I needed advice from my BFF. I called Trina to see if we could meet somewhere.

Chapter 8

Trina

I received a call from Evelyn telling me about Kayla showing up at her loft drunk, and then I got a call from Kayla asking if I would meet her for lunch. The one person who I hadn't gotten a phone call from was Keith. I was a little disappointed, too. By now, I thought that he would realize his mistakes and contact me to apologize. I felt as if I had been in the wrong too, and I intended to tell him that, if he called. But the no call meant that he didn't want to reconcile our differences. And if he didn't want to, neither did I.

Kayla wanted to meet at Bar Louie in the Central West End. I arrived a few minutes early, but shortly thereafter, I saw her coming down the street. She looked as if she'd lost a lot of weight. The wide-legged gray pants she wore were hanging on her. Her off-the-shoulder red sweater was pretty, and I loved her short haircut. With her weight disappearing, now she really looked like a runway model. As for me, I sported the usual because I preferred to be comfortable: had on a neon and black sweat suit with Nike tennis shoes. My layered hair was always on point, and my face was makeup free. I didn't get off into all the glam, but both of my best friends did.

Kayla walked into the restaurant and saw me sitting at a table. It had been awhile since we'd seen and or talked to each other. I had to admit that it was like a breath of fresh air to see my friend. I missed her, and by the wide smile on her face, I could tell she missed me too.

She walked up to me and we tightly embraced. Tears welled in my eyes, but I quickly blinked them away. I didn't like to get all emotional, but there were times when I couldn't hold back. We sat across from each other, and I was the first one to speak up.

"First things first," I said. "I don't want any apologies from you, and I will not offer an apology either. What's done is done. Let's focus on the positive, and whatever you do, please don't bring up Evelyn."

Kayla held out her hand and shook mine. "Deal, but you know I gotta talk about Evelyn."

We laughed and hurried to order our drinks and food.

"I'm glad you called me," I said. "I'd been thinking about calling you too, but I wanted to give you some space. If you don't mind me asking, how's Cedric doing? I had been talking to Jacoby for a while, but it seems as if he's been busy. I haven't been able to catch up with him lately."

"Yeah, he's been all right. Busy having sex in Cedric's house since I'm not there. Busy skipping school and spending way too much time with Adrianne."

"Sounds like the typical teenager, but the sex thing is a bit much."

"Yes, it is. As for Cedric, he's doing much better. I haven't officially moved back into the house, but I do stop by to check my boys. I hired a nanny to take care of things for me while I'm away."

"I hope she's not young, sexy, and available. If she was, you know that Cedric would have her in that bedroom and on her back in a minute."

I laughed, but Kayla found no humor in my comment. She stressed that Cynthia was an older Italian woman who wasn't Cedric's type.

"Forgive me for saying that," I said, correcting myself. "I was out of line."

She threw her hand back at me. "Don't worry about it. With his reputation, we all know that anything is possible. But, he has admitted to being a changed man. That's what I want to speak to you about, because I'm so confused. Do you believe people can change? Especially men who have the kind of reputation you mentioned? I don't know what I should do about my marriage. Sometimes I feel as though I want it to work, other days not so much. It's time for me to make a decision."

For the next hour or so, Kayla spilled her guts to me. She laid everything on the line about her feelings for Cedric, about her reasons for wanting to leave, as well as her reasons for wanting to stay. She even told me about how she wanted to slap Evelyn in the face with the news of her and Cedric possibly staying together, but then I decided to hit her with more news.

"She had an abortion. Got rid of the baby the second she thought Cedric was dead. That was why I told you to mention that to her. While I'm sad that she went that route, I figured that it would make things easier for you and Cedric. I really can't say if the two of y'all should work things out or not. That's a tough call, because you know how I feel about him. I'd be wrong to weigh in, but if I must say, I do believe that people can change."

Kayla's eyes looked as if they were about to break from the sockets. "She had an abortion? For real?"

"Yes. She told me that she couldn't afford to raise a child without his support."

Kayla shook her head. "What else did I expect from a woman like Evelyn? If she thought Cedric wasn't going to give her a hard time with that child, she was sadly mistaken. He wasn't even sure if the baby was his. If I didn't see the pregnancy test for myself, I wouldn't have believed her. I don't believe in abortions for any reason at all, but I can't say that I'm not happy about her no longer being pregnant with his child."

"So, does that change things? Does it make your decision to reconcile with him much easier?"

Kayla sighed. "I don't know. Cedric has hurt me so much. I think it would be almost impossible for us to put all of this behind us and carry on as if none of this ever happened. It would take years of counseling for us to get through this. I don't know if I have the time or energy and I don't believe he does either."

"Nothing is impossible. I mean, look at us. Our friendship has endured a lot too, but here we are, sitting here conversing and enjoying each other's company. Never say never, Kayla. You just don't know what the outcome will be."

Kayla agreed with me. The waitress came with more drinks and food, and that was when I started to tell her about my setback with Keith. I wondered if Kayla wouldn't weigh in on my issues with him, since I failed to go there with Cedric.

"I don't want to go there with you, Trina, but what are best friends for, if we can't be honest with each other and speak our mind? So, here it goes. Keith is a very nice man. I'd hate for you to lose him, and maybe, just maybe, you were confused about the condoms. Did you look at the expiration date? They could have been in there for a while. Maybe he forgot about them."

"If he had forgotten about them, he should have said so. And then to kick me out like that and not call me, you know that was foul."

"It was, but some men don't like to argue. He doesn't come off as the arguing type, and look at all of the wonderful things about him. Personally, I think you should call him. It was a petty disagreement that should have never gone this far."

"Evelyn said that I should kick him to the curb. She thinks that he's been lying to me, and to be honest, I'm not so sure about him and his ex. He had some deep feeling for her. I don't think he's quite over her yet."

"Well, Evelyn said that Cedric has the biggest penis ever and she lied. She said that he was in love with her, and she lied about that too. I wouldn't take any advice from Evelyn. As for Keith's ex, what would make you think he's not over her?"

I bit into a honey-glazed chicken wing and shrugged. "I'm not sure. I just know that he really cared a lot about her."

"So, in other words, you're fishing. Trying to find anything that you can to justify why you're acting this way toward him. All I can say, Trina, is that if you love him, and I know you do, don't let him get away. In my heart, I seriously feel as if he is the one for you. There is something about him that is intriguing to me. Don't blow it by listening to Evelyn. Her advice isn't worth two cents."

I kept trying to talk myself out of calling Keith or going to see him, but Kayla insisted that I do something fast. I took her advice, and after we ended our long conversation over dinner, she went her way and I went mine. We made plans to get together again, over the weekend.

Since Keith's house was only fifteen minutes away, I drove to it. I started to call and let him know that I was coming over, but I decided against it. Instead, I made my way to the front door and rang the doorbell. Several lights were on inside, and I heard a bunch of laughter. I then saw Keith step out from the living room with a happy-go-lucky smile on his face. When he saw me, his face fell flat. He opened the door, and that was when I could hear several people talking and music playing.

"I guess I came at a bad time," I said. "Maybe I should've called."

"It would have been nice, but since you're here, feel free to come in."

Since he'd said it like that, I started not to. But just to be nosy, I stepped inside and followed him into the living room. To my surprise, Bryson was there, two other friends of Keith, Jerry and Lance, and Evelyn. She sat close to Bryson with a drink in her hand. It looked as if they were playing cards, and according to Lance, they had a good game going.

"Why don't you join us?" Lance said to me. "Your man needs all the help he can get."

"Tell me about it," Evelyn said, laughing. "And hello, my dear friend. Had I known you were coming over, we could have ridden together."

Seriously? I couldn't believe this trick. Now, I had spoken to Evelyn several times this week and earlier today. Not once did she mention that she was coming over here, or that she and Bryson had hooked up. It was apparent that they had; otherwise, she wouldn't have been damn near sitting on his lap. It also pissed me off that Keith hadn't said anything to me about her coming over here either. I knew they didn't expect me to just grab a seat and pretend that everything was cool. I wasn't sure who was going to catch hell first. Then again, yes, I was.

"Evelyn, can I speak to you for a minute in the kitchen?"

She uncrossed her legs and rubbed her finger along the side of Bryson's face. "I'll be right back," she said. "Don't let them win, please. If you do, I'm going to cancel those plans we talked about earlier."

The men laughed and all eyes were on Evelyn as she paraded away in her mini-dress, which barely covered her ass. All eyes except for Keith's, who looked in another direction—only because I was there. I stormed into the kitchen with Evelyn in tow. As soon as we entered, I swung around and let her have it.

"Just what in the hell do you think you're doing?" I asked.

As expected, she played clueless. "Wha . . . what do you mean? I'm playing cards. That's what I'm doing."

"Playing cards inside of my man's house without telling me that you were coming over here? How many times have you been here without me knowing it?"

Evelyn rolled her eyes and caught an attitude with me. "Several times, but does it matter? I don't have to tell you everywhere I go. Like, where do they do that at? Stop being so freaking jealous and calm the hell down."

"Jealous? Uh, no. And hell yes, it matters, because I don't appreciate you being here while I'm not. This is real tacky on your part, Evelyn, and it makes no sense for you to keep running over here, even if it is to meet up with Bryson. He has a place and so do you."

"Yeah, we do, but Keith has the best place of all. You know that for yourself. That's why you're always over here. But I guess you're going to knock his brother for wanting to be over here too. How ridiculous is that?"

"Not ridiculous at all, especially when I smell a motive."

"Yeah, well, I smell something too, but it's not coming from me. It's a bunch of bullshit, coming from you. As a reminder, you were the one who called it quits with Keith. I happen to be trying to make a connection with Bryson, and he is the one who decided to come over here. I'm sorry if my little visit has rubbed you the wrong way, but for the last time, get a grip, please."

I wanted to punch Evelyn in her mouth, so she'd never be able to speak again. We continued to go at it, and as we got louder, Keith came into the kitchen.

"What's going on in here?" he asked with a twisted face.

Evelyn threw her hands up in the air. "Honestly, I do not know. Your ex-girlfriend is acting like she going through menopause. Otherwise, I can't explain this bizarre behavior of hers."

"You know damn well what my problem is, so don't stand there and play innocent. Like I said, I don't appreciate you being over here, and the fact that you don't even have any panties on concerns me."

Evelyn's mouth grew wide. "Whether I have on panties or not, that shouldn't concern you at all. You act like you want a piece of my pussy for yourself, but unfortunately, I have it reserved for Bryson. Now, if you don't mind, I'd like to get back to the card game. That's unless Keith prefers that I leave, and he hasn't said anything of that nature to me yet."

Evelyn looked at Keith and so did I. But before I gave him a chance to respond, I had to reply to Evelyn's comment. "Tramp, I wouldn't dare tamper with a pussy as used up as yours. Bryson can have it. I'm sure it won't be long before he throws it back into the water and searches for something more refreshing." I turned to Keith. "With that being said, we need some privacy tonight. Do you mind asking everyone to leave?"

Unfortunately, Keith wasn't having it. He moved his head from side to side. "If you want privacy, we can go upstairs. I'm not asking my guests to leave, and I would like for you to take your tone down a notch and stop all this cussing."

A smirk washed across Evelyn's face. She turned around and marched her prissy ass out of the kitchen. My feelings were bruised, and my anger was now directed toward Keith.

"I am shocked. I seriously thought you cared about me. Obviously not."

"Trina, stop being so difficult. If you have something on your mind, let's go upstairs and discuss whatever it is. I'm not going to stand here and discuss my business in front of everyone. Nor am I going to ask my brother and my friends to leave because you decided to show up without calling. For some reason, your insecurities are taking over, and you have no reason, whatsoever, to feel insecure around me."

I lifted my finger and pointed it near his face. "This has nothing to do with me being insecure. I have my reasons for not wanting my friends in your house, but . . . never mind." I moved around Keith and headed toward the kitchen's doorway. He reached for my arm to stop me.

"Calm down, all right? You have got to stop all of this madness. Please tell me what has got you so on edge like this."

I didn't respond, so Keith took my hand. He led the way, and as we walked past the living room, I saw Evelyn sitting close to Bryson again. She sipped from the glass of wine and laughed as if she was having the best time ever.

"You are a cheater," Bryson said to her. "I don't play with women who cheat."

That hookah was way more than that. If he only knew how she really was.

Keith and I went all the way up the stairs to his studio. I guess he didn't want anyone to hear me yelling or cussing him out. I hadn't intended on going there, until I sat on the couch and saw a sketch that was on his workstation. He tried to snatch it up, but his hands weren't quicker than my eyes.

"Please tell me that I didn't just see what I think I saw."

"What did you see?"

Why in the hell did he opt to go there? See, these were the kinds of games that I didn't have time for. He knew damn well what I was talking about. To stand there and try to play clueless infuriated me even more. I tried to snatch the sketchpad from his hand, but he held it up high so I wouldn't get it.

"Listen," he said as I stood in front of him. "I forgot all about this. The last thing I need is for you to get the wrong idea. This sketch is totally innocent, and I drew it spur of the moment."

I held out my hand. "Let me see it."

Keith sighed and gave the sketch to me. As I suspected, it was a sketch of Evelyn. I swallowed the lump in my throat and tossed the sketch on the couch.

"Do you care to tell me when you did that? Or did it happen during one of her several visits over here?"

Keith had a look on his face as if this was going to be difficult for him to explain. He massaged his hands together, shifted his eyes to the doorway, sighed, and then responded, "She stopped by to get Bryson's phone number. That's when I did the sketch."

"How does a person who stops by to get a phone number, wind up sitting on the couch in your studio with her legs crossed, and getting sketched?"

"I invited her to come upstairs to see my artwork."

"What else did you invite her to see? I mean, why not your bedroom?"

"Trina, stop it. It wasn't even like that."

"How do I know it wasn't? All of a sudden, she's showing up at your house, being all chummy and shit with you and your friends. Then I find out that she's been on the same couch that you done screwed me on time and time again. Not to mention that her phone number is on the sketch, too, Keith. This ain't looking too good, and I honestly don't trust you or her."

"If you truly believe that I've been having sex with your friend, then there is no reason for this conversation to continue. It's bad enough that you don't even trust me anymore, but to suggest that I'm fucking your friend is pretty low."

"Before you say anything else, all I ask is that you flip the script. Put yourself in my shoes. You walk into your friend's house and see a sketched picture of me on his table. Not once has he mentioned that I visited him before, but he took it upon himself to sketch a picture of me. How would you feel?"

"Honestly?"

"I wouldn't accept your response any other way."

"Honestly, I wouldn't be mad. If he's considered my friend, I would trust him. Just like I would trust that you wouldn't go there with him. I would think that he drew the picture for me, or something like that."

I was blunt. "Bullshit, Keith, and you know it. The question is, why did you sketch the picture anyway? I truly don't get it."

To me, he looked to be fishing for an answer. Whatever his explanation was, I wasn't buying it. "I sketched it for Bryson. I was going to play a joke on him by sending him the picture, since he said he couldn't resist her."

My eye twitched as I stared at Keith. "Apparently, you couldn't resist her. That was a bunch of crap you just said, but it doesn't even matter anymore. I'm out of here. I truly regret coming here to mend things with you."

I walked out, and as I had expected, Keith didn't come after me. I was pissed, too, and I couldn't wait to call Kayla to tell her just how wrong her advice was.

Chapter 9

Evelyn

Bryson and I had been seeing a lot of each other. Keith had given him my number, and I received a phone call later that day. We met up and clicked instantly, had a wonderful dinner at Outback Steakhouse; and then we went downtown to walk around. We talked about everything from his fiancée, who he wasn't really feeling, to his career that he loved very much. He and Keith were very close, and their parents, as well as their grandparents who had died and left Keith that house, were wealthy people.

Needless to say, I felt like I'd hit the jackpot. I explained my unfortunate financial situation to Bryson, and I told him how difficult it had been for me to find a job. Almost immediately thereafter, he got on the phone and made some phone calls. He set up an interview for me at the construction company he worked for. An administrative assistant position was open, and it paid $40,000 a year. That wasn't enough money to get overly hyped about, but I couldn't turn down the job right now. Plus, I had an opportunity to work close with Bryson. As the construction manager, he spent some of his time in the office, too. I was pleased about that. It would allow me the opportunity to keep my eyes on him.

Later that day, I drove to Bryson's condo for a quick dinner. I wanted to thank him for helping to get me a job, and he also loaned me $1,000 to assist with my rent. My landlord was happy to receive it. I told him I'd be starting a new job, so he backed off, knowing that I might be able to pay my rent on time.

Bryson popped a bottle of champagne and plopped down on the couch. He put the bottle up to his lips and guzzled down the champagne like it was water. When he finished, he slammed the bottle on the table and belched.

"Ahhh, you didn't want any of that, did you?" he said in a playful manner.

I moved closer to him on the sectional couch and threw my leg over his. I wiggled his tie loose and pulled it away from his neck.

"Champagne doesn't excite me as much as you do. And I prefer to have, or should I say give you a little something to show you how appreciative I am for the job and for the money you loaned me. I promise to pay it back, and I can't thank you enough."

Bryson smiled as I removed his tie and started to unbutton his crisp white shirt. We hadn't had sex yet, but there was surely a lot of sexting going on between us. I was eager to find out what he was working with.

"Evelyn, I have a feeling that you're going to get me in a whole lot of trouble. You're so damn sexy, and I'm looking forward to you serving me, every chance you get."

As I moved Bryson's shirt away from his chest and got a glimpse of his bulging muscles and tight abs, the pleasure would be all mine. There were no tattoos on his chest, like Keith's, and I had to admit that Bryson was a tad bit sexier. I maneuvered myself between his legs and got on my knees. While looking into his light brown eyes that were slightly slanted, I unlatched his leather belt. I pulled it away from his cut waistline and eased his zipper over the growing hump in his black slacks. Within seconds, his dick grew tall and escaped through the slit in his boxers. I touched the tip of it with my long fingernails then gripped it tight.

"Nice," I said. "And thick and juicy, just how I like it."

Bryson snickered and kept his eyes glued to me, awaiting my next move. That consisted of my mouth opening wide and covering his entire muscle. I saw his head drop back, and it wasn't long before his eyes closed. His hand touched the back of my head, and as I sucked him in to the back of my throat, he patted my neck and squeezed it.

"Mmmmm," he moaned and lifted himself just a little to stroke my mouth. It was moving pretty fast, along with my hands. My saliva covered every inch of him, and he was so far down my throat that I thought I'd choke. But sucking dick was my specialty. I knew how to make a man's eyes roll to the back of his head. I perfected how to make his toes curl, and it wouldn't take long for his semen to shoot up like fireworks. Bryson was no exception. Within two minutes, I felt his grip on my neck tighten. He also yanked my hair, and his thrusts into my mouth were now at a speedy pace.

"Suck that shit, baby. Swallow all of it and don't let one fucking drop go to waste."

My mouth swelled like a balloon as he released his juices inside of it. I didn't swallow all of it, but I licked some of the drippings from his pretty dick, which was now limp.

"Ahhhhh," Bryson moaned again. His six pack fluttered and sweat beads rested on his stomach. I licked around the minimal, smooth hair above his dick, and then sucked my fingers.

"Now that," I said, "was tasty."

Bryson sat up and leaned forward. He brought his lips to my glossy ones and our tongues danced for a while. During the intense kiss, he reached for my hand and placed it on his muscle. I felt it swelling, but it wasn't as hard as it was the first time.

"Stroke it," he said, backing away from my lips. "It'll get there."

"I'm sure it will, but I have a better idea."

I stood and unbuttoned the royal blue silk blouse that I wore. Within seconds, the blouse, my bra, and my tight skirt were in a pile next to me. All I stood in was a turquoise thong and my moisturized caramel skin glistened. Bryson's eyes scanned my plump breasts, which were sitting pretty. Then his eyes lowered to the tiny gap between my lips. My shaved slit was clearly visible, and it was inviting as well.

"You gon' make me hurt you, woman," he said. "Perfection. Pure perfection."

I couldn't have agreed with him more. He got up and laid me back on the couch. While bending over me, he reached for my panties and pulled them over my high-heeled shoes. He removed those as well, and tossed them over his shoulders. We both laughed, and before he did away with his slacks, he reached for a condom.

"You don't mind, do you?" he said, already putting it on. "I definitely don't want any children, and it's always good to be safe."

I agreed, but I damn sure wouldn't mind having his child. His wealthy parents would spoil the baby. I was sure I would somehow benefit too. Not to mention all that Bryson would probably do. But regardless, we went at it. He wrapped my legs around his back and positioned his dick at the crevasses of my hole. It wasn't long before he snaked his thickness inside of me, causing my pussy lips to spread wide. Probably wider than they had ever been before, because I could definitely feel his meat stretching my insides. I released one of my legs from his waist and poured it over his shoulder. I had to represent how flexible I was, so I pointed my leg out straight, as if I were doing a split. Bryson tackled my goodies down below, and with each perfectly planned thrust, my pussy juices ran over. His shaft was glazed from top to bottom. We both watched his insertions, and I was so hot and bothered that I began to massage my own clit. Bryson licked his lips to prevent saliva from dripping from his mouth. His eyes fluttered, his breathing increased and his soft moans let me know just how good my pussy felt to him. I reached around to grip his solid ass, and all I felt was sweat. At the pace we were going, things were starting to get heated. Our naked, wet bodies slapped together, and as he sucked the shit out of my breasts, a high arch formed in my back.

"Brrrryson," I cried out near tears. "I . . . My pussy would like to thank you for all of this. It feels guuuud, damn, you're making us feel sooooo guuud."

Bryson didn't have a comeback, but his actions let me know that he felt the same way. He eased out of me, and as a flood of my juices ran onto the couch, all he could do was shake his head. He sat up straight and positioned me to stand in front of him with my back to him. I did so with straddled legs. Cum trickled down between my thighs, while Bryson massaged them. He also massaged my ass then he held my waist and motioned for me to squat. His dick stood straight up, ready to aim and shoot.

"Ease down on it," he said. "And I won't complain if you drive me into overtime."

He must've known how I operated. I definitely drove us into overtime by riding him backward. I then got on my hands and knees on the floor, and allowed Bryson to have anal sex with me. An hour and a half in, we were spent. We passed out on the carpeted floor, and I wasn't sure who had more carpet burns, him or me.

I was still knocked out. Bryson was too, until we heard hard knocks on his door. My leg was thrown over his and the smell of sex infused the air. I was so sticky between my legs. A shower was definitely what I needed, but it didn't appear that I was going to get it anytime soon.

"Damn," Bryson said, getting off the floor. We both looked at the clock; it showed two thirty-five in the morning. The hard knocks continued, so Bryson turned to me.

"Do you mind going into my bedroom?" he asked. "I have a feeling that I know who this is."

"No problem." I got off the floor and moved into his bedroom. The king bed was neatly made and the soft comforter felt soothing against my naked body. I started to go by the door to listen in, but I could already hear the voice of a woman speaking.

"All day, Bryson," she said. "I've been trying to reach you all day."

"I had every intention of calling you back, but I got tied up. And I told you before about showing up like this. We agreed to go our separate ways for a while, and with you showing up like this, it doesn't help."

"It doesn't help you, because you're always up to no good. We will never be able to fix our relationship if you refuse to answer your phone so we can talk about it. And while we agreed to go our separate ways for a while, that didn't mean we were supposed to stop communicating, did it?"

I rolled my eyes at this stupid heifer. I mean, how many women had to beg and plead with a man to get his shit right? Bryson's ass didn't need space. What he needed was more excitement in his life and some more pussy. I had a thing for men like him, but, at least, I knew from the beginning what I was dealing with. And while the dick was always beneficial to me, it had to come attached with money. Good dick without money wasn't worth my time.

As expected, the tears came into play. I could hear the woman crying about how Bryson had been so mean and disrespectful to her.

"You haven't done anything for me. You played me. I saw you with her . . ."

The ranting went on and on about why he didn't do this or that, and he didn't seem to care anymore. If so, then why in the hell was she standing in his condo at almost three o'clock in the morning, eager to repair their relationship? I just didn't get it, and I despised women who were too stupid to realize that most men didn't give a damn about those tears.

"What else can I do?" she cried. "You say that you love me, and that we're going to get married. But when, Bryson? Please tell me when."

"N-e-v-e-r," I said in a whisper. According to Bryson, they'd been engaged for four years. If it hadn't happened by now, didn't she know she was wasting her time? I wanted to scream at the top of my lungs, but I didn't have to. I heard some tussling going on, and a few seconds later, the woman came busting into the room. I was surprised to see that she was white.

Her teary eyes fluttered as she saw me sitting on the bed with no clothes on. She looked as if she wanted to pass out. She covered her mouth, as if this was really a surprise to her. By how calm Bryson was, I could tell this wasn't the first time he'd been busted. He held her shoulders, massaging them, as she sobbed and appeared to weaken.

"Libby, go home," he said in a smooth, calm tone. "We'll talk about this tomorrow, okay? Don't do this to yourself *again*."

Libby choked up even more. The look in my eyes dared her to say anything smart to me. If she did, she would catch hell. She doubled over and held her stomach.

"Why?" she cried out. "Why do you keep doing this to meeeee?"

Was she asking me why? If so, her answer was simple. Because her dumb ass let him. I had no sympathy for her, but apparently, Bryson did. He eased his arms around her waist to hold her up. He continued to smooth talk his way out of this.

"Come on, Libby. Calm down, baby, and get yourself together. You don't have to do this. You know who I love. All I wanted to do was have a little fun, since we were separated. You know it wouldn't go down like this, if we were together."

"But you can have all the fun you want to with meeee. Why her, Bryson, why her?"

What did she mean by why her? Did she have to ask? I mean, look at me. All she had to do was look at how gorgeous I was. Damn.

Bryson continued to hold her by the waist. He escorted her into the bathroom so she could get herself together. On their way there, he looked over Libby's shoulder and shrugged. Behind the concerned expression on his face was also a smirk.

Some men got a kick out of this shit; it made them feel special. There was no question in my mind that Bryson was one of those men. It would be a cold day in hell if he ever got me to react this way.

While in the bathroom, he washed Libby's face and patted it with a towel. He insisted that she stay calm, and then he asked her, again, to go home.

"I'll call you first thing in the morning. We'll have breakfast, and how about I make you some of those favorite blueberry pancakes you like?"

She sniffled and slowly nodded. I swear I wanted to get off the bed and go knock some sense into her. I don't believe that God intended for some women to be this damn stupid. This chick was worse than Kayla, and I didn't believe it got any worse than her. Black dick had the minds of many all fucked up.

Bryson held on tight to Libby as he escorted her toward the door. She gave me a quick roll of her eyes, but didn't say one word to me. I comfortably sat back on the bed with my hands behind me, my breasts poked out and my legs crossed. Minutes later, I heard the front door shut, and Bryson rushed back into the bedroom.

"I am so sorry about that. That shit caught me off guard. I thought that she and I had an understanding."

"No problem. Handle your business, baby. As long as it doesn't interfere with what we have going on, I'm good."

He crawled on the bed and held himself up over me. "I'll tell you who has got it going on. You do. The way you're looking on my bed, all sexy and shit like this, makes me want to eat you alive."

"You may not be able to do that, especially since you have to get up in a few hours to make those blueberry pancakes. I don't like to be rushed, and I assume that I'll be asked to leave soon."

"Nope. As a matter of fact, I can make you some of those pancakes too. They're delicious, and for some reason, Libby can't seem to get enough of them."

Arrogant motherfucker, I thought. He was nothing like Keith was, but I had to settle. "Scrap the pancakes," I said. "Not interested. But I am interesting in seeing how well you can eat me alive."

"I can show you better than I can tell you."

Bryson parted my legs and buried his face between them. His eating skills were decent, but he damn sure was no Cedric. I closed my eyes and pretended, just for a few minutes, that he was. Then I went into a daze, thinking about how much fun Cedric and I used to have during sex. More so, how creative we were, even while Kayla was in the same vicinity as we were.

The more I thought about things I realized I'd have to go see about Cedric real soon, because men like Bryson just wasn't going to cut it. If I was going to involve myself with a real player, why not shoot for the best, or should I say, shoot for the player with the most money and the best sex? Compared to Cedric, Bryson was an amateur. I intended to toy with him for a little while longer, but his time would be up sooner than I originally thought.

Chapter 10

Kayla

After days and days of pondering, hours of lost sleep, going back and forth about my marriage, I'd finally made my decision. I was excited about it, too, and the first person that I needed to speak to was Cedric. We had a lot to discuss, so therefore, I made my way to his place.

Jacoby was at school. He and I had a long talk about how much he'd been skipping and his late nights with Adrianne. He admitted everything to me, and his excuse was him being affected, a little, by all that had been going on. He said that Adrianne had truly been there for him, and that he felt so much love when she was around. As for school, he said his work had suffered because he couldn't think straight. I understood everything he'd said, but I told him it was time for him to get back on track.

The same applied to me and Cedric. That was why I was at his front door. It was time to do this. I made sure Cynthia was out of the house, and when I entered, I went upstairs to find Cedric.

He wasn't in bed where he normally was, and when I checked the kitchen, family room, and his office, he wasn't there either. That was when I went to the lower level and saw him in the workout room, slowly jogging on the treadmill. He appeared to be getting himself back in shape, and I had to admit that he looked dynamite in his tan shorts. He didn't have on a shirt, and plenty of muscles bulged from his shoulders and toned calves. His beard was still a little scruffy, but his fade was intact. Every time I watched Scandal and would see Columbus Short, he always reminded me of my husband. Loud music played and Cedric looked up at the flat-screen TV mounted on the wall, as if he could hear it. I walked in and turned the music down.

"Good morning," I said then sat on a weight bench. "I see you must be feeling better."

"Much better."

He slowed down the treadmill then got off of it. He used a fluffy towel to wipe his face then stood in front of me. Sweat dripped from his body and the shorts hung low on his waist.

I could see the bullet wound on his chest, and all I could think about was how lucky he was to be alive. I reached out to touch the wound. "Does it hurt?" I asked.

"It's still a little tender right there, but not really. I've been taking good care of myself since then. Been eating right, exercising, and playing with my dick to keep it alive and active too." Cedric winked and laughed.

I rolled my eyes and shook my head. "That's too much information, but I'm glad you're feeling better. Looking much better, too."

He nodded and looked me up and down. I had on a simple pair of tight jeans and a button-down shirt that matched my yellow earrings. My hair had been trimmed, nails had been done, and my sandals showed my perfect pedicure.

"So do you," Cedric complimented. "And just so you know, I do love your hair like that."

"Thanks." I moved away from him and rubbed my hands together. I was a little nervous, but I assumed that he knew what I was there to discuss.

"Would you like to go upstairs to my office?" he suggested. "That way, you can sit on the couch and relax."

I nodded. "Yes. That sounds perfect."

I made my way up the stairs with Cedric following me.

"At least I know *that's* still in working order," he said.

When we reached the top stair, I turned with confusion on my face. "What did you say? I'm not sure wha—"

"I was talking about my manhood. It had a reaction when you were walking in front of me."

I moved out of the way and gestured for Cedric to go in front of me. "That's good to know. Maybe I'll have some kind of reaction too, walking behind you."

We laughed and made our way to his office. I sat on the couch, while Cedric stood with his backside against the desk and his arms folded.

"So, what's the verdict? Don't give me a long spiel either. All I need for you to do is hit me with your news and so be it."

"I don't know if I can sum this up as quickly as you may want me to, but the first thing I think you should know is that Evelyn had an abortion. She thought that you were dead, and since she couldn't provide for the baby, she terminated the pregnancy. I wasn't sure if you knew that."

Cedric didn't flinch. "No, I didn't know, but thanks for sharing. I'll toast later, but for now, I want to discuss you and me. What's the deal?"

"Cutting to the chase, the deal is, I want to proceed with the divorce."

This time, Cedric flinched. He cocked his neck from side to side, and I saw him take a hard swallow.

"That's your final decision?"

"Yes, it is. I just don't see how we can ever get this to work out, and I do believe that this is one of those cases where there has been too much damage done."

"I agree, but whatever happened to for better or worse? We had our worse, Kayla, and we had to kind of go through some things in order to get to this point. Now, don't get me wrong. I respect your decision, but I'm trying to get you to see that many things, a lot of things, have changed."

"I think they have, Cedric, but I don't believe that those changes will be enough for me. So, I'll just take my measly, little, tiny twenty percent and go on my merry way."

Cedric chuckled and rubbed his brow. "I figured you'd go there with that twenty percent. But, remember, if you stay, you can have waaay more than that."

"If I stay, that may be true. But then I'd have to deal with your late hours again, concern myself with who you're with, check your bank accounts, go through your pockets, hire private detectives, just to make sure you're staying on the up-and-up. I don't want to live my life like that anymore. It's time for me to be happy and live peacefully. I deserve that."

"You absolutely do, so I can't argue with you on that."

Cedric walked around his desk and sat in the chair. He typed on his keyboard, and seconds later, his printer sounded off. He removed the piece of paper and laid it flat on his desk. Whatever it was he signed it, and then brought the paper over to me. It was the last page of the dissolution of marriage agreement I had read time and time again.

"The signature you provided before wasn't acceptable because you were under the influence of alcohol. If you say what you mean, your signature is needed."

I took the paper from his hand and held it. "First of all, I'ma need you to change that twenty percent to at least forty percent, print off the whole agreement, and give me a signed copy, and then get a notary in here to notarize it, until our attorneys can confirm."

Cedric cracked up and walked back over to his desk. "I can't get you a notary right now, and there will be no problem with our attorneys confirming this. Also, I will be happy to give you a signed copy, but unfortunately, the twenty percent stands because you're the one abandoning me."

I stood and went over to his desk. "For a very good reason, I may add, so let's crank that amount up to, at least, thirty-eight percent for my troubles."

"Twenty-two."

"Thirty-six."

"Twenty-five."

"Thirty-three."

"Thirty and that's my final offer."

I sighed and released a tiny smile. "Thirty will do, and anything is better than twenty."

"Sixty-nine then. Over there, on the couch with you on top."

"No, thanks. And why are you being so nasty today? We're supposed to be down in the dumps today, sad and disappointed that we're ending this. You seem just as happy as I am."

Cedric looked at me with a blank expression. "Happy, I'm not, but I'm trying to make the best of this situation. I hope you are too."

"More than you know."

Cedric printed two copies of the document and we both signed it. "There you go, Miss Lady," he said. "After one lump-sum payment, I can finally be rid of you and have you out of my hair."

"I doubt that because we still have a son to raise. You know he's been getting away with murder in my absence, and I think we're going to have to put our feet down."

"I've seen his sneaky self in action. But let him go ahead and do what teenagers do. Eventually, he'll learn some valuable lessons that will either lift him up, or bring him down."

"Yeah, that's what I'm afraid of. Now come here."

Cedric stood next to me and I put my face next to his. I held up the agreement and told him to smile while I used my cell phone to take a selfie of us.

"You're crazy," he said with a fake frown. I was all smiles when I snapped the picture.

"I may need to send this picture to someone. Thanks."

Cedric moved away from me, but we stayed in his office, talking for about another hour. He agreed to wire the lump-sum payment into my account by tomorrow, but said that he needed to go directly to the bank in order to transfer that kind of money. We also talked about living arrangements. His intentions were to put the house up for sale and move into a smaller place. I was planning to get me a place as well. Jacoby was left to decide who he wanted to live with, and Cedric and I were fine with that. The truth was, I hadn't felt this good in a long time. I was glad that we'd gotten closure. Now I could focus on my own life. Holding on for so long had only crippled me.

I made my way to the front door so I could leave. Cedric was behind me. "I guess I'll see you whenever," he said.

I turned and gave him a tight hug. He rubbed my back and I rubbed his. I felt his hardness, but backed away from him.

"Now, who would've thought that my ex-wife was capable of doing this to me?" He looked down at his rising shorts. "All I can say is, baby, you're bad in every way possible. Why don't we seal the deal by indulging in some of that wild sex we used to have when we were mad at each other? You were always at your best when you were mad at me, and I would be thinking about that shit for days and weeks after."

I couldn't help but to laugh at Cedric's attempt to have sex with me. "Sex or no sex, the deal is sealed. And I'm not really mad at you now, so having sex would be a waste of time. So, good-bye, Cedric. I'm sure we'll be speaking soon. Please don't forget about the money tomorrow because I really need it. If you need me to take you to the bank, let me know."

I reached for the doorknob and Cedric smacked me on my ass; squeezed it too, and had the nerve to honk. I made my exit and closed the door behind me. But when I got into the car, I sat for a while thinking. I looked at the bay windows, manicured lawn, and two-story brick house that was one of the best looking houses on the block. Cedric had taken good care of me, no doubt. It was kind of painful to leave here for good, knowing that I would never officially stay in the house again. With that in mind, I wanted to leave my mark. I marched toward the front door and opened it. Went inside and made my way up the stairs where I could hear water running. Right at the bedroom's doorway, I removed all of my clothes and then swished toward the bathroom where Cedric stood naked, waiting for the tub to fill. His eyes shifted to me in the doorway, and a wide smile washed across his face.

"I guess this ain't really over, until it's over," he said.

"Oh, it's over, trust me. I just had an urge to seal the deal, like you suggested."

I walked into the bathroom and threw my arms around Cedric's shoulders. With our bodies pressed together, both of our hands roamed. Cedric touched my curvy backside, and I had my hand on his heavy, hard meat. Just as I was about to direct it inside of me, he stopped me.

"You'd better not tell your girlfriends about this. If so, they would think you're out of your mind."

"What I do with my life is my business. I don't owe anybody an explanation; after all, no one has walked in my shoes. If I want to screw my ex-husband's brains out, I will."

"Then g'on with your bad self. And you're right. To hell with them all. We got this."

I wasn't sure about the "we" thing, but I surely did have it. Got all of it and then some. And right after we finished having sex, I thanked Cedric for the good loving and made my exit with my divorce papers in hand.

This time when I got in the car, I drove off. I reached for my cell phone to call Trina and share the good news. She didn't seem as upbeat as she did the last time.

"Okay, what's going on?" I asked, feeling a little frustrated. Just once, one time, I wanted to talk to somebody who didn't have a lot of drama going on.

"If I told you, you wouldn't believe me. All I can say is I shouldn't have ever stopped by Keith's house that night. Then again, I'm glad I did because I discovered that your friend has been making her rounds."

My brows arched inward. "What friend? I don't have many, so who are you talking about?"

"Evelyn. Do you know she was at Keith's house when I got there?"

I had to slam on the brakes. "Are you kidding me?"

"No, I'm not. She's supposed to be seeing Keith's brother, but I found a picture that Keith sketched of her while she was sitting on the couch in his studio. He pretended that it wasn't a big deal, but Evelyn made it clear that she had been there, several times, when I wasn't. Keith thinks I'm overreacting, but you already know how Evelyn is."

"Yes, I do. And I'm surprised at Keith. I don't know what to say about Evelyn, but the two of us need to do something to put that chick in her place. I don't understand why you continue to be her friend. I am soooo done with her. That hooker can't say anything to me right about now."

"I question why I keep fooling with her too, but this last incident took the cake. She called and tried to apologize for upsetting me, but she wouldn't admit to doing the wrong thing. Said there was no harm in her going over there. When I inquired about the sketch, she said she didn't know Keith was doing it, until he was finished. She also said that he made some advances toward her. I'm so upset right now that I don't even want to bring any of this shit to his attention."

"I think you should. At least give him a chance to explain himself. Evelyn lies so much, Trina. You can't believe everything she says."

"I agree, but it's his reaction that has me more bothered than anything. He hasn't called, he hasn't apologized, nothing. I'm not going to reach out to him again, so it's whatever. Now, enough about my drama. What's going on with you? Did you make a decision yet?"

I shared with Trina everything that had gone down with me and Cedric, including the sex. She barked through the phone and laughed at my actions.

"You are so trifling, but good for you. You're sounding much better, and I think this calls for a celebration. Let's go somewhere this weekend and get our party on. Have a few drinks and just let it all hang out! We need some more fun in our lives."

"I couldn't agree with you more. Sounds like a plan to me! You name the place and I will be there!"

Trina said she would call me on Friday to let me know our destination. I was excited about hanging with my BFF, and I couldn't wait until the weekend. And before I forgot, I looked at the selfie I'd taken with Cedric. I typed in a number and sent it right over to Evelyn so she could see it. I was sure she would be just as happy as I was about the divorce.

Chapter 11

Trina

I hadn't been clubbing in a long time. The last time I got all dolled up like this was probably at a funeral. I wasn't sure what to wear, but I opted for a pair of stretch jean leggings, a navy cropped jacket, and a white tank. I could barely walk in the high-heeled pumps I had on, but they made my whole fit look sexier. My layered hair was swooped a bit to the left, and I accessorized with red and silver jewelry. I never liked to wear a lot of makeup, so all I did was gloss my lips and spread my lashes with mascara. My brows were already arched, and after several dashes of sweet perfume, I was ready to go.

I told Kayla that I would meet her at a jazz/R&B joint that was on Washington Avenue. Some of the other artists at the studio mentioned the place, but I hadn't ever been there before. To my surprise, it was nice. The crowd was thirty and older, and the loud music spilling through the speakers had many of people there up on their feet. I couldn't really see, but the spinning white lights from up above gave off some light. The club was decorated with purple, black, yellow, and silver. I always appreciated a colorful atmosphere, and the many colorful paintings on the wall impressed me. So did the humungous dance floor, where people from all races were dancing.

Kayla was supposed to be there at nine, but I didn't see her yet. That was until I looked over at a booth and spotted her sitting next to a white man who was all smiles. She saw me and waved her hand. I walked over to the table and the man sitting next to her stood up.

"You must be Kayla's friend, Trina," he said, yelling over the loud music.

"Yes, I am. And you are?"

"Chris. I saw Kayla when she came through the door and was like, wow. She damn near knocked me off my feet."

Kayla was all smiles. I was too, especially since Chris wasn't all that bad looking. Unfortunately, though, I knew my friend all too well. She wanted black dick, and would never settle for anything less.

"Now that Trina is here," Chris said to Kayla, "would you like to dance?"

"Sure." Kayla scooted out of the booth and made her way to the dance floor with Chris.

I eased into the booth and looked around at the drinks on the table. I could tell Kayla and Chris had been getting it in. She must've gotten here earlier than I'd thought. There was also a bottle of wine on the table, sitting in an ice bucket. I took it upon myself to pour some. Minutes later, an older black man with a slanted, mack-daddy hat on eased into the booth with me.

"I bet you a hundred dollars that you're going to turn me down," he said then sucked his teeth. "If so, please give me a Band-Aid, because I just scraped my knee from falling head over heels for you."

How weak was that? I thought. *Really?* But I had to admit, it was funny. "No, I don't have a Band-Aid nor do I have a hundred dollars. But I assure you that I'm like a Rubik's Cube: The more you play with me, the harder I get."

The nice-looking older man slapped his leg and laughed. "I figured you had a good sense of humor. And something told me to come over here and offer to buy you a drink."

I looked at the drinks on the table. "You know what, I'm good. But maybe if you stop by later, we can dance or something. By the way, what's your name again?"

"Chance. If you take a chance on me, you just may get real lucky."

I winked at him. "Okay, I got it. And thanks again for the sideshow. It's been real."

Chance said he would be back later to dance. As soon as he walked away, I looked for Kayla and Chris on the dance floor. Needless to say, it was hilarious. Kayla was a great dancer, but

Chris was all over the place. He was doing some mess that James Brown would do. Had his jacket pulled back and was moving his feet so fast that he was about to trip. I cracked up, and you best believe that after one dance, Kayla called it quits. I saw her say something to him, and then she headed back to the table alone.

Dressed in a white, wide-legged jumpsuit, Kayla eased into the booth with me. She was such a classy chick. I couldn't touch her style if I tried.

"What was that all about?" I asked.

"What? What do you mean?"

"I'm talking about the way he was dancing. Girl, he was all over the place."

"Yeah, he was. But he is . . . nice."

"Maybe so, but not nice enough for you to date, right?"

Kayla sipped from the glass in front of her then shrugged. "I might. Not sure yet."

I pursed my lips. "Don't even try to sell that mess to me. You know good and doggone well that a white man could never get it."

Kayla laughed and placed her finger over her lips. "Shhh, don't tell nobody. You already know that I love the brothas."

"Yes, I do."

We sat for a long while, enjoying each other's company, laughing and drinking. I danced, Kayla danced, and then we sang "Happy Birthday" with the people next to us who were there celebrating. I was tipsy as ever, and as the night went on, I was very flirtatious. I had just finished dancing with Chance, before plopping down in the booth and picking up another drink.

Kayla had a glassy film covering her eyes. She looked at me with a straw close to her lips. "I think you'd better slow it down," she whispered. "Somebody here is keeping a very close eye on you."

Regardless of who it was, I sipped from the glass of Patrón and whispered back at Kayla. "Who?"

"I'm not saying. If you look around, maybe you will see him."

I narrowed my eyes and scanned the room. Didn't see anyone I knew, nor did I notice anyone paying attention to me. "I repeat, who?"

"Look over by the bar. At the very end, there are three men standing together. One is a dark chocolate, and he is a sight for drunken eyes. He's rocking jeans, a V-neck shirt that's hugging those muscles and showing those colorful tattoos. I swear you'd better straighten up and get to him, before some of these other chicks do. Trust me when I say they're on it!"

I snapped my head to look over at the bar and squinted. Sure enough, there was Keith, Bryson, and one of his other friends. I hurried to duck in the booth.

"Damn," I said, pounding my leg. "I need to get out of here. Doooo, do not want him to see me. I wonder what he's doing here anyway."

Kayla leaned in closer to me. "Don't be mad at me, but see, you have a best friend who tends to poke her nose where it doesn't belong sometimes. I kind of reached out to him earlier and told him that we'd be here. I kind of felt like—"

I pulled my head back and held up one finger. "Uh, no. We don't go there, Miss Thing, and you were sooooo wrong for that. I could cuss you out right now for interfering, but I do not want to embarrass the hell out of us right now."

"Well, if you're going to do it, hurry up because we're about to have some visitors."

My eyes shot up, and Keith, Bryson, and their friend were heading our way. He looked so spectacular that my pussy started to get overly excited before I did. I crossed my legs and turned my head, just so I didn't have to look at him.

"Hello, ladies," Bryson said to both of us. "Y'all got a lot of room in this booth. Mind if we squeeze in, especially since there aren't many open seats?"

"Of course," Kayla said, scooting closer to me.

Bryson moved in next to her and their friend sat next to him. Keith sat on my other side, but his back faced me. He sat with his elbows on his knees, watching the crowds of people dancing. I guess his intentions were to ignore me.

"Kayla, right?" Bryson said to her. "You were the one at the hospital, correct?"

"Yes, I was."

"I remember. I told my knucklehead brother over there to hook me up. I was disappointed to hear that you were married."

Kayla blushed. She was happy to reply, "Not anymore."

Bryson licked his lips and moved closer. I quickly spoke up. "Where's Evelyn, Bryson? I spoke to her the other day, and she mentioned that you'd just left her apartment."

He tried to fire back. "I don't keep tabs on Evelyn. The fact that I was at her apartment doesn't mean anything. I'm here right now, in the presence of a beautiful woman who excited me from the very first time that I saw her."

I kept my mouth shut and let Kayla handle Bryson. He was such a dog, and even though Keith had his issues, they were the total opposite.

"Evelyn?" Kayla said, pretending to be surprised. "You've been dating Evelyn?"

"Nah, I wouldn't exactly say that we're dating. Just chilling and conversing from time to time. Stuff like that; nothing real serious."

"Well, any man who enjoys her conversation definitely wouldn't appreciate mine. Personally, I think she's a tramp, and any penis that has ever been inside of her will never get inside of me."

Surprise, surprise. I didn't know my best friend could be so blunt. Bryson's eyes bugged, Keith turned around to look at Kayla, and the other dude halted his conversation with the chick in the booth beside us to turn around.

"Sorry," Kayla said. "Did I say something wrong?"

"Hell no," I said, snatching up the glass of alcohol in front of me. "I wouldn't let a fool who been up in that touch me either. And if I ever find out that we've shared the same man, it will be bad news for him."

"Ladies, let's not talk about Evelyn right now," Bryson said in a smooth tone. He was eager to change the subject, but Kayla wasn't buying it. Her experience with Cedric left her with a lot of knowledge. It was easy for her to see through the bullshit.

As they talked, I was anxious to move away from Keith.

"Excuse me," I said to him so he'd move.

He stood and eased his hands into his pockets. Before I could get out of the booth, a mixed-looking chick stepped up to him. "Would you like to dance?" she politely asked.

"Sure," he replied. "Why not?"

He walked away and so did I. I tried not to keep my eyes on
him, but I couldn't help it. I kept seeing him whisper in the
chick's ear and they also kept laughing. I also watched Kayla
and Bryson. They appeared to be indulged in an interesting
conversation. Both of them kept smiling too. I hoped like hell
that she didn't go there. That was definitely a bad move, but
I trusted that after her experience with Cedric, she wouldn't
give Bryson the time of day.

I went to the restroom to use it then staggered my way
through the crowd to take a seat at the bar. It was so hot that
my jacket was now sticking to my skin. I was very uncomfortable. I removed my jacket and placed it on the back of a chair.
I then ordered another drink, but a young man with dreads
sat down next to me, offering to pay for it.

"Don't bother," Keith said reaching over him to place his
money on the bar. "I got it."

The dude looked Keith up and down then glanced at me. I
didn't say anything, so he shrugged and walked away. Keith
sat in his seat.

"So, you're not going to say anything to me," he said. "The
least you could do is speak."

"I spoke while we were at the table. You didn't hear me
because your back was turned."

"If you spoke, I would have heard you and replied. But
whatever. How's everything going with you?"

"Great. Can't complain."

"Hmmm, wish I could say the same. I have a lot to complain
about, but I guess now isn't the place or time to do it."

"You're right, it's not. And the thing is, I don't care to listen.
Buy that bitch you were dancing with that drink. I'm going
home."

I grabbed my jacket from the chair and walked toward the
door. Before leaving, I saw that Kayla was still talking to
Bryson. I figured that when I got in the car, I would send her
a text to tell her why I had to leave. Being in Keith's presence
didn't sit right with me.

I pushed the doors open and left the club. Several people were standing outside smoking and talking. One dude
whistled at me, but I didn't bother to turn my head. I kept it

moving, until someone came up from behind and snatched my arm.

"Okay," Keith said, turning me around to face him. "If a fight is what you want, then you're going to get it. If you want for us to stand out here and embarrass our fucking selves, then that's what we'll do. Throw in a few curse words, attack each other, and then go home still mad. Shall I start this or do you want to?"

I waved him off and kept it moving. "Fuck you, Keith. I don't have time."

He rushed up from behind me again. "Well, that's a start. Fuck you too, and why in the hell were you in there allowing those men to buy you drinks, feel all on you on the dance floor, and pass their numbers to you? I see you haven't wasted no time moving on, and you don't have to tell me again how great your life has been since we parted."

I sped up the pace to get to my car. "Sounds like you're mad. Good. And it's about time you started to show some interest."

"So, through your eyes, I show interest by yelling, screaming, cussing, and acting a fool. You are confused, baby. So damn confused about how a relationship should really operate. Maybe you do need to hook up with one of those men in there. They can probably offer you what I can't: drama."

I tried to upset Keith by agreeing with him. "Maybe so. And I should have hooked up with somebody, because I don't have a man anymore. See, my man is too busy having open condoms in his medicine cabinet, sketching pictures of my friends and inviting them to come over whenever they wish. Personally, I think his dick has been inside of her, but that's just how I feel."

"Get the hell out of here with that mess. You're just saying that to fuck with me. You want to upset me, just so we can continue to create this scene out here and you can then bring more attention to yourself."

I stopped at my car and removed my keys from my purse. "This scene that you're causing is too weak for me, so I'm going home. If you want someone to listen to your lies, call Evelyn. She knows where you stay. I'm sure she'll be happy to stop by and keep you company."

I unlocked the door and opened it. Keith rushed up to me and slammed the door so hard that it rattled the glass. He grabbed my arms and pushed me against the hood of the car.

"You want a bigger scene," he said through gritted teeth and with much anger locked in his eyes. I thought he was going to strike me, but instead he unlatched his belt, unzipped his jeans, and dropped them to his ankles.

"I'll show your ass a bigger scene all right."

Keith snatched me by the front of my jeans and lifted me. Damn near slamming me on the hood, he yanked at my zipper and attempted to unzip my jeans. I tried to force him away from me by pushing his shoulders back. He was too strong.

"You keep on bringing up that bitch Evelyn's name, but I'll show you who the fuck I want! When I tell you, you don't listen, so I need to show yo' ass the motherfucker who really excites me! Stop fighting back and allow me this one opportunity to create a scene your heart desires! I'ma do it right here, and you better not say shit!"

Keith wasn't playing. He was real rough with me, and when all was said and done, my ripped shirt hung off my shoulder, my jeans and shoes were in the dirt, and my backside was on the hood of the car. Keith was in between my legs and neither of us could catch our breaths. I had my fist tightened on the front of his shirt, grabbing it and telling him to let me go.

"Shut the fuck up. Just shut up and listen." He took deep breaths, but his voice was calmer. His forehead dripped with sweat and it was dotted with beads of sweat. "I have been so miserable without you. Sick to my damn stomach, trying to figure out where in the hell did I go wrong. All I asked was for you to move in with me. For whatever reason, that shit set off a firestorm. You've been coming up with every excuse in the book to fight with me and that scares me. Scares the hell out of me, and if you don't want this relationship to go any further, just say so, dammit. Say so right now, and I promise you that I will move on. You know I've been hurt before, Trina. The last thing I want is to be hurt again."

Keith didn't wait for a response. He pushed his dick inside of me and started to rock my body with his. "I love you," he said in a whisper. "Can't you see that? What do I need to do to get you to see how much I really love you?"

A slow tear rolled down my cheek. Deep down, I knew I had been giving him a hard time. I knew that I kicked up an argument, and kept it going because I was afraid to move in with him. The last time I moved in with a man, he'd hurt me so badly. He abused me and controlled my every move. I was afraid of that happening again, but I didn't realize that this was Keith. He had been so good to me. I suspected that some of this stuff with Evelyn was done to upset me. I was sure that he hadn't had sex with her. He wasn't that kind of man. Shame on me for insisting that he was.

I reached out and wrapped my arms around his neck. Kissed him like it was going out of style. Rocked my body with his and apologized over and over again for my foolish behavior.

"I'm sorry. Please forgive me. I love you too, and I promise to never hurt you like she did. Your ex was a fool. I'm not, so whenever you're ready for me to move in with you, I will."

Keith wet my juicy lips with his. We continued to fuck on the car, not caring who saw us on the darkened parking lot. I wrapped my legs around his back, leaned back as he sucked my titties and ground with him until I could grind no more. Hell, yeah, we put on a scene, and when I released an orgasm, you'd better believe that plenty of people who looked on heard about it.

Chapter 12

Evelyn

When I received the selfie of Kayla and Cedric, I pursed my lips and tossed my phone on the couch. How foolish of her to send that crap to me, like I was supposed to jump for joy or call Cedric to see what was up. Now that I wasn't pregnant anymore, there wasn't much that he could do for me. Bryson had helped with my finances, so this thing with Kayla and Cedric really wasn't a big deal. That day, I sent Kayla a text message, congratulating her for finally coming to her damn senses. If I had some extra money, I'd have flowers delivered to her, but that trick wasn't even worth one rose.

Then there was ol' crybaby Trina. She was just as crazy as Kayla was. The more she clowned on Keith, the better my chances were at getting to him. Yeah, I was still kicking it with Bryson, but he was just my little plaything. We had fun together, and the truth was, we couldn't stop screwing each other. My first day at work, we found ourselves in the bathroom stall getting it on. Then, we went to the park for lunch and started having sex in the car. Since Libby was still on her trip, I invited him to my place. We got busy in the shower, and then took our business to Keith's house the following day. Several of their friends came over, and Bryson invited me to come over. Like always, we played cards, listened to music, and watched TV. Bryson took me upstairs to one of the guestrooms and we indulged ourselves. Keith walked in on us, too, and Lord knows I wanted to ask him to join us. But timing was everything. All I wanted was one chance. Just one opportunity to be with him. There was something about him that I couldn't allow my best friend to keep all to herself.

Maybe if I suggested that the two of us do him together, maybe she'd get on board. After all, she used to be, or still is, bisexual.

It was three o'clock in the afternoon and work was almost over. I was kind of bored, especially since Bryson was out of the office and on one of the construction sites. I got up to go to the cafeteria for a soda and some chips. When I got there, I saw three black women sitting at a table gossiping. I could tell they were whispering about me, because their eyes kept shifting in my direction. I could also hear some of what they were saying. I heard words like: whore, tramp, Bryson, diseases, and white bitch. They laughed, and when I snapped my head around, fake smiles were on display. I got my snacks and walked over to the table.

"Hi, ladies," I said with a smile. "And FYI, all of you are correct. I am a whore, I am fucking and sucking the hell out of Bryson's disease-infected dick, and he is still planning to marry the white bitch. That's after I get finished with him, so keep on paying attention. I'm sure you'll all have more to gossip about soon."

Their mouths hung wide open. I started to walk away and couldn't believe what one of the women had the audacity to ask me.

"Did you clean up his sperm shots in the restroom? That's just nasty, and next time y'all need to get a room."

"Next time, and trust me when I say there will be a next time, please opt to use another restroom when that one is being occupied."

I rolled my eyes and walked off. Some women were so petty and jealous. Just like my so-called BFF's were. I guess I couldn't call them my BFF's anymore, because we had gone way beyond that. Maybe my FFF's. Fake Fucking Friends who I just didn't care about anymore. That included Trina, but I needed her "friendship" in order to accomplish some things.

When I got back to my desk, I saw that I'd missed a call from Bryson. I called him back and he quickly answered his phone.

"What's the play for today?" I teased.

"Nothing. I called to tell you that I'm working late and won't be able to come over tonight. Maybe tomorrow."

"Awww, that's not good news. But tomorrow will just have to do. Maybe we can meet at Keith's house since the game is coming on. He has that big ol' television that you like to watch."

"I thought about that too, but Trina will be there. I think they're trying to patch things up, so I don't want to keep getting in the way. For now, it'll have to be your place. You know Libby kind of acting up, and I don't want to put you in the middle."

"Please don't. Confirm everything with me tomorrow."

"Will do, Miss Sexy. Be good."

"Never," I said then laughed.

Bryson laughed too and then hung up. I couldn't believe that Trina had weaseled her way back in with Keith. I definitely had to call her to see what was up with that. I called her, pretending as if I didn't know they were back together.

"Trina?" I said, as she spoke in a low tone.

"What?"

"Are you okay?"

"Not really, but whatever. What's up?"

"No, the question is what's up with you? I haven't heard from you in a few days. I thought we were good."

"We are good, Evelyn. I'm just trying to sort through some things right now."

"Things like what? If you need to talk, I'm listening."

"I know, but I get tired of running to you with my problems. I can't ever seem to get my footing when it comes to relationships. All this back-and-forth stuff with Keith is driving me crazy."

"Have you spoken to him? The last time I talked to you, things were kind of sketchy."

"They're still sketchy. We tried to reconcile. Had sex and everything. I told him I was going to move in with him, but then I found out that he's still been talking to his ex-girlfriend. She reached out to me last night. Told me everything. I am so done with men. How many chances do I have to give them to get it right?"

"Well, women have their issues too. Maybe it's just Keith. I told you before how sneaky he was, but you refused to listen.

Why don't you just chill for a while, like me? Stop trying to force relationships on people who aren't ready."

"Maybe I do need to chill for a while. This is the last motherfucker I'm going to allow to hurt me. I've got to stop trusting people so much."

"I couldn't agree with you more. The way I see it, this is Keith's loss. You're a good person, Trina. If he didn't realize that, too bad."

"Kayla just said the same thing. I so wish the three of us could get together and go have some fun like we used to. Do you remember when we all went to Miami Beach together? We had so much fun. I swear those were the days."

Truthfully, I didn't have that much fun in Miami Beach with my BFF's, but if she insisted that we did, who was I to dispute it?

"Yes, those were the days. But things have changed and here we are."

"Right. But how did we get here is the question? We used to be soooo close, and our bond was unbreakable. But look at us now."

Sad, wasn't it? I had to admit that we did have some good times too. "Truthfully, we got here because of Kayla's selfishness and her thinking she was always better than us. I wouldn't have ever started sleeping with Cedric, if Kayla wouldn't have treated me like a nobody. As for us, we've had our issues too. But you already know how much I care about our friendship. It means a lot to me."

"You say that, Evelyn, but sometimes your actions don't show it. Where Kayla is concerned, no matter what, you never should have been sleeping with her husband. She may have been selfish, but that wasn't a reason for you to open your legs and get pregnant by Cedric."

"There you go taking her side again. I wish we would eliminate Kayla from our conversations. What's done is done. It makes no sense to keep harping on the past. Besides, she's supposed to be real happy now. She sent me a selfie of her and Cedric, holding their divorce papers. I don't know why she went there, but I guess you may know better than I do."

"That wasn't a bright idea, but whatever. I won't mention her name again, nor will I keep on bringing you my sob stories about Keith. I'm going away for a few days. Need some time to think, so I'm heading to an art show in L.A. this evening. I'll be gone for three days. When I get back, maybe we can hook up."

"Sounds good. Keep your head up, girl, and don't let no man stress you. Have a good time, and we'll hook up when you get back."

Trina and I left it there. I felt a little bad for her, but that's the way the boat rocks sometimes. Her news also had me thinking. If she wasn't going to be around for a few days, hmmmm. I sat for a few minutes, pondering. Then I got up and went into Bryson's office. I closed the door and hurried over to his desk. I'd seen several keys in his drawer, but one key had a piece of tape on it that read Keith. I assumed it was a key to his house. I searched Bryson's desk, but the only thing I came across were a bunch of pens and pencils, notepads, and a few pictures of unattractive women. I tossed the pictures in the trash, especially the one of a woman who had a pudgy stomach and a tattoo between her legs. Yucky. When I lifted a camera, that was when I saw a silver key and one with Keith's name taped to it. I tucked the keys into my pocket and hurried to get back to my desk.

Five o'clock rolled around; I couldn't wait to get home. I showered, changed clothes, then sat back on my couch. For some reason, I was a little nervous about reaching out to Keith, so I picked up a Newport and lit it. I took a puff, and then whistled smoke into the air. Took another puff and did the same. Before I knew, the cigarette was almost finished. That was when I picked up my cell phone to call him. My pussy thumped a little from the sound of his sexy yet sad voice.

"I hope I didn't catch you at a bad time, but I wanted to ask you a few questions about Bryson, if you don't mind."

"You're timing is cool. I've been painting all day and need to take a break anyway. Shoot."

"Well, I'm not sure if you know this or not, but Bryson and I have been getting a little close lately. I'm finding myself feeling him, a lot, but I'm also feeling someone else too.

Then there's the situation with him and Libby. I was at his place one day and she showed up. She was pretty distraught, and I felt terrible for hurting her like that. Bryson seems as if he cares for her, but a part of me feels as if I'm in the way. Do you think I should back off? Or do you think I should stop seeing him altogether and direct my attention to the other person I'm feeling?"

"First, I will say this to you. Libby and my brother have been together for a long time. Eventually, he's going to settle down, and if he does, it'll probably be with her. Then again, he's so hard to figure out. He is involved with several other women too. From what he's said to me, I'm sure you already know that, right?"

"Yes, I do. That doesn't bother me, as much as this thing with Libby does. To see her so upset like that really troubled me. I wouldn't wish the pain that she's going through on my worst enemy. A big part of me feels as if I'm contributing to her pain."

"In a sense, you are. But so are other people. If it's bothering you that much, back off. Chill for a while, and pursue the other person you're interested in. That's what I would do. At the end of the day, Bryson will be just fine."

"I think he would be too. I know his kind all too well. Now, in reference to the other guy, he's in a tricky situation as well. The woman who he likes is confused. She really doesn't know what she wants and she's a little drama queen. I think he's just about had it with her, but I'm not so sure. He's one of the nicest men that I've ever met, and I can't stop thinking about him. All I want is one night . . . one night with him and I would want no more."

Keith stayed silent for a moment. Then he cleared his throat. "One night to do what with him?"

"One night to have passionate sex with him. There is something in his eyes that says he wants me, but he's afraid. Afraid that what I intend to do to him will get back to his girlfriend. Thing is, it won't. My lips are sealed and I would take that secret to my grave. My question to you is, do you think I should pursue this man?"

Keith paused again. I heard his breathing increase then a sigh followed. "I don't know if he would risk losing everything for one night of passionate sex. You may have to offer him a little bit more than that."

"I would offer him anything he wanted. I'm feeling him that much, and if he wanted more, the sex could be viewed as a jumpstart."

"Anything?"

"Anything."

"I don't see any man rejecting your offer, but if the confused woman is a drama queen, shouldn't you be worried?"

"Women don't scare me. They never have. I always go for what I want, even though, sometimes, people tend to get hurt in the process. I like to deal with those situations as they come. They're always after the fact. After I've gotten what I wanted, and the other person has gotten what they wanted too."

"So, in other words, let the chips fall where they may."

"Exactly. Now, I'll ask again. Should I, or shouldn't I pursue him?"

Keith hesitated longer this time. "I . . . I think you should. Maybe you should go by his place tonight, around nine, and see what's up with him. If the door is unlocked, go to his bedroom where he'll probably be watching TV, since the drama queen who is causing him plenty of headaches will be out of town. Wear something real sexy to entice him and don't forget to bring condoms. You always want to stay strapped up, especially when you don't know what he's been into. I hope my advice helps, Evelyn. And let me know how everything turns out."

"You'll know soon."

I ended the call and hurried to call Trina, just to see where she was. She was already at the airport, waiting for her plane to depart.

"Have a safe trip," I said. "And be sure to call me when you arrive in L.A."

"Okay, I will. If I see a piece of art that you may like, I'll purchase it for you."

I laughed. "Don't waste your money. You know I prefer the cash over a painted picture any day."

"Right. Bye, girl. Holler later."

Much later, I thought.

I laid the phone on the table and tried to contain my enthusiasm for going to see Keith. I suspected that it wasn't going to be as simple as he'd made it, and I figured I'd had to put up a fuss to get him to give me what I wanted. I could tell so by the way he hesitated, but there was no question that by the time the night was over, Keith would be like putty in my hands.

If the man wanted sexy, I was going to give him sexy and then some. That consisted of me wearing nothing but my silky skin, underneath a coat. I changed into just that and left my place in a hurry.

As planned, when I arrived at Keith's house, the door was unlocked. I didn't even need the key I'd gotten from Bryson's office, but I still kept it. The downstairs was pretty dark. Upstairs was too, but I could see light from a television coming from his room. I sauntered up the stairs and heard soothing jazz music as well. He was apparently trying to set the mood, so I made my way to his doorway. I peeked inside and saw him sitting up in bed with a sheet covering him from the waist down. I knocked on the door and then walked inside. Keith picked up a watch from his nightstand.

"You're almost ten minutes late. I didn't think you were coming. I was about to fall asleep, because these shows on the television are boring."

"Then Evelyn to the rescue, right?"

I didn't want to waste any time with this. Keith appeared to be on board, and that was a good thing. His eyes locked on me as I removed the belt from my coat. When I peeled it away from my shoulders, I saw him suck in a deep breath. I stood before him, with no clothes on and ready to handle my business. Keith patted the spot next to him then cocked his head back.

"Come here," he said softly. "My brother said you were sexy as hell. I guess now I believe him."

I crawled on the bed like a courageous tiger. Moved face to face with him then leaned in for a kiss. This time, he didn't back away. He didn't reject me, and his mouth opened wide. I couldn't believe what a great kisser he was. No wonder Trina was hooked.

"Sweet lips," he said, holding the sides of my face. He lightly bit my lips a few times, and then backed away when the phone rang.

"Sweet pussy too," I replied. "Wait until you taste it."

The ringing phone interrupted us again.

"You may want to go answer that," I said. "Just in case it's you-know-who. The last thing you may want is her showing up here tonight."

Keith shrugged, but he took my advice. He snatched the sheet away from him. Lord have mercy on that body of his.

"I'll go get my phone, and why don't you run to the kitchen to get us some wine out the fridge?"

I really didn't want any wine, but since Keith was cooperating, what the hell? I went to the kitchen to get the wine, and then stopped by the bathroom to pee. I could hear Keith going off on somebody over the phone, but then his voice went silent. It was probably Trina. Then again, she was on a plane to L.A. Keith's ex-girlfriend came to mind, so I hurried out of the bathroom to eavesdrop on the conversation.

I returned to the bedroom with the wine bottle and two glasses in my hand. Keith was back in bed, lying on his side with the sheet covering him. The television had been turned off, and his cell phone was on the nightstand, ringing again. This time, he ignored it and didn't say a word. I set the wine and glasses down then crawled on the bed next to him again. When I pulled the sheet away from him, that was when I got the shock of my life. I eased away from the gun that was aimed right at the center of my forehead, which was starting to build up a sheen of sweat. The look in Trina's eyes was deadly.

"Bitch," she said through gritted teeth. "You got five motherfucking seconds to get your coat back on and get the hell out of my man's house! And if you ever, I mean ever, come back here again, I swear to God that I will blow your damn brains out!"

Trina didn't look like she was bullshitting, so I didn't bother to respond. I kept my eyes on the gun that trembled in her hand and carefully eased back on the bed. I bent down to pick up my coat, but didn't bother to put it back on. I waved at her, and jetted down the stairs so fast that I almost fell and broke my neck. Keith awaited me at the door. His face looked like stone, as he held the door wide open. I was too embarrassed to say one word. After I ran outside, he slammed the door so hard that it shook the house. Apparently, he wasn't down with my plans after all.

Chapter 13

Kayla

Trina called to tell me about her and Keith's plan for Evelyn. She had me laughing my tail off. I couldn't believe how desperate Evelyn had gotten. Since Cedric was no longer around, I should've expected something like that from her.

"I always knew she was scantless, but when Keith told me about her trying to hook up with him before, I couldn't believe it. This last thing was his idea. He wanted to show me what was really going on behind my back. When she called to speak to him about coming over, I was right there listening."

"Girl, I'm convinced that Evelyn is crazy. She needs some serious help. No woman in her right mind could be foolish enough to go into her best friend's man's house with nothing on and try to seduce him. Does she really think she's got it going on like that? And what about Bryson? Did Keith tell him?"

"Nope. He said he wasn't going to say a word, because Evelyn was going to get her feelings hurt, again, messing around with him. She's always running after men, but she'd better be careful what she wishes for."

"I know that's right. Right away I could tell Bryson was no good. He started talking all that mess at the club that night, but all I did was smile and listen. I had fun, but the truth is, I need to take time out and see about me. I'm not pursuing any relationship, until I get my stuff over here in order and make sure Jacoby is on the right track. Something seems to be troubling him, but I can't put my finger on it. Maybe it has to do with the divorce, but I explained to him that it was something I truly had to do for myself."

"I totally get that. He'll understand one day why you did what you had to do. And before I forget, thank you for interfering in my relationship. I'm glad you called Keith to come to the club. We needed to settle things down and talk through our differences."

"I figured the two of you would. I only interfere when I feel as though I have to. I didn't want you to make the mistake of losing him. Have you moved in yet?"

"Yep. Moved in a few days ago. I'm feeling good about this, too. Now, what about you? Have you heard from Cedric, and when are you going to start looking for another place to stay? Staying in that hotel must be driving you nuts."

"It is, and I'm getting tired of the ongoing noise, too. I think I found a place near Chesterfield. The rent is ridiculous, but I love how the apartment is made."

"Apartment? You're moving into an apartment?"

"Yes. It's a three bedroom, but it's humongous. It's perfect for me and Jacoby. We really don't need anything bigger than that."

"What about the house? Did Cedric put it up for sale yet?"

"He said he was going to next week. We've talked here and there, but more so about Jacoby and our finances. Cedric set me out. I must say that I'm very appreciative of the money we agreed upon in our divorce settlement."

"That's good. Seems like everything is working out for everybody, with the exception of Evelyn. Maybe she'll come to her senses and start doing the right thing. If she does, I'll never know about it because she would be too embarrassed to ever contact me again."

"Tuh, don't believe that for one minute. Sooner or later, you'll get a call. She'll be begging and pleading for you to forgive her. And I know you, Trina. You probably will."

Trina denied it, but among the three of us, she was the one with the forgiving heart. To a certain extent, I was too. But it would be very, very difficult for me to ever forgive Evelyn.

We talked for a little while longer, but since I was supposed to meet Jacoby at the apartment complex so he could see it, I had to let Trina go. I then called Jacoby, but he didn't answer his phone. I drove to Adrianne's house to see if he was there. He was, and I found the two of them outside arguing. I didn't like how heated the conversation between them seemed, so I got out of the car to go break it up. Jacoby was way too aggressive. I yelled for him to back away from Adrianne.

"Jacoby," I shouted again. "Didn't you hear me?"

He backed away with a mean mug on his face. Adrianne had been crying. This whole scene was kind of shocking to me because I thought things had been going well for them.

"Anybody want to tell me what's going on here?" I said.

"Tell her," Adrianne shouted. "Now is the time to tell her!"

Jacoby narrowed his eyes at her and shot daggers. "Shut up! Stay out of this, Adrianne, it's none of your business!"

I couldn't express how shocked I was. I put my hand on my hip and frowned. "Tell me what? Would somebody please tell me so that we can talk about whatever it is in a sensible way?"

"It's nothing, Mama. If you want to go see this apartment, let's go."

"If this is about the apartment, please let me know. I'll accept if you don't want to live with me, and you prefer to live with Cedric. We will always be a family, and you are welcome—"

"Tell her now," Adrianne shouted again. "She needs to know the truth!"

This was driving me nuts. I turned to Jacoby and let him have it. "The truth about what," I yelled. "What secret are you keeping from me?"

Jacoby had the look of fire in his eyes. He turned to walk away, but I ran after him. "Is she pregnant? Is that what you want to tell me? I told you about having all this sex, Jacoby, and the least you could've done was protect yourself. You haven't even graduated from high school yet and—"

"No," Adrianne said. "I'm not pregnant. And if you don't tell her what you did, I'm going to tell her myself."

I was floored when Jacoby reached out and grabbed Adrianne's face. He squeezed it tight and held his hand over her mouth. This time, I yanked him away from her and pushed him back. I pointed my finger near his face and gritted my teeth.

"No son of mine will ever put his hands on a woman like that! What in the hell is wrong with you? Who are you, Jacoby, and what in the hell are you keeping from me?"

Adrianne stepped back and blurted out the secret. "He paid Paula Daniels to kill Cedric. I begged him not to do it, but Jacoby wouldn't listen. We don't know why she hasn't said anything about it, but he's been so afraid that she's going to tell someone."

I stood as if cement had been poured over me. I couldn't believe what Adrianne had said. Things were just starting to look up for us, but now this.

"You did what?" I said to Jacoby. "Why . . . how . . . what made you do something so stupid? You didn't have to involve yourself in this mess, Jacoby. Why did you want your father dead?"

Jacoby stood with a frightened look on his face. Finally, he started to speak up. "I didn't want him dead. Well, at first I did, but then I changed my mind. I knew how much Paula despised him, and all she needed was a little push. I offered her the money and she said she would do it. But then things kind of settled down at our house, and when I went back to see her, she said the plan was already in motion and that I couldn't renege." Jacoby paused to take a deep breath. He placed his hands behind his head then turned around to face the other direction. Shame was written all over his face.

"I had already given her the money. She wouldn't give it back and she told me to get out. Then, Cedric was shot. I knew she did it, but I don't know if she's planning to tell the police about my involvement. If she does, they're not going to believe that I tried to stop her. Nobody will believe me. That was why I didn't want to say anything. I wanted to tell you the truth, as well as Cedric. But I couldn't. I just couldn't do it." Jacoby broke down in tears. He leaned against his car and cried like a baby.

I was numb about the whole thing, but this was still my son. I regretted not taking action sooner, regarding my marriage. Jacoby felt as if he had to step in and handle things for me. Thus far, Paula hadn't said anything. She pleaded guilty to the attempted murder charge and so be it. If she ever came back and tried to tell on Jacoby, we'd deny it. Even if she had evidence, we'd get one of the best lawyers in St. Louis to fight the case. But the person I was worried about was Cedric. What if he ever found out the real deal? Was it in my best interest to tell him, or should I leave well enough alone? I suspected what Jacoby's answer would be, when I suggested that we go see Cedric.

"We need to talk to him about this," I said while rocking Jacoby in my arms.

"Noooo," he cried out. "Please don't tell him, Mama. I beg you not to tell him. I know Cedric. He will turn me in. He will make me pay for this, and I don't want to go to jail."

Just the thought of Jacoby doing any time in jail pained me. Jail wasn't for my son. I couldn't let that happen, and as a matter of fact, I wouldn't let it happen. This was yet another secret that I'd have to keep to myself. Meanwhile, I had to hope and pray that this never got back to Cedric.

Later that day, I went to the new apartment complex to pay my first month's rent and security deposit. The quicker I got Jacoby away from Cedric the better. Jacoby had been through so much. When Adrianne told me that he'd contemplated suicide over this situation, I cried my heart out. Not my son. My focus was now on him. I didn't have time for anything else. He had two more years left of school, was a very bright student, and had always done well. For the past several months, he'd been consumed with my mess. Consumed with trying to keep this family together. I wanted to tell Cedric just that, but unlike me, he wouldn't understand. He would turn things around and make Jacoby seem like a murderer. He would disown him. Say that he was no good because Arnez's blood was the blood running through Jacoby's body, not his. Cedric would make our lives a living hell, and that was without a shadow of doubt.

After I left the rental office, I went to Cedric's house. Jacoby was supposed to meet me there, so we could start gathering his things and putting them in boxes. He wasn't there yet, so I called his cell phone. He told me that he was en route.

I used my key to unlock the door, and the second I walked inside, Cedric was right there. He looked even better than he did before, and this time he was dressed in one of his tailored business suits.

"Why didn't you tell me?" he rushed to say.

My heart raced, and I moved my head from side to side. "I . . . Didn't tell you what?"

"You could have told me, and shame on you for not saying one word."

Seriousness was in his eyes. Then all of a sudden he laughed. He patted my shoulder and walked over to the door to close it. "Why didn't you say anything about our anniversary? Did you forget that it was today or what? You should be ashamed of yourself, if you forgot. Then again, I won't hold it against you. I forgot too, right until the second you walked through that door."

I sucked in a deep, long breath and sighed from relief. "Uh, yeah, sorry but I forgot too. And are you sure that today is our anniversary? I thought it was a week from today."

Cedric shook his head and strutted toward his office. I followed. He sat in his chair and looked at the calendar on his desk.

"Sorry, baby. It's today. You got it wrong, and like always, I'm right."

"Okay then, Mr. Right. Where have you been? You dressed all nice, and I must say that you look awfully handsome."

Cedric smiled and leaned back in his chair. He propped his feet on the desk and placed his hands behind his head. His scruffy beard had been shaved and his skin glowed.

"I had a meeting with my business partners today, and I also met with my attorney. You did good with keeping up the payments on things, and I appreciate your efforts. All I can say is I'm glad to be back. Feeling good and ready to make some big moves. The house goes on the market tomorrow, but just so you know, when it sells, every dime goes in my pocket. Now, if you need any of this furniture, let me know. That way, I won't sell it."

"I'm good. I kind of want all new stuff."

"Well, you damn sure have enough money to buy all new stuff. And then some, Miss Husband-made Millionaire."

"Ooo, look at you. You sound bitter. Are you?"

"Not at all. There's more where that came from, and if things go accordingly, there will be way more. So, uh, getting back to our anniversary. Since you're here, would you like to throw some pussy my way and see if I'll catch it?"

Just then, we heard the front door open. I figured it was Jacoby, and it was confirmed when he came into Cedric's office. Jacoby barely wanted to look at him. His head hung low and he spoke in a soft voice to both of us.

"What's up with you, man?" Cedric said. "Looks like you got girl problems."

"Yeah, something like that," Jacoby said with a fake smile. "You know how it is."

"Hell, yeah, I know how it is. But don't sweat the small stuff, and always focus on bigger things. I got a lot to teach you, son, especially when it comes to women. Never let them get you down, and always stay up. You hear me?"

Jacoby nodded.

"Go ahead to your room and start getting some of your things," I said. "I have the key to the apartment, so we can move some of your stuff in tonight."

Jacoby left the room and did what he was told.

"Tell me again," Cedric said, sitting up straight. "Where is this apartment again?"

"It's in Chesterfield. Close by the Missouri River, got three bedrooms, two and a half baths, two fireplaces, a loft area, and a chef's kitchen. The clubhouse is off the chain, too. I can't wait for you to see it."

"To hell with seeing it. Do I get a key?"

"I'm afraid not, Cedric. How many times am I going to have to tell you that I'm your ex-wife? We don't get down like that anymore."

"Exes still be fucking each other, so don't stand there like those legs are locked down because we're not married any-more. If you want to keep holding out on me, don't be mad at me for going elsewhere. I'm starting to feel an urge."

"Have all the urges you want, just don't mosey your tail over to you-know-who's place. She's got enough trouble on her hands, and the last person she needs to drop back in is you."

"Who are you talking about? Evelyn?"

"Yes. Evelyn."

Cedric winced and blew me off. "Whatever. Evelyn is old news. Whatever trouble she's found herself in, it doesn't surprise me."

I couldn't help but to share what had happened between Evelyn, Trina, and Keith. Every chance I got, I wanted to make sure she looked bad through his eyes. I also wanted him to say that he had regrets about their relationship, but thus far, he hadn't said it. He sat in disbelief as I spoke. Couldn't stop shaking his head and cracking up. Then he slapped his leg and rubbed his chin.

"She that gotdamn trifling where she trying to fuck two brothers? They must have some money. Otherwise, I can't see her going out like that."

"Of course they do, but even if they didn't, she probably would have gone there. Trina is so pissed. We're to the point where we seriously believe Evelyn needs to see a psychiatrist."

"Yeah, maybe so."

He didn't seem too interested in talking about Evelyn, so I told Cedric that I was getting ready to go help Jacoby pack up some of his things. He stopped me at the door.

"When the two of you get settled into the apartment, do me a favor and have a long talk with our son. He's been a little off lately, and I'm worried about him. It could be about something with Adrianne, but usually, Jacoby don't let girl problems get to him like that. I think there's something else."

I started to bite my nails. "So . . . something else like what? What do you think is bothering him?"

"Not sure. He hasn't been right since I was shot. Maybe seeing me like that has done something to him. After you talk to him, I will. Okay?"

"Sure. I'll keep you posted on how the conversation goes. Meanwhile, happy anniversary, and please don't do anything that I wouldn't do."

Cedric held out his hands. "The sky is the limit. The last time I checked, I'm a free man. Unfortunately, since you're not interested anymore, I may be prompted to take another woman out to dinner and make love to her on our anniversary. Remember, I told you about my urge."

I threw my hand back at Cedric and left his office. At this point, I guess I didn't care who he spent his time with, as long as it wasn't Evelyn.

Jacoby and I spent the next few hours packing up some of his things. During that time, Cedric said he was going somewhere and left. Jacoby and I discussed, again, how all of this came about and how to move forward. He sat on the bed in his bedroom, shaking his head while I sat next to him.

"I know you want to say something to him, Mama, but you know your husband better than I do. My dad can be a monster when he wants to be, and nobody wants to find out they've been betrayed."

"I do want to tell him, but more than anything, I want to protect you. I definitely know how Cedric is; I've lived with him for most of my life. More than anything, I'm glad you got all of this off your chest. I can only imagine how keeping this inside has made you feel, but I wish you would have come to me so I could help you get through this."

"Trust me when I say I wanted to. Adrianne definitely wanted me to, but I didn't know how you would feel about me paying Paula to do something so horrific. At the time, my head wasn't on straight. I was so upset with my dad, and when I tried to reach out to him about how I felt one day, my timing couldn't have been more off. I saw him in a parking garage with Paula, doing some crazy stuff that no married man should be doing."

I could only imagine what Cedric was doing. The thought made me sick to my stomach. And then for Jacoby to witness it was awful.

"I don't need details, and reaching out to him was all you could do. You were not thinking straight, and I assume you used the money in your savings to pay Paula, didn't you?"

"Every dime of it. When I asked for it back, she laughed at me. I had no idea what kind of woman she really was, until I witnessed that evil look in her eyes. She hated Cedric with a passion. She was obsessed with him, but I can honestly say he created that monster."

He'd created several other monsters too, but I wasn't trying to go there right now with Evelyn. Jacoby and I finished packing, and a few hours later, we were on our way to our new apartment, ready for a new beginning. His secret was safe with me, and I intended to do whatever I had to do to protect my son.

Chapter 14

Evelyn

My feelings were a little bruised about what had happened, but oh well. You win some and you lose some. Trina had Keith's ol' weak self wrapped around her finger. For him to agree to do something so ridiculous was stupid on his part. I bet he was still thinking about that kiss, though. I tore up those lips. How could he ever forget about the sweet taste of my tongue?

The one thing that I was worried about was Keith telling Bryson about what had happened. For starters, I didn't want him to be so upset about it that I'd lose my job. I kind of liked where I worked, and it did bring in a little money to help me pay some bills. Then, I didn't want Bryson feeling as if I'd betrayed him. He'd been kicking me out every now and then. Not just sexually either. I never had to pay for dinner, never had to pay for drinks, and he even gave me some money to buy a purse that I had to have when browsing the mall with him the other day.

So in a nutshell, losing him would be a setback for me, especially since he was the only person I could really chill with and carry on a decent conversation with. I wasn't ready to go see what was up with Cedric yet, and the more I'd thought about it, I was skeptical about traveling back down memory lane with him. The last conversation we'd had didn't go so well and I wasn't so sure if he'd welcome me back with open arms. He hadn't called to say anything to me, and I wondered if Trina had told Kayla about the abortion, and if she'd told Cedric. I was almost positive that she'd mentioned it to him.

Then again, maybe not because I'd been left out of everything when it came to those two. It was a wrap in regard to my friendship with them. I didn't suspect that we would ever be able to have the bond we all shared, and at this point, all the damage had won the battle. So be it.

I'd been off work for about an hour. Bryson said that he was working late, but he promised to call when he got home. I wasted time by going to the grocery store and then I stopped at Walmart to pick up a few cleaning items. By the time I was done with that, it was almost eight o'clock. I still hadn't heard from Bryson, and to be honest, I was kind of getting a little irritated with him for telling me one thing, yet doing another. Like saying that he would call me. Sometimes, he never did. I wouldn't even stress him about it the next day at work, and he never provided an explanation as to why he hadn't called.

Well tonight, I wasn't having it. I left a message on his voice mail, telling him that if he didn't show up, I was going to stop by his place. I didn't see it as popping up, especially if I told him I was coming through. If anything, I figured that my threat would, at least, encourage him to call. It didn't. By ten o'clock, I still hadn't heard from him. I grabbed my keys off the counter, reached for my jacket, and threw it over my shoulder. Bryson's condo was about forty minutes away from my place. It wasn't long before I parked my car on the parking lot and prepared myself to go to his door. I saw his car, so I assumed he was home. But when I called his cell phone, yet again, he didn't answer.

With my high heels on, I strutted to his door and knocked. No answer. Rang the doorbell; nothing. If he was inside with someone else, the least he could do was come to the door and tell me. For whatever reason, he refused to do that. So, what I did was knock again. I put my ear to the door and heard loud music coming from somewhere. I wasn't sure if the music was coming from inside of his condo, but the music could have been his reason for not answering the door.

All of a sudden, something hit me. When I looked for Keith's key in the drawer, there was another key there as well. I'd taken both keys, and I wondered if that key was the one to unlock Bryson's door. I rummaged through my purse and finally found the key dropped inside of it. I slid the key in the lock, but unfortunately it wouldn't turn. That was when I realized that it was turned the wrong way. I turned it the other way, and yes, I was in business. The key turned and the door popped open. I pushed on it, causing it to squeak. Once I was inside, the music was louder. I also heard grunts, and that was when I figured that, maybe, this was a bad idea.

Still, I tiptoed my way forward. I saw a pair of lace panties in the middle of the floor. A bra was tossed on the couch, her shoes were right near the door, and the closer I got to it, I could hear Bryson's grunts more than I could hear hers. It was so apparent that she was putting it on him. So much so that it sounded like he was crying. He whimpered like a bitch, and the sound of naked, sweaty bodies slapping together got louder and louder. My heels sank in the plush carpet as I reached the door, and when I turned in the doorway, I got a shock that felt like electricity had ripped through me. My legs weakened, my stomach tightened, and I covered my mouth so I wouldn't throw up. My eyes witnessed Bryson bending over the bed with a tranny behind him. The tranny was wearing Bryson out. His grunts were louder than the music in the room. I removed my hand from my mouth, refusing to walk away and hold my peace.

"You nasty, stank-ass motherfucker," I shouted. "How dare you not call me because of this!"

Both of their heads snapped to the side. The tranny looked like a beautiful black woman with nice breasts and a round, tight ass. Thing was, she/he had a dick. A big one, too, which she eased out of Bryson who had already jumped away from the tranny like she/he was contagious.

"What are you doing here?" he yelled at me.

"No. The question is what in the hell are you doing? I mean, really, Bryson. Is this how you're doing it?"

Embarrassment, as well as shame, covered Bryson's face. He hurried into his sweatpants and ordered the tranny to get on his/her clothes.

"You do not have to tell Miss Thing to leave on my account," I said. "I'm out of here, sweetheart. My eyes have witnessed enough."

I got the hell out of there. My body felt grimy as hell. I couldn't help but to think about all of the sex Bryson and I had

had, and about all of the things that I allowed him to do to me. I had flashbacks of how he would touch me, and about how he requested that I touch him. He loved to have anal sex, and all of his little nasty ways now made sense. I definitely had no problem with gay or bisexual men, but I damn sure had a problem with the down-low motherfuckers who kept this kind of shit a secret.

I ran to my car and drove like a bat out of hell to get home. When I did, I stripped my clothes off and put the hot water in the shower on blast. I scrubbed my body with a sponge, but that felt like it wasn't working for me. What I needed was a Brillo pad, but unfortunately I didn't have any. I used the last one I had to clean the oven last week. I continued with the sponge and scalding hot water. My skin had turned red and my pussy couldn't get any cleaner. I finally turned off the water, and that was when I heard someone buzzing me from downstairs. I left the bathroom and turned on the monitor. The face that I saw was Bryson's.

"Say," he said in a whisper. "Why you leave so fast? I thought you wanted to see me."

"Oh, I saw you, but forget it. We have nothing else to talk about. I assure you that you never have to worry about me again. I will bring your key to the office tomorrow, and if you feel a need to have me fired, please do."

"I would never do that," he said, trying to smooth talk his way inside. That may have worked for Cedric, but damn sure not for him. "We don't even have to get down like that, do we? Why don't you buzz me in? I got a feeling that you're upset, and I need to provide you with an explanation about what you saw."

"Look, I don't need an explanation. Just go home, Bryson, and pretend that none of this ever happened."

"Can't do that right now. Besides, I don't want you to share what you saw tonight with anyone. If you do, that could swing a lot of heat my way, if you know what I mean."

All of a sudden, the sound of ca-ching went off in my head. I wanted to know what Bryson would be willing to pay for me to keep his dirty little secret. I had a feeling that it wouldn't be pennies. With that taken into consideration, I buzzed him in. The door was already opened for him to come inside, and when he did, I was sitting on the couch with my robe on. Another Newport was in my hand, and after I flicked ashes in the ashtray, I spoke up before he did.

"I don't want no explanation, I don't want any excuses, nor do I ever want you to touch me again. I am so disappointed in you, Bryson. How could a man as fine and masculine as you are holler louder than a bitch? I guess that's totally irrelevant right now; and the only question I need to be asking you is how much?"

"How much what?" he said with an attitude. He refused to take a seat, probably because his ass was still hurting from being bumped so hard.

I returned the attitude and snapped my head to the side. "How much are you going to pay me to keep my mouth shut?"

Bryson blew me off. He waved his hand and pursed his lips. The real bitch in him was starting to show. "I'm not paying you jack. You are not going to blackmail me, and if you tell anyone about what you saw tonight, they won't believe you. They'll think you're out of your mind, as plenty of people already think that you are. So rethink your plan, baby, or else."

I had to laugh at this fool. "How you gon' stand your greasy ass in here, trying to call the shots? They may not believe what I say, but they will believe me when I show them pictures that I took with my phone. You didn't see me take them because you were too busy getting got. I'm sure you don't want anyone to see you like that, especially not anyone at work, or your parents, and, uh, damn sure not Keith. He doesn't know about this, does he?"

I seemed to have Bryson's attention, even though I lied about the pictures. I wish I had taken some, but at the time, I was too in shock to even think straight.

Bryson walked slowly over to the couch and sat down. He rubbed his waves then cleared mucus from his throat.

"No," he said in a calmer tone. "Nobody knows. I've been hiding this for a very long time. I love women, no doubt, but

I like men too. It's been that way since I was in high school, but I was afraid to tell my parents. Didn't want to tell my brother because I wasn't sure how he would feel about me. So please don't tell anyone about this. When I'm ready, I will say something. I'm just not ready yet."

I sat back and crossed my legs. "That was a tear-jerking little story there, Bryson, and I have no problem keeping your secret. But it's going to cost you. You want to know why? Because you shouldn't have never put your dick inside of me, knowing that you also have a thing for men. If anything, you should have come clean about being bisexual and given me a chance to decide if I wanted to fuck with you. This down-low shit is a dangerous game to play. I hope to God that Libby knows what you're up to, and I guess that explains why you refused to settle down and marry her. At least you haven't been stupid enough to go that far."

"I haven't told her the truth yet, but one day I will. Then maybe she'll figure it out, since I'm refusing to marry her. Either way, I need to know that you're going to keep your mouth shut. I need to know your price, and if I give you any money, Evelyn, I don't want you reneging on me and putting my business out there. You have no idea how damaging something like this could be to me."

"If the price is right, I won't say a word. That price is a hundred thousand dollars. That's what it will take for me to keep my mouth shut."

"At that price, I may as well kill you then. I don't have that kind of money."

"Yes, you do. I saw the bank statements in your files. And if you don't have it, your parents do. Keith definitely has it, and all you have to do is ask him to sell one or two of those exquisite paintings in his studio. That's how you can get it and then some. As for killing me, don't bother. The word about you will still spread, because a good friend of mine already has those photos in her possession. She knows exactly what to do with them, if something happens to me. And we both know that, social media comes in handy when you need to use it to spread the word."

Bryson knew his hands were tied. He sat there and couldn't say shit. When he did open his mouth, he said exactly what I wanted to hear. I'd have the money by tomorrow. Certainly, that was good enough for me.

The next day, I walked into the office as if last night had never happened. I smiled at Bryson and he smiled back at me. He came over to my desk around noon, telling me that the money had been deposited into my account. I checked, and sure enough, sister girl was out of the negative. I was very happy about that. So happy that I wanted to go holler at an old friend of mine, so we could both celebrate our wealth. Hopefully, Cedric wouldn't refuse to see me.

Having a slew of money in my bank account caused me to pack it up and leave. My first stop was at the bank, where I withdrew several thousands of dollars to catch up on my bills. I prepaid my landlord three month's rent then I headed to the mall to purchase a pair of shoes and a pantsuit that I wanted. After that, I went to find a special gift for a dear friend of mine. Since I was going to stop by, it didn't make sense for me to stop by empty-handed.

I left the mall with several bags in my hands. Tossed them on the back seat, and then I made my way to Cedric's house. Upon arrival, the first thing I did was scope out the place to make sure Kayla's crazy self was nowhere around. I wasn't in the mood for another one of her slaps. My day had been on point, thus far, and I expected for it to get better.

Kayla's car was nowhere in sight and neither was Jacoby's. Cedric's BMW was parked in the driveway, and I was surprised to see a HOUSE FOR SALE sign in the yard. I figured that after the divorce was finalized, neither Cedric or Kayla would want to live in that house, especially since Cedric had almost been murdered in it. Something about that seemed creepy.

I was kind of excited about seeing Cedric, so I reached for his gift on the back seat and strutted to the front door. I rang the doorbell, and a few minutes later, Cedric opened the door. He looked fabulous and very clean cut in his business attire. I could always smell the dollars blowing in the air. His face, though, was without a smile. He looked me up and down, and hadn't invited me in yet.

The gift was behind my back, so I brought it forth to give it to him.

"Hello, handsome," I said. "I was at the mall today and I thought about you. I've been meaning to stop by and check on you, but time got away from me. Then I heard through the grapevine that you were putting your house up for sale. I'm very interested in purchasing it, but first, I kind of need for you to show me around. May I come in?"

Cedric stood for a moment, staring at me as if I had shit on my face. He then opened the door wider to let me inside. I tried to give him the gift again, but he wouldn't take it.

"Aww, Cedric, don't be so mean to me," I teased. "At least look at it. We both have good taste and creative minds. I'm sure you'll like it."

I forced the package his way again. This time, he snatched it from my hand and tore the shiny wrapping paper away from the box. When he opened it, inside was a protection kit that included Mace, a small pocket knife, and handcuffs.

I smiled at him and explained my nice gesture. "I thought those items may come in handy the next time any woman tries to come in your house and kill you. If you had those items in your possession, you could have sprayed that whore with Mace, stabbed her, and then handcuffed her until the police got here."

Cedric wet his lips with his tongue. He narrowed his eyes to look at the items then nodded. The next thing I knew, he reached out for my hair and pulled it tight. He then used his foot to trip me. I hit the marble floor in the foyer so hard that my ass hurt.

"Damn!" I shouted. "What in the hell did I say that was so wrong?"

Cedric flipped me on my stomach and pressed his knee into my back, damn near cracking it. He pulled my arms behind me and locked the cuffs on my wrists. I struggled to stop him, but to no avail. The cuffs were locked so tight that it felt as if they were cutting my wrists. While I was face down, he pulled my hair back to lift my head. He put the knife close to my neck and spoke through gritted teeth.

"Thanks for the bullshit gift. I'm glad that I could put it to good use. Let this be a warning to you that I'm not some motherfucking toy you can play with. I'm a changed man, and I promise you that I am nothing like I was before. You don't want to fuck with me, and to be clear, I don't have time for bitches like you. You couldn't afford to live here, so take yo' ass back to that rattrap you live in. I never want to see your face again. Got it?"

Well damn. Since when did I manage to get on his bad side? I didn't respond quick enough to his "got it" question, so he dropped the knife and slammed my head on the marble foyer, face first. I heard my teeth crack and my lip felt numb. I also tasted blood stirring in my mouth, and I could feel it dripping down my chin. This was a clear sign that his ass wasn't playing with me. I nodded to answer his question, but that wasn't good enough for him.

"Speak up, tramp! I can't hear you. You're not allowed to come here, call me, nothing . . . ever again! Do you understand?"

The loudness of his voice caused my ears to ring. I quickly answered before he slammed my face again.

"Yes," I cried out with tears rolling down my face. "I do understand."

"Good!"

Cedric lifted me off the floor and escorted me over to the front door. He opened it, and used the key to remove the cuffs. As I massaged my wrists, he shoved me outside. I fell on the porch, scraping my knees. While rubbing them, he threw the wrapping paper, box, and contents at me. I ducked to avoid the flying can of Mace. After that, he slammed the door and locked it.

Shit was getting a little rough for me. My good day had turned bad. And when I got in the car to look at my mouth in the rearview mirror, it wasn't a pretty sight. My mouth was bloody and my front tooth dangled. It hurt, too, so instead of going back to the mall to shop, I made my way to the dentist and thought about ways to make Cedric pay for this. He was out of control. He didn't appear to be the man that he was before. Something about him was different. Maybe, just maybe, it was in my best interest to leave his ass alone. Or, at least, until he shook off some of that madness.

Chapter 15

Trina

Keith and I were back on track. Moving in with him was the best thing I could've done. Just yesterday, I cleared out my entire apartment and turned in my keys. I called Kayla to see if she would come help me, considering that she had lived with me for a while too. She said that she was busy. She'd been acting kind of funny lately. I asked if something was wrong, but she insisted that she didn't want to discuss it. Good, because like she had mentioned to me, I got tired of hearing about the negativity too. Maybe it was a good thing that she was keeping whatever it was that was bothering her to herself.

I came to the conclusion that the reason she didn't have time to help me with my apartment was because she was moving into hers. I hadn't seen it yet, but she told me how fabulous it was. I hoped to see it soon.

Keith had gone to the studio on Delmar to do some work. There were more supplies there to work with. We'd been spending so much time in this house, he needed to get out. I wasn't trying to keep him cooped up in here, but it was nice to wake up with a sexy, fine man lying next to me. Especially one who was great at lovemaking and who appreciated having sex quite often.

While he was gone, I started to clean up. The house had gotten kind of messy since I'd been here. I cleaned the bathrooms, washed the dishes, and did the laundry. As I sat in the living room folding clothes and watching TV, I looked through the huge picture window and saw Evelyn parking her car. I couldn't believe that she had the nerve to show her face over here again. I guess she thought Keith was here alone, but unfortunately for her, he wasn't.

Seething with anger, I stormed to the front door and swung it open before she even made it up the stairs.

"Really, Evelyn? You must be insane. Either that or I guess you don't believe I'm capable of stopping you with that gun that was introduced to you the last time you were here."

Evelyn slowed her pace, and she didn't reply. She paced her way up to me with sadness written all over her face. Tears welled in her eyes. Almost immediately, I saw her bruised, puffy lips; and a deep cut was on her lip, too. She threw her arms around me and dropped her head on my shoulder. She started to cry and could barely catch her breath as she tried to speak.

"I'm so, so sorry about what I did to you. Pleeese forgive me, Trina. I need for you to forgive me because I don't have nobody in my corner."

I pursed my lips, unable to sympathize with her. I didn't even bother to hug her back, but I intended to offer her some comforting words. I backed away from her tight embrace and looked at her disheveled appearance that I hadn't seen before. Her clothes were slouchy, bags were underneath her eyes, her hair was frizzy, and her skin appeared very pale. Not to mention, again, her swollen lips.

"Come into the living room and sit down. You always have someone in your corner. I don't have to remind you who He is."

"God don't help people like me. I don't know what's gotten into me. Ever since I lost my friendship with you and Kayla, things in my life haven't been right. My life has been going downhill, and I don't know what to do to stop it from sliding."

Evelyn fell back on the couch, tucking her leg underneath her. I reached for some tissue and gave it to her before taking a seat. She wiped her nose and dabbed her teary eyes. I wasn't going to respond to her comment about our friendship yet.

"What happened to your lip?" I asked. "Did you get into a fight with someone or did you and Kayla have another conversation?"

"No, I haven't seen her. Cedric did this to me. I stopped by his house the other day to give him a gift and to see how he was doing. He went crazy on me. Started punching me, and he knocked me on the floor. Took his fist and punched me in the face, and then he pounded my head on the floor. He knocked out my tooth, and I had to go to the dentist to get a tooth implant."

Evelyn was known for exaggerating. She grinned to show me her new tooth. I saw that the inside of her mouth was swollen and bruised. I frowned from how nasty it looked. A huge part of me didn't believe her, though. For her to say that Cedric had done all of that to her was a bit much. A dog he was, but an abusive man he wasn't.

"I don't know if he did that to you or not, but why would you go over there? After all that has happened, why don't you leave Cedric alone and be done with it?"

More tears fell from Evelyn's eyes. She wiped them then crumbled the tissue in her hand. I got up to get her some more tissue then sat back down to listen.

"Believe me, I tried to stay away from him, but I got lonely. There was a time when I could always reach out to you or Kayla, but you already know where we stand. With that in mind, I ran to Cedric for friendship and conversation. I thought we were still cool, and I don't understand what I did to make him hate me so much. Maybe the abortion upset him."

I surely didn't want to hurt her feelings. "I doubt that, and please forgive me because I'm still having a hard time believing all of this. You are so good at fabricating stories and embellishing them, Evelyn. I don't know what to believe. I promise you, though, that I won't get caught up in your games again."

Evelyn closed her eyes and moved her head from side to side. "I know I've been a terrible friend, and I've lied a lot in the past, too." She opened her eyes and looked at me. "But I'm not lying about what Cedric did to me. I swear to you that I'm not lying."

She pulled out her cell phone and dialed out. Afterward, she placed the phone between us and hit the speaker button.

I heard a phone ringing. Seconds later Cedric answered. I guess knowing who the caller was, he tore into her right away.

"Didn't I tell you not to reach out to me again? I guess that ass kicking you got wasn't enough! If—"

Evelyn hit the end button and looked at me with more sadness. "See? I told you he beat me."

Damn. Why did I feel so bad for her? I tried my best not to let her know it. "He never should have put his hands on you. Maybe you need to press charges against him."

"I'm afraid to. He threatened me and said that he'd tell the police that I came over there to kill him, especially since this incident took place at his house. Considering what had happened with Paula, he assured me that the police would believe him. I just don't want any more trouble."

"Then stay away from there. If you needed companionship, friendship, or a conversation, why didn't you contact Bryson? Aren't you still kicking it with him? If not, what happened to y'all's relationship?"

Evelyn looked down and shook her head. She fumbled with the tissue then blew her nose again. This time, she stood and walked over to the picture window to look outside.

"I'll tell you what happened, but you have to promise me that you won't say anything to Keith. Is he here?"

"No, he's not. I can't promise you that I'll be keeping any secrets from him, though. We're striving to have a trustworthy and honest relationship."

"I get that, but this is something that you can't tell him. If you do, it will hurt him, and it could hurt me too. It involves Bryson and it's really, really bad. As for the two of us, I am so over him. It pains me to be around him every day at work, and I'm thinking about quitting."

Whatever it was sounded pretty darn juicy. I wasn't sure if I would tell Keith, especially if it was something that would hurt him. Regardless, I told Evelyn that I wouldn't say a word, just to get her to spill the beans.

"Promise me," she said, walking away from the window. "You have to promise me that you won't say anything. If you do, Bryson may hurt me even worse than Cedric did."

I was eager to hear what was up. "Okay, I promise. I won't say a word to Keith or anyone else."

Evelyn sat back down and went into great details about what she discovered with Bryson. The whole time she spoke, my eyes were bugged and my mouth was stuck wide open. When Evelyn was done, I flat out told her that she was a damn liar. That was when she told me about the money and showed me the deposit into her bank account.

"He begged me not to say a word to anyone. I don't even know if I should have told you about this, but it gives you an idea about how fucked up my life has been. I fell for a nigga on the down low, Trina. If I shared with you all of the things that I allowed him to do to me, or all of the things that I'd done to him, you'd throw up."

This was bad. Real bad. I couldn't believe that Bryson was on the DL. He had so many women in his circle, beautiful women, too. I'd seen him with chicks who looked as if they were Hollywood made. They loved Bryson's dirty under-wear and would do anything to be with him. I was outdone by this news. I figured Keith didn't have a clue about his brother. He and Bryson were very close, but I was almost positive that something like this wouldn't sit right with Keith.

Evelyn interrupted my thoughts. "I don't need any more trouble, Trina, so again, keep this between us. I get that you've been mad at me and you may not care what Bryson will do to me, if this gets out. But, please, have some concern for my well-being."

This time, I stood and paced the floor. Evelyn had put me on the spot. Maybe I needed to speak to Bryson first, before I decided what to do with this information. There was still a chance that Evelyn was being untruthful.

"Girl, if you're lying about this, shame on you. You need to seek help and—"

Evelyn pounded her leg with her fist. "I'm not lying! The truth is, I do believe that I need to talk to a professional who may be able to help me deal with all of this pain. I've been dealing with it for a long time, and I've never sought help from when I experienced my father beating me and my mother, him making us homeless or for having sex with me. I should have gotten help years ago, but I never did. Maybe all of this craziness wouldn't be happening, and maybe I could've figured out how to be a better friend."

Evelyn's words made me reflect to when she used to come to school with black eyes and with bruises on her arms and legs, compliments of her father. Kayla and I felt so bad for her. My mother even pitched in to help when Evelyn's father threw her and her mother out of the house. They stayed with us for a few months then went to live in a shelter. The people at the shelter found them a place to live, but it wasn't long before her mother let her dad back in. The abuse continued and the rest was history. I guess that a part of me couldn't blame Evelyn for being so screwed up. She wasn't lying when she said she needed some help.

"I applaud you for wanting to get some counseling, and it's not exactly a bad thing. I've had my issues too, and I just realized what was holding me back when it came to Keith. I talked to him about it, and I feel much better."

"That's the thing. You have somebody to talk to. I don't. I keep all of this stuff bottled up inside of me, and I haven't said much to you or Kayla about my issues because I don't want to be judged. Just know that I'm sorry for everything. No matter if you decide to forgive me or not, I'm sorry and please tell Keith I'm sorry too."

Right at that moment, the front door opened. Keith walked in with a smile, but it vanished when he saw Evelyn sitting on the couch.

"What is she doing here?" he asked with a frown on his face.

I didn't like his tone, but I understood where it was coming from. "She came over to apologize to us about what happened."

"Apologize? I don't need an apology and neither do you. What I need is for Evelyn to get off my couch and leave. Right now."

Evelyn blinked tears from her eyes and stood up. No words could express how bad I felt. She was so unstable. I didn't want her to leave here, feeling as if everyone was against her. I tried to settle this with Keith, but he wasn't trying to hear it.

"Keith, calm down. Let me finish talking to her, and then we'll—"

"I am calm, and I will remain calm, as long as she exits." He walked to the door and opened it. "Peace."

Evelyn blinked away her tears and her breath staggered. She was fighting back all that was inside of her. I wanted to tell her not to leave, but I didn't want to argue with Keith. Instead, I walked behind her and tapped her shoulder. She turned around.

"Give me a hug before you go. Stay strong and we'll talk soon enough."

She threw her arms around me and held me tight. So tight, as if she didn't want to let go. When she did, she barely looked at Keith who stood at the door with a mean mug. After giving him one last look, she left. I slowly closed the door and turned to him.

"I know what you're going to say, but she's going through a lot right now. I tried not to sympathize with her, but you know how I am."

Keith gave me a dirty look then walked away. He went into the kitchen and I followed. He opened the fridge, pulled out a beer, and popped the cap. The strange gaze in his eyes was still there.

"What is it?" I said. "Why do you keep looking at me like that?"

Keith guzzled down the beer and then wiped across his mouth. "I almost hate to ask you this, but something here ain't right. Were you and Evelyn ever lovers, or should I say, are the two of you still lovers?"

If there ever was a time when I wanted to smack the shit out of Keith, this was it. How dare he ask me such a question? What a gotdamn insult.

"You can't be serious," I snapped.

"I'm very serious. Because I don't understand how you could've let her back into this house. After all that she's done, her lies and games, you felt a need to open the door and let her in here? I don't give a rat's ass what she's been through. Hell, we all go through things, but we don't go around manipulating people, trying to screw people's significant others and telling lies about them, do we?"

"She's a little off, Keith. I suggested that she gets some help. Hopefully, she'll take my advice."

He slammed the bottle of beer on the table. "A little off? No, she is way off and wacky as hell. I don't ever want her in this house again."

"Yeah, well, you're way off too by suggesting that she and I are lovers. I guess you're a wacko too. And in case you forgot, I live here too. I don't tell you who is or isn't allowed in here, and it's wrong for you to try to tell me."

"What I say goes. She's not welcome here, Trina. If you don't like it, you know what you can do."

Keith walked past me and left the kitchen. The last thing I wanted was to get into another heated argument with him, so I decided to let him cool off and rethink his position. He went upstairs, and I grabbed my purse and keys from the couch. I looked like a bum in my jeans and half shirt, but I needed to get out of there. I also needed to go talk to Bryson. If what Evelyn said was true, Keith needed to know. I wasn't about to keep any more secrets from him.

Taking my chances, I went to a worksite where Keith and I had taken Bryson some lunch earlier in the week. It was a big project that he was working on, so I prayed that he was there so we could talk.

I arrived at the location, seeing several construction workers with hard hats on. It was rather noisy, and I started to think that maybe this was a bad idea. My thoughts were quickly washed away when I saw Bryson and another man standing real close to each other. They appeared to be indulged in a deep conversation, and I knew flirting eyes when I saw them. There was too much smiling going on and a bunch of lip licking, too. I parked my car, and as I moved toward them, I saw Bryson back away from the man. The second his eyes shifted in my direction, the man turned around to see who I was. Bryson said something to him, and he walked away.

"What's up, sis-in-law," he said with a smile. "You know better than to come out here without any lunch in your hand, and where is my brother at?"

"He's at home, mad as hell at me."

"What for?"

"I'll tell you in a minute. That's why I'm here. Is there anywhere private where we can talk?"

Bryson nodded and told me to follow him into a construction trailer that was piled with junk, including a desk, several folding chairs, and orange street cones. He invited me to have a seat in one of the chairs.

"Can I get you a bottled water or soda?"

"No, I'm fine."

Bryson got a bottled water from the fridge then took a seat behind the wooden desk.

"What's on your mind? Keith's been causing you some headaches?"

"No, not exactly, but one of my friends have been. That would be Evelyn. She came to see me today, and she said some disturbing things to me about you."

Bryson almost dropped the bottled water that was close to his lips. It splashed on his shirt and he wiped it. "What did she say that was so disturbing? I could say some disturbing things about her too, but I'm skeptical about going there because she's your friend."

"I'll get straight to the point. She said that you were on the DL. Claimed she caught you having sex with a tranny and showed me the balance of some money you put into her account to keep quiet. I totally do not believe her, but I needed to hear what was up from your mouth. Why would she say something like that about you, if it wasn't true?"

Bryson leaned back in the chair and scratched his head. "Because she's fucking crazy, that's why. I swear I be messing around with some weird-ass chicks. But this here takes the cake. I've never heard no shit like this before, and where do these women be getting their stories from? Books?"

I laughed because he had a point. "It's funny that you say that because I recently read a book by Nikki Michelle, *Bi-Satisfied*. It was along the same lines as what Evelyn claimed she saw you indulged in, so maybe she read the same book."

Bryson laughed. "Maybe so. But, uh, just so you know, I don't get down like that. Not me; never."

Bryson guzzled down the water, while tapping his fingers on the desk. As we talked, he tapped faster. His leg shook and he had the same shocking look in his eyes that I'd had when Kayla confronted me about what Cedric suspected about me.

When the direction of my eyes traveled to Bryson's fingers, he stopped tapping them and squeezed his hand.

I let him know what was on my mind. "Let me just say this to you, okay, Bryson? I don't know if Keith ever mentioned this to you before, but I used to be bisexual. My family disowned me, and until this day, they still do. I had a very difficult time telling anyone what was going on with me, and I kept that secret away from my friends for a very long time. You may already know that the chick who stabbed Keith was my lover. I have to live with that, and it still pains me to know that my lies could have killed him. I don't care what your sexual preferences are. You know that Keith and I will love you regardless. But do me a favor and please tell him the truth, if indeed you are having sex with men. I say that because hearing this from other people will be damaging. If Evelyn has any proof, or if what she's saying is factual, it's just a matter of time when your secret will no longer be a secret. All the money in the world will not keep her mouth closed."

Bryson looked away, swallowed, and then looked at me with a devious gaze. "Didn't you hear what I said? I told you that bitch was lying, and I'm not about to confess to something that ain't true. Keith told me about your little girlfriend, but if that's how you chose to get down, then don't come in here trying to push that shit off on me. I got a gang of women who can vouch for me. They know what I stand for. It's called pussy. That's what my heart desires, and unfortunately, your friend is only upset because hers wasn't good enough for me. Now, I have to get back to work. But before I do, you may want to tell your friend that if any of her lies leak elsewhere, well, I can show her better than I can tell her."

Seeing that Bryson was getting pretty upset with me, I stood to go. "If she is lying, then I guess you have nothing to worry about. If you are, then you're the one who has to deal with the repercussions. Thanks for listening to me, and you have my word that I will not bring any of this up to Keith."

"I hope not. And please keep that bullshit to yourself."

On that note, I left. I knew for a fact that Evelyn wasn't lying. Bryson was. But at this point, there was nothing that I could do but keep quiet until the shit hit the fan.

Chapter 16

Kayla

Evelyn told Trina what had happened and Trina told me. I wanted to laugh at what Cedric did, but to me, it really wasn't a laughing matter. Don't get me wrong. I despised Evelyn to the fullest. I would never be a friend to her again, but Cedric was out of line.

With that being said, I was going to contact him and say something, but I decided against it. I said that Jacoby was my priority and that he was. I'd been making sure that he handled his business at school, I limited his time with Adrianne a little bit, and the two of us spent a lot of quality time together talking, hanging out, and enjoying each other's company. I made it clear to him that I had his back and he now knew it, more than ever.

Jacoby and I had just gotten back from Froyo, getting some frozen yogurt. The second we got out of the car, Cedric was parking. He hadn't been over to see our new place, but I'd given him the address and told him all about it. He was in the process of looking for a place too. A few days ago, he mentioned that someone was interested in buying the house. I guess he'd stopped by to tell me all about it and to check out the new place we called home.

"Damn, that's how I get played?" he said, looking at our yogurt with his hands held out. "Where's mine at?"

"Jacoby bought this for me," I said. "Since I didn't have any money."

Jacoby said, "What's up," to Cedric and walked ahead of us. Since I'd known about the incident, he kind of shied away from Cedric. I told him to stop doing that because Cedric would pick up on it and say something, as he'd done before.

"No money," Cedric shouted. "Woman, please. If your money is gone, you need that ass kicked."

Jacoby had already opened the door to our apartment, so we followed and went inside. Cedric looked up at the vaulted ceiling in the foyer and checked out the spacious living room area with double bay windows.

"What kind of apartment is this?" he said. "How did you find this place?"

"By driving around. It's nice, isn't it? Let me show you the kitchen."

"I prefer to see the bedroom," he joked. I rolled my eyes at him. "Not to do anything with you, but just in case I may want to move in another unit around here."

"Please, no way. I don't want to be close to you, and I think it's best that you move waaaay on the other side of town."

Jacoby was already sitting at the kitchen table when we entered. He was eating his yogurt while watching TV. Cedric spoke about how fabulous the kitchen was, and then he sat at the table with Jacoby.

"What's up with you, man? Why have you been ignoring me?" Cedric asked.

Jacoby shrugged, looked at Cedric then looked at the TV again. "I'm not ignoring you. I was just looking at TV, trying to see if the game was on."

"That's cool, but, uh, how about we get together for the weekend. Go to one of the basketball games in Miami and see who's really bringing the Heat. A friend of mine got a yacht down there, too. He has a son around your age and we can hang out with them on the high seas and have a good time."

Jacoby nodded while rubbing his forehead. "Maybe so. I'll let you know for sure by tomorrow. Adrianne and I had plans, but I'll see if I can cancel."

"Adrianne can wait. Besides, she sees you more than I do. You need some space and time to just go do you, if you know what I mean."

"Like I said, we'll see."

I didn't want to interfere, but I could see how uncomfortable Jacoby was. "Jacoby, why don't you go call Trey back? He called earlier, saying that he needed some assistance with his homework. Go call him before it gets too late, and you get all wrapped up in that game."

Jacoby got up from the table and walked away. Cedric grabbed his arm, causing Jacoby to jump as if he were startled. All Cedric did was hold out his hand for dap.

"I can't get no holla later or hand slap before you head to your room? I'm not staying long, but don't forget to call me tomorrow."

"I won't," Jacoby said then slapped his hand against Cedric's. Jacoby also gave him a hug, too, and then he left the room.

"I'm telling you that something is up with our son," Cedric said. "I don't like it either, and I think he may need counseling. I also think that seeing me lying there almost dead has affected him in a major way. Every time I mention that day to him, he gets real uptight."

"I think you're making too much of this, Cedric. Jacoby has a lot on his mind with school and his girlfriend. Going away to Miami this weekend may be a good thing for him, but please be careful with my only child."

"Sure, Miss Too Overprotective. I wouldn't want him to fall off the yacht by accident and go missing in the water. You'd probably kill me."

My face fell flat after that comment. Cedric shot me a peculiar look and stared at me. Why would he make a comment like that? Did he know something that he wasn't saying? More than that, was his tail planning to kill my son? That comment rubbed me the wrong way.

I snapped my finger. "You know what? I just thought about something. I'm supposed to go take Jacoby for his SAT prep test this weekend. He's on the schedule to take it, and I don't want him to miss it. You may have to plan that trip to Miami on another date."

"All right. I'll check my calendar and see what's up."

Cedric's cell phone rang. He looked to see who it was. He excused himself and went outside on the balcony to take the call. I had moved to the other side of the kitchen, and I kept seeing him peeking around the corner to see where I'd gone to. I moved closer to the sliding doors, trying to make out what he was saying. All I heard was a lot of whispers. Whispers that made me nervous. So nervous that when he came back inside, I questioned him.

"Why were you out there whispering?" I asked while standing by the island.

"I wasn't whispering. And if I was, that's because who I speak to ain't your business."

"If it's not my business then it must have been Evelyn. Then again, it couldn't have been her because I heard you beat her like she stole something from you. I didn't know you'd gotten so violent."

Cedric shot me that peculiar look again then walked over to stand in front of me. He eased his hands in his pockets and jiggled his keys. "Yeah, well, when you keep on getting fucked over by no-good women who want your money one minute, then want to kill you the next minute, you kind of get tired of the shit. At some point, the only way you can deal with them is by being violent, because it's the only language they understand. The bottom line is, Evelyn got what she deserved. And everybody else who wishes to fuck me over will get the same thing too. With that, I'm out. I can't check out the rest of the place, because I have somewhere I need to be. Don't forget to tell Jacoby to call me, either way."

I nodded and watched as Cedric strutted toward the door.

"By the way, what about the house?" I yelled after him. "Any buyers?"

He turned at the door. "We'll talk about that the next time I stop by. Gotta go, but before I do, I wanted to let you know that I fired Cynthia."

"Why?" I said with a frown. "She was very nice."

"Nice, but too gotdamn nosy."

Cedric walked out. I hated to hear that about Cynthia, but was it possible that Cedric had already put two and two together? He was a very smart man, and the least I could do was try my best to stay on his good side, just in case his suspicions grew.

I was so worried about how much Cedric knew that I decided to follow him and go see what he was up to. I also thought it would be wise for me to stop by his house and do some snooping around. I had to be sure that he wasn't plotting against me and Jacoby. For some reason, he'd been extremely nice, which was kind of odd for Cedric. Yeah, he'd been near death before. That was definitely a reason to make someone have a change of heart. But what he'd done to Evelyn proved to me that Cedric wasn't the changed man he was claiming to be.

I rushed to Jacoby's room to tell him I'd be right back. He didn't bother to ask where I was going because he was on the phone. I hurried into my car, suspecting that Cedric would be heading toward the highway. Sure enough, he was. He had just made a left turn, and I had to go through a red light to prevent him from getting away from me. There were several cars between us, and I could barely keep up because Cedric was driving fast. I could see that he was on his cell phone. He didn't end the call until he got off at the Forest Park exit. That was where he exited his car and walked up to a white man who appeared to be waiting for him. They shook hands then sat on a bench, talking for a while. The man passed Cedric an envelope, but they kept on talking. There was no way for me to see what was inside of the envelope because I was too far away. As I moved closer and squinted, Cedric tucked the envelope into his jacket. He exchanged another handshake with the man then left.

After that, I followed him to a restaurant on Manchester. That was where he met a woman outside. She appeared to be a classy woman who kind of reminded me of myself. She was very tall and could have easily been a model. Truthfully, she almost looked like me, but I was healthier than she was. I watched as she and Cedric sat in his car and kissed. It was pretty intense, and then they exited the car. Cedric held her waist and patted her ass as they went inside. Less than a minute later, they came back out and headed to his car. With so many people waiting outside to be served, I guessed that the wait time was too long for them. Her back was against Cedric's car and he stood in front of her. I saw his hands creep up her dress, but she playfully smacked it. The way they acted toward each other, I could instantly tell that this wasn't a new relationship. Yet again, they shared a lengthy kiss then got into separate cars. Cedric followed her, and I followed him. I thought they were going to his place, but instead, they stopped at her place, which was less than a mile away from where he lived. It was obvious what they were getting ready to get into, since Cedric tossed his jacket over his shoulder and followed her into her house, while wiggling his tie away from his neck. After seeing that, I sped off. I was feeling some kind of way about my ex-husband being with this woman. Yes, a tiny part of me was jealous, but a huge part of me was delighted about the decision I'd made to proceed with the divorce. For him to bring up sex, when in my presence, was wrong on so many different levels. He knew better. I wouldn't dare go there with him again.

Cedric was going to be busy for a long time, so I drove to his house. I still had a key to let myself in, but I was nervous about going inside and snooping. The second I pushed the door open, my cell phone rang, causing me to jump. It was Trina. I hurried to answer, just so she wouldn't call back and rattle my nerves again.

"Hello," I whispered.

"Why are you whispering?"

I raised my voice up a notch. Didn't make sense to whisper anyway, especially since no one was there. "No reason," I said. "What's up?"

"Nothing much. I wanted to holler for a minute, about Evelyn."

Evelyn. Evelyn. Evelyn. I didn't have time to discuss Evelyn right now.

"Listen, Trina, I'm kind of busy. And to be honest, I'm getting kind of tired of hearing about Evelyn and her drama. I'm not trying to be rude, but can you please find someone else to talk about?"

Trina hesitated with her response. "Don't worry about it. I'll talk to you later."

Trina hung up on me. I surely didn't care. I mean, enough already with Evelyn and her mess. I seriously couldn't understand why Trina was still trying to hold on to their friendship. I was going to tell Trina how I really felt about this. But for now, I had a bigger fish to fry.

I dropped my cell phone into my purse. The first place I went to was where Cedric spent most of his time. That was in his office. The next thing I did was search through his computer. I examined his files and looked at the last links in his browser that he'd visited. I read some of his recent letters and scanned through his calendar to see if anything was out of the ordinary. Most of the things that I saw were related to business. I didn't find much on his computer, so I began to check his drawers. Yet again, much of what I found was business related, but I did find a porn magazine, condoms, and several pictures. I flipped through pictures of the woman he was currently with. They were naked pictures, and I found myself a little jealous because she had it going on. I also saw several "get well soon" cards from her. Touching messages were written inside and she stressed how much she loved him. Like I'd said, it was obvious that their relationship had been going on for quite some time. Joy made that quite clear in her letters and cards.

I came up empty with my drawer search, so I lifted the pillows on the couch and searched underneath them. I checked the bookshelves, and that was where I found a 9 mm that made me more nervous. I didn't dare touch it, but I walked away from the bookshelves and looked underneath a huge rug that covered the hardwood floors. Nothing. Nothing at all, so I left Cedric's office and went to his bedroom. Didn't have much luck there, but I found several more letters from Joy who was more than excited about our divorce. According to her, she couldn't wait for Cedric to sell the house, so the two of them could move in together. That way, she could take care of him, since I failed to do so. I wanted to go to her house and slap her, like I'd slapped Evelyn for being so stupid. Women sure didn't know how to stick together, and they would quickly throw you under the bus, when it came to a man. One day, I'd give her a piece of my mind and tell her what I really thought of the comments about me in her letters. She was on the outside looking in and didn't have a clue what it was like to be married to Cedric.

With an attitude, I continued my search. Went to the basement then found myself back in Cedric's office. I stood in the doorway looking around. My eyes shifted to a mail tray on

one of the shelves that I'd overlooked. Inside of the tray were
envelopes that contained bills. But there were also four envelopes wrapped with a rubber band. The envelopes hadn't been
opened, but there were letters inside. The letters came from
the correctional facility where Paula Daniels was at. They
were all addressed to him. Eager to see what she had written to him, I panicked as I tore open one of the letters. It was
short, and according to her, she needed to speak to him about
something important. She didn't say what it was until I read
the next letter. That was when she got specific and wrote that
it was imperative that she spoke to him about something with
Jacoby. She stressed how sorry she was, apologized for trying
to kill him, but said she felt as if he needed to know the truth.

I hurried to stuff the letters into my purse. Looked around
for more of them, but didn't find any. Searched for a few
minutes more then gave up. I left, feeling as if this situation
would, eventually, turn ugly. Maybe Jacoby and I needed to
get ahead of this and talk to Cedric? Seemed like Paula was
eager to bust Jacoby out, and it was best that Cedric heard it
from us, instead of her. I remained in the car in deep thought
about what to do. And when my cell phone rang, I grabbed it
from my purse and put the phone up to my ear.

"Hello," I said.

"I have a question for you," Cedric said in a serious tone.

My stomach twisted in a knot. I could feel a sheen of sweat
forming on my forehead.

"Wha . . . what is it?"

"Why are you in my house?"

This time, my stomach hit the floor. I had no answer; my
mouth was stuck.

"I have cameras in there," he said. "Didn't want what happened to me before to happen again. I've seen you going
through my things. And the only other question I have for you
is why are those letters from Paula any concern of yours?"

I was cold busted. Couldn't think of a lie fast enough to get
me out of this. I wasn't sure if my made-up explanation would
suffice or not, but I went for it anyway.

"The truth is, I still love you, Cedric. A part of me regrets
signing those divorce papers, and I could kick myself for

doing so. I suspected that you were on the phone earlier with another woman and I was jealous. After you left my house, I attempted to follow you, but I lost you somewhere on the high- way. I thought you would meet the woman here, so I came by to see what was up. You know how nosy I am, so I started looking around to see what I could find. Your relationship with Joy hurts me, and I didn't appreciate the letters I found from Paula. I hate her for what she tried to do to you, so I took the letters to dispose of them. You haven't been keeping in touch with her, have you? I truly hope not, Cedric, especially after what she did to you."

There was a crisp silence over the phone. I hoped that Cedric believed me, but maybe I rambled on too long. I waited with bated breath to hear his response.

He cleared his throat. "Hell, no, I haven't been keeping in touch with her. I couldn't care less about what she has to say, and I have no intentions to read those dumb letters. If she continues to write them, I'm going to turn them over to the police. I already have some people involved who will make those letters stop. As for Joy, she's a nice woman. I don't want you having any regrets about our divorce, only because I do believe you made the right decision for both of us. So don't sweat it, baby. You know damn well that you can have a piece of me whenever you want it. All you have to do is say the word."

Cedric laughed. So did I, feeling a bit relieved. Just a little, because I was still hoping like hell that the letters stopped.

Chapter 17

Trina

Keith's big dick was so far up in me that I couldn't even think straight. I couldn't move and I was on the verge of a shaky orgasm. Make-up sex between us was always the best. This time around, I apologized for the incident with Evelyn. I made Keith feel as if I were on his side, but the truth was, I was caught in the middle.

I'd spoken to Evelyn and expressed how sorry I was about Keith's ill treatment. I tried to explain his position, and Evelyn insisted she understood. What I didn't tell her, though, was that I'd gone to see Bryson. I didn't find it necessary to tell her my thoughts about what I discovered during our conversation. That would only give her more ammunition, and I didn't want to stir her up.

What I wanted was more of Keith. He was now down below, sucking my well dry. My thighs were locked on his face and my eyes were squeezed tight. I could barely catch my breath, and I pounded his back, letting him know how spectacular his tongue tricks felt.

"Baby, you are the motherfucking man! My man, so keep doing that shit, only how you can do it!"

I loved to stroke his ego. Seeing him smile always made me feel good. His tongue snaked in and out of my folds. He tickled my pearl then turned me over to tackle my goodness from behind. I kicked, screamed and begged for him to keep at, so I'd come again. Within minutes, my request was honored. I was spent; he was too. He crawled next to me in bed and lay flat on his back while taking deep breaths. While staring at the ceiling, he rubbed his chest.

"Did I tell you how much I love you today?" he said.

I turned sideways and rubbed my hand on his chest. "No, you didn't tell me, but you sure did show me."

Keith massaged my ass when I laid my leg across his. "I did, didn't I? But I'm gon' need for you to calm your hot self down. Just so you know, you are wearing my ass out."

"Good. And when I get finished with this shower, I'm going to wear you out some more. So get ready."

I got out of bed and headed for the bathroom to take a shower. I thought Keith was going to join me, but he didn't. With him not being in the shower with me, I took my time and indulged in a lengthy one. I shaved my legs and trimmed my toenails. It took me about an hour to get finished, and after I was done, I opened the door and could hear Keith downstairs talking. Better yet, yelling at somebody. I was so sure that Evelyn had shown back up, but as I jetted down the stairs, I saw Keith standing in the living room with Bryson. Their argument was pretty intense. I'd never seen them go at it like this before. They stood face to face with each other, talking shit.

"I'll say it again," Keith hissed. "Watch your mouth or I will drop your punk ass on the floor."

Bryson folded his arms across his buffed chest and a smirk appeared on his face. "Do what you must, little brother. The floor is all yours."

I quickly ran over and squeezed my short self in between them. "Whatever is going on here, it doesn't need to be settled with a fistfight. I know the two of you can do better than this, so calm down and chill."

Keith ignored me and inched forward, squeezing me more. "It can be settled when he gives our mother her money back. If not, I will handle you myself."

Bryson stepped forward and I eased out of the way. "I will give the money back when I choose to. This really ain't your damn business, and I'm getting tired of your threats."

"Maybe so. But here's a promise."

Keith reached out and slammed his fist right at Bryson's jaw. The blow sent him staggering backward, and he tripped over the table behind him and fell hard.

"How was that for a promise?" Keith said. "If you don't give the money back, another one of those punches will be coming your way."

Bryson tightened his fist and charged toward Keith like a raging mad bull. He wound up slamming Keith on the floor and they went at it tough. So tough that I had to scramble out of the way.

"Stop it," I yelled to get their attention. "Or else I'll call the police!"

My police threat fell on deaf ears and frightened no one. They kept at it and were pounding the hell out of each other. Keith was getting the best of Bryson, but then all of a sudden, the tables turned. He punched Keith in his mouth and I witnessed my man's blood splatter. I rushed in and started hitting Bryson on the back of his head to distract him so Keith could get the upper hand again. My interference distracted Bryson, but it didn't halt his punches. The next one he delivered landed right at my face, particularly at my right eye that throbbed and felt as if it had been knocked from the socket. I backed away and held my face. Keith lost it. But as he charged at Bryson, he sent Keith backing up with a hard blow to his stomach that dropped him to one knee.

"Now what, motherfucker?" Spit flew from Bryson's mouth and his chest heaved in and out. He pounded it hard then looked at me. "You dyke-ass bitch, stay the hell out of family affairs."

I was stunned by Bryson's actions, and I couldn't hold back all that was inside of me. My man was hurt and so was I.

"Screw you, you grimy, down-low-ass nigga. How in the hell you gon' call me a dyke, and yo' ass out there fucking men? Or should I say, allowing them to fuck you?"

The direction of Bryson's eyes shot over to Keith. His eyes, however, were locked on me. I could tell he was waiting for me to say more, but I fell back on the couch and held my eye.

Keith took deep breaths then addressed Bryson. "Get the hell out of here. Now! And don't you ever come back!"

Bryson stood for a moment, looking as if he wanted to say something or as if he wanted to apologize. Instead, he rushed off and swung the door open. He left, leaving it wide open.

Keith limped over to me while holding his side. "Why did you say that to him?" he asked. "Do you know something that I don't?"

I was about to tell him that my words had slipped, and I said them to upset Bryson. But then I decided against it. "I don't know if it's true or not, but Evelyn said—"

"To hell with what Evelyn said," Keith shouted. He shouted so loudly that my whole body shook.

"You're right," I hurried to say. "But please go talk to your brother. He has all the answers you're looking for."

Sweat was on the thick wrinkles that lined Keith's forehead. The mean mug was locked there, even when he rubbed my face and bent over to kiss my swollen eye. "Put some ice on that. I'm leaving to go find Bryson. I'll be back later."

Before I could say anything, he jetted.

I was so worried about Keith being gone. Hours had passed, and I kept calling his cell phone, but he wouldn't answer. My eye was bloodshot red, and by tomorrow it would be worse. I lay across the bed, wondering where my man was and if he was okay. I now regretted what I'd said to Bryson. Keith seemed very concerned about it, and that was the only thing that probably caused him to leave. If something happened to him again, because of me, I would never forgive myself.

I wasn't sure what time it was, but when I woke up, Keith sat on the bed next to me. He touched my face and apologized for what Bryson had done.

"You don't have to apologize," I said, slowly sitting up. "It wasn't your fault." I looked at the gloom expression on his face, knowing that he had caught up with Bryson. "So, how did it go? Did you talk to him?"

Keith nodded. "I did."

"And?"

"And I don't know what to believe. He told me about your visit. I was surprised to hear that you went to go see him, without saying anything to me."

"I wanted to, but I didn't want to confront you with something that may not have been true."

"Regardless, you should have said something to me. In not doing so, it makes me feel as if I can't trust you. I don't like secrets, Trina. I thought you learned your lesson about keeping them."

"I have, but this situation was different. With Evelyn being the source who provided the information, I wasn't sure how to handle things. That's why I went to go see Bryson, so that he could defend what she'd said."

Keith fell back on the bed and lay flat on his back. He put his hands behind his head and gazed at the spinning ceiling fan. "After speaking to him," he said, "what's your take on the matter? What conclusion did you come to?"

I lay silent for a while then slightly shrugged. I didn't want to say what I thought for real. I could tell Keith was hurt; I didn't want to hurt him anymore.

"The truth, Trina. I want the truth."

"Based on how I was when I tried to hide my preference from everyone, I have to be honest and say that I believe Bryson is on the down low. I'm not a hundred percent sure, but Evelyn was paid a substantial amount of money to keep her mouth shut. If your mother is missing some money, maybe that's the money Bryson gave to Evelyn."

"He has a gambling problem, and he's always taking money from the family stash. Just not that much. Either way, you didn't believe him when he told you he wasn't involved with men?"

"No. Unfortunately, I didn't."

Keith lay silent for a minute, and then he got off the bed. He opened the bathroom door then turned to face me. "Just so you know, I didn't believe him either."

Keith shut the door behind him, after he went into the bathroom. I shook my head, upset that there seemed to be no end to the drama.

Chapter 18

Evelyn

I was sitting on the couch, eating buttery popcorn and watching *Scandal.* I was so into it that I barely heard the knocks on my door. Whoever it was they were going to stay out there because, number one, the person didn't buzz me, and number two, *Scandal* was too good to be interrupted. I ignored the knocks then heard Bryson's voice, loud and clear.

"Open the door! You and I got ourselves a little problem!"

I rolled my eyes and continued to chomp on my popcorn. "Go away, Bryson! I'm busy."

I got back to watching *Scandal,* and minutes later, I heard a loud thud. The second thud was louder, and the third one caused the whole door to break off the hinges and come crashing down. I jumped and sent the bowl of popcorn flying at Bryson, when he rushed in. He resembled a madman in a horror movie. Sweat ran down his face, his teeth ground and his shirt was ripped. There was also a long scar on the side of his face. I quickly moved out of the way and jumped on top of the couch. I lifted my foot to keep him away from me and threatened to kick.

"Bitch, didn't I tell you to keep your motherfucking mouth shut!"

I played clueless. "I didn't say a word to anyone. What are you talking about?"

My eyes shifted toward the doorway. If I could just make it to the door and run to the elevator, security would see me. Then someone would be able to help me. But if I couldn't make it to the doorway, there would be no way out of this.

I took my chances and jumped over the couch. I sprinted toward the door, but this was one time I hated my hair was long.

Bryson grabbed my hair from behind, yanking it so hard that I fell backward. He straddled the top of me, and all I remembered seeing was him raising his fist and slamming it into my face. After that, I saw darkness, but felt numerous blows being delivered to my body. Blows that made my insides burn and hurt—hurt so bad that I seriously wanted to die.

I didn't know what day it was, how many hours had gone by or where I was at. For a while, I thought I was dead because of the numerous white lights that flashed before me. The last things I could picture in my mind were Bryson's angry face and his powerful fists. That was all, until somebody shook my shoulder and kept calling my name. I cracked my eyes open and everything in front of me was a blur. I could hear a voice, and the person in front of me looked to be a doctor.

"Next of kin," he said. "Any family members? If so, who would you like for me to reach out to?"

The doctor showed me a piece of paper and pen. He placed it on the table in front of me and I began to write. The person's name and number I wrote was Trina's. Underneath her name, I scribbled the word, sister. After that, my eyes shut again.

I woke up, hearing a bunch of chatter. My vision was still blurred when I opened my eyes. I could barely focus. I blinked and saw Trina standing next to me. She squeezed my hand with hers and kept calling my name. I wasn't sure if I was dreaming. Trina wasn't smiling and a deeply concerned look was on her face. She called my name again. This time, I nodded to let her know that I'd heard her.

"Can you hear me?"

I nodded again and spilled a soft, "Yes."

She released a deep breath. "Thank God. Thank you, Jesus." Apparently, she'd been praying for me. I opened my mouth to speak again, but it hurt so badly because of the tube in my mouth. With that, I stayed silent.

"Don't worry," Trina said. "You're going to be fine."

A slow tear dripped from the corner of my eye. My whole body was hurting. I tried to move around, but couldn't. Tried to move my arms, couldn't do that either. Attempted to move my toes, but no luck. I closed my eyes and had flashbacks of Bryson beating the shit out of me. This time, I didn't have to exaggerate like I did when Cedric attacked me. This was real. Everything that I played out in my head was real. Bryson tried to kill me. I wondered, who stopped him? Thought about if he was in jail. Hopefully he was, but I seriously didn't know.

What I did know was that he'd found out what I'd told Trina, only, about his down-low status. I had only shared that information with her. I begged her not to say anything. I knew that if she did, it would come to this. It was evident that she didn't care. It probably pleased her heart to see me laid up like this. She and Kayla always wanted to see me at my lowest point. Well, this was it. I hoped she was happy, even though she didn't look as if she was.

I opened my eyes and stared at Trina. This time, she displayed a forced grin. For some reason, I could feel her squeezing my hand again, but I couldn't feel much else but a severe headache. It was difficult for me to speak, but I had to ask her a question. I needed to know something, and I wanted to make her feel horrible for betraying me.

I stretched my mouth and mumbled to her. "Why?"

Trina inched closer so she could hear me. "Why what? What did you say?"

"Why did you tell Bryson what I'd told you? I begged you not to . . . to say anything. You promised me that you wouldn't. Why, Trina? Did you want him to kill me?"

A fast tear fell down Trina's face. She couldn't even respond. After a few minutes, she whispered that she was sorry.

Yeah, I was sorry too. Sorry that, eventually, she'd have to pay for running her big mouth.

Chapter 19

Kayla

I was in awe as Trina sat at my kitchen table, asking me to go to the hospital with her to see Evelyn. Trina claimed that it would brighten Evelyn's day and give her hope. Seeing me would be the best thing ever, and it would give us a chance to mend our friendship. There was no doubt that I felt terrible for Evelyn. I truly wished her well, but going to the hospital to see her was something that I didn't want to do. Trina acted as if she didn't understand why I didn't want to go. So, I had to remind her why I was standing my ground about not going.

"I'm sorry, but I'm having a difficult time forgiving a woman—no, let me correct myself—my best friend who slept with my husband, got pregnant by him, used his money, lied to me about it, stabbed me in my back, preferred that I be homeless, and told my son that I'd lied to him about who his father was. I could go on and on, Trina, but I won't. If you've forgiven her, that's on you. More power to you."

Trina massaged her forehead. "I know she's done some horrible things, but I feel so guilty about telling Bryson what she'd told me. If I'd kept my mouth shut, none of this would've happened. I'm stuck in the middle, trying to be there for her, and trying to be there for Keith who has taken Bryson's side. His defense is that Evelyn had a gun and threatened to kill him. Claimed all he did was go to her place to talk, but she pulled a gun on him. According to him, he was forced to defend himself because she was acting like a maniac."

"Well, you did say there were bullet holes in the walls, right? And how do you know that what he said happened isn't the truth?"

"Because I witnessed how upset Bryson was about being outed. And remember, I was on the receiving end of one of his rages too. He's still denying everything, and I don't believe anything he says. Keith and I keep clashing about this, too. I guess the truth will come out, during the trial."

"Maybe it will, but if I were you, I wouldn't put my money on Evelyn."

I got up and went to the fridge to get a soda. A part of me was livid with Trina for being so foolish. But I didn't want to say anything to hurt her feelings more. She felt responsible for this and had been running to the hospital almost every day to check on Evelyn. Trina said she was getting better, but Bryson had broken her ribs and given her a concussion. She could barely walk and needed therapy. Her headaches were severe, and Trina stressed how much pain she'd been in.

"I understand all of that, Kayla, but everything you just mentioned is in the past. You're not going to harp on that forever, are you? The last time I checked, Cedric was the one who caused you the most damage. If you can forgive him, surely you can forgive Evelyn. I think you should go see her."

I couldn't hold back any longer. "Trina, personally, I don't care what you or Evelyn thinks. I forgave Cedric because he was my husband. He took responsibility for his actions. In addition to that, he didn't leave me high and dry. So please don't compare Evelyn to Cedric. There is a big difference."

Trina pushed and cocked her head back to look at me. "So, let me get this straight. The only reason you forgave Cedric was because he put millions into your bank account? Damn, Kayla, how selfish can you be? How can you make this all about money, when your friend was in the hospital clinging on for dear life? Excuse me for thinking you were better than that."

The guilt trip was in full effect. And, no, Trina didn't just go there, did she? I slammed my soda on the island and walked up to her, darting my finger. "How dare you call me selfish because I refuse to break my neck and run out of here for a tramp who brought this mess on herself? You have no darn idea what I've been through. When I was down and out, nobody was there for me. Surely not Evelyn who put me out of her place, knowing that I had nowhere to go. So while you think I should run to her bedside, I don't get it. Please help me understand this, because I am deeply confused."

Trina didn't appreciate my tone or aggressiveness, as I'd moved closer to make my case. She picked up her purse and put the straps on her shoulder. This time, she was much calmer than I was.

"I can't say anything to help you understand. But what I will do is ask you to reflect on the bond the three of us used to have. We were like sisters, and a long time ago, we never allowed anyone to come between us. We used to be able to laugh and talk to each other for hours, without arguing, judging, or hating. Cried on each other's shoulders and could always depend on each other when one of us was in need. Then you married Cedric and things changed. You changed. We felt as if you left us behind because you did. Evelyn got jealous and she did everything in her power to be you and make you pay for what she considers you leaving us. I started to lie about who I was, and my secrets hurt everybody, including my immediate family. I say all of that to say that we've all made some mistakes. Every last one of us, Kayla, so no need to point the finger at one person. I'll let you sit on that for a while. If you choose to come to the hospital, do so. If not, don't. It doesn't matter to me either way, but I also had to make my case for why I believe you should."

Trina gave me a hug then she left. I stood in the kitchen, unsure about what to do. While she made some valid points, still, it was hard for me to go be by Evelyn's side.

For the next couple of hours, I paced the floor and pondered what to do. Things with Cedric, Jacoby, and me were going well, and Jacoby had been spending more time with Cedric. Today they were at a St. Louis University basketball game. I called to see how everything was going. Jacoby said fine. He hurried to end the call, saying that I was making him miss the game. I was happy about their relationship, but so sad about how my friendship had turned out with Evelyn. Sad enough to change my clothes and head to the hospital.

Before going to Evelyn's room, I stopped by the gift shop to get her a plant and a card. I didn't know why I was so nervous to see her, but I was. I had known her for most of my life, but there I was frightened, as well as hesitant to enter her room. I took a deep breath, before pushing on the door and entering. Instantly, my eyes connected with Evelyn's. She was sitting up in bed with her hair all over her head. Trina sat in a chair next to her with a book in her hand. A wide smile grew on her face, and the smile caused me to display a little grin too.

"Hello," I said, looking from Trina to Evelyn. "I hope I'm not interrupting."

"No, you aren't," Trina said. "I was just reading Evelyn this good book. Girl, it's juicy, drama filled, and hilarious. You may want to come in, sit down, and listen to this."

I walked farther into the room and set the plant in the windowsill.

"Yes, what Trina said is true," Evelyn added. "But good book or not, please stay. It's good to see you."

I cleared mucus from my throat and didn't reply to Evelyn yet. Instead, I walked up to the bed and gave Evelyn the card. She opened it and read my brief message inside that encouraged her to get well soon.

"I'm trying to," she said. "Every day I feel as if I'm getting better. Thanks to Trina for helping me with therapy, and thanks to you, right now, for making me feel as if everything will be okay."

I nodded and took a seat at the end of the bed.

"Can I finish?" Trina said, holding up the book. "At least let me get to the end of this chapter."

"Please do," Evelyn said. "I want to find out what's up."

Trina started to read and we all listened in. The books made the characters' lives seem so perfect, especially when our lives were all jacked up. I couldn't help but to feel as if this moment in time was special. Maybe it was the turning point we all needed.

Chapter 20

Evelyn

I had been in the hospital for almost a month. Trina came to see me almost every day, and after that amazing day with my BFF's, Kayla had stopped by several times too. She baked me my favorite: a German chocolate cake with a whole lot of icing. She also helped me with therapy. I was feeling much better and was one day away from going home. While I was definitely looking forward to it, I wasn't looking forward to my uphill court battle with Bryson. From what Trina had said, he was ready to fight me all the way in court. His wealthy parents had hired some of the best lawyers in St. Louis for his defense.

As for me, I couldn't afford an attorney. I had spent a substantial amount of the money Bryson had given me. Somehow, he got a hold of my banking information and withdrew the rest of my money. There was no question that the whole case would be interesting. I had a lot of solid evidence against Bryson that could prove he was guilty. But I was well aware that the attorneys his parents hired would tear my evidence apart and make me look like a thirsty, gold-digging whore. There was a chance I would come out on the losing end.

It was getting late. I sat in bed, finishing the yucky dinner that I hadn't finished earlier. As I ate my peas, I glanced at the numerous cards Kayla and Trina had given me. Kayla's plant had already started to grow, but Trina's balloon had deflated. I smiled while thinking about their kindness. I had to admit that my BFF's had come through for me this time. Never did I think we'd be able to repair all the damage that had been done, but putting everything else aside, it seemed as if we were well on our way to being the good friends we used to be, many years ago.

I finished my dinner and pushed the table away from the bed. Fluffed my pillow and then lay back to get comfortable. I felt myself fading a little, but when the door squeaked open, I widened my eyes to see who it was. From the shadowy figure, I could tell it was a man. My heart started to slam against my chest and beat faster. I thought it was Bryson, coming to finish what he'd started. Instead, it was Cedric. Seeing him put me a little at ease, but after him beating my ass, he was still considered one of my enemies.

He had a card in his hand and a smile was washed across his face. "Hey there, stranger," he said walking farther into the room. "Baby, how are you feeling?"

Baby my ass. Save it, I thought. "Better," was all I said, trying to keep our conversation short.

Cedric laid the card on the table then sat in the chair beside my bed. He crossed his legs and massaged his hands together. "So, when are you getting out of this place?" he asked.

My tone was very nasty. "In a few days. Why?"

"Because I kind of miss my partner in crime. Kind of need you to handle some things for me, and if you do, there will be some great rewards."

I was slumped down in the bed, but sat up to give him my full attention. "What kind of things do you want me to handle? And, I'd like to hear more about those rewards."

Cedric passed me an envelope and asked me to open the letter to read it. It was a letter from Paula Daniels, the woman I thought had attempted to kill him. According to the letter, she wanted to speak to Cedric ASAP about Jacoby's involvement. That was all she said, but she also assured him that everything wasn't what it seemed to be.

I slowly folded the letter and gave it back to Cedric. I wasn't sure what was going on, but I asked Cedric why he couldn't handle this.

"Jacoby is fragile and Kayla is weak. I don't want to hurt anybody's feelings, plus I'm always being lied to. That's why I need you. I need someone like you to check things out for me, and since Kayla is back on your team, maybe you can find out what's really going on for me."

A part of me didn't want to be used by Cedric again, but I still wanted to hear about those rewards. "If I do get involved, what's in this for me?"

"Depends."

"Depends on what?"

"Depends on what you want or what you need. Like a lawyer to help you fight your case, a new house, sex, whatever you want."

"Hmmm, but you haven't said the magic word yet. The one thing that energizes me and turns me into the woman I always wanted to be. A rich woman."

Cedric snapped his finger and smiled. "Oh yeah, that's right. I almost forgot and how could I forget about that. Money, right? However much your heart desires, as long as it's within reason."

I laughed and shot him a slow wink. "It's a good thing that you know me so well, Cedric. But let me think about this. When I get out of here, I'll definitely be in touch."

Cedric stood and straightened his suit jacket. He licked his lips then moved closer to the bed. He leaned in and planted a wet kiss on my cheek. Saying nothing else, he strutted to the door. It slammed behind him.

I, on the other hand, sat with a huge smile on my face, thinking about my best way forward.

BFF'S 3:

Best Frenemies Forever Series

1

Evelyn

After being beaten up and almost killed by my lover, I was finally home from the hospital. It felt good to be in my own bed, without anyone poking me with needles or trying to tell me what I needed to do to get well. I was already feeling better, especially after my ongoing visits from my BFF's, Kayla and Trina. I was delighted and super excited that we were able to put our issues behind us and become friends again.

Our friendship journey had been a long one. We had had ups and downs, even a few betrayals. It shocked the hell out of me that Kayla had finally forgiven me.

Then there was Trina. Lord knows, I had done some reckless things to her too. After giving it much thought, I had realized I was dead wrong for what I had done to my friends. Now that the dust had settled and I was feeling 100 percent again, it was time for me to handle some things. I had made a mess of my life and I was eager to clean it all up. Bryson was the top priority right now. He was going to pay for putting his hands on me.

My intentions were to sue the hell out of him. His rich parents had already hired an attorney, and they truly believed that I was some kind of broke bitch who wouldn't be able to defend myself. While I didn't have much money—well, honestly, I was broke and didn't have a job—I still knew of one person in particular who had cash and was willing to help me out of this mess. He had come to rescue me while I was laid up in the hospital, feeling sorry for myself and worried about my situation. While Cedric and I unquestionably had our differences, those differences had been kicked to the curb and set aside for another day. According to him, he wanted to help me. And if he was able to, then I had no problem helping him.

I lay comfortably in my bed, with a fluffy pillow tucked between my legs, thinking about his brief visit at the hospital that day. Who would have thought that he would be the one to ultimately save me from what I was about to face with Bryson and his family?

The fortunate thing was, I hadn't waited until I got out of the hospital to put a plan in motion. I had spoken to Cedric almost every day since his visit. He had already made contact with Bryson's parents, and a meeting to try to resolve all this crap was scheduled for this Friday. I couldn't wait to tell his parents my side of the story—they definitely needed to hear what kind of animal their son was, if they didn't already know. I figured that Keith would be there too. That way, he would finally know the truth about his brother and stop hating on me.

He and Trina stayed into it about who was telling the truth. Keith took his brother's side; Trina took mine. But no matter whose side anybody was on, for the time being, I was glad about Cedric having my back. I made him aware that I didn't want Trina or Kayla to know that he and I had reconciled some of our differences. If they knew we were friends again, I was positive that they would think I was trying to betray them again and that they would cut me off. Then I wouldn't be able to get Cedric the information he had requested about Jacoby and Kayla.

There seemed to be a big secret they had been keeping from Cedric. It revolved around him being shot. Paula Daniels was behind bars for the remainder of her life, but Cedric wasn't exactly sure that she was the one responsible for trying to take him down. If anybody knew the real deal, Kayla did. And if she had been keeping a secret, I was positive that I could get it out of her. Whatever information I found out, I intended to pass on to Cedric. It would be up to him to decide what to do with that information. After that, I wanted nothing else to do with him and our business would be done.

***

Friday was here before I knew it. I was well rested, and for the first time in a long time, I felt good about my future. I was currently unemployed, I didn't have much money in my bank account, and this apartment was starting to close in on me. I hated it here, but today I felt that a life-changing event was about to take place. Something inside told me that this meeting would work out in my favor.

Cedric was supposed to pick me up within the hour. I had been thinking too much about the outcome and wasn't even ready yet. Also, I'd gotten tied up on the phone with Trina. She had called earlier to check on me, and we had wound up spending thirty minutes on the phone, during which she'd bragged about her and Keith's trip to New York. While it had sounded like they'd had a good time, I had to cut her off quickly. I'd told her I had to go into the bathroom to shower, but technically, I'd needed to hurry up and get dressed before Cedric got here. He was a man who didn't appreciate waiting on others.

I didn't want to get left behind, so I hurried to straighten my honey-blond hair, which was parted down the middle. With so much body, my permed hair hung almost six inches past my shoulders and flowed midway down my back. My thin brows had been arched, and very little makeup covered my flawless light skin. I wore a sleeveless money-green dress that hugged my hourglass figure. It was made of linen and was cut slightly above my knees. A white cropped jacket really set my outfit off, but not as much as my gold high heels, which matched my accessories. I refused to go in front of Bryson's parents looking like a broke trick. That was what they probably expected. I had to represent, and when I looked at myself in the mirror, I was 110 percent pleased.

Right after I slid some shimmery nude gloss on my lips, I heard a light knock at the door. There was a time when Cedric had a key to let himself in, but times had surely changed.

When I opened the door and saw Cedric standing on the other side, I had a slight change of heart. Giving him another key could, indeed, be possible. He rocked a casual pair of black jeans that had that satisfying dick of his looking scrumptious and sitting pretty. A black leather jacket covered the deep blue button-down shirt he wore, and his Caesar cut was flowing with hella waves. His Hershey's chocolate skin was smooth, and I had to confess that he looked good enough to eat. He checked me out, too, before coming inside and asking if I was ready.

"Ready as I'll ever be," I said. "All I need to do is go to my bedroom and get my purse."

I pivoted and made my way to the bedroom. My hips purposely swayed from side to side. I was positive that my ass was doing all that it needed to do, and that Cedric wouldn't be able to resist checking it out. I wasn't exactly sure if he and Kayla were still intimate with each other or not, even though they were now divorced. But I would be sure to inquire about it the next time she and I spoke. Then again, maybe I needed to stanch these little feelings for Cedric and back off. I was just feeling a little horny, and the more I thought about it, the more I realized that nothing excited me about having sex with a man who had been shot up. He probably had numerous yucky bullet holes in his body, and from what I had heard, Paula Daniels had done some major damage to him. I had to see Cedric with all his clothes off before I made a decision to go there with him again.

After I got my purse, we left my place and headed to Cedric's car. He politely opened the passenger door for me, and the second I got inside, I got a whiff of his brand-new Audi. The leather seat hugged my body like a glove, and as he drove us to our destination, I almost fell asleep. That could have also been due to our boring time in the car. Our conversation was sporadic, until he asked if I'd had an opportunity to ask Kayla if she'd been keeping any secrets from him.

"No, I haven't had a chance to go there with her yet. We've spoken only twice since I've been home. She called to check on me, and then she called while she was at the grocery store and asked if I needed anything. She stopped by that day to drop off some of the things I requested, but she was in a rush. Said she had to pick up Jacoby from somewhere."

Cedric nodded while looking straight ahead, as if he were in deep thought. His grip on the steering wheel got tighter, and after he stopped at a red light, he turned to look at me.

"That's cool and everything, but hurry up and see what you can find out for me," he said. "I need something solid soon. I know you've been concerned about taking care of this shit with Bryson, but please don't forget about our agreement."

"I promise you that I won't forget. You have come through for me in a major way, and I owe you big-time. I will find out what I can, but I don't want to be so obvious. Kayla and I just started talking again. It may be a minute before she trusts me again. Just be patient, okay?"

The light turned green. Cedric drove off and spoke in a commanding tone. "I don't mind being patient, but after today you need to step it up a little. I need to know what's been going on behind my back. Just the other day, Kayla and Jacoby were whispering about something. I pulled her aside, inquired about it, but she said it was nothing. She was real nervous, and he's the same way when I come around. I also can't get the thoughts of her breaking into my house out of my mind. She was looking for something that day. What? I don't know yet, but I do know that you have a better chance of finding out what she was looking for than me."

Something wasn't quite adding up for me. Cedric was a smart man. He could easily do his own dirty work. There was more to this, and I also thought he was kind of upset that Kayla, Trina, and I were friends again. He couldn't stand it, and there was a possibility that he would do whatever he thought was necessary to destroy our friendship. That, to me, was obvious, and it could very well be his motive for getting me involved in this current scheme.

Several minutes later Cedric pulled into an arched drive-way that accommodated at least twenty cars. The ranch-style home to my right was breathtaking. Keith and Bryson's parents had it going on, without a doubt.

"Close your mouth," Cedric said, looking in the rearview mirror while brushing his waves. "Act like you've been to a place like this before, and remain calm, no matter what. I told them I was your uncle, and I'm here with you because I'm concerned about Bryson hurting you again. I can assure you that they don't want to see this mess play out in a courtroom, so they will throw some money on the table. Whatever their offer is, I want thirty percent for my troubles."

I tossed my head back, then let out a soft "Tuh." He was already filthy rich. What good was 30 percent going to do him?

"Thirty percent, Cedric? Really? You know that I've been suffering financially for quite some time. I barely have enough money to pay my bills, and you know that hospital bill isn't going to be cheap. Not to mention that I don't even have a job. I need every dime I can get. I don't know how much they will offer me, or if they will offer me anything at all. We don't know what kind of people we're dealing with, but agreeing to give you thirty percent may not work for me."

He shrugged, as if he didn't give a damn about anything I'd said. "Thirty percent, or I walk. Right here. Right now. I'll blow this deal wide open and let you go to court with a cheap, inexperienced lawyer and try to settle this. The choice is yours."

I sat thinking about what other choice I had. Cedric was a dirty muthafucka, and he'd taken greed to a new level. I finally responded by opening the door and getting out of the car. I guessed he figured that we had a deal, because he climbed out of the car and then walked to the front door with me, displaying a crooked smile on his face.

I reached out and rang the doorbell. Seconds later a prissy black woman with long salt-and-pepper braids answered the door. There was no smile whatsoever on her face, but she extended her hand to me first.

"My name is Netta," she said. "My husband and son are in the great room, waiting for you."

For the first time in a long time, I felt a little nervous. I shook her hand, then introduced myself, as well. Cedric followed suit. As we entered the house, I couldn't believe my eyes. The ceilings were roughly twelve feet tall, and that didn't include the great room ceiling, which was almost double. Swirling tan and white marble covered the floors, and someone's initials had been inscribed in the foyer in gold. The curved double staircases in the foyer were black and gold, and the crystal chandelier set everything off. The gallery was filled with black-and-white pictures of their family. Keith and Bryson appeared to be their only children, but there were also pictures of a little girl too.

The oversize bay windows in the far back lit up the whole place, and when I turned my head to the left, I could see a luxury kitchen with not one, but two granite-topped islands. This place was sick! It was in Trina's best interests to somehow or someway become a part of this family, and to do so very soon by marrying Keith. If Trina didn't already know it, she had hit the damn jackpot. I just didn't understand why she and Kayla were always so lucky. I had never been lucky enough to find a single man or one with wealthy parents whom I could benefit from.

Cedric and I followed Netta into the great room, where Bryson and his father were sitting. They stood as we entered, and all I could say to myself was, *Lord, have mercy on me.* Daddy was fine as fuck. It was no secret where Bryson and Keith had gotten their good looks from. He was tall, but just a little shorter than Bryson, who towered over all of us. There was a mean-ass mug on his face, and he looked at me as if he wanted to tear me apart. I ignored him.

Netta turned to introduce us. "Charles," she said, speaking to her husband, "this is Evelyn and her uncle, Cedric."

Charles politely extended his hand to me. When we shook hands, his soft touch sent chills up my spine. I was too ashamed to admit what effect it had on my pussy.

"Nice to meet you," he said. "Have a seat. Please."

He shook Cedric's hand too, and then we both sat in white plush chairs that looked as if they had just been purchased yesterday. Everything was so tidy, spotless, and clean. I hoped that the juices leaking from my pussy wouldn't ruin the chair, but looking at ole Charles just did something to me.

Charles sat on a sofa on the opposite side of the room, next to Bryson, while Netta made her way to another room.

"I'll be back with some drinks," she said. "Go ahead and carry on without me."

Drinks? I didn't think it was that kind of occasion. I also didn't know if that bitch would try to poison me, so there would be no drinking for me.

Charles rubbed his hands together while looking directly at me. "I'm glad your uncle reached out to us about discussing this little situation. Bryson has already informed us of his side of the story. My wife and I would like to hear yours."

Bryson placed his hands behind his head and pursed his lips. He then yawned, as if it was a waste of his time to be here. The smug look on his face irritated me. I hated to be in his presence, though the only thing it took me back to was the day I saw him getting screwed by that tranny, and the day he came to my apartment to hurt me. Nonetheless, I appeared relaxed and started to answer Charles.

"I'm not exactly sure what Bryson told you about what happened, but I'll start by saying that my encounter with him was one of the worst experiences of my life. I thought I was going to die, and there is nothing that a woman could ever do to a man to deserve a beating like the one I got."

Netta came back into the room, carrying several drinks on a tray. After she placed the tray on a table, she took a seat in a chair to listen in. I described what had happened, starting from the moment Bryson banged on my door, then kicked it down to get inside my apartment. I wasn't even sure if that was how it happened, but I made sure that what I told them was more dramatic than ever. Everyone was tuned in, and it wasn't long before disgust washed across Charles's face. Netta kept nodding her head, and there were a few shrugs here and there. As for Bryson, he kept biting down on his lip. His fists tightened at one point; then he released them and wiggled his fingers.

Tears rushed to the rims of my eyes as I spoke about how he had had his hands wrapped around my neck and how I had been unable to breathe. "He was too strong for me, and there was nothing that I could do to get him off of me. My vision was blurred, and after he removed his hands from my neck, all I could see were his fists pounding me over and over again in my face. My whole body felt numb. I—I kept choking on a bunch of blood that had filled my mouth. My head hurt so badly, and he was yanking my hair and beating me in the head at the same time. I didn't—"

Bryson slammed his fist down on the table in front of him. "Stop fucking lying, bitch!" he shouted. Spit flew from his mouth, as he was unable to contain himself. "You know it didn't go down like that, and if I had wanted you dead, trust me, you would be."

Charles's face twisted, and there were numerous thick wrinkles visible on his forehead. "Calm the hell down!" he yelled. "Don't you ever speak that way in front of your mother and me! And the last time I checked, we do have guests."

Bryson cut his eyes, then looked over at his mother, who was shaking her head. She didn't say a word. I was ready to continue, but Charles sent me in another direction.

"What brought all of this about, Evelyn? What did you do to him, or what did he do to you, other than beat you up? Something had to bring the two of you to that point."

Well, he asked, and I had already prepared an answer. I looked at Bryson's mother first. There was a chance that she might not want to hear this. It was obvious that Bryson was a mama's boy, and the last thing I wanted to do was hurt her little feelings.

"Miss Netta," I said as politely as I could, "I don't know if you want to stay in the room to hear this, but I came here to speak nothing but the truth."

"Then go ahead and speak your so-called truth," she said with a slight attitude. "We're all listening."

I figured that ole cockeyed bitch didn't believe me. No matter what I said, she was Team Bryson. I ignored her comment about me telling the so-called truth, and I kept my eyes on Charles. Bryson was in my sights too. The look in his eyes dared me to tell his parents that I had caught him getting dicked down by a man. I guessed he didn't think I would go into details, but I was prepared to.

"First, let me say that I have nothing against gay people," I stated. "My best friend, Trina, is bisexual, and I love her to death. With that being said, Bryson lied to me. He made me believe that he was straight. Did all kinds of things to me sexually, and the things I did to him I'm too embarrassed to say in front of my uncle. Had Bryson just been honest with me about his sexual preferences, we wouldn't even be here."

Bryson jumped up and darted his finger at me. "Bitch, I will hurt you for lying on me! What in the hell is wrong with you? Wasn't that beat down I gave you enough? You can't come into my parents' home and lie on me like this!"

He charged forward, but Charles stood and held him back. That was when Cedric stood up to protect me. I was surprised by his swift actions.

"None of that, so chill!" Cedric said to Bryson. "You've already hurt her enough, and you will not do it again."

"Man, fuck you! She's a goddamned liar! You don't even know the half of it!"

"Sit down!" Charles shouted at Bryson. "Or get out of here. I thought you'd be able to handle yourself better than this, but I see you're having some problems controlling yourself."

"It's hard to sit here and allow somebody to lie on me like this," Bryson muttered. "If you want to talk to me when she leaves, fine. I'm out."

Bryson stormed away. It was no surprise when his mother went after him.

"Sweetheart," she said, trailing behind him, "everything is going to be fine. Calm down, and don't you leave this house just yet. Go downstairs and cool off for a while. Your dad and I will handle this, okay?"

Bryson did exactly as his mommy had told him to. Babying a grown-ass man would do him no good. No wonder he wasn't about shit.

After he went downstairs to cool off, Netta returned to the great room. Charles and Cedric sat back down, and I was asked to continue.

I wiped a slow tear that was sliding down my face. "I never meant to hurt anyone, and the truth is, I had some very deep feelings for Bryson. By not telling me his status, he didn't give me a choice. I was upset about it, and I didn't know anything until I caught him having sex with a transgender man. I told my best friend about it, and that's when all hell broke loose. Bryson went on a rampage. He was determined to kill me."

"You can stop right there," Netta said, holding up her hand. "I don't believe a word you're saying, and shame on you for spreading vicious lies. You mentioned that your best friend, Trina, is bisexual, but isn't she the one who is dating my son Keith? If so, I met Trina before. We speak quite often, and I know for a fact that she loves Keith and only Keith."

Shit. Shit. Shit. I had totally forgotten about Trina being with Keith. In no way had I intended to mention her name or her past. I hoped like hell that this wouldn't get back to her. If it did, I knew that she was going to be very upset with me. I attempted to clear things up, but doing so made me look like a for-real liar, when in reality, I wasn't lying.

"Trina is my best friend, but a long time ago she expressed to me that she had a thing for women. I'm not sure if she was serious or not, but this isn't about Trina. It's about Bryson. Whether you want to believe me or not, your son needs to fess up and accept who he really is. His lies are going to hurt many more people, and from what I already know, he has already hurt plenty of the women he's dated."

Netta stood, then looked at Charles. "I've heard enough. You can do what you want to about this, but I'm not going to sit here and listen to all this craziness about my son." She looked at me with the evilest gaze I had ever seen. Her pupils grew bigger, and then her eyes narrowed. "You are one deceitful woman. I'm getting all kinds of negative vibes from you. Hurry up and finish with your lies, and then get the hell out of here before the devil in you causes this house to burn to the ground."

She walked off, leaving all of us stunned, even Charles, who sat wringing his hands together and looking down at the floor, as if he were in deep thought.

"I understand how your wife feels," Cedric said, trying to get back to the business at hand. "She wants to protect her son. I want to protect my niece too, so what are we going to do about this situation? Do we want a jury to decide who was in the wrong? Or can we settle this once and for all right now?"

Charles looked up. He stared at me and Cedric with his light brown eyes, which resembled Bryson's. He released a deep sigh, then sat back on the sofa with his hands behind his head.

"I love my son, and I am well aware that he has some issues. Issues that I don't want to discuss with the two of you, but I will say, Evelyn, that I don't believe everything you've sat there and told me today. I am, however, prepared to make you some kind of peace offering that will make this all go away today.

And after today, we don't want to hear anything else about it. A gag order will be included in our agreement, and if any word of this gets out, there will be major consequences. So, the next questions are, how much and can we make a deal?"

His words were like music to my ears. I had already thought about how much, and when I blurted it out, Cedric coughed, then cleared his throat.

"My niece is probably still feeling the effects of that beat down she got, because her head couldn't be on straight if she's requesting that kind of settlement. Add two more zeros to that amount for pain and lifetime suffering, and, we, sir, have a deal."

Okay. Maybe I did short myself a little. It wasn't until then that I realized just how important and helpful Cedric being here was.

Charles kept nodding his head, and then he stood up and extended his hand to me. "Deal," he said, waiting for me to accept.

I stood and happily extended my hand to his. "Yes. We have ourselves a deal."

Charles said he needed to call his attorney and would be right back. Within the next hour or so, I was asked to read over an agreement that would set me up pretty for the rest of my life. Needless to say, I was ecstatic. I thanked Charles before I left by wrapping my arms around his neck and pressing my breasts against his chest.

"I'm glad we could work this out," I said. "I thank you for doing the right thing, and please tell your wife that I thank her for her time, as well."

Charles patted my back, then backed away from the tight embrace. Cedric damn near had to pull me out the door to get me away from Charles. And when we got in the car, he chewed me out.

"Is that all you think about? Some goddamned dick? You almost blew it in there, and that woman wasn't playing with you, Evelyn. She looked like she was about to cut your fucking throat. I'm warning you. If that pussy of yours can't control itself, you'd better figure out a way to shut that shit down and stay the hell away from her husband."

I rolled my eyes at Cedric, even though he knew me all too well. Charles was on my hit list, and I didn't give two cents about his wife. For now, though, I had something else to be excited about.

"Forget all that mess you're talking about right now. I am rich! Did you hear what I said? I. Am. Rich! All I'm thinking about is shopping. Ole Netta can keep Charles, but she'd better hope like hell that I never come face-to-face with him again and she's not around. If not, I will fuck his brains out and send him back to her with my pussy juices all over his lips. Just like I may decide to send you back to your lover tonight. I'm in the mood to celebrate my new fortune."

I playfully placed my hand on his lap, but he quickly removed it.

"I don't know how to say this to you, but hell, fucking, no. You couldn't pay me to tamper with that coochie again, and quite frankly, I've already had enough of it."

We laughed, but Cedric quickly changed his mind after I lowered my head to his lap and damn near sucked the skin off his dick. It always tasted so good to me, and he could never resist my head game.

We arrived at my place several minutes later. He damn near broke the door down to get inside and have sex with me. I was so sure that Kayla wouldn't approve of this, but little did she know that Cedric just didn't move me the way he used to. As he lay on top of me, I stared at the ceiling, wondering how I was going to get rid of him.

2

Trina

I was exhausted from my trip to New York with Keith. We had attended an art expo, and it had let me know I had major work to do if I wanted to get serious about my art career. I'd seen artwork from some of the most famous artists in the world. Pieces that had me in awe and that I couldn't get off my mind. Some of Keith's work was comparable, but even he too felt as if his work wasn't up to par. He had discovered his gift when he was in his teens. His parents had sent him to some of the best art schools to learn more, and he worked almost every single day to perfect his skills. I, on the other hand, saw it as a hobby and a way to make a little cash here and there. That was until my trip to New York. I had realized how much love I had for art, so I intended to indulge myself much more, as well as to step it up on my interior decorating. I used to go that route, as well, but not so much lately.

While Keith was upstairs in the studio, I was in the kitchen, cooking breakfast. Things between us had been only okay, simply because Keith had been worried about the situation between Evelyn and Bryson. I had found myself caught in the middle. Evelyn was my friend; Keith was my man. I knew Bryson was guilty of doing what he'd done to her, and he continued to lie about what Evelyn had said when she caught him with another man. Just the other day, Keith and I had got into another disagreement about Bryson putting his hands on her. I couldn't believe that Keith condoned it and that he'd said that Evelyn deserved everything she got. I had a problem with that because I had seen her in that hospital bed, clinging to life. No one deserved that. The bottom line was Bryson needed to come clean.

We had gotten to the point where I didn't want Bryson over here and Keith didn't want Evelyn here. Keith had every right to be angry with her for trying to get him in bed with her, but that issue had been resolved. I had handled it, and Evelyn now knew that Keith was mine and only mine. She had apologized for what she had done, and even though a part of me still did not completely trust her, I was glad that we all considered ourselves friends again.

Mending our friendship had taken work. Faced with this work, most people would have said, "To hell with it." I had had a lot of convincing to do with Kayla, and we both had had to dig deep in order to forgive Evelyn. I thought about how I would have felt if she had died that day. If Bryson had killed her, how would I have handled it? We all had had unresolved issues, and I would have felt horrible for not working things out with her. We had been friends for too long. There had been ups, as well as downs. But thankfully, we had been able to focus on the true meaning of forgiveness and had pulled it all together and had remained friends.

I was just about done with preparing breakfast when I heard my cell phone ringing. It was on the kitchen table, so I walked away from the stove and went to answer it. I didn't recognize the number, but the voice sounded familiar.

"It's me, Sasha Bolden. One of the artists you met while in New York. You gave me your number to call you. Remember?"

I snapped my fingers, then smiled. "Yes. I remember now. How are you?"

"I'm doing well. Thanks for asking. I'm glad you made it home safely, and I wondered if you gave more thought to what I mentioned to you while you were here."

In New York Keith and I had been in an art class together, learning new things, and there we'd met Sasha. I had mentioned to her that I originally saw my art as a hobby, but after observing a portrait I'd done, she'd felt that I had major potential, and she'd encouraged me to do more. She'd insisted that she could help me. She'd also said that she could get my paintings in front of some serious art buyers and help me make money. I'd told Keith about it, but he hadn't seem as enthused about it as I was. New York was definitely a place where I could make a lot of money if I wanted to, but I wasn't up to traveling there more than once or twice a year. Sasha had mentioned that I should travel there more to showcase my work.

"I've given it some thought," I said. "But I'm not sure what I really want to do yet."

"Would that be because of Keith? If so, let me say this to you. You can't let anyone hold you back. If you have an opportunity to get your work out there more, jump on it. I can help you out a lot. Just give it some more thought and then let me know what you decide."

"I'm not letting anyone hold me back. If I believe this is going to be a good opportunity for me, I will definitely jump on it. I need time to think about it, though. I'll let you know something soon, and thanks for calling me."

We ended the call on that note. I stood there in thought while tapping the phone against the palm of my hand. I was confused about what to do, but I sure as hell didn't want to turn away money or mess up an opportunity to become a well-known artist. There was also something else that weighed heavily on my mind. I was a little bit attracted to Sasha. She was a beautiful black woman who was very likable, hilarious, and fun to be around. Her natural fro was beautiful, and her curves weren't nothing to play with. I could tell she worked out a lot, like I did, and I appreciated how knowledgeable she was about art. She had spent a lot of time with me and Keith while we were in New York. I liked her style, and I'd been a little sad when we all parted ways. I wondered if Keith had seen me checking her out. Had he noticed lust in my eyes? I was glad that she lived in New York and I was miles and miles away in St. Louis. If she lived here, God help me. I would probably be at her doorstep right now, trying to see what these feelings would lead to.

The crazy thing was, I thought that I was done with women, especially after what had happened between me and crazy-ass Lexi. After she wound up trying to kill Keith, I had promised myself that I would never lie to him again about my feelings. But there I was again, holding back on how I felt inside. I guessed it wasn't a biggie, and I didn't think it was necessary to mention a simple crush. The bottom line was, I loved Keith to death. And one day I intended to be his wife.

As I entered the upstairs studio with a breakfast tray in my hands, I could see Keith sitting behind a tall canvas. His legs straddled a stool, and with his shirt off, the numerous tattoos covering his biceps were on display. I had myself one of the sexiest men in the world. I could kick myself for thinking about being with another woman, but seeing him in his boxers surely made my thoughts switch gears. I stepped forward, and the second he saw me with the tray in my hands, a wide smile appeared on his face. His pearly whites showed, and he reached out for my waist. I placed the tray on the floor, then sat on his lap.

"You are so sweet," he said. "But if you plan on interrupting me, you'd better make sure you're bringing me more than just breakfast."

"I'm bringing you breakfast and then some. Take whatever you wish. . . . I'm all yours."

Keith planted a soft kiss on my shoulder, then reached for the glass of orange juice on the tray. As he took a sip, I looked at the painting he'd been working on since we'd gotten back from our trip. It was an abstract design that displayed numerous bright colors. I loved it.

"Your painting is coming along well. I'm feeling the abstract look of this, and it's good to see you venture away from what you normally do," I remarked.

"I'm trying," he said. "New York was a wake-up call for me, and if I want to compete, I have to do much better."

"Me too. You know I've been thinking about stepping up my game too. After the call I got today from Sasha, I think I may let her help me out. I'll see what she can do to get me to the next level."

Keith shot down my comment real quick. "I doubt that she'll be able to help you, Trina, so don't get your hopes up too high. People are always talking about what they can do to help your career, and most of the time, all it is a bunch of talk. I sensed that from her. If you ask me, she talks too damn much."

I was surprised by Keith's response, but he'd been this way lately. Kind of on edge a little and real blunt about certain things.

"I get that some people make promises that they can't keep, but I have a feeling that she's genuine."

"Genuine? No, I wasn't feeling a genuine person when she was around. As a matter of fact, the word *genuine* was far from what I felt."

I released a deep sigh, then continued. "I'm not sure what you're sensing about her, but whatever it is, you didn't seem that way while we were in New York. You were talking just as much as she was, and the two of you seemed to get along just fine."

"I know how to handle myself when it comes to business, but I didn't go to New York to make new friends. I just don't want to see you get your hopes up too high, and maybe you should focus more on trying to enhance your skills first."

Keith had always believed that he was more talented than I was. Whether that was true or not, I didn't like where we were going with this conversation.

"I do need to improve my work, but so do you. And when all is said and done, if I can get paid for my work, I will."

I stood, only for Keith to pull me back down on his lap. "Listen," he said. "I'm not trying to insult your work or anything like that, okay? There's just something about that Sasha chick that didn't sit right with me. She seemed very nosy. And I didn't know that you had given her your phone number."

"I gave it to her because she said she could help me. I didn't get the same vibes from her as you did, but if I ever sense that something isn't right with her, you know I'll back off."

"Just like you did with Evelyn, huh? She hasn't been out of the hospital for two weeks, and she's already causing trouble."

A frown covered my face. I surely didn't know how we'd got from Sasha to Evelyn. It seemed like Keith was purposely trying to kick up an argument with me.

"How is Evelyn causing trouble? What has she done now?"

"I'll let her tell you all about it. I'm sure she will, but then again, maybe she won't remember to tell you that she told my parents you were bisexual."

"What?" I shouted. "When . . .? Why would she tell your parents that?"

"She met with them to discuss that situation with Bryson. During their conversation, she felt that it was necessary to mention that you were bisexual. My mother called me, and so did Bryson. I've had it with your conniving-ass BFF, and I wish you would wake up when it comes to her. She is trouble. When will you and Kayla ever learn?"

I was shocked that Evelyn would bring up my name while talking to Keith's parents. What in the hell was she up to now? I couldn't wait to call her, but for now, I had to find out what Keith's response was to his parents.

"I will deal with Evelyn later, but what did you tell your mother?"

"I told her the truth. I don't want you to ever feel as if you have to cover up who you are, and I'm not ashamed of the woman I fell in love with."

His answer put a smile on my face. I was so lucky to have a man like Keith in my corner.

"I love you too, and thanks for keeping it real with her. Did she say anything after that?"

"She did, but I don't want to talk about it right now. What I want to do is eat breakfast before it gets cold and get busy again with painting. I also want to go to the fitness center to work out, but only after we get a little workout here first."

"Count me in, as always."

We ate breakfast, scratched sex for now, and then changed to go to the gym. I couldn't stop thinking about what Keith's mother now thought about me. Some people had no love for individuals like me, and even though Bryson was who he was, his mother didn't seem like she was the type who would embrace something like this with open arms. If she ever asked me what the deal was, I wouldn't deny it. And if her feelings about me had changed, so be it.

Meanwhile, I was highly upset with Evelyn for putting my business out there. While Keith was upstairs, putting on his tennis shoes, I went downstairs to call her. She answered the phone, sounding as upbeat as ever.

"It's funny that you called," she said. "I was just at Foot Locker, trying to decide what size shoe you wear. I saw these cute tennis shoes that have your name written all over them. They're only eighty bucks, and they're green, gray, and navy. Are you still a size eight, or have your feet grown?"

"I wear a size nine, but aside from the tennis shoes, can I ask you a question?"

"Sure. What's on your mind?"

"Why did you tell Keith's parents I was bisexual? That's none of their business. If I wanted them to know, I would have told them myself."

"I get that, but the truth is, it slipped. I didn't mean to say anything about you, but as I was talking to them about Bryson accepting who he is, I accidentally mentioned your name. I apologize, but at the same time, if you were or if you still are bisexual, I don't want you to be ashamed of it. You kept your secret long enough, and to hell with Keith's parents if they don't approve. That mother of his is a real bitch. I don't see how you've been able to get along with a woman like that."

Evelyn was trying to change the subject, but she was right about his parents. To hell with their feelings about me.

"I'm not ashamed of who I am, but that doesn't mean that you have to spread my business to the whole world. Keith's mother and I get along very well, so please don't refer to her as a bitch. You must have done or said something to her that really pissed her off. You also never told me that you were planning to meet with them about your situation with Bryson. How did that turn out?"

"All I can say is well," Evelyn replied. "It turned out very well, and everything worked out for the best. I can't say much more than that, because of a gag order, but I'm sure Keith will provide you with more details."

"I'm sure he will too. Meanwhile, get back to whatever you were doing, and we'll chat later. Glad you're feeling better."

"Much better. And when you have time, I want to take you and Kayla to dinner. It's the least I can do, so let me know what you're up to this Sunday. I know church isn't on your agenda, but maybe some time after two or three will work."

"Why are you over there trying to throw shade? Church isn't on my agenda, and I'm sure it's not on yours, either, you sinner. "

Evelyn laughed. "Aren't we all? But you're right. It's not on my agenda. But I serve the same God as you. He's sho' 'nough been good to me, and I'm thankful for my new blessings."

I didn't bother to reply about her new blessings. Evelyn had things twisted. It was obvious that she'd managed to swindle some money out of Keith's parents. I wanted to know how much, so on the way to the gym with Keith, I asked him if he knew.

"I know, but I'm not supposed to talk about it. I'm so angry about the whole thing, and I'm sick and tired of my parents bailing Bryson out of these situations. We made up after the fight, but certain things will never be forgotten. I don't like how he treated you, and he has no respect for our parents."

"I know how you feel about him. I feel the same way about Evelyn. She has a big mouth, and I told her that I didn't appreciate her telling your parents about me. But it is what it is. I just hope that they don't look at me differently now."

Keith didn't respond.

I was sure he was holding back on what his mother now thought of me, but the past was the past. I couldn't do anything to change who I was, but I was worried about speaking of my sexual desires for women as if they no longer existed. There was something stirring inside of me again. First, there were my surprising feelings for Sasha. And when we got to the gym, I jogged on the treadmill and observed a woman's nice, heart-shaped ass in front of me. Keith jogged beside me, and even though I'd seen him take a quick glance at her butt, my eyes were glued to it more than his were. I tried to play it off by watching the TV mounted on the wall, but my eyes kept traveling back to the same place—her ass. Dirty thoughts swam in my head, and I visualized her ass cheeks spread across my face. I was so disturbed by what I was feeling that I stopped the treadmill to go cool off.

"Where are you going?" Keith asked, still jogging. I looked at the sweat dripping from his sexy body, and all I could think was, *Shame on me.*

"I need some water. I also want to work with the weights, so I'll be over there."

"Give me twenty or so more minutes on the treadmill and I'll join you."

He continued his workout on the treadmill, while I moved on over to the weights. I kept taking peeks at the beautiful woman, and when she got off the treadmill, I saw her walk over to a man who was doing sit-ups on a mat. They kissed, and a few minutes later they left together. Out of sight, out of mind. I was left thinking about my relationship with Keith. I certainly didn't want to lose him, but how long would I be able to curb my desires?

3

Kayla

I seriously thought I'd gotten rid of my problem. After divorcing Cedric, I had figured my little world would be peachy keen. But now I had a bigger issue to deal with—drinking too much alcohol. It had started off as a casual thing. Then I had found myself drinking just to take away the pain. The pain had never really gone away, especially since this thing with Jacoby reaching out to Paula Daniels for her to kill Cedric was still fresh in my head. I wished like hell that she hadn't followed through with the plan. I was on edge every time Cedric stopped by. He kept questioning me about my demeanor, but I didn't have the guts or the courage to tell him that Jacoby had been involved in planning his demise.

As for Jacoby, he seemed to be doing much better than I was. But there was no doubt that he was just as worried as I was about Cedric finding out the truth. We knew what kind of damage Cedric could do if he ever found out, and there was no question in my mind that he would have Jacoby arrested. In no way could I see my son in jail. He wasn't that kind of kid, and he didn't deserve to be put behind bars. The other prisoners would eat him alive, and it made me sick to my stomach when I thought about my baby being in a place like that. At the end of the day, I viewed this as being my fault. Had I handled my business with Cedric a long time ago and divorced him when he first cheated on me, we wouldn't be in this predicament right now. But for many years, I had held on for the wrong reasons. I'd caused my son more damage than I'd realized. He'd felt as if he didn't have a choice, and I totally understood why he'd wanted Cedric dead.

Jacoby had felt that I was weak and that he needed to stand up for me. Now I had to stand up for him too. If I had to lie and say that I was the one who had put him up to it, I would. I would go that far and do jail time. I was prepared for wherever the chips fell, but meanwhile, I needed something to help calm my nerves and enable me to cope with all that was unfolding around me. For now, alcohol was, indeed, my best friend. I was afraid to talk to Trina or Evelyn about my problems, and I did my best to keep up a good front. They both thought that from the outside looking in, my life was still perfect, even without Cedric. I had money to do whatever, a son who loved me to death, an ex who now respected me, and two friends who were as close to me as sisters. After all that had happened, they were still like sisters to me. Evelyn had turned over a new leaf, and maybe it had taken her being on her deathbed to realize her mistakes. We all got those wake-up calls. It seemed as if hers had come right on time.

While Jacoby was at the mall with his girlfriend, Adrianne, I was at home, watching TV. My new condo was decked out, and I had recently hired an interior decorator to hook up my kitchen and hearth room. She had jazzed it up with a new color palette: olive green, tan, and white. My flat-screen TV hung above a wall-mounted fireplace, and an array of beautiful art covered the walls. All my furniture was traditional, and I was very particular about people coming over and putting their shoes on my sofas, especially Evelyn, who disrespected my place no matter where I lived. In the past, if she wasn't somewhere in my home fucking Cedric, she was somewhere with her feet propped up on my furniture or with a lit cigarette. I had called her out on that mess too, and it was good to know that we were now on the same page.

She had called earlier to tell me she had something for me and was on her way over. I hadn't seen her since I left her place the other day, and I didn't mind her coming over. I was bored and needed someone to talk to. And with her being here, I wouldn't think about drinking so much. It seemed like whenever I was alone, alcohol was the only thing on my mind.

With an empty glass in my hand, I looked at the clock on the wall. It was a little after two in the afternoon, and there

I was, still in my pajamas. I figured I'd better go into my bedroom and put on some clothes, so I stood to go do just that. As I walked past the bar, I looked at the almost empty bottle of vodka. There was only a little swig left, so I decided to get another glass and finish it off. After pouring it, I tossed the liquid down my throat, then swallowed hard. My eyes watered from the burning sensation in my throat—a feeling that I had gotten used to. I felt a little more upbeat, so I turned on some music, which played throughout my condo, and listened to Jill Scott break it all down for me.

While singing along, I changed into a pair of tight jeans and a ribbed tank top that revealed my tiny nipples. I wasn't in the mood for a bra, nor was I in the mood to put on any makeup. My dark skin was flawless, and I loved the way my short hair had grown on me. I kept it cut low and lined to perfection. Cedric hadn't had anything nice to say to me when I first got it cut, but he had later admitted that it was the best thing I could have done to show off my round face and doe eyes. I appreciated his compliments more than he knew, especially since he had barely had anything nice to say to me when we were married. I had never thought we'd be able to get along as we did, but I guessed it was like that because we were no longer under the same roof.

As soon as I closed the blinds in my bedroom, the doorbell rang. I made my way to the door, thinking that it was Evelyn. Instead, it was Cedric. His pop-up visits annoyed me a little. Since his office and his new home were close by, he often stopped by to check on me and Jacoby.

I opened the door with a fake smile on my face. "It would be nice for you to call before coming over, Cedric. We're not here all the time, and I would hate for you to waste gas."

He walked inside, bringing the smell of Clive Christian cologne with him. His tailored suit was always on point, and as usual, his waves were flowing.

"I came to see what Jacoby was getting into this weekend. He's been dodging me, and we've never gone this long without spending some father-and-son time together. Every time I suggest that we go somewhere, he comes up with excuses. Haven't you noticed?"

I closed the door, then made my way toward the kitchen. Cedric followed.

"No, I haven't noticed. But he's a teenager, Cedric. I'm sure he doesn't want to be doing things with you all the time. Besides, Adrianne keeps him quite busy. He spends a lot of his free time with her."

"I get that, but I also know that he's been avoiding me. And it's not like I'm trying to just hang out with him anywhere. What teenager wouldn't want to go to an NBA championship game? Who would turn down going to Dubai or taking a trip to Hawaii? I even suggested that he bring Adrianne along, and he still made excuses. I know that finding out I wasn't his real father upset him, but at the end of the day, I'm the one who raised him."

Cedric was making this more difficult than it needed to be. He needed to back off and give Jacoby some space.

"You can't force him to do what he doesn't want to do. And to be honest with you, I think that he's been struggling with this whole father thing. You and I did a lot of damage to him. I'm not sure if he's completely over it."

Cedric opened the fridge, then removed a bottle of water. He unscrewed the cap, then looked at me. "Correction. You did a lot of damage by not telling either of us the truth. Don't put me in that mess, and please take responsibility for your actions."

I rolled my eyes. He didn't have to go there, did he? Yes, I had messed up by not telling Jacoby the truth about his real father, Arnez, but I wasn't going to beat myself up about it.

"I have taken responsibility for my actions, and I'm going to encourage you to do the same. As a matter of fact, I don't even want to talk about this right now. Jacoby is gone, and he won't be back until later."

Cedric guzzled down most of the water, then placed the bottle on the island. He licked across his lips to moisten them.

"I guess I'll call him later to see what's up, but I'm sure I'm going to get the same ole song and dance. As for you, what's been up? It smells like a brewery when I walk in here. And just so you know, I am paying attention. The liquid in those bottles over there is getting lower and lower by the day."

I turned my head to look at the numerous bottles on the bar. I didn't know that Cedric had been paying attention. Was the smell of alcohol really that prominent in here?

"I'm doing fine. I was vacuuming the other day, and I hit the liquor cabinet over there with the vacuum cleaner by accident. Some of the bottles hit the floor, and the liquids spilled on my carpet. I need to call a carpet cleaning company to come clean the carpet."

"You do that," he said, finishing off the water. "And while you're at it, you may want to attend a few AA meetings too. I can't believe you would try to feed me that bullshit you just said, but I can say that it doesn't surprise me. The one thing I can say is, you do always do your best to cover up a lie."

I wasn't sure what Cedric was referring to, but I tried not to make much of his comment. Either way, his words upset me. He was always coming over here, trying to run my and Jacoby's lives. He seemed to make my alcohol problem a bigger issue than it was, but I didn't know why I was surprised by that. Anything to belittle me was the name of his game.

I tried to change the subject. "Whether you want to believe it or not, I have things under control over here. What you need to worry about is your new home and the woman you now have living with you, Joy. When are the two of you getting married? She couldn't wait for us to get divorced, so I know she has already gone out and picked out her dress."

"Breaking news, baby. Marriage is not in my future again. In my eyes, women are only good for one thing and one thing only. No offense to you."

His eyes traveled to my tiny breasts, which were visible underneath my tank. I snatched the bottle of water from his hand, then tossed it in the trash can.

"I am highly offended, and I can't believe you would say something like that. If that's how you truly feel—"

Suddenly the doorbell rang.

Saved by the bell, I thought when I heard the doorbell. This time it had to be Evelyn. It had been a long time since we were all in the same room. I wondered how the two of them would react upon seeing each other. The last thing Trina had told me was that Cedric had knocked out Evelyn's teeth. I didn't want any chaos to go down today, so I warned him that that was probably her at the door.

He shrugged, then followed behind me as I made my way to the door. "I'm surprised that you're still friends with that bitch, but that's your choice. I'm getting ready to go. Tell Jacoby I'll holla later."

The second I opened the door, Evelyn's bright smile vanished. Cedric walked around me to make his way outside. He didn't say one word to Evelyn. She stood with her mouth wide open. Several bags were in her hands, and it looked as if she'd just gotten her hair done. Long curls hung past her shoulders, and the short dress and high heels she wore made her look as if she was ready to go party.

"Ugggh," she said, looking at Cedric as he walked off to his car. "What's his problem? Or should I be asking, what is he doing here? Are the two of you getting back together?"

Honestly, I didn't feel comfortable discussing Cedric with Evelyn. She didn't need to know the purpose of his visit, and if we were getting back together, she would be the last person I would tell.

"Come on in here and stop asking me questions about Cedric. I don't want to talk about that man. I'd rather talk about how you've been doing."

With a smile back on her face, Evelyn trotted into the living room with her bags. She placed them on the floor and then sat on the sofa, crossing her long legs.

"I've been doing great, but come sit by me so the two of us can talk."

I walked into the room, watching closely as Evelyn checked me out from head to toe.

"You've lost more weight," she said. "Girl, what are you trying to do? Model again?"

"No, not at all." I sat beside her. "Just been eating healthy, exercising a lot, and trying to raise my son to the best of my ability."

"Well," she said, patting my leg, "you've done a great job with Jacoby. If I had a son, I would want him to be just like him."

I smiled, but her comment made me think about her being pregnant by Cedric. I truly needed to let go of the past, but a tiny part of me couldn't.

"Okay," Evelyn said, rubbing her hands together. "I bought you some thank-you gifts, and before I give them to you, I have a few things that I want to say. First, thank you so much for being there for me when I needed you. You and Trina are truly the best, and I don't know what I would have done in that hospital without your support. I know that forgiving me wasn't easy, and if the shoe were on the other foot, I don't know if I could have done it. But you've always been a better person than me, Kayla. I'm working on myself, and I must say that I'm embracing the new me and loving all the goodness that has come my way."

This certainly seemed like a new and reformed Evelyn in front of me, but as always, it was wise not to trust everything she said. While I did believe that the whole situation between her and Bryson had changed her, it was yet to be seen if it was for the good or the bad. Either way, I reached out to give her a hug.

"Apology accepted. Now, stop trying to make me cry and tell me what's in those bags for me. I see Jimmy Choo bags on down to Michael Kors. What did I do to deserve all of this?"

We laughed, and when all was said and done, Evelyn had outdone herself. She certainly knew my taste. From the purses to the fabulous shoes to the watch, I loved it all.

"Thank you, my dear friend, but you really didn't have to do all of this. You know I'm about to ask where you got the money from, but you don't have to tell me if you don't think it's any of my business."

"Look, my business is your business. While I can't tell you how much they gave me, I will say that Bryson's parents hooked me up! They knew he was at fault, and they were willing to do whatever to make sure I didn't put their son's business out there. I'm pleased by how everything turned out, and as long as I don't ever have to ever see him again, I'm good."

"That's good. I'm glad you all were able to settle everything without going to court. Put the money they gave you to good use, and please keep much of it in a savings account. Shopping is nice, but if you don't budget your money correctly, you'll find yourself in the hole again."

"I am making smarter choices, but I had to go splurge a little on some of the things I've always wanted. I also wanted to do something nice for my BFF's, especially you. I borrowed from you until I couldn't borrow anymore. I want to pay back some of the money you gave me, and since you and Cedric aren't together anymore, I suspect that things may be a little tight around here."

I wasted no time setting the record straight. While Evelyn might have gotten a substantial amount of cash from Bryson's parents, I doubted that the money would last a lifetime. It would surprise me if she still had any money six months from now. I wasn't hating. Just being honest.

"Girl, with or without Cedric, I will be just fine. You know I wasn't about to walk away broke after our divorce, and I'm happy to say that he was willing, and able, to give me everything I asked for."

Evelyn clapped her hands. "That's wonderful. And now we must celebrate. Not only on Sunday, when I'm planning to take my BFF's to dinner, but right here and right now too."

She removed a champagne bottle from one of the bags. I went to the kitchen to get wineglasses, and within the hour, we found ourselves drunk, giggling, and delving into a conversation that I didn't want to have with her.

"I needed this," I said. "Lord knows, I needed to let go and feel free again."

I raised my arms in the air, then waved my hands like a bird.

"Fr-free?" Evelyn slurred. "Free from who or what?"

"From my past. I feel so much better, but there is one little thing that is still bugging the heck out of me." I fell back on the sofa after I took another sip of the vodka I had put on ice.

Evelyn crawled on the floor, then maneuvered her way into one of my wingback chairs. "If it has anything to do with me," she said, woozy and pointing at me, "let it all out. Don't hold back, 'cause I totally understand if you still got some problems with me."

I sat up, then waved my finger in front of me. "Noooo. Not with you, but with my ex and my son. What am I going to do about them?"

Evelyn sipped from her wineglass, then slammed it on the table in front of her. "What? Exactly what do you mean? Stop talking in riddles and spill it!"

I placed my finger over my lips, then whispered, "Shhh. If I tell you, you can't say one word about this to anyone. Not even Trinaaaaa."

"Yo . . . your secret is safe with me. Maybe not with the old Evelyn . . ." She laughed. "But definitely with the new Evelyn."

I laughed too. I smacked my leg, then laughed even louder. "Right. That old Evelyn was something else. But the new Evelyn, I'm kind of liking this bitch."

"Ooh, girl, stop. Shut yo' mouth and keep on talking. I'm listening too, bitch."

I pointed my finger at her. "Tyler Perry gon' get you for biting his stuff. But, anyway, as I was saying, Cedric and me . . . we still been screwing around from time to time."

"What?" Evelyn shouted, then sat up in the chair. "Are you telling me that you still been giving that man all your precious goodies?"

I held up one finger. "Ju-just one time, but he keeps coming over here, trying to get into my panties. I don't know if I should let him in again or not, but when I tell you that man knows how to make my juices flow, I mean he really knows how to make my juices flow. I don't know who I'm gon' find to replace him."

"Hey, you ain't talking to a woman who don't already know how skillful he is, but trust me when I say there are other men out there who know how to make the pussy pop too. In my opinion, Cedric is good, but I know a man who delivers nothing but greatness."

"Well, you've definitely had more sex partners than me, so I can't argue with you on that. And if whomever you're speaking of is that great, maybe you should send him my way."

Evelyn sucked her teeth, then moved her head from side to side. "No way, sweetheart. We will not share another man, and it's a damn shame that we shared Cedric. But it is what it is, and at least you know now what kind of man you were really married to."

"I do know, thanks to you." I paused to take another swig of the vodka. "But like you said, it is what it is, and the past is the past. The future is yet to be seen, but I got a feeling that I'ma need another one of those toe-curling orgasms he provides real soon. You gotta admit that the man definitely knows how to chomp down on the cooda."

Evelyn jumped from her seat to give me a high five. "Bam!" she exclaimed as she slapped her hand against mine. "I'll give him that for sure. That tongue of his be all up in there, and, girl, don't let that mutha slither near yo' ass or take a swipe at it! Boom!"

I giggled, then fell back on the sofa while kicking my feet in the air. "Yes! Yes! Yes! That tongue is fierce! I'm getting all hot and bothered just thinking about it, and I can't help but think that he's only a phone call away. Do you think I should call him?"

Evelyn moved her head like a bobblehead doll. "Yep. 'Cause he's just a phone call away. You should call him to come over tonight. Let him bend you over like this, and call you bitches and hoes while slapping yo' ass." Evelyn bent over the chair and slapped her butt. "He be smacking hard, and . . . and he'll bite that ass too."

I laughed my butt off. He'd never cursed at me, nor had he taken a bite out of my ass. But I was so sure that Cedric had *explored* many interesting things with the tricks he had cheated on me with, including Evelyn. In no way was I offended by this conversation. Cedric's dick was always on point, but after our last sex session, I never wanted him to touch me again. I was strictly talking smack because I was drunk, and I had always wanted Evelyn to discuss freely what had happened between them. I had to let her know that it didn't anger me one bit.

"Girl, you are a mess," I said, throwing my hand back at her. "I can't believe we're talking about ole Ceddy like this, but you'd better believe that if it were two men, they'd surely be talking about the woman."

"Right. And I don't know how we ventured here, because you were about to tell me something about Jacoby, weren't you?"

I scratched my head, thinking about Jacoby. It was getting late, and I hadn't heard from him. It wasn't like he often called to check in, but there were times when I worried too much about him.

"It wasn't important," I said. "But I do need to call and check on him. Where in the heck is my cell phone at?"

Evelyn stood to look around the room. She staggered a bit, then let out a loud belch. She slapped her hand over her mouth, and when her cheeks blew up like a balloon, she rushed off toward the bathroom. Unfortunately, she didn't make it. Puke sprayed on my plush carpet, and some splattered on my table. She slowly turned while holding her stomach.

"Sorry," she said in a whisper. "I'll clean it up."

"Yes, you will," I said, then shook my head as she ran the rest of the way to the bathroom.

While she was in there, I attempted to gather myself so that I could look for my phone. It was in the kitchen, and when I called Jacoby, he didn't answer. I left a message for him to call me back, and after ending the call, I dialed Cedric's number to see if he'd had any luck with reaching him. I guessed he heard the slurring of my voice.

"Yes, I talked to him, but like always, he said he would let me know. On another note, you really need to get some help. I'm concerned about you."

"Don't be. I'll be fine."

I hung up on Cedric, hoping that I would be fine, as I'd professed.

4

Evelyn

Being with my BFF's on Sunday was fun. First, we went to dinner at Outback Steakhouse, and then we went to a little hole-in-the-wall nightclub to have some drinks and to dance. Trina didn't drink as much as Kayla and me, only because one of us had to drive. Kayla was sloppy drunk, and we had to hold her up as we carried her through the door of her condo. When we entered, we found Jacoby and his girlfriend in the living room area, watching TV. They looked like they were up to no good, causing Kayla to straighten her back and wave her hands around.

"Up, up. Hands in the air," she ordered, slurring. "I need to make sure y'all are not over there doing any of that freaky stuff."

Jacoby's girlfriend laughed, but he sat there with an embarrassed look on his face. Kayla blew him a kiss before we carried her off to her bedroom and laid her back on the bed.

"Stop making such a big fuss over me," she said, trying to push us away. "I'm fine. Get out and go home so I can get some sleep."

Sleep was exactly what she needed. Trina pulled back the sheets, and after tucking Kayla in bed and turning off the lights, we left her bedroom. As I closed the door behind us, I listened to Kayla sing Mary J.'s "No More Drama," which played on the intercom.

"She's a mess," Trina said, turning to me. "Y'all had too much to drink, and I'm surprised you're still standing."

"I'm good. I knew when to stop, even though my head is banging."

As we made our way toward the front door, we stopped to say good-bye to Jacoby and his girlfriend. She was kind of on the thick side. I was surprised to see Jacoby with a chick who had so much weave too. As tall and as handsome as he was, I expected better from him.

"We'll lock the door on our way out," Trina said. "Check on your mother in a few hours and call me if she doesn't seem okay."

"She'll be fine. She's like that all the time. By morning, she won't remember a thing."

Trina and I looked at each other. It appeared that Kayla was starting to have a serious problem with alcohol. Cedric had mentioned it to me, but I hadn't taken his claim seriously. But after witnessing her toss back all that alcohol tonight, I knew she had a problem.

We stood at the door, about to leave, but I stopped and asked Jacoby if he would get me a few aspirin. I didn't have any at home, and I didn't want Trina to have to stop and get me some. As I waited for Jacoby, Trina told me to meet her in the car. Seconds later, he came out of the bathroom and handed the aspirin to me.

"Thanks," I said.

He didn't reply. I could sense that he was still bitter about my actions from the past. As he looked down at the floor to avoid eye contact with me, I reached out and lifted his chin.

"I know this may seem a little awkward for you, but just so you know, I'm sorry for everything that I did. I never meant to hurt you, but I was stupid, and I did some crazy things just to get money. That's all in the past, okay? And just as Trina said to you before leaving, if you ever need anything, let us know. We're like family. A little dysfunctional at times, but we love each other, nonetheless."

Jacoby nodded. "Thanks for saying that. Take care, and I'll tell my moms to call you in the morning and let you know she's okay."

"Is she really okay? I'm a little worried about her. Should I be?"

He shrugged, then took a hard swallow. "You'll have to ask her. I don't know what's going on in her head."

I didn't think that I could get Jacoby to speak up about what was really going on, so I left it there. I walked to the car, thinking about my interesting night with my BFF's. It had been a long time since we'd kicked it like we did tonight. It had felt good to get turned up. Trina and I laughed about it in the car, but our conversation quickly got serious when we talked about Kayla.

"When is the last time you saw her sober?" I asked. "She's been working that bottle, and she really did consume a lot of alcohol tonight."

"Yeah, but so did you. I think tonight was long overdue. Kayla was out to have a good time. She stays cooped up in that condo a lot. Her whole life revolves around Jacoby, and I think it felt good for her to get out tonight. We need to do that more often."

"I agree. And I do understand what you're saying about Kayla, but let's keep our eyes on her. It seems as if she may be going through something, and I don't think it has anything to do with Cedric."

Trina tapped her fingers on the steering wheel while driving. "If not, what do you think it is?"

"I don't know. I was hoping that you'd be able to tell me."

"I can't tell you what I don't know. Out of all of us, Kayla has always been the private one. I hope everything is okay, and if there is something severely wrong, I'm sure she'll eventually tell us."

We continued to talk about Kayla, but then our conversation switched to her and Keith. I had a few questions about his father, but I didn't quite know how to get the information I wanted without seeming too nosy or as if I was up to something.

"I just wish Keith would lighten up and look at things from a different perspective," Trina said. "He's so narrow minded, and it drives me crazy sometimes."

"That's how most men are, so don't trip too hard. Keith loves you and you love him. The two of you will be able to work through whatever."

"I truly hope so. Lord knows, I hope so, 'cause I do not want to lose him."

Trina was always talking in circles. I could tell she wanted to tell me something, and if not today, she would spill her guts to me at a later date. She wasn't as private as Kayla was.

"Why do you think you may lose him? Something must be going on, but if you don't want to share, I'm good with that. I already know how you feel about me knowing your business."

Trina stopped at a red light, then glanced at herself in the rearview mirror. She moved her short bangs away from her forehead, then wiped her finger across her dry lips.

"There's nothing going on with us. There's more going on with *me*. While we were in New York, we hung out with this chick named Sasha. I've been chatting with her over the phone about some of my paintings, and she insists that she can put some money in my pockets and help me make a real name for myself in the industry."

"And? What's so wrong with that?"

Trina shrugged. "Nothing, I guess. Except that I'm starting to think about her maybe more than I should be."

When the light turned green, she drove off. She didn't dare turn her head to look at me. I totally didn't get my BFF's. They both had it all, but they always managed to fuck things up. As far as I could see, Keith was the best man that any woman could hope for. He was fine as fuck, sexy as hell, and God fearing, and he had money. He had his own crib, owned three cars, and had a career. But there Trina was, talking to me about catching feelings for a bitch in New York that she barely knew. I wasn't sure how to respond. The last thing I wanted to do was come off as being too judgmental and harsh.

"You can think about whomever you wish," I said. "But I hope you're not planning on pursuing this chick. Keith would be devastated, and after what happened to him because of that other crazy broad you was dating, Lexi, you may want to rethink those feelings you're having."

She had the audacity to catch an attitude with me. Her head snapped to the side, and she tried to pull back on what she'd said.

"It wasn't like I just told you I was falling in love with someone else. I know that Keith would be devastated, and I will never forget what Lexi did to him. All I said was I'd been thinking about her. A thought never hurt anyone. I have no intentions to pursue a relationship with her, and all I'm doing right now is rambling."

"Are you sure about not trying to pursue a relationship with her? If you're going to allow her to, as you put it, help you with your career, how do you know what that will lead to?"

"It will lead to nothing. Nothing at all, because I love Keith, and that's all there is to it."

I wasn't convinced. And people always saw me as the bad person. Hell, yeah, I was, but I wasn't about to give Trina a pass on this one. She wanted a bitch like me to come along and steal her man. And while I failed at trying to get him on my team, that didn't mean another woman would fail. I left well enough alone and tried to change the subject. I was sure she would appreciate me doing so.

"How long have Keith's parents been married?" I questioned.

She shrugged. "I'm not sure. Maybe twenty or thirty years. All I know is for a long time. I think they were high school sweethearts. Why?"

"I was just asking. I had no idea you were dating a man with wealthy parents like that. That's great, and I often think about what people do to make that kind of money. What kind of work does his father do, or was the money inherited?"

"Some of it was inherited, but very little. I think a lot of his dad's money comes from investments and business deals that he's made over the years. He also works for the government, but I can't really say what he does. All I know is that whatever it is, it's legal."

"I would hope so. I mean, does he have an office or anything like that? Or does he work from that beautiful house they live in? And speaking of that house, why haven't you said anything to me about it? It is off the chain, and talk about somebody who was shocked."

"I know. I was stunned when I first saw it too. Keith kind of kept it a secret from me. I guess he didn't want me to know how much money they were sitting on. His father's office, though, is in Chesterfield, right across from the mall. It's a tall white building with mirrorlike windows on it. Keith and I stopped by there a few times to drop him off some things.

Like I said, I don't know exactly what he does, but that office he sits in is sick too."

I didn't want Trina to get too suspicious, so I left it right there. I had been thinking about paying Charles a visit. Now that I knew where he worked, maybe I would follow through with my plan. For now, though, Charles had to wait. I had to deal with Cedric, who showed up at my apartment ten minutes after Trina dropped me off. He never called to say he was coming over, and we had to be careful, because I didn't want Trina or Kayla to know he and I were involved.

I hurried to let him inside, then quickly shut the door.

"What is it, Cedric? It's late, and I need to get some beauty rest."

"I stopped by to see if you've made any progress with Kayla. Has she told you anything? You stopped by to see her the other day. Y'all had dinner, then went out to kick it. I'm sure she told you something."

"She was too drunk to say anything. I will say that she mentioned something about you and Jacoby, but she didn't elaborate on it."

He didn't like my response. His face twisted and he winced. "What in the hell is that supposed to mean . . . ? She mentioned something? What did she mention?"

I folded my arms and caught a quick attitude with him too. "First of all, lower your voice. What I meant was, she said that something about you and Jacoby was bothering her. That could have been anything. I tried to get her to say more, but she was so drunk that she changed the subject and started talking about you and her having sex with each other recently. I had no idea you were still fucking her."

I was sure he didn't want to have this conversation, and even if he was or wasn't, I didn't care. In the past, it had bothered me. I had wanted it over between the two of them, and I had done my best to make sure Cedric kept his sex life with her down to a minimum. Today it was a different ball game for sure.

Cedric waved me off, then went into my bedroom. My thoughts about him not wanting to hear this were confirmed. I followed behind him, only to listen to more of his bullshit.

"Who I fuck is no one's business," he said, wiggling his tie away from his neck. "The bottom line is, we had a deal. You got what the fuck you wanted, and I'm still waiting to get what I wanted. What in the hell is taking you so long to find out what she and Jacoby are up to?"

"I told you this will take some time. Kayla doesn't completely trust me yet. I'm working hard at getting her back on my team. You never gave me a specific time frame to get this information to you, so you just have to wait, unless you want to do some type of investigation of your own."

He sat on the bed and started to remove his leather shoes. "Investigation, my ass. I took care of you, and now it's time for you to take care of me. You got two more weeks, Evelyn. Two more weeks or else."

"Or else what?"

He snatched my arm, then pulled me to him. As I attempted to pull away, he pushed me back on the bed, then lay on top of me. "I can show you better than I can tell you. Just keep that two-week time frame in your head while you open your goddamned legs."

Cedric attempted to pry my legs open with his, but I resisted. He stopped, then gave me a hard kiss on the mouth. While kissing me, he flipped up my skirt and slipped a few fingers underneath my panties. Several of his fingers entered my pussy. A high arch formed in my back, and I squirmed around as he worked his thick fingers in and out of me.

"How was dinner tonight?" he asked while fingering me.

I answered with my eyes shut tight, trying to pretend that I was enjoying this, just so this night wouldn't turn ugly. "Good, but never better than this."

"Well, I have something even better. Keep your eyes shut and enjoy."

He lowered himself and took oral sex to new heights when he fucked me with his tongue. I couldn't deny that Kayla was so right. He was pretty good at this.

The next day, I put the thoughts of what had happened between Cedric and me behind me. I was excited about going to pay Charles a visit. I had a burgundy, V-neck, fitted dress on that showed a healthy portion of my cleavage. A thin black belt was secured around my waist, and I had topped it all off with red-bottom shoes. My straightened hair fell past my shoulders and was parted down the middle.

As I strutted into his office building, I worked my curvy hips from side to side, causing both men and women to turn their heads in my direction. I wasn't sure if Charles would take time from his busy schedule to see me, but the second I got off the elevator, I spotted him conversing with two men, who were standing close to him. When they turned their heads, so did he. The expression on his face turned flat. He squinted to make sure I was the same woman who had come to his house. I confirmed who I was when I walked up to him and asked if we could go somewhere private to talk.

"Sure," he said, then excused himself from the other conversation.

As we walked past the receptionist's desk, he stopped to address her. "Hold my calls for about fifteen or twenty minutes. I'm going into a meeting."

"Yes, sir," the receptionist said. "Will do."

He motioned for me to follow him, and I had no problem doing so. I checked him out as we went. He was wearing black leather shoes and black slacks with suspenders that looked like they were straight off the rack at Armani. His well-pressed burgundy shirt showcased his muscles, and his coal-black waves, which showed a hint of gray, had sharp lines. I had no words for his trimmed goatee, and I loved men with rich black skin. His whole persona turned me on. Today he looked more like Keith, without all the muscles and tattoos, than like Bryson. I knew that I had to have my shit together when confronting Charles, and knowing that time wasn't on my side, I decided it was in my best interests to get straight to the point.

"Have a seat," he said as we stepped into his spacious office. To the right of his mahogany desk sat a sofa and two chairs. A glass table stood in the middle of the seating arrangement, and on top of it was an array of business magazines. Many plaques covered his walls, and pictures of him and his wife, as well as their family, were propped up here and there. His entire office was surrounded by windows that afforded a view of Highway 40 and part of the city of Chesterfield.

We both sat on the sofa, but before he actually took a seat, he asked if I wanted a beverage. "I can ask my secretary to get whatever you'd like," he said politely.

His secretary couldn't give me what I wanted. Only he could. But instead of saying that, I crossed my legs, then cleared my throat. "No, thank you. I already had lunch, and the cranberry juice I had with it was fine."

"Okay. Now, tell me why you're here. I hope your visit doesn't have anything else to do with Bryson, and I also hope that it has nothing to do with you asking for more money. My wife and I aren't prepared to give you more than we've already given you. The agreement was very clear. You did understand it, didn't you?"

"Of course I did. And I wouldn't dare come here to ask you for any more money. You've already given me enough. I'm very appreciative of your generous gift. It has changed my life in many ways."

Seeming relieved, he released a deep sigh. He rubbed his hands together and then wiped one across his forehead.

"I also didn't come here to discuss Bryson," I continued. "I haven't heard one word from him, and I'm very pleased about that."

"Let's just say that he's on an extended vacation. You won't be hearing from him anytime soon. His mother and I have made sure of that."

That pleased me. I hoped he was somewhere burning in hell. But after speaking to his mother, I was sure that Bryson was somewhere on an island, relaxing and stirring up more trouble.

"The reason that I'm here goes a little something like this," I said. "I honestly cannot stop thinking about you. From the second I laid my eyes on you, I have felt something strange. Something I've never felt before, and I refuse to ignore what I'm feeling inside. I had to come here and share this with you. I'm a very confident woman, and I was always taught to pursue my dreams. Like the one I had about us the other night. I would love to tell you all about it, but only if you want to hear how things went down."

Charles remained silent as he sat next to me. I had a difficult time reading him. There was no expression on his face whatsoever, and he damn near looked like he wasn't even breathing. He was still. Calm. Cool and very collected. I figured he was pondering what to say, and while he was in deep thought, I continued.

"I don't know how things are with you and your wife, and quite frankly, I don't care. All I would like to do is spend one day with you. Just one, and if you demand more time with me, you're more than welcome to it. If not, so be it. I'll move on and pretend that this conversation between us never took place."

Charles still hadn't said anything. He did, however, get up and strut over to his desk. He opened a drawer, then pulled out something that looked like a plaque. He observed the plaque while sitting on the edge of his desk.

"I just got this the other day," he said, still looking at it. "The inscription reads, 'Charles Vincent Washington, MVP.' This is, like, my tenth award, and as you look around my office, you can see for yourself that I'm quite a successful man. I am saying that to you because I need a few minutes to gather myself before responding to what you just said. I'm searching for the right words, just so I don't, you know, hurt your feelings.

"While I think you're one sexy-ass woman, I have to ask if you are out of your goddamned mind. I didn't get this far in life by fucking around with tricks like you. I've always had a very supportive woman by my side, one whom I love and one whom I would never betray. My family means everything to me, and I've raised my sons to be outstanding men who make smart decisions and who don't need side hoes like you to make them feel good. That's why I'm highly disappointed with Bryson, and you—"

He had gone too far, so I quickly stood to cut him off. "That's right. Speak for one of your sons and not the other. One may very well be a man, but the other one comes off as a spoiled rotten bitch with no morals or values. I didn't come here to hurt *your* feelings, but insulting me was the wrong thing to do. I am way more than a side ho or a trick, and if you had taken the opportunity to get to know me better, you would know that. But thanks for letting me know how much you love your wife and how would never betray her. That's a beautiful thing. I applaud your dedication to her, and kudos to you and all your success. Keep up the good work, Charles. I'm sure I'll see you again, and maybe next time you'll be singing a new tune."

"There won't be a next time. Get the hell out of my office, and don't ever come back here again."

His nastiness was totally uncalled for. No wonder Bryson acted a fool as he did. He had got it all from ole dad. That was how I knew Charles wasn't the so-called loving husband he claimed to be.

With my feelings slightly bruised, I walked out of his office and headed to my car. I was less than two blocks away when I heard my phone vibrating inside my purse. I reached for it, then looked to see who it was. The caller came across as unknown, but I answered, anyway.

"Hello," I said with a sharp tone.

"Evelyn," the woman said. "If you thought my son beat your ass, I assure you that what I will do to you is a whole lot worse. Stay away from my damn husband or else."

I laughed at him for telling her about my visit, and at her for being so insecure as to call me. Without replying, I hung up on her. What she was unware of was the fact that I loved a challenge. And had she not called, I might have left well enough alone. It was time to carry on, and I was now in hot pursuit of Charles.

5

Trina

I was wrong, and I knew it this time. For the past two nights, while Keith was asleep, I had been on the phone with Sasha. At first, our conversations had been all about business. But then things had taken a turn when she told me about her girlfriend and her having problems. Tonight I shot her some encouraging words, and before I knew it, we began to click. She thanked me for listening to her, and she said she wished that I was there to help take away some of her pain.

"Whether I'm there or not," I whispered to her, "please keep your head up. I get how frustrating relationships can be, and nobody's relationship is perfect."

She sniffled, then said, "Not even your and Keith's? The two of you seem so happy together. I watched the two of you while you were here. I could sense the love. I can only wish for a relationship like that, but it's been real hectic around here. Diamond is never home anymore. When she is here, all we do is argue. She speaks real ill to me, and I think she's cheating on me with a man."

I thought I heard someone on the steps, but when I got up to see if someone was there, I didn't see anyone. I returned to the sofa and tucked my legs underneath me, sitting on them.

"If it's that bad, Sasha, then end it. Life is too short to be unhappy. I never would have thought that a woman as beautiful as you are would be in a relationship like that. You came across as having it all together. If your woman is preventing you from being all that you can be, then you know what you have to do."

"You're right. And again, thanks for listening to me. It's been one of those days, but I'll get through this. In the meantime, you really should come to New York. We can have ourselves a lot of fun, and I want to introduce you to some people who can really help you. I showed them some of the paintings you did while you were here. They were floored."

I couldn't help but smile. "I haven't decided when I'll be coming back that way, but it may be soon. I'll let you know for sure. Meanwhile, keep your head up and do you."

"Okay, my sista. Stay pretty and we'll talk soon."

"You too."

After we ended the call, I sat on the sofa, in deep thought. I needed to take that trip to New York just to see if Sasha and her friends would really be able to help me like she claimed they would. It would be foolish of me not to go and see what was up—too foolish—even though Keith wouldn't approve.

I went into the kitchen to get some water. While guzzling it down, I glanced at the clock on the wall, which showed that it was almost one o'clock in the morning. I hadn't realized that I'd been talking to Sasha for that long, and I was sure that by now Keith was in a deep sleep. I climbed the stairs in my sweatpants and tank top, which was cut above my midriff. Keith and I had gone and worked out earlier, and I still hadn't taken a shower. My muscles were a little sore, so instead of jumping into the bed with him, I tiptoed by the bed and made my way to the bathroom.

Before entering the bathroom, I stood near the doorway and looked at him in bed as he snored. A thin white sheet covered his bottom half, and I could see a sizable hump where the good stuff was. His colorful tattoos showed on his arms and chest, and I had a serious desire to kiss those thick lips. I hurriedly showered, and dripping wet and without any clothes on, I quietly climbed on top of him. As I massaged his chest, his eyes began to open. A slight smile appeared on his face as his eyes scanned my body, and his hands began to roam my curves. He traced my hourglass figure, then sucked in a deep breath.

"Sexy, sexy, sexy," he said while now massaging my breasts.

I could feel his dick rising to the occasion, and I was eager to remove the sheet that stood in our way. I pulled it away from him, then comfortably straddled his lap again. He flexed his neck from side to side and closed his eyes as he started to tickle my pearl. Within seconds, my juices started to flow, causing me to put a slow grind in motion.

"Your pussy is so sweet, juicy looking, and perfect for me. And did you know that I love to watch your fluids drip and ooze right into the crack of your ass? That's why I can't keep my mouth off of it."

I laughed, then lean forward to finally kiss his thick lips. "Yeah, well, then maybe you should take action and do something about those juices. Better off in your mouth than on the sheets."

"I concur. So I suggest that you lie on your stomach and let me enter as I please."

"Of course."

I removed myself from his lap, then lay on my stomach. Keith lay beside me, with one of his legs crossed over mine. His cold fingertips ran up and down my spine and through the crack of my ass, giving my whole body a tickle.

"That feels sooo good," I said, with my head on the pillow and my eyes closed. "There is something about your touch that sets me on fire."

Keith was a gentle lovemaker. On very few occasions was he rough with me, and that was normally when he was upset with me or mad about something else. His soft lips touched my shoulders, then my back. From my back, they traveled to my ass. That was when he moved from beside me and kneeled between my legs. He then buried his face in my ass and sucked my juices that flowed near my anal hole. I hiked my butt up high just so he could have as much access as he needed. From one hole to the other, he set my entire body on fire. I shivered all over and cried out his name when he turned on his back and carefully placed my pussy lips over his mouth. His tongue traveled deeper. He brought it out to toy with my belly ring, and then he locked my pussy in place and tore it up. I was out of breath as I ground on top of him. My legs quickly got weak, and my curled toes were squeezed tight.

"I lovvve you," I cried out. "Damn, I love you, and I don't ever want you to stop loving meee."

He couldn't respond, as he had a mouthful, but it wasn't long before he fired back at me. By then his dick was as far in me as it could go. I was on my back, with my legs poured over his broad shoulders.

"I love you too," he said while looking down at me with so much passion in his eyes. "And I will never stop loving you."

I was so emotional. Tears seeped from the corners of my eyes as we rocked our sexy bodies together. Keith and I were perfect for each other. I couldn't ask for more, and I made a silent vow in that moment never to converse with Sasha again.

The bright sun rays came through the window, letting me know that morning had arrived. With a slight headache, I turned in bed, only to see that Keith was gone. On the night-stand was a beautiful red rose, along with a note. I reached out to see what it said. It read: *Had some errands to run this morning. Didn't want to interrupt your beauty sleep. See you around noon. Love you.*

I smiled, then pulled the sheets back to get out of bed. My whole body was sore from the workout we'd gotten in last night. I needed a long, hot shower, so I staggered into the bathroom to handle my business. I must've stayed in there for about thirty minutes, and when I turned off the cold water, I heard my cell phone ringing. I wrapped my body with a towel, then walked over to the nightstand to answer my phone. It had stopped ringing, but I could see that I had seven missed calls. They all were from Kayla's phone. I hurried to call her back, praying that everything was okay. When Jacoby answered, I held my breath.

"Can you come over here, please?" he said, with frustration in his voice. "My mother is passed out on the kitchen floor. I've been trying to get her up, but she keeps going in and out. I've never seen her like this, and I'm starting to get worried."

"Does she need an ambulance? I'm on my way, but maybe you need to call an ambulance."

"She's drunk as shit," he said. "I don't think she needs an ambulance. She needs to talk to someone who can help her. I tried talking to her, but she won't listen to me."

"Okay. I'm on my way. Thanks for calling me."

I rushed to put on some clothes, then made my way to Kayla's place. On the way there, I called Evelyn to see if she could meet me.

"What's going on with her?" she asked.

"I don't know. But she's putting a lot of stress on Jacoby. I can sense it in his voice. I think it's time for us to step in."

"I was on my way to the nail shop, but I'll meet you there within the hour."

"Thanks. See you soon."

Right after I ended my call with her, my phone rang again. I thought it was Jacoby calling me back, but instead, it was Sasha. I didn't bother to answer. Eventually, I would tell her that I wasn't interested in her help, and that I wouldn't be coming to New York. I just didn't need anything or anyone to interfere with my relationship with Keith. Even though I could surely use some additional money, a visit to New York just didn't make sense right now.

Financially, I had to do something, though. I hadn't been to the studio to get any work done in about three months. Keith was holding down most of the bills, and we both understood that if we didn't sell our artwork, we basically didn't have money. It had been a long time since I'd had any interior-decorating gigs too. I thought about putting out an ad to spread the word about my services.

When I got to Kayla's condo, I saw Evelyn's car parked in the lot. She must've rushed to get here. When I got inside, I saw that she and Jacoby had put Kayla on the sofa. They were trying to get her to snap out of it by shaking her. Her arms flopped around, and she kept slurring a bunch of nonsense about the sky not being blue.

"It's actually purple, if you look hard enough, and no . . . no one can deny that it's a *beautiful* day in the neighborhood, isn't it?" she said, smiling at me.

Her eyes were bugged out, and if I didn't know any better, I would have thought that Kayla was on drugs. The flimsy dress she wore hung off her shoulders, and we could all tell that she had lost a lot of weight. She squinted, then threw her hand back at me.

"Trina, girl, is that you? I almost couldn't tell with that ugly ole frown on your face."

She laughed, but my frown deepened. I hated to see my best friend like this. It tore me to pieces, and I would do whatever I could to help her get back on track. But first, she needed to come clean and tell us what was really going on with her.

We all helped her off the sofa and escorted her to the bedroom. Evelyn headed toward the bathroom to run her some bathwater, but I told her that I didn't think a bath was a good idea.

"She's too weak. Maybe a shower would be better. She can sit on the seat and wash herself."

Jacoby went to get us some towels, as well as some clean clothes that she could change into. I hated for him to see his mother like this, so when he returned to the bedroom, I suggested that he leave the house.

"We can handle her from here," I said. "Go hang out with your friends or something. I'll call to let you know if we need anything else."

"Are you sure?" he said, looking at his watch. "I'm supposed to be at band camp right now. But I didn't want to leave her like this."

"She'll be fine. All she needs is a shower and some rest. Maybe a little counseling too."

"I agree. I'm leaving, but don't forget to call me if you guys need anything."

Jacoby left. Evelyn and I lifted Kayla from the bed—she had fallen asleep that fast. We carried her into the bathroom, and after sitting her on the seat in the shower, with her clothes on, Evelyn turned on the cold water. The water sprayed all over Kayla, causing her to snap out of it and cover her face with her hands.

"Wha . . . what are y'all doing? Turn that cold water off!" she shouted, then stuck out her hand to touch the faucet. She couldn't reach it. I turned the water to warm so she would sit still.

"Relax," I said. "When you feel that you can stand, take your clothes off and wash yourself. Evelyn and I will be in your bedroom, waiting for you, when you come out."

"Waiting on me?" she spat. "Ugh! That's nasty. I don't do women, and you already know that I'm only interested in men. There is no reason for y'all to be waiting for me in the bedroom."

I ignored her comment. After all, she didn't know what she was saying. We left the bathroom, but from a short distance, we could see Kayla struggling to take off her clothes. She kept cussing and fussing about something. And when she finally got her clothes off, she fell back on the seat and started to cry. Seeing her cry brought tears to my eyes. I looked at Evelyn, whose eyes were filled with tears too, but she hurried to blink them away.

"Do we allow her to get it all out or go in there with her?" Evelyn said. "I feel horrible for her. She really needs to get some help."

I agreed, then went into the bathroom with Kayla. Evelyn followed me. I kneeled beside the shower door, while Evelyn stood close behind me.

"What is it?" I asked Kayla. "Why are you doing this to yourself? If you're going through something, please tell us and stop trying to act as if everything is okay. We're your friends. We're only here to help."

Still seated, Kayla wiped her flowing tears, and then she wiped snot from her nose. She squeezed her eyes together, then lightly banged the back of her head against the glass.

"Please leave," she said. "I don't want nobody to see me like this. I want to be alone."

"We're not going to leave you like this," Evelyn said. "Take your shower, and when you're done, we're going to be right here waiting for you."

"Right," I added. "Say what you want and get mad if you wish. We're not going anywhere."

Kayla didn't even look our way. She just sat there, releasing her emotions. We went back into her bedroom, and as I kept my eyes on her, I could see her starting to wash up. Within an hour, she came out of the bathroom with a pink robe covering her. The first thing she did was walk over to a small cabinet that had liquor inside of it.

"Where's Jacoby?" she said in a soft tone. She lifted an almost empty bottle of Hennessy, then twirled it around.

"Please put that down." I stood to go remove the bottle from her hand. She snatched it away as I reached for it, and held on tight to it.

"Don't come into my home, trying to tell me what to do. If I want to have a little drink, I will do it."

"She's not trying to tell you what to do," Evelyn said from her perch on the bed. "She's just trying to prevent you from making a big mistake."

Kayla snapped her head to the side and gave Evelyn a look that could kill. She narrowed her eyes, then gritted her teeth. "Don't you dare talk to me about mistakes, especially when you've made plenty of them, missy."

Evelyn hopped up from the bed, then snatched up her purse. "I figured all of this had something to do with your feelings about me. And there is no need for you to pretend that you've forgiven me, when you haven't. If being around me is causing you this much pain, then I'll leave and never come back here again. I know what I did was wrong, but damn. How many times am I going to have to apologize? How many times will I be attacked for doing what I did with Cedric?" Evelyn's voice started to crack. "I'm tired of this crap, and forgive me for thinking that we had left what had happened in the past." Now Evelyn was crying.

I wasn't as emotional as the two of them were, and like always, I was caught in the middle. "Calm down, Evelyn. We came here to see about Kayla and find out what, exactly, is troubling her. I'm sure you want to know too, so let's not make this all about you."

"All about *me*?" Evelyn said, pointing to her chest. "It's never been about *me*, Trina. Ever since the day I was born, it hasn't been about me. As I sit here watching Kayla, all I can think about is my drunk-ass mother. How she ignored me and gave all her attention to my father. How all I was to him was a punching bag and a sex toy. I'm not trying to make anything all about me, and I'm not going to stand here and take the blame for everybody's damn problems. My mother blamed me for hers, you blamed me for yours, and now Kayla is standing there, once again blaming me for hers. This is just . . . just too much."

Evelyn charged toward the door, but Kayla reached out to stop her. She grabbed her arm real tight but spoke with a calm voice. "I'm not blaming you as much as I blame myself. You will never understand what it feels like to lose everything that you had and have to start all over. While I'm glad that my divorce from Cedric is final, this shit still hurts. We spent many years together, and it's hard on me to wake up every morning alone. It feels funny doing everything by myself, and I hate that Jacoby doesn't have a father figure around."

Kayla went on. "Some days are good, but other days are bad. And like Trina said, this has very little to do with you. Yes, I'm still a little bitter about what you did, but I also know that Cedric used you. He saw a broken woman with an unfortunate past, and he took advantage of your vulnerabilities. It had nothing to do with his love for you, and I know that now."

"Then why do I feel as if you still hate me?" Evelyn said tearfully. "I know you, Kayla, and things are not the same as they used to be. The way you look at me says it all. Given how you speak to me, I can tell you're still angry. I don't want to be here if you don't want me here. But the truth is, I love you and Trina. I just don't know how to show the two of you how sorry I am for everything that I did."

"The first thing you can do is stop apologizing," I said. "We hear you loud and clear. It's just that we got our own problems too. And when we tend to think about all our problems, we may focus too much on where those problems originated from. Kayla can't think about her failed marriage without putting you into the equation. You played a big part in that, even though Cedric had been messing around with numerous other women, as well. What Kayla has to do is come to grips with it being over. She needs to celebrate her departure from him and realize that it really is a good thing. That may take some time, but during the process, it will take time for her to have that trusting and loving friendship with you again."

"I couldn't have said it better," Kayla said with a nod. "Just give me more time. I'm almost there, and the truth is, I'm on a downward spiral because of something that is bothering me about Jacoby and Cedric. If I tell the two of you about it, y'all probably won't believe me. I'm so worried about my son, and

I don't know what Cedric will do if he ever finds out the real deal behind him being shot."

Kayla sat down on the bed, in tears, and then told us about Jacoby's plot to have Cedric killed. He was the one who had gone to Paula Daniels and had asked her to do the dirty work. She was paid a substantial amount of money, but when Jacoby went back to her to call off the deal, Paula moved forward. She wanted Cedric dead, and there was no changing her mind. Kayla had no idea why Paula hadn't said anything about it to anyone yet, but she knew that Paula had been trying to get Cedric to come see her in jail. Kayla truly felt that if he found out the truth, Cedric would contact the police and have Jacoby arrested. And to her, that could happen any day.

"I'm just so worried," Kayla said, barely able to catch her breath as she cried. "I want to tell Cedric, but I can't go behind my baby's back and do that. What if he goes to jail? He would never make it in there, and I do not want to lose my only child."

Evelyn and I sat down on the bed and embraced Kayla.

"You're not going to lose him," Evelyn said. "We'll think of something, and we need to do it fast, especially if Paula is trying to reach out to Cedric."

"I agree," Kayla said. "It's just a matter of time before Cedric changes his mind about going to see her. I know that she's been writing him, but he never opens her letters to read them. What if he decides to open them? What if she writes to him and tells him exactly how things went down?"

"I guess I must have too much faith in Cedric," I said. "I don't believe that he would contact the police and have Jacoby arrested. After all, he does consider Jacoby his son. He loves him, and would never do anything like that to destroy him."

Kayla and Evelyn snapped their heads to the side and looked at me as if I were crazy.

"You don't know Cedric," they said in unison.

"He would put his mama behind bars if he thought she'd betrayed him," Kayla said. "I'm well aware of the man I was married to, and ever since he got shot, Cedric has been a changed man. I can see it in his eyes. In my heart, I truly believe that he's up to something."

We all sat silent for a while. I then tried to convince them that Cedric wouldn't harm Jacoby, but then I got to the point where I was trying to convince myself. This was one big mess. Now I understood why Kayla had been doing so much drinking. We discussed her new habit, and she said that it was under control. I didn't believe her, and Evelyn and I promised to check on her every single day.

6

Kayla

I felt a little better. Trina and Evelyn left a few hours later, and right after they left, I called Jacoby to find out where he was. The two of us needed to talk, and the first thing I needed to do was apologize to him for the way I'd been acting. I knew that seeing me drunk all the time was affecting him. I just couldn't stop causing my son harm, and that made me feel horrible. I told him that as I spoke to him over the phone, and I asked him to come home soon.

"I don't like to see you that way, but stop worrying so much about me," he said. "And if you don't mind, I won't be home until later. Some of the fellas and me are going to hang out at the mall. After that, Adrianne's mom wants me to help her paint their kitchen. I told her that I would."

"Okay. Have a good time, and please know that I can't help worrying about you. You definitely know why. Have you spoken to Cedric again?"

"I have. I told him I'll try to catch up with him next weekend. Maybe I do need to start doing some things with him again. That way he'll get off my back."

"That may be a good idea. It makes him suspicious when you distance yourself. He continues to ask me what is wrong with you, and it makes me feel awkward when I have to keep telling him that I don't know."

"Well, whatever you do, don't tell him anything. I'm thinking that maybe I should say something to him myself. If he hears it from me, maybe he'll understand."

"No. He would never understand, and I would never want you in a situation where you're alone with him, talking about what you did. I don't trust Cedric. He's a vicious man when he wants to be, and you already know that."

Jacoby said that he wouldn't say anything to Cedric, but he also could have said that just to get off the phone and get back to his friends. His social life was much better than mine was. I couldn't believe how much I had been cooped up inside since my divorce. I had had so much fun with Evelyn and Trina the other night. I needed to get out more, so I decided to put on some clothes and go have a few drinks. Many of the bars downtown were open because of the baseball game. It was the perfect time to meet people and watch the game somewhere near Ballpark Village. I'd thought about asking Trina if she wanted to go, but she had already taken enough time away from her day to see about me.

So within the hour, I was dressed in my Cardinals' T-shirt and skinny jeans. My hair had a shine to it, and with a little makeup on, I felt good. It was almost time for me to have my long lashes redone, but tonight they worked for me. I climbed in my car and headed in the direction of Ballpark Village. I spotted a bar and grill less than two blocks from the stadium and Ballpark Village. I parked and went in.

On the inside, the place was packed. I saw a few empty chairs at the end of the bar, so I made my way to it and sat right in front of four African American women who looked to be having a good time. They spoke to me as I took a seat and waited for the bartender. I spoke back, but my attention was focused on the bartender, who was spending way too much time waiting on someone else. I was eager to get a drink.

Almost ten minutes later, he came over to my side of the bar. He laid a napkin in front of me, then asked what I wanted to drink.

"Vodka and cranberry juice, no ice. A double shot, if you don't mind."

As the bartender made my drink, my eyes scanned the crowded place. There was a diverse group of people there, but the majority were white. I spotted a few brothas sitting in the far corner, by the restroom, and another group sat by a jukebox. Most people, however, were tuned in to the game, and plenty of drinks, wings, and burgers were being served.

"Here you are," the bartender said. "Your drink has already been taken care of by the gentleman over there."

The waiter pointed to a white man who was standing at the other end of the bar. He lifted his glass, then nodded with a smile. I didn't hesitate to smile back. After all, he was very handsome. A little young for my taste, but he had the looks of Adam Levine written all over him. His jet-black hair was spiked on top, and his beautiful light brown eyes hooked me right away. I blushed as he continued to look at me, and within a matter of minutes, there he was, standing right before me.

"Tell me," he said, "what modeling agency do you work for?"

"Oh, I wish I could tell you. There was a time when I wanted to be a model, but then life happened, and those dreams went right out the window."

"I'm sorry to hear that. But you are stunning. I hope you don't mind me buying you a drink. It's the least I can do for such a beautiful woman."

Yes, he was putting it on pretty darn thick, but I didn't care. I loved every bit of it. It was so refreshing to sit next to a man who filled my head with compliments and who had on some smell-good cologne. The black V-neck T-shirt he rocked melted on his muscles, and I could see how cut his abs were through his shirt. He was rather thin, though, but his jeans seemed to fit him in all the right places.

"I don't mind you buying me a drink, but the next one is on me. Thank you, and I do appreciate your compliments."

"Then I'll keep them coming. But before I do, my name is Justin. Justin McIntosh."

"I'm Kayla. I don't give out my last name unless I really know a person. That has always been one of my rules."

He pulled back the chair next to me, then took a seat. "I get that. Truly I do, but I'm hoping that when all is said and done, you'll get to know me much better. And if you have any more rules, I certainly want to know all about them."

We both laughed, and for the next hour or so, we indulged in an interesting conversation that revealed much more about him. He was only twenty-nine years old, he lived in an apartment complex that was less than fifteen minutes away from where I lived, and he had a degree in computer science. He had a four-year-old daughter, and he'd never been married.

I gave him the scoop on me, and I told him that I had recently divorced.

"You don't have to go into the details about why that happened, but he had to be a fool to lose a woman as sexy as you."

"Well, being sexy doesn't keep a man at home and faithful these days. Not that it ever did."

"No, it doesn't. But there seems to be something real special about you. I haven't put my finger on it yet, but when I do, I'll tell you what I'm referring to."

No doubt, he was saying all the right things to me, stuff that I needed to hear, but trust me when I say I was no fool. He wanted something from me. I also wanted something from him. And after we had shared several more drinks and more laughter, I was ready to put it all on the line.

"Justin, why don't we get out of this noisy place and finish this conversation in a more private setting? Do you have a problem with that?"

He lifted his glass, then tossed the remainder of the alcohol down his throat. "I don't have a problem with that, and I thought you'd never ask. My question to you is, my place or yours?"

"Neither. Let's go somewhere and get a room."

Justin was all for it. We broke out of the restaurant like two bats coming from hell. Several hotels were close by the stadium, and when we entered the lobby of one of them, Justin went right to the counter and paid for a room. Things got a little heated in the elevator when he swung in front of me and planted a soft kiss on my lips. My breasts rose against his chest, and after staring into his eyes, I opened my mouth wide and sucked his thin lips with mine. The juicy kiss left me as horny as ever, and when the elevator opened, I followed his sexy self to the room.

He used the key card to open the door, and the moment we entered the room, there was a rush to remove our clothes. We didn't get far before Justin pinned me against the door while he kissed my face and neck. He ground hard against me, and as I attempted to unzip his jeans, he pulled at my shirt, ripping it open. My breasts popped out, giving him a clear invitation to suck them.

"Mmm," he moaned while licking my nipples. By now I had his jeans lowered, and my hands were pressed into his tight and muscular ass. I couldn't believe what I was about to do with this young man, and I doubted that Trina or Evelyn would believe me. I wasn't exactly drunk, either—tipsy for sure, but definitely not drunk. He was, though. But he was absolutely in control.

He pulled his mouth away from my breasts, then took a few steps back to look at me as I stood there with my back still against the door. Not only did my shirt hang off my shoulders, revealing both breasts, but now my jeans were unbuttoned, showing my purple lace panties.

"I know your pussy is going to be good," he said. "How in the hell did I get so lucky?"

When he kicked off his jeans and pulled his shirt over his head, I wondered the same thing. His package was mouthwatering. I couldn't believe the thickness of that thing, and the width of it made me a little nervous. I watched as he eased on a condom, and then he reached forward to secure my waist. He pulled me on the bed with him, and the first thing I did was give him a ride. I could feel my coochie being stretched far apart as I slowly guided myself up and down on him.

"And . . . and you have the nerve to rave about me," I said. "This dick is so worthy of my time."

"Then take as much time as you need. It's yours."

I did as I was told and used my time wisely. Justin and I screwed around for hours. He twisted my body in every position he could think of, and my favorite had to be when he tackled the goodies from behind. One of his feet was on the floor; the other on the bed. I was bent over and could feel every inch of him working me over.

"I could do this with you every day for the rest of my life," he strained to say. "Your pussy is so warm and tight, just how I like it."

I liked the way he felt too, but this was not something that was going to happen every day. It was a one-night stand for me, and I truly didn't believe that he would have a problem with that. Meanwhile, I wasn't about to run from this feeling. Apparently, neither was he. We were both caught up in the moment.

With his dick still resting inside of me, he lifted me from the bed. My entire backside was against him, and my legs were straddled wide. He used his strength to hold me up. His fingers brushed against my clit, and he took several soft bites on the side of my neck. I was seconds away from coming again, and this time, he released his energy with me.

"Fuck!" he shouted while thrusting faster inside of me. "Where in the hell did you come from?"

I should have asked him the same thing too, but I was too busy biting down on my lip to calm the feeling. I felt my juices flow all over him. His dick thumped inside of me, and just so we wouldn't hit the floor, we both crashed on the bed. I could feel Justin's heart beating fast against my back. His rock-solid body was covered in sweat, which dripped on me as I lay underneath him. I had been sweating too, and when he suggested a shower, we found ourselves doing the nasty in there too. He had me up in the air, with my back pinned against the wall. My legs straddled his waist, and for whatever reason, I just couldn't get enough.

"Damn you, Justin," I whispered. "I'm not supposed to be doing this with you. I don't do this kind of stuff, but it sure in the hell makes me regret that I didn't step out of the box sooner."

"I believe you about not doing this with anybody. I'm just glad you decided to do this with me."

Enough said, enough done. We wrapped up our sex session almost an hour later. Justin was beat, and he fell asleep. I quietly crawled out of bed, looked for my clothes. After giving him a sweet little kiss on his cheek, I jetted.

I left the hotel on a serious high. I couldn't wait to tell Trina and Evelyn about my little adventurous night with Justin, and I wanted to let them know that there was still some hope for me. Trina didn't answer her phone, and when I drove by her house, it was pitch black inside. I didn't want to wake her and Keith, so I made my way to Evelyn's place. To my surprise, when I swerved into a parking spot, I saw a car that I knew all too well. It was Cedric's car. Why in the hell would he be parked outside of her complex if he wasn't inside with Evelyn?

My heart dropped to my stomach. I started to feel ill. I knew that trusting that hoochie again had been the wrong thing to do. And even though I felt so much hurt inside, I refused to go to the door and confront them. I just wasn't going there again, and at this point, I thought, *To hell with them both*. They could have each other, and they deserved to be together.

The second I got home, I did the norm and went straight to the liquor cabinet. Almost a whole bottle of vodka was there, and you'd better believe that I tore into it. I didn't want Jacoby to see me, so I made my way down the hallway and into my bedroom. I plopped on the bed, turned the bottle up to my lips, and thoroughly enjoyed my new fix.

7

Evelyn

Cedric and I were to the point where all we did was argue. I wholeheartedly regretted having had sex with him again, and after being at Kayla's house and seeing how torn she was, I wasn't about to go through with telling Cedric anything. Yes, the information about Jacoby was damaging. Cedric needed to know, but he damn sure wasn't going to get any info from me. I was done with him. I continued to tell him that Kayla hadn't said a thing to me about Jacoby or him.

"Stop lying, Evelyn," he said while sitting comfortably in my living room. He was casually dressed in tan slacks and a peach shirt. His loafers had a shine, and so did his chocolate skin. It was late, so I was dressed in a pink, see-through pajama top that cut right at my thighs.

"I'm not lying to you, Cedric. She told me that she didn't trust me. Said that she was still bitter about what happened. I can't get the information you need, so you're going to have to think of another way to get it."

"You think so, huh? Now that you have a little change in your pocket, you feel as if you don't need me. You feel as if you don't have to come through for me, like I came through for you, right?"

"You're making me feel as if I made a deal with the devil. I can't tell you something that I don't know. If you want me to lie to you, I will. There is no way for me to force Kayla to have a conversation that she doesn't want to have. My suggestion to you is this. Go talk to her. Ask her about the letter you got from Paula that mentioned Jacoby. Maybe she'll tell you something. Anything that will help you make sense of all of this. I'm just getting to the point where I can't help you. I've done all that I can do, and when all is said and done, you did get a nice chunk of the money from Mr. and Mrs. Washington too."

"Fuck money!" he shouted. "I don't need no goddamned money! What I need is for you to step up and do what the fuck you told me you was gon' do! You're running out of time, and I've given you plenty of it. There will be consequences if you don't follow through, bitch, and I'm just being honest."

Like I'd told Kayla and Trina earlier, I was sick and tired of this. Tired of Cedric and his shit. And the name-calling was totally uncalled for. I stood, then walked to the door. With my hand on the knob, I turned to him.

"Cedric, please leave. I'm not doing this with you tonight. I'm tired as hell. I'll keep talking to Kayla, but I don't know what good it's going to do. And if she says something to me that may interest you, I'll be in touch."

While wringing his hands together, he slowly got off the sofa and stretched. He strutted my way with narrowed eyes, then stood close to me at the door.

"Since you can't seem to deliver on one thing, you will deliver on another. I've had a long day at work, and I need my dick sucked tonight. Bow down now, and watch your teeth."

I moved my head from side to side. "I'm not in the mood tonight. Go home to Joy and ask her to suck your dick. I'm sure she's wondering where you are, and your late nights in the streets probably concern her."

Catching me off guard, Cedric reached back, then brought his hand forward to slap the shit out of me. He slapped me so hard that my hair shifted to one side. I was also moved a few inches away from the door.

"Don't worry about what my woman can and will do for me at home. When I ask you to do something within reason for me, you'd better do it! Now, I've been real patient with yo' ass, Evelyn. Real patient. Stop with the games and give me a little something in return."

There was a time when I thought I was in love with Cedric. I had wanted to spend my life with him, have his children, and spend his money. Now I hated him. I hated everything about him, and his dick didn't move me one bit. I lifted my finger, pointing it near his face. A mean mug was on my face, and I spoke through clenched teeth.

"Don't you ever put your hands on me like that again! You got away with that shit once before, and now you think I'm down with it. I'm not, and trust me when I say if you do that shit again, I will cut your balls off, stuff them in your mouth, and watch you choke on them."

He smirked at my comment, and then gave a loud laugh. "I believe you, 'cause you are one bad bitch. But get on your knees and send me out this door with some kind of smile on my face. That's the least you can do after failing to give me the information I need. Maybe I do need to seek other alternatives. Tonight, though, I want some head, and I need some pussy. Joy is being kind of stingy with the goods. She suspects that I've been fucking someone else, but none of that matters. Her ass is on the way out the door real soon."

It wasn't as if he was doing me any favors by kicking her out. Cedric was a mess, but like always, in order to keep the peace, he got what he wanted from me. I didn't drop to my knees until we were in the bedroom, and as I held his package in my hand, I started to get him back for slapping me earlier. But now wasn't the time or the place. I locked my mouth on his shaft and sucked him until my jaws got tired. I had a headache from bobbing for so long, and I was thankful when I looked up and saw that he had fallen asleep. This was another opportunity for me to get back at him. It was such a shame that he underestimated me. He wasn't the only one who had done so, and I lay there thinking that it was time for me to pay Charles another visit.

Two days later I found out about a grand opening event that Charles was expected to attend later that day. A new technology company was opening in St. Louis, and the company Charles worked for was one of the big donors. This time around, I had to pretend that I wasn't there to see him.

Basically, I was there for support, and plenty of people had been invited to come out and attend the all-white dress party to celebrate new jobs for our youth. I wasn't sure if his wife would join him or not, but her presence wouldn't bother me one bit. I was on a mission, and whenever I wanted something, nine times out of ten I got it. Money used to be the exception, but all I could say was, "Look at me now."

I spent the whole day looking for the perfect dress. My hair had already been done, and it was still dark blonde. It was similar to Beyoncé's, as were my curves. When I found a white dress that was sheer in some areas and covered with pearls and silk fabric in other areas, and had a plunging neckline and a long slit up the front, I suspected that Charles would rethink his position. The shoes I found were like Cinderella's glass slippers. The crystal-like heels were almost five inches, and there were tiny diamond studs near the front. I was pleased with the whole outfit, and when I got home to try on everything, I felt ready for Hollywood Boulevard.

I tucked my purse underneath my arm, grabbed my keys, then headed to the event in my new silver Mercedes. I arrived at the Renaissance Hotel almost an hour late. Traffic was a mess, and because I didn't want to be delayed any longer, I gave my keys to the valet and let the nice gentleman park my car. I headed to the ballroom where the event was being held, and right outside the door I saw groups of people dressed in white. I figured it would be difficult to find Charles, and I became totally convinced of this when I entered the ballroom and discovered that it was filled to capacity.

Several dressy round tables had been set up, a long buffet stretched from one corner of the room to the other, a band was playing music in another corner, and many of the people there were tuned in to a PowerPoint presentation that provided more information about the new technology company. I pretended to be tuned in too, especially since so many eyes were on me. Yes, there was a bunch of women standing around, hating, and none of them looked as good as I did in my dress. Several men nudged each other, and I saw one woman catch an attitude because her man kept looking in

my direction. I guessed I was grateful to my mother for something. I definitely had her good looks. There was no question
that she was, indeed, a beautiful woman. Too bad she didn't
know how to take advantage of what God had blessed her
with, and it was such a shame that she had allowed my father
to use her until he couldn't do it anymore.

A little while later, along with everyone else, I waited in
a long line to get some food. I started to converse with two
ladies who stood in line with me, and then I joined them,
along with several others, at one of the round tables.

For the next several minutes, I got my grub on and chat-
ted with the women and the men at our table. The room filled
up even more, and when I saw some of the VIPs take a seat up
front, that was when I spotted Charles. My mouth dropped
open. When I said he was sexy as hell, I truly meant it. The
white tailored tuxedo he wore set his black ass off. Keith and
Bryson didn't have shit on ole dad, and judging by the way he
strutted around and flashed his Crest smile, he knew he was
all that. I searched the room, looking for Netta. There wasn't
a chance in hell that she had let him attend an event like this
alone. If she was as supportive as he said she was, I was sure
she was somewhere lurking in the crowd. As I sat there in a
trance from looking at him, I felt a hot breath next to my ear.

"Do you mind if I ask you to step outside in the hallway so
we can talk?"

I snapped my head to the side, only to see a brotha with
long dreads and too much facial hair standing next to me. He
was cute, but not cute enough to steal my attention away from
Charles.

"Maybe later," I said. "I'd really like to hear what's going on,
and I think some of the VIPs are about to speak."

"Sure," he said. "You're looking good, girl, and I for sure
want to catch up with you later."

Two proper-talking women went to the podium and spoke
first. Then Charles stepped to the podium and gave his little
spiel about donating. The first person his eyes connected with
was me. He squinted just to be sure that it was me. Then he
turned his head in the other direction.

A hot and bothered, nosy woman next to me had to open her big mouth. "Why does he keep looking at you like that? Do you know him?"

"Uh, no, I don't. But he sure is good to look at, isn't he?"

"Girl, you ain't said nothing but a word. That man if fine as hell! I would certainly enjoy some that."

I hit her with "Exactly," then got back to watching Charles.

It was a good thing that the band was still softly playing music and that the PowerPoint presentation was still keeping many people occupied. Charles was still speaking, but I ignored pretty much everything he said. I focused on those sexy lips, and every time he licked them, I felt a jab in my pussy. I looked at his big hands and visualized them touching my body. His dick print was on point, and when he stepped away from the podium for a few minutes, I got a clear glimpse of it. Most of the women in the audience looked like zombies and seemed to be in a trance, as I was. Their eyes were glued to him, and I was 120 percent positive that I wasn't the only woman in the room with dirty thoughts in her head.

"So we're very excited about this new venture," he said. "And I welcome all of you, each and every one of you, to get behind this company and watch our youth grow."

Applause erupted. Before walking away from the podium, Charles took one last glance at me. The music kicked up again, and numerous people rushed over to the buffet line to get more food. Charles made his way through the crowd, but he was stopped by so many people who wanted to talk, mostly men who sat in the VIP section. I saw several of them step into the wide hallway with him. That was when I got up and proceeded to make my move.

Displaying much confidence, I paraded down the hallway with my head held high. My hips swayed like Olivia Pope's from *Scandal*, and my heels clacked on the floor. From a distance, I could see several of the men who were standing with Charles look my way.

As I approached the VIP circle of men, they began to part like the Red Sea. Heads turned, eyes zoomed in, and many of them wet their lips. Charles turned around too, and as soon as I walked by him, as if it was in the plan, a thirsty man spoke up.

"Slow down, beautiful, and drop your name on me," he said.

"Forget it, man. She don't seem like the kind of woman who would be interested in you. Maybe I need to introduce myself instead," another man declared.

They laughed, and I stopped to flash a smile.

"Evelyn," I said while observing some of the wealthy black men in my presence. I could smell the money, but only one of them was of great interest to me. "My name is Evelyn, and I am really happy to be here. I love what you all are doing for our youth, and, Mr. Washington, the speech you gave was simply amazing."

He was the only one who wasn't smiling. I didn't want to entertain his little attitude right now, so I hurried to wrap this up.

"Gentlemen, please enjoy the evening. And thanks a million for the compliments."

I strutted away, knowing for a fact that every last one of their eyes was on my backside. I had no panties on, and I was sure someone, maybe even Charles, had noticed. I went into the ladies' room to check myself in the mirror. "Fucking fabulous" was written all over me. I washed my hands, dried them with a paper towel, and then left. As I made my exit, I ran right into Charles, who stood close to the door. His hands were in his pockets, and that same blank expression was on his face.

"Wha-what do you want from me, Evelyn? Is this how it's going to be? Are you going to keep showing up at places where you know I'll be, until I give you some attention?"

I kept it real with him. "You already know what I want, so no need to ask. And if you think I'm some kind of stalker, please rethink your thoughts. I'm here with a friend of mine tonight. He invited me to attend this special occasion with him. I had no idea you would be here, and quite frankly, I was shocked to see you. Now, if you don't mind, I need to go back inside the ballroom. I've been gone for a while, and I'm sure my friend is looking for me."

I attempted to walk away, but he snatched me by the arm. I looked at his hand tightly squeezing my arm, then shifted my eyes to his. He stared me down, then lifted his other arm to look at his gold watch.

"One hour," he said. "In one hour meet me out front. You'll recognize what kind of car I'm in, and if you're not there in an hour, I'm leaving."

I didn't bother to reply. When he let go of my arm, I turned around and proceeded to walk, with a slight smirk on my face. All I could think to myself was, *Got him.*

I pranced around the ballroom, talking to people whom I did not know. Some of the conversations were interesting, but many were stirred up to waste time. And before I knew it, the long hand hit twelve and my hour was up. I said a few good-byes, exchanged numbers with several people, and promised this one lady whom I had been talking to that I would make a donation to her organization. After that, I walked outside. Sitting behind the steering wheel of a muthafucking Maybach was Charles. Dark shades covered his eyes, and with the slightly tinted windows, I could barely see him. I walked his way, and he unlocked the passenger door so I could get inside the car.

"Hurry up and close the door," he said.

I shut the door, giving us all the privacy we needed. The soft leather seats were so comfortable that I felt as if my body was melting. I had never ridden in one of these cars before, and this was something special.

"Here's the deal," Charles said with arrogance. "I give you what you want, and I never want to see your face again. I thought that I'd already taken care of you, but obviously not. I don't want you to mention anything about Bryson, and please don't say anything about my wife. Got it?"

"I clearly do, but don't sit there and pretend that you're giving me everything that I want, when you know darn well that this is something that you want too."

"Do I need to repeat what I just said?"

"No. And like I said . . . nice car."

For the first time, Charles smiled. "Good girl," he said. Then he sped off.

I wasn't sure where we were headed, but it looked to me as if we were heading toward his office. He was speeding like crazy, and as we drove by many cars, people were trying to get a peek at who was inside his. Once we hit the highway,

Charles tore it up. That was until we saw flashing lights behind us. He pulled over, and I watched through the side mirror as the cop got out of the car.

"You are in major trouble," I said playfully. "And don't ask me to help you pay that ticket, because it's going to be very expensive."

"I assure you that I won't be getting any tickets today."

"Would you like to put some money on that? I don't care how much you're worth. Your skin is still black."

Charles lowered the window to address the officer. The first thing the officer did was peek into the car.

"License, insurance, and registration, please."

"For what?" Charles said.

"You were speeding. Fast."

"No I wasn't. What I was doing was trying to keep up with the flow of traffic."

"You were way ahead of traffic. Now again, I need to see your license, insurance, and registration."

Charles tapped a button that opened a small compartment between us. He pulled out his license, then gave it to the officer. "I don't have my insurance card on me, and my registration is in another vehicle. See what you can do to work with that."

The officer took his license and then bent down to look at me again. "Good evening, ma'am," he said. "What's your name, and can I get some identification from you too?"

I reached for my purse, but Charles reached over and touched my hands. "You don't need any identification from her. She's not driving this car. I am."

I didn't want no shit, but it seemed to me as if Charles knew something that I didn't.

The officer walked away with a slightly red face. I could tell he was pissed.

"See? You done really made him mad. He's going to write you several tickets. And why would you not carry your insurance and registration papers with you?"

"My insurance and registration papers are right in this car. And I would have given them to him had he not approached my car with an attitude," Charles replied, raising his window.

The officer came back in less than two or three minutes. Charles lowered the window again, and the officer handed him his license back.

"Have a good evening, sir. And slow it down a bit."

"Will do," was all Charles said, and then he looked both ways before taking off.

"Hold up," I said. "What in the hell just happened back there? You were supposed to get a ticket. But all you got was a 'Have a good evening, sir.'"

"Hey. Some of us got it, and some of us don't. They definitely know who does, and that's all I'm going to say about that."

It left me pretty speechless too. I did, however, talk to Charles about Keith and Trina. He didn't tell me that I couldn't say anything about them. And all I asked was if he liked Trina and if he thought she would one day be his daughter-in-law.

"That's for Keith to decide, not me. I don't have an opinion about her one way or the other."

"Do you think she's cute? She's a good friend of mine, but I promise not to tell her if you think she's cute enough for your son."

"If my son thinks she's cute, that's all that matters."

"Do you expect me to believe that you don't have any influence on your sons and their relationships? I don't believe that for one minute, Charles. To me, it seems like you're the kind of father who can say, 'Jump,' and they respond, 'How high?' Bryson is spoiled by his mother, not you. Am I right?"

"See, I asked you not to go there. I don't discuss my family with strangers, so let it go and focus on something else."

"I'm real focused. Focused on what I want and what I intend to get from this one night. The one thing that I would like for you to tell me is if you're hard already or if you got a sock in your pants that's making your *thingy* down there look massive."

Charles didn't want to laugh, but he did. Shook his head, too, and then pulled into the parking garage at his office building. He turned to me with his index finger pressed against his temple.

"How can you say something like that to a grown-ass man? And for the record, the only socks I have on me are on my feet. You're a mess, Evelyn, but there's something intriguing about you that I like. And even though I like it, I don't want no parts of it after today. Promise me that you won't continue to pursue me."

"I'm bad with promises, and I often break them. Besides, even if I did make you that promise, you wouldn't believe me."

"No, I wouldn't. But I will make you a promise that I intend to keep. If my wife or sons ever find out about this one-night adventure, I will, indeed, make you disappear."

I ran my fingers across my lips, zipping them. "Your secret is safe with me."

I followed Charles inside the building, but instead of going up in the elevator, we went down. Down into the basement, which made me a little nervous. For a minute, I thought he was tricking me. I also thought he was going to do something horrible to me, until we stopped in front of another door, which prompted him to provide a code. Charles quickly punched in a few numbers, and the door slid open. I didn't know where in the hell we were, and I couldn't believe this Negro had some kind of underground bunker that was set up like a real apartment. That made me even more nervous, and I hoped that he wouldn't break out with any *Fifty Shades* bullshit. I wasn't into whips or chains. Just didn't get down like that, though I meant no offense to people who did.

I watched as Charles entered another code, which secured the door behind us. Talk about a nigga being discreet . . . He definitely was and then some. I was sure that Netta had no idea about this place. And that was why I didn't buy that bull-shit about him loving his wife and never betraying her. Most men with money, like Charles, did what the hell they wanted to. There wasn't enough love in the world to stop them from delving into a piece of pussy if they desired it.

"Well, well, well," I said, looking around at the spacious area that was hooked up like some shit right out of a James Bond movie. There was a lounging area, a bar area, and a section that had a Jacuzzi and a TV. A small boardroom was behind a wide expanse of glass, and a beautiful aquarium surrounded the entire space. If I told anybody about this, they wouldn't believe me. Cameras were everywhere, and I also saw a room that monitored several different places. I had no idea what those places were, but as I began to look harder, Charles picked up a remote and shut that room down, turning it pitch black.

"Let me guess," I said. "CIA, right?"

"No. RTF," he replied, then took off his suit jacket and tossed it on a leather circular sofa.

"It will take forever for me to figure that out, and I think I may need some help."

"Yes, you do."

He stepped forward to remove my dress. After moving the top of it away from my shoulders and exposing my breasts, he asked me to turn around so he could unzip it. I did so, and when my dress fell to my ankles, I stood naked. He walked in a circle, observing every inch of my body as I stood there.

"Flawless," he said, stopping in his tracks. "Unquestionably flawless, and I am so RTF."

It took me a minute, but as he grabbed a nice chuck of my ass and shook it, I finally got it. "I'm ready to fuck too. Lead the way and allow me to serve you."

Charles took my hand and directed me down a short hallway that led to a bedroom. I stood in awe as I looked at the huge round bed that was fit for a king. I honestly did not know what in the hell this man did, but I had to admit that it felt good being in his presence. The whole room was shaped like a circle. The bed sat elevated in the center of the room, and a spacious tub was to my right. To the left was a curved TV, and another bar area was beside it. An open shower was visible too. Glass surrounded it, and it was large enough for at least twenty people to stand inside it. This was so breathtaking, and as I stood with a shocked look on my face, Charles crept up behind me. He massaged my breasts together, and I couldn't even explain what the feeling of his gentle hands was doing to me.

"What are you thinking?" he whispered in my ear. "About my sock?"

I laughed, but trust me when I say that it was no laughing matter when he dimmed the lights, removed his clothes, laid me on that bed, and introduced me to his sock. I had never in my life tampered with a dick so big. I had to back away from that thing, because I thought he was trying to slip something else inside me.

"Wait a minute," I said, scooting back. "What is that?"

Charles stood with pride. My eyes traveled to his package, and all I could say to myself was, *Lord, have mercy on me.* I had never witnessed anything like it. He planned to rupture my insides with that motherfucker. I quickly had second thoughts about this.

"Listen," I said while sitting up on the bed, "I don't know if I'm ready for this. You are not about to put all of that in me. I assure you that it won't fit, and if it won't fit, I must acquit."

"I'm not going to let you do that, because you went through so much trouble to get me here. And now that I'm here, you don't want it? The least you can do is try to work with it. As creative as you are, I'm sure you can come up with something to help you cope."

I had a feeling that this was the end of my sex life. A dick that size could damage me for life. Nonetheless, after he put on a condom, I took my chances. I allowed Charles to take it real slow, but after he journeyed eleven or twelve inches deep, I couldn't even move. My whole body stiffened. My pussy felt as if it was being stretched far, far apart. How in the hell was Netta able to handle all of this? She was brave, and I had to give her props. How could she have had two kids by this man, and why had she agreed to spend the rest of her life with him? This was too much! He kept planting soft kisses on my neck to calm me, but those kisses didn't do much good. I touched his chest to push him back.

"I—I can't do this. As much as I want to, I have to admit that I am *way* out of your league."

Frustration was written all over Charles's face. "Stop talking about what you can't do, and show me what you can do. I'm going to ease it out and let you take control of this. Whatever you do, don't waste my time. Please. And thank you."

Well, since he had put it like that, I put my big girl panties on and did my best to take control. I started by getting on top of Charles. My legs straddled him, and as I looked between my legs, I could see his long, hard pipe, which damn near surpassed the top of my breasts. My wet coochie lips coated one side of his shaft, and when I was ready to take in a few inches, I lifted myself up high. One inch went in, then two. Two turned into five; then five switched to ten. He was about twelve inches deep again when I started to feel the pain.

"Don't get greedy," he said, helping to guide me. "Take it easy, and after a few more inches, you'll be just fine."

Shit. Not in this lifetime. I worked with what I could for a while, and I doubted that I would be able to take him all in. My pussy was sore as fuck. Even though his strokes felt nice, it was very difficult to enjoy a man this size. I could hurt myself by chasing this dick, and I now knew why this room was in a bunker, where no one could hear. Any woman who was brave enough to come down here and fuck him had to scream and holler. There was no way to stay silent, and as I moved up and down on him, my mouth stayed open. I had to catch my breath after spewing words like "shit," "fuck," and "damn." Every time I made a safe landing, there I was, singing vowels and saying words that echoed loudly in the room.

"Ooh, mmm, aahhh, noooo. Please don't move, and give me a minute."

As Charles halted his thrusts inside me, I remained still. I released several deep breaths; then I tackled him again.

"Aahhh, yesss, yes, baby, yes! I think I'm ready for more!" I yelled.

Charles lifted his hand and covered my mouth. "Let's try something different," he said. "You may not like the idea of it, but it's going to help you get through this a lot easier." He removed his hand from my mouth.

"I don't know what else I can do, but I'm listening," I said.

"Allow me to secure your arms and legs. That way you can't stop me. You won't be able to prevent me from doing all that I want to do to you, and all we have is a few more hours together. Why not take advantage of the time and enjoy ourselves a bit more?"

I was hesitant, but what the hell? You only lived once, and I was eager to get to a point where I could thoroughly enjoy this. I held my arms together in front of me.

"Secure me. And try like hell not to hurt me."

I slid off Charles and watched as he got off the bed and went into another room. He came back with four ropes, which he used to tie my wrists to the bed, and with my legs spread wide, he tied my ankles.

"You can get loose if you struggle hard enough, but please don't try too hard. I want you to withstand as much pain as you can, and then you will discover how much easier this will be."

This time, Charles lay on top of me and pecked my lips, giving me a soft kiss. I wanted to rub the back of his head, but I couldn't. I also wanted another kiss, so I lifted my head and stuck my tongue into his mouth. The kiss was all of that and then some. I didn't know why he held back on me, but it definitely relaxed me. So did the feel of his tongue as he licked down my neck, journeyed between my breasts, and landed in my belly button. He entertained that spot for only a few minutes, and then his tongue turned up the heat in my pussy. A very high arch formed in my back; then I pulled tightly on the ropes. The feeling was so intense that I attempted to free my legs so I could wrap them around him.

"Oh, my *God*," I said, squirming around. "Help me, *please*."

Charles backed his tongue out of me, making sure I was soaking wet. He turned the tip of his thick head against my hole, as if he were about to screw it in. The feel of it made me tremble all over, and without breaking down his insertions so that he went inch by inch, he rammed the whole thing inside me. My whole body jerked forward. My stomach was in so much pain. I let out a scream that was sure to bust his eardrums. Tears ran from the corners of my eyes. That was when he leaned in and planted a soft kiss on my cheek.

"Warning," he said. "I need to do that again."

He backed out and went full force again and again. I grunted loudly after each thrust and tugged at the ropes to attempt to free myself. No such luck. He repeated his actions, and each time he went in, it felt like I was being operated on without being given anesthesia. His dick touched something in my body that I didn't know was there. But eventually, it started to feel real good to me. My grunts got softer and softer, and my pussy juices rained on him like never before.

"I told you, you could handle this," he said while rubbing my trembling legs. "It's in there, baby, all the way in there, and there's no need to fuss anymore. Relax and let your legs fall apart so I can give you what you wished for."

Charles gave me just that—a good ole dick beating, along with multiple orgasms. His strokes started off smooth and slow, but as things started to loosen up more, he didn't hold back. My sweaty body squirmed all over the bed, and several times I fought hard to jump off it. The ropes helped to keep me in place. And after almost twenty minutes of being beat down by his penis, I finally felt some relief. I ground right along with him. Locked my coochie on his muscle and didn't want to let go. When he freed my hands, I got on my hands and knees to show him just how courageous I was. But no matter how hard I tried to please him, he wound up defeating me. Broke my pussy down to an all new low. Had me spewing made-up words that were no part of the English language. I couldn't be mad, because I had asked for this, all of it, and he'd given me that and then some.

At almost four in the morning, it was over. Done. Complete. And there was never supposed to be seconds. I could barely walk. Pussy felt loose, and my back hurt like hell. Charles walked behind me as we made our way back to his car.

"I know a good doctor you can go to, if you need one," he said in a playful manner.

I was exhausted and barely had enough strength to laugh at his joke. "No, thank you. Keep your doctor, and you can keep that dick too. I won't be needing anything else like that for at least another year or two from now."

"I doubt that, and all I will say about that is we'll see."

We got into his car, and almost forty-five minutes later, we were back at the hotel. He dropped me off so I could get my car and go on my merry little way. As I slowly exited his car, he reached for my arm.

"Damn. A man can't have one last kiss before you go? You shouldn't even be like that, especially after all that I gave you tonight."

I could barely lean in for a kiss. It was a quick one too, and so was my final good-bye. I waved at him, then shut the door. Walked slowly to my car, drove slowly home, and took a long, hot bath when I got there. I damn near fell asleep while closing my eyes and thinking about this night, which I would never forget. Too bad I couldn't share it with my BFF's. Trina, for sure, would kill me.

8

Trina

It was so easy to say one thing yet do another. I had been on the phone with Sasha again. She'd called me the other day, in tears. I couldn't ignore her calls. During our conversation, she had asked if I would come see her. Said that it wasn't solely because she wanted to see me, but that she also wanted to get me some money, which I so desperately needed. I wanted to tell Keith, but then again I didn't. I knew how he would react, and I had been doing my best to prevent any arguments with him. He still seemed on edge about some of the things that were going on with his family, and in order to clear his head, he was spending more time painting and going to the gym. He had also started hanging out with some friends of his, but since he always invited me to go, I didn't trip. He had come in at around three in the morning last night. And I had just gotten off the phone with Sasha. I had pretended to be asleep, so he hadn't bothered me.

The next morning, while Keith was still resting, I searched for airline tickets on the Internet. Sasha had asked me to come to New York soon, so I checked the prices to see which day was the best one to go. I found a good deal for this Thursday, for a flight departing St. Louis at eleven and arriving in New York at a little after three. There was a deal on hotels too, so I search for one that was close to where Sasha lived. I didn't think it would be appropriate for me to stay with her, especially since she already had a girlfriend. And if things didn't pan out like I intended them to, I could always go back to the hotel, pack, and bring my tail back home. Without further ado, I booked the flight and paid for three nights at the hotel.

I didn't have a lot of money in my account, so I pulled a few hundred dollars from Keith's account and put it into mine. I did that often, and I was sure that he wouldn't trip.

After booking my trip, I called Kayla to check on her. She had been calling me, but every time I called her back, she didn't answer her phone. I had started to go by her condo to check on her, and I would do so if she didn't answer this time around. Thankfully, she did.

"Girl, where have you been?" I said.

"Here and there. At the movies, at Jacoby's school, over at his girlfriend's house, and in a hotel room with a young white man who showed me what I've been missing out on."

"What? Stop playing. And something like that would happen only in your dreams."

"I am very serious. You know I wouldn't lie to you about anything like that."

"You sound serious, but what made you go there? I've never known you to just up and have sex with someone you barely know."

"Well, sometimes you get tired of the same ole, same ole. I wanted to explore something different, and I'm glad I did."

"I can't be mad at you for that, and I hope it was good to you."

"It was, and you won't hear any complaints from me."

"Anything serious brewing? Have you spoken to him again or not?"

"Nope. But I'm good with that. I don't need the hassles, and there are times when I prefer to be alone."

"I know you do, but on another note, how have you been doing with the drinking thing? Be honest, Kayla, and you know I can tell when you be lying to me."

"The truth is . . . I've been doing okay. Not drinking as much as I was, but I've still been drinking here and there. The key is to keep myself busy and stop worrying so much. I also realized that there are certain things that I can't change, and that refers to other people too. I stopped by your place the other night to tell you about the guy I met. It looked like you and Keith were asleep, because the whole house was dark. I left your place and went to Evelyn's. You're not going to believe whose car was parked outside."

I pondered this for a quick second and then stared at the bookshelf in front of me in disbelief. "Please don't tell me Cedric was over there."

"Yes, he was. It took everything in me not to go to the door, but then I asked myself what for. He's not my husband anymore, and he's free to screw around with whomever. If Evelyn is who he wants, so be it. I don't have much else to say to her, because I'm sick and tired of being played like a fool and lied to. I thought she was sincere this time, and more than anything, I thought she had learned a valuable lesson."

Hearing Kayla tell me this just broke my heart. I had thought the same thing too. I didn't think Evelyn was that in love with Cedric, but maybe she was. Maybe he was in love with her too, and neither of them knew how to come clean about their feelings. This was so messed up. I really didn't know what to say to Kayla. Never again would I ask her to forgive Evelyn.

"I'm glad you're not taking this too hard. And I feel bad for forcing you to move on from the past when she keeps slapping you in the face."

"That's all I'm saying. And you didn't force me to do anything. I thought that forgiving her was the right thing to do, but sometimes you just have to let go."

We both agreed on that. I asked Kayla if or when she planned on telling Cedric about the situation with Jacoby. With her spilling her guts to me and Evelyn, we knew it was just a matter of time before she ran back and told him everything.

"I've been thinking about that too," she said. "Jacoby's been bugging me about allowing him to explain the situation to Cedric, but I just don't know. It looks like that conversation may have to take place real soon, and to be honest, I've already been searching for an attorney to represent him."

"That's good. If I can do anything to help, let me know. Keith's parents know a lot of people, and I don't mind reaching out to them and asking for their help. I don't know how his mother is feeling about me these days, but I'll do whatever to help."

"What happened between you and Keith's mother? I thought she liked you."

I explained to Kayla what Evelyn had done while she was over there, trying to settle things between herself and Bryson. Kayla didn't have anything nice to say about it.

"Trina, you are too darn nice. How much damage are you going to let her do to you? That kind of mess didn't slip, and she intentionally said that to tell your business and put you on blast. She doesn't want his parents to like you. It was her way of making sure his mother views you in a different light."

"I never know what Evelyn's intentions are, but if his mother holds that against me, then she never liked me, anyway. I haven't spoken to her since then. Normally, she calls to check on me and Keith, but she's been reaching out to him on his cell phone, instead of calling the home phone."

"How do you know she calls on his cell phone, and why are you checking his messages? Only insecure women do that, and please don't tell me that you have a reason to be insecure."

"I don't, but I do look at his calls from time to time. A woman can never be too sure, and after all that has happened, you know how difficult it is for me to trust anyone. There are times when I don't even trust myself."

"I know exactly what you mean. But tell Keith I said hello, and if his mother doesn't call you, call her. Don't let Evelyn's nonsense come between y'all."

I told Kayla I would call Keith's mother, but a huge part of me was afraid to. Netta was good at reading people, and I didn't want her to question me about my experiences with women. I would wait to make that call. After Kayla and I hung up, I made a mental note to contact Evelyn about what Kayla had told me. The fact that she was screwing Cedric again was a big disappointment. It was yet another blow to our friendship.

Keith woke up around noon. I was upstairs, sketching a picture on a small canvas, which I intended to ship to Sasha before I left.

"I'm going outside to cut the grass," he said. "Maybe we can go to the movies or something later. I want to check out that new comedy movie, and if anybody needs a good laugh, it's me." He looked tired, and it also seemed that he had something weighing heavily on his mind.

"What's wrong? Do you want to talk about it? If so, you know I'm here."

"I know, but I don't want to discuss it right now. I get tired of talking about my family, and one of these days, I'm going to move away from here and be done with everything. You gon' move with me, aren't you?"

"Where you go, I go. I'm riding this out with you all the way to the end."

Keith walked farther into the room to give me a kiss. He then left the room and headed outside to cut the grass. I felt horrible inside. I knew that I was about to lie to him—I was going to tell him that Evelyn, Kayla, and I were going to take a trip somewhere together—and I decided to wait until later to do it. While he was outside, I called Kayla back to make sure she would cover for me, just in case.

"What? Why are you lying to that man like that? And where exactly are you going?"

"I'll tell you all about it another day. Right now I'm going outside to help my man cut the grass."

"Please do call me back. I want to know what is up with you."

I told Kayla that I would call her later, but just like when I spilled my guts to Evelyn, I feared being judged. Some people just didn't understand how difficult it was when you just hadn't discovered yet who you were or who exactly you wanted to be with. It was a scary feeling to know that loving someone just wasn't enough to fill the slightest void inside.

I put on my sweat suit and went outside to help Keith cut the grass. Afterward, we showered together, indulged in a quickie, and then went to dinner at Applebee's. During dinner I finally told him about the fabricated trip I was taking to Las Vegas with Kayla and Evelyn. He seemed okay with it, and I was shocked that he didn't even gripe about me going with Evelyn.

"You must have something really heavy on your mind," I said. "I can't believe that you didn't complain about me going somewhere with Evelyn."

"I don't have time for Evelyn right now. Besides, all I want is for you to have a good time. You need to get away, and I'm happy that you'll be spending some time with your friends. Maybe this is what y'all need."

"Maybe so, but what about you? Are you ready to tell me about what is bothering you? I don't know why you always try to keep things about your family a secret. You know you can talk to me about anything."

"I do, but some family matters have to stay in the family. When you become my wife, then I'll tell you."

I smiled. "Is that a proposal?"

Keith scooted close to me, then wrapped his arm around my waist. "No, it's not, but I assure you that it's coming." He pecked my lips, then rubbed my nose with his. I swore that I loved this man. I truly did, but it was difficult to express what I was going through.

"You say it's coming, but I have a little feeling that your mother is trying to stop you. Am I right, and are her comments about me starting to bug you? I noticed that she hasn't called me ever since Evelyn told her about me. And I also know that she's been in touch with you."

Keith released his arm from my waist. "I have to be honest with you about this, so yes, she has been making comments that I don't approve of. But my mother is set in her ways. I can't do anything about that. She has these issues with you, but what she needs to do is have a real talk with her son. Bryson continues to lie to her, and just the other day, I got a call from his daughter's mother, telling me some crap about what he did to her while they were in London. He's out of control. I don't know what it's going to take for my parents to stand up and put him in his place."

"Bryson is a grown man, Keith. You all speak about him like he's some kind of teenager. Your parents have no control over what he does, and if that's how he wants to live his life, so be it. His girlfriend shouldn't be calling you or anyone else. She has put up with his mess for a long time, and what she needs to do is end it. I don't get why so many women stay in abusive relationships like that. She knows that he goes both ways too, and I guess she's in denial, like he is."

"All of that could be true, but it still doesn't stop my mother from calling me and crying about it. She's upset about not seeing her only grandchild, and I'll sure be glad when we have a baby. I really want you to stop taking your pills. Are you ready to have a baby with me, or would you prefer to be my wife before we venture there?"

I almost choked on the water I was drinking. This was a conversation that I wasn't looking forward to having. Of course I wanted to have his baby, and one day I wanted to be his wife. Now . . . today I wasn't ready for that. I didn't know how to say it, but I replied in a way that I didn't think would offend him.

"I want to have your baby, but you know I have to get myself together financially. I don't want to depend on you for everything, and you need a wife who has a solid career and who can contribute to the marriage."

"Money is not an issue, and you already know that. I don't care if you contribute one dime, and there are other ways that you can contribute without dishing out money. It may be years before you feel as if your career is solid. The art industry is a tough business, and it took me almost eleven years before I started to make some decent money on my paintings."

Damn. Why did he have to go there with this? I was forced into a conversation that required me to be on the defensive.

"Money isn't an issue for you, but it is for me. And while I know you can and will provide for us, I still want to contribute more than good pussy. I have no desire to be barefoot and in the kitchen with a lot of babies. That's not me, and I think you already know that. At the moment, it's easy for you to make ten or fifteen thousand dollars on one painting. I'm not there yet, but I'm trying to get there too. Just be patient with me. In time you will have everything you want, and so will I."

Keith didn't reply. He picked up a buffalo wing, then bit into it. After tossing back another drink, he said he was ready to go home. The movies were squashed, and we spent the rest of our evening watching TV and not saying much at all to each other.

9

Kayla

I had put the bottle of alcohol down and had got serious, especially after seeing Cedric's car at Evelyn's place. She had left several messages for me, but I had ignored all of them. Instead, I had got motivated to deal with this situation with Jacoby and come up with the best solution. I didn't want to waste much more time on this, and I had a feeling that it would be just a matter of time before the police were knocking at my door to take my son away. Thanks to Evelyn.

Last night Jacoby and I had spoken to a lawyer, who had seemed very helpful. He had encouraged us to do our best to work this out with Cedric. "The truth," he'd said, "will set you free," so I had decided to invite Cedric over and let Jacoby tell him what he'd done while the two of them were in my presence.

After Jacoby got out of school and was done with band practice, I called Cedric at work. He sounded as if he was busy, so I hurried to tell him the purpose for my call.

"Jacoby and I need to talk to you about something very important. If you can come over after work, I would appreciate it very much."

"I don't mind coming over, but it may be around six or seven. Do you care to tell me what this is about?"

"I will once you get here."

"I don't like surprises, Kayla. Did Jacoby tell you why he has distanced himself from me, or are you going to tell me that I'm going to be a grandfather? I'm not ready to be one of those yet, and you need to stop him from spending so much time with Adrianne."

There he was again, telling me what I needed to do. I rolled my eyes, then sighed. "No, you're not going to be a grandfather, and I love his relationship with Adrianne. She has been there for him through thick and thin, and he is blessed to have her."

"Thick and thin, my ass. You shouldn't put that much trust in her, and neither should he."

"Why? Because you know something that we don't? I guess you're going to announce that you've been screwing her too."

There was silence. I could tell that my tone annoyed Cedric, but I didn't care. I couldn't help it.

He finally spoke. "She's not my type, and I'm surprised that he's stuck with her this long. Her head game must be fierce."

That about did it for me. I didn't have anything else to say other than "I'll see you later."

After that, I moseyed on by the liquor cabinet, thinking hard about making a drink. I needed a little something to calm me before Cedric got here, but after I began to pour myself a drink, I stopped. I poured the liquid down the drain, then rinsed the glass. To keep myself busy, I started to clean up. I vacuumed the floors, washed a few dishes, and then cleaned Jacoby's bathroom. I noticed two condoms in his trash can, and I was kind of pissed that he and Adrianne had been having sex in his room. I wasn't sure if I was going to call him out on it or not, especially since tonight would wind up being hectic for all of us.

When Jacoby came home, he kissed my cheek, then rushed to get something to eat in the kitchen. As he sat at the kitchen table, eating two hot dogs and some chips, I sat with him.

"Are you nervous about this evening? Cedric said he would be here around six or seven."

Jacoby shrugged. "I'm a little nervous, but I'm ready to get this over with. Whatever he decides to do is up to him. And whatever my punishment may be, I'll accept it."

"There will be no punishment. You've already suffered enough."

"Unfortunately, Mom, that won't be for you to decide."

Hearing him say that made my stomach hurt. Now I needed that drink even more than I had needed it earlier. Jacoby seemed much calmer than I was, and when the doorbell rang almost an hour later, he still seemed calm. I was flustered. I almost tripped on a rug as I made my way to the front door, and when I swung it open, it was not Cedric. Instead, it was Justin. I hadn't seen him since we had sex at the hotel, and we had talked on only one occasion after that. For him to show up at my door was a total surprise. His timing couldn't be more off, but I didn't want to be rude.

"Normally," he said, "I don't just pop up like this, but I was in your neighborhood. Just thought I'd stop by to say hello and find out what you were doing this weekend. There's a jazz concert at the park. I remember you telling me how much you like jazz. We don't have to go as a couple or anything like that, but it would be nice to hang out with you again."

I didn't mind hanging out with Justin, but I had to let him know that this thing between us wasn't going anywhere. I told him just that as I invited him inside and asked him to have a seat in the living room. I closed the French doors just so Jacoby wouldn't hear our conversation.

"I suspected that it wasn't that serious for you," he said, raking his hair back with his fingers. "And that's fine with me. You're fresh off of a divorce, and I get that the last thing you want to do is jump into another relationship."

"I'm glad you understand. Feel free to call me on Friday. If I'm not doing anything, I would love to meet you at the park. It sounds like fun, and jazz music is my favorite."

Justin started to tell me about some of the artists he loved. I enjoyed his company, but as it was nearing seven o'clock, I tried to rush him out the door before Cedric got there. My attempt, however, was too late. Cedric knocked on the door, and when Jacoby opened it, he came inside. I could see him from where I was sitting, and he could see me. The person he couldn't see was Justin, until he came closer to the French doors and opened them. His eyes shifted to Justin, who had stood right along with me.

"Justin, this is my ex-husband, Cedric. Cedric, this is a friend of mine," I said.

Justin politely extended his hand, but all Cedric did was look at it. "Friend of yours?" he said. "Since when did you start having friends that I don't know about?"

I was taken aback by his tone and his comment. And his poor treatment of Justin really disturbed me. "I'm not required to tell you about any of my friends. How dare you come in here like you live here or something?"

He pointed his finger right at the tip of my nose. "Don't disrespect me. I may not live here, but you'd better believe that it was my fucking money that bought everything up in here. I paid for that sofa he's been sitting his ass on, and I got a problem with you inviting muthafuckas up in here who don't help to pay the bills."

To say I was in shock would be putting it mildly. I didn't know where all of this was coming from. He needed to correct himself quickly or else. Justin just stood there, as if he didn't know what to say or do. He appeared even more shocked than I was.

"You need to apologize to my guest. If you don't, you need to leave and try this again at another time. I don't understand how you think you pay all the bills around here, and just in case you don't know, my bank account has my name on it, not yours."

"Excuse me," Justin said. "I—I think it'll be best if I just go. I didn't mean to cause any trouble, and, Kayla, I will see you at the park this weekend."

"Yeah, it is best that you go," Cedric said. "And don't you ever bring yo' ass back here again."

This was too much to swallow. I stopped Justin from exiting, then stood face-to-face with Cedric. "He's staying right here. And you're the one who needs to go. I don't know what has gotten into you, Cedric, but you will not come over here and try to run anything."

Jacoby stood by the door, trying to calm the situation, which was minutes from boiling over. "Dad, why don't you just go? I'll call you tomorrow, and we'll talk then."

"I'm not going no damn where!" Cedric yelled. "This sucker got one minute to get the fuck out of here, or else he's going to find my foot in his ass."

"And you're going to find mine in yours," I fired back. "Stop this madness and get out! Now, Cedric, before I call the police on you."

Justin didn't want any part of this. He took a few steps forward to leave, and I got the shock of my life when Cedric lifted his foot and punted Justin in his ass. I gasped as Justin turned around and swung at Cedric. He ducked, and before I knew it, the two of them were going at it. This was unbelievable to me. I yelled for them to stop, but my screams fell on deaf ears. Cedric held on tight to Justin's neck as he was bent over, and then he rammed Justin's head into my French doors. Glass shattered, and one of the doors fell off its hinges.

Justin kept punching Cedric in his legs to weaken him, but he was no match for Cedric. He lifted Justin up high, then slammed him down in the foyer. As Cedric punched him in the face, I saw blood splatter everywhere. Jacoby and I tried to pull Cedric off Justin, but Cedric was in a rage. He shoved me back so hard that I fell and almost bumped my head on the table. Justin attempted to get away from him, and that was when Cedric and Jacoby started to argue.

"Stop it, Dad! Now!"

"Back the fuck up, Jacoby. You don't want none of this, trust me!"

Cedric refused to let Justin get out the door. He punched him in his chest, then lit up his stomach with several hard blows. As Justin dropped to one knee, Cedric punched him so hard in the face that I thought I heard something crack. I cried hard as I jumped on his back to stop him. That was when I saw Jacoby lift his shirt and remove a gun from the inside of his jeans.

"Push her again, and I'll shoot." Jacoby held the gun near Cedric's temple. "Now, do like she said, and get the hell out of here. You ain't got no business coming here and doing all of this. In case you didn't get the memo, the damn marriage is over!"

There Jacoby was, trying to defend me again. I removed myself from Cedric's back, and he stood up straight with caution and ease.

"Put it away, Jacoby," I said, looking at Justin, who seemed to be in a lot of pain as he swayed back and forth on the floor. "Put the gun away. This is ridiculous, and I'm calling the police."

"Call them," Cedric said, with calm in his voice. "I can't wait for them to get here. Ain't no telling who will go to jail, though, and it very well may not be only me."

His eyes shifted to Jacoby. The look in Cedric's eyes told me that he knew what Jacoby had done. Cedric reached for the gun, demanding that Jacoby give it to him. "You shouldn't be carrying anything around like that. Guns are dangerous, and people can get hurt by them. Trust me, I know. I have the scars to prove it, and you wouldn't want to be put in a position where you have proof too."

I rushed up to Jacoby and snatched the gun from his hand. It was better if it was in my hands than in his or Cedric's.

"Go, Cedric. Please go," I pleaded. "You've done enough tonight. You should be ashamed of yourself for carrying on like this in front of your son."

"Trust me, I'm not. I'm no more ashamed than you should be for fucking this young punk and allowing him to come to a place where I pay the bills at. You can do better than this, Kayla, and before you bring any motherfucker up in here again, in front of my son, you need to seek my approval. If not, I will kick ass again, just like I did his."

Before he walked out the door, Cedric lifted his foot and kicked Justin in his face. I was crushed, and even though I wanted to call the police, I couldn't. I rushed over to Justin to comfort him.

"Jacoby, go get me a wet towel and some ice. Hurry."

I helped Justin up off the floor and held him up as he limped over to the sofa.

"Hey," he strained to say while holding his side, "it's not as bad as it looks."

To me, it looked pretty bad. His face was bruised. Right eye was almost shut, and blood ran from his nose. I saw bruises on his neck, and I could only imagine what the rest of his body looked like.

"If you want, I can drive you to the hospital and take you to the police station so you can press charges against him. I am so sorry about this, and I feel horrible that this has happened to you."

Jacoby came into the room with two wet towels and a bucket of ice. He also offered to take Justin to the hospital.

"No," Justin said while squeezing his head with his fingertips. "I'm okay. I just need to get cleaned up. That's all."

I did my best to clear the blood from his face. I also put ice on it. When I helped him remove his shirt, I saw that his chest and his side were bruised.

"I can't let you sit there like this. Let me take you to the hospital. Please."

He refused. Said he didn't want to go, but he did go to my bathroom to clean himself up better than I had. While looking in the mirror, he touched his swollen face.

"Damn. He's good," Justin said, then released a chuckle. "He banged me up pretty bad, didn't he?"

"I don't see how you can find humor in all of this. I can't, Justin, and I want you to press charges against him."

Justin ignored my request. I didn't know if he had warrants out or not, but he refused to go to the police station. He also refused once more to go to the hospital, and it was almost two hours later when he decided to leave and go home.

"Thanks for taking care of me," he said. "I still hope to see you on Saturday, but if not, I won't be mad at you."

I refused to put him in a situation like this again. Lord knows, I was hurt, and yet I had to admit that this was on me.

"I may or may not see you at the park, but please go home and take care of yourself. If you change your mind about going to the hospital, call me. I'll take you, and I will do anything else that you need me to do."

Justin reached out and gave me a hug. He squeezed me tight, then gave me a kiss on the cheek. I took that as a sign that I would never see him again.

After he left, I went to Jacoby's room to talk to him. He was on the phone and acted as if he didn't want to be interrupted.

"Not now, Mama. Please. I just need to chill."

"Where in the hell did you get that gun? I don't like you carrying that thing around, and I had no idea that you had it."

"I got it to protect myself."

"Protect yourself from who?"

"From whoever."

"Well, you won't have it to protect yourself from whomever it is that you're protecting yourself from. I have it now, and you won't be getting it back."

"Fine. Now, is there anything else you'd like to get off your chest?"

"Plenty of stuff, but I'm not going there with you tonight."

I left his room, upset with him for having the gun, furious with Cedric for clowning as he had tonight, and livid with Evelyn for telling Cedric my secret. I was anxious to speak to Cedric again, but I intended to wait a few more days to let things cool down. I grabbed a bottle of Hennessy Black and took it to my bedroom with me so I, too, could chill.

10

Evelyn

I was starting to get bored with shopping. Over the past several weeks, I had spent at least two hundred thousand dollars on material bullshit that didn't make me feel better. The car I had purchased was included, and after driving my new Mercedes for one week, it felt like any other car to me.

The only thing I was excited about was moving . . . and the time I'd spent with Charles. I couldn't stop thinking about that man. I couldn't remember the last time I had felt this attached to someone. With Cedric, it was all about the money. I put up with that fool because I wanted his money, and I was trying to secure a future with a man who had it. Charles being wealthy was a plus, but it didn't matter to me either way. There was something about him that moved me big-time.

That was too bad for me, because I wasn't supposed to reach out to him again. I had promised him, as well as myself, that all I needed was one day. One day to do exactly what we'd done, but I was to the point where I wanted more. I hadn't heard from him, but that didn't surprise me. He didn't have my number to reach me, but I was 100 percent sure that if he wanted to get in touch, he would.

For now, I went into chill mode and turned my thoughts to moving. First of all, I wanted a bigger place, but more than anything, I wanted to get the hell away from Cedric. My apartment had too many bad memories. Memories of Cedric, of Bryson, and of some of the other useless men I'd brought there from time to time. I needed a fresh start, and the new town house I had found was in a peaceful neighborhood, and only twenty minutes away from my BFF Kayla.

I was a little perturbed because I hadn't heard from her. I had called to check on her several times, but she hadn't replied. When I'd reached out to Trina, she hadn't called me back, either. I wondered what was up with them, especially Kayla and her little drinking problem. A huge part of me felt terrible for her. My original plan had been to tell Cedric everything, but I just couldn't do it. I didn't want to keep hurting Kayla and Jacoby, and I had realized that they had been hurt enough not only by me, but by Cedric, as well. Together, we had caused enough damage.

He just couldn't stop, and he got carried away. He had started talking slick and taking advantage of me again. Treating me like shit and putting his hands on me wasn't the route to go. I had an idea about how I was going to deal with him, but the one thing that I wasn't going to do was tell him anything about Jacoby trying to kill him. The truth was, something inside of me felt as if he already knew. In my heart, I believed that Cedric had put this little scheme together to cause more chaos between me and my BFF's. He was too much of a wise man to sit back and wait on me for information. That just didn't seem right, and whenever I saw him again, I intended to share my thoughts.

The movers were at my place, boxing up everything for me. I was so ready to get out of here, and I had already taken some of my things over to the new place. I called Trina and Evelyn to see if they wanted to come see my new town house, but the only person I got in touch with was Trina.

"Of course I want to see it, but you and I have some things that we need to discuss. If I come over there, will I be in the way?"

"No. The movers are almost done, and the majority of my things won't be moved out of here until tomorrow. Come on over. I'll be here."

Trina told me she was on her way. While waiting for her to come, I went into my bedroom and started to put some of my shoes in a box.

"I'll get those," one of the movers said. "I'm just working on your other closet right now."

"That's fine. You work on that one, and I'll work on this one. I don't mind helping."

He got back to work, and so did I. But the whole time I packed, I couldn't shake my thoughts of Charles. It still *felt* like his dick was inside me, only because every time I thought about it, there was a throb that came from deep within. I wanted so badly not to think about him, but something strange was happening to me. Something that I knew I wasn't ready for. Something that felt kind of scary.

I finished up in the closet, then thanked the movers who had been there to help me.

"We'll be back around eight in the morning," one of them said. "Is that too early for you?"

"No, that's perfect. How long do you think it will take?"

"Probably about three or four hours, drive time included. But keep in mind that if you're not happy with our services, you don't have to pay."

"So far, so good. I'll see you guys in the morning. And thanks again."

As they were leaving, Trina was on her way in. She looked really cute in her soft pink sweats and a crop top that showed her tight abs. Out of all of us, she was the one who kept herself real fit. She had muscles, but not the ones that made a woman look manly. Her short, layered hair swerved to one side, and her bangs rested on her forehead. As she passed by me, I smacked her big ass, which looked to be growing.

"No wonder Keith is in love," I said playfully. "And it looks to me like he's been working that thing out."

"All day, every day," she said, then made her way into the living room and took a seat on the sofa. "And while he's been working me out, I hope like hell you aren't still working Cedric out."

Her comment stunned me. I had thought that my secret was safe with Cedric. Did Trina know something that I didn't?

I sat down on the sofa. "What do you mean by that?"

"What I mean is, you have some explaining to do. Kayla stopped by your place the other night and saw Cedric's car over here. If you expect me or her to believe that y'all were in here building blocks, then I'll have to ask you to come again."

I wanted to lie to Trina, but I decided to come clean. I told her about him visiting me at the hospital, and about him asking me to give him information about Kayla and Jacoby. I also admitted to having sex with him again.

"After we left Bryson's parents' house, I went there with him again. I also had sex with him a few more times after that, but that's because he keeps coming over here and making demands. He is out of control, and I fear that he may do something to me or Kayla."

Trina's lips were pursed the whole time I spoke. "You don't expect me to believe you, do you? I mean, come on, Evelyn. Cedric can't make you do anything that you don't want to do. And why would you agree to tell him anything about Jacoby and Kayla? So what you're telling me is you were being fake with her. You were around only to pump information from her?"

"No. I've been hanging out with y'all because we're friends, and that's what friends do. At first I was on the fence, only because I felt as if I owed Cedric. Then, after seeing Kayla break down like that the other day, I just couldn't do it. I haven't told Cedric one single thing, even though I know what Jacoby did."

"Please forgive me, but I'm having a hard time believing you. Yet again, Kayla is so upset with you, and I can't say that I blame her. You need to stop this, Evelyn. I don't know what you're trying to gain by your constant betrayals, but when will enough be enough?"

Trina was starting to upset me. I didn't know what else to say to her, especially since I was speaking the truth.

"I don't know how long I'm going to have to pay for my mistakes. Yes, I've done some dirty things, and as you can see, I'm trying to make up for those things. I have no reason to sit here and lie to you. It was difficult for me to admit that I've still been screwing Cedric, but I told you that because I want to be clear about how I feel about him. I do not love him, I have never loved him, and the only reason I messed around with him was that I needed his money. I know that sounds crazy, but it's the truth."

"And you're still messing around with him because you need his money, right? How could that be the case when you're supposed to be over here, sitting pretty with the money Mr. and Mrs. Washington gave you? All I'm saying is, something doesn't add up."

I just shook my head. I swore I needed some new friends. What was so difficult to understand about this?

"It may not add up to you, but it adds up to me. I just said that the only reason I started fucking with Cedric again was that he helped me out of a situation that I had no way out of. You know darn well that I didn't have a dime to defend myself in court. Bryson's parents were about to eat me alive, until Cedric reached out to them. He turned that whole situation around, and I had to promise him something in return."

Trina sat silent. She rolled her eyes at me a few times and then released a deep breath. "Instead of telling me all of this, why don't you call Kayla? You really need to have this conversation with her, not me."

"I'm having this conversation with you because you said you wanted to talk. I don't mind telling Kayla what I just told you, but I assure you that I'll get the same response. She will not listen to me, and she is set on me being a horrible person who can't be redeemed."

Trina didn't say anything, but she knew I had spoken the truth. And at this point, I just didn't care anymore. I was sure Trina would relay everything I'd said to her to Kayla. If she wanted to talk further about it, I was sure she would reach out to me.

"I did say that I wanted to talk," Trina finally said. "And if that's going to be your explanation for all of this, then so be it. On another note, when can I see your new town house?"

"We can go over there now. Do you have time?"

Trina said she did, so we got in her car and left. On the drive there, she was real quiet. I asked what was on her mind. That was when she mentioned her trip to New York tomorrow.

"So you decided to go, huh?" I said.

"Yep. I need to stabilize my career, and I'm due to meet with some important people on Friday."

"What kind of important people?"

"I just told you. People who may help me stabilize my career."

"So you have to go all the way to New York to find people who can help you stabilize your career? That makes no sense to me, and like you told me earlier, I think you may need to come again."

Trina swallowed and continued to speak to me with an attitude. She did that often when she felt guilty about something. "If you don't mind, I don't want to talk about my trip. I have a lot of things on my mind right now, and talking about it isn't going to help much."

"Okay. I won't push like you push me when I don't want to talk. But I do have to ask how Keith feels about your trip."

"He thinks I'm going on a three-day vacation with you and Kayla. So, whatever you do, please don't call me at home, don't call my cell, and do not call him."

Trina was playing with fire. And she had the audacity to try to make me feel bad about my situation with Cedric. He wasn't the one she should be concerned about. If she wanted to be mad at me, she should be mad at me about having sex with the one who could be her possible father-in-law. Since she didn't know about us yet, I guessed she couldn't be mad.

"I won't call Keith, and as a matter of fact, I have no reason to call him. While I don't approve of what you're doing, I'm not going to sit here and judge you like you judge me. Especially when I . . ." I paused, then changed my mind. "Never mind. Forget it. Make a right at the light, and at the first street, make a left."

"Forget what?" Trina said, following my directions. "What were you going to say?"

"Nothing. Now, drive all the way to the end of the street, and my town house is on the left."

Trina drove farther down the street, then parked her car. She looked at the town houses, then nodded. "These are nice. Must have cost you a fortune. But what were you about to say?"

"I said never mind."

"And I said tell me. I hate when you do that, Evelyn. You need to quit it."

"I'm hesitant to tell you because the last time I told you a secret, it got back to Bryson, and he wound up beating my ass. You do remember that, don't you, my dear friend?"

Trina looked down; then she started fumbling with her nails. "I'm sorry about that, but I had no idea Bryson was that kind of man. And even though you told me he would hurt you, I didn't think he would go that far."

"You mean, you didn't believe me. Just like you don't believe what I just told you about me and Cedric."

"Let's not go there again, but go ahead and tell me what you were about to say. I won't say anything to anybody, especially not Kayla."

"Kayla's not the one I'm worried about. I'm worried about you telling Keith."

"I don't like to keep things from him, but you already know that I have been keeping some secrets. Whatever your secret is, if you don't want him to know, then I won't say anything."

I paused for a few seconds, then let it out. "Even if it's about his father?"

A tiny frown appeared on Trina's face. "His father? Is there something he should know about his father? If so, Evelyn, you'd better tell me. I don't want Keith to get hurt again, like he did when you broke it down about Bryson."

"I wouldn't want Keith to get hurt again, either, so my lips are sealed."

Trina wasn't having it. She wouldn't get out of the car unless I elaborated more. "You are so wrong, Evelyn. Did you see him with someone? And please don't tell me that you saw him with a man too."

"No, trust me when I say it was nothing like that. He is, indeed, one hundred percent all man. I can assure you of that."

Trina looked as if she had stopped breathing. Her mouth dropped open, and she sat up straight in her seat. "Evelyn, please don't tell me what I think you're trying to tell me. Are you fucking Keith's father?"

I looked straight ahead, then zipped my lips. "I have nothing to say."

"Like hell!" Trina shouted. "Tell me now. Then again, no. Don't tell me. I don't want to know. 'Cause if you did, I would definitely have to tell Keith. But as far as I'm concerned, this conversation didn't happen. I don't want to know anything, and please take me inside to see your new place."

"I will. After I tell you how freaking big his dick is. Girl, that thing is about this damn long, and he beat the shit out of me with it." I tried to show Trina the measurements with my hands, but she turned her head and covered her ears.

"Nope," she said. "I didn't hear a word you said. All I heard you say was, 'The weather sure is nice outside.'"

I laughed, then pulled her hands away from her ears. "Huge, girl, and your dear friend is hooked! It only happened one time, but I can't stop thinking about him. Are things that serious between him and his wife? Do you know if the marriage is solid or not?"

Trina started to hum. She tapped her feet on the floor of the car, then covered her ears once again. That was when I opened the car door.

"Fine then. Let's go inside," I said.

I got out of the car, and so did Trina. As we made our way to my front door, she walked behind me.

"You know what?" she said. "I think there is a motive behind everything you do. You knew that if you told me about you and Mr. Washington, I would tell Keith. And Keith would tell his mother and confront his father. A whole lot of shit would get stirred up, and then Mr. Washington may come running to you. That's what you want to happen, but just so you know, I'm not telling Keith one word. The holes you dig keep on getting deeper. I promise you that he is not the kind of man you want to fuck with."

I didn't respond, but Trina knew me all too well. I did have a motive for telling her, and it was just that. While she said she wouldn't tell Keith, in my heart, I felt that she would.

The next day I was all moved into my new town house. It was sweet. Had a spacious loft area, three bedrooms, two and a half bathrooms, and a luxury kitchen. I had so much room, and I intended to use one of the bedrooms as an office. In order to keep myself busy, I had to start a business or invest in one. Whenever I was ready, I had the place to do it.

Most of my furniture had been delivered, and this go-around I had gone the classic contemporary route. The walls were a light gray, and most of my furnishings were soft yellow and silky white. I was totally impressed by some of the things I had picked out. The interior designer I had hired to hook up everything for me had said she couldn't make it over until the weekend. I had wanted to ask Trina to help me, but I didn't like her taste. She liked loud colors—colors that could blind a person when they came into a room. I hoped that she wouldn't take offense at me for not asking her and hiring someone else.

After the sun went down, I sat on my new plush sofa and thought about calling her. Then I remembered what she had told me about going to New York. I was worried about that little situation, but I figured that Trina and Keith would someway or somehow work it all out.

I got up from the sofa to go turn on some music. Kayla wasn't the only one who could afford to have an intercom that played music throughout the home. I was now balling too, and it certainly felt good. So good that I got me a cigarette, poured a drink, and then went outside on my balcony. I took a few puffs from the cig, then whistled smoke into the air. Thoughts of Charles quickly invaded my mind. I visualized myself on that bed, getting the royal treatment again. The way he held my waist from behind and gave me inch by inch had felt spectacular. I had gone crazy and had never leaked that much in my life. My thoughts of him got so deep that I backed up to the wrought-iron lounge chair and let my silk robe fall to the side. I smashed the cigarette in an ashtray, then cocked my legs open. Hot and more than bothered, I slipped two of my fingers inside my pussy. I closed my eyes while sliding my fingers in and out of me. They felt nothing like Charles, and a few minutes in, I gave up.

I went inside, snatched up my cell phone, then punched in his number. On the second ring, he answered. His masculine voice uttering a simple word like "hello" made my pussy dance.

"Charles, this is Evelyn," I said in a soft tone.

There was a pause. Then he responded, "What do you want?"

"You. I want you. I need to see you again."

The only thing I heard was the call drop. I wasn't sure if he had done it intentionally or not, but when I called back, his phone went to voice mail. I tried three times, and after that, my number was blocked. I was completely taken aback. I guessed he meant what he'd said about going there only once, and I was highly upset about it. I didn't know what to do about his ill treatment, but surely I'd think of something.

11

Trina

The big day had finally arrived. I had stayed up late last night, packing and making love to Keith, and afterward, I hadn't gotten much sleep, maybe an hour or two. When I woke up, I found him in the kitchen, cooking breakfast. He was in his black Calvin Klein briefs that melted on his perfect ass. His colorful tats were on display, and his smooth chocolate skin made me want to have him again for breakfast. When he turned around, my eyes dropped to his mountain of love, which appeared to be hard.

"What are you thinking about, other than my breakfast?" I teased.

"I was thinking about how bad you put it on me last night." He laughed, then slid my pancakes on a plate. "I couldn't let you leave here hungry."

"Thank you," I said, walking up to him to give him a kiss. "But I only have time to eat one. I'm running behind, and I really need to get out of here. Kayla and Evelyn are already on their way to the airport."

"Do you need me to drop you off?"

"No. I'm going to drive and leave my car in the parking lot. When I return, I don't want to wait for you to pick me up."

"Okay. We'll hurry up and eat. Give me some suga and go."

I wished I had time to give him more than that, but I didn't. I ate the pancake and a few pieces of bacon. Guzzled down some orange juice, then gathered my luggage, which was already at the door.

"Let me help you with that," Keith said as I put the straps from one of the bags on my shoulder.

"I have only two bags. I got it, but thanks."

I puckered my lips for a kiss, Keith obliged, and that kiss instantly turned intense. Keith was the one who backed away from it.

"Don't start nothing you can't finish," he said. "Have fun, and don't forget to call me when you get to Vegas."

I assured him that I would call. I surely intended too, and the second I got on the plane, regret and guilt washed over me. I wasn't sure how this trip was going to pan out. For one thing, I knew it wasn't all about business.

I was in New York in no time at all. Was glad I didn't have any layovers and the plane was on time. I had asked Sasha to meet me at LaGuardia, and, sure enough, while as I was waiting for my luggage, she appeared.

My heart skipped a beat when I saw her, but I tried to play down my enthusiasm. Her beauty couldn't be denied. I loved her Afrocentric style. And she was one sexy woman.

The first thing she did was walk up and give me a hug. Her breasts pressed against mine, and her sweet perfume drew me right in.

"No words can express how delighted I am to see you," she said. "Thank you so much for coming."

"No, thank you for inviting me. I'm waiting on my luggage. It should be here in a minute or two."

We waited for almost fifteen minutes for my luggage to come. Afterward, we walked together to her car, and within thirty minutes, we were at my hotel.

"You don't have to stay here, you know," she said. "The last thing I want you to do is waste money."

"Well, hopefully, I'll be in a position to get some of that money back. I'm excited about the meeting on Friday. Did you get those pictures I shipped to you?" I had shipped three of my paintings to Sasha so she could share them with the individuals I planned to meet tomorrow.

She confirmed that she had gotten them. "They arrived late yesterday, so I haven't had time to show them to anyone. But they are breathtaking. You certainly have talent, and your pictures need to be on display in museums."

I'd never gotten compliments like that about my work. Not even from Keith. And even though I was good, I didn't think I was that good. Then again, yes, I was.

Sasha helped me unpack my things, and then we headed to the sandwich shop in the lobby so I could get something to eat. Sasha couldn't join me, so we parted ways outside the sandwich shop.

"Don't eat that much," she said. "I'm taking you to dinner later, and then we're going out to have some fun, before we take care of business. Try to get some rest, and I'll pick you up around seven or eight tonight."

She gave me another hug before prancing away. I felt good about being here, and when I returned to the room after having a sandwich, I quickly called Keith to let him know I had arrived.

"We're here," I said, lying my ass off. "It's steaming hot, but we're going to go walk the Strip and see what's up."

"Try to stay cool and drink plenty of water. How was your flight?"

"A little bumpy, but we made it. Evelyn and Trina are already arguing, but you know how they are."

"Yes, I do. Don't get in the middle, and if they start fighting, you need to come home. I'm missing you already."

"Yeah, me too. What are your plans for today?"

"I'm going to hang out with Chris and Shawn at the pool hall tonight. We also have plans to go to a strip club," he said, laughing.

"Strip club, my ass. You'd better not be spending your time at a strip club, especially when you have all of this."

"I agree. I was only kidding, and I'm well aware of what I have. Love you, baby, and I'll see you soon."

"Yes, you will."

I hung up, then fell back on the bed. I drifted off as I thought about our relationship, and then my thoughts shifted to Evelyn and Keith's father. Since yesterday I'd been pondering the question of whether I should tell Keith, but that would give him another reason to hate Evelyn even more. I also felt as if it was none of my business, but then again, Keith was my business. The last time I had thought that way was when I discovered that Evelyn was having sex with Cedric behind Kayla's back. Keeping that from her had been the wrong thing to do. I just wasn't sure if spilling the beans was the right thing to do this time, but I did know that keeping all these secrets wasn't good for anyone.

I fell asleep while in thought, and when I woke up, it was already several minutes after six. I quickly got up to shower, and since Sasha said we would be going out tonight, I decided to put on a mustard-yellow pantsuit I'd brought. The jacket buttoned at my waist, and the pants fit like leggings. Even though I didn't like to wear heels, I rocked them, anyway. I swooped my layered hair to the side, spiked the front a little, then sprayed a dash of perfume between my breasts, which were visible due to the low-cut jacket. The only thing I had underneath it was my bra, which you could barely notice was there.

Sasha had told me to meet her in the lobby. By the time I had gotten all dolled up, she was already there. She still had on the skirt and the accessories from earlier, but instead of the tank, she now had on a jacket. From a short distance, I could see the lust in her eyes as she scanned me from head to toe. A wide smile appeared on her face, and a compliment followed.

"You are so beautiful," she said. "Anybody ever tell you that you look like Kelly Roland?"

"Trust me, I hear it all the time." I laughed.

I made my way to her car with her. The club we went to was less than five miles away, and when we got inside, it was jam-packed. Sasha had reserved a table for us. We sat close to a stage, but nothing was happening there yet.

"What's going on here tonight?" I asked, then took a seat.

"You'll see. It's a surprise."

A waiter came over to the table to ask what we wanted to drink. I wasn't a heavy drinker, so I ordered a wine cooler. Sasha ordered a Long Island Iced Tea.

"I'll be right back," the waiter said. "We also serve food. Would you ladies like anything else?"

"Yes," Sasha said. "I want my friend to try the Strawberry Shrimp. The chicken is good too, so I'll order chicken also."

The waiter left to place our order, and after he came back with our drinks, we delved into a conversation about Sasha and her girlfriend. Things seemed pretty rough, but when we turned the page to Keith and me, I had nothing but nice things to say. Jealousy was trapped in Sasha's eyes, and it made me kind of skeptical about her, because I had seen a similar look in Lexi's eyes whenever I spoke of Keith. Regardless, I told the truth and let her know that everything was good with us.

"He's the best," I said. "I have no complaints about my man whatsoever, except that he doesn't always put the toilet seat down. I can certainly live with that."

I laughed, but she didn't. The expression on her face was serious.

"Do you *want* to live with that? What I mean is, are you happy? Are you fully committed to him, and if so, why do I sense that you want to pursue something with me?"

I sipped from my drink, then sat the glass on the table. "I am happy, but sometimes, I just want to see what else is out there. I don't think that I've allowed myself an opportunity to figure out why I still find myself attracted to some women."

"It's because you fit the definition of *bisexual*. It's that simple, and your only problem is that you are trying to fight it. Embrace it and learn to accept it."

"Yeah, I guess. Been fighting it for too long, but I seriously thought that falling in love would make me swing one way or the other. I feel as if I'm in the middle."

"That's because you are. Maybe one day you won't be. But one thing I'm certain of is this. If you're still in the middle, as you say, then Keith isn't the one for you."

I disagreed, but I didn't say it. I didn't want to spend the evening defending my relationship with Keith, so I moved on to our plans for tomorrow. "What time are we supposed to meet tomorrow?" I asked.

"They'll be at my place around noon. I can't pick you up, because I need to set up everything. I have some other displays that I want to show them, and I didn't have time to lay everything out today."

"Just be sure to give me your address again. I'll take a cab."

Sasha wrote her address on a napkin. We conversed some more and ordered a few more drinks to wash down our food. Rap music thumped in the background, and when a famous rapper came through the door, many people rushed over to get his autograph, as well as his attention. A few minutes later the black curtains on the stage opened, and out came two female strippers with nothing on but thongs. With us sitting front and center, I saw everything. One of the strippers blew Sasha a kiss, and she waved at her.

"That's Black Pearl," Sasha said to me. "A good friend of mine. I've known her for years."

I felt uncomfortable sitting up close, and on a for-real tip, this wasn't my cup of tea. I watched males and females have their way with the strippers, making money rain on them. There was no question that the ladies had it going on. My eyes were glued to them, and I even had some nasty thoughts swarming in my head. Still, I couldn't get with this, especially when Black Pearl came over to us and Sasha started licking her nipples. I stood and told Sasha I was ready to go.

"What's wrong?" she said, looking shocked that I wanted to leave. "I brought you here to have some fun. Why is this setting bothering you?"

"It just does."

I walked away from the table, and after Sasha said something to Black Pearl, she followed me out the door. When we got to her car, she seemed slightly upset with me.

"Look, Trina. There was nothing wrong with us being in there. You just made me feel like shit. I had the whole night planned out for us, but now I guess you want to go back to the hotel, right?"

All kinds of thoughts were running through my head. It would be hypocritical of me to think that I could kick it at a strip club but Keith couldn't. I would have a fit if he did, and in addition to that, I was starting to feel bad about this whole thing.

When I was in thought, Sasha leaned in and pecked my lips. She waited for me to reciprocate, but I didn't. She softly kissed me again, and then she lifted her hand to my breast and squeezed it.

"If we go back to the hotel, can I join you? I don't want our night to end here, and it is my goal to make sure you have a wonderful time while you're here."

I licked my lips, just to see what hers tasted like. They were sweet and very inviting. Without responding, I leaned forward to kiss her. I touched her breasts, though I knew I shouldn't. Rubbed her soft legs, which I couldn't resist. Invited her to slip her fingers into me, and when I opened my legs, she reached inside my panties and did just that. The moment was extremely intense, and I had to take a deep breath and back away from it.

"Give me time to think about this, Sasha. I don't want to be rushed into this, okay?"

I was surprised that she didn't push. "Sure, Trina. Whenever you're ready, you know I'm here."

We climbed in the car, and she started it and then drove back to the hotel. We were there in no time. I thought she was going to go up to my room with me, but instead, she stayed in the car.

"I'll see you tomorrow. Have your sales pitch prepared, and get ready for what may be a new start for you," she said as I got out.

That made me feel better. Changed my whole demeanor. I was looking forward to tomorrow so I could hurry back home to my man. While I was feeling Sasha and her touch had aroused me, there was something about her that stopped me from going any further with her. I saw what Keith had seen, and I really didn't trust her.

The next day, I took a cab to the address Sasha had given me. The cabdriver parked in front of a brownstone that had an array of plants on the porch, and I paid the fare and climbed out. The small lawn in front was well manicured, and when I reached the porch and looked through the huge bay windows, I could see plenty of artwork covering the walls. I walked over to the tall door. I could see that it was open, but I still knocked. Nobody came to the door.

"Sasha," I called, then knocked again.

I could hear loud music coming from inside, so maybe she didn't know that I was at the door. I pushed the door open wider, and when I stepped inside, I saw my paintings, along with several others, propped up on easels. There were also a few folding chairs in front of a fireplace, and the smell of burning incense infused the air. Before going any farther, I called out to Sasha again but didn't get a reply. Then I heard something coming from another room. It sounded as if she was hurt. As if she was crying and needed help.

I rushed down a small, narrow hallway and then turned right. There was a room with an open door about ten steps in front of me. Didn't know what I was getting myself into and was nervous as hell. I had managed to grab a knife from the breakfast buffet I'd eaten at earlier, just in case. It was in my purse, and I held it close to me as I approached the open door. When I looked inside the room, I saw that Sasha was getting it on with Black Pearl, one of the strippers from last night. They both were moaning and groaning while caressing each other. Sasha stopped for a second to address me, with a smile on her face.

"What took you so long to get here?" she said while licking Black Pearl's neck with her curled tongue. "You're late, and we've been waiting on you."

I'd be lying if I said that seeing their near-perfect bodies in the bed, naked, didn't turn me on. I would not be telling the truth if I said I hadn't thought about being in a position like this with two other women. I couldn't deny that there was something in me that wanted to jump in that bed and have at it. But, deep down, I had to admit that there was something inside of me that outweighed all my thoughts. This just didn't feel right.

"I'm not late. You told me to be here at noon. Are we meeting some potential buyers or not?"

Sasha got off the bed in all her nakedness. She was as sexy as sexy could get. Lust was definitely in my eyes, and it made her smile when she noticed the attention I was giving her.

"They're going to be here, but not until later. We have plenty of time to explore each other, so why don't you take off your clothes and join us? I already told Black Pearl all about you, and from the look on her face, you can already see how delighted she is that you're here."

My eyes shifted to Black Pearl, who was kneeling on the bed, toying with her pussy. I was angry yet still slightly turned on. I attempted to be as nice as I could about the situation, since I didn't want to disrespect Sasha in her house.

"I didn't come here to explore sex with you or anyone else. I came to meet the individuals you said could possibly help with my career and would maybe purchase some of my paintings from me. If that's not going to happen, then I think I should leave."

Sasha stepped forward, leaving no breathing room between us. "I didn't say it wasn't going to happen. It just may not happen today, because, unfortunately, they called to cancel."

"Bullshit," I said, not holding back. "All you wanted to do was get me here to do this. Go ahead and admit it, Sasha. All you wanted was for me to come here so we could fuck."

With a smirk on her face, she reached out to touch my breast. I slapped her hand away, then moved backward.

"You do not have permission to touch me," I said. "Now, back the hell up and go back over there, where you're wanted."

Sasha turned to Black Pearl and pouted. "You hear that, baby? She doesn't want me. She's mad, and it looks as if I'm not good enough."

"If she doesn't want you, I do. Come on back over here so we can finish what we started. Let that bitch go back to wherever she came from."

Sasha sashayed back to the bed and wasted no time getting back to her lover. I swallowed the oversize lump in my throat. It wasn't until that moment that I realized just how stupid I was for coming here. I walked away, feeling awful. Didn't even bother to grab my paintings on my way out—just left empty-handed. Went back to the hotel, only to lie on the bed and listen to a voice mail from Keith.

"Hope you're having a good time, baby. But it's sad that a brotha can't get a phone call or nothing. Be sweet, and when you get back, I have something magnificent waiting for you. Until then, love you like the teddy bear I couldn't let go of until I was almost ten years old. I told you that story, but then again, I shouldn't have." He laughed, then ended the call.

Stupid me, I thought. *Stupid, fucking me.* I could have kicked myself in the ass for being here, so I hurriedly packed and got out of there. I had to pay a little extra to change my flight, but no ifs, ands, or buts about it, I was on my way back to St. Louis.

I sat at the airport for hours, waiting to get out of there. My phone kept ringing, and to no surprise, it was Sasha. My intention was to block her calls, but not until I told her how I was feeling.

"I don't know what you could possibly have to say to me after inviting me to come all the way to New York for this. You were wrong on so many different levels, and I do not want you to call me ever again."

"Trina, had I known you were so insecure, so stuck up, and were not willing to go there with me, I never would have asked you to come here. I guess I got the wrong impression of you from our conversations, and if so, I apologize. Now, why don't you come back to my place so we can talk? Black Pearl is gone, and it will be just you and me."

"Do I look that fucking stupid to you? Hell, no, I'm not coming back. You are out of your mind. And in reference to our conversations, you also understood that my main purpose for coming here was to meet with the people you kept talking about. I seriously thought you would be able to help me, but you know it was all a lie."

"It wasn't. I—I thought I'd be able to help you, but when I showed your paintings to a few people, they thought your stuff was basic. Basically, there was nothing really special about it, and the more I looked at it, the more I started to feel the same way too."

I hung up on that bitch, then blocked her number. Was she kidding me? Was she for real? I couldn't wait to get my ass back home, but unfortunately for me, as soon as I got back to St. Louis and was heading for my car, I looked up and saw Keith leaning against it. His arms were folded, and I surely didn't know that the look on his face could get that ugly. I smiled to play it off, but his face remained flat.

The only thing he said to me was, "How was your trip to New York?"

12

Kayla

I stood on the porch, with its five big columns and a wrought-iron, glass double door that offered a view of the interior of Cedric's new house. He'd sold the property where we used to live, and this was what he called downsizing. I had been here only once before, but I knew it was ten times better than the place in which we used to live. I guessed he had decided to go all out now that he was a bachelor.

I wasn't here to discuss any of that, though. I wanted to break it all down to him about Jacoby and also find out how much he knew. He obviously knew something. The way he had looked at Jacoby that last time said so. Then there was the issue of Justin. Cedric needed to do something . . . anything about that situation, and I was going to make sure that he knew where we stood. He couldn't come to my place anymore. I was done, and as far as I was concerned, I never had to deal with him again.

I rang the doorbell and could see Cedric's girlfriend, Joy, as she headed toward the door. There was a scowl on her face, and she had to be one of the saddest-looking women I had ever seen. I didn't understand why until she opened the door and I saw her blue-and-black eye, which looked real nasty. Seeing it almost took the breath out of me, and before I could say anything, she gave me an explanation.

"I know it looks bad, but I was in a car accident. I'm so thankful that I'm okay, but my car is completely totaled. Does Cedric know you were coming here today?"

"No, he doesn't, but is he here? Also, I'm sorry to hear about your accident, but I'm glad you are okay."

I had no problem with Joy, even though she had dated Cedric while we were married. I didn't find out about her until I broke into his house that day and saw her letters. The way I saw it, he was her problem now. Not mine.

After she let me inside and told me to have a seat in the living room, I saw Cedric coming down the hallway. He had on a blue silk robe and house shoes. A cigar dangled from his mouth, and as expected, there was no smile on his face. He evil eyed Joy, then cut his eyes at her. Without saying a word, she timidly walked away.

"You should have called before you came," he said.

"Yeah. Just like you do when you come to my place. I'm sure you were expecting my visit, so don't pretend that you weren't."

I was still standing, and he invited me to have a seat, but I didn't bother. I stood with my arms crossed, ready to let him have it.

"I need for you to tell me what you know," I said. "I do have some explaining to do, and I'm willing to do that, provided that you tell me why you're still having sex with Evelyn and how you found out about Jacoby."

He played clueless. "Evelyn who? Your best friend, Evelyn? No, I've had enough of that pussy, but I will say that she has shared some important things with me over the past few weeks. Things that shocked me and made me want to watch my back more than I'd been doing."

"Stop beating around the bush, Cedric. Important things like what?"

"I don't know, Kayla. Why in the fuck don't you tell me? I know you didn't come all the way over here to stand there and look pretty while talking shit."

"Keep you freaking compliments and save them for your hoes. I asked you a question, and I want some answers."

Cedric took a seat, chewed on the tip of the cigar, and then he laid it on an ashtray. He invited me to have a seat again, but I stayed right where I was at, all the while tapping my foot on the floor.

"Fine. Then stand your crazy ass there and be mad all you want to. If anybody should be mad, it should be me. I'm the one who's been lied to and plotted against. I'm the one who made sure you and Jacoby had everything y'all needed after our divorce, only to find out what the two of you had planned to do to me. I thought we could get along well as divorcés, and I am highly disappointed that I was wrong."

Lord knows, I was pissed. He had known and hadn't said a word.

"We were getting along well, until you started showing up at my place like you owned it. And what you did the other day was foul. You didn't have to do that young man like that. I am still trying to convince him to press charges against you."

"What a good way to change the subject and ignore what I just said. I don't give a damn about that fool coming to your place. He just happened to be in the wrong place at the wrong time. He caught me in one of my moods, and since I couldn't beat yo' ass like I wanted to, I settled for his."

"Beat my ass for what? I've done nothing to you. You're the one who has done everything to me. I haven't forgotten about all of it, Cedric. I may have forgiven you, but I have not forgotten how you treated me when I was married to you."

Cedric got up, then tied the belt on his robe tighter. He casually walked up to me and stood close. "Let's get real here," he said. "This has nothing to do with the way I treated you while we were married. The question is, do you really want me to stand here and explain to you what you did to me, or do you want me to pretend that I've been blind and can't see?"

"You have been blind if you—"

When I was in mid-sentence, Cedric lifted his fist and punched me clean in my right eye. He caught me so off guard that I stumbled back in my high heels and then fell hard on my ass. My eye felt as if it had been knocked from the socket, and my head throbbed. I placed my hand over my face and squeezed my watery eyes shut. Cedric stood over me, with his finger pointed near my face.

"I've waited a long time to do that. You have gotten away with too much shit, Kayla, and your biggest mistake was lying to me about Jacoby being my son. You want to talk about for-giveness? I will never forgive you for that. 'Cause you see . . . my son, my own flesh and blood, would never plot my demise.

He would never want me dead, nor would he pay someone to kill me. You taught Jacoby to hate me. You wanted his plan to fall into place. That way you could have everything in life that I worked so hard to get, so that you could sit on your lazy ass, just like you're doing now, and do nothing. I know all about it, baby. Evelyn told me all about it, and it's too late for you to come over here and try to tell me anything. I don't want to hear one word from you, and you can tell Jacoby the same thing too."

With tears pouring down my face, I looked at Cedric with so much hate and anger inside of me. "Don't you dare talk to me about Jacoby! You are the one who destroyed him! You made him hate you by bringing all your tricks around him and by dogging his mother out. He felt like he had to do something to stop you. And I don't care what you've been told, but he didn't want to go through with it. He wanted to tell you, but I wouldn't let him!"

Cedric grabbed my neck and pushed my head back on the floor. I had never seen him like this. When we were married, not once had he put his hands on me. I didn't know who this man lying over me was. He had the look of a killer in his eyes. I tried to fight him and get him off of me, but he grabbed my arms and punched me in my face again. I felt blood trickling from my nose and flowing over my lips.

"That's your fucking problem now. You're always treating him like a baby, and you won't let him grow up and be a man. When a man wants to confront somebody about his wrongdoings, you need to move your ass out of the way and let him. But once again . . . ," he said, tightening his grip on my neck. He lifted my head, then slammed it hard on the floor. So hard that the back of my head stung. I didn't know if it was bleeding or not. "Once again, you felt it was best to keep secrets from me. You thought your way could save us all, and you were wrong, wrong, wrong!"

He banged my head three more times before letting me go. I rolled over. I was in so much pain. I seriously thought Cedric was going to kill me. I needed to get out of there fast.

He continued his tirade. "Then you bring your ass over here, talking shit about Evelyn. Hell, yeah, I'm still fucking her.

Your pussy was never good enough, so a man gotta do what he must. You will never be better than her, and if it wasn't for her, I would still be left in the dark. I owe her my life, as well as a little more dick too."

I lifted my head and felt real dizzy. My eyes were blurry from crying, but I could see Joy a short distance away, biting her nails. She looked too afraid to say anything, and I now knew exactly where her black eye had come from. Cedric had lost his mind. Trying my best not to say anything else to him, I crawled my way to the door and reached for the knob. He grabbed both of my arms, then pulled them behind my back so hard that I thought they would break.

"You will not leave here without telling me you're sorry!" he yelled. "I want to hear you say it, and you damn well better mean it. Because if you don't, I am going to call the police right now and have them go to your place and arrest Jacoby. I have all kinds of proof about what he did, and I may even concoct some shit to have yo' ass arrested too."

My arms were hurting so bad that I had to say something. "So . . . sorry. I'm sooo sorry," I cried out, blood now dripping from my chin. "Now, please let me go, Cedric. You're hurting me!"

"Good! Now you know what it feels like to hurt. Tell me again, and this time, mean it! Leave all that other shit out of the mix!"

I swallowed hard, then lowered my head. "Sorry. Truly sorry for what I've done."

He let go of my arms, then pushed me away. He then opened the door and grabbed me by one of my arms. The next thing he did was toss me outside and slam the door behind me. My nose and my hands were bleeding, and so were my knees. I could see that my knees were bleeding through the holes in my jeans. I limped to my car, and if I could've called the police, I would have. I wanted to go home and get the gun I had taken from Jacoby, but if he saw me like this, I was sure that he would use the gun this time. I was a complete mess as I drove away, and I was mad as hell at Evelyn. She was the one who had told Cedric everything. I was going to make sure that she paid for running her big mouth.

Within an hour, I had stopped at a gas station to clean myself up and then had driven to Evelyn's apartment, only to discover that she didn't live there anymore. I had forgotten that Trina had told me in person that Evelyn had moved, and she had also told me so in her voice mail messages. But I didn't know where she had moved to. I called Trina to ask for Evelyn's address, but she was real short with me.

"I'll have to text it to you. Check your phone in five minutes," she said.

I could hear a male voice yelling in the background, but I didn't bother to ask if something was wrong. I just waited on her text message, and when I got it, I drove to Evelyn's new place, which wasn't too far from where I lived. It angered me that she was this close to me. And I hoped that this would be the last time I ever saw her face again.

Still banged up from what Cedric had done to me, I walked slowly to Evelyn's door, rubbing my sore arms. I knocked, and it wasn't long before she opened the door. As soon as her mouth opened, I slapped her across it. I then rushed inside and jumped on top of her. I pounded her head with my fists and yanked at her hair.

"Are you crazy!" she yelled out as she squirmed around on the floor. "Bitch, have you lost your mind!"

I didn't say a word. Just kept pounding away at her until I got tired. She tried to grab anything on me, but the only thing she could get ahold of was my shirt. She pulled on it so hard that she tore it off my body. After that, she bit my arm, then scratched the side of my face. That caused me to fall off of her. And when I did, she scurried into another room. I went after her and was met at her bedroom doorway by a nine millimeter. She aimed it at my head, trying to catch her breath. Her hands trembled as a tear rolled down her face.

"Put your hands on me again, and I will kill you, Kayla! What in the hell are you thinking?"

I wanted to go for the gun, but I already knew how unstable and jealous Evelyn was. She would blow my brains out, and somehow or someway she would make herself look like the victim. Afraid of that gun as I was, I still showed no fear as I told her how I felt about her betrayal.

"How dare you tell Cedric what I told you about Jacoby! You have caused my son great harm, all over a lousy dick that you just can't get enough of. I will never forgive you again, and this time you have really and truly gone too far. I don't even know how you sleep at night, Evelyn! Please tell me how in the hell you can live with yourself. You are the worst of the worst, and damn me for ever considering you my friend!"

Evelyn was breathing real hard, and her chest kept moving in and out. "I don't know what Cedric told you, but I did not tell him about Jacoby. He's playing you, Kayla. Playing you like a fool, and you're too blind to see it. I told Trina all about his plan, but I see that telling you will do no good. You are looking for someone to blame for all of this, and like always, that person is me."

"You're doggone right it is! And if you didn't tell Cedric about Jacoby, then who did? After all, you are the one who is still fucking him, aren't you? I guess you're going to lie about that too."

"I'm not going to lie about it, but I had my reasons. You—"

"Shut up!"

I wanted to break that heifer's neck, but when I moved forward, she squeezed the gun tighter and gave me a warning.

"Think before you make another move. As a matter of fact, turn around and get out of here. If you want to believe Cedric, fine. I have nothing else to say. What I know is, I'm not going to allow you to put your fucking hands on me again."

I was done with Evelyn and Cedric. I hadn't really wanted to come here, but I had to. This was the last straw. Everybody had a breaking point. This was mine. I walked out her door, vowing never to let her back in my life again.

13

Evelyn

Wow. In all the years I had known Kayla, we had never fought like that. She was on a rampage. I was so confused by what Cedric had told her. I hadn't said one word to him, but there he was, lying on me again. I had figured he would do something like this, and when I called to chew him out, he laughed about it.

"You made your bed, so you need to lay in it," he said. "I told you that if you didn't get me the information I wanted, shit was going to start happening, didn't I? My only question to you is, did Kayla beat that ass, or did you beat hers? I would have loved to have been a fly on the wall to see who got the best of who."

"You're truly the devil, Cedric, and this is what I get for dancing with you. It would be so nice if Paula had killed you when she had the chance, and I should go straight to that jailhouse and slap her for not finishing the job."

"Awww, don't be so nasty, sugar pie. You weren't talking all that shit when I had my dick up, and just a few weeks ago, I was the best thing ever. I saved your life and made you a rich woman. According to you, you owed me big-time. Now, all of a sudden, my name is dirt. I'm not worth two cents, and you wish I was dead. That's no way to speak to a man who is on edge right now. And you'd better watch yourself, because I will give you a dose of what I gave your friend earlier."

I hung up on Cedric. He was cuckoo. I didn't know what he said or did to make Kayla believe him, but she should have known better. Why didn't she just come over here and ask me? I would have told her everything, even though I'd have figured that she wouldn't listen to me. I was concerned about

Cedric winning this battle, so after I cleaned myself up and brushed my hair into a sleek ponytail, I called Trina to see if she had spoken to Kayla about our conversation.

"What is it?" she yelled when she picked up her phone. "I'm busy right now. I'll have to call you back!"

She hung up, and that was that. I guessed Kayla must've gotten to her before I did, and they were, once again, on the same team. I threw my hands in the air and then got back to what I was doing before Kayla came barging in here and interrupting me. I was in my office, doing research on the best way to invest my money. I knew that I couldn't keep spending it at the rate I was. If I didn't want it to get away from me, I had to start doing something that would make my money grow. I searched the Internet for a few hours or so. I also set up an appointment with a financial adviser, but I wasn't meeting with him until tomorrow. I then figured that Charles might be able to give me some good advice too, so I called his phone to see if my number was still blocked. After hearing his voice, I knew that I was back in business.

"Please do not hang up this phone," I said.

"You're hardheaded, Evelyn. I told you not to call me."

"I know what you said, but unfortunately, I don't always listen. Can I stop by your office tomorrow to see you? I have certain things on my mind, and I want to ask you some questions about investing the all-mighty dollar."

There was a long pause before he finally responded. "Your time will be limited." After that, he ended the call.

For now, I intended to take whatever time I could get.

The next day, I left the financial adviser's office around two o'clock and then headed to Charles's office. Like always, I made sure I looked good, smelled like a bed of roses, and was at my best. I strutted into his office, looking like a movie star. Heads turned as I asked the receptionist to buzz him, and when he came to the lobby, we immediately stepped into a nearby boardroom that had a round mahogany table with eight chairs surrounding it. Charles sat down in one of the chairs, while I closed the door and stood by it.

"My first question to you is, why are you playing games with me?" I said. "You know I've wanted to see you again."

"I'm too old to play games. And a whole lot of people want to see me. I don't make myself available to everyone. You shouldn't, either."

"Trust me when I say I don't. But I do make exceptions for special people. Don't you?"

He looked at his watch, then shifted his attention back to me. "Don't I what? What did you say?"

Unfortunately, he wasn't paying me much attention, so I spoke louder. "I said, 'I do make exceptions for special people. Don't you?'"

"I don't know of many special people, so no, I don't." He looked at his watch again.

"I guess with you constantly looking at your watch, that means you have somewhere to be and I need to hurry this up. Right?"

"Exactly. We've been in here for almost five minutes, and you still haven't told me the purpose of your ongoing calls."

"You know the purpose of my calls, so stop trying to pretend that you don't. I want to play with your sock again. I really and truly do miss it."

"My sock doesn't have time to play. And what would make you think that you can just snap your fingers and have it available to you?"

"Because I have it like that, that's why."

His brows rose, and he stood up. "There is only one person in this room who has that much power. Breaking news, baby. It's not you. It's me, and I say my sock is busy."

"What makes you think that you're the one with all the power? I'd like to know, and if you can spare five more minutes of your time, please tell me."

"I'll tell you in less than a minute. You're here because you want me. You want to feel me again, and if you do, the only way you're going to get what you want from me is if you get on your knees, crawl over here, and come get it. There's still no guarantee that I will switch the power to you, but you have to start somewhere."

I wasn't sure if he was joking or not, but he was out of his damn mind if he thought I was going to get on my knees and crawl to him for some dick. I hadn't met a man yet who made me want to do that, and even though he was top-notch, that was a no-no.

"You can't be serious, and if you are, I may have a few words for you that you may not like."

He walked toward the door, then opened it. "Words are just words. When you're ready to do as I asked, call me. If not, don't bother."

He left the room and was gone in a flash. It looked as if I wasn't going to be getting any more of the good stuff anytime soon. If I had to crawl for it, I definitely didn't need it.

I stopped at the mall to pick up a customized purse I had ordered, and then I stopped to get some groceries. I thought about Trina not calling me back, and it made me kind of mad that she had cut me off earlier and hadn't even called back to apologize. That was just how things were in my world. I felt as if it was time to start removing more people from my circle. Cedric and Kayla were already gone, and Trina was the next one on my list. Instead of moving to a new town house, what I should've done was moved out of town. I needed to get away from everyone, and not even a seven-day trip would do me much good.

When I got home, I threw a TV dinner in the oven, popped some popcorn, and then prepared to watch a movie on Netflix. I was thirty minutes in when someone knocked on the door. There were only two people who knew where I lived. Either it was Trina or Kayla, obviously here to cause more trouble. I guessed Evelyn hadn't gotten the message from yesterday, when I had told her what I'd do if she didn't cut the crap. I meant every word.

I went to my bedroom to get my gun before going to the door. When I asked who was there, there was no answer. I looked through the peephole, and that was when I saw a big white man standing outside my door.

"Yes?" I said. "I think you're at the wrong door."

The man didn't budge. He knocked again, and when I pulled the door open, he looked me up and down.

"Mr. Washington wants to see you. You have to leave now."

A frown covered my face. I didn't have to do anything, and if Mr. Washington wanted to see me, then he'd better come here. I didn't mean to display an attitude, but what in the hell was going on here?

"Please let Mr. Washington know that I'm in the middle of watching a movie. If he wants to make arrangements to see me, then he needs to call me in advance."

The strong man lifted me and threw me over his shoulder. He reached for my door to shut it, and as I kicked, screamed, and hollered out in my pajamas, he put his hand over my mouth. He tossed me in the back of a black Escalade and then closed the door. He sped off, and when I kept asking him where he was taking me, he ignored me. I tried to unlock the doors, but to no avail. I screamed, "Help!" and banged on the windows, but it did me no good. I finally calmed down a little when I realized that the Escalade was on the way to Charles's office, or to his bunker, I should say.

Several minutes later, the man parked in the garage. When he opened the car door, I slowly got out. Taking the same route as I had with Charles, I found myself deep in the bunker and waiting for the man to get access by entering a code. When the doors opened, I followed him inside. He pointed toward a room.

"In there," he said, then walked away.

I made my way toward the room, and when I opened the door, Charles was there all by his lonesome self. He was sitting on a long sofa, with no clothes on. The room was rather dim, but I could see a bottle of champagne to his left and an array of stronger alcohol to his right.

"You know," he said, "I've been kind of thinking that that one little, measly time we spent together just wasn't enough. And since you keep calling and showing up at my job, I thought that maybe if I give you another chance to show me what you can really do with this, you'll decide to step up to the plate. The thing is, though, my comment from earlier still stands. If you want it, there is only one way to get it."

The whole time Charles spoke, my eyes were focused on his muscle, which rested on his leg. I had dreamed about being with him again, and all kind of thoughts had swum in my head about what I would do if or when I was given another opportunity.

"I have a problem with getting on my knees and crawling to you, and I also have a problem with you sending someone to my home to get me. How do you know where I live, if I haven't told you?"

"I always know where those special people are in my life, and even though I wasn't willing to admit it earlier, you are, indeed, special, Evelyn. Real special."

I didn't want to waste much more time on this, simply because I was so ready to tear into this man. And since he'd met me halfway by sending someone to my home to get me, I figured I could meet him halfway too. I dropped to my knees, and then I slowly crawled over to him. He watched, leaning slightly to his left, with his index finger against his temple. His eyes were narrowed, and his dick grew longer with every inch forward that I took. When I reached him, I maneuvered my body in between his legs. He sat up straight and then lifted my pajama top over my head. I was naked underneath. He cupped my exposed ass with his hands and squeezed it.

"This is it, Evelyn. Make it count for something."

I tried my best to do just that, but once again, I found myself being beaten down and defeated by Charles's dick. He tore me up on that sofa, and as he bent me over the back of it, I was punished for not abiding by his rules.

"No more, baby. You hear me?" he said, spewing his words while grinding way deep in the jungle. "This is it, and the next time I give you some of this, I'm going to make you pay for it."

"Whatever you want," I couldn't help saying, as I was on the verge of an orgasm. "You . . . you keep fucking me this good, and you can have whatever you want."

"I know. That's because I have the power, don't I?"

"Hell, yes, you do. All of it and then some."

He slapped my ass hard and then turned up the heat when he squatted behind me to catch my fluids in his mouth. I damn near jumped over the sofa, but he held my legs to stop me.

"Don't fly away until tomorrow," he said. "For the next few hours, you're mine."

Yes, I was his, and after he was done with me, he called his driver and had him take me home. I was in a daze as I walked through the door and bumped into a wall. My hair was a mess, my whole body was sweating, yet my pussy was so pleased. I lay on the sofa, cuddling my pillow. The only thought that was embedded in my brain was, *Charles*.

14

Trina

My heart started to beat faster, and I was totally speechless, after Keith asked how my trip to New York was. Did he make a mistake, or did he really know I had gone to New York to see Sasha? I had to pretend that I didn't know what he was talking about, because I simply wasn't prepared for this.

"New York? You mean Vegas."

"I didn't stutter. I said New York. You went to New York, not Vegas."

My face fell, cracked, and shattered into a thousand pieces. I opened my mouth, but nothing came out.

"I'ma give you time to think about how to approach this," he said. "Meet me at home."

He walked away and got into his car. After he drove off, I put my things in the trunk, then got inside my car. On the drive home, I was a nervous wreck. I had to tell him the truth about everything, and that included my feelings for Sasha, which had been all washed away. I felt like a complete fool. Keith didn't deserve this. If I lost him over this, I didn't know what I would do.

I parked my car in front of the house, and as soon as I entered, I saw numerous trash bags at the door. I could also tell that many of my belongings were inside the bags, and that made me ill. My stomach hurt so badly. I wanted to throw up, because I couldn't believe that while I was in New York, he was here packing my shit. I turned to address him as he sat, with a twisted face, in the living room.

"What is this?" I said, pointing at the bags. "Are you putting me out of here? Is that what you're doing?"

"You're damn right I am. You don't belong here, Trina, and shame on me for thinking that you did."

Now, that hurt. I swallowed the lump in my throat and did my best to clean this up quickly.

"Okay, look. I'm sorry for not telling you about my trip to New York, but I was sure that you wouldn't understand. Every time I brought it up, it seemed as if you weren't interested in hearing about it. It's like you don't think my work is worthy of being on display, and Sasha was telling me all the things I needed to hear."

"That's bullshit, Trina, and you know it. Don't you stand there and blame me for your lies, especially when you know damn well that I wouldn't have had any problem with you going to New York if it were strictly about business."

"It was about business. That's why I went."

He looked at me as if he wanted to get up from that chair and choke the life out of me. I was holding back on saying much more. I didn't want this situation to turn ugly, and I damn sure didn't want him to put me out of here. I had no money, nor did I have anyplace to go.

"You know what gets me?" he said.

Right then, my phone rang, and it was Kayla. I hurried to answer, just in case I had to go to her for a place to stay. Sounding very unstable, she asked if I had Evelyn's address. I told her I would text it to her, since Keith was starting to get louder in the background. I ended the call and quickly texted the address to her.

"You thought I was that damn stupid," he went on to say. "Do you really believe that? You paraded around here like everything was all good, made your secretive phone calls, thinking that I was asleep. Then you told me every lie that you could possibly tell me to make me think you were going on a trip with Evelyn and Kayla. If that wasn't enough, and through all your deception, you had the audacity to tell me you loved me. What in the hell kind of love is that?"

It was apparent that he knew more than I had thought he knew. I walked into the living room and tried to explain what I'd done.

"I do love you. I have always loved you, but sometimes, it feels as if it's not enough. I'm still a little confused about certain things, and there are times when I do feel attracted to women. I didn't intend to act on those feelings, until Sasha called me out of the blue and started talking about helping me. Our conversations took a turn in another direction, and when she asked me to come see her, I felt as if I should go and work through these feelings inside of me, and also see what I could do to enhance my career."

Keith chuckled, then shook his head. "You sound like a damn fool. And you've been confused since I met you. I asked you to marry me, but you can't, because you're confused. I asked you to have my children, but you can't, because you're confused. I asked you to move in with me, and even though you evidently did, your initial reaction was that you couldn't, because you were confused. You're damn right you are confused. And a confused woman should not be living here with me. So, I have taken it upon myself to pack your bags and allow you to go find yourself. Take some time to figure out who or what you really want. Right now it's apparent that it's not me."

Tears started to well up in my eyes. This shit hurt, especially since I had to admit that it was all on me. I couldn't blame him for anything, not one single thing, and he had every right to be angry with me. I moved closer to him and knelt down in front of him as I attempted to make my case.

"I know what I want. I don't need to go figure out anything else, and I'm staying right here with you. We're going to work through this, Keith. I'm not letting you walk away from me, and that is something I am sure of."

"You weren't so sure when you happily walked your ass out of here and went to New York. I watched you these past few weeks with so much pain and hurt in my heart. Even while we were in New York, I saw the way you and Sasha looked at each other. I noticed how there was something sparking between the two of you, and I get tired of going places with you, and you are looking at women harder than me. From day one, I knew what you were plotting to do. I didn't say one word, because I wanted to know how far you would go. The last thing I want is a sneaky-ass woman. I'm not doing this with you, Trina. I can't ignore how much this is affecting me, and as far as I can see, we have no future."

His words stung. I dropped my head on his lap and started to cry. He knew that it took a lot for me to express my emotions, but I couldn't hold back. I needed Keith more than he ever knew. And while he was so right about my attraction to women, it didn't mean that I didn't want to be with him. It didn't mean that I wasn't in love with him. I loved him with all my heart. It was just that I had needed a little more time to explore what was inside me. Only a little. And after going to see Sasha, I knew that being with another woman was not where I wanted to be.

"Don't say that to me," I sobbed. "We do have a future, and I can't lose you, Keith. I can't, and you've got to understand why I did what I did."

"Thanks for letting me know that you fucked her."

He shoved me away from him and stood up. As he tried to walk away from me, I tugged at his arm. I begged and pleaded for him to give us another chance.

"Please, Keith. I did not have sex with her. I promise you I didn't. You have to believe me."

"Believe you? After you've been doing all of this lying to me? Woman, please. I don't believe shit you say, and you'll say anything just to stay in this house, living confused."

He snatched his arm away from me and started walking. I called after him, but he ignored me and jogged up the stairs. I followed behind him, with so much hurt in my eyes. I was disappointed that I couldn't get through to him. He walked into the bedroom.

"Will you please listen to me?" I said, entering the bedroom. "What do I need to say for you to listen to me?"

"You don't have to say anything. Now, I've been nice and very calm about this. In a minute, I'm going to lose it. I want you out of here, Trina. Nothing else needs to be said."

I stood and looked at him without saying a word. He turned his head to look in another direction. I knew I could get through to him, but he was so stubborn at times.

"Keith, I'm begging you not to end this with me. I will marry you. I will have your children, I will do whatever it is that you need me to do. But what I need is for you to forgive me. Please forgive me, and don't do this to us."

He shook his head in disgust, plopped on the bed, and kept massaging his hands. "Now you want to marry me. Now you want to have my baby. This is some funny shit, Trina, and you must really think I'm a damn fool. Go marry your girlfriend in New York. Go fuck her some more, and just maybe, maybe she can help you with your career."

"I did not fuck her!" I screamed. "All we did was kiss, and that was it! I didn't want to go any further with her, because I wasn't feeling her like that! It was a big mistake, and I'm so, so sorry!"

"Don't raise your goddamned voice at me, especially after you're the one out there, fucking cheating on me! And you didn't make no mistake. What you did was fuck up." His voice went up a notch.

I could tell my time was running out.

"You fucked up, Trina, and you won't get another chance!" He got off the bed and stood directly in front of me. My head was lowered, but he lifted my chin so I could look at him. "You know why you don't get another chance? Because your lies already caused one of your bitches to put a knife in me. Your lies almost killed me before, and your lies had me lying up in a hospital bed for three weeks, not knowing if I would ever be right again. I'm not going to sit here and wait for another one of your bitches to come and attack me. There was something in Sasha's eyes that told me she didn't have all her marbles. You didn't notice that, because you were too busy trying to figure out when and where you wanted to fuck her. But you know what? My thanks go to ole dad once again for confirming everything that I needed to know."

Keith had it all figured out. With Mr. Washington working for the government and somehow or someway being affiliated with the CIA, it wasn't hard for Keith to get ahold of my phone records, bank records, flight information, whatever he needed. I felt horrible, and at this point, there was nothing else I could say.

"Now, Trina," he said, "it's time for you to go."

I tried to swallow the oversize lump in my throat, which felt stuck. It wouldn't go away, so I wiped my tears and then pivoted away from him. My legs were so weak that I could barely walk down the stairs. And when he slammed the bedroom door behind me, my whole body shook. One by one, I carried the trash bags containing my possessions to my car. And just as I grabbed the last bag, my phone rang again. This time, it was Evelyn. I was so frustrated that I put down the bag, answered the call, and yelled at her.

"What is it? I'm busy right now. I'll have to call you back!"

I threw my phone down, almost breaking it. This was not good for me, and I knew it. I looked up the stairs and softly called Keith's name.

"Are you listening to me?" I said. "I hope you are, because all I can say to you right now is that I love you. With all my heart, I truly do."

Unfortunately, there was no response, so I left, taking the last bag out of Keith's house.

I drove around in my car for what seemed like hours, thinking about what had just happened and trying to figure out where I should go. I could probably go stay with either one of my BFF's, but I didn't feel like discussing all that had happened today. Instead, I pulled my car over to the curb and cried my ass off. I wound up falling asleep, and when I woke up, it was morning. I wiped my mouth and then decided to go to Evelyn's place, instead of Kayla's. Jacoby was still living there, and I didn't want to inconvenience two people. I was sure that Evelyn would have her gripes too, but when she opened the door at her place, she had a smile on her face.

"Come in and tell me what happened," she said. "Did Kayla tell you about our fight? I hope you're not mad at me, because that was her fault, not mine."

"I—I don't know what you're talking about. I haven't spoken to Kayla. I'm here because when I got back from New York yesterday, Keith put me out."

"What?" she shouted as I walked inside and plopped down on the sofa. "Why did he put you out? Then again, never mind. I warned you, Trina. I warned you about this, and I told you that going to New York wasn't a good idea."

"I know, and I made one big fool of myself. All Sasha wanted to do was have sex. She lied about people wanting to help me. Nobody wanted to help me. All she wanted to do was help herself."

"Duuuh! You didn't know that? Some women are just as bad as men. You have to be careful out there. You're lucky that she didn't cut yo' ass up and leave you in a trash can somewhere, stinking. I'm surprised that you fell for her games, Trina. This is not like you. What exactly were you thinking?"

"I know. Crazy, right? That's why I'm so mad at myself. Keith is never going to forgive me, and he made that perfectly clear."

"It is a hard pill to swallow, but how did he know you went to New York? And whatever you do, don't go pointing the finger at me. Everybody wants to blame me, and I assure you that I have not spoken to Keith."

"I'm not accusing you of anything. I'm sure he did some little investigations on his own, but I'm also sure that his dad gave him some information too."

"How could his dad give him information about you? He doesn't know you like that, does he?"

I sat silent for a few seconds; then I spoke up. "He knows everything about everything, in case you didn't know that. The man works for the government, and without going into details, he is privy to a lot of information."

Evelyn's eyes bugged out. "Is he really CIA? I knew there was something about him, because don't no regular person have access to underground bunkers."

"Bunkers? What are you talking about?"

"I'm talking about going underground to work and do other great things. It's where he takes me to screw my brains out, and I must say that last night was spectacular."

I shook my head, then massaged it, because it hurt. "Evelyn, you need to stop. I don't think you should make a move in that direction, and I'm just telling you that for your own good."

"Yeah, like I tried to tell you about going to New York. You didn't listen to me, so please don't sit there and tell me what I should or shouldn't do. With that being said, I guess you came here because you need a place to stay. I don't mind you staying here, but even though this place is paid for, I still want you to contribute something. It's out of respect, if you know what I mean."

"That's nice of you, and thanks for letting me stay here. I can honestly say that this is a side of you that I could get used to."

"I'm not all that bad, trust me. Besides, I do get lonely over here sometimes. It'll be good to have you around. But please don't overstay your welcome."

"I won't. As soon as I can figure out a way to get back on my feet, or get back into Keith's house, I'm out."

"I don't know how long that will be, and if he's stubborn like his father is, you could be in for a long wait."

Evelyn and I started to talk about how she had got hooked up with Charles. We also talked about the fight between her and Kayla. I was stunned. I wanted to believe that she was telling the truth, and if I had to put my money on her instead of Cedric, I would. His dirty ass was out to destroy our friendship and everything about us. I wasn't sure if Kayla was aware of that or not, but since Evelyn said she thought Cedric had jumped on Kayla, maybe she was starting to open her eyes.

"I still haven't spoken to her," I said. "I've had a lot going on myself, but I was going to call her. I don't want to suggest that we all get together and talk, but sooner or later, we're going to have to get together and do something about Cedric. He is out of control, and he should be arrested."

"I agree one hundred percent. But Kayla is the one who holds the key. She needs to deal with him fast."

Maybe she would, and if it was true about him putting his hands on her, I was sure that Kayla had something in store for him.

15

Kayla

I had been so drunk that I could barely see straight. All I remembered was stumbling and then falling on the floor and almost hitting my head. Jacoby had said something to me, but I hadn't been able to make out what it was. I hadn't cared. At this point, I didn't care about anything. I hated my life, and I had to figure out a way to escape from it.

What Cedric did to me had left me bitter and angry. It had got me to a point where I wanted to remove him from this earth and this time get it right. With him being gone, Jacoby wouldn't have to worry anymore about going to jail. I wouldn't have to worry anymore, and he would be out of our lives for good. The more I looked at my face in the mirror, the angrier I got. I had to do this, and if it meant jail time for me, so be it. I already felt as if I was living in hell. All the money in the world wasn't enough to take away this pain, and it sure the hell didn't make me happy.

Now, hours later, I crawled on the floor, removing myself from the vomit I lay in. It felt like someone was beating a hammer against my head, so I sluggishly walked toward the bathroom to take some aspirin. Afterward, I removed my soiled clothes, then took a hot shower. Once I was done, I changed into some clean clothes and made my way back into the living room area to clean up my mess. As I was on my knees, scrubbing the carpet with a towel, Jacoby walked up to me.

"What happened to your face?" he said. "How did it get like that?"

"Do you have to ask? I was so drunk that I can't remember. All I know is I had a hard fall last night and I hurt myself."

"Did you go see Cedric?"

Yet again, I found myself lying, because I didn't want Jacoby to know that Cedric had done this to me. The last thing I needed was for him to go over to Cedric's place. I was sure—no, positive—that Cedric would do the same thing to Jacoby as he had done to me and Justin.

"No. I called him, but he refused to talk to me. I guess when things settle down, we'll talk."

"Or I'll go talk to him myself."

"No!" I shouted, then calmed my voice. "I don't want you to do that now. You saw how Cedric acted the other day. He knows something, and I fear that he may hurt you."

"Yeah, well, I'm not afraid of him anymore. He and I need to have a talk, and it's time that you moved out of the way and let that happen."

I was getting frustrated with Jacoby. He just didn't know when to listen. If he thought for one minute that Cedric was going to embrace him with open arms, he was sadly mistaken. That simply wasn't going to happen.

I threw the dirty towel on the carpet, then looked at him. "I've been in the way because I'm your mother, and you're all that I have. I can't just sit back and do nothing, Jacoby. I do hope that you understand that, and if you do, please listen to me and forget about going to see Cedric."

"I do understand, but you're losing yourself. Look at you, Mama. You're a mess. I get tired of coming in here almost every night and seeing you passed out on the floor and laying in your vomit. When are you going to stop this?"

I stood up and put my hands on my hips. "If you get tired of coming in here and seeing me like this every night, then your solution is simple. Don't come home. If it's that bad, Jacoby, you really don't have to be here."

"I agree. That's why I'm moving in with Adrianne and her mother for a while. I get way more peace there than I do here."

He had just pissed me off without even knowing it. Sometimes kids said the wrong things when they should have just kept their mouths shut.

"Fine, Jacoby. Go ahead and run your tail to your girl-friend's house. They have the perfect life over there, and you'll fit right in."

He shrugged his shoulders, then walked away from me. Minutes later, he came back downstairs. I was in the kitchen, drinking water. A heavy duffel bag was on his shoulder, and a pair of his tennis shoes was in his hands.

"I'll check in with you later," he said.

I rolled my eyes and tried my best not to show how hurt I was. Funny how when he needed me, I was there for him. But when I needed him, he walked.

"Don't bother, Jacoby. No need to bother."

He walked away, and when the door slammed, I was crushed. I went right over to the liquor cabinet and snatched a whole bottle of whiskey from the shelf. I opened it, and as I started to guzzle it down, the liquid ran down my chin and spilled all over my clothes. I gagged and then threw the bottle so hard that it cracked on my kitchen floor. Shards of glass were everywhere.

I went into the living room and fell back on the sofa, wondering how in the hell a woman like me had got here. The first thing that came into my head was, *Lies*. Maybe, just maybe, if I had told Cedric the truth about Jacoby not being his son, we wouldn't even be here. Maybe if I had told him about Jacoby trying to kill him, we wouldn't even be here. While I didn't take responsibility for him cheating on me, I had to know that some of this was on me too. Still, it was too late to fix it. I had helped to create that monster. I sat for a while, thinking about how to disable it. I got a little help when Cedric called with some more of what he called "breaking news."

"I slept on what happened over here, and I called to say I'm sorry. Sorry for not taking action sooner. Before the end of the week, *your* son will be arrested. I'm gathering all the information Evelyn and Paula have provided me with. Once I have my ducks in a row, lives will change."

He hung up, leaving it right there. That was the last straw. I stumbled into my bedroom, changed my wet shirt, which reeked of alcohol, and then reached for the gun underneath my bed. In that moment, I was so mad at Paula for not doing away with Cedric when she had the chance to. *Damn her*. Why did she leave it up to me to finish the job? I had to be the one to finish this, and no matter what, I would get it right.

I stood up straight, with no fear in me whatsoever. I tucked the gun in my purse, then took one last swig of alcohol from a bottle in the liquor cabinet before heading out the door. I rushed to get into my car and headed to Cedric's place, which was only several minutes away. I was speeding so fast through my neighborhood that I could hear my tires making a whooshing sound. And just as I was about to make a right onto the main street, I saw a little girl run into the street to go after her ball.

I gasped, then slammed on the brakes. My tires screeched loudly, and my whole body jerked forward. I looked up and saw that the front of my car was within inches—only inches— of the little girl's body. She cried loudly as her mother charged out into the street and let me have it. With her daughter clinging to her, she pounded the hood of my car with her fists, overcome by much rage and anger.

"You stupid bitch!" she yelled. "Didn't you see her? Why in the hell were you driving so fast! Slow the hell down! Nothing is that damn important where you have to almost kill my freaking child!"

She was so right. I dropped my head on the steering wheel and broke down. This was definitely God's way of trying to save me. He had put a little girl in my way to stop me. I needed help, and I needed it now.

16

Evelyn

In my world, everything seemed to be going well. My financial adviser had shared some good ideas with me about increasing my wealth, and I had taken heed of everything he said. I had left an enormous amount of money in the bank, and I had also given Trina a few thousand dollars to help get her back on her feet. She was a total mess. I had never seen her this emotional, and it was kind of strange to see her crying all the time. I wanted her and Keith to work things out, and even though he would never, ever listen to me, I decided to stop by his house and tell him exactly what Trina had been going through. Maybe he would understand and decide to give her another chance.

I arrived at Keith's house at a little after four that afternoon. Lord knows, I hated the cold weather, and it was starting to turn cold. A gusty wind blew my hair all over my head as I headed up the sidewalk to his front door, and I could see just a little snow starting to fall. This was crazy because it was only early October. Winter hadn't officially arrived yet, but St. Louis weather was always tricky like that.

I rang the doorbell, and minutes later, through the window I could see Keith coming down the stairs in jeans and a T-shirt. Unfortunately for Trina, a female trailed right behind him. She looked okay, but quite frankly, she didn't have anything on Trina. I wasn't sure who she was, but when he opened the door, she made an exit.

"Thanks, Keith," she said. "You are totally the bomb. I'll keep in mind what you said."

"You do that, and I'll see you again tomorrow."

The nappy-headed bitch didn't even speak to me. Just walked right past me as if I wasn't even standing there. I swore that some people were just so rude. Either way, I flashed a smile at Keith, but his expression was flat.

"Why are you here, Evelyn?"

"Trina is at my place, and I need to talk to you about her. May I come in?"

"Talking to me about Trina will do you no good. I don't want you to waste your time."

"Aw, come on, Keith. People get cheated on all the time, and they learn to forgive. You know Trina loves you. She just made a mistake, and the last time I checked, we all make them."

"Yeah, we do. And you should know all about those mistakes, Evelyn. Especially since you keep on making them. I honestly can't wait until you get yours. You are so deserving of all that you have coming, and you're too blind to see that an earthquake is coming your way. The last thing you need to concern yourself with is my relationship with Trina. What you need to concern yourself with is your relationship with my father. I hear it's been fun, but all good things do come to an end."

I guessed Trina must have told him about me seeing his father, even though she'd said she wouldn't. I suspected that it would just be a matter of time before I heard from his mother, or maybe he hadn't said anything to her yet. He was probably on Team Dad, and this was their little secret too.

"I am having a lot of fun with him, and during the process, I am still concerned about my friend. Don't let a good woman pass you by, Keith. All she did was kiss the darn girl and exchange a few feels with her. You act like she went all the way with her. And when it comes to lies, we have all had to fib a little. You're not perfect, and you shouldn't expect her to be perfect, either."

"Evelyn, talking to you is a waste of time. I have work to do, so good-bye."

"Yeah, whatever. But what am I supposed to tell Trina in the meantime? I at least want to give her some hope. Is there anything you would like for me to say to her?"

He stroked his chin, as if he was in thought, then snapped his fingers. "As a matter of fact, there is. I've been doing a lot of thinking over these past few days, thinking about what I would say to her if I saw her. That would be . . . to go to hell. You can go there too."

Well, damn, I thought when he slammed the door in my face. Through the window I saw him jog back up the stairs. *Vicious and nasty.* He was beyond mad at Trina. I hadn't known he was that serious. If Trina was ever going to call this place home again, she had her work cut out for her.

I returned home, only to find Trina weeping as she lay in the guest bedroom. I guessed when you realized how badly you had fucked up, it was a hard pill to swallow. I sat next to her on the bed, then pulled her to me.

"Stop this, okay?" I said. "I know it hurts, but you have to know that what is meant to be will be. Keith isn't the only good man out there, and you are not a bad person. Still a little confused, though." I laughed. "But certainly not a bad person. Stop beating yourself up about what you did."

Trina dabbed her eyes with a tissue and then sat up straight. "I miss him," she said. "I miss him so much, Evelyn. I don't know what I'm going to say or do to get him back."

I didn't want to go there, but I had to get Trina up and out of this bed and energized to get her man back.

"Well, you won't get him back by staying in bed all day, crying. If you don't get up, there are plenty of women out there, ready to make a move. I ran into one chick as I went by his house today to talk to him. I was only trying to help, but there was someone else there with him."

Trina cocked her head back. "Who?" she said. "What did she look like?"

"She was kind of tall, had short hair and some really wide hips. She mentioned something about him helping her, and he told her that he would see her again tomorrow."

"That must have been Latisha. She comes by sometimes so that he can help her with her paintings. I have never trusted that hoochie, though, and if she knows I'm out of the picture, she will definitely do whatever to slide right in."

"Hell, who wouldn't? On a scale from one to ten, it ain't like Keith a five. That man is ten all the way, and I'm not just talking about his looks."

"Ten and then some," Trina said softly. "It's funny how you see a clear picture when you've broken up with somebody. All I can think about is where I went wrong."

"Yes, wrong, wrong, wrong. And you were also wrong for telling Keith about me and his father. I wanted you to do so, but I didn't expect for Keith to mention it today."

Trina had a puzzled look on her face. "He knows? I didn't say one word to him about you messing with his father. I was going to, but I decided against it."

Now we both looked puzzled. "If he does know, who told him?" I said. "I just can't see his father telling him anything like that, especially since he made it clear that I'd better not open my mouth."

"I don't know. I can't see him telling Keith, either."

I got off the bed and headed to the door. "The only way to find out is for me to call Mr. Washington and see who's been talking."

I went into the kitchen to get my purse and cell phone. When I punched in his number, he answered on the third ring. I didn't even get a chance to say hello.

"Evelyn, this is the last call you will ever make to me. Good-bye."

"But wait!" I shouted. "Why did you tell Keith about us? You know he knows, don't you? I'm just trying to warn you."

The call ended. I called back but didn't get through, and after I tried several more times to reach him, with no success, I spoke with the operator, who said the phone number had been disconnected. I couldn't believe it had been disconnected that fast. I was so curious, and I needed some answers. He could stop me from calling him, but he couldn't stop me from being face-to-face with him. I rushed to the guest bedroom and told Trina I was leaving.

"Where are you going?" she said.

"I'll be right back. I need to go see someone."

"Who? Mr. Washington?"

"Yes."

"I want to go. I'll stay in the car or whatever, but I just need to get out of here."

I was hesitant. After all, I didn't want Trina around, just in case he wanted me to crawl for him again. But I also knew that Charles was a late-night lover. He liked to wait until business hours were over to do his dirt. Then again, so did I.

"Come on, Trina. Hurry up and put on some clothes. I'll wait for you in the car."

Trina got out of the bed, and I went to my car. I even called Charles's phone one more time, just to be sure that it was disconnected. It was.

Minutes later, Trina came outside, looking like a slouchy bum in an oversized shirt and pants. It was a good thing that we weren't going to see Keith, with her looking like that. And wherever we ultimately wound up going, I had to be sure that she stayed in the car.

I drove to Charles's office, and after I parked, I told Trina that I would be right back. She yawned, then laid her head back on the headrest.

"Don't be too long. And after we leave here, can we please go get something to eat? I'm hungry."

"Me too, but be patient. I'll be back as soon as I can."

I closed the car door and then went inside the building. Something about this day felt really strange to me, and when I got off the elevator, went up to the receptionist, and asked to speak with Charles, she told me he didn't work there.

"Excuse me," I said to the receptionist, whom I had never seen before today. "I know he works here. I've come here to see him many times before."

"I'm sorry, ma'am. You must have the wrong floor. There is no Charles Washington in this office."

"Do you mind if I go back to the office where I normally meet him at? I can go get him for you. I think that since you're new, you don't know who he is."

"No, I've been working here for almost four years. I was on vacation for a few weeks, but I can assure you that no Mr. Charles Washington has ever worked here."

I scratched my head, and a look of anger washed over my face. I wasn't sure if I would get myself in trouble or not, but I rushed away from the desk and stormed down the hallway. I could see Charles's office from a distance, and as the receptionist called after me, I kept going. I quickly opened the door and stepped inside the room. There were four white men in suits standing in the office, talking business. Three were sitting in chairs, while the other one was standing and pointing to a diagram on the wall.

"May I help you?" said the one who was standing.

"I—I'm looking for Mr. Charles Washington. This is his office, isn't it? Is he here?"

"Charles who?" the man asked, with a disturbing look on his face. "No, this is my office, and I don't know him."

I thought I was going crazy. I walked out the door, and when I slowly walked past the receptionist, with a bewildered look on my face, I barely heard what she said.

"Leave now, or I'll call security."

I walked to the elevator, feeling numb. What in the hell was going on? Surely, I was at the right building and on the right floor. There was no way that they didn't know Charles. Instead of going back to the car, I got on the elevator and hit the button for the lower level, where the bunker was located. But as I made my exit, I discovered that there was a wall to my left and a wall to my right. Short hallways were on both sides, but that was it. I could go no farther, and in that moment, I truly felt as if I had lost my mind. Just to confirm that I hadn't, I went back to the car to question Trina.

"Something really strange just happened in there," I told her after I climbed in the front seat. I was still in awe. "They told me Charles doesn't work here. I went to his office, and he wasn't there."

"Did he quit or something? Maybe he quit."

"No. The receptionist told me he has never worked there. That was a total lie, and you know it. You yourself said that you and Keith brought him something here before, didn't you?"

"Yes, we did. He used to work here, and whoever told you he didn't was lying."

"Yeah, there seems to be a lot of that going on lately. And all I can say is, something doesn't feel right, Trina. All of a sudden Keith knows about me and his father, but you didn't tell him. Not to mention that he didn't tell you he knew. I don't like the feeling of this, and I'm starting to feel real weird."

"I agree that something isn't adding up, but it could be that Charles just doesn't want to have anything else to do with you. Men get like that, and it may be to the point where he's trying to protect his marriage. I'm sure you call and bug him a lot, Evelyn. I know how you are, and you can be quite demanding."

"Yeah, whatever, but it still doesn't explain the whole bunker thing. That bunker in the basement is gone. It has a whole new look down there. You can go see for yourself."

"I've never seen this bunker you're talking about, but I do know that Mr. Washington has worked here before. I'll let you figure out what is going on, and I'm sure the two of you will be in touch soon."

I started the car, with a puzzled look locked on my face. I wasn't so sure that Trina believed everything I'd said, but I had to be clear that I wasn't crazy. "You don't think I'm crazy, do you, Trina?"

"I'm not saying that you are crazy, Evelyn. What I've said all along is that you shouldn't be messing with Mr. Washington. He's a real private man, and to be honest with you, whenever I've been around him, it has kind of scared me. He's too darn observant. Looks as if he's studying people all the time and taking notes in his head. He makes me nervous, even though he is a nice man. I honestly do not know if he's in some way connected with the CIA or not. Keith has never confirmed that either way. But I do know that he has a lot of power and influence in our city. That, I can confirm."

I thought back to when Charles got pulled over by the police. Shit was starting to make sense to me, and I couldn't help but wonder how this was going to unfold.

17

Trina

Evelyn and I ate dinner together at a restaurant, but the whole time she appeared to be in a daze. She picked at her salad and kept staring off into space. I waved my hand in front of her face, in hopes that she would snap out of it.

"Come back, come back from wherever you are," I said.

She shot back a fake smile. "I'm sorry. I can't help myself. My thoughts are all over the place right now."

"They should be. And I hope you're coming to the conclusion, like I have, that you shouldn't have gone there with Mr. Washington."

"I don't know how I feel about it right now. The outcome of this has yet to be seen. I'm sure I'll hear from him, and whenever I do, he's going to get an earful."

Evelyn told me about the white man coming to her door and whisking her away to the bunker. I myself was starting to feel not so good about this. Was there a chance that Evelyn was lying? Yes, Mr. Washington did work in the building we had gone to. But something wasn't adding up. All this talk about bunkers, limos, and overly big dicks wasn't quite clicking with me. Evelyn's mother had a history of mental illness. A tiny part of me was starting to think that it had rubbed off. I didn't dare say that to her.

By nine o'clock that night, we were done eating and on our way back home. When we got back to her place, Evelyn parked her car, and then she popped the trunk.

"I put a trash bag in my trunk earlier," she said, in a somber mood. "I forgot to take it to the Dumpster, so I'm taking it now. Here are my keys to let yourself in."

"I'll take the trash to the Dumpster. Go inside and lie down. You look like you could use some rest."

She released a deep sigh. "Yes, I could. Thanks, Trina. I really appreciate it."

She walked toward her town house, and with the trash bag in hand, I made my way to the Dumpster, thinking about my BFF's. We were seriously going through some things. But we always had a problem rallying around each other for support. Either Kayla was mad at me or at Evelyn. Or she was mad at both of us, or I was in no mood to be around them. We had to do better than this, and even though I didn't want to force anything on either of them, we had to try again to work things out. I wasn't giving up on my friends, and the truth of the matter was this: we were all we had.

I dumped the trash and then made my way back to Evelyn's town house. From a short distance away, I heard something like moaning going on. I thought someone was having sex in a car, until I approached Evelyn's door. When I opened it, there she was on the hallway floor, with her skirt flipped up and Cedric on top of her. His hand was clamped over her mouth, and she was squirming around on the floor, moaning something and trying to get away from him. He punched her in the stomach to try to get her to be still.

"You can't run from me, bitch! I know your every move, and I told you there would be consequences if you didn't do what I told you to do!" Cedric yelled.

I was shocked by what I saw. I had never witnessed Cedric in action like this, and I moved a little closer to make sure it was him. He didn't see me, but I was positive that Evelyn did. Her watery eyes, with mascara running from them, shifted to me. That was what made him turn around. Without saying one word, I picked up one of Evelyn's statues on a shelf in the hallway and slammed it against his head. The hard blow was enough to knock him out cold, and it damn sure caused him to get off of her. She crawled backward and then got up off the floor and rushed to her bedroom.

Cedric got up slowly, holding his head. His eyes fluttered a few times, and he peered at me with a devilish look in his eyes. "I . . . I've been waiting on a piece of you for a long time too," he said softly, then looked at the blood on his trembling fingers. Thick blood started to run slowly down the side of his face, and his eyes fluttered again. He looked dizzy, as if he was seconds away from collapsing and dying right in front of me.

Did I hit him that hard? I wondered. I started to get real, real nervous, and even more so when Evelyn appeared in the hallway with a gun in her hand.

"Get out, Cedric! And don't you ever bring your ass back here again!" she shouted.

He stumbled as he turned around and looked at her, and when they made eye contact, she moved closer and fired one bullet into his chest. His blood splattered all over her clothes. He fell forward, and as he leaned on her, she pumped two more bullets into his stomach. She growled, as if doing this hurt her more than the bullets hurt him.

"Die, bastard! Die!" she said through gritted teeth.

I was numb all over. Couldn't move, didn't breathe. Didn't take one step. Just stood there and watched Cedric's body hit the floor like a bloody piece of meat. My body trembled as I watched Evelyn. It was as if she were another person when that gun was in her hand. After she snapped out of it and began to fall apart, she dropped the gun and fell beside Cedric.

"OMG, Trina! What did I just do? Come help me with him. We've got to save him!" She spoke in a panic. As she struggled to turn Cedric's body over, it was obvious that he was, indeed, dead. "Help me!" Evelyn cried out. "What did I *do*?"

I stared at the huge gash on his head, knowing that my blow had probably mortally wounded him and that he would have died even if Evelyn hadn't shot him. I wasn't sure if Evelyn knew it too, until she looked at the gash and covered her mouth. She looked at me with wide eyes.

"Did this gash . . . how . . . what?" She was crying so hard, she could barely get out the words.

I finally snapped out of my trance and rushed over to them. "Should we call the police?" I blurted, all the while thinking about my situation and about going to jail. This was so fucked up. I couldn't believe how people's lives could change in an instant. I began to cry.

Evelyn ran her bloody fingers through her hair, pulling it back. "Uh, let me think. Let me think. Let me think about this." She looked at Cedric again, which caused her to cry harder. "Oh, my, God! What did we do to him, and what should we do?"

Both of us couldn't stop the tears. We were in a severe panic, and we definitely knew that someone had heard those gunshots.

"We have to get out of here," I said. "Let's get out of here and go . . . go somewhere and think. I can't stay in here with his body lying there like that." I slowly backed away from Cedric's body, and so did Evelyn.

"But we, we can't leave him here like this, can we?" she screamed. "Trina, damn it! We have to call the police!"

"Stop screaming, would you? We *will* call them, just not right now. Right now we need to think hard and come up with the best story that will help to clear us. This isn't good, Evelyn. Trust me when I say this isn't good."

She clawed at her chest and kept looking at Cedric's body. "I know this isn't good, but what if he's still alive? We need to call an ambulance and see if they can get here and save him."

I didn't know what Evelyn was thinking, but with his eyes opened wide like that, it was clear that Cedric was dead. He was gone, and there was no bringing him back this time.

"Calling an ambulance won't save him. And calling the police won't save us. We've got to lock up your place and go."

Finally, Evelyn agreed. She tiptoed over Cedric's body, washed her hands in the kitchen, and then snatched up a jacket to cover her bloody clothes. Hoping that no one saw us, after Evelyn locked the front door, we ran to my car.

"Where are we going?" she said.

"To Kayla's place. We've got to go there."

Evelyn seemed reluctant, and while we were in the car, she told me that she thought going to Kayla's was a bad idea. "Trina, Kayla would love to see me behind bars. I know she would, and I don't think we should go there."

"What makes you think that you'll be the one locked up? I think it was my blow that ultimately killed him. He was mortally wounded before you put those bullets into him."

She was quiet for a few minutes, as if she was pondering something. "You don't know that for sure. And even if you were the one who killed him, you can't go to jail. I won't let you do it. I won't let you take the blame."

I swallowed hard, thinking about my situation again. "I don't have a choice. What choice do I have?"

"We *do* have a choice, and the last thing you're going to do is have that baby in jail. He or she will need you, Trina. You can't be a mother to your child if you're in prison."

I didn't know how Evelyn knew I was pregnant, because I hadn't told anyone. She must have seen the pregnancy test in the trash bag.

"Yes, I know," she said. "I saw the pregnancy test. We have to figure out a way to spin this, and we have to do it real fast."

I couldn't even think straight. It was in our best interest to go somewhere and chill for a while. I couldn't think of a better place than Kayla's. I tried to convince Evelyn to go there with me.

"We have so much to explain to her. She doesn't know what you told me about Cedric, does she?" I said.

"I tried to tell her, but she didn't listen. If she didn't listen then, she won't listen now."

"Please, just follow my lead on this. Just this one time, Evelyn, do it."

Evelyn's legs kept shaking, and she didn't say another word. When we got to Kayla's place, she remained in the car.

"I'm not going in there, because all she'll want to do is fight me," she said. "I'm not in the mood for it, so I'm staying right here. You can go in there and talk to her."

"No, Evelyn, we both need to go inside. Please do this. I can't think of a better time for us to come together and figure out what to do."

Evelyn finally listened to me and went to Kayla's door with me. We knocked several times, and almost five minutes later, Kayla opened the door. She appeared calm, but there was no smile whatsoever on her face, especially as she looked at Evelyn.

"Trina, I told you not to do this," she said. "Don't bring her over here. All I want right now is peace."

"I do too, but . . . but something just happened that I think you need to know about. It's important, Kayla. I wouldn't be here like this if it wasn't."

Kayla let us inside, and when she turned on the light in the foyer, she finally saw some of the bloodstains on our clothes, especially on Evelyn's. Kayla covered her mouth, then stepped back.

"What happened?" she said in a high-pitched tone. "Where did all this blood come from?"

"Cedric," I didn't hesitate to say. "Cedric is dead."

Kayla's eyes bugged out. She took a few more steps back. "How . . . ? When? And who—"

"I'll tell you all about it, but I want you to come with us," I said. "Please come with us so that I can explain everything to you."

This time, it wasn't Evelyn who was hesitant. It was Kayla. "I'm not going anywhere. Tell me what is going on right now!"

Tears were on the brink of falling from her eyes. This was one gut-wrenching moment, but I needed Kayla, as well as Evelyn, to cooperate.

"Evelyn and I are going to be in big trouble," I said. "Cedric made us do this. He was like an out-of-control madman who couldn't be stopped. If you had seen him, you would know what I mean. We had to do something to stop him."

Something snapped Kayla out of her resistance mode. She opened the front door, then wiped away a tear that had fallen down her face. "I know what you mean, but take me to him," she said. "Tell me what happened in the car and take me to him."

I didn't want to go back there and stare at him again. But when I asked Kayla if we could just chill at her place for a few hours, she wasn't down with it.

"No, Trina. Let's go now. I want to see him. Staying here won't do us any good."

I didn't want to argue with Kayla, and neither did Evelyn. We all got in the car, and as I took a circuitous route back to Evelyn's place, just to waste more time, we gave Kayla more details about what had happened before and after this incident. I couldn't remember some of the missing pieces, so Evelyn spoke up and told Kayla everything. She spilled her guts about Cedric coming to the hospital, and about him forcing himself on her. She mentioned his threatening phone calls and her suspicions that he was trying to destroy our friendship. She also gave specific details about what had just happened at her town house. She made it seem as if her shooting him had killed him. I then told Kayla that I thought his death was due to what I'd done. Kayla was speechless the whole time we spoke.

There was a long silence before Kayla mentioned what Cedric had done to her. "I didn't know who he was," she said tearfully. "I never thought he would do me like that, and I'm still in shock about it."

Not only was she in shock then, but she was in complete and utter shock when she walked through the door of Evelyn's town house and saw Cedric's dead body lying there. At a slow pace, Kayla walked up to him and then fell to her knees.

"No, no, no!" she cried out. "How dare you do this! How dare you cause me so much pain and suffering and then lay your ass there and die!" She pounded his chest with her fists, causing it to rise a little.

I had no idea what was going through her head right now. She and Cedric had a long history together, and they had been together since college. As much as Kayla might have despised him, I was sure that it was hard on her to see him lying there like this. It was hard on all of us, and when Evelyn walked up to Kayla, she lost it.

"I am so sorry, my dear friend," Evelyn said softly. "I didn't want to kill him, but I had to. I had to do it, Kayla, and you just don't understand what kind of man Cedric was. Maybe with you he was different. With me, he wasn't. He treated me like shit, and I had my own reasons for accepting it. I wish I could bring him back. Lord knows, I wish I could, but I . . . I'm sorry."

Kayla didn't respond to Evelyn. She laid her head on Cedric's bloody chest, sobbing uncontrollably. All we could hear was her cries. Other than that, the room was silent. There was something in the air that sent chills all over my body. I wasn't sure if Evelyn or Kayla felt it, but I surely did.

I stood there without moving, looked at my BFF's, who were torn beyond repair, and couldn't find the right words to say to either one of them. I just allowed them all the time and space they needed to get through this very frightening moment.

"What are we going to do?" Kayla finally said, with tears streaming down her face, as she looked from Evelyn to me. "We can't leave him lying here like this."

I stepped closer, but my legs were so weak that I could barely stand. "I guess we need to call the police. But what are we going to say?"

Evelyn sucked in a deep breath, then released it. "We're going to tell them that it was self-defense and that I shot him."

"But what about the gash on his head?" I questioned. "This doesn't look good, and I doubt that the police will believe it was self-defense."

Kayla slowly stood and started to wipe the tears from her face. "Trina is right. They're not going to buy that. I hate to say this, but I think we may need to take his body somewhere and dump it."

Evelyn's eyes bugged out. "Are you out of your mind!" she shouted. "We can't do that. Someone may see us, and if his body is ever found, we could all be facing jail time."

I agreed with Evelyn. "I don't like the idea of removing his body from here and dumping it somewhere. I do think we need to call the police, and we need to be on the same page when we tell them what happened."

"You're right," Evelyn said. "And I think it would be wise for us to tell the cops that when you came into the room, Cedric was on top of me, choking me. He got distracted when he saw you, and that's when I was able to reach for the statue and hit him across the head. He fell to the side, and I rushed into the bedroom to get the gun. He continued to charge at me, so I shot him. That's not completely the truth, but it's close enough to it."

I moved my head from side to side, refusing to put all the blame on Evelyn. "We've got to come up with something else. You know darn well that I'm not going to let you take the fall for this. Can't we just say that we came into the house together, we thought he was an intruder, and I hit him across the head? Then you went to get the gun, and without knowing who he was, you shot him?"

"That makes no sense," Kayla noted. "The police would never believe that, but they may believe that I did it. I took pictures of what Cedric did to me. I could say that I came here to confront him about being with Evelyn and we got into a fight. I could put my fingerprints on the gun and say that I shot my ex-husband, who had been threatening me and had become very abusive toward me after our divorce."

"No, no, no!" Evelyn shouted. "Stop this, okay? My story makes the most sense, and it's closest to the truth. I know the police will probably arrest me, but I'm sure they'll set a bond and I'll be released. I can get a lawyer who can defend me and help me explain why I did what I did. This may not be as difficult as it seems, as long as we all agree to stick to the exact same story. Now, are y'all with me on this or not?"

I looked at Kayla, who seemed to be still on the fence, like me. We didn't have many choices, so for now I decided to go with the flow.

"I don't like it, but I'm with it," I said.

Evelyn turned to Kayla. "What about you, Kayla? Are you with me on this or not?"

Kayla remained silent for at least a minute. She then walked up to Evelyn and gave her a hug. "I don't know what the outcome will be, but I do know that we allowed Cedric to cause a lot of damage in our lives. I hope and pray that this is the right thing to do, and that we will be able to finally move on from this. So, yes, I'm with it too."

Evelyn nodded and swallowed hard as she backed away from Kayla. She took a deep breath before removing her cell phone from her purse and dialing. Within seconds, she went into panic mode and yelled into the phone.

"Hello! Can you please send an ambulance to my apartment! I—I just shot a man who tried to kill me! Hurry, please!"

Evelyn provided the 911 operator with her address, then ended the call. We looked at each other with fear in our eyes. Kayla turned her head to glance at Cedric, and then she started to ramble on and on about his threats and her attempt to go kill him one day. Like me, she was still plotting other options in her head before the police got there.

"I thought that the two of you were on board with me," Evelyn said, with a look of frustration on her face. "We're running out of time. What must I say or do to convince y'all that this is the only real choice that we have? Dumping his body won't work, lying about a fight between Kayla and Cedric won't work, and admitting that Trina struck him on the head will make it look like she and I were out to get him. I know the two of you still have trust issues with me, but this is one time when I'm asking for both of you to follow my lead. Please listen and promise me that we're in this together."

Kayla and I had to make Evelyn that promise. I reached out for their hands, and as we stood in a close circle, we began to pray for guidance. Sirens could be heard in the background, and when we opened our eyes, we looked at each other again.

"Showtime, ladies," Evelyn said. "Let's do this."

Minutes later, numerous police officers swarmed the place. To say that all three of us were nervous as hell would be an understatement.

18

Kayla

As Cedric's body was taken away in a body bag, I was numb. I had flashbacks of when I first met him; of when we were at the hospital, waiting for Jacoby to be born; of when we purchased our new home; and of just the other day, when he beat the crap out of me. So much was going through me now that I couldn't even explain it. I just couldn't explain it. It was as if I was having an out-of-body experience. This all felt like a dream, and in a matter of minutes, I would wake up, feeling a little better. But that didn't happen. This was my reality. Cedric was dead, and they had just put his dead body in the back of a van.

Just like the last time when Paula tried to kill Cedric, people were standing outside, trying to figure out what had happened. Crime-scene tape surrounded the area. Many police officers were walking around, asking questions, and it just so happened that the same evil officer who had been there when Paula Daniels attempted to kill Cedric was there again. But just like the last time, I wasn't guilty. This time, Evelyn and Trina were, but I was hopeful that our story would hold up.

I totally understood how Evelyn felt, and neither of us wanted Trina to get arrested. She had done too much for us. And to be honest, after all that had happened, I didn't want either one of them to go down. Before the police had arrived, I'd told Evelyn and Trina about my plan to shoot Cedric that day. They'd been in awe by what had stopped me, and once again, we had agreed that Evelyn's story was the most believable.

A moment ago she had finished telling two officers how everything had supposedly gone down. Now the officers addressed me and Trina. Trina vouched for her, and so did I. I even lied, saying that I had entered the apartment and had witnessed Cedric charging toward her.

"So you didn't see Mr. Thompson attack her in any way?" one of the officers questioned, with a notepad in his hand, as he looked at me.

"What I saw was my ex-husband rushing toward her with his fist in the air. I didn't see the initial confrontation, but I can assure you that he was in a rage. She had to do whatever she could to stop him," I said.

The two officers looked at each other, then back at us. We all displayed much attitude, because, as we had expected, they were giving us a difficult time.

"Where were the three of you coming from again?" the other officer asked.

Trina quickly spoke up. "Evelyn and I had dinner earlier. We asked Kayla to meet us here. She arrived shortly after we did."

"And the only reason you didn't enter the home at the same time as your friend was that you dumped trash in the Dumpster, correct?" asked the first officer.

Trina nodded. "Right. After putting the trash bag in the Dumpster, I came inside and saw Mr. Thompson choking my friend. I yelled for him to get off of her, and that's when he turned around and saw me standing in the doorway."

"Sure. What was in the trash that you took to the Dumpster?" asked the second officer.

Displaying a frown, Evelyn crossed her arms and quickly spoke up. "Does that really matter? I put one small trash bag in the trunk before we left earlier. I forgot to put it in the Dumpster. If you would like to go to the Dumpster and sift through my tampons, dinner from yesterday, and Diet Pepsi cans, feel free."

The officers were being real jerks. One of them made Evelyn take him to the Dumpster to show him the bag Trina had dumped. Trina and I continued to get hit with several more questions, but, finally, within the hour, the officers wrapped up the questioning.

With sadness in our eyes, we watched a police officer cuff Evelyn's hands behind her back. Trina was standing closer to Evelyn than I was, and filled with emotions, she reached out to Evelyn, grabbing her tightly around the neck.

"I'll be okay," Evelyn said, unable to hug Trina back. "Stop all of this, 'cause I assure you that everything will be fine."

Evelyn had her game face on, but I wasn't so sure that she would be okay. One thing that I did know was that if it weren't for what she and Trina had done, Jacoby could be on his way to jail. Cedric had made that quite clear, and I had certainly taken his word for it.

With that on my mind, I walked up to Evelyn and reached out for her too. Trina had backed away, and I was surprised that the officers didn't separate us from each other. While hugging Evelyn, I leaned in and whispered close to her ear. "We're going to do everything in our power to see that you get released. So no worries and hang in there."

Evelyn displayed a forced smile and nodded. The cops finally pulled us apart and then put her in the backseat of a police car. As it slowly drove off, we watched with heavy hearts as the sight of our BFF faded away.

The next several days were some of the most difficult days of my life. I was left to take care of Cedric's funeral arrangements, and I learned that Joy had cleaned out the majority of his bank accounts and was nowhere to be found.

Evelyn's bond had been set at two million dollars. I had a lot of my money tied up in investments, so I really didn't have access to that kind of money right now. The money Evelyn had in the bank, she couldn't even get to. Her assets had been frozen, and we all were very puzzled about that. We couldn't even question anyone about her funds, and since she didn't have a POA listed on her accounts, we were shit out of luck.

The same thing applied to Cedric's house. I wanted to go in there, clean it out, and sell everything. But I couldn't get my hands on anything, unless I trespassed and broke in. I still hadn't decided if I was going to do that yet, but it was an option. Thankfully, he had already paid for his burial;

he had requested to be cremated. All I had to do was make sure everything was finalized. Not only that, I had to tell Jacoby that this time, Cedric was truly gone.

Like me, Jacoby had mixed feelings about Cedric's death. There had been good times, as well as bad times. We loved the old Cedric, the Cedric in the beginning. But somewhere down the road, he had got lost. So had I.

"I don't know what to say, Mama," Jacoby said while standing outside, by his car. He scratched his head, then looked down at the ground. "This whole thing is just horrible. How did we get here, and what is going to happen to Evelyn? Are you worried about her?"

"Yes, I'm very worried. But Trina and I are going to do everything that we can to help clear her name."

"Are you sure you want to do that? I mean, she was still fu . . . screwing around with Cedric, wasn't she? I can't believe that after everything he did, she was still messing around with him. Not to mention that you had forgiven her too. The two of you were friends again, weren't you?"

"Yes, we were. It's a long story, and I'll explain it to you later. But her messing around with him or not, Cedric turned into a madman. I think that what Paula Daniels did to him hurt him even more. He wanted revenge, and he didn't quite know where to go to get it. So he took what happened to him out on everybody, even Justin, who just happened to be at the wrong place at the wrong time. Cedric also jumped on me. When I told you I had fallen that day, I'm sure you know I lied."

Jacoby shook his head. "I figured you did. And don't be mad at me for saying this, but this may be a good thing, after all. Eventually, I think we all would have paid the price, and he wouldn't be the only person dead."

"I'm not mad at you at all. I feel the same way. Somebody had to stop him."

Jacoby sighed, then looked directly into my eyes. "Yeah, they did. I guess we should be thankful for Evelyn, huh?"

I agreed. Jacoby came inside and stayed the evening with me. I cooked dinner for us, and then we watched a movie. It felt good spending this time with my son. When I asked how things were going at Adrianne's house, he had nothing nice to say.

"All I can tell you is, I'll be moving back here real soon, if you don't mind. Only for a little while, because it's almost time for me to be on my own. As for Adrianne's mother and her boyfriend, they argue just as much as you and Cedric did. But they argue over the phone a lot. She be accusing him of this and that. Mad at him because he won't come over. Crying because he said this or didn't say that. I mean, does every household have to be like that?"

"No, it doesn't. And every household *isn't* like that. Some people love and respect each other enough, and they have very little problems living together. It's all about finding the right person to be with, and it looks to me that you have found that person in Adrianne. Have you?"

Jacoby smiled. "I think I have. And if we're still together after college and all that stuff, I really want her to be my wife. She's been there for me a lot. I can honestly say that the only two people that I love with all my heart are her and you."

That was a beautiful thing for Jacoby to say. I gave him a squeezing hug and told him that I loved him too.

Two days later I sat in the small sanctuary, paying my final respects to Cedric. Jacoby sat next to me, and even though I shed some tears, he did not shed one. He held my hand the whole time, and when it was over, we shook hands with the fifty people who had shown up and thanked them for coming.

"I'm so sorry for your loss," one of Cedric's business partners said to me. "Be well."

He kissed my cheek, and then another man stepped forward to pay his respects. I didn't know who half these people were, but they all claimed to be some of Cedric's business partners.

"He was a good man," the second business partner said. "A very good man. I can't believe this happened to him."

All I did was nod. A good man, Cedric was not, but I just kept it moving to the next person.

"We lost a gem," his new secretary said. "Cedric was so funny, and our office will never be the same."

Gem? Funny? Now, she had taken it too far. I stood there and heard it all. What I knew was that Cedric had given these people much more respect than he had given me. They didn't even know the man that I knew, but out of respect for him, I stood there without saying a word. Even when one of his tricks walked up and tried her best to hurt my feelings. I didn't know who she was, until Jacoby whispered in my ear that he had seen her with Cedric.

"I'm going to miss Cedric," she said, barely touching the tips of my fingers to give me what she considered a handshake. "We really had a lot of fun together. He sure knew how to keep a smile on my face, and I don't know who I'm going to find to take his place. He's definitely irreplaceable."

"Your search shouldn't be that hard," Jacoby said to her. "Thanks for coming, and good-bye."

All I did was smile. Smiled at her and at everyone else who continued on with their loving stories about Cedric. I seriously wanted to throw up, but this was his moment, so I let him have it.

After it was all over, I picked up the urn and Jacoby grabbed all the photos we had on display. We put everything in the car, then hopped in. I drove, and right at the Missouri River was where I stopped. We got out of the car, and I watched as Jacoby pitched the urn into the dirty, murky water. We gave each other a hug, then watched as the urn drifted away.

May my dear ex-husband now rest in peace, I thought.

19

Evelyn

I could no longer keep my game face on. And after being in this place for almost a week, I was about to go crazy. My bond had been set at two million dollars, cash only, and I had been coming up short. I didn't know how or why all my assets were frozen. It just didn't make sense, and I needed that money like I had never needed it before. I talked to my attorney and Trina almost every day. She was the one who was trying her best to get me out of here. As for my attorney, it seemed as if all his job was, was to figure out how much money he could get from me. Thankfully, however, he had taken my case—in hopes that whenever I got out of here, I would be able to pay him every dime he requested. I hoped so too, but first, I had to come up with the money to post my bail.

There was no question that I had a long way to go with the trial and everything. But if there was a way for me to break out of here today, I would. This jail cell was no way for anyone to live. The so-called beds were hard as hell, the toilets were nasty as ever, the walls and floors were filthy, and don't even let me comment on the smell. There were two other chicks in the cell with me. One of them appeared to be just as scared as I was, and the other thought she was a badass. She had been here and done this before, but like me and the other chick, she was waiting to post bail or get a court date.

"So, you're a murderer," she said while sucking her stained teeth and looking at me as I sat, disgusted, on the bed. "Killed your man because he was dicking down another trick, huh? I don't know why you dumb broads keep finding yourselves in situations like this. Do you know how many women are incarcerated for doing what you did? No dick is worth all that trouble, is it?"

The heavy white chick with long red hair and freckles on her face didn't know what in the hell she was talking about. I started off by not saying a word, but she didn't know anything about me, and so I had to set the record straight.

"It didn't happen like that," I said, rolling my eyes. "I don't kill men over dick problems, but maybe you do."

She got up and stood in front of me, trying to intimidate me. "I don't kill slime-bucket-ass men, either, but I do kill bitches with smart freaking mouths. Would you like to see how I do it?" She slashed across her throat with her finger, then laughed.

Trying to let her know that she couldn't intimidate me, I stood up to confront her. With much force, she pushed me back down.

"Get up again," she said, still sucking those rotten teeth, "and you will never see daylight again, pretty girl."

Just then, a guard walked by and saw her standing in front of me. She tapped the bars with a billy club and gave the fat bitch a warning. "If I come back again and you're still causing trouble, Niecy, I'm going to take you out of there and put you in a place where you belong."

Niecy backed away from me with her hands in the air. "Pretty girl is the one in here harassing me. I ain't said nothing to her, and she's the one who keeps looking at me like she's crazy or something."

"Pretty girl," the guard said to me, "leave Niecy alone. All she wants is some attention, but don't give it to her."

I took the guard's advice by turning myself around to face the wall. Niecy continued to chastise me and the other young lady, as well. I ignored her by closing my eyes and doing only what a place like this would allow me to do—think. I thought about everything, from my ongoing betrayals to Charles. I didn't even know if I would ever get a chance to spend time with my BFF's again, and that was real scary. I couldn't even imagine my life without them. And what about Trina's baby? Would I even be there to see it come into this world, like I was when Kayla had Jacoby? We had all been so tight then. Nothing had been able to keep us apart. I had been so happy for Kayla then, as I was right now for Trina. Just didn't know if I would miss out on everything. I couldn't help but think that there was a chance that I would be in a place like this for the rest of my life. It sure was no picnic, and I was positive that there were more jealous women in prison like Niecy, waiting to start some shit.

My thoughts then turned to Charles and how he had just vanished. I was still puzzled about that situation, but Trina had said she didn't know what was up, because she hadn't been in touch with Keith. I had even asked if she would borrow some money from him. She'd said that she would reach out to anyone that she could, and to my surprise, so had Kayla. Her intentions were to put up some money, but I didn't think she had enough to cover my whole bail. It was a lot for anyone to come up with, and I was so thankful to my BFF's for doing whatever they could do.

I lay sideways on the bed, still facing the wall. It was hot as hell in the cell, and my forehead was dotted with numerous beads of sweat. I curled into a ball, my eyes started to flutter, and I fell asleep.

That night I dreamed that I was free. Dreamed that I was back at home, and Charles was there with me. We were having sex, while Cedric stood at the door, watching us, drinking alcohol from a bottle. He laughed at the thought of me not being able to handle Charles, and Charles laughed too. But as I got up to go curse Cedric, he lifted the bottle he was drinking from and poured the alcohol all over my face. My eyes burned, and when I attempted to open them and escape from my dream, my face was being sprayed with water. That was what I thought it was, until I opened my eyes and saw a bushy-ass, nasty pussy staring at me.

"Oops," Niecy said, laughing. "It's dark in here. I thought you were the toilet."

I totally lost it. I threw that fat bitch off of me and then jumped on top of her. Gripping her hair with my hand, I pounded her damn face, turning it fire red.

"Bitch, do not fuck with me!" I yelled. "Do you hear me? Stop fucking with me!"

Our other cell mate tried to get me off of Niecy, but by that time, several guards had come into the cell to pull me away from her. I kicked and screamed as they dragged me down the hall and then threw me into a tiny-ass room that had filth running down the walls and another shit-stained toilet in the corner.

"Pretty girl, you haven't been here that long to be causing so much trouble," one of the guards said. "It looks as if this may be your permanent home for a while, so you'd better learn how to clamp your mouth shut and cope. 'Cause if you don't, I'll tell you what. You are going to have a difficult time, more than what you will ever expect."

The guard slammed the door, leaving me there with my thoughts. I sat with my back against the wall and my knees pressed against my chest. All I could think about was how fucked up this was. My father might have been proud of this, but surely not my mother—may she continue to rest in peace. I leaned to the side, and with my face on the concrete floor, I had flashbacks of my friendships with my BFF's and thought about all I had done to them. First, I reflected on all of the messed up things I had done to Kayla. Back then, I hadn't even recognized how wrong I was.

No words could express how I felt right now. Then I started to think about how I had betrayed Trina too.

I thought Keith was alone that day, because Trina had told me she was going out of town. I arrived at his house; the door was unlocked. I didn't even need the key I'd gotten from Bryson's office. The downstairs was pretty dark. Upstairs was too, but I could see light from a television coming from his bedroom. I sauntered up the stairs and could hear soothing jazz music. Apparently, he was trying to set the mood, so I made my way to his doorway. I peeked inside the room and saw him sitting up in bed, with a sheet covering him from the waist down. I knocked on the door and then walked inside. Keith picked up a watch from his nightstand. He was expecting me.

"You're almost ten minutes late. I didn't think you were coming. I was about to fall asleep, because these shows on the television are boring."

"Then Evelyn to the rescue, right?"

Tears welled up in my eyes as I thought about everything. I didn't deserve to have any friends at all, and I was so grateful for Kayla and Trina for sticking by me. Lord knows, they didn't have to. I couldn't even be mad if they decided to scrap all their plans and leave me in here. I deserved this. I had to take the fall for everything, and it was my responsibility to try to make this right. I just didn't know if it was too late for me. Maybe it was.

20

Trina

I was running out of options for Evelyn, but I didn't want to tell her that. Money, money, and more money was what we needed. But since Evelyn had gotten herself into a fight with someone behind bars, I wasn't even able to speak to her. For days Kayla and I pondered what to do next. She had been contributing most of the money, and she was to the point where she couldn't afford to give much more. The only other person whom I could turn to was Keith. Yes, he needed to know about our child, but he wouldn't learn about my pregnancy today. After what Evelyn had done for me, I had to put that situation on the back burner and figure out what I could do to save her. I also didn't want Keith coming back to me because I was pregnant. I wanted him to forgive me totally because in his heart, that was what he wanted too. Since I hadn't heard one word from him, it was obvious that he wasn't there yet.

Keith had money, but it was nowhere near what Evelyn needed. Every little bit helped, so I went to his house to see him. I rang the doorbell, then waited with bated breath for him to come to the door. Looking in through the window, I could see him coming down the stairs. His eyes shifted to his bedroom, then back to me. Before he opened the front door, he looked upstairs again. He then unlocked the door and opened it an inch, wearing nothing but a pair of jeans. A black do-rag was tied around his head, and his colorful tats were in full effect.

"Yes?" he said through the cracked door.

"I need a favor."

He opened the door wider, then stepped outside on the porch with me. It was chilly, but the cold didn't seem to bother him.

"What kind of favor?"

"Before I tell you what it is, I need to elaborate on some of the things you've probably heard on the news about Cedric's murder, and to tell you about my involvement. Do you have time to listen?"

He answered with a nod, and I began to tell him about everything that had happened since I left here. He kept shaking his head and turning it away from me, as if he was disgusted.

"How did you manage to get yourself caught up in that mess?" he said when I finished telling my story.

I started to tell him that I wouldn't even be in this mess had he not put me out of his house. However, I quashed that line of reasoning and went another route instead.

"It just happened, and we both had to defend ourselves. I feel horrible that Evelyn is in there, and the truth is, I should really be in there too. Can you help me with some money to pay her bail? Her attorney is going to want a lot of money, and neither of us has it."

"Evelyn has it. She has it all. Didn't she tell you?"

"I know your mother and father gave her some money for what happened with Bryson, but her accounts are frozen. We can't get access to any of her money, and the banks won't even talk to Kayla or me about those funds. Our hands are tied, and I'm to the point where I don't know what else to do."

Keith was silent; then he released a deep sigh. "Go talk to my father. He should be at home. And if you can't work out anything with him, come back here. I may be able to free up some money somewhere, but it won't be anywhere near what you need."

"I know, and whatever you can do will be much appreciated. Thank you."

Just for the hell of it, I reached out to hug Keith. It sure felt good to be this close to him again, even if it was only for a few seconds. He backed away from me.

"Good-bye, Trina."

My heavy heart just wouldn't let up. I turned around to walk away, but then I pivoted around once again and called his name before he entered the house. This time, I ran up to him and locked my lips on his. I held the back of his head, pulling him to me as I forced him to kiss me. To my surprise, he didn't reject me. But he also didn't allow the kiss to go on for very long. He backed away, but I continued to hold his head and gaze into his eyes.

"I know someone is in there, and I don't care who she is. I don't want to know who she is, but I can assure you that she won't be in your life for long. I'm coming back. You are taking me back, and all I need right now is for you to give me a little hope. All I need is a little hope, and it will surely help after all I've been through."

He stood in silence while looking at me. And when he spoke up, yes, indeed, he gave me hope. "I love you, Trina. I will always love you."

That was enough for me. I left on a serious high. Seemed like I'd waited forever to hear him say those words to me again. I knew he was still trying to cope with what I had done, and it was too soon for me to push. Another woman had him in her possession today, and all I could say was that she'd better enjoy her time with him while it lasted.

I rang the loud doorbell, and its chime was like a song being played. It was my hope that Netta wouldn't come to the door, only because I didn't want her looking at me all crazy and questioning me about what had happened between me and Keith. I was sure she knew all about it. But unfortunately for me, I didn't get my wish. She opened the door, displaying a fake smile that I could read through.

"Keith called and said you would be coming over," she said. "Charles's office is upstairs, the second room on the right. But before you go up there, I want to say this to you. When you hurt my sons, you hurt me. And if or when he forgives you, it doesn't mean that I have to."

She walked away. I couldn't even say anything to her, because if any woman had done to my son what I had done to Keith, I would probably be bitter too.

I climbed the curved staircase, which led to numerous rooms on the second floor. Before going into Charles's office, I knocked and he buzzed me in.

"Come in, Trina," he said. "I've been waiting for you."

I entered the office, nervous as hell. Charles sat with his back facing a huge bay window that stretched from one side of the spacious room to the other. Fancy drapes hung from high above, and the old-fashioned desk that he sat behind looked as if it had come straight from the early 1900s. Bookshelves lined the walls, and several computer monitors were all over the place. None of them were on, but CNN played on the TV mounted above the stone fireplace. An American flag on a pole was next to it.

He swung his chair around to face me. Without a doubt, I knew how easily Evelyn had gotten herself caught up. Charles looked just like an older Keith, one without all the muscles and with much more power.

"Have a seat," he said, his eyes scanning me like radar.

I wondered what in the hell he was thinking, but I quickly sat in the chair in front of his desk and started to tell him the purpose of my visit. As I spoke, he kept switching positions in his chair, sighing, and looking at me as if he were looking through me. Not once did his gaze venture away from my eyes. That made me even more nervous.

"That's why I need your help," I said with a cracking voice when I was done recounting my tale of woe. "I'm just as responsible as she is, and I feel obligated to do something and help her out of this."

Charles cleared his throat, and then he sat up straight. He clenched his hands together while resting them on his desk. "You may be at fault for fucking over my son, but you're not at fault for what happened at Evelyn's place. The way I see it, she is one hundred percent to blame for everything, and I haven't made up my mind yet as to how I'm going to deal with her. You see, that woman came into my home with her lover and attempted to extort money from me. I allowed her to think that I wanted that little problem between her and Bryson to go away, but anyone who knows me knows that if I want a problem to disappear, I can make it do so just like that." He snapped his fingers and then got out of his seat.

As he walked over to the bay window to look outside, he slipped his hands into his pockets. "That day, I gave her some money and told her to be gone. I knew that money would eventually wind up destroying her, as that's what happens to people who believe that money can save them. But what she did next really took the cake. She thought she was so good, so special, that she could whip her pussy on me and control me. Yet again, I decided to let her have at it. By design, I messed with her head to put her under my spell. She was definitely hooked, and when I tried to set her free and let her off the hook, she still wouldn't stop there. So now here we are. I have two choices. Would you like to hear what they are?"

I slowly nodded, though deep down I had a feeling that I wasn't going to like where this conversation was going. "Please proceed. And I thank you for sharing this with me."

"You're welcome," he said, then sat in his chair again. He leaned back in it and held up one finger. "I can make everyone believe that your friend is delusional and suffers from a mental illness. It runs in her family, so I won't have a problem convincing anyone that she killed Cedric because he was seeing other women and he didn't want anything to do with her. I will get people to go on that stand and tell a jury that she fantasized about me and our relationship—that it was all made up, that I had never worked where she said I did, and that all of it, every single thing, was part of her wild imagination. And I will say that even though she claimed we had sex, we never did, and she was plotting to kill me too, because I wouldn't get with the program. That, for sure, would send her to a mental institution for the rest of her life."

My stomach hurt so badly, and my throat ached. My heart went out to Evelyn, because this was not looking good. Charles sipped from a glass of water on his desk; then he reached for a pack of gum in his drawer.

"Have some," he said, offering me a piece and then putting one in his mouth.

"No, thank you."

He folded his arms across his chest, then continued. "Option number two goes a little something like this. I can have all her assets unfrozen and allow you to take that money and get her out of this. I would also appreciate it if some of that money got returned to me, but I'm sure—no, positive—that the majority of it will have to be used for her defense. I will put women on the stand who can vouch for her. Who will allow that jury to see what kind of animal Cedric really was and how he deserved to die. Evelyn will look like an abused, distraught, and destroyed woman who had no other choice.

"Even so, I want to be very clear about something. If I decide to go that route, your friend will still have to do some time. I don't want to let her off the hook that easily, and sometimes, people need time to sit and think about all that they've done. When you keep on rescuing them and forgiving them for their mistakes, they tend to take advantage of that. I think that a year in prison . . . maybe two to ten, will do her some good."

I wanted to break down right then and there and just cry. I didn't know how to tell her this, but it was as if there were no other options. I knew she was probably already losing her mind up in there, and I had lost sleep, knowing that she was probably in some kind of hole for getting herself in trouble.

"Mr. Washington, she will not survive in there. I know that she won't, and I'm asking that you please reconsider. She will give every dime of your money back. I will make sure of that, and you will never have to worry about her again. She's had a very difficult life, and many of those things done to her in the past cause her to be this way."

"Believe me when I say I know all about her and her past. And I don't worry about Evelyn at all, nor have I ever lost any sleep thinking about her. Her past is exactly what it is, her past. She used that as an excuse to hurt people, and that kind of shit doesn't fly with me. Being in jail causes people to see things in a different light. I have faith that Evelyn will find that light, and she'll come out of there a reformed person. Stronger, smarter, and humbler than she has ever been before. Nonetheless, I'm delivering my final words to you. They are that there will be no option three. Overnight, I will decide what I believe the best option to be. I'll call you in the morning, or no later than the afternoon. Now, if you don't mind, I have other serious matters to tend to."

In fear of pissing him off and making him change his mind about option two, I remained silent and stood to leave. As I approached the door, he said something to me that made me slowly turn my head.

"Sasha is sweet, isn't she? Good thing you found out she wasn't for you. And just so you know, my son is. Tell him about the baby. He needs to know."

My mouth dropped open, but I didn't bother to elaborate on Sasha or the baby. All I did was reply from my heart, "I know he is for me. That's why I love him with every fiber of my being."

He nodded, then buzzed the door so I could exit.

21

Kayla

Trina came over this morning to tell me about her conversation with Mr. Washington. I was shocked. I hadn't even known about any of this. Yet again, Evelyn had been screwing around with somebody else's husband. I tried not to be so harsh about this, but I knew we all made our own beds and we had to lie in them. I found myself still on the fence about so many things, but there was no question that Evelyn needed my help.

There was a side of me that felt so bad for her. Even one year in prison seemed like a long time. Like Trina, I surely didn't think Evelyn would be able to cope. I was worried about her trying to kill herself and about never seeing her again. I guessed my life wouldn't seem complete without her around, and at this point, at this very point in my life, I started to feel like we were a small yet unique dysfunctional family.

Trina and I waited, on pins and needles, for Mr. Washington's call. I had never met him a day in my life, and I couldn't believe how much authority he had. This was something that you saw on TV or heard about from those who felt that juries were tainted and that people were purposely put on the stand to fabricate stories. If I hadn't heard it from Trina, I wouldn't have believed any of it.

Trina looked at her watch while sitting at the kitchen table. "It's almost one o'clock. Do you think I should try to reach out to him?"

"Do you have his number?"

"No, but I could call Keith to get it."

"Let's wait. If he doesn't call by three, call him."

The next two hours seemed like a whole day. We tried to keep ourselves busy by watching TV and even doing a little exercising. As we sat on some mats, doing yoga, I told Trina how happy I was about the baby.

"I'm happy too. I can't wait, and I don't care if it's a boy or a girl."

"With Jacoby, I didn't care, either. I've always wanted a girl, though, but you know how that story goes."

"I do, but who would have thought that it would end like this?"

"End? Girl, it's just the beginning, especially for you and Keith. You need to tell him that you're pregnant, and whatever your reasons are for not telling him, I'm telling you that they're not good enough. All you're doing is setting yourself up for more chaos between y'all. He's going to be upset about you not telling him, and then y'all will be fighting about that. Keeping secrets has already cost us enough damage, only because one day those secrets all come out."

"I agree, and I will tell him after all this stuff with Evelyn is over. I'm too stressed right now, and believe me when I say that I'm not trying to keep any secrets from him. If I was, Mr. Washington would bust me out. I don't know how he knows so much, but I swear that he knows everything about me, about Evelyn, and probably about you too."

"It sounds like he does, and he's probably thinking that I really need to get a life. In due time I will."

Trina and I started talking about our future plans, but there was no question that Mr. Washington's call was on our minds. And just as we finished exercising, Trina's phone rang.

She snatched it up and hit the speakerphone button so I could hear.

The only thing Mr. Washington said was, "Option two. She'll be released on bail by six o'clock this evening." After that, he ended the call.

"How much time in prison?" Trina yelled. "Damn it! Don't hang up! Tell me how much time!"

Trina had been through so much with her BFF's. If there was any one of us who stood by the other one's side, it was her.

She had fought hard to keep our friendships together, and I had rarely told her how grateful I was for her support. In the moment, she seemed very overwhelmed. I reached out to hug her, and she broke down in my arms.

"I want this to be over with," she cried out. "When will all the pain end?"

"Real soon. It will end soon, but we have to stay prayed up and continue to be there for each other. I thank you for always trying to make things right. I know I haven't said it in a long time, but I thank you for everything, Trina. With all my heart, I love you, and you are the best friend any woman could hope for. I know for a fact that Evelyn feels the same way."

"I love you too," Trina said, wiping her eyes.

Sometimes people just needed to hear those three words.

When six o'clock rolled around, we were outside the jailhouse, waiting on Evelyn to come out. Like clockwork, the doors opened, and there she was. A small bag was in her hand. I had never, ever seen her look the way she did. Her eyes looked swollen, her hair was matted, her clothes were slouchy, and her lips looked dry as hell. Not to mention her very pale skin. Trina and I tried to play it down by smiling at her. We hadn't even had a chance to tell her how everything was supposed to go down, and that she would have to spend *some* time in prison. At this point, we still didn't know how much time, but *some* time was set in stone.

We met her halfway, and the first person she hugged was Trina.

"Thank you," she said in a light whisper. "Thank you for everything."

"Thank you too," Trina said. "And you already know why."

Afterward, Evelyn and I hugged too. I hadn't done nearly as much as Trina had done for her, but she knew that I had put up a substantial amount of money for her attorney fees and bail. We were sure that even her attorney would be replaced and that Mr. Washington would assign an attorney who could make things go according to his plan.

"I'm going to get your money back to you," she said to me. "And like always, I owe you."

"Don't worry about it right now. We have other things that we have to deal with. Trina and I will tell you about them in the car."

On the drive back to my place, Trina broke it all down for Evelyn. She remained real quiet. Didn't say much at all. Just listened and listened some more. By the time we reached my place, her only response was, "I guess I just have to do what I have to do."

After that, there was silence.

22

Evelyn

As Trina and Kayla broke it all down for me in the car, I felt numb. All I could say to them that day was, "I guess I just have to do what I have to do," but I didn't feel that way at all. Not after being in that cell with a bully like Niecy. Not after staring at four walls all day, lying in filth, eating garbage, and sitting my ass on those nasty toilets. No, I wasn't ready for that, and I didn't have the guts to tell them how scared I really was. That would worry them. I didn't want to keep stressing them out, and Lord knows, they didn't need any more stress, especially Trina. If something happened to her baby, I would never forgive myself.

So, no question, I needed to take action and do it fast. I was sure there were many more Niecys in prison who couldn't wait to get their hands on me. Therefore, I had to do something . . . anything to get Charles to change his mind. I knew that I was taking a big risk by confronting him, but I didn't have a choice. Trina and Kayla had done so much, and they really couldn't do much more. It was my time to stand up for me, and if Charles had that much control over the outcome, I couldn't sit around doing nothing.

I allowed things to settle down a bit, and a week after I was released from jail, I headed out to find Charles. I had to be careful about going anywhere near his house, but since he was no longer at the office, I basically didn't have a choice. I wanted to catch him when he was by himself. When Netta wasn't around, or Keith or Bryson. It was a Sunday afternoon when I saw the garage door go up and his white Mercedes back out. Thankfully, he was alone. I followed his car, but in no way was I too close. He was too observant, and I knew he would see me, even with my dark shades on and a scarf tied around my head. I had a nice little dress on, as if I had just come from church. My face was makeup free, but I did have on loud red lipstick, which gave me a different look altogether. I glanced in the rearview mirror to make sure no one was following me, and then I looked straight ahead, where I could see Charles making a left to get on the highway.

He drove for about twenty minutes or so and then got off at the Delmar exit, heading toward the Loop. Minutes later, he parked his car and then went inside an Italian restaurant. I waited for a few minutes, just to see if he would be dining with someone. But as I looked through the window, I saw him sitting alone. He glanced at his watch, and when I saw him look toward the door, I figured I'd better hurry up, because maybe he was waiting on someone. I went inside, and as Charles's head was lowered—he was looking at the menu—I slipped into the booth. He slowly lifted his head, and as usual, the pearly whites didn't show.

"I figured you were coming," he said. "I just didn't know when. What do you want, Evelyn? And please make it quick, because I am expecting someone."

I was a little nervous, but I came to say what I had to. "I don't know how quick I can make this, but I really need your help. Trina told me how all of this is supposed to play out, but I can't do this. I can't spend any more time in that place, and if we can work out some kind of deal where I don't have to go back there, I—I will do anything."

"I'm sorry to hear about what you can't do, but there's really not much else that you can do for me. And the last time we tried to work out a deal, it was in your favor, not mine. I don't like to keep negotiating with people who continue to make me feel like a loser. At some point, I have to come out a winner."

"But this isn't about winning or losing. This is about my life." I couldn't help that I started to get emotional. "My life, Charles, and I want it back. I've changed. This entire experience has changed me. I totally get it now. Going to prison will do me no good. It will destroy me and make me bitter. Right now, I'm good. I'm so good, and all I want to do is go live my life in peace."

Charles removed several napkins from the napkin holder, then gave them to me. There was a soft spot in him, for sure. I was trying my best to reach it.

"It's too late for tears, Evelyn. You've been given too many opportunities to correct yourself, and you haven't. I said the same thing to Bryson, and when shit starts to affect me, and I have to inject myself into these little petty matters that I don't have time for, well, it upsets me. I get angry, and, unfortunately, some people have to pay."

I wondered what had happened to Bryson after our meeting that day, because I hadn't seen him. I really didn't have time to inquire about him, but I still asked.

"How did Bryson pay? Where is he? And please know that I have already corrected myself. You just don't know how different I am. I'm loving the new me, and you would be proud of how much I've changed. My friends are proud of me too, and I know you've spoken to Trina about me. She told you everything, didn't she? She believes in me, and I need for you to believe in me too."

Charles snickered, then rubbed the long hair on his chin. He stared at me. I stared at him. Seconds later, he got up and stood next to me. Immediately, my eyes shifted to his package, then to his lips, which found their way to mine. As his tongue entered my mouth, I made mine dance with his. The kiss was intense, and with my eyes closed, I savored every minute of it. I hoped that he did, as well.

"What was that for?" I said softly when he backed away from me. He sat back down, then released a deep sigh.

"As expected, you failed the test, and my point should be much easier to grasp now. The new you won't be discovered until you hit rock bottom. You're not there yet. I assure you that you're not there. You're just trying to say and do all the right things to get me to change my mind. Allowing me to have my way with you is not the route to go. Throwing your pussy at me won't work, Evelyn, and you need to stop believing that it can get you whatever you want."

"I did not just attempt to throw anything at you. You're the one who kissed me. I went with the flow because I'm always happy to see you and I do have some feelings for you. What's the big deal here?"

"I'm sorry if you're too blind to see what it is, and I don't have much time to help you figure it out. The bottom line is, no matter what you say or do, my decision stands. I will not change my mind, but I do have a few suggestions for you. Don't spend the next several months of freedom worrying about where Bryson is. Like you, he was given an opportunity to correct himself, and he didn't. He's somewhere thinking real hard about his mistakes, and I'm going to give you a chance to do the same.

"Until then, make a bucket list and tackle some of the things you have always wanted to do. Spend time with your friends and enjoy your freedom, while you have it. Don't waste another day by following me around, and if you're really a changed woman, get on your knees every day, afternoon and night, and thank God for your friends. Thank Him that you're still alive after all the dirt that you've done. None of us are perfect, Evelyn, but you still have a lot of soul-searching to do. Good luck, and be sure to choose your battles wisely while you're incarcerated. Doing so will help you stay alive."

Charles exited the booth, then left the restaurant. I sat there, as if cement had been poured over me. In that moment, it finally hit me that this was, indeed, a done deal.

The next several months played out exactly as Charles wanted them to. An attorney was hired to represent me, and he coached me on everything to say, especially when I was put on the witness stand to defend my actions. During the trial several ladies whom I didn't even know and had never seen in my life got on that stand and cried their hearts out about what Cedric had done to them. Charles even went to the extreme of putting Paula Daniels on the stand. She really put on an act. She had the jury in awe when she cried as she told the courtroom about how badly Cedric had beaten her one day.

"My entire body was black and blue," she said. Her lips quivered as she spoke. "He tried to stomp the life out of me, and if it wasn't for my neighbor, I would be six feet under."

Some of the jury members, the ones who hadn't been bought, had tears trapped in their eyes. Paula became so overwhelmed while telling how things had gone down between her and Cedric that a police officer was asked to carry her out of the courtroom.

Kayla was then asked to take the stand. She spoke about how loving Cedric was and then confessed to him beating her too. "I didn't know what was going on," she said. "He turned into a man that I hadn't witnessed the whole time I was married to him. I truly believe that my ex-husband would've killed me that day, because something inside of him snapped. I don't know what it was, but he snapped."

"Did he ever threaten you or put his hands on you after that?" my attorney asked Kayla.

"No, but he called to threaten my son. I was also worried about Cedric hurting my son."

"Thank you, Mrs. Thompson. Thanks for your time."

The arrogant prosecutor approached Kayla with a spiral notebook in his hand. We already knew how all of this was going to play out, and he did his best to make it look good for the jury members who weren't part of the plan and simply for the record.

"Mrs. Thompson, you sit there and act as if you hated your husband. But the fact is, even up until he was murdered by your best friend, you still loved him, didn't you?"

"I loved him as a person, but I wasn't in love with him anymore."

"Really now? I read from a journal that you wrote in prior to his murder, and you say right here that you love him with all your heart. That you wished the two of you had stayed married, and that's why you would never give up your married name."

"That's not true. I decided to keep that name for financial reasons and other reasons that have nothing to do with still being in love with him."

"Maybe that's not true, but it is true that you and your friend shared your husband, isn't it?"

"At one point in the marriage, yes, I did share, without knowing it."

"And that same friend killed your husband, didn't she?"

"Yes."

His voice got stern and louder. "Mrs. Cedric Thompson, did you have anything to do with your husband's murder? Did you pay your friend to pump three bullets into his chest, bash his head, and kill him!"

Kayla remained as calm as ever, just as she'd been advised. "No. No, I didn't have anything to do with my ex-husband being killed. And in future, please do not address me by his name."

The prosecutor rolled his eyes, then looked at the judge. "No further questions."

My stomach was tight the whole time Kayla spoke. She did good, and I was so relieved. I awaited my time on the stand, and it happened later that day. At first I was nervous, but my attorney helped to put me at ease. He bombarded me with question after question. He asked me to explain how it all went down that day. He also asked me to speak about my ongoing relationship with Cedric. You'd better believe that I made it sound horrific. I saw one of the jury members clench her chest and another shake her head. Even though Charles had crafted this trial, I seriously thought that when all was said and done, the jury would find me not guilty of murder in the second degree. However, less than a week later, they did.

I still did not know my ultimate fate, and I guessed that Charles intended to put me on pins and needles as I stood before the judge, who was responsible for delivering my sentence. He gave his spiel, which went in one ear and out the other. All I wanted to hear was the number of years I would get for murdering Cedric.

"I sentence you to five years in the—"

After hearing the words *five years*, I fainted.

23

Trina

This past year had been interesting. Keith and I were taking things one day at a time, and I was so grateful to him for giving me another chance. He wasn't completely over what I had done to him, but he was thankful, as well as excited, about his newborn son. I hadn't seen Keith this happy in a long time, and it made me regret that I hadn't gotten my act together sooner. I, too, was happy, and our little boy changed our lives in ways that neither of us had thought was possible. Our anniversary was in one month. I was one sista who was hoping and praying that my man would propose to me. I kind of sensed it, and you'd better believe I was keeping my fingers crossed.

As for Kayla, she had stuck with her Alcoholics Anonymous classes and had been sober for months. We were spending a lot of time together while Evelyn was away, and my bond with Kayla was stronger, as well as unbreakable. She and Jacoby had been getting along better too. He was trying to finish up school, and I suspected that he was ready to move out of Kayla's house for good and live on his own. Kayla had said that he hadn't mentioned much else about Cedric, and she had also mentioned that he wanted to have his last name changed. She felt some kind of way about it, but I reminded her that it was time for her to let go and let Jacoby do him.

Evelyn's situation, however, had been turned out to be much more complicated than we had originally thought it would be. We were disappointed about the five-year sentence, especially since the bottom line in the case was that it was an act of self-defense. I'd felt that there was no way that I could sit back and let Evelyn do five years for something I'd had my hands in too, and so as soon as she was to have visitors, I'd spoken to her and Kayla about coming clean and telling the police about my involvement.

"Hell, no," Evelyn said, looking at me tearfully that day as she sat behind the thick glass. She was dressed in an orange jumpsuit, there were bags underneath her eyes, and stress was written all over her frowning face. "This is over with, Trina. It's time for us to move on, and five years will come and go just like that." She snapped her fingers, but I wasn't buying what she was trying to sell me.

"You don't have to put on your game face for me. All I'm saying is—"

She quickly cut me off. "All I'm saying is people are listening, so it's best that we talk about something positive." Her eyes traveled to my stomach. She cracked a tiny smile. "Have you decided what you're going to name the baby yet? I'm good with picking names, and if it's a girl, feel free to name her after me."

Evelyn was trying to change the subject, but I needed her to be on the same page with me when I decided to go to the police and tell them what had really happened.

"I haven't decided on a name yet, but I have decided to go to the police. We—"

"If you do, I'll make you look like a liar. And if you say one more word about this, Trina, this conversation is done."

I ignored Evelyn's threat, and as I continued to make my case for wanting to tell the truth, she glared at me through the window before placing the phone on the hook. She swallowed hard, then moved away from the window. I sat, full of emotions, not knowing what else to do. Kayla was in the car, waiting for me. After her prior conversation with Evelyn, Kayla had advised me to stick with the plan.

"If she doesn't want anyone to know the truth about what really happened that day, then let it go," Kayla had said. "Going through another trial will be difficult for all of us, and the outcome could be even worse than it is now."

That had, indeed, been a possibility, but remaining silent had been difficult to do, especially after I'd started getting letters from Evelyn that were nothing nice to read.

She kept talking about wanting to kill herself, and about her ongoing arguments and fights with others. And after being in the hole so much, it appeared that she had begun to realize that she just wasn't going to win in a place like that. There were too many women trying to be the boss, and she had to sit back and give them their crown. I had responded by telling her how much I regretted not telling the police the truth. I'd also mentioned that it was not too late for me to speak up, but after my third letter to her in which I declared my intentions to do something, her letters stopped, and the fourth one I wrote came back marked RETURN TO SENDER. I thought that something bad had happened to her, but it was obvious that she wasn't down with my plan and had decided to ignore me. I had nowhere else to turn but to Keith. He had been against me going to the police, as well, and had kept reminding me of the dire consequences.

"This is one time I will have to agree with Evelyn," he said as we discussed my options one day. "What's done is done. Evelyn will be okay, but you won't be if you keep stressing yourself like this. You've got to take care of yourself, baby. And what about us? We deserve to be happy, and for once, I want you to think about how important it is for you to be at your best for our child."

I squeezed my aching forehead, trying to soothe a headache that wouldn't go away. "I'm trying to be the best person I can be, but this is hard, Keith. I wish there was something I could do to get her out of there sooner. I don't think nobody understands how painful this has been for all of us. Kayla and I both feel as if we haven't done enough. Yes, Evelyn brought a lot of this on herself, but the truth is, we're like family. They are my family, Keith, and we have been through so much."

Keith could see how wounded I was. He embraced me, then planted a soft kiss on my forehead. "I do understand. Some bonds can never be broken, but I want you to make me a promise. If you promise to start taking care of yourself, and our child, I'll reach out to my father and see if there is anything he can do. I don't know if he can do anything, but we'll see."

I rested my head against Keith's chest, praying for some kind of miracle.

The miracle arrived almost a year and a half later, when Kayla and I were informed that Evelyn would be released. With much enthusiasm, we drove to the prison to get her and parked right outside the gates through which she would soon walk free. I couldn't wait to see my BFF, and as we stood outside my car, waiting for Evelyn, we tried to guess how she would look.

"I bet she done cut off all her hair," Kayla said while holding out her pinkie finger. "How much do you want to bet?"

"No way. Evelyn's hair is probably somewhere down her back. I'm sure her nails are all polished, and she may come out here with a suit on."

"See, I disagree. I think she done gave all that up."

"Girl, this is Evelyn we're talking about. I don't care where she's at. You know she is going to do her best to look good."

We laughed, but as time ticked away, Kayla bit her nails, all the while keeping her eyes on the door through which we expected Evelyn to exit. She was getting just as nervous as I was, especially since another prisoner had made an exit about thirty minutes ago. We were so sure that Evelyn would be coming soon. But after fifteen or so more minutes, we started to get worried. I didn't know who to call in order to find out why this was taking so long, but just as I was reaching for my phone to call Keith, the steel door to the prison came open. I could see Evelyn from a distance, and just as I had predicted, her hair was parted down the middle and she sported a long ponytail that stopped midway down her back. She wore a white T-shirt and a pair of baggy jeans that did nothing for her figure. She also looked as if she had picked up some weight, but it wasn't a lot. A smile was on her face, and as she got closer, she started to laugh while strutting on the pavement.

"I's free!" she shouted as the gates parted. "Y'all hear me, ladies? I's free!"

She started skipping her way to us, and then she stopped to do the cabbage patch. We could see that her sense of humor had improved. That made us feel good, and the smiles on our faces showed it. She held out her arms, then grabbed me and Kayla around our necks when she reached us. She kissed my cheek first, then Kayla's.

"I missed the hell out of y'all," she said tearfully. "I dreamed night after night about this day, and all I wanted to do was wrap my arms around my BFF's again."

Totally relieved, we knew exactly how she felt. Our arms were wrapped tightly around her, as well, and what an amazing day this was for us. I mean, if our friendship could be mended after all that we had endured, surely, other friendships could be too. Not all, but certainly some. . . .